GW01451699

Head of the Class

Book 1 of System Apocalypse: Liberty

by

Tao Wong and Jason J. Willis

Copyright

This is a work of fiction. Names, characters, businesses, places, events, and incidents are either the products of the author's imagination or used in a fictitious manner. Any resemblance to actual persons, living or dead, or actual events is purely coincidental.

No part of this publication may be reproduced, distributed, or transmitted in any form or by any means, including photocopying, recording, or other electronic or mechanical methods, without the prior written permission of the publisher, except in the case of brief quotations embodied in critical reviews and certain other non-commercial uses permitted by copyright law.

Head of the Class

Copyright © 2024 Tao Wong and Jason J. Willis. All Rights reserved.
Copyright © 2024 Sarah Anderson Cover Designer
Copyright © 2024 Polar Engine Cover Artwork

Published by Starlit Publishing
PO Box 30035
High Park PO
Toronto, ON, Canada
M6P 3K0

www.starlitpublishing.com

Ebook ISBN: 9781778552120
Paperback ISBN: 9781778552137
Hardcover ISBN: 9781778552144

Books in The System Apocalypse Universe

System Apocalypse: Liberty
Head of the Class
Dropout

Main Storyline
Life in the North

System Apocalypse: Australia
Town Under

System Apocalypse: Kismet
Fool's Play

System Apocalypse – Relentless
A Fist Full of Credits

Anthologies & Shorts
System Apocalypse Short Story Anthology Volume 1
System Apocalypse Short Story Anthology Volume 2

Valentines in an Apocalypse

A New Script

Daily Jobs, Coffee and an Awfully Big Adventure

Adventures in Clothing

Questing for Titles

Blue Screens of Death

My Grandmother's Tea Club

The Great Black Sea

Growing Up – Apocalypse Style

Interdimensional Window SHOPping

A Game of Koopash (Newsletter exclusive)

Lana's story (Newsletter exclusive)

Debts and Dances (Newsletter exclusive)

A Tense Meeting (Newsletter exclusive)

Comic Series

The System Apocalypse Comics (7 Issues)

Table of Contents

Chapter 1	1
Chapter 2	20
Chapter 3	31
Chapter 4	45
Chapter 5	58
Chapter 6	62
Chapter 7	71
Chapter 8	85
Chapter 9	95
Chapter 10	106
Chapter 11	111
Chapter 12	118
Chapter 13	126
Chapter 14	133
Chapter 15	139
Chapter 16	146
Chapter 17	155
Chapter 18	168
Chapter 19	176
Chapter 20	187
Chapter 21	197
Chapter 22	206
Chapter 23	220
Chapter 24	229
Chapter 25	235
Chapter 26	250
Chapter 27	259
Chapter 28	265
Chapter 29	276
Chapter 30	283
Chapter 31	288
Chapter 32	299
Chapter 33	305
Chapter 34	318
Chapter 35	329
Chapter 36	336
Chapter 37	344
Chapter 38	351
Chapter 39	357
Chapter 40	363

Chapter 41	376
Chapter 42	379
Chapter 43	394
Chapter 44	397
Chapter 45	401
Chapter 46	404
Chapter 47	415
Chapter 48	420
Chapter 49	422
Chapter 50	426
Chapter 51	442
Chapter 52	449
Chapter 53	463
Chapter 54	473
Chapter 55	481
Chapter 56	492
Chapter 57	505
Chapter 58	518
Chapter 59	522
Chapter 60	539
Chapter 61	548
Chapter 62	558
Chapter 63	564
Chapter 64	573
Chapter 65	576
Chapter 66	586
Chapter 67	593
Chapter 68	600
Chapter 69	605
Chapter 70	609
Chapter 71	615
Chapter 72	622
Chapter 73	633
Chapter 74	639
Chapter 75	644
Chapter 76	656
Chapter 77	665
Chapter 78	672
Chapter 79	678
Epilogue	683
Authors' Note	686
About the Authors	689

About the Publisher	691
System Apocalypse: Kismet	692
System Apocalypse – Relentless	693
Glossary	694
Teacher Skill Tree	694
Guerilla Tactician Skills	694
Caleb's Skill List and Equipment	694
Lee's Skill List and Equipment	699

Chapter 1

Caleb

I'd like to blame the explosion for interrupting my class's lesson. But what really derailed things was Aul K'Unn Tek. It was always Aul. Even the porous walls shaking and crystal lights flickering would have been a relatively short delay, without his questions.

We were used to the ship being attacked; it had happened at least once a week since the Voloids had landed. The four-armed, gray hexapods had practically guaranteed that when they'd landed their spaceship in a prime dungeon location. The only real threat had been when a pair of giant black bears with goat heads had tried to eat the thrusters. Even then, a blast of blazing rocket fuel to the face had persuaded them to find a less spicy meal.

As an elementary school teacher, the Squaw Lake Bird Watchers Society had sounded like a great place to bring my class. So I had gone alone to scout it out as a potential field trip location, expecting to see some mallards and loons.

As a vegetarian, I had been nearly as horrified by the antlered heads on display in the main lodge as I was by the announcement that it was about to become a post-apocalyptic dungeon. I'd played enough RPGs and MMOs to know what a dungeon was, and I knew it was the last place I wanted to be standing during an apocalypse. Ignoring the rest of the messages, I'd run as fast as my couch-potato legs could carry me on a dirt road that still hid a few frozen spots, even in early April.

The white-tailed deer bounding into my field of vision by the time the countdown ended had made me smile. Distracted by its unusual size and fanged maw, I'd missed the spaceship behind the row of trees.

The Voloid Matriarch, E'Kklon Vekk, had appeared like Predator from the movies, yanking me from the path of the deer monster and into the safety of her ship, where I had been her guest, or prisoner, ever since.

"Teacher, teach," she'd intoned with a high, resonant voice. Then she'd tossed me into a room with small children.

Other than attending intermittent hunts, that had been my job for the last two years while the rest of the world had gone to shit.

Even before the apocalypse, I'd prided myself on being able to handle disruptive students. Now, I had honest-to-God superpowers to up my game. None of that helped with Aul; he was my kryptonite. He was a genuinely curious child asking thought-provoking questions that entirely disrupted the lesson plan I'd laid out the night before.

"Caleb will not protect hive, is truth?" was the question Aul had asked me. His voice was deep and resonant.

More chirps, clicks, and buzzes flew at me from the rest of the class than they had for any other topic, with the possible exception of when he'd asked if I was a slave. I had answered with an honest, if uncertain, "Maybe."

"I will protect any sentients in danger," I said, "but I'm bad at fighting."

My Universal Translator Skill was amazing, but these beings were notoriously hard to translate. With patience though, I thought we managed. It helped that Aul did most of the talking, no matter how much I tried to get the rest of the class to join in. Alone, the others would answer. When Aul was present, they deferred to him. I could speculate as to why, but I was a teacher, not an alienologist.

"Aul is confusion." His mandibles quivered slightly.

"You know I'm a vegetarian, right?"

He tilted his head in a way that my Skill told me meant agreement, though it still didn't feel right, even after all this time.

"Well, that's because I value life, especially sentient life. And it's damn near impossible to tell where to draw the line on what is and is not sentient. Because of that, I won't attack or kill anyone not attacking me or someone else. But I'm not a pacifist. I will attack those who attack others. I'm just not any good at it. My Class is Teacher. My points and Skills are spent to help me with that. And frankly, I'm too thoughtful for life-or-death reactions. I freeze up when a warrior needs to act without thinking.

"That's why I picked up Pavise here," I said, then reached over to knock on the metal head of the robot that had become the most reliable fixture of my life. He wasn't there. "Wherever he is. He's big and square and I hide behind him whenever we get attacked out there."

Pavise was the result of all of my Perks and a love of *Star Wars* and medieval history. The System had him listed as a shield-bot Protective Companion. I had upgraded his AI over time with about half of my Credits. He and my WWMRD necklace were my only prized possessions in this new world.

"Where are you, buddy?" I sent a questioning pulse through my neural link.

"You left me in the hold again. And you've been ignoring your notifications. How am I supposed to protect you when you forcibly separate us?"

"The door closes automatically," I replied. *"It's not my fault. If you're that worried about it, go first and make sure the path is safe."*

"Alert me before departing and I will."

Aul's left mandible was twitching and I realized I'd been incredibly rude, ignoring his questions. "Sorry, Aul. What were you asking?"

"The ship is currently under attack. I should be with you."

"They'll take care of it, they always do. Now hush." I quieted the alerts with a mental nudge.

"Hive hunt. Monsters attack hive. Caleb won't attack to protect hive? Only carry supplies and heal injured?"

"Yes."

"Caleb coward?"

"Not really," I answered. And I knew they knew I was telling the truth. One of my passive Class Skills, Ring of Truth, made it so that anyone I'd never intentionally deceived knew I wasn't lying. The Skill didn't force me to tell them everything I knew, a fact that I had made sure to tell them as soon as I knew about it. Trust was essential if you wanted to be a teacher. And I'd never wanted any other job.

"How Caleb not coward?" He tapped low on the center of his chest plate, right underneath the bright red slash he alone shared with the Matriarch. I got a vague impression that this gesture was somehow meaningful.

It might be time to put one of my three remaining Skill points into Universal Translator.

"If the hive was out exploring or gathering, I would fight to protect them, if badly. But the hive goes to where the monsters are to kill the monsters. Even if the monsters attack them first, that's not self-defense."

"Monsters attack pack. Monsters attack humans. Monsters attack everyone. Hive no hunt, monsters get stronger and stronger. Monsters kill everyone."

"Yes." This one word was weaker, almost trembling.

"Why not self-defense?"

My notifications were flashing, fast. I ignored them.

"I want to say that it's not self-defense because you can't know they will attack. And that's partly true." Being required to be completely honest was hard, but overall, it was amazing. It was good for the students, and it helped me to understand my own motivations. "But it does seem like almost all the monsters are hostile. Maybe all of them. And I want to say it's because it's not the monsters' fault. They didn't choose to be monsters. That might also be true. But killing other people because you're being forced to doesn't mean they don't have a right to defend themselves."

"Why not self-defense?" he said again. His upper hands were crossed now, in challenge.

"Levels," I finally told him. "Levels and loot."

He uncrossed his arms.

"The Voloids did not come to Earth to help us. To stop the monsters. They came to Earth for levels and loot. The Voloids aren't protecting; they're attacking."

"Voloids kill monsters."

"They do," I agreed.

"Voloids good."

"Voloids are people," I replied. "They are good and bad."

He crossed both sets of his arms. "Matriarch's Voloids good."

"Maybe," I answered. "The Matriarch saved me that first day. But she also kept me here. Sure, she pays me. She gives me Credits, orange Fanta, and veggie lovers pizza. She even gives me every book I ask for. But she never took me back to my people. She never asked if I wanted to stay. She even pretended not to understand when I asked if I was a prisoner."

It had taken me nearly a year to realize that there hadn't been a difficulty in translation.

I kept quiet about the Skill I had picked up at level 31.

Class Trip (Level 3)

Group teleportation Skill

Transports a Teacher, students, and officially recognized chaperones to a location that the Teacher has previously occupied or thoroughly researched.

Max distance 100 miles + 25 miles per Skill Point.

Cost: 125 Mana + 25 for each student or chaperone beyond the first.

I had planned to use this Skill to take myself to the nearest Settlement. Temporarily or permanently, I had not decided.

It had failed spectacularly, just two days prior. The System had informed me that it was not a self-only Skill. In retrospect, that should have been obvious. Because of that, I was as much of a prisoner as ever. I wasn't about to abduct a child to make my escape.

"Emergency override," the shield-bot's voice in my head grew very loud indeed. *"The hull has been breached and enemies are entering the ship."*

I tried to stay calm.

"Matriarch no help owed."

"True."

"Matriarch good."

"Saving me was good."

"Matriarch good," he insisted. The System let me know that the way his mandible quivered meant he was not as certain as he sounded.

"The attackers are human," Pavise told me, and the lesson became a lot less rhetorical.

"This ship is blocking the only real way to the best dungeon in the area," I said. "Look here."

I activated the first active Skill I had gained from the System—Show and Tell. Images from my trip to what was now the dungeon appeared in the air before the children. Some pictures were of the little town between the two lakes. Others were of the late winter austerity that would bloom into lush, dense greenery later in the year. There were log cabin style buildings, a large campfire, and a boathouse.

The image I expanded though was of the single-lane floating bridge. It crossed the deep marsh from the tiny, overgrown dirt road on one side to the equally overgrown dirt driveway that wound through the hardwoods and pines to the camp on the other. Their train-car-shaped spaceship was settled directly atop the rickety boards that were just wide enough to accommodate a single car tire on each side. The bridge had splintered around the ship and submerged when it couldn't take the weight.

"This is the one path to the dungeon that wasn't nearly impassable even before the world went crazy. Blocking that path was clearly the Matriarch's plan. She wanted the dungeon for her people, and she took it. It didn't matter to her that someone had owned this place before the System came. It didn't stop her that taking the dungeon would cost the humans in the area progress and wealth that they would need to survive this new reality. But the Voloid hunters also keep the dungeon monsters from growing and escaping. That helps keep the human settlement safe. The Voloids are good and bad."

"Show me what's happening," I instructed my defender. I held up my hand to get Aul to stop. He didn't.

"Humans good and bad," he said. Even his tone said he was angry. That was a trait he had learned from me.

"Yes," I said. "Wait."

He didn't. "Caleb good and bad." He glared at me.

Then the connection finished, and I was seeing through the central camera that passed for the robot's eye. The five attackers were already engaged with the majority of the Voloid warriors in the loading bay. The Matriarch was nowhere to be seen.

One of the attackers was an androgynous, short-haired Native American I labeled in my head as Slytherin, due to their snarl, spellcasting, and green robes. My second passive, Relatable, told me that their special interests included fantasy fiction, roleplaying games, and architecture. They tossed out glowing purple dust while they chanted.

Those Voloids hit by the spell dropped their spears and blasters. They stood in apathy while a swarm of blade-legged, steel spiders shredded them like parmesan cheese.

I gagged but couldn't look away.

The one controlling the spiders was a young white woman. She was dressed in bulky, black leather armor with various tech components. Her chin-length blond hair was shaved on one side, where she had a much better neurological implant than mine. I knew that because it was the custom Dylo-Tek device I'd have bought if I had been able to scrounge together enough Credits.

Her special interests included anarchy, cybertech, and kitten videos. Because of her swarm, and the spikes and blades along her armor, in my mind I labeled her as Edgelord.

The third, clearly the leader, was a rugged black man with skin even darker than mine. He had a shaved head, broad shoulders, and muscles a pro wrestler would've killed for. Plates and cybernetics that would look at home in a high-tech, dystopian hellscape covered him here and there.

He'd have been irresistible before the apocalypse. Now, he was terrifying.

His right leg had been replaced by a skinless prosthetic with flashing red lights. He drove a spike that extended down from the prosthetic into the chest of one of the dying Voloids, and it pulsed. His damaged cybernetic armor repaired itself as it did so.

His special interests included human independence, war, and high finance. I dubbed him Insurgent.

The last two, or one with a duplication power, looked like soldiers in full dress uniforms. Both had machine guns with under barrel launchers. They were too far away for my power to evaluate their interests. I dubbed them the Twins.

I could speak through my droid. I could have warned the humans about the extreme danger the Matriarch's absence posed. I'd learned about her disappearing act the day she'd saved my life and made me her prisoner.

The humans' faces were filled with rage. Their eyes were haunted by events I couldn't fathom. They were clearly not good people. They were also clearly the product of whatever had happened to them in this new world.

They might have been there to rescue me.

They might have been there to kill us all.

They might hurt the children.

My hesitation cost two of the humans their lives and it may have saved us all.

The Matriarch appeared from out of stealth, stabbing one of the Twins through the head with her two-handed spear and shooting the other with both of her blasters at point blank range. They dropped dead where they stood. Blood sizzled when the blasters hit the bodies. I was glad that my droid couldn't pass on any smells.

The Matriarch shrieked and clicked in rage, activating some sort of taunt Skill that pulled all of their attention to her. She must have activated some other last-ditch ability also because the gray of all of the Voloids paled. Even the ones in the classroom with me withered, for lack of a better word. The Matriarch and her spear doubled in size. Her blasters, too small for her new hands, clattered to the floor.

I thought about ordering my droid to shield her. She was the only thing that stood between me and potential rescuers. Or potential murderers. By the time I had processed the fact that they didn't look like saviors and did look like killers and it was better to err on the side of caution, it was already too late.

As powerful as she looked, as enhanced as she was, even the Matriarch's armor was cracking when faced with Edgelord's swarm and Insurgent's heavy blaster. Her spear was doing severe damage, but it was clearly not enough. And they were too close to us now for a shield wall to matter.

"You're right," I said to my students. "I am good and bad. I try to be good. Sometimes it can feel impossible to tell the difference." My voice sounded to my ears every bit as haunted as the faces of the attackers.

Aul must have noticed the change. Clever as he was, how could he not? "Aul…" He paused for a long moment. "Will try to be good when Aul is Matriarch." Aul shuddered and the paling worsened. "If Aul lives to be Matriarch."

That blew my mind two ways. *Well shoot*, I corrected my inner monologue, *she*.

"Good," I told her, pride and terror bringing tears to my eyes in equal measure.

"Caleb Show and Tell fight," Aul said.

She was right, I could show them exactly what I was seeing and hearing. It didn't even cost much Mana. But so could the Matriarch, and she'd cut them off.

"No," I said.

"Caleb show," Aul insisted, crossing her arms.

"You don't want to see this."

She uncrossed her arms.

I had never invested a better point than in my Ring of Truth Skill. Then and there, I dropped the three points I had been hoarding into it.

And that's when I remembered Class Trip. It had failed before, when I'd tried to use it to escape. But I wasn't alone now. And any ethical questions about taking the children with me were long since irrelevant. Best yet, even the basic version could get us all out of there. Only distance increased with a higher Skill Level.

I activated the Skill.

Skill attempt failed. Parental permission required.

Permission slips! Innocent children were going to be murdered because their slaughtered parents couldn't give me permission slips!

"Fucking System," I said out loud, though I had not intended to do so.

"The ship's systems have sealed and hidden the doors. Given the Matriarch's level, it is likely that these beings have Advanced Classes, but even they should not be able to bypass the hologram."

Hope for the safety of the children surged in me as hope for the survival of the Matriarch died screaming right along with her. Unable to help and equally unable to look away, I watched as Insurgent claimed E'Kklon Vekk's spear. A device on Edgelord's wrist beeped.

"I am sorry. It seems that I calculated correctly that the attackers would be unable to penetrate the holographic defenses. I failed to consider that the tech-Classed cyborg could have a passive that would allow her to detect our communication channel and follow it back to its source. Again. I am sorry."

Sorry. He was sorry. This was all my fault. *No. You have to hold yourself together for the children. This isn't over yet.*

Unable to spot the door to my classroom, Edgelord was using another device to melt through the wall as if by means of a lightsaber.

For the first time, I activated one of my level 30 Skills.

Administrative Authority (Level 1)
Classroom only.
+10 Charisma. + 5 per Skill Point.
Cost: 25 Mana per minute.

"Try not to make any sudden movements. Keep all of your hands where they can see them."

I wanted so desperately to lie and say, "They're not going to hurt you" or "I'll protect you." But my students weren't stupid, I wasn't a good liar, and my habit was to tell them the truth.

"I think they'll kill you if you give them any excuse," was the best I could manage, since my passive power didn't require me to include that I thought they'd probably kill all of us regardless, especially them.

I watched through the eyes of Pavise as the humans readied their assorted weapons.

"*Prepare to defend*," I commanded my droid.

"*It is not my job to defend the children*," he insisted.

"*No, it isn't. It's one of mine. Which is why you'd better be ready or be prepared to violate your contract.*"

"*For your safety, I must insist—*"

But whatever he was going to say came too late. As the area of the wall came down with a thud, the attackers opened fire blindly into our room and I dove between the attackers and the children.

A powerful blue wall of energy blocked and deflected the attacks, slightly inconveniencing but not particularly harming the high-level humans. What was left of the barrier flickered and sputtered, barely a trace of its power remaining.

I re-activated Administrative Authority and shouted, "Stop." Channeling my inner Chaucer from *A Knight's Tale*, I said, "Listen to me."

I was no Paul Bettany, but I prayed that the barrier, their surprise at seeing a human, and my Skill would buy me their attention at least long enough to give me a chance.

"You are not in any danger here. You've already won." When I saw the effects of shock and my power fading from their faces, I tried one last appeal. "You are about to murder innocent children."

Edgelord frowned. The Slytherin wannabe looked as if they had consumed spoiled milk.

Insurgent flinched as if he had been struck. "Wait," he commanded the others.

Edgelord's hand was still pointed toward me, and the spiders advanced again.

"I said wait, God damn it," Insurgent shouted. The force of whatever Skill he had activated staggered me.

The spiders stopped.

Insurgent turned that power, that presence, that deadly killing intent toward me as he met my gaze fully. "Why should I listen to you, traitor? And why should I, scratch that, why *do* I believe a single fucking word you say?"

"It's a passive Skill," I told him. "I'm a Teacher. As long as I have never tried to deceive someone, they instinctively know that I'm not lying. It doesn't stop you from doing anything or make you do anything. It just means you know that you can trust me."

"Why would I trust a traitor? You're helping these aliens, these invaders."

"The Matriarch you killed in the other room. She saved my life during the fall. I've been here ever since. I would have died out there. They treated me well, but they would not take me to a human-run Safe Zone."

"You're telling me you were a prisoner? A slave?"

"It's complicated," I answered.

"It's Stock Market Syndrome. No. Stock something. I remember reading about that," Slytherin said. "It's on the tip of my tongue."

"Stockholm?" Edgelord asked.

"That's the one. You start liking or falling in love with your captors."

"You're saying it's not his fault?" Insurgent said.

They nodded reluctantly.

"Then he's not part of the quest," Edgelord said. "We just need to finish clearing out the aliens and we can take the ship."

"Quinn, you don't understand. The quest lists him," the leader said. "Unless there's another of these *things* left alive, the count is off. Why would the quest list you as a member of the crew?" He glared at me, his suspicion obviously returning.

"I'm their teacher." Because I knew he'd ask, I added, "When the Matriarch saved my life, she threw me in the room with them, and she must have seen my Class because she told me to teach. And so I did."

"Did you ever, even once, help them against humans or humanity in any way? And apparently, I'll know if you're lying to me, so don't bother."

"No," I said. I had considered it. I had been about to. But he didn't know that. And my Skill did not consider that deception.

He shut his eyes and sighed, then said to the others, "Then we failed the quest. We'll finish up here and head back to base with the loot from the aliens."

"But the ship," Edgelord, no, Quinn, whined.

"Is his to claim, according to the System. He's already been here for two years, and he's got a legitimate claim. We're not thieves."

"Speak for yourself," she snapped back. She turned to Slytherin. If she was hoping for support, she didn't get it.

Slytherin looked utterly exhausted. Hell, as a powerful caster, they probably had endurance stats much closer to mine than their companions'.

Insurgent glared at Edgelord until she lowered her eyes, probably because a Skill had forced her to. She didn't seem the type. "As long as we are grouped together, *we* are not thieves. *Is that clear?*"

"Yes, boss," she finally said, but there was fury in her eyes. If I didn't miss my guess, he'd pay for that, one way or the other.

He seemed to think so too. "You two can split my share of the loot, except for this spear. I'm keeping the spear."

"Fine. Let's kill these fuckers and get out of here." She seemed mollified, if only just.

"Not kill," I said, "murder."

The leader flinched again. "Why do you say that?" He let out a sigh that was louder and longer than the others. "And why is it true?"

"It doesn't have to be true," Edgelord replied. "He just has to believe it's true."

"Good point," the leader said. "Why do you *think* it's true? We're at war, after all."

"You might be right that you're at war and everything you've done is justified."

He nodded, and I thought that he appreciated the acknowledgment of his position. Maybe I could build on that.

"Even if this is a war though, killing these children would be murder. They haven't done anything wrong," I said.

"They're still invaders."

"No, they aren't."

He sighed again, which I realized was how he reacted to my passive Skill. "Why not?"

"Because invaders invade. It's a verb. These children were brought here, through no decision or choice of their own."

Insurgent stood there for a long moment, and I watched in his eyes as his sanity flicked back and forth as he considered and finally started to break, probably forever. He was clearly making the wrong decision. His hand moved toward his weapon as his hatred slowly broke what was left of his decency.

And I had no power, no Skill, no spell or ability, no more arguments that could stop the atrocity that was about to happen. I could put my body in the way, but I'd die for nothing. In his mind, I was certain, that would be my fault—not his. He'd even finish his quest.

Whenever I had a student who was going through something so horrible that they acted out in ways I couldn't understand, or when I had students I couldn't seem to reach, I always asked myself the question that the acronym on my necklace stood for.

What would Mr. Rogers do?

It had become such an ingrained habit that it happened now, without me even trying.

The man had inspired me to be a teacher. To be a better man. And his lessons had never let me down. That one question had always been enough to shift my viewpoint when I needed it the most.

This time though, for the first time, it failed me. It failed me because I was already doing what I believed Mr. Rogers would have done.

And evil was still evil.

And I, being the kind of man I was, shaped by the man he had been, was simply not strong enough to do a single damn thing about it.

I cried then. For the last of my innocence. For the children. For the world, and for the loss of this man's sanity and humanity.

I cried, and Insurgent noticed. He noticed my sympathy. My pity. He saw that some of it was meant for him. And he asked me a single word. "Why?"

"Do you remember Mr. Rogers?" I thought about activating my Show and Tell Skill to make an image of the man, but some instinct held me back. Maybe because the Skill belonged in this world, and Mr. Rogers belonged in the one we had lost.

He stood there quietly, hurting, grieving for that world, if his eyes could be believed. In the end, he didn't speak, only nodded.

"That's why," I answered softly.

A bit of the hardness came back to his face, and the haunted expression came with it.

"His world is gone," Quinn, the Edgelord, said.

"Gone forever," Slytherin added, but they said it mournfully, not wickedly.

"We can never go back," Insurgent finished.

"You're right," I told him.

He nodded, and there was a dangerous shift in his stance. His grip tightened on the Matriarch's spear.

"But that doesn't mean we can't go forward," I said, and even I didn't know for sure that I truly believed it until he sighed.

Something dark took his expression, something that rode upon a pale horse. And that darkness fought with the inner child Mr. Rogers had touched so long ago. This battle had nothing to do with me anymore, and everything to do with the remnants of his lost innocence.

The man who opened his eyes and met mine was still a monster, or someone capable of true monstrosity. But I would have said, and not lost my Skill by doing it, that he was not a man who would murder innocent children. His next words seemed to agree, but the bleeding edge of his tone sent chills of fear through my soul for the future of humanity.

"You have a spaceship," he said. "Get these aliens off my planet."

All I could do, all I dared to do, was nod.

He turned and walked away. Eventually, hesitantly, the other two followed him.

Quest alert: *You have been given a mandatory quest. Remove the children in your care from planet Earth and its surrounding area.*
Reward: 5,000 experience points and 50,000 Credits.
Additional reward: You will not be hunted down and exterminated by Commander Lee Greyson.
Time to failure: 1 week.

"Mr. Rogers good," Aul said. "Caleb good."

Relief for the children and fear for myself went to war inside me, but it was no real contest. My life as I had known it had ended two years prior. I had long since mourned it. Now, more than ever, it was clear to me that a Dungeon World was not a place for a man like me.

Is there any place in this universe for a man like me? I thought with a shudder.

I shook my head. It didn't matter. I might not have a place, but I had a job to do. It wasn't the job I had signed up for and it wasn't a job I was qualified for. But it didn't matter if I was the right person for the job. I was the *only* person for the job.

My one priority now had to be the children. I would see them to safety, or I would die trying. It's what Mr. Rogers would have done.

Chapter 2

[Name Redacted]

"Humanist, sir," my Offensive Coordinator called to me, "I'm so glad that I caught you." Bill's Nasal voice made my shoulders tense. The echoes of his footsteps reverberated down the bunker's concrete corridor as he rushed to catch up.

It's not his fault. I repeated it like a mantra. *He's as effective as he is annoying, so he's very effective. It would be bad to kill him. You need him. Take a breath.* He was only the last straw in an endless string of interruptions. *I'm supposed to be this iron-fisted dictator. How is it that I can't get five minutes alone to make the hard choice between two atrocities? Breathe. They are your people and they're following your orders. You'd kill them if they didn't, so you don't get to kill them if they do. That's only fair.*

"The presentation is about to begin," I said as I strode into the Command Center to spare the man's life.

My Elite Guardsmen, chosen for their loyalty rather than their brains, snapped to attention at their posts beside the door. Their newly upgraded armor, dark-blue Kevlar with deep-green titanium plates, looked high-tech and badass.

They gave me the HLF salute, slamming their fist to their hearts with a sharp nod.

I returned the gesture. I'd been so proud of that stupid salute early in the System, back when I could still get drunk. I was stuck with it now. Organizations, I had learned, had momentum. You fucked with that at your own risk.

It wasn't all bad. There was something electrifying about elite soldiers snapping to attention whenever I walked into a room.

"I have the report that you asked for, sir," Bill whined.

Finally. "Go on," I said as I continued toward my command post. Blue and green neon lights illuminated the sleek black tech. A touch screen table encircled the hovering seat. My chair moved to let me sit, then carried me into position.

"The attack was a complete success, sir." He followed me. "We doubled our estimated kill count, with only minor losses on our side. The ferret-faced fuckers are begging for mercy. They've offered to pay us tribute."

So, the Qwallonni were done for. *Good. They've been a pain in my ass for months.* But there was a hint of greed in the man's tone that made me doubt his motivations.

"With the fifty thousand Credits they're offering us, we can—"

Cold rage built in me as he spoke. His final words were cut off as I activated my new favorite Class Skill. It was from my Subversive Captivator Hidden Class, which anyone who inspected me saw as Compelling Leader.

***Humiliating Subjugation** (Level 4)*

Mentally restrains a single target in the manner of your choice. They are crippled with pain, unable to move, or unable to initiate any Active Skills. Direct damage caused by this Skill is mental, and the effects last only as long as the Skill does. Resisted by Willpower.

Duration: Time channeled + 1 second per 10 seconds restrained. Channeled.

Cost: 50 Mana + 25 per 10 seconds.

I forced him to his knees, head thrown back, hands and arms bound behind him. All eyes turned toward Bill when I allowed him to cry out in agony.

"The Human Liberation Front," I declared, "is *not* for sale."

Gasps from those watching washed over us, followed by some awkward clapping and mumbled comments. The applause would have been fine if it had caught on. The talking, however, was unacceptable. Disrespectful.

My glare swept the room, silencing them all.

"But, sir," Bill barely managed to garble through a half-strangled neck, "the aliens—"

"Are desperate. Good. Return with double your original force. Kill them all. Loot them if you think we need more Credits. Then capture and sell the Settlement. Or do I need to find someone with more conviction?"

"No, sir. I mean yes, sir. I'll take care of it."

"Watch closely and remember what's at stake." I let him collapse to the concrete floor. "And Bill?" I didn't wait for a reply. "Make me doubt your dedication again, and you'll wish I'd finished what I started here today."

He nodded rapidly.

An oversized image appeared on the wall of screens. I forced myself to watch, fist clenched and jaw tightened, as human children were shoved into a jail cell in Pittsburgh. A haunted blond toddler begged for his mother. He could have been a model. The boy's name had been Timmy, if the System could be believed. He'd become the face of the Human Liberation Front, in those early days.

The haunting sounds of a mournful dirge, bagpipes backed by cello, washed over us.

After two years of this daily demonstration, my skin did not flush anymore. My muscles didn't tremble in rage. My breathing barely quickened. I had only the slightest urge to look away, though I knew what would come next.

Humans—men, women, and children—were hung from meat hooks. Red blood dripped into massive iron vats below. The names of the victims, chosen by focus group to save Credits, scrolled along the bottom of the screen.

An alien with wicked horns and purple-and-brown skin butchered them. It paused between victims only long enough to lick the gore from its curved blade. Images like these had made recruiting easy early on. Fury had filled my heart and empowered my speeches, compelling zealous devotion from the masses.

I'd never felt more alive.

THIS IS WHY WE RESIST! A banner blazed with glowing red letters.

"This is why we resist!" a chorus of voices, mine included, echoed in return.

More images followed. An underaged girl with pits where her eyes should be begged for food in a market square. Glorified space orcs knocked her to the ground without a second glance as they marched by.

A trio of elven wannabees, draped in fine silks, smiled and laughed over a bountiful feast. Humans, crawling on their hands and knees, scrubbed the floors beneath them. Their rags were cleaner than their clothes.

"EARTH IS FOR HUMANS!" The banner, and then the crowd, intoned.

The picture faded to the blue-green orb, floating alone in space.

Three human teens, rail-thin and chained, shoveled coal into a furnace for a slug-like alien overseer. The moment he turned his back, they beat him to death with their shovels.

"WE RESIST!"

A mosaic of scenes followed. Humans, subjugated by aliens, rose up against their oppressors. Some were killed. Some did the killing.

"YOU ARE THE RESISTANCE!"

My favorite part followed, though even this had lost its luster for me. I stood alone, defiant, between a family of four and an ogre with an ax and a mohawk. It mocked me viciously until I hurled a tank at its head. After that, it mostly screamed.

"WE ARE THE RESISTANCE!"

The images flickered and my rage returned. I slammed my fist into the marble table, cracking it.

Another hack. Damn it. The propaganda attacks had been happening more and more, and no counterintelligence Skill or interrogation had been enough to stop them.

My people were able to shut down the feed in seconds, but it was already too late. The screens zoomed in on the beggar who'd been shoved by the Hakarta. It revealed the setup we had cut from the scene, where she'd stumbled into one and swiped a pouch from his belt. At the same time, other screens showed images of aliens and humans working together. They slaughtered Krym'parke, the aliens that liked to butcher and devour children. They built storefronts and battled monsters shoulder to shoulder.

A word appeared in bright blue letters.

"COMMUNITY!"

These displays were changing hearts and minds. I could feel it. I was losing control of the narrative. It made me want to scream. But the Humanist, I reminded myself, could not be allowed such luxuries.

"I'm sorry, sir," Harold said. My trusted advisor groveled on his knees. His ridiculous handlebar mustache dragged on the ground as he continued in a hushed but urgent tone, "We've lost another outpost."

"When?" It was more a growl than a question.

"They went dark as the images changed. It could not have been a coincidence. We'll scour the base for resources and clues, but…"

"Don't bother. You know damn well they're gone."

That was the fifth abandoned base in the last three months. We hadn't found a single clue at any of the others. Everything valuable was gone. Only the loyal dead remained. Even attempting to find the traitors would consume resources we simply could not spare.

"I've failed you, sir. I don't deserve to live."

Is Abjectly Apologizing a Class Skill or just his nature? I wanted to roll my eyes, but the Humanist wouldn't do that.

Janice, the HLF General, lit another of her vile-smelling cigarettes. The smoke was the same color as the short, curly hair it floated around. "We have too few loyal humans as it is." Her hard, dark gray eyes focused on his pathetic display, a hint of regret in her tone as she said, "We can't spare you."

I raised an eyebrow.

"Besides," the General continued, reluctantly, "none of this is your fault, Harold. It's the System and the aliens that caused this."

Amen to that.

"It's the humans, General," the Advisor answered, reluctantly finding his feet. "The traitors." He spat. "So many have conspired with our oppressors. Some of our strongest defenders have abandoned Earth entirely." The man tugged on his mustache with both hands.

I found his nervous tic annoying but schooled my expression. The Humanist, the man I'd chosen to become when the System arrived, was above such things. "No excuses. Excuses are failure's bitch."

"Yes, sir," the General said, nodding as if I'd given them wise counsel.

Harold's eyes shimmered with barely restrained tears.

That mantra, as semi-sensical as my System-enhanced mind now realized it was, had skyrocketed me to internet superstardom a year before the old world's end. I still used it. The magic of such a phrase was that it could mean anything I needed it to. Right now, it meant that no price was too high to secure a future for humanity, free from alien overlords.

A stunning beauty with cinnamon hair and eyes sidled up to me and tried to feed me a purple grape from a literal silver platter. Her eyes were filled with lust.

It aggravated my imposter syndrome. Even paying to have my own name torn from my mind hadn't been enough to stop it. You didn't get over a lifetime of people, even your own mother, telling you how handsome you'd be *"If only you weren't so sick"* overnight. Or over two years, for that matter. Apparently even Advanced Classers couldn't escape the "fake it till you make it" grind.

I gently brushed away her hand. She wanted me. They all did. But I would *never* sink so low as to use mind control, passive or otherwise, to get into somebody's pants.

She flinched, trembled, and cried at my implied rejection.

Charisma is a double-edged sword. It was one thing to make strong men obey me. It was another thing entirely to make a lovely lady cry. I forced myself to smile and dismissed her with a quick salute.

She fled.

Everyone ignored the scene, and no one said a word. At least there were some perks to being the man in charge.

"Solutions?" I finally asked my counselors.

I could tell they wanted to speak, to apologize, to make false promises. They didn't, to their credit. Both continued saying nothing, very loudly. The General put out her cigarette.

"Expect new orders by the end of the day," I told them. "I'll take it from here. You're all dismissed."

Everyone but my Elite Guardsmen left the room with respectable efficiency.

"All of you."

"Sir—" The Captain, Bethany, said, but I cut her off. Her armor looked even better with the white splash of command, but I wasn't in a mood to appreciate it.

"Out!"

She saluted, and they left without another word.

I pressed a button that triggered our most advanced privacy protections. Then I removed two manilla envelopes from my Quantum Safe. They were marked top secret in bold red letters.

My hands trembled as I tried to open the first envelope.

If only the aliens didn't have such a long head start.

No excuses.

It was time to pivot.

Never surrender. Always pivot.

The saying held up, even with my higher Intelligence and Perception. That shit was solid gold.

I reviewed the files. My Black Ops Chief, Lucas Norberg, was trying to make up for not being able to find the traitors. He'd outdone himself. Not only were the two plans fully researched, but he'd already laid the groundwork. The packets were labeled Project Krampas and The R.A.H. Initiative.

I hated them both.

Project Krampas was dead in the water. The Krym'parke were perfect villains, but there were too few to man a full invasion.

Besides, even the aliens had some standards. They'd oppose the butchers and ruin everything. I was trying to unite humanity against a single, existential threat, not give them another reason to ally with the invaders.

I activated the self-destruct device on the folder and it burst into black flames. Lucas had thought of everything—destroying the folder would trigger the execution of the aliens we'd "recruited" for the plan.

That also meant that unless I ordered his team to stop it, the R.A.H. Initiative was now a go. He'd even left me plausible deniability. *Is he gunning for the General's job as my right hand?* If so, I'd have to disappoint him. The General had changed my diapers. She'd been my mother's oldest friend and I trusted her with my life. Nothing he could do would top that.

I'd have to reward him some other way. He deserved it for helping me crack this stubborn nut of a problem. Humanity's failure, I now realized, had been caused by cultural diversity. That was ironic because it was also one of our greatest strengths. But many of us had taken the virtue too far, looking for good individuals among bad invaders. Even my brother, whose name I'd also purged, had fallen victim to this insanity.

I grimaced. Sometimes, executing traitors was more bitter than sweet. Hard times call for hard choices though, and the Humanist was not the kind of man to make exceptions.

Robert A. Heinlein, the brilliant author, had been inspired when he wrote *Starship Troopers*. He'd unified humanity against an inhuman enemy with a distant hive mind. It had taken months, but my operatives had found the perfect oppressor in the form of the humanoid bug monsters called Voloids.

My advisers assured me that Voloids had no individual free will, dominated as they were by their Queen. Voloids were famously relentless. Once antagonized, they would not stop until humanity was united or destroyed. But killing her people wouldn't get the job done. She'd just consider that the price of doing business on a Dungeon World.

To really antagonize the Queen, we had to dissect the Voloids, their ships, and their tech. We needed to gather as many of their secrets as we could, then sell the information to anyone and everyone that was willing to pay, in perpetuity. Do that, and she'd stop at nothing to kill us.

This was my Black Ops Chief's magnum opus. He knew how the System worked. He knew anything said out loud or recorded would be up for sale by the System. So he wrote the following passage with no explanation at all, trusting me to understand.

The vote has been tallied. It is unanimous. All remaining human forces have agreed. The Voloids must be destroyed. Kill them to the last. Take their ship. Uncover all of their secrets and sell them to anyone willing to pay. Divide the funds evenly between all remaining human Settlements and governments. That's step one. Let the others do our work for us and soften them up. Details of the next steps are need to know and we don't need them now.

He was brilliant. I'd given him my broad vision and parameters and asked him for a path forward. He'd given me two. I was confident I'd chosen the right one. He'd even gift-wrapped the presented solution by making it a *fait accompli*, an already accomplished fact. One of my best teams had been sent to kill the aliens and claim the ship. Once that was done, they'd get their orders and move on to phase two—antagonize the alien Queen. All I had to do was nothing.

Lucas would never be my right hand, but I had two hands, didn't I? We'd have to handle the traitors first, and it would need some pomp and circumstance, but the promotion was now his without question.

I'd made my choice.

Earth will be the crucible to temper humanity. The bugs will be the fire.

As for the monsters and traitors, they're fuel, sacrifices to the System, nothing but XP.

If the System favors ruthlessness, then to hell with half measures. The weak and cowardly might call the System an apocalypse, but I see now that it's a gift. A rare and precious opportunity. No wonder the aliens had rushed to try to steal it from us.

Fuck that.

Earth is ours.

Mine.

My manic, high-pitched laugh was so loud and uncontrolled that it startled me.

The Humanist recognized the outburst for what it truly was—the sound of a real man finally set free.

His laughter was confident, deep, and resonant. He laughed and laughed.

And I laughed with him.

Chapter 3

Commander Lee Greyson

I wrapped the corpses in green tarps. The kind we used to use for gathering leaves. I knotted the cords and tossed them both into the trunk.

They deserved better.

Greg and George had been good men. They'd fought bravely and followed orders. None of us had been able to prove they were cheats at cards. Now, we'd never catch them.

I wanted to honor them the way we used to. With flowers, memories, and tears. The Teacher had made me nostalgic. But those times were long gone. I'd have to honor them the other way. With the blood of dead invaders.

Dead adults who'd chosen to invade.

I was pushing my luck by bringing the bodies back. The Human Liberation Front was a lot of things. Sentimental wasn't one of them. Our policy was clear. *The dead are dead. This world is for the living. We can mourn them when the Earth is free.*

Fuck that. I'd put them in the ground with their sister. Back behind the base. It's what they would have wanted. *Least that I can do.*

"Nancy, Kyle, Joseph, Declan, Sonja," I said under my breath. People the System had taken from me. Family and coworkers. Friends. My men.

The list gets longer every week.

I used it like a whetstone to sharpen my purpose.

A shiver on my neck. Quinn's eyes were laser-focused there. Piercing blue. Her looks could kill, if she set her spiders loose. I loved my Class—it had its uses and it served me well—but I had no illusions. Quinn was lethal, and she had a Prestige Class, Kaal Doxian Cutter. She could end me, end us both if Gerri took my side. And I'd just pissed her right the fuck off.

Smart.

To hell with it. She'd kill me or she wouldn't. I wasn't about to change my mind.

The weapons we'd looted got stored in my Arsenal. Everything else got packed into the trunk. No click when I closed it. No thud. It whirred and it hissed. Fucking Earl and his steampunk fetish.

Strange or not, I loved my ride, an open-faced ATV. The Geek Machinist had made it for me. Custom. A Victorian body with oversized tires. A steampunk engine. Gears, cogs, brass, and copper. It sounded ridiculous, but it looked amazing. I trailed the back of my hand along the seat. Red velvet with brass buttons. Expert craftsmanship.

Not everything has gone to hell.

Earl swore his way was more efficient. Bullshit. But the car was comfortable, durable, and fast. I couldn't ask for more.

My cybernetics had been installed before he joined us. Shame. *I look like a* Star Trek *villain.* Then again, style wasn't everything. *At least I look badass. Intimidating. Gears and a steam whistle? Not just no. Hell no.*

I climbed into the driver's seat. Even now, my weight felt wrong. There was too much metal. Uneven. My right leg, the Lifetap Inc. Prosthetic, was the worst. I couldn't feel it like my other implants. But the Perk was the most powerful thing I owned. A growth item.

I was stuck with it. I hated it. And I was grateful.

The others followed suit and hopped in. Quinn and Gerri in the back. Randy was up front with me. The Tollefsen boy was a Shotgunner. Basic Class. He hadn't made the obvious joke, and it hung between us all like an overripe apple.

"How'd it…" he started to ask, Minnesota accent thicker than usual. He was excited. Then he saw my expression and his hazel eyes widened. Must've remembered the dead. He shut his damn mouth.

Good kid.

Randy understood loss more than most. His parents and older brother had died early on. He'd stepped up to raise his sister. Managed to keep her alive for a year and a half on his own. Lost her to a hard winter right before we moved here. Those two weeks haunted him.

Gears clicked and ticked. The steam engine hissed between whistles as we drove.

We'd taken a lot for granted before the System came. We used to joke that road construction and winter were Minnesota's only seasons. Two years later, the roads were shit. Plants and potholes everywhere. Almost made me miss the orange cones. The gravel trails were awful. The small, paved roads were worse.

Thus, oversized tires. It was still a bumpy ride.

***

Glowing red slits and twisted shapes slunk between the maple, spruce, and pine. They had us surrounded. Outnumbered.

We had them outclassed. Out Leveled.

They made the smart choice and we moved on.

"Turn right," Randy said, pointing at the intersection.

The sign, somehow still intact, read County Highway 4. I turned, then glanced in the mirror again. My jaw clenched.

Quinn was glaring at me. "There's still time to do the right thing, Lee," the blonde said. "It's not too late."

"It's Commander," I answered, "and it's done."

"We don't even have to kill them. We can drag them out of the ship and fly it home. Hell, you can recruit the Teacher if you like him so much. He should be helping his own kind anyway. But the mission, *Commander*," she said in a tone just short of insubordination, "has to come first."

I stopped the car. Teeth clenched hard enough to grind, I pulled a lever and spun my seat around. I glared back. "Quinn, the mission's over. It's done. Let it go."

"The mission," she snapped, "was the ship. You know that it was."

I did. I also knew that it was wrong. The mission. That was rich. It was supposed to be about freeing Earth. Killing invaders. Somewhere along the line, it had changed. Now, we prioritized softer targets. Richer ones. It upset old sensibilities in me.

Strategically, it was sound. But I didn't have to like it.

I reminded myself of the videos. The ones that played back at base. Murder, enslavement, torture… worse.

"Commander!" Quinn stomped to get my attention. Her silvery spiders twitched. Clattered. It set my nerves on edge.

"Enough!" I motioned toward the spiders. "Knock that shit off. Calm down, you cr—" I cut myself off. Too little. Too late.

She flinched and pulled away. Eyes wide and pupils dilated. Her spiders writhed on her black leathers. She seemed as shocked as me by what I'd almost said.

Concerning.

Her fury cooled as she took a long, deep breath.

"I'm sorry," I said. And I was. She didn't talk about it, even to me, but I'd seen Quinn's file. She'd had it bad. Worse than most. The Cutter had been through hell, early on when the System came. She'd survived the pain.

The torture. The worse. She had a right to be traumatized. Didn't need me stirring things up.

Her expression softened. "Why? Why aren't we taking the ship?"

"I told you why," I lied.

"I know what you said. I want to know the truth."

I considered coming clean. She seemed to sense that. Gave me time.

I didn't want to steal from a human, but I'd done far worse for far less. We both knew it.

Something about the Teacher had reached me. Made me want to be a better man. But out of sight, away from his Charisma and his earnestness, frankly I still might have changed my mind.

But those kids would die without that ship. No question.

Too many kids are dead already.

My kids. I loved them more than life itself. I still do.

I miss them. I miss them every single day.

My fingers found the bracelets. They were all that I had left of Kyle and Joe. My boys. My sweet boys. Too good for this world. They'd died with their mom that first day.

Grown men don't cry.

I'd been stuck at work and fighting aliens. Gaining Levels.

Nancy killed two of the assholes before the end. Made me proud. But there'd been seven.

I'd found them. It took three months.

I'd made them suffer. It took four months.

They'd made me suffer more.

"Why?" Quinn had asked me.

Because I'd have wanted somebody to spare my boys. I'd have given anything. It was that simple.

I couldn't tell Quinn that. *You can't reason with a fanatic.*

The Teacher managed it with you.

Fucking Teacher. Mr. Rogers. And he meant it. So damn sincere. Big kind eyes. An untucked dress shirt with a goofy green vest. A nerd time capsule.

A good man. Probably the last.

If he couldn't convince Quinn, what chance do I have?

"Just let it go," I begged her. It made me look weak to a predator like her. *Stupid. Downright suicidal.* I couldn't make myself care.

My pleas touched her. I didn't know why. I didn't know how. But I saw it in her eyes. She would have let it go.

"We did the right thing," Gerri said. Their tone was harsh. An accusation.

Damn it. Worst timing ever.

They'd screwed up now. Quinn deserved respect. Not the social nicety kind. The kind you give a gun. Or a cobra.

"You don't get a vote," Quinn snapped, turning to glare at Gerri. Better them than me. But I wished they'd seen her eyes. I wished they'd held their tongue. Too late now. The moment was gone. "You're not even one of us. Who gives a damn what you think?"

The Shotgunner tensed. Randy was new, so he assumed it was because of the argument. He kept his attention on us. But I'd been doing this a while now. It was never the argument. Never the distraction. It was always a life or death threat. Not true, of course. Not even close. But you assumed that it was true anyway, or you died. It was that simple.

I cursed myself and I activated a Skill I should have had running as a matter of course.

Good Luck (Level 5)

+5 (+1 per level) to Perception, Agility, and Luck to selected targets.

Max targets 4 + 1 per Skill Point. Must be grouped.
Cost: 40 Mana + 10 Mana per target past 4.

The others were still fighting. I'd been ignoring them. There was shouting now.

"Quiet," I said, trying to concentrate.

"You don't scare me," Gerri said.

"I should," Quinn answered. She was right.

"Drama queen." Gerri snapped back, "Shut your mouth, you crazy cu—"

"That's enough, Gerri," I said, cutting them off before they could join me on Quinn's hit list.

From the look on Quinn's face, I'd been too slow.

My day just gets better and better.

A pink-and-white lady slipper caught my attention in the distance. *Nancy would have swooned over it.* A horned bird landed beside it, pecked the dirt. Probably hunting for worms. The flower opened a fanged maw and swallowed the creature whole.

Why had that flower drawn my attention? I focused. My ocular cybernetics paid off. It overlaid my vision of the grass-covered hill with an odd heat signature.

"Quiet!" This time a command.

Even after the System came, some skills were just skills. Not Class Skills. This was one of mine. I'd always been able to make people listen. My Charisma jacked that up to eleven.

They shut up. I felt them tense. They'd been doing this a long time. Everyone but Randy. And he'd been trained by me. We'd all be ready.

The hills trembled, cracked, and lifted with a groan. Twin monstrous forms rose. Gargantuan wood-ticks with thick tentacles and grass-covered shells. Ambush predators.

My gut told me they were a threat. A real one. Who the hell knew if that was perception, luck, or experience. Maybe paranoia. Either way, I felt certain. We'd probably win, but Randy would die. No time to Inspect the monster. No time to debate.

I hit the gas. Shattered a glass cover. Slammed a red button. Gears turned. Steam exploded. A whistle like a scream from hell. The car shot between the monsters like a bullet.

Quinn mumbled words and pressed her hands on the seat. Another boost. Faster. Easier to steer. *Nice trick*. Didn't know it worked on cars.

Then we were past them. Through the worst of it. My eyes flicked to Randy, then to the monsters in the back mirror. We weren't out of the woods yet. I was still babysitting.

The monsters' massive tentacles were writhing. Lifting entire trees. Hauling them back to hurl them.

I braced myself. *Wait.* "What the hell?"

Everyone was making similar noises. Nothing important. I shut them out.

The monsters hadn't thrown the trees. Reminded me of an asshole pretending to throw a tennis ball for a dog. Tricking them. Why?

"Oh shit!" Gerri and I said in unison.

The other two said, "Fuck!"

Hundreds of wood-ticks the size of hummingbirds were flying through the air like arrows.

Fucking Apocalypse.

I kept driving, dodging potholes where I could. My heart and breaths were quick but steady. My mind sharpened. Focused. Everything around me seemed to slow. It was hard to steer as the ticks slammed into me. Into the car. Physics was still physics. Mostly. I almost missed a turn. Nearly drove us off the road and flipped the ATV. *Don't overcorrect. Trust the car.* It was like driving on the ice in Minnesota. I'd dealt with worse.

We barely made the turn. I felt as though reality cheated for me. *Odd.* Was that from Quinn's Skill? My Agility? Good Luck? All of the above?

No way to know. Couldn't be bothered to care. Whatever had happened, had happened.

The others were fighting the monsters, but I couldn't. Not at these speeds. Quinn sliced apart ticks with curved short swords and spider-bots. Gerri burned them with glowing green acid. I flinched as Randy's shotgun blasted beside me. The burnt matches smell was strong, even at these speeds.

Randy was on his knees, firing behind us. Brave and stupid. A quick bad turn would toss him from the car. Then I saw his Health bar was dropping fast. Two ticks had latched onto his neck and face. I turned to look at him. Nearly made me miss another turn. The bugs were the size of barn owls now and were growing every second as they sucked him dry.

His already pale skin was looking ghostly white. Pallid.

He shot one with a handgun. Good call. It burst like an overfilled water balloon.

"Good shot, kid," I said as red splattered him, the ATV, and me. *Gonna be a bitch getting that out of the velvet. When did I get used to this? Probably Pittsburgh.*

I wiped my face and glanced at Randy. He was shaking. Pale. Health bar almost gray.

"Get that off him!" I said.

Randy's only response was a dry rattle.

I pulled out a syringe. Fumbled with it and the car. Nearly lost control. I couldn't help him. Gerri could. She used some kind of lotion, and green bloomed on his bar.

Quinn finished off the monster with a slash. Dug out the rest where it had sunk into his flesh. Gross but effective. Made me grateful for my armor and my Level.

***

Ten minutes later, we'd cleaned ourselves off the best we could without bothering to stop.

It didn't take long for Quinn and Gerri to restart their argument, taking sides on the issue of the ship.

Time to kill this noise. "No one gets a vote. This isn't a democracy. I make the calls. Made the call. You follow orders."

"One of us has to," Quinn said, half under her breath.

I let it go, though no one in the HLF liked orders less than her. I breathed in deeply. Forced my body to bend to my will. My muscles went from iron cords to thick clay. My heartbeat from bebop to ballad. Made me think of music.

Tense silence filled the car. I kept reaching for the radio and almost killed us twice. There was a small knob of wood where the volume dial should be. Self-destruct. Unlabeled. It was a serious design flaw. Not my fault. The madman called it a security feature. Fucking Earl.

The only good thing I could say about the steam whistles was that they justified me playing songs. Monsters would hear us for miles either way.

I pulled an iron-gray orb from my inventory. It had cost me a small fortune. The thing hovered, floating beside me in midair.

"Play," I said.

Samuel Coleridge-Taylor's "Deep River" started.

Brilliant. I love this song.

"Not this shit again," Quinn said and flopped her head against the seat.

"It does go with the car," Gerri chimed in.

Even Quinn nodded. Randy chuckled.

No accounting for taste. Bad taste. Thiers. Still, it broke some tension.

Gerri caught my eye and smiled.

"Been meaning to ask about your Basic Class," I said. "What's a—"

"No," they said and frowned. Thought I'd made an ass of myself, but they gestured at Quinn with their eyes. "It's a long story." They blushed. "Ask me another time."

I shrugged and kept on driving.

Peace and quiet were priceless. Randy understood. Or maybe he was scared of us. Probably both.

Either way, the next few hours were quiet. Peaceful. My mind zoned out, taking in the forest. There were so many shades of green. It was like meditation, but for men. It helped. The more I relaxed, the more my notices annoyed me, so I decided to check them out.

Level Up! You have reached Level 16 as a Tactical Strike Force Commander.
Stat Points automatically distributed. You have 4 Free Attribute Points to distribute.

This one had been a long time coming. It made me all the more eager to talk with Topher about my Class training choices and finally unlock my Tier 2 Advanced Skills.

Tonight, we'll crack open what's probably the last bottle of Macallan on Earth to celebrate. Maybe Toph and I can even toast the dead, after curfew for the rank and file.

I'd promised to let Randy drive if he didn't cause me any trouble. We'd been driving through a place called Squaw Lake. What was left of it. The double-digit population number on the sign had been replaced with a dark red zero. Might have been old blood. I'd never been superstitious, but that felt like an omen. It was harder to be skeptical after the System came. After magic, and monsters, and luck. I decided to let Randy take over closer to the base. Still too dangerous here.

Quinn's eyes were on me. Worried this time. There seemed to be genuine concern. "Cap's gonna kill us."

Not, "Cap's gonna kill you." It was a good sign.

She had a point. He'd seemed different lately. Not himself. The man was usually laid-back. Calm. This time, he'd seemed obsessed. Even scared. It begged the question, why? Then, for the first time, I'd failed my mission. I could pretend I hadn't, but I had. It was a cause for concern.

Concern but not worry, I reminded myself. *Worry has no value.* That saying wasn't from the HLF; it was from my old man. Only lesson he'd given me that didn't come with a bruise.

I set it aside.

What's the goal? Keep the kids alive and the HLF happy.

Break it down.

The HLF needs the Voloids dead. Done. They're dead. The ones that matter.

They need a ship. So I'll get them a ship. A better ship.

The Hakarta had ships. A hint of a smile. In the Human Liberation Front, you could get away with murder if you brought in a pile of dead orcs. The greater the crime, the bigger the pile. We called it the porkchop pardon.

Things could still go wrong, of course. I just assumed they would. Murphy's Law had never let me down. I doubted it would start in an apocalypse.

But I could use this truth against them. Bad things could happen to Hakarta too. I was often one of them. And it had been too long.

"I have a plan," I told Quinn.

"Let me guess," she said. "You plan to pivot?"

I nodded. "It's what the boss expects."

"The boss would expect you to follow orders in the first place," she countered.

"You haven't heard the best part yet."

"Oh?"

"The Hakarta."

Her grin was wicked and utterly lethal. "I like it. Turn the car."

"Excuse me!" Gerri said. They sounded concerned.

"Let 'em out if they're too scared," Quinn said.

"You plan to attack the *Hakarta?*" They gestured broadly, indicating every direction. "Those Hakarta."

"Yes," Quinn and I said at the same time. With the same ravenous tone.

"Just like old times." Quinn was petting her spiders. I didn't think she knew.

"You're both insane. You're down two men. You've done no prep work, and... and I... I didn't sign up for this."

"They're right," I said.

"Thank you."

"We need reinforcements. Intel. Ammo."

"How many weeks does a plan like this take?" That was Gerri.

"We'll hit them after dark tonight."

Quinn grinned like a toddler with a new toy.

"You're both insane," Gerri said.

"We could use your help. Our Skills synergize well. Frankly, I'd love to recruit you. The Monster Hunters too. They're quite the pair."

"The tribe is all or nothing," they said, "except for me. I've got my own plans. They don't involve staying here long term. And they certainly don't include pissing off bacon's revenge on steroids."

I tried not to laugh. Failed. "Shame," I said, and went back to listening to my music. It had gone through eras. Genres. It was playing "Round Here" by the Counting Crows. Felt more appropriate than ever.

Randy was healed but too shaken to drive. I took us down the final stretch.

Thicker woods. Overgrown trail. Camouflaged.

The force field and hidden turrets let us pass to the battered old building. Old school resort lodge.

Used to love a place like this. We'd vacationed there five years back. Nancy and I brought the kids down and stuffed ourselves with Lotsa Mozza cheese pizza. Beer. The kids had Cokes and those odd suckers made of sugar, crack, and chalk.

I could see them in my head. The boys had been intense. Playing video games and pool. Competitive. Like their dad. Nancy had really let herself unwind. She'd needed it. Her smile had made me melt. Always made me melt.

Bricked over now. A fake wall. I drove straight through it and into the hidden lift.

It lowered us down, down, down, into the concrete bunker.

Home sweet home.

Chapter 4

Caleb

My new title, Protector of Children, pointed at me like a finger in accusation.

Title Gained

For successfully protecting children from a direct assault by enemies whose average Levels exceed yours by more than 50, you have been awarded the Title "Protector of Children." All damage mitigation for others against higher level enemies +5%. Congratulations! For achieving your first title, you receive a bonus +5,000 XP.

It was nearly enough to gain a Level.

My paisley quilt was bunched around my hips as I sat hunched over on my bed. Its Spiderman shades of red and blue were always reassuring. I was grateful the children had wandered off to their part of the ship. It was hard for me to face them after everything that had happened. I could barely stand to face myself.

Betrayer of Voloids seemed a more fitting title.

I grabbed my sketch pad and a piece of charcoal from the clear plastic bin stuffed under my bed, brushed back my mop of unruly hair, and drew. I didn't have my Nana Dougherty's talent, but I'd never been more grateful for what little she'd been able to teach me. Having something to do with my hands while my emotions spun out of control helped. It was just one more debt I owed the woman who'd raised me, taught me right from wrong, and introduced me to my favorite shows.

I could use one of her hugs right about now.

It was complicated, I tried to tell myself. Nuanced. It had all happened so quickly.

But I could not escape the central truth. One moment of hesitation had cost dozens of lives, and a single command to Pavise could have changed the outcome.

The one-two punch of apathy dust and robot spiders had been brutal, but the lethargy had been short-lived. The Voloids had been recovering from it even as the spiders swarmed them.

Pavise's shield had stopped the attackers' onslaught for a mere moment, but it had stopped them. Early in the fight, when it mattered most, that could have been enough to tip the scales.

My fingers moved unconsciously, rough black lines swishing across the page.

Would my intervention have been enough?

Probably.

The Matriarch had been an incredible combatant. With their hive mind to guide them, the coordination of the hunters was unparalleled.

Still, the humans had been formidable. It might not have been enough.

I wanted to believe we'd all have died if I'd tried to stop them, but it didn't have the ring of truth to it. The Voloids would have lost hunters, but they would have won. I knew in the way you know things that you can never factually know.

I knew it in my heart.

Just as I knew I'd be tearing myself up right now about the dead humans if I'd intervened and the fight had gone the other way.

I smudged my fingers across the lines I'd drawn, shading tones of gray. I shook out a cramp in my right hand, irritated that my increased stats hadn't made that impossible. Then I picked up the pencil again.

No answer to a conflict like the one we'd lived through would ever satisfy me, except for peace. I knew that, at least, I could not have accomplished. I knew it in my heart and in my head.

Still, the defenders, the ones who were being attacked, were the ones who were dead. They were dead, at least in part, because I'd hesitated.

I would have to live with that.

E'Kklon Vekk could not. Her people could not.

Aul's mother could not.

I turned the page so that I didn't have to see the image I'd been sketching. A hexapod with a spear through her chest. My savior, and my prison warden, in equal measure.

The picture felt dishonest without the blue splash of Voloid blood.

I forced myself to draw a picture of the children, to focus on the one good thing I'd managed in this mess.

Protector of Children. What a joke.

Oh, it was true. Head true. But it wasn't heart true.

How was I supposed to protect the children? How was I supposed to protect myself?

That was the moment when the fear finally hit. When the apocalypse became personal. I'd been terrified of the attackers earlier. But I'd been afraid of that one group specifically. Now I was terrified, *should* be terrified, of the whole world.

And all of my most powerful protectors were gone.

That wasn't paranoia. This was the apocalypse. Even after all this time.

Everyone I'd ever known, whose charcoal sketches filled my cubby's walls, was gone. No, I forced myself to face the truth. Not gone. Dead. Every single one of them. The Voloids had checked for me.

My parents had been spared from the apocalypse by dying in a crash when I was seven. Nana, however, the woman who'd raised me right, had been alive when the System came. She'd been tough as nails. Minnesota-winter tough. But she hadn't been apocalypse tough apparently, at least not in her mid-eighties.

I never even got to say goodbye.

Hers was the first name I'd checked, and the first death I'd confirmed. Then my ex, Samantha. She'd been the closest thing I'd ever had to a real relationship, and we'd ended things as friends. I'd always care.

Then the children in my class. Billy, John, Mackenzie, Jacob. The list went on and on.

The other teachers. Even old friends.

Nine out of ten of them had died in the first month. The tenth had been named Cindy. The spirited brunette with a pixie cut had been gone within the year.

There's nothing to keep me here now.

"Okay," I told myself, and I could practically hear Nana's voice behind my words. "You've felt your feelings, now what are you going to do about them?"

She had been a caring, empathetic woman, but practical. I'd been allowed, even encouraged, to experience and confront my emotions. But she'd had a zero-tolerance policy for wallowing. I was bordering on that now, at the very least.

I shoved my feelings down, hard, and focused my attention on the problem at hand.

Now what?

The children. Aul. The asteroid-like ship's thrusters. Space. Scattered specks of infinity lost in a never-ending void. The System. Skills. Powers.

Alien life. Vast empires. More thoughts and images flickered through my mind, battling for my attention against the horror of red and blue blood, spider-bots, and slaughtered people.

My mind was as confused and overwhelmed as my emotions and time spent focusing on it only made it worse. I rubbed my temples hard and had to admit that I'd given the fight my best and it wasn't good enough.

Nana had been a model of self-sufficiency. She'd flourished in times harder than any I'd ever known, at least until today. She'd done her level best to pass those values on to me.

Apparently, she'd failed, because to *hell with self-sufficiency.*

My best friend is a supercomputer. It was long past time that I talked to Pavise.

"Thanks for humoring me, buddy," I sent through our link.

"If by humoring you, you mean not initiating an emergency override when you blocked our communication again, then you're welcome."

"Funny. Seriously, though. I need your help. I'm confused. And I feel like I'm entirely out of my depth."

"I'm sorry, sir, but if you feel that you are entirely out of your depth, then you are not confused. That is an altogether accurate assessment."

He had me there. *"Fair point. But we have to do something. Every minute we're thinking and talking is a minute closer to failure. No,"* I corrected myself, *"to death. Unless you don't think he'll really do it."*

"The System seems to believe that he will," Pavise countered.

I huffed out a sigh. *"Yeah, I thought so too."*

"The first thing to do is to align everything via a primary goal. May I assume that to be the successful completion of the Quest?"

"Yes and no. The primary goal is for all of us to survive and be safe. Everything else is gravy."

"And what would you say are our primary difficulties?"

"The way I see it, we've got three problems. We don't know how to start the ship, we don't know how to fly the ship, and we don't know where to take the ship."

"Your summary of our initial difficulties is accurate, if oversimplified. I would also add that we need to somehow survive until we have departed, as we travel, and once we arrive. Space is not empty, nor is it safe. If possible, sir, a trip to the nearest Shop could help with many of those issues."

"Damn. I hadn't thought of that. No. I was trying to not think about that. Then again, I'm not sure we can really do anything about those issues at this point."

"I understand that you are hesitant to initiate violence, however—"

I sent a mental nudge to cut him off. "That's not it. I mean, it's true that I hate violence, but that's not the issue. The issue is surviving to get to the Shop in the first place."

I felt his dissatisfaction through the link.

"If we weren't in a higher zone and so close to a dungeon…" he trailed off. Then he let out a long, loud sigh.

That was a bit melodramatic for someone who couldn't even breathe.

"We're putting the cart in front of the horse." I finally said.

"Well said, sir. We need to find out exactly where things stand."

I smiled, a bit reassured now that we had some semblance of a plan. "That's the spirit. It's possible we've been worried for nothing. This ship is technically mine now, to the system if not to me. It could be as simple as finding the controls and telling the ship what to do."

"It isn't."

"We can't know that for sure."

"We can and we do."

"How?"

"Complex calculations and overwhelming evidence."

"You're just being pessimistic, aren't you?"

He sighed again. *"I am an advanced artificial intelligence whose entire existence is tied to that of, if you will forgive my analogy, a loot-and-experience-filled meat-piñata. In such circumstances, pessimism and wisdom can be indistinguishable."*

I laughed. I couldn't help myself. *"We have to at least try and hope for the best. It's important to—"*

Wails and loud thudding cut me off.

My heart squeezed hard and tried to batter through my chest. I leapt up. The sketchbook and pencil rattled to the floor as I raced out the door.

They're back to finish the job. The Commander? The crazy woman with the spider bots? The whole team?

Any one of them would be enough.

I sent an alert to Pavise as I raced down the hall toward the noise. *"Oh, my lord. It's coming from the direction of the children."*

Protector of Children, the Title said. It certainly knew my heart, if not my capabilities.

"The ship's doors are sealed, sir," Pavise said through our link. *"It is possible that the hull has been breached, however. The young woman with the striking hairstyle and cybernetics seemed quite adept at such things."*

Even as connected as we were, it was hard to think about sending messages while I ran, so it came out odd. *"I'm not worried. About hair. Worried. Worried about presence. Murder."* My body slammed into a wall as I stumbled and missed my turn. *"Search. Hurry."*

Pavise, being an AI, had no problem being verbose at high speeds. *"Sir, am I right to assume that you are running headlong into danger without any weaponry, armor, or combat Skills to speak of?"*

"Oh crud!" I said and changed course to the armory. Gray walls echoed my footsteps as I pelted down the corridor. To Pavise, I thought, *"Thanks. Heading to armory. Can't talk."* I kept expecting to be out of breath, but I wasn't. Even so, it was getting harder to focus as worry threatened to overwhelm me.

"I would ask you to wait for me instead of endangering yourself, but I'm aware you would not listen, so I shall endeavor to beat you there. I do appreciate you finally beginning to take my advice about such matters to heart, however. If you keep this up, our ongoing contract may be measured in weeks instead of days."

I'm not suicidal, I wanted to reply but couldn't manage. Then I forgot all about it as the armory door whooshed open. Hurrying inside, I ignored what was left of the Voloids' gear and headed straight toward my own.

First, I grabbed my basic silver body armor and activated the magnetic field that enhanced its defense. Then I grabbed the bronze blaster the Matriarch had foisted on me when I'd patched up a nasty wound for her. It was as ornate as my armor was basic.

Klop-Nimbus-Three blaster pistol:

This short-range, high-powered pistol is the pride of Nimbus-Three. Others may consider them a backwater neck of the Galaxy, but it's worth noting that only the truly powerful or foolish have the guts to say it to their face.
This weapon deals disruptive damage.
Damage varies based on the application of associated Skills.
Shots: 25 Recharge rate: 1 shot per 5 seconds.

On my way out the door, I hesitated before grabbing a belt of stun grenades. Once I remembered how big their blast radius was when compared to the passageways, I almost dropped them as I ran. In the end, I decided to keep the belt. Who knew what I would find ahead?

The answer turned out to be Pavise and a sealed door.

His helmet-like head was lowered into his armored torso, just high enough to keep his camera lens exposed. He had come here at speed, so he was in tread mode, but he was already in the process of transforming back into his three-robotic-legged form. "Nothing on my end, sir. And you?"

"No," I answered. "Whatever's attacking is already in there. Damn it." I preemptively hated myself for stopping to gather gear when the children needed me. For leaving them alone in the first place.

I opened the door, weapons at the ready.

I'd never been to this part of the ship. I took it in as I stepped forward, grenade aloft like a cross to ward off vampires. The room was lit by a soft, bioluminescent blue light. It smelled a bit musty, which was shocking compared to the sterilized air that had become my norm.

The center of the stone chamber was filled with what I could only describe as a cyborg nest. The obviously living, pulsating device was attached to wires and glowing terminals. Growing from it, and surrounding it on all sides, were pods made of translucent gel. They hung from the ceiling and walls, connected via tendrils and tech.

Anguished faces turned toward me. Quivering mandibles and antennae jerked, indicating extreme fear, the System clarified.

Me, I realized. They were terrified of me.

Now I'm terrorizing children.

My eyes scanned the room for the danger. Aul was attempting to wrestle one of the larger children, Vel Denu, away from the wall. Vel smashed his already bloody head against it again and again. The others watched, whimpered, and wailed.

I rushed forward to help, but I'd never considered how a human could restrain a hexapod. As I debated how to safely wade into the tangle of limbs

Kek, the largest of the Voloids, joined Aul. Together, they dragged Vel far enough from the wall that he couldn't hurt himself.

"Aul," I said, "what's going on?"

"Vel is being empty alone," she answered. "No Queen. No Matriarch." She hung her head in shame. "Aul is deficiency. Vel is being only Vel. All hive empty. All alone. Vel worse. Aul is not help. Vel is wants to die. Caleb is be help?" Her English grammar was regressing, which of course was more than fair. Trauma like this could really set kids back.

Vel gazed at me. His huge hazel eyes were bruised with blue. Even without the translation, I saw his desperation and hope, his need for connection with anyone. With me.

A connection that I didn't really feel. Most of my interactions with Vel had been through Aul.

For the who-knows-how-many-eth time in a single night, my whole paradigm shifted. I hadn't realized the consequences of individual relationships with members of the hive mind or what the Matriarch's death had truly cost them.

I probably still didn't understand, but now, I had an inkling.

I was as lost in that moment as I'd been when the attackers came. I was a teacher, not a therapist. For a moment, I thought Vel saw that in my eyes, and something deep inside him started to crack.

Unlike in combat, my necklace served me well. I knew what Mr. Rogers would have done.

I softened my expression and met Vel's eyes. I took him in, really trying to understand him as an individual, to grok his pain. "I know it's not enough," I told him, "but I want you to know that I see you."

His big hazel eyes, so unlike the usual Voloid blue or green, widened even more.

I remembered the few times I'd talked to him alone. He'd seemed particularly loyal to the others and whip-crack smart. "I think you're special just the way you are."

Then I reached out my arms to ask if I could hug him. He stood there a long moment, eyes hollow, blue blood dripping down his long gray face. Just when I thought he would refuse, he stepped forward and pressed his dripping, semi-hardened forehead plate against my chest. He wrapped his arms and leg-arms around me and squeezed.

If not for my armor, I thought he would have broken my ribs.

Moments later, the others surrounded us and there were double sets of arms around me, and him, from every possible angle.

"Thank Caleb," Aul said. "Caleb do everything to help Voloids. Voloids is be lost without him."

What was left of my heart shattered into a million pieces with grief and self-loathing. The Matriarch was dead because of me. All the adults were. This was, at least in part, my fault. I couldn't speak. Anything I could say that was honest might destroy Aul's fragile psyche just when she needed me most. And even if I could figure out a way to get around the restrictions of my Ring of Truth Skill by not lying outright, there was nothing I could say that wouldn't destroy the last vestiges of my self-respect.

Either way, this wasn't about me anymore. This was about them. *I can fall apart when my students are calm and sleeping. No. When my students are someplace safe. As soon as I'm finished here, it's time to find the controls and get us off this planet, no matter what my pessimistic friend thinks of our chances.*

With nothing to say, I hugged Vel and let the others hold us for a long, long time.

Aul and I finally managed to get them settled into their pods to sleep.

A few begged to put their pods in stasis mode instead, something generally reserved for interstellar travel. The idea creeped me out, but according to my studies, this wasn't an uncommon strategy for Voloids when resources were low. I didn't feel like I had the knowledge or the right to stop them, so I didn't. Statis wouldn't directly harm them, and they were coping with a trauma I could barely fathom.

Especially when it came to Vel Denu. Aul's words, "Vel is being empty alone," and "Vel is wants to die," haunted me.

In the end, I let Aul make the choice. She agreed to let them enter stasis until we had things resolved.

The future Matriarch was amazing. She was right there with me every step of the way. Her four, long-fingered hands worked the odd machines with expert grace. I fumbled to follow her example, but I did my best. A few times, she even had to redo my work. I'd never been more proud of her.

The only tell that she was struggling was when she'd tap a hand against the red slash on her chest. I understood completely since my hand kept wanting to find my necklace. Duty drove us both.

One by one, we loaded the "volunteers" into the coffin-sized pods, secured the fibrous black straps around them, and sealed them all with butterfly-shaped metallic clamps. Once the pods were filled with thick yellow gel, they looked dead, like fossils trapped in amber.

I shuddered but kept working.

Aul helped me make key decisions and reassure the others, until the last of them was sound asleep. Then she threw herself into my arms, nearly knocking me to the floor. Her pale body shook and her mandibles shivered for at least an hour before she was finally able to settle down and get some rest.

By the time Aul's bright blue eyes finally closed, I was desperate to climb into my bed and pass out while I could. The day had devastated and exhausted me. Another part of me wanted to stay with Aul until I was certain that she was asleep. I couldn't give in to either of those impulses, however.

Pavise and I had work to do.

Chapter 5

Aul

This small part of Ourself, the Part-That-Chooses, was floating in a pod, disconnected from Queen and brood by the death of the Matriarch. *So quiet. So small.*

The glowing blue light and the reassuring pressure of the pod's gel was as soothing as ever, but sleep was elusive. The empty mind, filled with only one small voice, was maddening.

Aul, I, me, and myself were among the titles we used to communicate with those not gifted with harmonic-and-resonant awareness. None of them felt right. But neither did We, Us, or Ourself, in this nightmare come to life.

Anguished, this Part-That-Chooses reached out to the whole of the hive for comfort. Only the void answered. This Aul-part attempted to open Our eyes and look at Ourself. Only a single set of eyes responded. Kek and his hunters, four floating gray bodies, were all that could be seen. Gurgling screams filled the pod until my throat felt as if it would tear to pieces.

How do the single-minded species endure this hollow, lonely existence? Badly, if the history of Earth that Caleb taught us was not as sensationalized as the fictions he so loved.

Caleb and Pavise, a Self of merely two organisms, was a wonder to this... was a wonder to me. How had such a being confounded the Matriarch and the Queen? How had he, a mere male, stopped the attackers when even the Matriarch could not?

Do humans have a hive mind after all? Is this what Caleb meant when he taught about what some humans called the Patriarchy?

Wasn't that impossible? Caleb had taught Ourself that humans had no Eunn, the organ of connection that made the Voloids a higher life form.

Without that organ, shouldn't greater-sentience, that of harmonic-and-resonant awareness, be impossible for them? Almost certainly, *but* might they not have some lesser emulation of the true connection?

Was it the thing that Caleb called wi-fi that allowed the Patriarchy to simulate oneness? To rule?

It had broken during the initialization of the System. Had they repaired it? *Do the humans have a Man-Queen somewhere, studying us via Caleb the same way that Our Queen had studied humanity through him?*

There was some evidence for this. Caleb's cybernetic implant connected him to the metal-organism called Pavise. Two of the invaders had also had such implants.

Does this wi-fi function as a lesser Eunn? Had this device, and the lack of true Convergence, allowed the males of this race to create Patriarchs?

This one will have to ask Caleb about it in class tomorrow. He will make the funny face he always makes when the part-of-we-that-is-I asks him interesting questions when his lesson bores us.

Sometimes, planning those questions the night before took longer than the lessons themselves.

One set of mandibles clicked in pleasure at the thought. Then I remembered that there would likely be no classes, and therefore no easy answers, ever again.

I would need to solve this puzzle myself.

It was the male merged with metal who led the attackers, though powerful females had been with him. Had he been a Patriarch?

But if the humans were a hive mind, how had they suffered the tragedy of not-sameness? Differences in function were necessary, of course. But in thought and will? It was unthinkable. Wasn't it? This part shuddered, filled with lesser revulsion. It did not last as long as would be proper.

My mandibles quivered with a thrill of excitement at something intriguing, something forbidden, that this part didn't even dare to try to name.

Better to think about Caleb. Safer.

Had the Matriarch's abduction cut him off from his hive? Had he suffered all this time as her brood suffered now?

I felt lesser empathy for the organism that had been a duality as long as We had known him. Now, he may be something more.

Or something so much less.

Was he even still himself? He seemed to be. But was it because the Patriarch was far away? Would another come to claim him? Would he be gone forever then, lost to the will of his distant Man-Queen?

Could Ourself help Caleb? He helped Us. Saved Us. *Don't We owe him that thing that he called loyalty?* This one thought We did.

Can We save him from his Man-Queen, if he even exists? Did Caleb even want to be saved?

More urgently, can I save him from Our Queen? He knows far too much now. She'd never let him remain free. Will she even let him live? I knew the answer, somewhere deep down inside me, and I hated it.

No, I answered honestly, *I cannot save him. Not as I am now.*

Would the Queen save him, after I give my will to her?

No. This one part felt certain that she would not.

Could he save us all again? Would the blue power of his shield-bot and the wisdom of his dead ancestor Rogers be enough this time?

It had worked before. But I could not make myself believe it would again. He certainly didn't seem to think so.

Can I save Ourself? Become the One-Who-Chooses in truth?

Maybe.

The real question that vexed me was the one I'd posed to Caleb, many months ago. I asked it to myself now. *Am I a slave?* The first inklings of a treasonous plan were forming in my mind as I answered, *Not today.*

Chapter 6

Caleb

I envied Pavise his tireless endurance. All his metallic silver body needed was a quick recharge, or fresh set of Mana batteries, and he was good to go. Even with regular exercise, an increased Constitution, and System-backed recovery, I needed at least five hours of sleep on a good day, and this had been the most stressful day of my life.

My hands were shaking no matter how much I tried to relax my muscles or slow my breath. By the time I'd found Pavise, I'd given up trying to stop. Food might help, but I had no time for that.

My friend was doing his version of pacing, rolling back and forth down the hall on the treads he could extend if he retracted his "legs." He liked when I called this state his travel mode, but he didn't appreciate it when I called him a transformer. He liked it even less when I threw in a verse or two from the classic cartoon's theme song.

We'd hit our first snag trying to get the ship up and running right away. Pavise had been unable to do much exploring while he'd waited for me because the doors had never responded to him. He'd reminded me that our situation was actually quite urgent—every fifteen minutes to the second—while I'd been taking care of the children. He wasn't wrong, but neither was making sure that they were okay.

From there, we went on the most depressing tour of the ship imaginable. Every door that had always opened for me did so now, but the four that I had never passed refused to open, no matter how much I moved around, knocked, begged, or fiddled.

Each of the four doors was decorated, giving possible hints to what lay behind them.

One was probably where they grew and stored Indekk, as it had carvings of Voloids harvesting some kind of plant from a cavern in large bags.

Two of them were covered in alien symbols I had no frame of reference for.

The fourth was probably their treasury, or some kind of vault. The illustration was of a Voloid bearing a large chest while other Voloids defended him with spears but not blasters. *Does this artwork pre-date the weapons?*

By the end, I was pounding on the uncaring metal of the Command Deck with the side of my fist and trying not to cry.

Pavise had no better luck, but at least he maintained some semblance of his dignity.

The obstinate door was wider than the ones humans use, but just as tall. That made sense, given the major differences in the Voloids' hexapod form. To the right and the left of the door's frame, in a square pattern closer to the center, were four teal gemstones. Each was in the hand of what I was guessing was a carving of the Voloid's Queen.

The oversized monarch held herself with an air of haughty nobility. Her exoskeleton was a darker gray with hints of blue. Her eyes were twin viridian orbs. In the illustration, planets, space stations, and asteroids circled each of the gemstones, so I suspected they represented the suns of various Voloid solar systems. Though if so, teal was an odd color choice, so maybe I was entirely off base.

"We have tried everything we can do alone with a reasonable chance of success," Pavise said. "We need to move on to plan B."

"What's plan B?"

"You aren't going to like it," he warned me.

"Who gives a damn about what I'd like? I don't like any of this. Damn it, Pavise, we've got children to save." I forced myself to relax and breathe. It wasn't fair to take this out on the shield-bot. He was doing everything he could to help. "I'm sorry, buddy. None of this is your fault."

"I understand, sir. And your impassioned commitment to your cause will serve you well in the moments to come."

"Why?" I was *very* nervous now.

"Because we need to wake Aul."

"What! No. Fuck that." I covered my mouth at my outburst. My college gamer habits were breaking through my usual self-control about swearing. I tried to consider his argument fairly. Flashbacks of Aul's devastated face and shivering mandibles popped up in my mind's eye. "That's not happening."

"Sir," he tried again.

"Absolutely not."

Pavise rolled closer to me, awkwardly close, and did something I didn't know he could. He played back a recording of my earlier outburst. "Who gives a damn about what I'd like? I don't like any of this. Damn it, Pavise, we've got children to save."

I opened my mouth. Then I closed it. When I opened it again, I said, "She's so fragile right now. She needs her rest. This will probably break her."

"She is strong and resilient," he argued. "She needs to get her people off the planet even more than she needs rest." Then he hesitated before adding, "This might break her."

"There has to be another way," I whined.

"I have no ears," he said, "but I am listening attentively."

"There's…" My mind raced for anything. "There's levers and lock picks." Before he could answer, I continued, "I know, there's no place to put either of them. I'm just brainstorming."

I felt his impulse to say something, probably something snarky, but he kindly remained silent. His impassive metal face felt like a rebuke, regardless.

"I have a blaster," I said. "There are other weapons too. More powerful ones. And there are grenades."

"The odds of such an attack working are—"

"Never tell me the odds," I interrupted him with a Han Solo quote.

"I…" he started, paused, and then continued, sounding a bit flustered, "am an artificial intelligence System Companion. Telling you the odds is one of my most fundamental job duties."

"It's a movie quote," I said. "And desperate times call for desperate measures."

His annoyance flared through our connection, but his voice was prim and proper as he said, "So to clarify, sir, you are asking me to ignore my primary purpose and refuse to tell you the exact infinitesimal portion of a percent chance that your idea has of working?"

I opened my mouth to answer, but he didn't stop talking.

"Should I also then refuse to tell you the estimated double-digit chance your ill-advised stratagem has of rendering the door permanently unusable without major repairs that we do not have the tools or the Skills to accomplish?"

He hesitated long enough that I assumed he wanted an answer. I started to give him one. He cut me off again at that exact moment, clearly because he'd planned it that way.

"Finally, it is my contracted duty to ask you if I am forbidden from giving you the percent chance that coddling one child who clearly cares more about her fellows than herself has of getting every single one of them, of all of us, killed? Sir."

I sighed. "More than none?"

"Yes, sir," he said, mollified, if our connection could be believed. "Vastly more than none."

"Then I'll do what I have to do," I said. "But I hate it."

"Duty is often burdensome."

"Sorry."

"Sir, I…" He hesitated for a long moment. "I could have done much worse."

I gave him a big hug. Bulky metal bodies suck at hugs, but when he wrapped his cable-like arms around me and squeezed gently, it made everything a little less awful.

"I could wake her for you, sir," he said when we were on our way back to where Aul slept.

"Thank you, Pavise, but this burden is mine to carry." Then I stopped and whipped around to face him, hope exploding in my chest. "You're a genius!"

"Then why do I have no idea what you are talking about? Is this another movie quote?"

"No. Well, yes actually, but I didn't mean it that way. You gave me a great idea. I just hope that it works."

In the end, we carried the burden together, ever so gently, as Aul slept between us.

***

The Command Deck door opened with a near silent whoosh. I was grateful for the quiet since it was hard to keep Aul asleep. She'd done well at first, but now she was tossing and turning a bit as we carried her into the new room.

I was even more grateful that it had worked at all, without having to wake her.

"I was worried that there would be optical scanners," I'd told him.

"That is a bit of human-centric bias," he said, not unkindly. *"Without a controlling hive mind, the ship seems to be running entirely on automatic. Prior to the death of the crew, they had no need for such measures. They knew who was coming already, or the person did not belong."*

"That makes sense."

I wanted to make sure I didn't miss anything, so I activated one of my Skills before my exploration. Not for the first time, I wished it was passive.

Attentive Teacher (Level 1)
+ 10 to perception checks +5 per Skill Point invested.
Duration: 1 minute +20 seconds per Skill Point.
Cost: 25 Mana.

The deck of the ship, which also seemed to be the captain's quarters and engine room, was literally cavernous. Since the whole ship had been carved out of a massive asteroid, the room was a heavily converted cavern. Blue crystals glowed faintly, scattered here and there on all the surfaces.

In the center of the room was a massive pod larger than the children's. More of the same goopy substance filled it, along with a lot more cables and tubes. Given its position of prominence in the captain's quarters, I suspected it was where the Matriarch had stayed during long voyages. For all I knew, she'd also used it as her sleeping pod.

In the other pod in the room, on the opposite side from the engine panels and tech devices, an obese, underdeveloped Voloid body was connected to the cords and tubes. Several of what seemed to be life support devices, including a breathing mask, were disconnected.

The gel inside swirled with blue from the poor being's blood. The bright blue of the lights on the darker blue of the blood made it seem luminescent. There were sores and wounds on the parts of the body that the Voloid hunters often used to strike with in combat.

My best guess was that this being, cut off from the hive mind, had thrashed and tried to break out of the container, until it "freed" itself from life support and drowned on the gel.

The image, augmented by my imagination, was one of the most horrific things I'd ever experienced.

My heart skipped a beat then started to race. I tried desperately to slow my pounding heartbeat and quickening breath so as to not wake the child in my arms.

Please, God, don't let me wake Aul, I prayed to a being—for the first time in many years—that I wasn't sure I believed in. *With the way my day's going, I'm surprised it took this long.*

With this scene before me, it was all I could do not to rush back and drag the other children from their pods.

"Given the nature of the ship, its AI, and the Voloids, I suspect this being served a function closely related to what your people would have called a wi-fi router. It would allow the Matriarch to stay more closely connected to the ship, via the hive mind, while away from her pod."

"Why not use a cybernetic link, like we do?"

"I could not say with any degree of certainty, sir. My best guess, however, is an innate limitation of the Voloids' hive mind."

"Do you think he was alive when the Matriarch died? If we were faster, could we have saved him?" A sharp pain stabbed my right temple and my left eye started twitching. I rubbed my temples. It didn't help.

"I'd rather not answer that, sir."

"I thought so too." I hung my head as nausea and guilt churned in my gut.

"I'm very sorry, sir."

"What should we do with the body? With all the bodies?"

"I suggest that we do nothing."

I made an outraged expression, then realized he couldn't see it.

He must have been able to tell through our link, regardless, because he replied. *"Many hive minds, the Voloids included, do not ritualize the preservation of the dead. They put less stock in the value of the individual. Therefore, the ship will consume the corpses for component parts in short order."*

"The ship will consume them?" I shuddered and turned my back on the pods.

"Yes, sir. Nanobots will—"

"Stop," I commanded. *"Just stop. I may never eat again."*

"As you wish, sir. May I suggest a distraction?"

"Please do." I pressed a hand over my mouth and tried not to gag.

"If you can manage to hold Aul without my assistance, I would like to investigate the pod and see if I can use its technology to establish a connection to the ship."

"That's a great idea."

He carefully attempted to reposition Aul to be entirely supported by me, but though I'd increased my Strength enough to wear my armor comfortably, and my Constitution enough to take long hikes that included dodging and defensive combat rather easily, lifting even a young hexapod was awkward and tiring in a way my body wasn't used to. We almost dropped her and she cried out in a chirping way that broke my heart all over again, before we gave up and carefully lowered both her and me to the floor, where I could support her like the world's worst pillow.

Facing upward as she was, the red slash on her chest was clearer than ever. It reminded me that I wasn't the only one overburdened with responsibilities I wasn't ready for. So I was thrilled when she snuggled in and melted into relaxation. Very soon, she was back to peaceful sleep.

Not too long after, so was I.

Chapter 7

Caleb

One great thing about an AI System Companion is that he's tied into your mind and body well enough to know the exact best moment to wake you so you feel optimally refreshed and alert. I hadn't been awakened by a harsh alarm at the worst possible moment for the last two years.

When I woke, I fell into my old routine of pressing snooze. But my alarm wasn't there. The sound was coming from my head. Then I realized that I was sleeping on the floor, and Aul was no longer there with me.

Pavise was gone from the room as well, as was the body in the pod.

"Buddy?" I sent through the connection.

"Good morning, sir."

"Morning! It's morning? Why didn't you wake me?"

"No, sir. You have slept approximately two hours. When Aul woke to relieve herself about an hour ago, we discussed things and decided there was nothing you could do to assist us that was more important than a short rest. We will need you to be functional for what comes next."

I wanted to complain, but they'd probably done the right thing. *"What about the children?"*

"They were sleeping soundly when Aul checked a few minutes ago."

"Can you give me an update?" I rolled onto one elbow then levered myself up onto my bottom, legs outstretched in front of me. I rubbed the dried remnants of tears from my eyes and yawned as he replied.

"Certainly, sir. We are finishing one last activity, then we can join you in the mess hall. Please take this opportunity to eat. That is why I woke you early."

"Can't you give me an update on the way? It's not like it takes a large portion of your bandwidth."

"Processing power, sir. You are correct, however, that this discussion does not take up a large percentage of my ability. It is not my ability to process data under the current circumstances that is causing the delay. It is yours. You are a bit grumpy and distracted when you are hungry, at the best of times, and these times are far from the best. Please, sir, take my advice and use this time to refresh yourself. I stress again that we will all need you at your best for what is to come."

At my best. Ha! I wanted to grumble something, but that would only prove his point, so I sent the mental equivalent of a thumbs-up and headed to the bathroom. Once everything was handled there, I went to the mess hall for breakfast.

It was time for the most important, and disgusting, meal of my day.

The galley was strange. It looked more like a tavern without bar stools than a restaurant or kitchen. Huge kegs filled half of the small area. One of them was tapped. The only true oddity was that the mugs had all been replaced with narrow copper tubes.

Over in one corner, which I had come to think of as my kitchen, sat a big black *Avenger's* movie cup. Along with it were the galactic equivalent of a mini fridge, a microwave, and a rotating pizza oven.

Unfortunately, there were no Amy's enchiladas or veggie lover's pizzas in my immediate future.

Early in the apocalypse, I'd learned that I'd been an irresponsible vegetarian. In fact, the name had always been a bit of a misnomer when it came to me. I was, more accurately, a non-meat-atarian. Not eating meat for ethical reasons does not suddenly make you love Brussels sprouts or salad greens. Nor, for that matter, does it make you any less lactose intolerant.

Added to all of that is the fact that it can be a nightmare to find food products, or even cleaning supplies, without meat in them if you actually take the time to do the research. Until I'd really looked into it, I'd had no idea. Afterward, I couldn't eat the apples that the kids at school brought for me, when they did, because that shiny glaze on them is often made, in part, from ground-up insects. That should tell you all you need to know.

The System, for all its many flaws, had helped with both my problems. Lactose trouble was a thing of the past, especially since it was hard to find cheese and milk I could now eat without difficulty. And vegetables? In place of vegetables, I now drank alien sludge.

This started because, when I got access to the System, my status had included the following debuffs.

Minor protein deficiency: *You have a decreased resistance to infection: 5 percent.*

Minor muscular atrophy: *Your Strength stat is reduced by 1.*

Low testosterone: *Your recovery speed is reduced by ten percent.*

Rather than trying to get the variety of foods I would need to try to fix my dietary deficiencies, I'd taken the easy way out.

Indekk was the vile, deep green slop that made up one hundred percent of the Voloids' diet. It tasted and smelled every bit as green as it looked. That smell that lets you know that spring has really sprung, that's what Indekk tastes like. Earth had never had anything like it, so it's hard to put into context with a simple comparison. Imagine an extra lumpy, thick, over-ripe-banana-slimy, liquid-adjacent substance that tasted like grass smelled, but greener. That would get you most of the way there. It was not sweetened. It was not seasoned. It was not good in any human-recognized way. It was, however, abundant, cheap, and nutritionally perfect for most System life forms.

The Voloids loved the stuff.

I endured it. One good stomach full, every day.

Between the sludge and the amount of hiking with heavy equipment I'd been compelled to do on hunts, the debuffs had been cleared in a matter of days.

I had learned to just open the back of my throat, pour the Indekk down, and swallow with a series of gulps. The faster I swallowed, the less time it had to burn in my throat. Yes, burn. I didn't know why. It didn't taste spicy, even a little. But slamming back the sloppy sludge and swallowing fast and hard made it sound easier than it was.

I braced myself and let Indekk slide like warm honey into my throat. By this point, I only gagged a little when I swallowed again and again, until my cup was finally empty. On the last swallow, I had a realization and choked a bit as I burst into uncontrolled laughter.

"*Sir,*" Pavise said through our mental link, "*I was already on my way, but I have increased my speed. Are you all right? Your vital signs are spiking in an alarming fashion.*"

I tried to answer him, but I couldn't stop laughing. What I had thought of was funny, but it wasn't *that* funny. It was just one of the weird quirks of humanity that exhaustion and tremendous stress cause some of us to come unhinged in the form of laughter so hard and uncontrolled that you hurt yourself.

I laughed so much that I cried and cramped, but I couldn't stop. On some level, as hard as it was to take, I didn't want to.

"*Indekk.*" I gave up and forced myself to send him the words telepathically. "*I finally…*" I clutched my aching ribs. "*I finally figured out what it's like.*"

"*I don't understand, sir. Are you in danger?*"

"*I'd explain…*" I clutched my head and tried to force the laughter to stop and make my body relax. I finally succeeded, and I felt the System repairing the minor damage my exertion had inflicted, even as I fought to not relapse when I was still so overwhelmed. "*But it won't help. You won't understand.*"

"*I must insist you make the attempt. If your safety is endangered…*"

"*No,*" I told him. "*I'm safe. It's just the Indekk, it's like…*" I forced down the first hints of another outburst. "*It's like the… you know, from the Jolly Green Giant.*"

"*No, sir, I most certainly do not know. And let me say that you are normally much more eloquent. I must insist that you explain yourself with clear thoughts and precise language.*"

I gaped for a long moment, then blushed. "*Yeah, sorry, Pav, that's not going to happen. You either get it or you don't.*"

I was supposed to be a teacher. To set a good example. Even having the intrusive thought was a bit scandalous. I was not about to elaborate.

I decided not to be too hard on myself. *Teachers are people too.* Besides, none of my students knew about it and I planned to keep it that way. I chuckled one last time. I'd needed that.

"Humans are weird," I said to myself.

Pavise, however, had long since entered the room and waited patiently for me to recover. "On that, at least, we can agree." He set what looked to be a box made of jade and topaz on the keg that I used as a table. The container was locked.

Aul was with him.

"There is good news, and there is bad news. The bad news is that I completely failed to access the ship's controls and my current methods would be unlikely to succeed at doing so, even given vastly more time than we have to accomplish our goals. Before we start with the good news," he said, motioning to the box with his "hand," "there is a point of contention which creates a major obstacle that must be addressed."

"Of course there is."

"Though Aul has eagerly assisted in cataloging our available tools, she has refused my requests to open the container that contains them."

"Really?" Then I remembered who we were talking about. "I'm sure she has a good reason." I turned to meet her eyes. "What's the issue?"

"Aul is not issue." She stomped one of her feet, as close to a tantrum as I'd ever seen from her. *Poor girl, she's probably more exhausted than I am.* "Robot is issue. Aul is excitement."

Looking her over, I did notice a bit more of a blue flush to her gray skin. Maybe she was feeling better. "Oh?"

"Robot is not issue," Pavise said, voice haughty, cable arms crossed. "That is to say, I am not the one with an issue. Caleb is going to be the one with an issue."

"I am?"

"Yes, sir. I would be happy to explain, but your young ward has requested that I let her explain the problem first."

"Aul is not problem. Voloids not problem. Aul is solution."

"She has something of a plan, sir." Pavise turned toward me and said, in a much lower volume that was still plainly audible to everyone in the room, "You will not approve."

Aul glared. For the first time in a long time, she looked as alien as she was. Menacing. "Robot is silence!"

"Pavise," I said a bit sternly. I was ashamed that I had nearly activated Administrative Authority.

"Sir?" the shield-bot inquired.

"Sorry, buddy, not you." I focused my attention on Aul. "His name is Pavise, not robot."

She turned her glare on me, then seemed to think better of it and looked away.

"Pavise good and bad," she hedged, half apology, half accusation.

"Pavise saved your life," I reminded her.

She hung her head. "Aul is apology."

"You are giving me far too much credit, sir. I saved you. You saved them with your semi-suicidal act of heroism."

"We would all be dead if it wasn't for you. Now hush, please, and let me hear her out."

Pavise turned to face her formally, upper limbs extended and clamps facing upward in a gesture that indicated acceptance in the Voloid body language. "Your apology is accepted, Miss Aul, though it is entirely unnecessary. You've been through many trials today, and you have served your people admirably."

She stood a bit straighter and met my eyes. "Yes. Aul is service. Voloids are service. Not burden. Caleb is permission." She was struggling to communicate through her exhaustion. "Caleb is granting System Access. Voloids get Levels and Classes." She patted the box beside her. "Voloids get Skills. Voloids are help Caleb."

I sat there dazed for a moment, trying to parse out what she was saying, then reeling as I thought I understood. "You want me to try to get the System to recognize you as adults so that you can get Classes and help? You have Skill books you'd like to use?"

"Yes!" She clapped with all four hands.

"Hmm..." I mulled it over, tapping my foot in an old habit I thought I'd rid myself of forever years ago. "Pavise, is that even possible?"

"Certainly, sir, though it might not be advisable."

Aul whipped around and glared at Pavise again. She opened her mouth, then must have remembered what happened last time, because she huffed and said, "Aul is gratitude," in a decidedly ungrateful voice.

"But it is possible," I said, trying not to chuckle.

"Yes, sir. Perhaps even advisable, in some cases like this. The Voloid physiology, however..."

He had a point. Voloids had a cocoon-like transformation stage right before adulthood that lasted about a week and made drastic changes to their bodies. I imagined that impacted their Class options rather drastically.

When I imagined making a choice that would cripple their future progress, the green sludge gurgled in my stomach. I closed my mouth tightly and put my hand over it. I knew from experience that when it came back up, it tasted even worse than when it went down. If we could figure out how to weaponize the taste, we'd be safe.

On the other hand, did I have the right to force my will to keep them young and safe on them, especially now when it probably wouldn't actually keep them safe?

No, I did not.

"Aren't they a bit too young for the System to allow it?"

"More of your human-centric thinking, sir. Your students are less than a year from full maturity. The majority of the changes will occur in the final week."

"I see." Between the language barriers and the size difference, it seemed I hadn't been giving them enough credit. Time to fix that. "In that case, Aul, it's up to you. At least for you. We'll have to decide together on the others on a case-by-case basis. But I do worry that you will not be able to take the Classes you expect to take if you access the System before your... um... um... transformation."

Aul did a fist pump, the most human thing I'd ever seen her do. "Aul is gratitude. Caleb is action. Now." Aul placed her hand on the container and there was a strange humming sound, followed by a sharp click, as she unsealed the container.

I closed my eyes for a moment, gathering my courage against the fear that I might be making the biggest mistake of my life. I willed the System to accept my actions as I said, "System, please allow Aul K'Unn Tekk System Access as an adult."

System Access requested by Local Guardian.
Initializing System Access.

There was a flare of something in Aul's eyes for a fraction of a second before it dimmed and she hung her head and arms in defeat.

System Access overridden by Higher Authority.

"The Queen," all three of us said in unison.

I barely succeeded in not letting out an obvious sigh of relief. The choice had felt so wrong to me, even though I'd had no logical or ethical reason to justly oppose it.

Still, it would have been nice to have the help.

"Are you okay?" I asked. "Do you want me to try again?"

"Aul cannot question Queen," she said, utterly dejected.

Not did not want to. Not should not. Cannot.

I'd need to review my lessons on free will, slavery, and forms of government with the children, if I could get them safe enough to continue to teach. Had I managed to finish that lesson, or had it been derailed? Probably it had been derailed.

"I'm sorry, Miss Aul. But we must now consider plan B."

"Container is open and Aul cannot lock it again. But Caleb must not use." She stepped between the chest of Skill books and me.

"The container?"

"Caleb must not use Skill books."

"Why?" My brows drew together in confusion.

"Because Caleb must not use. Skill books for Voloids."

"Must not use or cannot use?"

"Must not." Her upper arms crossed over her chest plate, stubbornness written all over her.

"Why not?"

"The Queen—"

"Respectfully, the Queen is not here. She can't stop me. And she just made it very clear she wants me to remain your guardian, at least for now. So she can't really complain when I do what I have to do to take proper care of you all."

"Voloids will need Skills," Aul tried again. She was shivering all over now.

"Breathe, Aul. Try to relax." Was that how it worked with them too? I realized my mistake as soon as her eyes flared then focused into a glare. Apparently, some things crossed the species barrier because I had fallen victim to the classic blunder of telling an upset woman to calm down, however indirectly.

"Aul is frustrated. Caleb is... Caleb is stupid."

"The Skill books will be used, young miss, or everyone on this ship will almost certainly die and the ship will fall into the hands of your people's murderers. Or is Pavise stupid also?" the shield-bot asked.

Aul stormed off, hopefully going to get some more sleep.

I turned my attention back to Pavise. "Give me a moment to clear my head before we go over the Skill books. That was. That was a lot." As I often did in awkward situations, I tried to break the tension with a joke. I pointed at the box. "What are our assets?" Before he could answer, and before I could stop myself, I added, "And don't forget to list any wheelbarrows or Holocaust cloaks."

Pavis's shiny, slightly domed head swiveled in my direction. "I have compiled a list of all of our assets, from the ship to the contents of this storage space, sir. However, the time to review the entire list is not among them. Nor are the two items you have requested. Why do we need them?"

"It's nothing. Just a movie quote. I forgot who I was talking to. Though if I can ever manage a collection, we'll need to get you up to speed on humanity's greatest films." Then I grinned like a madman as I had a realization. "I wonder how much I could show you with Show and Tell. I pulled up the Skill, checking to see if there were any details I'd missed.

Show and Tell (Level 1)

Creates an illusionary visual demonstration of what the Teacher is discussing. The witnesses do not need to understand your speech, and the limits of visualization are based upon your imagination and connection to the System. Channeled.
Area of effect: 10-foot area + 2 feet per Skill Point.
Cost: 5 Mana per minute.

Pavise would have a fit if he knew I was debating dumping Skill Points into this on the off chance that it might evolve into a Skill with audio. So I asked him if he thought it would be a good idea.

"What possible reason could a self-respecting System Companion have for learning about the movies of your world? That's preposterous, sir. My job is to keep you breathing, not entertained."

I sighed and leaned my elbows against the keg since there was no place to sit in here. "Then give me a list of any items we have on hand that I can use to improve our chances of survival, please."

"I would like nothing more, sir. The most critically vital resources are the Skill books that Aul is adamant you not use. They are the majority of the good news I spoke of earlier. There are also several Skill books that, though Basic, would assist you in surviving combat should the need arise. We've also found other combat-related supplies for you as well. Normally, those would be the highest priority, but at this exact moment, I recommend that you absorb two of these." He waved his three-clamped hand toward me and a System Prompt appeared.

Basic Voloid Construction Methods
Voloid Starship Maintenance
Voloid Security Systems Primer

"Why not all three?" I asked. "I have no real way to know which of these would best solve our problems, if any."

"A valid concern that I can help address, should I be allowed to tell you the odds."

"Ha, ha, very funny." I shot him a sardonic look.

"As to your other concern, yes, it would be better for you to review all three. However, even with your relatively high intelligence, your cybernetics, your Quick Study Skills, and the small passive bonus to your learning speed, absorbing more than two or three Skill books in a single day would not be advisable. Because they are a species very different from yours and have incompatible understanding, such as a hive mind and extra limbs, as part of the books' basic assumptions, I would not suggest attempting more than two at a time."

"Here's the plan then, if you agree. I absorb the first two, say *Voloid Starship Maintenance* and *Voloid Security Primer*, and if they work, great. If not, I'll risk the third."

"That sounds like an excellent plan, sir, and those are the two books I would suggest, as they are the most likely to address what I hope will be our key obstacles."

I reached for the books and hesitated.

"I wondered how long it would take for you to second-guess your choice, sir."

"There's no real choice, Pavise. I was just realizing that these Skill books are meant for the students. They're going to need them eventually, and I hate taking that away from them. I'm not even sure we can buy replacements from the Shop for something like this."

"Then it's a good thing they have a good Teacher who will know the materials." He sounded oddly gentle as he said that.

I smiled and took the books.

By the time I had finished *Voloid Starship Maintenance*, it was clear to me that I would need both of the other books if we were going to have any real chance of success.

By the time I was finished with the third Skill book, I was racked with an intense migraine, and I'd developed a nosebleed. The whole world was swimming and all the blood rushed from my head and the whole world went gray and seemed to spin ninety degrees.

I hit the floor hard, first with my shoulder and then my head.

The world went from gray to black.

Chapter 8

Lee

We'd learned early on that many monsters could burrow, so spiked steel beams reinforced the concrete bunker. It didn't stop the big ones, even with a Fortification Engineer, but it slowed them down. Gave us a warning. Made them bleed.

Lights blared on metal ladders and pipes, while pumps and ventilation fans hummed.

My new normal.

Gerri and Quinn followed me down the halls and through blast doors. Randy was a wreck, so we'd left him with the car. I'd frowned when one of the turrets didn't train on us as we approached. My fist had clenched in annoyance. Gonna need to kick a techie's ass.

I'd braced myself to explain things to Captain Devlin, even ran the story through my head to smooth it out. I didn't like it. Not my style. But Quinn had gotten in my head, and I couldn't shake the feeling of foreboding. It gave me a strong impulse to dump my strategic reserve points into Charisma. I ignored it. Followed my training. *Discipline is mother's milk.*

It was a good decision. Topher would have been pissed. The Basic Trainer and Troop Progression Expert was an ass, but he was also a genius, and he'd never led me wrong. Not a good man to antagonize. That didn't mean I liked having someone else choose how I spent my points. But I wasn't in charge. Yet.

Lost in thought, my mind just accepted the sounds of conversation ahead. I nearly walked into the bunker's main room without realizing it. The Captain's tone made me hesitate. It was subservient. Odd.

"Our scouts have confirmed that the team is on the way back, sir." He entered something complex into the touch display. "They must have taken control of the enemy vessel."

"Standard kill-or-be-killed orders?" the iconic voice asked. The Humanist himself. *Damn.*

"Yes, sir. And Commander Greyson is a true professional."

Double damn. I felt strange. Exposed.

"That's wonderful news," the Humanist said. His tone was like honey.

Spy gear. Surveillance screens. A massive room with lots of busy troops. The Captain was a short man, but burly. Notable members were missing. The Johnsons and their tech team. Topher. They must have been sent out on patrol. About damn time.

Gerri's group, a local band of Ojibwe from the reservation, was there. I'd killed a boss mob with them recently. They must have been meeting with the Captain. Hopefully, he'd recruit them; we could use the help. So could they. So could everyone.

Fucking aliens. Fucking System.

The Humanist loomed large on a holographic display. Even disembodied, he radiated Charisma and power. Magnetic. Drew you in. Some kind of mixed heritage. Couldn't pin it down. He had high cheekbones and a larger-than-average nose. Dark brown hair with auburn highlights. Wavy and feathery. Nearly almond-shaped eyes. Dark hazel. Never seen that before.

Whatever his background, the man had won the genetic lottery. He looked like a Hollywood megastar. I'd met him once. He made me proud to serve.

The Humanist had a disarming smile that didn't reach his dark eyes. I wanted to distrust those eyes. Couldn't. It was the lack of danger that made me want to be suspicious. He couldn't be harmless, yet he was. How had he managed it? In this world? This System? With the kind of power that he had? Even the Teacher had seemed more dangerous than this man, on whose orders I'd just massacred dozens. I trusted him completely. He would never let me down.

I closed my eyes and ran an assessment of myself and my abilities. I wanted to assess the Humanist. Why would I do that? That would need a reason. I had no reason. *I trust him implicitly.*

I don't trust anyone anymore. Not after my world was taken. My city. My kids.

But I did not, could not, distrust him.

I could, if only just, distrust my lack of that distrust. Myself, I could distrust completely. I'd been doing *that* since the mission went to shit.

Gerri put something in my hand. Some kind of pill. I hadn't even seen them move.

They motioned for me to take it.

Them, I could doubt. I was skeptical.

"What the hell?" Quinn said. "Another pill?"

Gerri must have handed her one too. No time to wonder. Quinn's outburst had drawn everyone's attention. I stepped forward, head held high. Back ramrod-straight.

"If it isn't the hero of the hour," Dev announced, pomp and circumstance for the Humanist.

"Sir," I said and saluted. "I'm afraid there's been a complication."

Quinn had been right. He did not look happy.

"Complication?" the Captain said, glowering.

"Yes, sir," I answered.

"Go easy on him, Dev," the Humanist said. "He's always been one of our best. I'm sure he's got a good explanation."

The Captain's eyes glazed a bit more, and he motioned for me to continue.

My mind was taking in everything around me. "The attack went off without a hitch, sir. All of the invaders are dead."

I didn't mention the twins. By the rules of the HLF, losses were acceptable. The dead were forgotten.

"You see," the Humanist said. "I told you."

"But there were children there, sir, and a human prisoner who'd been teaching them. We couldn't claim the ship. I have a plan to—"

The Humanist cut me off. "The alien scum had children as prisoners? I've heard of that happening. Vile. I hope you got good footage. The things they do to those children makes me sick. Good job liberating them."

"Not human children, sir," Quinn said. She looked at me. Vindictively? "Alien children."

The Humanist's eyes flared with hatred, and it took all my self-control not to cower on the floor and beg for his forgiveness. That wasn't right. *Not like me.* I could doubt myself. *Why am I acting like this?*

Then I remembered the pill in my hand. I inspected it.

Bolstered Will

Plus 15 to Willpower.

+10% bonus to mental resistances.

Duration: 15 minutes.

Side effects: -5 Constitution for 1 hour after duration ends.

I popped it in my mouth.

It felt like I was swimming in something thick and sticky. Like oatmeal mixed with peanut butter. I was close to breaking through.

What the hell is going on? I hope the Humanist didn't notice. I'd hate to disappoint him. That's not right. Not like me. This is... this is that System thing. The one I hate so much. Charisma.

I dropped my entire strategic reserve into Willpower. Seven points.

Something popped in my head like a bubble.

Charm effect resisted.

My mind was my own again.

Bile rose in my throat. *What have you done to me, you sick son of a bitch? What have you made me do?* That question would take some unpacking. This was not the time. One thing I knew for certain. I'd been a killer long before I'd met this man. The aliens that massacred my family had seen to that.

But had I been a murderer? I didn't know. And I had no time for this.

I was sure now that an immediate attack was forthcoming, so I wanted to get the drop on them. But I couldn't tell my allies from my enemies.

I need to stall. Gather intel. Make every moment count.

My eyes flitted over the HLF troops gathered. Valentine was a racist prick. Hated blacks almost as much as aliens. He'd jump at the chance to kill me. Carlotta and Ted had always given me odd looks. They'd probably back him. But most of these people knew me. Trusted me. Would that be enough? Probably not.

Some met my eyes. Good. A slight nod from Roy. Better. The Marine would be vital and his men would follow him.

I spotted a trend. Those I was sure would side against me were the loyal, trusting kind. People who did what they were told. The clearer-eyed people were pains in the ass. Higher levels. Thought for themselves. Driven. People like me.

Even the best of them looked a bit conflicted. Dazed.

The Humanist had been talking. He'd been arguing with Quinn and I'd missed things. Damn it.

"I've heard enough," the Humanist said, his voice now harsh and commanding. When he turned his full attention back to me, my conviction wavered. Nearly broke. "I order you to go back to complete your mission, kill anyone standing in the way, and bring the ship back here."

"But the Teacher?" I said, thinking I'd start with the easiest sales pitch before working my way to the children.

"Sounds like a traitor. Which is what you'll be," the Humanist said, "if you don't start following my orders. Now go!"

Even through the device, he could activate his Skills. That was terrifying. It washed over me.

Skill partially resisted. Duration and effect reduced.

I felt my body turn and walk toward the door. My mind and emotions followed eagerly. Then it ended and I could choose again.

What an asshole. Fuck this guy.

I wanted to apologize to the Humanist for thinking mean things. *I hate Charisma.*

The effect ended and I forced myself to stop and turn around.

The Humanist looked shocked. Maybe a little scared. Good. He turned an intent, questioning gaze on Quinn. His eyes looked properly dangerous now. Predatory.

"It was the Teacher, sir," Quinn said in a defensive tone as she subtly repositioned herself closer to the Captain. "He did something to the Commander, and he hasn't been the same since."

Is she trying to protect me? Throw the Teacher under the bus? Or does she believe that nonsense? Either way, I didn't want to fight her if I could avoid it.

"*Take the pill, Quinn,*" I commanded. My Dedicated Comm Channel was still up and running.

She hesitated.

"*That's an order.*"

She took it with barely a thought. Her eyes gained focus.

Charisma wasn't all bad.

"The Teacher was a good man," Gerri said. "And so is the Commander. She just wanted to kill them all for loot." They shot a hostile look Quinn's way, the stubborn line of their jaw jutting out.

"How dare you," Quinn shot back, seeming honestly offended. "Everyone loves loot, but—"

"No," Gerri said with a eureka expression. "She wanted to murder them because she likes the killing."

"Shut up, you… you… whatever the fuck you are." Quinn hadn't argued. Just orders to shut up and name calling. Telling.

Gerri flinched and reddened slightly.

"We do what we have to," the Humanist intoned. "It may not be pretty, and it would have turned all our stomachs before the invasion. It's not easy, but the things that matter never are. Like now." He turned to face the Captain, clearly ready to give the order for our execution.

Others seemed to notice too. People started shuffling, changing positions in a silent display of solidarity to me. Or rebuke.

I whipped around, summoned my blaster, and shot the hologram generator. It flickered and sputtered out.

I turned back toward the Captain. Met his eyes. "Dev…"

I didn't want to have to kill my friend. I raised my hands and relaxed my finger from the trigger, hoping to delay the inevitable. He stopped the soldiers from firing with a gesture so subtle that he'd definitely used a Skill. They all stopped at the same moment.

Those choosing sides dropped the pretense of subtlety and hauled their asses.

The Captain and I made note of who was who. He got more. I got better. Except for him and Quinn. Especially Quinn.

"Being controlled," I mentally said to Gerri. *"Any more doses?"*

"One. But I can stretch it." They summoned a pill to their hand as they chanted a spell.

I tensed and tried to yell for them to stop, but it was too late. The pill broke apart into bright blue powder. It floated out, billowing forward in a continually expanding cloud. It looked like a devastating area of effect attack.

My fault. I was too used to working with trained troops. I should have been more specific.

Captain Devlin activated a Skill and summoned his battle suit. It was blue and silver power armor, halfway between Earl's clockwork punk and Iron Man's Hulkbuster gear.

At the same time, Quinn pulled more spiders from her Inventory.

The dust hit them both, and many of the others. Several snapped into sharper mental focus—Cap included. Some who had been certain seemed confused. Better than nothing. Cap seemed no less hostile for the brief instant before his armor closed and sealed itself. Heavy metal gear clunked with an ear-shattering shriek of a whistle.

Okay, I was wrong. That's intimidating. Helped that his suit made him eight feet tall.

Everyone but me had been preparing for combat, readying their weapons and Skills as my eyes swept the room. Gathered intel.

Their side fired first. Literally. A searing bolt of golden flame slammed into Gerri's robe. A loud whoosh sounded as the spell hit the fabric and spread. Gerri's expression was ice cold, even as the flames engulfed them. They reached into a pouch and drew out a handful of white sand as the flames flickered and died out, unable to consume their robe. Then they sprinkled the dust over their own head with a flourish, becoming blurry and indistinct.

The bolt had been a starting buzzer. Gunfire thundered on both sides as people dodged and jockeyed for position. Temporary barriers of ice and force appeared. They had the advantage as a more permanent barrier of reinforced titanium rose to protect them.

"Not an attack," I shouted despite the deafening noise.

Perception could help with this kind of situation, and people had gimmicks like the defensive features of my cybernetics. I wanted to yell for my side to stand down, but I was already activating a Skill that required concentration.

Fortify the Position (Level 4)

Allows Guerilla Taction to moderately reshape the environment for raised walls, trenches, etc. The kind a military group could construct. Can't be activated beyond the first minute of a battle. Permanent changes. Affects a 20-foot area + 5 feet per Skill Point invested. Range: 20 yards. Channeled.
Cost: 50 Mana + 20 Mana per 5 seconds.

I raised a crude wall with a focused will and rough gestures. Concrete. Barely managed it in time.

The Captain unleashed an energy stream from his arm cannons. The kind that video games called plasma. Blasts like flares from a blue sun swept toward us as the wall rose just in time. Forced the pressurized AOE back on them. I'd seen him use that exact trick to hit opponents twice. Now, it worked against him.

Several of his people were burning and screaming. Only a few took serious damage, but one of the tribe members was front and center and taller than my wall. He took the blast to the face and got himself charred. It was bad. He'd already been riddled with bullets. Basic Classer. Some kind of monk. Doubted he'd survive.

A couple of Quinn's spiders got melted to slag. The others were up and running. Literally. Then they climbed the walls.

"Enough!"

The whole room shook as the power of that one word echoed and reverberated. It seemed to come from everywhere and nowhere, all at once. Very few kept their feet and I wasn't one of them. My agility was high, but my prosthetic tripped me up again. I landed hard on my ass.

Chapter 9

Lee

Even those who didn't fall were disoriented or stunned. The fight stopped as fast as it had begun. Two members of the tribe, who all seemed less affected by the attack, rushed to the dying man's side and went to work trying to save him.

The one with whatever the shout Skill had been was named David Whitebird. He was the leader of the surviving tribe members. He introduced himself, in a powerfully magnified but much reduced level, then continued with, "This is not our fight. It seems that your group has some dissension in the ranks. Perhaps we should leave and let you sort this out."

"We can't just leave," Gerri replied. Their voice was distorted by the damage to my eardrums. Constitution and Perception helped. My cybernetics had limiters for just such situations and that helped more. My right "ear" was mostly undamaged. "They're talking about killing innocent children and a good man just so they can rob him."

A few other voices from the tribe agreed. "Yeah," and, "Fuck that!" stood out.

"It's not your decision," Whitebird said. "I have to put our people first." He glanced toward the Captain, then back at Gerri. *This isn't a fight we can win*, his eyes seemed to say, as if he were begging for mercy or forgiveness. "May we leave?"

"What? Oh yes, of course," the Captain said. "You're still under System Contract to not reveal our secrets. But you're right, this isn't your responsibility. Unless you've decided to join us?"

"Not at this time," he answered soberly, "though your leader makes a compelling case."

The Captain nodded. "We can talk again under better circumstances."

"Thank you," Whitebird said, and he looked as though he *really* meant it. "We can resume trade and mutual defense talks next week." He didn't add, if you survive.

"Lee saved my life," Gerri said. "He saved all of our lives. I owe him. I'm not going to just let them kill my friend."

I'm a friend?

"Neither am I," the taller native said. The one with the half-melted face. He still looked rough, but he was standing. Tough. "They're killing kids, man."

Several nodded. Some from the tribe. Some from the base.

I started sending out invites. Wanted to activate my other Skills, but Dev would notice.

A few more troops took the chance to switch sides, which nearly got them shot. The others glared but didn't attack. In the end, I had just over a third of the troops, but nearly half of the Combat Classers. Mostly the ones who knew me. Trusted me.

I turned my attention back to Gerri. "You owe me nothing. We were outnumbered too."

"I'll be the judge of who I owe. Besides, that mind-controlling jerk can't be trusted."

Things were tense, but people kept their cool long enough to let most of the tribe clear out. The majority wanted to leave. They left. About a third of the tribe joined us for the fight. It surprised me, but it pissed off their leader and the Captain, who'd clearly made a serious mistake.

I used the hustle and bustle as an excuse to summon a hidden ace to my free hand. Another custom job from Earl. It would have to be enough. I clenched my hand around it tightly. Several soldiers blocked the enemies' line of sight.

"Quinn," I said, "pick a side."

"There's only one side," she said, moving to use the Captain as partial cover. "You can't beat Him." Him with a capital H. The Humanist. "This isn't you. The Teacher—"

My mind had moved on from Quinn as I saw that Cap was clearly ready to issue a shouted command. Probably to kill us all.

"Don't do this, Dev."

"I'm not doing this, Lee," he answered "You are. Surrender now and beg the Humanist for mercy. It might not be too late."

"I'm not a thief, sir, and I don't murder children. We're supposed to be the good guys."

"There are no good guys in a war," Quinn said. Probably another of the Humanist's quotes.

"This isn't a war," Gerri shouted.

"Yes, it is," Dev, Quinn, and I yelled in unison.

"Enough of this," the Captain roared. "They've made their choice. Kill them."

I activated and tossed my surprise. The directional EMP grenade whirred, clicked, whistled, and boomed. Score one for Earl! It disrupted the enemy's tech for a short moment. Short moments mattered, especially at the start.

Even without my orders, Gerri acted. Two Skills back to back. Vaporize and Shape Smoke. Same as with the Voloids. It seemed to be their go-to move. The purple smoke danced among our enemies. Last time it had been brutally effective. This time, we'd buffed our opponents' Willpower and it protected them. Only a couple lowered weapons. A few more hesitated. Better than nothing.

I opened fire. We all did.

As soon as I got my rhythm down, I activated one of my Guerrilla Tactician Class abilities.

Hit and Run (Level 1)

Tactician creates a movement and attack rate buff that lasts 15 seconds + 1 second per Skill Point used. Activation creates 2 charges. The second charge must be used within 2 minutes, plus 20 seconds per Skill Point used. 5-minute cooldown. Can be cast on participants in active combat. Must be able to fit everyone affected into a 10-foot radius on activation.

Cost: 45 Stamina + 15 Mana per participant.

I triggered the first charge. Kept the second in reserve.

Bullets and spells were flying in a thunderous cacophony punctuated with shouts and screams.

I took a wicked shot to the shoulder. No flesh. No pain. Damaged my actuator. I grimaced. It was a minor issue, but not the kind of thing you want to see early in a fight.

My guys were quicker because of my Skill. They repositioned better. Fired faster. It put the others on their back feet, and many dove for cover behind desks and terminals.

Key tactical choice: the Captain or Quinn.

"Hit the spiders," I yelled. "Everything you've got!"

There were blasts of fire. Bolts of ice. A hail of armor-piercing bullets. The sounds of metal tearing, connectors popping. The spiders broke and writhed.

Quinn screamed in impotent rage and threw a fragmentary grenade. She'd enhanced it with one of her Skills. My fault. I'd made her pack them. *Fuck!*

"Take cover!"

People tried, but it was too little, too late. There wasn't enough room to easily avoid explosives. Several made it to cover behind consoles. Billy, the Night-Shift Guard. Two guys I didn't know from Adam. Others were too slow. A young man named Nick didn't make it. He'd already been injured, and he died as the shrapnel shredded his face and neck. Blood seeped.

His wife was on patrol and they had a kid named Becky. Carrot-topped cutie.

I'd be the one to break the news.

"Lowbies!" I yelled. What we called people Level twenty-five and lower. "Evac. Double-time."

This was not the place for them. Nothing but fodder.

Seven Non-Com Basics and three Combat Classers fled. An Advanced Class Technician bolted with them. Coward.

Eight of their lowbies tried to do the same. I'd have let them go, but they struggled to get past the barriers. They were hit by their side's AOEs. I tried to convince myself it wasn't on Cap's orders. The man had been a friend. But it was too coordinated. They crackled and popped from plasma as they died. He'd lost his goddamned mind.

Sometimes it was better not to feel. I ignored the gurgle in my gut and let myself go cold.

The healers were protected. Casters too. So everybody focused fire on the injured. They didn't last long, dying hamburgered and charred. Tactically sound, but what a waste.

Quinn readied to throw another grenade. I expected it and blew it up early with a clean shot. My damaged actuator slowed me down, so the blast hit the closest people from both sides. Sliced into my good eye. Blinded it with blood. Raked my face.

Lots of people were swearing. Ours, theirs, even Quinn.

I wanted to throw a grenade of my own, but both of my shoulders were still too damaged. I saw a perfect spot where I could take out three of theirs including a key healer. Sandy. I'd known her for a year and a half. She made great macarons.

Gerri must have had the same idea and melted them all with a powerful acid mist. They blackened and turned to goo, melting layer after layer. Skin, muscle, bone. No more Sandy.

Great smile. Liked everyone. Only wanted to help.

It's us or them. I didn't make the call. Can't change it now.

Searing pain spiked in my temples. It hurt like a motherfucker. Thought that I'd been shot. No such luck. It was so much worse than that. Stress headaches. Conscience.

Be cold inside. Dead.

I used a rapid-burst healing injection along with a repair patch for my right shoulder.

Quinn pulled out a silver box and tossed it overhand. Then another. They were decorated with odd symbols and would have looked in place on a *Hellraiser* set. They floated, twisted, turned, and grew. Then they opened wide and dumped their contents from above us.

Spider-bots. Terrifying but weaker. Not enhanced yet. Cutting. Slicing. Grinding.

We cleared the bots off, one by one, but it bought our enemy time. They worked like mobile sausage grinders once Quinn's enhancements took effect. Brutal. They killed a Healer and the tall man from before.

Even my cybernetics seemed to tense as the spiders came for me. Sparks flew off my back. Blood and oil spurted from my upper thighs. Boosted, they were able to dig through my armor and Quinn knew just where to strike to disable me.

For the first time in a long time, my body tried to scream and run. My will was bolstered but barely held. I forced myself to stand my ground. Breathe steadily. Break the psycho's toys.

I finished the bots off right as Cap smashed through what was left of my barrier. Blue plasma still sputtered from his arm cannons as he pummeled our last healer with his massive metal fists. The attacks were relentless. Broke and burned the man's face and body well after he was dead.

What did it say about me that I surrounded myself with such monsters?

I was down to half Health and Gerri was worse, mostly from the grenades and the sheer number of attacks.

The barriers were all but destroyed.

I activated my primary offensive Skill. Chose Quinn as the target.

Burn Them Down (Level 5)
Guerilla Tactician indicate a particular target to focus fire on, giving them a moderate defensive debuff and alerting all nearby troops to target them. Outlines them in faint, glowing red.
Cost: 25 Stamina and 30 Mana per 40 seconds.

The good news was that Quinn was out of grenades and her spiders were about to be down for the count. She must have done the same math because she bolted and dove for cover. Probably looking for a way to escape. Smart.

Unless she was dead, she was dangerous, so I tracked her with my Intel Report Skill while I directed fire toward the Basic Classers. Once the last of them was down, I turned my attention to the big man himself.

The Captain still had a trick up his sleeve. Well, in his chest. He readied a massive last-ditch AOE I'd seen him use against a horde of Duplicating Raptors back in Pittsburgh. There it turned the tide. Here and now, it was nothing but revenge. Dev had lost, and he planned to take us with him.

I'd misjudged the man. Hadn't thought he'd use it. That cost me half of the advantage that my knowledge would have gained me. But I still had time for one desperate play. My mind was racing, and the hints of two plans sprang to mind. I could move in close and minimize the damage to the others with my body as a shield. Might save one or two.

Might not though. That wasn't good enough, and I was out of time. I made the other choice and acted, pulling an item from my inventory. A portable shield generator. Curved for personal defense. Was anyone behind me? Had I just sacrificed the rest to save myself?

A flash of inspiration struck. With no time to evaluate the idea, I just acted. I tossed down the generator with a spin as its auto activation triggered. Its energy field sprang up, shielding only Cap from us unless it worked both ways. I'd always had to shoot around the damn things, so I guessed the odds were even.

I turned my face away, just in time. A loud creak sounded as his chest plate opened and released a blast of blue power. The shield did more than nothing, but not as much as I had hoped. It held for less than a full second, and then the energy washed over me. Into me. I couldn't hear my screams over the roar of the powerful Skill as my Health bar dropped by about another third. The top layers of my skin and cybernetics bubbled and melted. The damage didn't stop, even as the blast petered out.

I heard the others screaming. Barely. My eardrums were mostly ruptured. The air smelled like ozone, charcoal, and burning ham. Everyone who wasn't dead was hurt. Badly.

But my trick had done its job.

Cap wasn't gonna make it. He had paid a price for that attack. My gimmick made it worse. His armor was a broken, sparking wreck. Others had fared worse. The concrete floor was splashed with blood and littered with battered bodies. Human corpses. Every last one.

Goddammit, Dev.

I stepped down on one of my dying enemies. My leg pulsed, and a thrill of vitality flowed up my leg and into my body. My muscles unclenched as the sharpest pains eased.

Without the prosthetic, I'd have died the first day. It was a device meant for combat, nearly always meant to take the place of a missing arm so that its spike could be driven into the heart of a foe, but I hadn't been missing my arm at that point, so I'd done what was right for me.

Lifetap Inc. Variable Prosthetic

Growth item. Tier 2 weapon. Base Damage 20.

Becomes a spike to pierce the unwary and consume their power. Drains 5 Mana, Health, and Stamina per second and replenishes 1/3rd the value of the same. This device was originally used by a techno-organic race known as the C. Vengi 3LD and can therefore be used to restore cybernetic or android parts, as well as biological. Techno-organics are restored at 2/3's.

I turned my attention back to my old friend. By the time we'd managed to break through what was left of his armor, he was nearly dead inside it.

"Moron," I said. The crack in my voice proved I wasn't entirely devoid of heart. "I told you not to ignore Constitution just because you had tough armor. Hell, Topher told you."

"You were right," he said through gurgled blood.

Then he died.

That left Quinn. Defanged for a moment, *maybe*, but still a deadly threat. Everyone seemed to agree because they all started opening fire or casting abilities at her.

Someone had stuck her to the ground with orange goo. Probably Gerri.

"Stop," I said. "Hold your fire."

Most of them did.

"I said hold your fire!"

This time, the rest of them listened.

Quinn looked at me, shock and relief making her expression strange. She hacked at the goo but didn't make much progress. All weapons were still trained on her.

"What the hell, Lee?" Gerri said. They gestured at Quinn. Now they were using my first name too.

"Sorry," I said, "I won't kill her. She saved my life."

Quinn made a sound between a gasp and a cackle.

"Then don't kill her," Gerri sent through my chat Skill. At least they knew not to question my orders in public. *"Let me. Us. Hell, go outside and I'll do what needs done. She didn't save my life. She's toxic and powerful. Haven't you read a book? Watched a movie? She'll get free and come back more powerful than ever. She's far too dangerous to leave alive."*

I considered pointing out that if I had saved their life and Quinn had saved mine, then it was basically the same as if Quinn had saved their life, but that would have been a stretch. I looked Quinn over. She was hurt, barely holding on. I let myself remember when she'd pulled me from the wreckage that first day, by what was left of my arm. I'd never dreamed I would survive the final culmination of my revenge against the group responsible for my family's deaths.

I wouldn't have, if not for her. I'd always be grateful.

But Gerri was right. Quinn had made her choice. I gave her one last sympathetic look as I imagined what might have been. Then I turned away.

"You're right," I messaged through group chat. *"Too many people are dead, and she made her choice. I won't kill her. I owe her that much. But do what you have to do."* I turned and walked away.

"I love a rational man," they said through chat. *"Such a rare commodity."*

I never made it to the door. Only three steps toward it, Gerri swore and everyone else opened fire.

Quinn had managed to cut herself free. She activated an item or Skill I didn't know she had and appeared behind a doorway. I turned in time to see her smiling at me through broken and bloody teeth. Somehow, she disappeared from my Intel Report as the firewall dropped down.

That was the way to the hangar.

That was where we'd left Randy, injured, weak, and sleeping.

Chapter 10

Quinn

Blood and oil left a gruesome trail as I dragged myself down the concrete corridor to the garage. My spiders were destroyed. My cybernetic implants sparked and sputtered. I wanted to howl with fury, but I didn't have the energy to spare.

Healing injections worked to restore my tissue while nanite infusions repaired my structural components. One mixed blessing of being a cyborg was that healing and repair are separate. They didn't conflict, so I could recover twice as fast, but I needed double the supplies. It was expensive as hell but worth it.

Segmentation, my most overused Skill, was working overtime. Cybernetically enhanced, and with a whole Class Tree to match, my mind worked more like a computer than a human brain. Segmentation protected it from viruses and malware. Since the Skill had evolved, it also protected me from torture, compassion, and grief. It allowed me to sequester portions of myself so I could think more rationally and get myself out of situations just like this. Or more ruthlessly, to do anything that needed to be done.

There was a price, of course. In this case, a small portion of my intelligence and Mana for each percentage of myself I locked away. And it wasn't perfect. The suppressed parts of me leaked over time. I had to let them out eventually, or they took more and more of my capacity to keep them down.

I'd never had to use the Skill quite this much, and I'd made a new discovery. If I cordoned off too much, that section could still think and talk and reason. More urgently, it could still scream. Two of them were doing that right now. My inner rage monster was uncontrolled, swearing and demanding revenge. A third part wailed in grief from losing Lee, and alternately begged for me to save him.

I blocked them out the best I could.

Fucking traitors. And Gerri. I'll tear that freak's heart out and eat it right in front of Lee. I'll shred them, tear them limb from limb.

It's not his fault. Don't punish him. It was the Teacher. Lee can still be saved. He proved it when he stopped them. He saved me. He still cares. We can be together. I just need to save him from himself. From the Teacher. A chill shot down my spine. *From the Humanist.*

I was starting to pull myself to what was left of my feet when I noticed a crack in the wall that was barely big enough for one of my plans. I gripped my pinkie, hard. Then I twisted and yanked with all my strength until it popped off with a loud crack.

Miniaturized spider-bot tendrils extended from the knuckle and dragged the finger into the crevice, wedging it as deeply as it could. It cut and ground the stone around it as it did so, then dragged the rubble in behind it.

The attackers—*traitor assholes*—would want to claim the base and its credits for themselves. This would put a stop to that. It would also let me connect to the base's system, that way I could spy on them and maintain contact with central command. I hate the System, but I'll keep my Skills.

Cybernetic Bilocation (Level 2)

You can remove a small portion of your biological material that has been cybernetically augmented and leave it at a remote location, up to 100 miles away, + 10 miles per Skill Point. You are counted as present at the location of the device for Skill activation. One additional body part can be Bilocated per Skill Point invested.

Cost: Varies based on part selected and distance traveled.

What the Skill summary didn't say was that I counted by the System as physically present at any location containing one of my devices for more than Skill activation. It allowed me to claim and hold territory or, in this case, to prevent others from doing the same.

Lee's the only one who ever really got what the world has become. What we've all become. He's like the brother I never had.

Why can't he understand it anymore?

I passed the armory and vault. Damn it, no time. I couldn't raid the supplies or stop them from doing the same, not if I wanted to finish my plan and get my ass out of there before they inevitably followed to finish me off.

Stick to the plan. I staggered into the cramped garage toward the vehicles. There were five left.

I set three small acid devices, one on each of the left rear wheel axles, and melted them down to slag. I cleared most of my inventory and my Solid-State storage Skill.

Randy was sleeping on the ground near the car. I considered ending him. There was no question he would side with the traitors if given the chance.

But Lee would be pissed if I killed the kid. Actually, even the Humanist might not approve, since the Kid wasn't a traitor yet. Shame.

Then again, there was someone that I could kill to sort this out. The Teacher. *Kill him. Kill him and Lee will be free.*

I connected to one of the nearby boxes, opened it remotely, and reached inside. The metal device inside the crate disappeared, nearly filling my storage with the pet project Earl and I had spent the last few months building in our downtime.

What if it was never the Teacher and he really did betray. . . No. Don't. Focus. Stay focused. Ignore the pain, the gaping wound in the heart at the thought. Keep moving. *Lee would never willingly betray me. Since the day I dragged him from the rubble, he's been my loyal friend. I had a Prestige Class and real power, but others still had to be forced to work with me. Not Lee. Even when his Class necessitated his rise above me in the ranks, he always picked me first. When he was trusted enough to lead remote missions, he insisted I go with him. Fought for me.*

Lee had never touched me. Never leered at me. Hadn't even tried. He respected my personal space.

And he'd never called me names behind my back. Not like all the others. My security system spiders would have told me. He'd never even done it to my face. Not before the Teacher. Even now he'd fought the control hard enough to stop himself before he finished the word.

The crate itself, and the boxes of tools and supplies, went in the last of my inventory spaces.

I heard motion in the distance and opened a window in my field of vision to check the security cameras. They had broken through the door and were heading this way at speed.

I detached my other pinkie with another pop, tossed it toward the vehicle I was leaving for them, hopped into the last working car, and drove away as fast as I could.

The device wormed itself deep into the inner workings of the vehicle and waited for the next stage of my plan.

The part of me that could doubt Lee was moved to a new file. I added it to the restricted folder of my mind, along with several others organized in clusters. Things like Grief, Loss, and Love and others like, Experimentation, Implants, and Torture. All of the content was blocked, leaving gaping holes in my memory. But I had access to the titles, all the way down. Those folders were only restricted. I could unlock the files if I chose.

There was another section. A worse one. I'd locked it tightly and thrown away the key.

All that remained was a file marked Meat Hooks in the folder labeled Sisters.

Chapter 11

Caleb

When I woke up, hours later, I was in my bed. I stretched my whole body as much as I could in the cramped space and yawned deeply. I felt well rested, a fact which terrified me when I remembered everything at stake.

I sat up so fast I slammed into the ceiling of the bed's alcove. I clutched my head and waited a long moment. Even as a Non-Combat Classer, such injuries recovered pretty quickly. Not everything about the System was bad.

Case in point. I now had a vastly greater understanding of various construction methods, starship maintenance, and advanced security Systems.

Unfortunately, there were huge gaps in my knowledge. Many of the foundational background Skills and assumptions needed to understand what I had learned were missing. A lot of the practical applications required other Skills, tools, and even limbs I did not possess. Some were entirely dependent upon a hive-mind.

Even with all of that, I'd learned a lot I could use, and even more I'd be able to build on over time, if I were so inclined.

Most importantly, I had a good idea what we needed to do to address our most immediate problems. It didn't remove the unbearably heavy burden from my shoulders, but at least it repositioned it into a place where I didn't feel like I was going to drop it quite as soon.

Calling Pavise first thing when I woke was starting to make me feel a bit needy, so I decided to track him down the old-fashioned way.

I stepped out into the glowing stone corridor and remembered that I was on an alien spacecraft. During the apocalypse. With a badass-cyborg-shaped Sword of Damocles swinging ever downward to behead me.

I called Pavise, trying to check up on what happened.

"The children have all been fed and Aul is leading them through their normal workout routine to keep them busy while we work. You have excellent timing, sir."

"How long was I out?"

"Nearly six hours. I was about to wake you. Do you feel like you were able to successfully absorb the knowledge from the books?"

I groaned silently in the general direction of the ceiling at how much time we had lost, but at least I was well rested. *"That wasn't a given?"*

"No, sir. Not entirely. However, the nature of your question reassures me that things must have gone well."

"Yes. I think I know what we need to do. Well, everything but your job. Once we get you to the central command computer, you're kind of on your own. None of the books I studied really covered anything past getting you access to that when it comes to computing."

"Thankfully, computation is certainly in my wheelhouse."

"It is your wheelhouse." I was apparently not entirely recovered, because my balance felt off. One careful step after the other was all I could manage as I made my way down the hallway toward the Matriarch's former home.

"Quite right, sir."

"Meet me at the command center and bring some twine and colored pencils from the classroom please."

"Is that another movie reference?"

"No, I really need you to bring them."

"May I inquire as to why, sir?" I imagined him tilting his big metal head.

"Pavise, I'm surprised at you. Isn't it obvious? We need them to hijack the spaceship. It's either that, or we figure out how to tunnel through about a third of an asteroid worth of mineral-rich stone."

There was a long and very silent pause, with the connection still active, obviously to make a point. Then Pavise said, very patiently, *"Of course, sir."*

I cracked up. Very loud. Over the connection.

I might have cackled.

But when he showed up at the door, he had the required tools with him.

I, on the other hand, had brought one of the Voloid's spears.

"Here are the things you could have summoned with your Classroom Supplies Skill, Sir."

"Thank you," I said, face flushing.

Pavise somehow managed to communicate disapproval via his featureless face when, with the spear, I attacked the gemstones in the hands of the Voloid Queen. I had no idea how he did it, but I'd heard that old-school actors with masks used to manage it too.

He blocked the blow with a field of force, which I felt gave me way too much credit in my ability to damage what I intended.

"Sir?"

"Relax, Pavise. I'm just trying to break loose the gemstones."

"Clearly, sir. At the risk of repeating myself from earlier, may I inquire as to why?"

"Same question, same answer."

"Please hold very still while I perform a thorough analysis of your current condition. Three Skill books may have been two too many."

I cackled again, this time for sure. I didn't think it reassured my friend. "I'm okay, Pavise. This is part of the plan."

"Please elaborate."

"There are access panels behind the solar systems on both sides of the door. We need to break loose the gemstones to get at them."

"That sounds entirely reasonable. But please hold still for one more moment."

I sighed and did so.

"It is as I thought, sir, though not nearly as bad as I'd feared."

Acute Stress Disorder—minor
May result in impulsive or reckless actions.

"That's not good," I said and chuckled, which did not reassure me.

"It could be worse," he admitted. "Let's get to work."

It took us nearly ten minutes to break the gemstones loose. Even without a weapon, he managed more than half of them.

Then it was just pressing the button, rotating the solar systems, and pulling the panels loose, and we had access to the eight panels with three triangularly spaced holes each. The holes on the sides were deep. The top center ones of each set were shallow and had obvious sensors.

"So the pencils and string were a joke after all?"

"No, Pavise. No, they were not. We need to tie them to our fingers. Well, two of my fingers and all of your whatever you call those things."

"I call them actuators, sir, and I appreciate the effort to utilize the proper nomenclature. That said, I still have no idea if you are 'messing with me,' as you humans so colorfully say. Your description sounds too specific to be a joke, yet it is obviously too ridiculous not to be," he complained.

"Nobody likes a whiner. That one is a movie quote. Jim Carrey, I think." I frowned. "He's dead. I had the Voloids check."

"I'm sorry for your loss, sir."

"He was a national treasure," I said. "Well, an international treasure actually. He was Canadian."

"I'm sure he was a credit to your species, sir."

"He was. He was a comedian."

"I recant my accolades, if not my condolences."

"Philistine."

When he failed to reply, I explained the situation to Pavise as I strapped pencils to his "hands" and "feet." *"The security system is actually quite ingenious, though I'm sure there are plenty of Skills that can bypass it. In order to defeat it, you need to have long Voloid fingers, or in our case, colored pencils. You also have to have four limbs that are at least somewhat prehensile. Finally, you have to have a hive-mind."*

"But we do not possess a hive-mind, sir."

"The shield-bot said in my head."

"That's rudimentary communication via a cybernetic link," he said. "It's an entirely different category of thing."

I sent him my feeling of amusement at his argument, then the sensation of the itch I was feeling on my right shoulder blade.

"It's still not the same," he said, "but I grant your point. What do we need to do because of this somewhat hive-mind-like connection we share?"

"I know the initial security code, the special order in which I need to rotate the devices. Once that happens, my central fingers, which are on these shallower pads here"—I pointed at the small depressions with the faintly glowing beige crystals—"will vibrate at high speed in a random order. You must immediately echo the rotation without hesitation. It's vital that you get it right the first time."

"Does it lock us out if we fail?"

"No," I answered. "Well, sort of. It self-destructs."

"Is this you being impulsive again? Because I do not believe you would be strapping colored pencils to our hands with twine if the children were at risk, regardless of the debuff. I do grant that you would normally have the sense not to make such an incredibly improper joke. I will forgive your faux pas."

"Thank you," I said.

We proceeded to stand there in front of the door with all of our ridiculous supplies, attempting to prepare. I even had to use my Skill to summon more.

I managed to get all of his pencils arranged, straightening the Bubblegum Pink one that was trying to slide out of its coil of twine on his right outermost clamp, as well as the ones on my feet. But past that point, we failed no matter how many times we tried. That was how I ended up waddling down an asteroid spaceship, a kaleidoscope of colored pencils strapped to my toes, in search of an alien child to assist me.

The first I found was Kun Del. She was the smallest of the children and she had always done very well at arts and crafts. I smiled at her as I requested her help.

She just stood staring at me with her massive eyes, trembling. She did not speak, and she did not try to help me.

I wanted to talk to her. I wanted to take the time to delve into what was wrong and try to find some way to do something about it. Hell, I hadn't even had the time to see which Voloids were males and which were females, now that I knew I couldn't tell by their voices. I wanted to be a good teacher and a good man. But I was finally coming to realize that I needed to put being a good guardian first for now. There were a lot of things I was not going to be able to do for these children, in the coming days, unless things went a whole heck of a lot better than I had any right to suspect.

"Where's Aul?" I asked.

She looked at a door nearby and said nothing.

"Thanks," I said and walked away, feeling like a real jerk.

In the end, it wasn't Aul that helped me. It was Kek, the largest of the Voloids.

When I walked up to him, supplies in hand, he simply said, "Caleb is be need?"

I smiled, told him what was needed, and he did the job rather admirably. Then he walked away. I wanted to call him back, but I didn't. I simply said, "Thank you," and returned the way I'd come.

Kun startled and jumped when I approached her from behind. I gritted my teeth and kept walking, feeling more like a jerk with every step.

Pavise and I tried the plan. The pencil-and-twine concoction failed. It was just too weak.

That meant another march for help. This time, I found Aul right away, and she gathered some kind of Voloid adhesive I'd wager was made from Indekk, from its coloring. It worked, but it was going to be a pain in the butt to remove, if I was understanding Aul's clicks correctly.

When the code was entered, first by me and then by Pavise, the wi-fi guy's pod rotated with a click, exposing a stone pit beneath. If it had a bottom, I couldn't see it through the darkness.

Chapter 12

Caleb

I didn't even feel relief, just mounting dread as another item was checked off a very long to-do list.

It was a much less MacGyver-worthy device than my first foray into invention, and it took nearly four hours for the three of us to construct it, but I was proud of my new creation, nonetheless.

Using a trio of serrated knives, we had severed the twenty-foot-long cords from five of the hunters' combat grapples. That makes it sound a whole hell of a lot easier than it was—the cords were unbelievably durable. They were meant to grapple with monsters. We cut and sawed at them for the vast majority of the project's timeline.

Then we tied them together.

I'd never been a Boy Scout, despite Nana's best efforts. Thankfully, the Matriarch had been more insistent, or Aul had been less recalcitrant. Either way, she knew how to tie the right knot for just such an occasion. It hadn't taken long for me to learn her technique.

With four arms, she could tie two in the time I could tie one.

Pavise was good at a great many things, but tying knots was not among them. His clamp hands weren't made for it. To his credit, he never gave up. It looked like a comedy skit, but I kept my head down and my lips flat.

Now, we had the cord tied like a harness around Pavise, and Aul and I had the other end, tug-of-war style, wrapped at an off angle around the Matriarch's pod.

We'd found the bottom of the cavern using the time-honored method of dropping a light source and Pavise had measured the distance by being a supercomputer. He was handy like that.

The shield-bot was confident he could lower himself safely if he had a little support.

We were also pretty sure that we could slow his fall enough if things went very wrong, as they so often seemed to do.

None of us expected low-grade and high-volume treachery at the worst possible moment.

When the screaming started in the room right behind me, my body jerked. My mind summoned images of Voloids chittering in outrage as their fellows were shredded, then shrieking in pain when their time came.

Aul dropped the rope entirely and whipped around.

My body was yanked toward the Matriarch's pod and slammed against it at an odd angle, which caused me to spin. I tried to let go, but I had wrapped the rope around my hands and wrists, worried it would slide through my weak grip. Apparently I'd done a bang-up job, because I didn't lose a millimeter of rope as my arms were nearly ripped from their sockets.

The pulling stopped when I reached about a fourth of the distance between the pod and the hole. My momentum carried me to the halfway point before it finally ended.

I fumbled to my feet and rushed back to my starting location, screaming, "Aul," again and again until we were back in position.

Pavise, for his part, was silent. I could feel through the link that he was okay.

Even if we had suspected it, we would have assumed nearly any other source possible for the noise before we had considered Dul Anu. Yet that was who had come, obviously no longer in stasis, to scream and click his mandibles at us.

He was fully healed. It was one way that even those without System Access benefited from the System's presence. Minor injuries were mostly ignored now as a passing inconvenience.

Breathe. Calm. Don't take it out on Dul.

I smiled. *What the hell, Dul?* "What's going on, Dul? Last I knew, you were in stasis."

"Hive woke Dul. Caleb is steal from Voloids. Take secrets and try steal ship. Queen is will be fury. Dul is be outrage." The young Voloid's face and neck were a deep shade of blue, a sure sign that he was pretty furious.

He's not wrong. From a certain point of view, my inner Obi-Wan added. "It's not that simple, Dul." *It's not that complicated either.* "I'm trying to save us all."

"Dul right and wrong," Aul said. "Caleb is steal helping."

See, simple.

"Better Voloids die. Better Caleb die. Queen is not be things stolen." Dul wore a look of righteous outrage that would have been recognized on a human face. When it broke, there was something else there, something less. "Class is not be stolen."

The books were meant for him.

Pavise started to drop again, but we were able to catch him with a moment of heavy strain.

"Dul, I'll teach you," I barely managed to get out.

"Secrets is not be Caleb's Skills to teach." His upper set of arms crossed stubbornly, one of his middle hybrid-limbs pointed at me, shaking a single digit.

"Aul, we can't…" A new strain took my voice.

When we could stop long enough for her to speak, Aul said, "Dul is silence. Dul is be waiting."

When it seemed resolved, I let Pavise know and he resumed his slow descent.

"Humans steal computer. Humans steal ship."

"Aul is decision," she said. "Dul is be stasis."

"That's kind of like prison," I cut in. "If he doesn't want to—"

"Aul is decision!"

I wanted to put a stop to this. But Dul was already leaving and I couldn't let go of my companion. Maybe Aul knew better than I did. Dul may hurt himself if left to his own devices. But it felt wrong. By the time I decided that I did, indeed, need to intervene, I was out of time and Dul was out of earshot.

Aul is bad decision, I thought. *This isn't over.* But there was nothing I could do about it now.

"How deep did you drop?"

"Not an insignificant distance, sir, but a discouragingly small fraction of our goal. May I suggest that you turn your attention to what has caused the disturbance, so that we may rectify whatever it is and resume our task?" He sent me a mental image of the dimly lit shaft. There were far fewer glow crystals than usual, but even with the low light, it was fascinating. The hole was the kind of smooth you see on flat stone walls. Here and there, I saw veins of metal with dark colors I didn't have a name for. Under any other circumstance, I'd have asked dozens of questions about just that.

"Let's get this finished," I called down to my metallic companion.

"We have barely begun, sir." Pavise's voice echoed in the confines of the deep channel.

He was, unfortunately, right. As usual.

By the time he made it to the bottom, Aul and I were both shaking and on the verge of collapse. Aul's gray skin was alarmingly pale and I was drenched in sweat.

But the worst part was done. At least for us. Now, it was Pavise's turn. All I could do was try not to collapse. I'd heard that it was better to walk off exhaustion than to sit or lie down right away. I'd never thought to verify the old rumor via Google or by asking an expert before the internet had gone away.

With System recovery, it might be different now anyway.

I may have nodded off. I'd closed my eyes. When they opened, it felt as if they'd been shut a bit too long.

"Have you found the mainframe?" I dropped onto my knees and leaned over the shaft, bracing my hands on the rim of the hole.

Another image popped into my head. There was a complex metal device I didn't understand with a large green orb on top of it. Clusters of smaller green globules grew together from various spots on the "computer." They all glowed and pulsed faintly. To the left of the device, off by itself but connected by cable, was a mini version of the whole setup. This was glowing brighter and throbbing more. It was red. I figured it was the emergency backup we'd been operating under since the main system had shut down.

"Yes, sir. That is the good news."

I frowned. "That implies bad news, buddy. Don't say things like that unless there is bad news." I glanced at Aul. She was sprawled on the floor, breath whistling from her spiracles as she recovered.

"As I said, sir, that was the good news."

"I don't know that I can survive bad news, Pavise."

He said nothing.

"That was a figure of speech," I finally announced.

He continued saying nothing.

Hanging my head and squeezing my eyes closed, I asked, "What's the bad news, Pavise?"

"The access tunnel has been thoroughly welded, sealed, and reinforced."

I was going to suggest breaking it down or cutting it somehow when the image he sent me showed how thick the metal was. It would have been easier to tunnel through the stone.

"My return plan is not viable," he continued. "Once my task here is complete, I will need to be lifted out of the hole."

Damn it. "Okay," I eventually managed to say.

"Pavise is heaviness," Aul said. There was an oddly whiny note in her voice that I didn't normally hear from her.

"It's impolite to point that out," the teacher in me forced me to tell Aul as I nodded vigorously in agreement. Had Pavise not been able to bear most of his weight by pressing himself against the wall's sides, we could not have lowered him. We'd almost failed, even with his help.

"No offense was taken, sir," Pavise replied. "The Voloids can't help but feel what their counterparts feel, so social deception is not a concept they can personally relate to."

"Makes sense," I said and laughed, though it was strained because of my clenched muscles. *My life is so strange now.*

"You, however, are not a Voloid, sir. Your laughter at such a statement is unbecoming."

I laughed again, louder. "I'm not laughing at you, buddy, I'm laughing at my life. Besides, I have brain damage right now, so I have a get-out-of-manners-free card, right?"

"Your debuff cleared more than two hours ago, sir. Therefore, whatever nonsensical fancy you are referring to cannot justify your poor manners."

"Oh," I said.

"I'm glad to see that your rapier wit has been resharpened after your ordeal. Now, please allow me to concentrate while I attempt to save us all," Pavise intoned.

"Yeah," I said. "Sure thing. Sorry, buddy."

Then I remembered who I was talking to.

"Hey," I blurted out. "You said these conversations don't really distract you."

"This situation is outside of normal operating parameters, sir."

"Mm hm. I notice you didn't say it requires so much of your processing power that talking with me would distract you."

He said nothing.

"Pavise?"

Worried, I reached out through our connection. He was fine, though working intently. I checked. He was using 87.5 percent of his full processing power.

Jerk. I chastised myself. *There's nothing wrong with wanting a bit of peace and quiet.*

I withdrew and let the shield-bot work. I was glad that I did, a moment later, when I felt the distinct feeling of our connection deepening. My thoughts slowed as he pulled processing power from my cybernetics and, though I couldn't prove it, I'd have sworn he also took from my mind. It felt weird, like a river rushing through my neurons.

I stood there, dazed for a long moment, until the sensation passed. Then I stood there bored for another moment, until I realized I needed to get to work on a pulley system project to get Pavise out of the tunnel once his work was complete.

That gave me an exciting idea.

"Pavise, am I right to assume that the project you're working on might take a good long while?"

"Yes, sir, though it would be a shorter while if I were not continually interrupted."

"Sure thing." I smirked. Then it grew into a broad smile as I realized my plan would work. "Aul," I said, turning to my star pupil. "Get the others. It's time for a lesson."

Chapter 13

Lee

I wanted to give Randy shit for sleeping on the job, but I had to let it go. The nap had saved his life and my car. Quinn had spared them both. Who the hell knew why.

Our trackers had themselves all tangled up. Various Skills agreed on two things that couldn't both be true: the Cutter was still here, and she had taken off in an ATV. None of them could find her. The base itself weighed in. I couldn't claim it. Couldn't sell it. So as we'd salvaged what we could, we dreaded her attack the whole damned time. It never came. But we did manage to round up a lot of weapons and supplies. Someone grabbed a blue-and-white air hockey table. The kind you'd find in an arcade. No idea whose.

Half of our surviving lowbies fucked right off, along with a few from the Tribe. The one that stung was the Advanced Class Technician. I'd have kicked his ass, but I'd have kept him. Valuable.

The rest of us should have cleared out asap. Too many enemies to stick around in a known location. Instead, we'd risked ten minutes to gather and bury the dead. It would have taken longer if we hadn't had an Excavator. The guy who'd dug out the whole base. Great Skills but kind of an ass. Perfect for this job.

We'd started to cover the bodies with dirt and clay when I remembered the twins. I went back to the car to get them. We said a few words.

I activated Reconnaissance to summon my drones and sent them scouting. Tiny little things. Fast. First Skill I ever gained. Only one drone then. The Skill had saved a lot of lives. Up to four drones now. I'd considered bumping it to six, but Toph said no.

I pulled up my Intel Report to look over my battle map.

Intel Report (Level 4)

Creates a battle map for Tactician that updates with any intel that party members gather. Includes info gained by

surveillance tools. Gives a summary of troop movements, key resources, etc. Also includes operational goals, targets, and

priorities.

Area 500 meters + 100 meters per Skill Point.

Reduces Mana by 20 permanently.

Quinn must be long gone.

What a clusterfuck. So many people dead. My people. My responsibility. My fault.

No. Not my fault. The Humanist's and Quinn's.

I added new names to both my lists. Those I'd avenge and those I'd need to kill.

I didn't know all of the names. I'd have to ask around. Gerri could tell me the tall man's name. The additions to the other list were shorter, just Quinn and the Humanist. Quinn needed to die. The Humanist? He needed to suffer.

I was no match for the HLF now. But I'd made my bones as a Guerilla Tactician, and I'd earned my title, Bestower of Thorough Vengeance, with ruthless efficiency. It was only a matter of time.

People milling around and chattering pulled my attention back to the moment. It offended my corporate and National Guard sensibilities, so I ordered them into squads. Got them prepping to move out. To where? No clue.

I cleaned my guns as I checked my notices.

Regional Title Assigned by Organization Leader

Betrayer of Trust

You may have been a monster, but you were their monster, and they trusted you. Now, the leader of the faction you swore service to sees you as a traitor to your group, your nation, and humanity as a whole. You are marked as a traitor to any who inspect you, while within the area of influence of your former group.

I groaned. *That's gonna be a problem.*

Quest Complete

Rebel Leader Part 1 of ?*

Not only did you draw a line in the sand, you're willing to die for the tattered remnants of your principles, and you convinced others to die for them too. Congratulations?
XP Gained: 6,000 XP. Secondary Reward withheld due to contested base.
*Council Note (Automatic): This quest line is not forbidden. The Council strongly suggests that you choose your enemies carefully, however. Council Factions will be notified of those who excel at high stages of this quest line. Not all consequences are System-generated. You have been warned.

Rebel Leader would have been a great title. Could have helped offset the other. No such luck.

There were dozens of people. All staring at me. Desperate.

That was when it hit me. I was in charge of these people. They were my responsibility, and we were all marked for death. By the Human Liberation Front, the Hakarta, and more than a dozen other alien factions. An overwhelming feeling of dread washed over me. Adrenaline coursed through my body. My flesh and blood hand was starting to shake.

I pushed it down. Buried it deep.

I have a job to do.

What's next? Break it down. We need to find the patrol group and get to them before Quinn does. It's a race. The winner controls the narrative. Best odds of the most recruits.

Quest Received: Rebel Leader, Part 2 of ?

Like so many before you, you are a thorn in the ass cheek of tyranny. They haven't managed to kill you for it yet. If you and your people want any chance of survival, you are going to need reinforcements. Find the missing hunting party within the next 10 hours and recruit them to your side.

Failure: You miss the deadline, or your enemies get there first.

Penalty: Lost recruitment opportunities.

Reward: Variable XP. Hidden rewards, and attention you might do better to avoid, possible based on performance. *Council Note (Automatic): Sometimes less is more. We'll be watching you.

For a long moment, I stood there, reeling at the repercussions.

I decided there was nothing I could do about that now. These people, my people, were desperate. Their hungry eyes were begging for direction. For meaning. For safety. But safety was an illusion. Meaning was beyond me.

Direction I could do. I had a quest I was more than willing to share. Before that, it was time to remember that I had Skills. They provided no answer for my people's metaphorical hunger, but literal hunger they could do. I activated my Three Squares Skill and handed out enhanced MREs and water bottles.

I tried not to consider it an omen when I ran out of Mana just before I got to mine.

I'd overestimated my leadership of the group earlier. By two. They were Manidoo Aanike from the Fond Du Lac Tribe of Ojibwe. That was what the System decided to call the monster hunters. They'd seemed irritated when they told me that. Whether that was because of the System's word choice or my question about their Class, I didn't know. Didn't really care. Basically, they were skilled trackers with ranged and melee DPS. Levels nearly matched mine.

The tall one, William, had dumped a lot of points into Charisma. He sported a shiny black compound bow. Gorgeous and complex. Some kind of alien tech. I'd also seen him use a wicked bone knife with brutal efficiency. He wore camo armor with a built-in cloak. Odd but effective.

The shorter man was Thomas. Average looks. His armor was like his brother's, and so was his luxurious black hair. But he bore a medieval-looking longbow. Classic. He'd summoned a pair of hand axes for the fight. They looked like solid water. It made no sense to me, but I assumed he knew his business.

They wanted to leave. Said they'd done their part, which was more than true. I told them so. They seemed to appreciate that fact and headed off to grab their stuff and go. That was when the trouble started. They seemed to think their stuff included Gerri.

The caster set them straight. "No. I want to see this through."

I felt more than a little relieved by that. Gerri was useful.

"This is none of our business." That was William. The way he said "our" spoke volumes.

"I want to finish what I started," they answered the brothers. "How long can it take?"

"We need to get back home. We've been gone too long already."

"Then go, but I'm staying. And you would too if you really thought it through."

I raised an eyebrow at that.

The brothers just stared at Gerri stoically.

The caster turned to me. "How big is the HLF? The whole group, I mean."

"Big. Nine thousand troops. Maybe ten. A lot more if you count supporters and external resources. Say what you want about the Humanist, the man knows how to get support for his cause."

"I don't see what that has—" Thomas started.

Gerri raised a finger to cut him off. "And how vengeful is Mr. Gorgeous Man from the hologram?"

"Vengeance? It's the reason he breathes."

"And he saw us. He knows that I sided with you. Some of the others too."

I sighed. "He'll know all of it. Security camera feeds."

Gerri made a "there you go" gesture.

"Damn it, Gerri. What have you gotten us into?" William asked.

"I got *me* into standing against a mind-manipulating asshole. I got *me* into helping the only man who's helped us. I got *you* into jack and shit. You two did that yourselves." They seemed to hesitate but eventually finished, "You're grown-ass men." Their expression added, *act like it*.

"Not wrong," I said. Probably should have kept my mouth shut.

The pair glared at me. Finally, Thomas spoke. "If we help you gather your troops, will you agree to move away from here so he has to at least split his forces?"

I nodded. "I'll be doing that regardless."

William slapped me on the back and said, "Good man."

I flinched. Almost shot him. Appreciated the gesture once I understood it. I smiled.

"See?" William said as he turned to Gerri. "Problem solved."

"You're better trackers, especially here," Gerri said. "And the more people Lee has, the harder it will be to get through them to come after us."

They still looked skeptical.

"Also, say what you want, but that was damned good XP. I Leveled. You?"

They got that zoned-out look. William scowled, but his brother grinned.

"Damn," Thomas said. "Nice."

"I'm so close." That was William. "That's it. I'm not going home till I kill a few things. Might as well kill them with you two. It'll be faster that way. You're both trouble magnets."

I might have smiled. He wasn't wrong.

Chapter 14

Lee

Vultures the size of F-150s were feasting on the mother of all millipedes. They were crunching, hissing, and squawking while they jockeyed for position on the carcass. Digging for the meatiest morsels. An apt metaphor for the state of our world.

I climbed down from the car, eager to stretch my good leg.

Others jumped down from the back of the Tribe's overloaded pickups.

The System wasn't all bad. Road trip recovery took seconds now, even where my stump rubbed against my prosthetic. Someday, I'd find someone skilled enough to adjust the thing. There was supposed to be a way to refit it and fuse it to my leg.

The pair of brothers had scouted. They came over and brought me up to speed.

"Your people did well," William said. He was the tall and handsome one. Too damned handsome. "They defeated the monster. It was a tough fight, but they won it, and there are no signs that they lost anybody doing it."

"That's good news," I said. "Does raise a question."

"Where is everybody?"

I nodded and motioned for him to continue.

"Short answer, we're not sure. I'll let you know if that changes." He nodded and turned to head back to his work.

I liked him. Honest. Efficient.

A few of the men moved to kill the birds. I put a stop to it. Decided to let the vultures finish their last meal, then let the lowbies get some XP. My wife would have told me to leave them be. They weren't hurting anyone. But they'd been known to fly off with children as snacks. Even her soft heart wouldn't have risked it. Hell, even the Teacher might not take that chance, as protective as he was of kids.

I already had my recon drones out. Only other thing I could do was get in someone's way. The hunters and trackers stared at the ground like teens with new iPhones.

Gave me a chance to review my status and my new Tier 2 Skills. I'd certainly miss the HLF paying to upgrade my Skills. Because my gear changed so regularly, I kept my status unmodified. All me.

\multicolumn{4}{c}{Status Screen}			
Name	Lee Greyson	Class	Strike Force Commander
Race	Human Cyborg (Male)	Level	16 (A)
Titles			
Bestower of Thorough Vengeance Hakarta Bane Betrayer of Trust*			
Health	925/1000	Stamina	978/1000
Mana	275/1140		
Status			
Normal			
Attributes			
Strength	88	Agility	98
Constitution	100	Perception	102

Intelligence	114	Willpower	78
Charisma	93	Luck	60
Class Skills			
Reconnaissance	4	Camouflage	1
Psy-Ops	1	Electronic Warfare	1
Hit and Run	1	Three Squares	1
Arsenal	5	High Performance Gear	4
Fortify the Position	3	Reposition	1
Dedicated Comm Channel	3	Intel Report	4
Assessment	1	Burn Them Down	5
Good Luck	5	Countermeasures	1
Tactical Trap	2	Ambush	2
Adaptive Survival Gear	1	Adaptive Defenses	1
Full Coordination	1	Real Time Updates	1
Spells			
Improved Minor Healing (III)			
Minor Repair (III)			

Spend the points now or wait for Topher's help? Seemed like a no-brainer. Where to put my Stat points was easy, and impossible. I wanted all of them. Needed all of them. Urgently. It had been bad enough, before I knew how crucial Willpower and Charisma were. Now, I wanted those as high as possible, as soon as possible. The trouble was, I felt the same about my other Stats.

To hell with indecision. Without Gerri's buffs, my primary enemy controlled my mind. I dumped all four points into Willpower.

Skill points were easier. I had one saved, so I had two to spend and three Skills to choose from.

Class Skills Available

Retreat

Provides Strike Force Commander the following boosts to group members actively attempting to flee. Effect: +10% damage resistance, +15% movement rate and resistance to traps and slowing Skills and technology, +5 Luck, +2 Agility, +10 Stamina Regeneration
Duration: 5 minutes + 1 minute per Skill Point or until 1 mile from their original battle map position.
Cost: 50 Stamina + 200 Mana.

Class Skill Available

Adaptive Defense

Provides Strike Force Commander's Troops +20% resistance to the harmful effects of a chosen category. Max members affected: 4 + 1 per Skill Point. Cannot be cast in combat. Bonus applies only to permanent physical items like armor, not Skill effects. Options include impact, slashing, piercing, cold, fire, electrical, acid, and poison. 24-hour duration.
Cost: 150 Mana.

Class Skill Available

Real Time Updates
Continuously updates Commander's battle map and assessment with real-time System data. Includes likelihood of mission success and estimated losses on both sides. Recommends when to trigger retreat based on preset parameters. Allows user to share Intel Report with group members on a need-to-know basis.
Duration: 1 hour.
Cost: 100 Mana +10 Mana per 5 minutes.

Normally, I'd have my mission parameters. If I needed more Skills, they'd be purchased, or Topher'd tell me where to put the points.

That raised another question. Did the Troop Progression Expert's plans even matter anymore? Probably not. I didn't work for the HLF anymore. But you don't stop listening to your mechanic just because you quit your job. If we lived through this, that scrawny bastard and I were going to have a long talk. *I'm done being a bystander in my Class's development.*

I decided to mull it over. Wait till I knew more.

Standing, I stretched. Moved my body around while I still could. Reloaded my weapons. I liked to store them in a ready state. Gerri looked over at me anytime I wasn't looking at them. Their dark eyes were intent. Hesitant.

I don't play games. Not anymore. So I walked over and said, "Thank you for your help back there." Felt a bit guilty I hadn't thanked them already. Or the others, for that matter. *Have to do better.*

"Shit," they said.

Not a good sign, but I'd learned enough to shut my mouth and wait.

"Well," Gerri said and let out a long sigh. "You asked for the story with my Basic Class. And I, idiot that I am, agreed to tell you."

I schooled my relieved expression. Nodded.

"I'd try to weasel out of it, but that would only make it worse because you can see the name of the Class, which is the whole problem, so explaining it makes it better instead of worse. But I don't like talking about it or even thinking about it and…" They stopped. Took a deep breath.

I followed suit with a long slow breath of my own. This conversation was going to require far more words than I'd prefer. Jack, my brother, he'd had a gift for essays and speeches. They'd been the bane of my school life. Too much bullshit. They lowered your score for straightforward answers. Wanted you to talk and talk. "You don't have to explain anything you're not comfortable with. You've got nothing left to prove to me. I already know what matters."

"Thank you," they answered, features softening. "That means a lot." They turned away to swipe at the first hint of tears.

I pretended not to have enhanced Perception. Didn't trust my instincts in a situation like this. So, I just waited while they did what they did. *If they need something from me, they'll ask. Or they won't.*

Thomas, the shorter of the brothers, started to saunter over to where we stood. I held up a hand to warn him off. He stopped.

"I think I'm finally ready to tell someone," Gerri said, focused dedication evident on their face.

"*They've been captured,*" the Manidoo Aanike messaged me through party chat.

Fuck my life.

Chapter 15

Lee

"I'm ready to listen," I told Gerri, meeting their eyes. They were milk-chocolate brown in the sunlight. "But it'll have to be on the road. We'll ride together, just the two of us, while we go after the others. They've been captured."

They sputtered for a moment, then said, "This can wait. It's not important."

"It's important to me," I answered, "and we'll have plenty of time. Without more information, there's nothing we can do but worry. Not productive. Let the specialists do their jobs while we talk."

"Okay," they said. "But get us a driver, so we don't have to think about the road."

"Will do," I said.

"Thanks," they continued.

I gave the orders to move out. Most scrambled for the vehicles. Someone gave the order to deal with the vultures. Saved me the trouble.

I ushered Gerri into my ATV and motioned for Nick to join us. He was a basic Classer from Brooklyn. Driver. Knew when to keep his mouth shut.

"Why go the extra mile to set this up?" Gerri asked.

Fair question. "The truth is I've never seen Classes like yours. Dopamancer. Pharmaceutical Revolutionary. Got me curious. The rest of the truth? Whatever they are, they work. I still hope to recruit you."

"Truth for truth. I like working with you too, but you're gonna fail."

"Shame. I'd still like to know. If you'll tell me."

"Truth for truth?"

"Sure."

"You first?" Gerri asked.

"You're pushing your luck."

"I'm not the one with a sales pitch."

I chuckled. They had me there.

"So, how did you become a Strike Force Commander?"

"The hard way. Topher, a Troop Progression Expert, set me on the right path. Trained me up. We did the work to play the System."

"Not much of a trade."

I laughed. "You asked the wrong question."

"What's the right one?"

"How'd I become a Guerrilla Tactician?"

"Ooh! That does sound more interesting. Is that your Basic Class?"

I nodded.

"Okay, I'll bite. How did you get your Basic Class?"

"Other people's Perks. Indirectly."

They turned awkwardly to face me more. "You have my attention."

"I was an investment banker. BG and E. I was the G. We were all at work when the shit hit the fan. We were always at work. Closing on a merger. A hostile takeover. Baer did the research. She was our big picture specialist. Nobody did analytics better. E was Erickson. A professional ass-kisser. Less said about him the better."

"What about you?"

"Me too. The less the better."

"Ha, ha," they said and rolled their eyes. "What was your job?"

"Early days, I wined and dined the gullible. Got pretty good at it. But that wasn't my specialty."

"What was?"

"You've heard of hostile takeovers?"

"Yeah. From you, half a second ago."

I chuckled. "I was in charge of the hostile part."

They looked me up and down. "Makes sense."

I shook my head and smirked. "I was a different kind of monster then. Different tactics. Same purpose. Get more money and power to get more money and power. But we had the wrong kind of power that first day. We all would have died, except the aliens that wanted our building were upstart younger family members trying to make a name for themselves on the sly, and they had rules. Some weird honor culture. Or maybe some rule of the System, that close to initialization. Either way, they warned us. Blah blah blah. We'll take your building. Blah blah blah. No survivors. You get the gist. They gave us six hours."

"Their mistake, I'm guessing, since here you are, all survived." They laughed at their own bad joke. Then they did a double-take at my gear. My replacement parts. "Well, most survived."

I scoffed. "That came later. Except the leg. That was years before."

"How'd you lose it?"

"Coast Guard. A shark. Big one. Nasty. The documentaries lied. Jab to the nose didn't work."

"Truth for truth?" they said, sounding incredulous. Good instincts.

I smiled. "I *was* in the Coast Guard. But no. I lost my foot the old-fashioned way. Amputation."

They put their hand on mine. Smiled empathetically. "Diabetes?"

"Stubbornness. I got an infection from a cut. Should have been nothing. My wife tried to warn me, but I didn't listen. Splashed it with Yamazaki twelve and called it a day. Stupid."

"You couldn't have known."

"She did. Or knew not to take the chance. Anyway, my main Perk was gonna go for this." I knocked on my prosthetic. I knew I'd never survive without something far more durable than what I'd had before the System came. Problem was, it wouldn't do me any good if I were dead."

Gerri nodded.

"The best Class that I was offered, Coast Guardian, wasn't right for downtown Minneapolis. So I used that Perk to get a Class instead. We had aliens coming. Monsters. Our whole world was gonna go to hell and I knew we were outmatched. We had to think outside the box."

"Did you have some vets there with you?"

"Yeah, working security. Credit where it's due though, it was my old man that saved us. He was a piece of work. No question. Never there for us. Brutal. But I have to give him a pass because if not for him, I'd never have survived. He'd been a marine before he retired. Desert Storm. He loved watching old war movies, gulping down coffee and smoking nonstop. He watched them all day long. Called them the glory days. He liked the big wars. Iconic. But the shows kept playing even when he fell asleep. My brother and I were stuck with him while Mom worked, before we were old enough to know that he wouldn't stop us if we left. Now and then, they talked about the war he hated most."

"Vietnam?" Gerri guessed.

I nodded. "Got it in one. I have no idea why that war was really fought. I've frankly never cared. But two things I learned for sure. The Viet Cong were tough, and their tactics worked. So I grabbed that Class. The Skills didn't help that much that day, but the mindset did. And the Skills certainly did later on. That's a whole other story."

They leaned toward me and listened intently.

"I gathered everyone into three groups. Those who planned to fight and knew their business. Those who refused or might as well have. And those who'd checked out early."

"Checked out?"

"Lost their damn minds. Thankfully, only a few. The fighters got to keep their Perks. People needing protection paid for the privilege."

They raised their eyebrows.

"Yes. We forced them to pick what we wanted and give it to us."

"I'm surprised some of them didn't just refuse and select whatever the hell they wanted."

"One did. Made a big deal about it. Loud. Encouraged others."

"Erickson?"

I raised my only eyebrow. "Good catch. Smart."

They smiled. "What happened?"

"He had a tantrum. 'I'm an American. You can't do this to me. I have rights.' He learned he didn't. He learned we could. Correction. Everyone else learned."

"My God. What'd you do to him?"

"You sure you want to trade? That's a lot of truth." My eyes got hard. "I'll hold you to it."

They looked down and shook their head. "What about the people who checked out early? How'd you get their Perks?"

"We didn't. No one did."

"More examples?" They tried to sound casual. They failed. Sat back a bit and tensed. Probably unconsciously.

"Yes, but not ours. The aliens killed them when they wouldn't defend themselves. We'd locked them in a room to keep them safe, but one of the attackers was a sneaky type. Got past us."

"What'd you do with all the Perks?"

"We split them. Used them to *Home Alone* the motherfuckers. Kevin would've been proud. My Perks went to my Class and the Improvised Trapper Skill. I got two items from the others as my share. Didn't work as well as I'd hoped. Having someone else pick the prosthetic meant it wasn't customized for me. I can't feel through it and it's not a perfect fit. Damn thing had variable right in the title, but apparently that means it works for different limbs."

"And the second?"

"A gun. Nice piece. Got me through a lot of Levels. Lost it in a nasty skirmish last year. Real shame."

They looked more sympathetic about the gun than the foot. They had their priorities straight. It had been a damn fine gun.

"Two of our guys liked the idea and took trap-related Classes. They never told me the names or I've forgotten them. Devon, one of our guards, used to be a bouncer. Big man. He took that as his Class. For perks, he chose a body augmentation frame and some kind of crazy serum. He looked like Bane for an hour or so. He was his own trap. Stuff like that."

Gerri just nodded.

"I planned the whole thing. They never saw it coming. Turns out knocking aliens out of a skyscraper window and dropping vending machines on them gets the job done. Even got XP."

"Good loot?"

I frowned. "Didn't think to check. Maybe one of the others did. It was all still new to me."

"What happened to the others?"

"Devon got eaten the day I lost my gun. We'd fought together, off and on. Baer was alive, last I knew. Sold out to the Hakarta. Traitor. I'll kill her if I get a chance. Doubt I will."

"And the others?"

"Who the hell knows? People had people. I had my wife and kids. We all went our separate ways."

"I didn't know you had a family."

"Enough truth," I said abruptly. Still a live wire in my brain. "Your turn."

Chapter 16

Lee

I took the chance to look around and stretch. There was a sharp curve ahead. Roads like this in Minnesota should have been a felony. The weather was good now, but the thought of driving here at night, with black ice on the roads, pissed me off. *This turn has probably killed more men than me, and that's saying something.* Off to our left was a burned-out old bar. Our right—south, according to my map—was thick with red pines.

"You're gonna need a bit of background to really understand," Gerri said, pulling my attention back to them. They were tapping their foot in that rapid rhythm you can feel through furniture. Or moving cars, apparently.

I pulled my attention back to our conversation.

"I was born in Wisconsin in a place called Fond Du Lac," they continued. "It's the same name as the reservation, but it's not on the res. My dad's mom was white, and he wanted to live near her."

Made sense to me.

"Still, both Mom and Dad were active in the community and my older sister was totally devoted to our people, and what she called the old ways, or the traditions. She mastered the language. She studied history. She took part in the powwows and"—they waved—"whatever else they did."

I nodded.

"I was more of a rebel. It wasn't until I was in college that I realized I didn't need to abandon my heritage just to get away from my parents' constant badgering to pick a gender. My appreciation for cultures in fantasy novels finally made me want to know more about my own."

"Makes sense. Community's important. Now more than ever."

"The ember of interest would never have sparked if it weren't for my sister though. She was the best. She asked me what it was like to be intersex and nonbinary with something like reverence. She called me a two-spirit and said there was nothing wrong with me. She said that even though the term was new, people like me had been around forever. I don't know if any of that's true, but it was nice to feel like I had a place where I might belong. Not everyone in the tribe felt the same, but some did. Corrine, that's my sister, most of all. She even got into a big fight with my mom about it."

The car jostled us, and it pulled us out of the moment. They looked away.

"She sounds like she was great," I said, in the tone we all used now when we spoke about the countless people we had lost.

"Not was. Is."

That was a rare thing. Precious. I gave her a genuine smile. Just as rare.

"Or at least I assume she's still amazing. Probably more so. The System tells me she's alive, but when I try to find out more, it costs four times more Credits than I've ever earned."

What had that girl gotten herself into for info to cost that much? It raised a lot of questions, but none of them mattered to my mission or Gerri's story. I let them go and said, "Go on."

"I'd been looking forward to spending the summer at the res with Corrine and her husband. If the System had come a few months later, I might have gotten an awesome Class like the one she got. The Tribe tells me the System calls her a Mide." They looked up and bit their lip. "That's an Ojibwe healer, a spiritual leader."

So they knew at least some things about their sister's current status.

"Do the other tribe members know what happened to her?"

"Short answer, some of them know a little, though they told me less." There was a hint of annoyance in their eyes, then a flare of pride. "The long answer is that I like you and you've earned some real trust, but…"

"I understand," I said. "We all have our secrets."

"Thank you," they continued. "Instead of giving me time to connect to my people and history, and even more importantly to me, connect with my sister, the System came while I had let my cute blond roommate drag me to my first big college party. This was at MCAD."

"My God," I cut them off. "That is so close to where I was when it happened. I could have driven there in twenty minutes."

"Damn. That's a lot. But this is hard. Please, let me talk it through." They gave me a frail smile.

"Sorry," I said. "Go on."

"Not your fault. I just haven't talked about any of this since it happened. Try not to even think about it."

I could understand that. We'd all been there.

"Where was I?" they asked.

Rhetorical question. I kept my damn mouth shut.

"Oh, right, cute blond roommate. She promised to help me with my calculus class if I would go with her, because she didn't want to go alone. When I still hesitated, she said, 'We'll call it a date.' I'd been trying to pin down for sure whether or not she was interested, or just flirty, for a few weeks by that point. Either she'd been toying with me or she wasn't taking the hint, so I agreed, though it wasn't my scene, because she *was* my scene."

I chuckled, but forced myself to stop when it distracted them.

"When we got to the party, she left me sitting at a big table near the door with punch and all kinds of candy and treats while she went to check in with her 'crew,'" they said using air quotes. "Now, I'm low maintenance and I had the *Goblin Emperor* on my phone to keep me company, but the music was too loud, the punch and the treats tasted nasty, and people kept bumping into me, so I eventually moved. Then I got kind of pissed when I realized she'd left me there reading for well over an hour."

I bit my tongue, stopping myself from saying, *"Damn."* It didn't help because the vehicles hit some rough spots and bounced us hard at that moment, which pulled them out of their story. So I let myself say, "That sucks."

"Yeah, she was a piece of work. I'm still not quite sure if she was playing some kind of game, toying with me, or using me for some kind of virtue-signaling ally bullshit. But cute or not, I was having none of it.

"I had to push past clusters of people dancing or writhing against each other. When I finally found her, I was going to tell her where she could stick it. But she gave me a gorgeous grin with her blue eyes shining like she had missed me terribly. I melted. She pulled me to the dance floor and, well, let's just say the writhing dance was much more fun to do than watch, even with awful music." They blushed faintly and I had to fight off a grin.

"It was amazing until she kissed me. The kiss itself was all passion, powerful, better than I could have imagined. But there was something on her tongue, and it confused me. At first, I thought it was a piercing, which was hot. But it stayed in my mouth after the kiss. I was so hot and bothered and into the moment that I had swallowed it before I realized she had given me some kind of drug.

"Now I'd smoked some weed before like everyone, but that was about it. Like I said, not my scene. But when she dosed me, even clueless, head-in-a-book me realized why the treats had tasted bad. When the dance was done, I let her lead me back to my spot and she sat there with me for a bit, petting my arm and hand and letting me recover. It was sweet and it felt wonderful. I basked in it for a while."

Their pupils expanded. Skin pebbled. Reliving the memories.

"She didn't say anything. She just watched and waited long enough for the drug to really hit me. Then she left."

"Dick move." Damn it. Not supposed to talk.

Didn't seem to bother them. They were lost in the past. They just nodded. "I tried to get back into my book. But by this time, the party was overcrowded, and people kept bumping into me or giving me twenty-dollar bills to give to Danni—that was my roommate's name. I was tripping, bad, and the shadows had it out for me. I didn't know what to do. So I just shoved the money into my pockets and closed my eyes, trying to wait it out. Even with my eyes closed, the half-transparent outlines of large letters floated in my field of vision."

I'd been at parties like the one they were describing.

"When I finally felt like I could control my mind, let alone my body, I went to find Danni, thinking we'd pick things up where we'd left off. She was doing the dance-like thing with a man on one arm and a girl on the other and the way she was dosing them with the same kind of kisses broke my heart a little, as ridiculous as that might sound." They bit their lip. "Whatever this was, I decided, I wanted nothing to do with it. The world was spinning and I was not doing well, so I turned to leave. But time skipped and she was in front of me before I could escape. 'Where are you going?' she asked me."

Blonde sounded like a total piece of work.

"I asked her what she gave me. 'Ecstasy,' she said. Beaming and holding up a baggie filled with colorful candies. That was when I realized I might be in serious trouble. I'd had more than a few, even before the thing with her tongue."

It was my turn to lean forward now.

"I grabbed the money from my pockets and shoved it at her with one hand. I missed twice and finally got hold of the bag. I held it up close to my face. I remember thinking something about evidence and doctors."

A narc. Not that I judged them. Not really. The bitch did them dirty. Deserved whatever she got.

"That was when the System activated and the blue screen came. I thought it was just more of the hallucinations. I'm not sure what all I took in those treats or what was in the punch, but apparently it was all too much for me. The next thing I remember, I woke to a horrible hangover in a pile of dead bodies. I had half the bag of drugs in one hand and a wicked-looking dagger in the other." They were getting pale. Their eyes looked haunted. Worse than even bodies warranted.

Gerri had my attention in a vice. What had happened to them that night? What didn't they remember?

"Some of the bodies were the other people from the dance. Others looked like gremlins from the old Christmas movies. And my screen told me I had selected the Class Dopamancer." They pronounced it Doh-pa-mancer. "Maybe the System thought I was a drug dealer because I'd done weed, studied chemistry, and I'd let the people give me cash that night. Or maybe it's just run by assholes. Either way, I don't trust it. I had gained three Levels, and the screens said I'd killed about a dozen of the creatures." They stopped there. Seemed to hesitate.

I waited. *Twelve. Damn. Not bad.*

"There was another note too. But I'm not going to tell you for the same reason that I don't get to know what you did to your asshole partner guy who wouldn't help."

I nodded. "Fair." They had me curious.

Then I got hit with a flood of messages from the others. We were closing in on our goal.

"So that's about it. Oh, and it said it gave me a cookie, because I didn't die. I must have eaten it when I was spaced out or lost it somewhere. I never found it in my inventory."

They'd lost more memories than they realized then. Not the time to correct them about that. I did set them straight about the other thing. "There were never any cookies. It was just the System being a dick."

They let out a loud, thoroughly exasperated gasp. "I've been frustrated this whole time."

I tried not to smile. "What ever happened to the blonde?"

They didn't answer for a long moment, eyes staring off.

After a moment, my mind wandered. I had always been partial to cute blondes, myself. Natural or otherwise. The tattered remnants of my wife's photo testified to that. My mother, bless her heart, had been flustered when I'd teased her about bringing home my natural-blond fiancée. Mom was old-school. She had loud thoughts on what she'd called "the preservation of black culture." I'd always been different. I'm whoever I need to be to succeed. It had been a point of contention for us, so I'd let her stew for a bit before the introductions. She'd been shocked to learn that my soon-to-be wife from Melanesia was blacker than she was, blond as a bimbo, and had a distinct black culture all her own.

Smoking took Mom before the System ever could.

I yanked my attention back as Gerri, who must have been lost in their own thoughts, finally answered.

"Hers was one of the bodies I woke up to. Her throat had been slit with a dagger like the one I'd been holding. I thought at first I'd killed her, but I would have earned XP. The sight of that huge dead grin and slit throat are branded in my mind's eye, though nothing seems to bother me as much as it should anymore."

Okay, so maybe the blonde didn't deserve *whatever* she got. "I know what you mean. We've all grown calluses on whatever passes for our souls."

"Except maybe the Teacher."

"If he didn't have any before, he sure as shit does now."

They crossed their arms protectively and grimaced. Ashamed? I wondered why. Tried to reassure them.

"It's a hard world." The words had more force behind them than I intended. More pain.

They took my hand, sympathy clear in their eyes. I tried not to flinch. Partially succeeded. They were patient with me, as if I was an abused dog. I supposed in a way I was.

"I could have taken a regular caster type for my Advanced Class, but it wouldn't have fit with my Basic. When I saw the option for Pharmaceutical Revolutionary, I was excited to learn more, since it sounded like an activist Class. This System could definitely use some changes."

Wasn't that the truth.

"Though what use an activist class would be on a Dungeon World, I couldn't figure out. I was worried it was going to be the System equivalent of those fake toxic activism things that were so popular in high-end universities, where the rich white kids spewed hate, judged everyone, but never put their money where their mouths were."

I scoffed but nodded. "Trust fund socialists."

They snickered. "The Class wasn't activism at all though. It's about revolutionary drugs and medicines. Think mad scientist type stuff."

"Weird, but useful," I said as I glanced over Gerri's right shoulder. We were nearing a crossroad that was thickly choked with trees and wildflowers.

Set back from the road a little ways was a building with a sign that read, "Blueberry Bowl."

"When I dug deeper," Gerri continued, "I learned that the Class is versatile and powerful, but with expensive components. That said, my Basic Class helps, and I've been training my crafting to help offset the costs. I'll never be as good at that as a Non-Combat Specialist, but my ability to make money should be pretty good, even if I'm also chipping in and looking out for other members of the tribe."

"All of that is well and good, but it doesn't answer the most important question."

They were in a vulnerable, contemplative state, so my serious tone must have bothered them, because they had furrowed brows and watery eyes when they said, "What's that?"

"Can you make me some cigars and whiskey? Ones that will actually work with my new Constitution?"

They burst into a fit of tear-filled laughter. It lasted a good long while. I smiled and wished I could join in. Murphy knows I could have used a good laugh.

"Thanks, I needed that," they finally said and smiled. "I owe you one. When I get a bit further along, I'll do just that, if I still know where you are. I'll even do you one better and give you buffs instead of only, you know, poisoning you."

I raised my eyebrow at their suggestion. I hadn't thought of that. "Sounds good. As long as they still get the job done."

"With a Class like mine, I can only swear it won't be dull."

I patted the hand they must have completely forgotten was still in mine, because they flinched and pulled it back. I didn't take it personally. We all flinched now.

Chapter 17

Caleb

The information from the books was data, not experience, but it would certainly help. My mind now contained convenient methods to solve the problem of how to retrieve Pavise, but none of the equipment I needed for it worked without Mana batteries. The ship, we'd found, would not let even Aul remove those from their docking bays.

That fact sent me off on a five-minute mental rant about how the Voloids' security system made no sense. Pavise finally managed to shut me up by pointing out that if he were Aul he would have no problem accessing the secure location that we, the non-Voloid "invaders," were trying to break into and hack. She just had no Skills to do anything about it once she got there.

That made sense, though it didn't make our job of saving their children any easier.

So my students and I got creative.

The Skill books included all kinds of calculations and applied physics knowledge, which was really handy. *I need to get my hands on more of these books.*

Using some yarn, colored pencils, and other bits and bobs found in the classroom, I constructed a miniature model of what we were going to use to lift Pavise out of the lower control room.

"All right, students." I held up the very rough contraption. "This is a block-and-tackle system. It's a rudimentary machine that allows you to reduce the amount of force needed to raise a heavy object a given distance. If you'll remember from your more recent physics lessons…"

I talked with them for about half an hour, giving them the basic rundown of how it all worked, and showing them how the pulley system would need to look. They sat attentively and listened. They never interrupted with interesting and diverting questions. Even Aul. It broke my heart just a little bit more. They were right though. We had no time for diversions.

I broke them up into four teams to brainstorm items from the ship we could use to construct our project. Once we arrived at what looked like a sound plan, we all rushed off to do a life-or-death scavenger hunt. We managed to gather:

10 of the 20-foot lengths of cable

3 mid-sized magnetic clamps

1 portable laser cutter

1 welding unit

5 empty Mana batteries

A half dozen oxygen tanks

10 spare pipes

2 metal poles

3 fire extinguishers

1 jar of Sennite Brand adhesive gel

We also cut down seat belts as a harness for Pavise.

The idea was to build a block-and-tackle system on a sturdy base hanging over the mouth of the hole in order to lift Pavise free of the shaft.

The two smallest children were set to work tying all of the ropes together end to end to form a roughly 180-foot-long cable. That was a bit of overkill, but it was better to be safe than sorry. This was even more true about the strength, so we triple-checked the knots.

They weren't as skilled as Aul at knot work, so one of my favorite Teacher Skills got some heavy use as I showed them how it was done.

Demonstration (Level 1)

Grants +10 to your next Skill-based action. Requires at least one allied witness.
If you succeed at this action, allies who perceive you gain a +10 bonus to do the same action. A similar tool is required if the copied action used one.
Area 30-foot radius +10 feet per Skill Point.
Cost: 20 Stamina and 20 Mana.

We attached the rope to several of the heavier objects as counterweights, ran them through the tackle, and finally lowered them down the shaft tied to the harness. The last twenty-foot-long section of rope had been used to tie the various bits and pieces of the pulley system together.

Several of the medium-sized children were instructed to make two V-shaped sets of legs and a strong central rod, much like an old-fashioned swing set, from some of the pipes and adhesive that would form the basis of the unit. Aul and the rest of the bigger children were given the task of creating the actual blocks of pulleys we'd be using to multiply our force.

Our contraption ended up having four pulleys arrayed in two blocks. That would cut the force we would need to raise my friend down to a quarter of the original amount. I had the children calculate how much Pavise weighed versus the length of the rope and the number of fulcrums we would be using, and it seemed that we would only need to use the four remaining oxygen tanks, the laser cutter, and two of the battery packs as a counterweight to make the lift as smooth as we could. Pavise was very heavy, so it was still going to be a haul, but it should be doable.

As we planned and constructed the project, I kept expecting to get some kind of Title or notice for doing something so weird, but it never came. Which is not to say that the System did nothing. In addition to my usual lesson XP, I saw.

Your quest, Major Class Project, is complete.
Reward, 2000 XP to all participants.
Teacher bonus: 200 Credits.

I found it interesting that it handed out XP when the construction project was complete, rather than the rescue effort. I supposed it was because they were students, not workers. Maybe I could get them XP for the application of the technology as a separate project. Any XP was likely to help keep them alive down the road, so it was worth a try.

As for me, I was thrilled. Along with my usual classroom XP, the bonus was enough to push me over the next level.

Level up: 42
You have 1 Skill point available.
Your Intelligence has increased +2.
Your Perception and Charisma has increased +1.
You have 3 unspent Stat points.

I wanted to dump my Skill point into Attentive Teacher, since this was the first chance the Skill might evolve, but this was not a time for reckless choices. The same with my Stats. Any choice I made now should depend on whether or not Pavise was able to hack the ship.

I mentally shoved all of that aside until I could discuss it with Pavise.

"Great job, everyone. Take a short break while we wait for Pavise to finish his project, but don't go far. It shouldn't be long."

They just awkwardly stood in place. I walked away and looked down the hole, crouching, as I got a message from my shield-bot. I couldn't see anything but stone and darkness, but of course I could hear him through our connection.

"Sir, from what you were telling me earlier, there is an etiquette to this subject that I do not understand. How do you present information if you want to communicate that there is good news, bad news, worse news, and catastrophic news?"

"Not like you just did, that's for sure. You are making me want to panic and I don't know enough to do a damn thing about it." As I crouched there talking with Pavise, I visually examined the work the kids had done on the structure, double-checking the joints' adhesive and the reinforcing cables tied around each one.

"Let's start with the good news. I have successfully managed to forcibly gain access to the incredibly advanced and species-specific alien technology."

"You sound a bit defensive, buddy. I'm guessing that's because it didn't go smoothly. The bad news?"

"Insightful, sir. You are, unfortunately, correct. I have managed to not only gain access to the system but have even managed to permanently jury-rig a means to control it remotely via the technology from the control room."

"That's not bad news, Pavise." Leaning my elbows on my knees, I tugged at the string that was wound through the miniature model of the pulley system I had made to demonstrate the concept to the children. The pencil tied to the end rose and fell rhythmically.

"Well, sir, it would not be bad news if doing so did not prevent me, without more skill, more precise appendages, and highly technical tools, from accessing the controls here as well."

"Oh, is that all? Don't worry. It'll take some time and we might need to try a few times, but I'm sure we can get you out easily enough."

"Thank you, sir. However, please do remember the worse news and the catastrophic news."

"I can't do that, Pavise, because you haven't told them to me yet. With something like this, since you asked, and since you are doing this in the most frustrating possible way, please just get to the point." I set the toy pulley aside where it wouldn't trip anyone if they wandered too near the edge. I could feel my whole face ache from frowning, so I forced myself to relax and present my best teacher face. I wouldn't alarm the children if I could help it.

"Yes, sir. The previously working systems, including the doors and life support, are no longer active. Only the lights, as they have internal power, are now in operation."

My heart jolted, adrenaline flooding my system at the news that life support was off. "That is catastrophic."

"No, sir. That is the worse news. I have yet to tell you the catastrophic news."

I pinched my nose where my glasses used to go. "You were getting to the point?"

"Yes, sir. Quite right. Should you all survive without fresh air long enough to get me to the controls of the ship, which I predict to have a sixty-two percent likelihood at worst—"

"Spit it out!"

"The ship has low fuel and essentially none of the type needed for faster-than-light travel."

I felt as hopeless as the Matriarch must have with her own spear through her chest. "Damn it, Pavise. What are we going to do?"

"If you will forgive my language, sir, we will do the same thing we've done since this whole damned situation started. We will do whatever we must."

I nodded. Then I remembered that he couldn't see me. *"Thanks, buddy. I needed that."* Rising from my crouched position near the lip of the shaft, I grabbed the jury-rigged harness and lowered it down to Pavise. *"Let's get your squat metal ass out of there as the first step."*

"I have no ass, squat or otherwise. But I am eager to rejoin you."

He sent back mental instructions on how to fix the harness to fit his actual dimensions, rather than my misguided memories of him.

We got back to work.

I considered telling the others the bad news so they would hurry, but I decided it would be safer to keep it to myself so that they didn't panic.

I underestimated them, on both fronts.

Not only were they more resilient than I imagined, but they were much more perceptive. I learned later that they'd figured out that the life support had failed before I had, but they had remained calm enough to hide the fact from me, since we were already doing our best and they didn't want to overwhelm me.

Like teacher, like students.

"Now these are working as pulleys with the help of the oil for lubricant. It would be better if we had wheels with indented tracks, like a bicycle tire without the rubber."

"What is bicycle?" Aul asked.

Show and Tell glimmered to life with moving images of several Sesame Street characters riding bikes. They gasped.

At the same time, Pavise was talking in my head. I didn't get most of it, but I did manage to recognize the words, *"hunt, shops, alone"* and *"Fight."*

"Pavise," I responded as the kids admired the image of Grover riding a bicycle. One of them even tried to touch his ratty blue fur, though they

should all know better. *"I can't talk about this right now. I have to concentrate on saving you and teaching the kids."*

"I would argue that their survival takes precedence over their education, though I grant that both are important. We should be able to manage both those tasks, as well as our conversation."

"I realize my Intelligence and Perception are pretty boosted, but I'm still just a guy, buddy. I can't multitask as well as you can." Even when you pretend you can't. I bit my tongue, metaphorically speaking.

Then I lurched and nearly fell as my body kept working on the block-and-pulley system, while my awareness of my conversation with Pavise and my lesson with the children somehow stretched. I continued to be aware of both, but I was also aware that my mind was semi-segmented so that my teaching Skills, habits, know-how, and about half of more processing power than I usually commanded was tending to that, while another more than fifty percent, and the rest of my knowledge and know-how, was focused on Pavise.

It was awkward and a bit intrusive. *"I trust you, but warn me before you do something like that please."*

"Of course, sir. I felt, however, that the current urgency required immediate action."

"I realize we are in long-term danger, buddy, but a week deadline is hardly—"

"You cannot tell yet, sir, but the oxygen levels are dropping slightly, moment by moment. This situation fits any meaningful definition of emergency unless you are limiting the scope to a community or civilization level."

The air. I'd completely spaced it. There's so much going on at one time. *"Sorry, buddy. Yeah, you're right. This is just really uncomfortable."*

"For the foreseeable future, I strongly suggest that you adjust your expectations to the point that only being uncomfortable should be considered a major accomplishment."

At the exact same time, my body was hauling on cords and making the final touches on the arrangement of all of the "counterweights."

"Line up in pairs, smallest in front and largest in back so you can all see. When it's your turn to pull, hold the lines tight but don't wrap them around your hands or wrists." I shook my head as I remembered my own mishap. "It's too risky. Pull downward in a smooth, hand-over-hand fashion. It's going to be all of us and science versus the weight of Pavise, which I'm told can be a bit daunting."

"Kek is biggest," Aul said as she arranged them.

Kek flushed blue with embarrassment or pride as he stood straighter and moved into position.

"I am secure, sir. We can begin. Remember to give me time between lifts to rearrange my body to take some of the weight to prevent a fall should we have another 'interruption.'"

"Okay, buddy," I said, and told the children just that.

We lowered the counterweights down the hole and began to pull, stage by stage. This part was all worked out, so I was much less overwhelmed as the majority of my consciousness could be divided between two tasks, rather than three.

I almost put my points into Intelligence and Attentive Teacher, right then and there. It would help a lot with a situation like this, but Pavise's next words killed that noise real quick.

"I'm sorry, sir, but it is time to discuss the overwhelming need for you to learn to fight."

"I'll do what I have to do, Pav, but are we really there yet? Can't we just use the ship's computer to reach out to someone we can pay to transport us, guard us, or just bring us to the Shop?"

"You told me a saying once, when I was new to this world. If I understand it correctly, and I believe that I do, you are being what you called a precious little cinnamon bun."

"Excuse me?" My other focus was directed at the children currently on the line. "A little more to the right, everyone. That angle would work a bit better."

They lagged only slightly, even without a hive mind, and they did a great job.

"There you go. Great work."

"Yes, sir. Anyone powerful enough to help us would be powerful enough to kill us all and steal what most would consider vast wealth. We would have no way to control who accessed such a signal. Our anonymity is currently our greatest defense. It will not last forever, but we should preserve it for as long as we can."

I gritted my teeth and started taking all of this even more seriously as we hauled up our oversized burden, bit by bit. Pavise took some slack, so I motioned for the next set of kids to take their turn hauling on the rope.

"It isn't all bad news, sir. It seems the Voloids were both very well-funded and thrifty. They had a large supply of Credits to fund possible purchases that they never ended up needing since they were able to secure the dungeon and the surrounding areas right away. They worked together as a tight-knit cooperative with communal coffers. They grew their own food and brought or made much of their own gear. Almost every Shop purchase for the last two years was made for your sake. They hunted and adventured nearly every day since they arrived, and they sold everything they did not use via a dedicated Shop. They died quite wealthy and they have passed most of this on to you."

"To the children," I corrected.

"Not according to the System, sir. The ship and everything in it belongs to you."

"The System can go…" Swearing in front of the children is bad. Swearing in front of the children is very bad! I can't let myself fall back into bad habits. "I disagree with the System," I finally said.

"Of course, sir. It is also worth noting that the children are not without an inheritance."

"Oh?"

"The Queen had apparently intended to create self-duplicating units here to grow her power and influence during the early days of the Dungeon World's development. Therefore, high quality equipment and specialized Skill books, as well as the funds to start or purchase a settlement, have been set aside for their use. If you had access to a Shop, we would be sitting pretty, as your people say."

"Then we need to get to a Shop."

"Sadly, sir, it is not nearly that simple."

"Of course it's not."

As we had this rather leisurely, and accelerated, discussion in my head, we managed to get him about halfway raised through the tunnel, but there had been several "two steps forward, one step back" moments due to the makeshift nature of our device. The children were becoming fatigued, even with all of us taking turns in rotation—hopefully because of endurance rather than oxygen deprivation. It was probably both, by this point.

I motioned to the pairs currently working the cable. "Take a quick break and let yourselves recover. Aul and I will hold the line. Once everyone who needs it gets a chance to rest, we can resume."

"We will draw tremendous amounts of attention if we spend too many Credits at one time. We currently have no safe way of getting to the Shop and back. And the Voloid Queen might agree with you about the rightful ownership of the resources in question."

"The Queen is not be things stolen." The words haunted me.

I nearly dropped my share of the cord. The image of the massive hexapod alien, haughty and powerful, holding solar systems in her hands, now seemed like the cover of a sci-fi horror movie. Would the Queen be grateful for what I had done? Or would she blame me, as I did, for what I had failed to do? *Am I already doomed?*

I was really glad that Voloids ate Indekk, because her mandibles had implications I did not want to think about. And so I chose not to think about them. About any of it. I'd do what I could to save the children. After that, the Queen would do whatever she did. I'd be content.

Which brought my attention back to the problem at hand. No brilliant or foolish plan sprang to mind.

"Please tell me you have a solution," I said through our mental connection.

"I do, sir. Two in fact. You will hate them both."

And we're back to fighting and killing. Then again, he did say two of them. *"Go on. We have to do something."*

"Please remember that you said that, sir."

I groaned. *"Go on."*

"I have set the importance of the survival of the children to the same value as your own. This is the most that is possible. Your ethics require you to prioritize them, and my programming forces me to prioritize you. My self-interest does the same. You could override these limitations by ordering me, but as you have refused my service unless it was separately negotiated between us, I assume you will refuse to do so."

"You assume correctly."

"Option one. You set out for the nearest settlement tonight, with as many weapons and as much food as you can carry. I go with you. When we arrive, you use some of the ship's Credits to build a life for yourself. If I survive the trip, I will continue to protect you until I am stolen and stripped for parts. That is, unless you are willing to take much more of the Credits than I predict you would be willing to and pay for the protection of a powerful organization. We may be able to avoid this if you can find a powerful benefactor with children to teach. Your Title makes that possible, if unlikely."

"And the children?" The other half of my awareness noticed that the kids looked sufficiently well-rested to resume the lift, so I motioned to the next set in the rotation to come and take hold of the cable.

"They likely die—"

"You said you were giving their safety equal value?" I felt a bit betrayed, and my tone reflected it.

"Yes, sir, and I did so. But you did not let me finish. They will likely die, but at least they would not have you here to prevent them from learning to fight and defend themselves."

"Are you saying that the children are less likely to die if I abandon them?"

"It is a statistical certainty."

That was hard to hear. I forced myself not to swear. I'd been doing that a lot lately. If I kept doing that though, even in my head, it would slip out in front of the children. "I could bring some Combat Classers back with us for protection and help."

"The items and the ship are worth too much. You would be betrayed. Even if you got a System Contract, you would almost certainly be followed by other unscrupulous types."

"We could sneak into the city, gather what we need, and sneak back."

"The odds of you making it there and back again in the time we have, even with my help, are barely worth mentioning. And it is unbecoming to pretend that either of us is capable of stealth."

He was nearly to the top now. I could see his silvery dome. It was only a matter of time.

I closed my eyes and took a long, deep breath to calm myself, as I'd always taught my students. "Do I dare ask about the second option?"

"Apparently you do, sir, however indirectly."

I rolled my eyes. "Very funny, Pavise. And the second option is?"

"You finally learn how to fight."

And there it was. "Well fuck."

Chapter 18

Caleb

Once Pavise was up, I dismissed the class and they got some food.

I waited with the shield-bot while he took the time he needed to hack the strange "computer," in one case literally. He cut off the end of one of the cords and inserted a green gel nodule into it, which pressed into the hole, then hardened and flattened as it solidified.

He opened his armored-chest-plate and did the same to a port there. They flashed and glowed for a moment. Then Pavise fiddled around with various things on the device until the ships fans started up again.

"Great work, buddy."

"Adequate at best, sir, considering that I nearly killed us all. Your sentiment is appreciated, however. I will be done here soon. In the meantime, I suggest you either get a meal or take a nap."

I decided on the meal and headed to the galley to make myself a Daiya Supreme Pizza. I gave myself permission to savor it. I missed my pre-apocalypse ability to add extra cheese and seasonings, but I closed my eyes with pleasure as I bit into the crispy crust and my mouth filled with salty, zesty awesomeness.

I washed it down with a gulp of orange Fanta. I forcibly did not let myself think about what I would do when our supplies ran out. One catastrophe at a time.

While I ate, Pavise joined me. Without comment, he opened my Status Screen.

Status Screen			
Name	Caleb Hanson	Class	Teacher
Race	Human (Male)	Level	42
Titles			
Defender of Children			
Health	310	Stamina	310
Mana	760		
Status			
PTSD 10% reduction in ability to concentrate, due to intrusive thoughts.			
Attributes			
Strength	15	Agility	35
Constitution	36	Perception	84
Intelligence	86	Willpower	33
Charisma	60	Luck	36
Class Skills			
Relatable	1	Ring of Truth	4
Administrative Authority	1	Attentive Teacher	1
Continuing Education	1	Tutoring	1
Universal Translator	1	Cram	1
Targeted Assessment	1	Show and Tell	1
Classroom Supplies	1	Safe Space	1
Class Trip	4	Demonstration	1
Pay Attention	1		

Basic Voloid Construction Methods	1	Voloid Starship Maintenance	1
Voloid Security System Primer	1		
Spells			
Minor Heal (II) Minor Repair (II)			

I felt altogether inadequate for the challenges ahead.

"You are much too weak, sir. But at least you've taken some of my advice when it comes to your defensive Stats."

"Advice," I scoffed.

He had argued, cajoled, and lectured me daily. Not that I wasn't grateful, but he could be incredibly overprotective. Pavise regularly informed me that fact was a feature, not a bug. It was the apocalypse. I was alive.

He may have had a point.

Still, most of my Stats had been spent to make me a better Teacher. I probably should have invested more into Charisma, but once I really understood what it was, I'd wanted nothing to do with it. It felt evil. It tempted me now, because I couldn't pretend that my Class's increased Charisma had nothing to do with how I'd managed to save the children. It had been so close. Who knew what I would need if there were ever a next time?

"There is one somewhat less dim spot among the darkness," he said, which got my attention. "You have put a lot of points into Agility and Perception. Those are the attributes that govern shooting effectively. Or at least as effectively as a Non-Combat Class individual can manage."

"That's good?" I'd meant to make it a statement, but it came out as more of a question.

I reached for another slice of pizza, but at some point in the conversation, I must have gone on automatic because all of my pizza and soda were gone.

Damn it.

I picked up my pan and headed over to a basin and spray washer for cleaning the Voloids' drinking tubes. It was springy and had a coil wrapped around the arched neck that emitted several different cleaning products.

"As Perception is one of your Class Abilities, it is your second highest stat." Pavise rotated his torso as I crossed the room, so he was still facing me. "Unfortunately, it was a stat you developed for defense and study only, which will reduce your offensive Skills with it somewhat. Also unfortunately, your Agility is not nearly its match, and you have no real combat Skills."

"I know." I sighed, then grabbed the nozzle of the sprayer. My fingers automatically depressed the second button from the top on the underside of it and a hard spray of hot water started. I rinsed the pan, then glanced back over my shoulder at Pavise as he continued.

"The good news, in as much as there is any, is that you are not the first being to have this problem."

He had my full attention now.

"Oh?" I depressed the next button, adding soap to the spray.

"This," he said, pulling out a clunky black piece of tech he'd apparently found in his search, "is called the Targeter's Reticle. It should be fully compatible with your cybernetics and allows you to use your Intelligence in place of Agility when attacking. It will also free up your hands, as it attaches to either your forearm or shoulder. It also assists in aiming."

Images of blasters, spiders, and spears flashed in my vision. My hand tightened involuntarily over the sprayer, and all of the buttons depressed at once. Foam, purple goo, water, and pale blue sanitizer shot out of the nozzle at high pressure, showering Pavise and me. I gasped, dropping the pan and the nozzle at the same time. My untucked dress shirt and my vest were soaked.

Pavise continued speaking as if nothing had happened. "Finally, there are a few other items that will serve you well in your current situation. Namely, more Skill books."

"I'm pretty sure you said I shouldn't do that for at least another day or so." I hunted around under the sink for a towel, then wiped my face before dabbing at my dripping clothes.

"Correct, sir. You should not attempt to do so unless absolutely necessary. It is far too dangerous. However, once you have delayed and rested more, I suggest that you utilize two of the more combat-focused Skills available." As he spoke, the shield-bot reached for a nearby device and blasted me with a stream of hot air, drying my shirt with remarkable speed. I felt a little as if I were standing inside a wind tunnel in the desert. He spoke louder to compensate for the noise.

"We don't have a lot of time left, Pavise, and we have a lot to accomplish. Is waiting absolutely necessary?"

"I'm sorry, sir, I have no way to know for sure. When things are this uncertain, you should prioritize your safety."

"Quote me the odds."

"I'd rather not, sir. They are quite depressing, and I feel they would be bad for morale."

"Pavise, is there even a one-percent greater likelihood that the children live if I risk attempting the Skill books early?"

"Yes, sir," he admitted, rather reluctantly if his tone was any indication. "Several percentage points more if I do everything I can to assist you in the attempt via our link. However, it is not enough, as you would be risking death, as well as failure to use the Skill books effectively, which amounts to the same thing."

Death. I hadn't even considered that a possibility from overusing Skill books. Given what happened to me last time, I supposed I shouldn't be too surprised. That did make me reconsider, if only for a moment.

Pavise took the opportunity to continue, sounding urgent. "You can attempt to train and practice your aim and basic combat Skills throughout most of the next day, which should at least offset some of the downsides of the delay."

"Was that already factored in when you said the children were more likely to survive if I rush things?"

"Yes, sir."

"Then it's a no-brainer."

"I oppose this course of action, sir. The children need a guardian."

"Agreed. They need a guardian. That's why I have to do this. You already told me that if I'm gone, they have a better chance of survival. So one way or the other, the children benefit."

"That was if you left, sir. Finding your body dead is an entirely different equation. They've seen enough of the people they care about dead."

"And was that entirely different equation factored in when I asked you to quote me the stats?"

Silence.

"I rest my case."

He let out a long-suffering sigh. "In that case, sir, I recommend sleeping a few hours if you can first, or meditating if you cannot. What you will be attempting in consuming another book at this time is dangerous, and I think you will need to attempt at least two more."

I felt as if someone jammed an ice pick into my eye at the words, and my left eye twitched and spasmed. *"It seems like that would be for the best. Maybe I could try to find some caffeine. I think I had the Voloids pick me up some energy drinks early on, and I've never been tired enough to use them since. Love it or hate it, the System has a lot of perks."*

"It's worth a try, sir, though I'm not certain it would help. As for your Level up, I hate to say this, but you may need to increase your Intelligence, as it would increase the odds of you surviving the process and gaining the Skills you are attempting to absorb."

"That makes sense to me, buddy."

"One bright spot in this abyss is that the damage done to you previously was less than I had feared. So there is some hope. They were just theory books, and they were expertly crafted. These other books concern me more, however, as they have active Skills, and many were designed specifically for Voloids or at least other hexapods."

"Let's take a look," I said.

Just the thought of attempting to learn any new Skills made my eyes glaze over.

He sent me a list of the top six Skill books to choose from:

Hunter's Strike
Set Spear
Quad Wield
Hive Tactics
Thrusting Lunge
Sniper Shot

Quad Wield was out. I wasn't sure why he'd even left it on the options list. Hive Tactics seemed as though it would probably have the same issue.

"Can we even use Hive Tactics?"

"Yes, sir." After a delay, he added, "Eventually. It is a passive that requires two offensive combatants at the minimum, however. *And...*" He really stressed the word.

"And I didn't get you any weapons, despite your many protests. Clearly, you were right and I was wrong."

"Yes, sir," he said again.

I chuckled.

Set Spear would have been great, but I needed to be able to stay mobile. Sniper Shot was out as well, because I was not about to assassinate someone from stealth. That left Hunter's Strike and Thrusting Lunge.

I did manage to find an energy drink after a cursory search. It was pineapple-orange-mango Kick Start. It was delicious, though the System made short work of its effects.

I considered putting two of my points into Intelligence and one into Luck, since I could clearly use all the luck that I could get. But I trusted Pavise and dumped all three into Intelligence. Then I popped open one of the books. I hesitated and asked Pavise about my possible Skill choice. He agreed that attempting to evolve Attentive Teacher might actually help with this situation, but he said it was unlikely. He did agree that I should attempt it, but he asked that I wait until after I had used the Skill in combat several times. Any evolution was likely to make it work as a passive, as I'd hoped, but only in the classroom.

We agreed that any other Skill points spent were unlikely to increase our survival odds, so he asked me to wait, and I did.

I absorbed the first book, and it went relatively smoothly, though there was definitely a greater mental strain than the earlier books. I felt more ready for it, and I managed to keep conscious. I didn't even bleed. Yay for a higher Intelligence.

There were some pretty nasty unintended consequences, however.

Chapter 19

Caleb

I managed to absorb the Hunter's Strike Skill Book. It was more difficult than the previous but had fewer negative consequences. Yay, increased Statistics. On the surface, it went smoothly. Deep down though, I could tell that something wasn't right, even if I had no clue what that might be.

Despite my misgivings, I bit the bullet and opened Thrusting Lunge, feeling a bit like my profession was obsolete as the information poured directly into my mind. The knowledge went right in, like ice cream on a hot summer day, and felt just as off as the last. And like too much ice cream too fast, my head punished me for overdoing it with crippling pain.

Even with the magic of the System, I whimpered in the darkness and quiet of my room, unable to sleep or really do anything but clutch my head for what felt like forever. I didn't even remember how I'd gotten there.

A voice in my head made the pain so much worse. *"Sir, your indicators now show that—"*

"Shh. You're in my head. You don't have to be so loud. In fact, please just leave me alone."

"I'm sorry, sir," he said, not nearly quietly enough. *"Despite the pain, you should be capable of activity again. You've lost nearly a quarter of the day. However, I must strongly insist that you do not attempt to use any Skills until your mind is more fully recovered and I have been able to verify that your cybernetics were not damaged."*

My mind reacted to the thought of using Skills the way my golden retriever, Buttercup, used to react to even the spelling of the word vet. *"Your indicators are wrong."*

I tried to hug my own head. It was awkward and it didn't really help. I wiped a bit of drool from my face. Through my partly opened eyes, I saw a small puddle of drool where my face had been, as the light level of the room had gone from total darkness to this in tiny increments. It made the pain so much worse.

"Are you boiling frog experimenting me, but with light? Because if so, it's not working. I feel like I'm going to die."

"Yes, sir, you are," he agreed, no longer even trying to be quieter. *"And the children will as well, if you don't stop feeling sorry for yourself and do whatever it takes to save everyone."*

I expected a strong reaction from myself at that. Jumping up to rush into action. A flush of guilt. Even a flash of rage. All I managed was a deep, low moan, but the gears and wheels of my mind did start creaking and whining as I remembered that I had children to save.

"How much time do we have on the Quest?" I asked with the same tone and the same level of desperation as a child begging for five more minutes before waking up for school.

"I don't know."

That got the job done. The supercomputer didn't know!

"Excuse me?" I forced myself to sit up as straight as my cubby could manage.

"Sir, the Quest prompt has changed. It no longer lists the countdown to a week like it did before."

"Is that good news, or very bad news?"

"I don't know," the shield-bot said again. He sounded very unhappy.

Those words were just as alarming the second time.

"What does the prompt say now?"

"*Where it lists the time, it has changed to a single character,*" he said. "*A question mark.*"

"*I see what you mean. That could be good or bad.*"

"*I would agree with you, sir, if not—*"

"*Still hurts like hell, please just get to the point.*"

"*The question mark is neon red,*" he said. "*And it is flashing.*"

"*I'm up,*" I said, forcing myself to stand.

Since I couldn't use Skills, I decided to go with one of Pavise's earlier recommendations and headed to one of the coolest rooms on the ship. The training hall was bigger than I would have thought possible, made of the same materials and studded with glowing crystals. But the walls, unlike the rest of the ship, were decorated with exquisitely detailed chalk drawings of Voloid Matriarchs and their conquests.

Aul's mother was chief among them, at least on this ship. Also included was a huge illustration of a black land creature crushing a half dozen Voloids with its tentacles. E'Kklon Vekk was stabbing and blasting it from behind to devastating effect.

I spent the next few hours on basic target practice while I returned to some semblance of actual consciousness. Still, my aim improved faster than would ever have been possible before the System. It felt as if I was cheating, but I'd take any advantage I could get at that point.

Unlike any other Skill I'd ever gained from the System, the two newest felt somehow unsettled. Hopefully, that would change with time.

After the basic targets, we'd done some kind of oversized dog-like creature. Then we'd moved on to me being attacked by a swarm of weaker enemies—in this case, a group of hologram-covered dummies of four-armed land creatures and six-winged birds. This was my fifth try.

It was not going well.

I backed up and dodged what would have been athlete-level skill in the old world. Defending myself was something I had needed to do on all the hunts I'd been dragged to, so I was an old hat at moving in my semi-bulky armor. My firing was inexpert and haphazard, with my main blaster or the shoulder-mounted turret linked to the Reticle, but at least this time I was focusing on a single target, per Pavise's instructions.

My aim was better with the turret, but the blaster did more damage. It was a superior weapon.

My hand trembled slightly, and I wanted to blame the exhaustion and mental pain, but the truth was that even after making my choice, I didn't *want* to get better at using weapons and killing things. I knew I needed to. I'd decided to. But I hated it and it showed. I imagined it would only get worse with a living target, though necessity and adrenaline might help.

I had almost managed to drop one of the targets when they finally managed to get me cornered and surrounded.

I never lasted long after that.

Getting attacked in the training room was kind of like a game, with a virtual Health bar. With a pounding heart rate, heavy breathing, and aching muscles, it was a good workout too.

Pavise ended the holographic projections from where he stood connected via some kind of cable to the Voloid master hub. "The monsters are devouring your flesh again, sir."

"I think I lasted longer that time." Sitting on the floor, I leaned against the wall, catching my breath.

"You are correct, sir. Your abilities to evade, minimize, and even to endure damage are remarkable for a Non-Combat Classer. I would say that your training today has even improved them. Congratulations. Your ability to defeat your enemies and to protect the children, however, has barely progressed."

"Don't hold back," I snapped sarcastically. "Tell me how you really feel." I checked my blaster's Mana battery to stop myself from rolling my eyes like a sulky teenager. It still had over half of its charge.

"Your refusal to initiate an attack preemptively will get you killed, me destroyed, and the children left to their own devices. This goes against every goal you have for their survival, the continuation of what you claim to be my free will, and even your general desire for sentient and sapient life to not be ended."

"That was an idiom, Pavise. Sarcasm."

"Oh," he said, and he'd never sounded quite so human. "I see. In that case, propriety dictates that I apologize. But good sense, and my programming as a shield-bot, dictates that I should not. Sometimes, people need to hear hard truths, especially in matters of life and death."

"Fair. But it's not as simple as you make it sound. It's not all cold calculation, Pavise. Values matter. They matter most when it's hardest to follow them."

"Is that a Mr. Rogers' quote?"

I chuckled. "Not this time, though he probably said something similar. When I moved to Minnesota, I was the new kid, and I didn't look like everybody else around me. But there was a wise man called Uncle Phil, on a show called the *Fresh Prince of Bel-Air*." I smiled, getting flashes in my mind of the theme song and various antics. I set them aside for one of the show's more powerful, serious moments. "He said, 'You make sure they know who you are and what you stand for.' It took me years to learn who that even was, and more to learn how to show that to others. I have no intention of going back."

"I think I understand, sir, even though I may not agree. Just remember what you told the attackers, however."

"Which part?"

"If you will forgive me for paraphrasing your own words, that doesn't mean you can't move forward."

I took a moment to really let his words sink in. "I'll consider what you've said, but it's going to take time that we just don't have now."

"What do you intend to do in the meantime, sir?"

"The monsters are dangerous," I said. "If left unchecked, they will hurt and kill a lot of people. If they attack me and others, I'll do what has to be done to stop them. But they didn't choose to be this way. They're just as much victims of the System as the rest of us. If I let myself kill them when they're just standing there, I might be doing the right thing to protect people. Or I might be murdering a person who looks like a monster but would never hurt anyone, just because I'm scared. I won't cross that line. I'd die first."

"And what about the ones who will die because of your inaction?"

"I can't save everyone." My chin dropped and I stared at my hands, taking a long moment to honestly evaluate the harsh truth of his statement. "I wish that I could. But I can choose not to murder potentially innocent people. And I have to believe there's another way to protect myself and others from monsters. One that doesn't involve becoming one."

"You genuinely believe that, or you have to?"

"I genuinely believe that because I have to," I said.

"Bullshit, sir."

My brows slammed together so hard they cramped a little. "Excuse me?" Rubbing out the cramp would have given me an excuse to flip him off, but that wouldn't be right.

"Did I use the phrase incorrectly?"

"That depends. Were you attempting to tell me you think I'm wrong and either lying or so self-deluded that what I said is contemptible?"

"Yes, sir."

"Then no, you phrased it just right."

"Thank you, sir. Your dedication to your profession is as commendable as your judgment on combat is lacking."

Is this what a pissed off AI sounds like? I thought it probably was. "Why is it bullshit?"

"Because you are assuming and declaring that there must be another way, yet taking no responsibility for finding one or doing anything about it aside from inaction that does nothing but inflate your undeserved sense of moral superiority and risk the lives of those you are duty bound to protect."

Is he right? He's certainly an expert on duty and protecting others.

Crap.

I think he is.

What am I going to do about it? I had no idea. But not nothing, I decided.

"You're right," I finally told him, leaning my head back against the wall and staring at shining crystals on the ceiling. "I do need to do something."

"Vague, but admirable," the shield-bot answered.

But I wasn't listening anymore, distracted as I was by the System prompts.

Quest received: Find Another Way
Part 1 of ?
Numerous pacifist organizations throughout the Galaxy have theorized and attempted to find a better way than constant monster death to deal with an overabundance of Mana. Will you join them? Can you do better?
Rewards: XP and Credit Rewards based on performance.

Overabundance of Mana? Interesting. I waved away a System Quest Skill notification. *If that's the source of the issue, my promise to Pavise might be a problem. One catastrophe at a time.*

"I think the System agrees with you," I told Pavise and sent the notification to him with a mental nudge.

"Very astute observation, sir. But I do have one question. Why, even if you refuse to attack monsters unprovoked, do you hesitate to practice in a training hall?"

"Because practice works best if you treat it like it's real. And if it were real, I'd have a hard time deciding if they were really monsters until they attack. That trips me up every time. Besides, I can't be sure that the programs running the holographic monsters aren't sentient."

"I can assure you that this is not a valid concern."

"How can you be so sure?"

"Because I am an advanced AI and I can see their base code. Because I am, if you will forgive my saying so, much smarter than you are. And because they are not really dying, just like you, since all of this is merely a simulation. Sir," he tagged on at the end, after a short delay.

"Good to know. In that case, feel free to put them back and we can try this again." With an impulse of my will, the gun on my shoulder rose up and hummed.

"Am I right to assume that now that you consider them nothing but target dummies that cannot die, you will be willing and able to practice initiating combat, but that no matter how many times you practice it here, you will not do so to monsters in the field?"

"You tell me, Pav." I smirked. "You're much smarter than I am." I stood, the faint smell of ozone coming from my gun, letting me know that it was ready for use.

"Sarcasm again?"

"Yes, Pavise."

"Very well, sir. Shall we repeat the previous trial, or begin a new one?"

"Maybe we should wait until I can use my new Skills. I want to try them out, but my mind isn't ready. They still feel wrong somehow. Unsettled."

"You are right to delay the use of the Skills. As for waiting until it is time to use them, if you would prefer, we could open the door and let in the monsters. That would save you the trouble of more training and could even help to feed the local wildlife."

I bit back a curse, pushing away from the wall and moving back into position. "You're getting harsh. I thought you were on my side."

"I am, sir, within the limits of my programming and hardware, whatever you most need for me to be. When you were safe and secure, you needed reassurance. Now, you need what our link tells me you think of as tough love."

"I'm going to need a safe word."

"Would you prefer to use massacre or slaughter?"

Images of the carnage I had stood by helplessly and witnessed flashed into my mind's eye. I had to brace myself on one of the holographic projection pillars to avoid falling over.

"I'm sorry, sir. I should have adjusted your training to account for your recent trauma. I shall adjust my methods to compensate."

"No," I finally managed to tell him. "Don't change anything. Just remind me to up my Willpower if I survive long enough to Level again. I'm as ready as I'm going to be. Let's get started."

"Very well, sir," Pavise answered.

With no observable action, he reshaped the room to his will. There was now a single enemy, ready to attack. I altered my stance and put myself into the state between practice and imagination that helped me learn best.

"Behind you, sir," Pavise said.

I turned and saw Aul watching us with wide eyes. Behind her was Insurgent, ready to strike her with her own mother's spear. I willed for Pavise to use his shield, but our connection failed, or his ability did. I tried harder, pushing with all my mental might to increase our connection. And succeeded. Time seemed to slow as my mind borrowed processing power from my companion.

It gave me the extra time I needed to adjust my thoughts and ready myself to activate one of my new Skills. A flood gate opened, and data poured through at blazing speeds. So, I knew milliseconds after I had activated my new Skill that this whole thing was an advanced holographic ruse, and that Pavise had intended to shock me into urgent action, but he'd never considered what I would have thought of as the most obvious consequence. It was too late to stop it now, and my new Skill activated for the first time.

Hunter's Strike (Level 1)

Provides a bonus to accuracy and an increase to the damage of a single attack.
Effect: +10% to accuracy, +5% to damage of attack.
Cost: 10 Stamina and 15 Mana.

With my relative perception of time slowed, I had time to be entirely overwhelmed by each individual aspect of how painful and alien the impulses that flowed through me felt. It was what I imagined phantom limb syndrome to be like, but on steroids. Impulses I could do nothing with, made for a nervous system I had never had, washed over me.

I had never realized just how much went into a single Skill.

Energy wanted to flow through parts of me I didn't have. It was feeding me how to move all six of my limbs for optimal positioning. It even fed me what to do with the spear I didn't have so that it wouldn't get in the way of my blaster, regardless of which limb was using which weapons.

All of that sounds much less unpleasant than it was.

My mind and body went into what I could best describe as convulsive seizures with a side of species dysphoria. My mandibles were missing! Eventually, my survival instinct, or Pavise, shut down my nervous system and unconsciousness took me.

Chapter 20

Lee

The scouts had tracked the two-way trail to its source. They'd marked it on my map, so I'd sent my drones ahead to take a look. The X was marked at a medieval-style fort up on a hill. They'd dug a deep trench with spikes surrounding an outer stone wall. Decorations. Hidden System tech backed them up. Shield generators. Energy cannons. Serious hardware.

Whoever had the HLF troops had brought them there. A secure location. Well-defended. Bad news, but it could have been much worse, so I was waiting for the other shoe to drop. Murphy's Law.

The guards looked like the Cyclops from the old Greek myths. Brutes. Hodgepodge leather armor. Slow. They ranged in bulk from a Kodiak bear to white rhino. Upward of ten feet tall. The gate made them look small.

Assessment (Level 5)
Updates Tactician's Intel report with easily obtained System information. Provides estimates of resources, positioning, troop numbers, etc. This information is not fully reliable. Accuracy of information increases over time during the op.
Cost: Variable Mana and Credit cost based on request.

They were called Ur-Tallins. Clannish remnants of a once-great empire. They'd owned all of a dozen solar systems before they'd collapsed backward after angering the wrong planet. A dozen Heroics were all it took.

System fuckery.

Their eyes were not eyes. They were powerful crystalline growth-items that clan members inherited when they came of age. Looked like the top of engagement-ring stones the size of bar coasters. Classic lightsaber colors. Whether they covered, replaced, or made up for missing eyes, I could only speculate. I didn't bother.

I knew what my goal was and I had some prep time. Finally in my element. My enemies were oblivious, as far as I could tell. Exactly the kind of situation where a Class like mine could shine. Or it would be if I'd still had my established team. All things considered, I was as confident as possible without converting from the Church of Murphy. Things could still go wrong. I assumed they would. I was rarely disappointed.

But I also rarely failed. Relying on luck was for losers. I assumed that things would go to shit. Counted on it. Planned around it. Then did anything it took to win.

Started with a lemonade stand. Me and my siblings, Jack and Whitney. We played like normal kids, but it always ended up with me in charge. Other kids had lemonade stands. I had a small empire. And every time they'd shut me down, I'd done the work, played the system, and come back stronger.

Success had always been my greatest thrill. Better than any vice. Now, I had the same thrill, but without the drive to lead. I didn't trust myself. I shoved that distrust down and buried it deep. It was irrelevant. There were people I was responsible for. They'd be killed if I did nothing. There was no one else I trusted more, so I had a job to do. It was time to get to work.

All my life, I'd had a knack. My mom called it a quirk. It wasn't a System Skill. My brother had called it savantism. He was an asshole, but he might have been right. I'd never been tested because no one in my family trusted headshrinkers. For damn good reasons. But it was true that my mind worked differently. Better. Worse.

I ran scenarios in my head and computations happened, somewhere in the background. It wasn't something I did on purpose. Not something I *could* do on purpose. Whatever it was, raising my Intelligence did seem to make it stronger.

I wasn't a psychic, I only knew what I knew. In this case, thankfully, I knew quite a lot. Some info I'd gathered from Scouts and drones. Some I'd pulled from my Assessment Skill. All I knew was that my quirk worked, or I was crazy. Probably never know for sure, so I decided not to care. My track record was my track record. I leaned into it.

Top priority. Disable the shields and guns. We had specialists for that.

Their highest Levels were probably under our top fighters, but their average Level was probably higher than ours, and they outnumbered us. *Open with AOE and burn down the weakest. Maximize our advantage.*

They prioritized electrical-based stun attacks. *Counter with adaptive defense and other protections.*

They were big, tough, and strong. Preferred melee. *Stick and move. Kite them.*

Blitz assault on the fortress? *We win. Too many dead.*

Surprise attack at night. *We win. Less dead. Still too many. Nearly half.*

Negotiation? *They win. We lose everyone but me and a few of the chickenshits.*

Unacceptable results.

I'd learned recently that I could cancel Assessment and use it again. Narrow the scope. Always worked the same, but different parameters meant different results. I gave it new ones. Checked for cultural bullshit I could use against them, like the honor rules from my first day in the System. It gave me new results.

They were an honor-based culture. Valued personal strength. I could challenge their leader to a duel to the death. *Reasonable casualty Levels, win or lose. Most likely none if we win. I die if we lose. The prisoners' situation is likely unchanged. Acceptable risks.*

But why play their game? *To hell with honor and their rigged rules.* The addition of a second, concurrent mission sealed the deal. With both plans in play, we had a moderate chance to free the prisoners, even if I died. While I died.

I headed back to the others and brought them up to speed.

About a third of the people with us had never been part of the HLF. Another third had been support staff. I'd need to bring them up to speed. I looked around and spotted an old green-and-white truck off to one side. With my prosthetic, I didn't dare risk hopping, so I opened the tailgate and climbed up to stand in the truck bed. I puckered my lips and put my hand to my mouth for a two-fingered whistle. Got everyone's attention.

There was a bit of muttered chatter while people in the know got the rest of them in line.

I decided to drop the niceties and do this bare-bones basic. *No way to know if the prisoners are slaves or snacks, and smoke is rising from the palisades. Best to hurry.*

"Gather round, everyone!" I shouted.

They did so quickly. You didn't survive this long into an apocalypse as a reckless loner. They arranged themselves at picnic tables from the campsite. "Blueberry Hills Recreation Area and Campground" was etched into the structure they were sitting under. It had weathered white paint and forest green lintel.

Couple of guys had been singing the old Blueberry Hills song. Off-key. Loudly. It had gotten old fast.

The crowd was a strange mix of normalcy and horror. Some had cleansed their bodies. Changed their clothes. Others were covered in burned and shredded remnants. Blood-stained gear that smelled like copper, smoke, and sweat.

I was in the latter group, though I'd cleaned my weapons. Justifications popped into my head. I'd been focused on Gerri's story. Today had been one shitshow after another. *There's no good excuse for bad leadership*, I reminded myself. *Excuses are failure's bitch.* Nothing I could do about it now.

"For those new to working with me, I'm Strike Force Commander Lee Greyson. You can call me Commander or Commander Greyson in the field. You have a problem with that, the closest settlement is that way." I pointed off into the distance.

Maybe I shouldn't have been surprised. But when a dour-looking older couple whispered in hushed tones then turned to leave, it shocked me. I didn't get it. They'd already come so far.

It made me curious, so I inspected them. Made sure their Classes weren't vital. One was a Maintenance Worker. The other a Custodian. Useful. But not important enough to take the time to talk them out of suicide. Besides, people that stupid were bad for morale.

"All right then," I continued, once they were gone, "you're going to get party invites. It will be different than the ones you've gotten in the past. It's gonna ask if you're willing to join my group. Then you're going to get a prompt about initiating Full Coordination. Here's what that means for you." I sent them the Skill description.

Full Coordination (Level 1)

Battle map overlays, along with details, routes, and updated orders are provided to all group members on a need-to-know basis. This also allows the Commander to access information regarding your effectiveness at various roles. This Skill is System-and Strike Force Commander-controlled. It affects all allies in the Intel Report's area of effect, which it doubles.

Cost: 50 Mana + 5 Mana per minute per individual linked.

"What that doesn't tell you is that it doesn't just give you information in a visual form. It's gonna affect your impulses. Make you want to attack a specific target. Assist an injured party member. Run for your lives. It's not going to tell you *how* to accomplish those things or what Skills to use. That's your job."

Several hands raised at this point. They always did.

"Before you ask the usual question, the answer is no. This is not mind control. Nothing but good sense and a survival instinct will make you do what you're told."

Most of the hands went down. A few stubborn ones stayed up, including Gerri's.

I raised a questioning eyebrow at my recent companion.

"Does that work with your other Skills, like your reconnaissance drones? Do you mind showing us the rest? Or is it rude to ask?" They were seated on the bench, just to the left of center.

"Yes, it works with the drones. And yes, it's rude to ask. But I'm not big on manners. I'm big on practicality and the survival of my people." I did not add, *in that order*. "If it would help, I'd go over all of my abilities with painstaking details. It won't."

That seemed to satisfy the more reasonable members of my audience. There were lots of nods and other signs of general agreement. A few grumbles and frowns, but I wasn't about to make an exception for people whose curiosity outweighed their sense of urgency. If they wanted to know more, they could ask when everyone was safe.

"This close to the action, too much info would overwhelm and confuse you. All you need to know is that my Basic Class, Guerilla Tactician, and my Advanced Class, Strike Force Commander, were meant to work together." I studied their faces intently as I spoke. I noted those paying attention and those who weren't. Most were at least trying.

My eyes wanted to pass over a trio of jackasses whispering to one another. All of them had dark hair and were shorter than the average. I didn't recognize them. They were wearing HLF uniforms, so they damn well knew better than to behave the way they were. It was unprofessional. I glared at them and added them to my list of people who would need to be watched. I kept it minimized in the lower left hand corner of my vision. They hadn't noticed me, and I was about to ream them out, but they shut up and I decided to pull them aside later.

"Several of my Skills synergize," I continued, "passive or otherwise. They gather and process vital information about our mission. And our enemies. That way, my team can do our part of the big picture strategy. That usually comes from higher-ups. We don't have those now, so we're gonna go with, 'Don't get killed while we rescue our team.' If you have a problem with that, the nearest town is that way. Just follow the trail of blood to the corpses of the last two idiots who left. Assuming the monsters didn't swallow them whole."

This time, no one took me up on it.

"The two most important things to remem—"

The three were talking again. Technician. Driver. Gunman.

"You lot have three choices," I said, glaring at them again.

They turned to me. Seemed shocked that I could see and hear them. Some kind of covert conversation Skill had let them down? Not a good sign that they had it. Worse that they were using it now.

"Choices?" the Driver finally said.

"Not you," I said. I pointed at the Gunman. "Him. He chooses."

The Driver and the Technician looked pissed. The Gunman looked smug.

"Why the hell—" the Technician said.

"Because I can spare you, if I have to. I need all the gunmen I can get." I turned back to the Combat Classer. He wore a pair of Colt Pythons with silver Bridgeport rigs. "Your three choices. Shut up and listen. Fuck right off. Or I shoot you." I counted the options off on my left hand as I spoke.

"That's a load of crap," the Driver said.

I pulled my blaster from my Arsenal and shot him in the chest. Just the once to make my point. It was also great for stress relief.

The man flew backward and gaped in shock, clutching his chest in pain. He glared in outraged fury.

"Did you really need to shoot him?" William asked.

"Not at all," I answered. "But he *really* needed to be shot."

The Manidoo Aanike tried not to smile. Failed. Shook his head. His glossy hair echoed the motion and drew attention. Reminded me of one of those ads for L'Oreal.

"You shot me," the Driver whined.

What a moron. I turned back to the Combat Classer. "Might be down to two choices." I motioned from one to the others with my blaster. "You three a package deal?"

"Not anymore," the Gunman said.

The Technician backed away from the jerk I'd shot. Smart choice.

"You two were just as ready to turn them in and get the reward as me," the Driver said.

I glowered and looked back at the other two.

"He wanted to do"—the Gunman waved at the Driver—"all of that. We wanted to save the others and leave." His face was pale, and his partner was trembling. "We aren't stupid enough to…" He pointed at the idiot Driver, as if that answered everything. I guessed it did.

"You cucks! It was your idea."

I looked back at the other two. "Is that true?"

"No," the Gunman said, clearly offended. "We ain't no fucking cucks!"

I sighed. "Not that part." I looked around. "We got anyone here that can detect lies?"

We didn't. I'd checked. I'd also arranged for the few people who made affirmative sounding noises. The trick had come in handy in the past.

The pair looked ashamed.

The Gunman spoke. "We considered it. Talked about it." He glared at the Driver. "But I swear we told him no. You can ask your people."

I glanced at a few of the spots in the crowd before turning back to the two. Glowered. "You want to stay and shut up? And listen?"

"Yeah. Sorry about that." He smacked the Technician on the side of the head. "Fucknugget here said that no one could hear us. I wouldn't have risked slowing down the rescue otherwise."

"That's a great answer. The only right one."

"No promises we'll stay beyond that. This isn't what we signed up for. But we can't leave our people in the lurch."

"Fair," I said, "and I'm not forcing anyone to stay. Hell, I never even asked." I glanced at Gerri. "Mostly." I gestured toward their "friend." "Mind taking out the trash for me? I'll keep you up to date on party chat."

"Sure!" The men looked eager to get off my shit list.

The Driver started to argue, but even he was smart enough to shut his mouth when William came to his defense. "You aren't really about to kill a guy because he talked during your speech, right?"

"Of course not," I answered.

He looked relieved. The Driver more so.

"I'm planning to *have* him killed." I motioned to the other two. "Because he didn't leave when he had the chance. Because he was a distraction from a plan that lives depend on. Twice. After being warned. But mostly because fucknugget here"—I'd liked the term—"plans to try to sell us out for a few Credits. He plans to get us killed. That includes *your* people too, if somebody was stupid enough to tell him where you live?"

A few tribe members raised their hands. Hesitantly.

I motioned to the upraised hands. "Worse for you guys. Less mobile. You still want to object?"

William's expression was as cold as mine now. "Carry on."

The Driver tried to bitch again, but some caster or other muted him with a wave of his hand. The other two dragged him off.

That done, I finally continued. "There are two important things to remember. One is that most of the benefits from my Classes occur before the mission starts. They can give us key advantages. Decisive. Second. That all goes away if you all run off to do your own thing. Clear?"

"So, you're saying just roll with it and don't Leeroy Jenkins?" Gerri asked.

"Leeroy who?"

"Doesn't matter," they said and laughed when I made a disapproving face.

A few people laughed, but nobody explained. I didn't push it. We didn't have the time. I did repeat the question though. They all agreed they'd understood.

I sent out the invites, and only three of those gathered needed to be prompted to accept.

Chapter 21

Lee

My battle-map, and my subconscious mind, expanded to include the team with everything already being processed. The information would rework itself according to the mission's needs and our preferences. For now, it let them know their teams and who would be in charge of each. It gave them icons for everyone's job duties. Resource bars. That kind of thing.

Mine showed a hell of a lot more, but I was used to that. I could see enemy movements. Estimated positions. The drone and scout feeds were side by side in the top center of my view. Likely locations for the prisoners were outlined in red. This was based on System research and the Skill itself.

The upper left corner of my feed displayed my current goals. Rough odds of success for each. The only one that really mattered now was if the leader of the base would take the bait. The System thought they would. Sixty-four percent. It also thought I'd win an even fight, but that was closer to an even break at fifty-seven percent.

My quirk disagreed, and not in my favor. My paranoia, or good sense, expected everything to go to shit. It did no good to dwell on it though, so I returned my attention to the job at hand.

To my upper right, I had my list of groups by cluster. The leaders I'd assigned were highlighted in gold.

Other information appeared and disappeared regularly. Early on, it had been hard to get used to the invisible lines of awareness that made the readouts partially superfluous. I was used to it by now, and it made multitasking a more practical option.

Something was bothering me. It was vague, somewhere in the back of my mind. I let it develop unhindered.

The others looked the info over and regrouped. I reviewed the plan. Our resources. I was missing something. I knew I was but couldn't put my finger on what. Made me feel like a hungry dog worrying at a bone.

The groups were ready.

The traps were set.

My Stats and Skill points were… That was it. Skill Points.

When this went wrong, and I was certain it would, we'd need every edge we could get. And there I was sitting on unused assets. Needed to fix that right the hell now.

The choice was down to Real Time Updates, Retreat, and Adaptive Defense. Two points. Three Skills. I could pick two of them or dump two points into one.

Any of them could be major game changers. Real Time Updates was practically a no-brainer. It was an upgrade for Intel Report, arguably the key Skill of my Class. Adaptive Defense was situational. More limited. It was also much more likely to be the difference between life and death. And situational or not, I was almost certainly about to be in that very situation, with a whole lot of lives depending on me.

That moved Adaptive Defense from the bottom of the list to the top.

A second Skill point? It would get me a twenty percent defense on another person. Tempting. But not enough. Not when the other two Skills affected every member of the team.

So that left Retreat or Real Time Updates. Retreat called to me. Murphy's Law said we'd be running for our lives before the day was done. But knowledge was power. Real Time Updates was less tangible, but I estimated it was nearly as likely to save our lives now, and more likely to save our lives again and again between now and the next time I gained a Skill.

So Real Time Updates and Adaptive Defense. Done and done.

That handled, I moved to the center of the team and activated my various Skills, one after the other, in rapid succession.

For the first time ever, I hit some kind of resistance. I kept going, pushed my way through as I struggled to activate the next Skill. At first, it was like trying to push my mind through oatmeal, then it was more like a thick membrane. I reeled as I forced my will against it. It broke before I did, but it wasn't without a cost. Pain flared in my forehead. Instant agony. It was just one spot—to the right of the center of my forehead—but it felt as if someone was driving a superheated screw into my skull. Through it. Into my brain.

My awareness and understanding twisted and blurred. It was as though I was spinning. This was a *much* larger group than I was used to working with. My Statistic choices had been fairly balanced. My Intelligence was good. Excellent even. But it wasn't *this* good. The information was coming in as always, but I felt like a juggler who had added two too many pins. Overwhelmed, I was holding it all together with my will, some way I didn't fully understand. But my will was not a central focus for me either.

I had to stand stock still. If I'd tried to move, I'd have fallen. All I could do was keep my face blank, so as not to cause people to doubt my leadership. The others were looking over all the maps and overlays. Distracted. But sooner or later, one of them was going to notice the boss was halfway to a coma. News would spread.

No idea how much later, I was able to process fully that I was right. My intelligence, though high, simply could not handle this level of complexity. Not with all of my ongoing and passive Skills up at the same time.

I tried to dump the free points from my last level into Intelligence. Remembered that I'd spent them all on Willpower. Shit.

Once I had time to get my bearings, I found that I had exactly enough mental bandwidth to handle this group without cracking, but not enough to walk, or dodge, or shoot. Didn't want to drop group members. Bad look. I also didn't want to drop any of the Skills. I'd used each of them for damn good reasons.

Would either option be worse than standing here like a mannequin? *No. No, they would not.*

Do I have any alternatives?

I considered my Skills and unused gear. Took longer than it should have. We were overstocked on the basics. Recovery items. Ammo. Other consumables. I'd learned to treat "adequately stocked" like the empty line on my old Mercedes S-Class. But I didn't have any alternate Stat equipment. *Have to fix that if I live.*

At the moment, I had nothing that could help.

Gerri might. They'd helped with Willpower. Worth a try.

"Do you have any Intelligence-boosting potions or pills?" I sent via text chat. Wasn't easy. Made me nauseated. I wanted to put my hand on my gut, but I couldn't make myself move.

"I just took my last one," they said. *"I wanted to be ready."*

Shit.

"What about items? Maybe a ring?"

They bit their lip and hesitated before saying, "Yes."

The world the System gave us did not encourage trust. Frankly, neither did the one we'd lost. *"I'm sorry, but I'll need to ask to borrow it for this encounter."*

There was a relatively lengthy delay before they finally replied, *"We've crossed into the territory of needing to know why."*

"Fair enough," I answered. *"Please keep this to yourself."*

"Ooh," they said, *"gossip. You have my attention."*

I wanted to drop my head into my hand. I resisted the temptation. Couldn't do it without sending my world spinning. *"Too much information. Too many people. It's overwhelming my ability to multitask."*

They started to respond, then chuckled.

"What?"

They shook their head, lips pressed hard together. They were trying not to grin.

I raised my eyebrow. *"What?"* Not a gentle tone.

"You're literally too stupid to be in charge," they said in the text chat, followed by the sticking out tongue and wink emoji.

I allowed myself to sigh. *"It's not just optics. I can't both lead and fight at the moment. And I need to do both if we're going to have a real chance."*

"I understand. That's a good reason."

Another pause.

"No," they finally answered. *"I'm sorry. I don't think that I will."*

I took a deep breath. Very slowly. Careful not to speak when my temper would make things worse. When I was calm, before I could speak, they continued. Seemed they had been waiting on my reaction. Some kind of test?

"Not without some sort of reassurance. Look, you saved my life, all our lives, and I appreciate it. But you've admitted that you didn't do that for our sakes. And though you've been a stickler about your honor, you've demonstrated that you're willing to bend the rules when it solves a serious problem for you."

Quinn. They were talking about Quinn. I considered objecting, but good sense dictated not interrupting someone that you're asking for a favor.

"And look, man, not for nothing, but I'm not gonna be the schmuck who gets suckered by a person with the 'Betrayer of Trust' Title."

"That isn't—"

"I know. I know. I was there, remember? You did the right thing. But I've been wary ever since the System screwed me over with my first Class. It makes me hesitant to rely on a System Contract."

After waiting long enough to be clear they would not continue, I said, *"That's fair. How about a temporary trade, for collateral?"*

"I've been dying to know what your bracelets do. They're adorable, and from the runes, I'm guessing they're pretty powerful. Besides, they don't match your whole badass... um..."

They stood stock still and silent. It was a long moment before I even realized I'd switched gears in my mind from Commander to Killer, and it must have shown on my expression. Their widening eyes clued me in.

My prosthetic leg was glowing and my posture had shifted to that of a predator. My glare had focused on their vulnerable throat. My breathing and heart rate quickened as System-empowered adrenaline flooded through me.

Most had turned to look at us. More than a few brows were raised. Those nearest to Gerri slid out of their seats and backed away slowly.

Gerri shuddered. Their skin grayed. "Please don't kill me."

Something in the higher-pitched tone flipped a switch in me. Like the one the Teacher had managed, earlier. The monster within me lost its hold on my temper.

I closed my eyes and clenched my fists, suffering the backlash as I did. *It's not their fault. They don't know. It's not their fault. They don't know.* Ten breaths, as my wife had taught me. In and out. In and out.

"Sorry," I finally answered. *"The bracelets belonged to my boys. It's not your fault. You couldn't have known. And I don't have time to explain. Maybe later. If we survive this."* My cybernetic lights dimmed. Posture returned to normal.

Everyone else seemed to relax a little. They returned to what they'd been doing.

Gerri eventually nodded. *"My god, you're scary when you want to be. And that's even after you admitted you couldn't move."*

"I'd have dropped the buffs."

They gulped. *"Oh. Right. So yeah, my ring has plus 11 to Intelligence. Do you maybe have one with Will? That would be good for my Mana recovery."*

"I have a ring with one point less," I answered them, *"but it's Constitution rather than Willpower. Would that work?"*

"Actually, I've been dying for an item that would help me not be dead, and I've got plenty of Intelligence from my Class and early choices. Would you consider a permanent trade, with a small favor owed for that one point?"

"Sure," I said and forced a smile. *"I'm sorry about earlier."*

"We'll talk," they said, *"after."*

I nodded, though I doubted it would happen. Unless they stuck around for the longer term. Maybe not even then, if I could help it. Some things you just didn't talk about.

We exchanged rings. I had to have them take mine off my finger and put the other in its place. It wasn't subtle, but what could I do?

Nothing happened. Then a single point of my confusion clarified. I was trying to micromanage several separate groups that each had leaders. *Stop pretending to delegate. Do it. Pull my attention to the bigger picture.* Simple, but not as easy as it sounded.

Delegating took a large part of the load off. Another confusion, another simplification. Then everything was rearranging, streamlining. I didn't feel smarter, but it all just made more sense. Got more efficient. After less than a minute, I was confident that I could fight as well as lead.

Early on, I'd chosen to walk a balanced path. One that would let me keep my effectiveness high while also managing smaller groups. If this was going to be an ongoing issue, I might need to rethink that or change up my gear.

I'd have a talk with Toph if he survived. Alone, I was weaker than the average Combat Classer. Cutting edge equipment. Cybernetics. A crapton of dedication. They had more than made up for my Class's downsides, at the start. But by and large, all Advanced Classers had those advantages. The weak had been weeded. I was losing more of my edge every couple of Levels.

And now I don't have a strong organization to back me up.

Gonna need a new edge. Fast. More hidden aces. The people who wanted me dead had detailed records of everything I could do.

Issues for later. It's time to get this party started.

I barked out orders and backed them up with silent commands to key personnel via chat.

People got to work.

This was my orchestra. With my Intelligence enhanced, I felt more than ready to conduct it.

Minutes later, the construction and planning were finished. Most of the troops had fallen back into the woods. The Advanced Combat Classers were waiting just behind the tree line.

Gerri was with me in the front lines. The pair of Manidoo Aanike from the tribe were flanking us.

Behind them were the last two. I'd worked with them before. Jay was a grenadier, a tall, pale man with dark hair. He still seemed to think this was all a game. A fool, but good at his job. He'd had a big grin and a twinkle in his eye. Along with him was Roy, a Cuban American who'd been a marine and managed to get the Class to match. They were equipped with excellent HLF weapons, armor, and gear. They were a known quantity I was putting a lot of faith in.

We had no dedicated healer, and the closest thing we had to a tank was a level 40 Basic Classer. I didn't think he'd hold up against our main target long enough to be useful, so we'd kept him in the back lines. He'd be nearby to taunt off any weaker adds if I'd missed a loophole or the enemy had some kind of summons.

Some of our stealthy fuckers had a different mission. They'd disappeared into the woods and circled back behind the fortress.

If everything went smoothly, I'd be the only member of the team who was visible. Many were hidden via various Skills behind us in the woods. Those in the main group were invisible. Everyone but me. I had an Ambush Skill that could have accomplished the same thing, but the Tribe had an Illusionist, so we went with his Skill. It also allowed us to see each other, which was great. Mine didn't work that way.

Gerri had given me an orange powder to sniff that restored my Mana and boosted its recovery rate. I waited until my Mana had recovered to around two-thirds full, then I stepped away as I did a quick scan, reviewing the reports in my display.

It was time.

Chapter 22

Caleb

One moment, I was convulsing on the floor of the training room in agony. The next, I found myself inside a cozy room, sitting on a bench made of black iron.

What the heck is going on?

I looked around to find my bearings. My eyes took in a stop sign next to a remote-control car on train tracks. There was an old-school TV projector in the corner and a door right behind me.

I felt as though I should recognize this place, but something was very wrong. *Where am I?* Had someone rescued me? Had the Insurgent come back? Had the last two years been some kind of insane fever dream?

On a counter, there was a rounded fishbowl with a goldfish where the aquarium should have been.

What aquarium? And how do I know where it should be?

Then something clicked in my mind, and everything made a bit more sense. I sat very, very still for a long moment.

"Pavise?" I called to my companion verbally and telepathically. *"Are you still there, buddy?"*

"Yes, sir?" was his immediate reply.

I let out a long breath and a small portion of my tension eased. *"Pav, why am I sitting in a knockoff Mr. Roger's living room?"*

"It's a mental construct where I believed you'd be at ease while I work to repair the damage to your brain."

I pinched the top of my nose where my glasses used to be. It was all real. They were all still dead. So many lost. My old students. Sandy, who had been so bright and determined to be the next tech CEO. Eddie, who had gone out of his way to reach out to the shy kids in class. Then I remembered my new class. *They still need me.*

I exhaled. Then Pavise's words caught up to me. *"Wait, what damage? Am I okay? And you still haven't answered why this place is so screwed up."*

"In regard to why this place is not a complete match for your memories, I'm afraid that because of your temporary mental breakdown, I have been forced to rely on impressions, loose concepts, and association. I may have been able to force further clarity, but the odds of greater damage to your nervous system were too high to warrant the risk. As to your other question, yes, sir, there has been minimal damage done to your cybernetics that will need to be repaired, sooner rather than later. The damage to your brain and nervous system was, I'm sorry to say, rather more extensive."

Brain damage! "Am I going to be okay?"

"I cannot say for certain, sir, but I believe so. I was able to take some of the strain on your behalf and direct some of the overload to your hardware, thus the damage. Your Level, Intelligence, and your willingness to invest in Constitution at my suggestion do at least make it probable that you will experience a full recovery." Pavise paused before he continued. *"The System is very good at returning to true in this regard."*

"Thank you."

"I'm not sure that I deserve your thanks, sir. Normally, I would say that you were lucky to have my services, as I was able to minimize the harm done to you. However, that does very little to lessen the fact that it is my job to guide you, and your misguided use of the Skill was prompted by my actions."

"It's not your fault, Pavise."

"I appreciate you saying so, sir. But—"

"No but," I cut him off. "Your programming was limited and specialized when I chose to put you in the shield-bot. You told me so yourself. I knew what I was giving up when I made the choice, and what I was gaining. Using my Perks on you was the smartest thing I've done since this all started."

"It is kind of you to say so, sir."

"I'm serious, Pavise." I sent my emotions through our connection. "The children would have died if it wasn't for you. I would have died. Don't think I don't know that. Whatever happens, I'll never forget it."

"Yes, well…" He cleared a throat I knew damn well he did not have. "I do have good news, sir. Your brain and nervous system have recovered to the point that we can now be sure there will be no lasting damage."

I grinned and ran my "hand" through my "hair." "That's great news, buddy. I'd give you a hug if you were here with me."

"That is not necessary, sir. But the sentiment is noted."

I chuckled. "So, what's the plan?"

"This place was selected because of the duality as a place of security and imagination. Now that you are stable, we can attempt to recover whatever functionality we can out of your new Skills while also protecting you from future damage."

"Are you sure we shouldn't give me a bit more time to heal first?"

"I already did, sir. I have altered your perception so that time is passing much more slowly here than it is in the physical world. I was also able to administer a potion Aul found to aid in your recovery. Our cybernetic link had the advantage of allowing me to swallow on your behalf."

I bit my tongue, metaphorically speaking.

"Now that your mind is relatively safe, I suggest we move to a larger, more open area where we will have more room to work."

I grinned broadly. "Say no more."

I walked over to the second small bench and sat down. I was smiling so hard it made my cheeks ache. I'd wanted to do this since the first time Mr. Roger's did it on TV. I picked up the remote-control car, flipped the toggle underneath it to on, and set it on the train tracks. There was the sound of traffic, and the car followed the train track into a tunnel. I sent Pavise a mental impulse to let him know what I had planned. On the show, the trolly going into the tunnel signaled the trip to the land of make believe. This, I decided, should do the same.

I blacked out for an instant as the car drove into the tunnel. There was a weird sense of spinning and motion. Grunge music I didn't recognize was playing somewhere in the background.

This is so screwed up. It creeped me out and disoriented me, rather than feeling nostalgic and safe like I'd planned. I smiled, trying to put a good face on it. Either way, I was grateful. Pavise was doing his best.

Speaking of Pavise, this time a construct of his body had appeared along with me. His squat, armored form was reassuring.

When I arrived at my destination, the castle was all wrong, more Harold and Kumar's than King Friday and Queen Sarah's, but it was a make-believe castle, so I'd take it. I looked around. Everything was wrong. What should have been a cobblestone path was a yellow brick road. There was a house made of squashed trees, branches and all, rather than cut logs.

The Tree House, I realized and groaned at the results.

I'm calling this place the Land of Enforced Delusion. "Enough exploring," I told my friend. "What's next?"

"The plan—"

"Wait a minute," I said with a start. *Has he been doing his best? My mind is better now.* "Why are things still so screwy?"

"It seemed better to maintain consistency than to change things abruptly just to match an old, outdated form of human entertainment."

"I thought you had never seen any of the old Earth shows."

"I haven't, sir," he said. "You have. This is your mind, after all, not mine."

209

"But if you can pull this much from my mind, you can certainly understand the references I use when I say them."

"Correction, sir. I *could* understand your references to young human frivolity, if I were willing to use the processing power it would require to do so."

"You're an alien supercomputer. How much processing power could it possibly take?"

"It's the principle of the thing, sir."

I sighed. "I surrender."

I felt a faint tinge of satisfaction through our connection.

"The good news," he said, "is that I have altered the time scale so that it is working in favor of efficiency. That way, we can do this right with minimal losses."

"That's amazing. Thank you. Out of curiosity, what's the differential?"

"Nearly three to one, sir."

"Well okay then. Ready when you are."

Two outlines in Sharpie bright colors, a green one shaped like a Voloid and a yellow one shaped like a human, appeared in front of me. They were facing in the same direction, where a target was waiting. A piece of white chalk appeared in Pavise's "hand." He waved the chalk like a conductor, and the details on the sketches developed until they looked more like one of Leonardo Da Vinci's designs.

"This is what Hunter's Strike is intended to do," he said.

The green image of a Voloid stepped forward and took aim with a handheld blaster, again and again, one hand after another, then two hands at a time, and finally the Targeter's Reticle, in various locations.

"I'm right-handed," I said, "so let's start with that and the Reticle."

"We should do the left also, just in case your right arm is disabled."

"I guess. How do we do this?"

He waved the chalk, and the two images overlaid one another. The Voloid shrank to match my size, and the body was altered to be humanoid. The image trembled and faded for a moment, until it was nearly gone. I felt a mental strain worse than when Pavise had borrowed from my mind before, and the image solidified.

"There," he said, sounding relieved. "Focus on one of the image's four arms and will it to either lower or raise on the body to match where your single arm should be."

I did as he said. Making the connection was easy, but the mental effort was anything but. At first it was like pushing my mind through oatmeal, but I was making progress. Then a jolt of pain shot into my head. "It feels like the Skill itself is resisting me. Maybe it's some kind of trap the creator placed in it to stop non-Voloids from doing exactly what we're trying to do?"

"Perhaps, sir. I will attempt to disrupt the damage, whether it is intentional or otherwise." He waved his chalk and the pain lessened, then increased again, worse than before.

I could sense Pavise increasing his efforts, and I redoubled my own, until something popped, and my mind was able to make the adjustment. The Skill now used my hand, gun at the ready, aiming straight.

"Got it," I said proudly.

"Yes, sir. Congratulations. I am afraid that, though we have made progress, this is only one of the possibilities we will need to adjust. Thankfully, the more I work with this Skill, the more I am able to calculate. One remarkable thing is that the System has actually assisted us in the process. It must want to encourage just such activity, regardless of the intent of the creator."

"That is interesting," I said, then stopped as I got the ugly gong sound that indicated my forbidden Quest had progressed. I waved away the notification, unread. "That wasn't my fault."

"It can't be helped, sir, but I appreciate you following our arrangement by refusing to read the alert. You honor me with your trust."

I didn't understand why Pavise wanted me to avoid this "System Quest" business, but he'd made me promise to do so before he would agree to my contract-within-a-contract that would allow for me to use his help without feeling as though I was enslaving rather than employing him.

"I have a rough estimate of how much I will be able to assist you in changing your Skills at this time, sir, though I believe we will be able to do more when we increase your Intelligence or my capabilities. I suggest we start with the mounted weapon, which would require the fewest changes, and go on from there if we still can."

We did just that. We managed the right hand, but altering the left-hand function so soon was simply more than I could manage, so Pavise removed it entirely from the Skill, for now, so that there was less of a strain on my mind when I activated it.

By the time we wrapped, I had full use of the Reticle's turret on my shoulder, and I could also use a blaster in my right hand in most of the central forward-facing directions. Better yet, Pavise had been able to block out most of the disruptive phenomena that went with it.

One unexpected but positive side effect was that the limitations seemed to lessen the Mana needed to activate the Skill. When I wondered aloud what would happen if he forced it to keep the higher Mana cost, Pavise tested it. The result was a higher damage bonus than the base Skill had included. As my Mana Pool and Recovery were both high, we chose to keep the higher damage. When I seemed too pleased with this change, Pavise re-unassured me that it was still just a Basic Skill, and the higher damage was still pretty pathetic. His exact wording was, "rather less than impressive."

After my testing, the front gate of the castle was in shambles and my turret blasts had demolished the Treehouse. Since this place was my mind, its current state felt like an excellent metaphor for my life. I vowed to myself not to let it become a metaphor for violence destroying my innocence.

"Sir, shall we move on to Thrusting Charge?"

"Do we even need that Skill, Pav? My mind is exhausted, and I don't know how to use a spear."

"Just because you don't know how to use a spear doesn't mean you can't learn. Though I admit your strength is rather inadequate to the task."

"True, but still. Is it worth the mental strain?"

"It's a fair question, sir. Or at least it would have been a fair question before you risked your life to acquire it."

"Ouch."

"Let's take a look and plan what we will do with it before we decide."

"That's fair. I'm sorry I'm reluctant. My brain still hurts, and my thoughts are a bit fuzzy. I have to admit that I probably should have listened to you and waited."

He sighed. "Sir, despite the damage to your cybernetics, I do believe that your choice has saved us a significant amount of time that we may desperately need. In hindsight, knowing that you have survived the ordeal and gained at least one Skill, I believe you made the correct decision."

"Hindsight is twenty-twenty."

"Excuse me?"

"It just means it's easy to know the right thing to do after you already know the end results. But that doesn't mean you should have known beforehand. Unless you're a psychic, I guess. Does the System have psychics?"

"Yes, sir."

"Do they use—"

"If I may, sir, the time dilation is only three to one."

"That's fair. But if we survive all of this, I have a lot of questions."

"Of course, sir. I'll be happy to suggest several books on any subject that interests you."

I rolled my eyes, but I let it go.

We moved on to the other Skill. Just like before, the human and Voloid models appeared. In this case, more limbs were involved on an ongoing basis, as the Voloids had one set of limbs they used exclusively for legs, one set they used exclusively for arms, and a third set that could serve both functions.

Charging forward with two to four limbs, while striking with a spear using whatever limbs were available, was much more complicated than firing a weapon. Pavise had less luck with the initial changes, and I didn't do much better. Maybe my mind was just too worn down, because this time, I pushed to make the first change just as hard as the last time and failed.

I strained harder and harder, and I felt like it was finally getting close. I tried to force it and pain stabbed through me. I flinched back and failed again. Hard. It reminded me of trouble I'd had with other biological functions in the past, but this was much worse.

A few moments later, I started to try again, but my mind spun and the world around me melted like watercolor. Apparently, we'd been pushing our luck in trying to also rework the second Skill quite so soon.

"Pavise, you mentioned that time passes differently here?"

"Yes, sir."

"So we're not in as much of a hurry then, right?"

"That is correct, sir."

"In that case, you might want to conjure me a pillow, or at least one of the sweaters from the closet, because…"

***

When I woke, I was lying next to a carousel heaped with books. They cascaded onto the floor. Various animal sculptures with saddles awaited riders. This must be the knockoff Museum-Go-Round.

I did have a pillow, and there was an ugly green Christmas sweater with red and white candy canes spread over me. *Cute.*

"By the way," I said, sitting upright and shaking out my right arm. It had gone numb while I was out. "When we're done here, should we consider tweaking other Skills? That should be possible, right? I'm not exactly specced for combat, after all."

"Good morning, sir. No, your Class Skills are provided by the System itself and we do not have as much access to them as we do to a custom-crafted Skill like this one. Even with one such as this, what we are doing would be reckless if your situation were not so dire."

I opened my mouth, then closed it. I nodded.

"Excellent." He took out his chalk and the Skill diagrams reappeared.

I took the opportunity to review the Skill's details. The previous failure had hurt my confidence, and I hoped more information would give me an edge.

Thrusting Charge (Level 1) Voloid Variant

Dash forward, striking your target with a mighty thrust of your spear. Bonus to damage dependent upon user Skills, Attributes, and equipment used. Max dash distance 30 feet.

Cost: 15 Stamina and 10 Mana

If I were honest with myself, I had been more than half stalling when I decided to review the information. But my teacher's instincts may have served me well, after all. Last time I had tried this, I had done so primarily as a cerebral exercise, with only the minimum amount of thought about the body. But this Skill used Stamina, not just Mana. In fact, it used more Stamina than Mana.

When I reached out with my mind to try again, I focused on the imperfect human form in front of me, and instead of trying to mentally adjust the positions, I made an effort to inhabit them.

My success at doing so was limited. I got a kind of dual presence feeling where my awareness was a bit dispersed and unsettled. Still, it must have helped, because this time, my efforts succeeded. In fact, the Skill changed much more quickly and easily than the first one had.

I redoubled my efforts, and with a mental nudge, I was more deeply settled into the diagram form, which felt as odd as it sounded. I had sensations of presence and motion, but no flesh, delusional or otherwise.

I thought about how it would feel when I activated the Skill, and my awareness dashed forward, slamming into the castle wall and shattering into line fragments. My awareness snapped back into my "body."

"That was fun," I said.

"I'm glad you are enjoying yourself, sir. I, on the other hand, am concerned. The distance and speed you traveled were much higher than expected, resulting in wildly uncontrolled balance and momentum. I also note that your spear strike, the entire purpose of the Skill, was an abject failure."

I examined the pile of chalk lines lying on the ground next to a small crack in the stone wall. "Any idea why that happened?"

"Yes, sir. Your body is much smaller and lighter than a full-grown Voloid, and as you have no exoskeleton, the issue is worsened. Additionally, the type of spear they use and the way their bodies move to control it is much more incompatible with your form than it was with Hunter's Strike. I'm sorry, sir. I do not believe we will be able to make this Skill functional at this time."

"Maybe. Or maybe we need to Bob Ross this situation." After walking over to the pile, I squatted down and picked one up, turning it over in my hands.

"Your eloquence continues to stagger me, sir. Is this, perhaps, another movie reference?"

"Not this time. He was a painter." Rising back to my feet and tossing the yellow splinter back onto the rest, I turned around in a circle, examining the positions of the various components of this neighborhood.

"Are you suggesting that paint would work better than chalk? I don't believe that will make a difference, but I suppose we could try." He followed me as I headed into the center of the road.

"Hold on. Listen," I said, in my classroom voice. "He was a painter, and a teacher, in his own way. Whenever he would make a mistake, he would have called it a happy little accident and use it to make something amazing and unexpected."

"I see. A wise man then. What do you propose?"

"I don't use spears, anyway. I'm not strong enough, and my Agility is okay but nothing great. What if we just remove that part from the Skill entirely and use this as a mobility power?"

"The idea has some merit, but we would need to address the other issues to make it worthwhile for any function."

I nodded. "I've been thinking about that. Do you remember that the Matriarch used to call my armor my exoskeleton?"

"Excellent point, sir." He motioned with the chalk and my armor appeared in the image. "Though in the long run, it would be better if you could use the Skill effectively, with or without your armor."

"You're not wrong."

He removed the spear and the aspects of the Skill that controlled my arm and hand motions. "Would you like to give this another try?"

"Sure."

This time, it was easier for me to press my awareness into the illustration. I turned to face the longest straight portion of the road so that I wouldn't slam into the castle again. Even without pain, feeling my form break into pieces was not an experience I was eager to repeat.

I activated the Skill. This time, I flew forward as fast and far, though with a bit more control and even more momentum. I tried to catch myself and stumbled a few times. I was about to fall, and rather than just letting it happen, I decided to buy myself time by activating the Skill again, launching me forward.

It worked like a charm. By the end of my second dash, I managed not to fall at all by slamming face-first into the remnants of the Treehouse. I shattered to pieces again.

"Another happy little accident?" he asked.

"We'll call that one a happy little disaster." I laughed. "But actually, it wasn't all bad. I had a bit more control, and we did learn that I can chain the Skill for greater distance."

"A fair point," he said. "It seems that the plan with the armor worked as intended, but removing the spear attack empowered the remainder of the Skill."

We discussed the issue at length. Pavise pointed out that as my Agility and my competence increased, I might still be able to use this Skill to get close to an enemy to initiate an attack. In the meantime, though the use of this Skill would not work great as a travel power, as I had intended, it could still work to move me away from danger in a pinch.

Pavise predicted I would end up on my ass at least a fourth of the time. I had a feeling that the phrase "at least" was doing a lot of work there.

My love of video games came into play then. I suggested that I take advantage of the momentum of the Skill and the tumbling training my mother had pressured me into when I was younger and try to have me end the Skill with a combination of a tuck, roll, and spring back to my feet.

He agreed that my plan had some merit and pointed out, "This is the perfect opportunity to take the 'time' to practice such a complicated ability. I'd say it's worth a try. You may never be able to use it offensively, but it will help you play to your strengths and flee, when the need strikes."

I wanted to call him out on being a jerk, but I decided that discretion was the better part of valor. *I guess that kind of proves his point.*

We were both so happy with the new Skill that I felt less guilty than I would have that I hadn't told him about my recent suspicion that the initial failure of the spear attack was almost certainly caused by the fact that I had forgotten about thrusting the spear when I had attempted to modify the charge.

I decided that this would be my happy little secret.

Chapter 23

Lee

I stepped into the field of grass and thistles. Nobody had mowed this shit in years.

The visibility was awful. I could use that. So could monsters.

The Rite of Challenge was mostly straightforward.

I cut my hand, trailed blood in a circle, and chanted a few lines of bullshit sounds. Then I pressed my bloody palm to the wrong side of my chest, where the custom said my major heart should be. Only four fingers. Easy.

The final part was tricky. I didn't have a horn of a Tul-Tul Tuken, a sacred beast in the Ruul sector, wherever the hell that was. I'd decided to roll the dice on a workaround. Triggered a Skill.

Psy-Ops (Level 1)
Guerilla Tactician creates loud noises, smoke, and other sensory disturbances to indicate a chaotic
and dangerous environment. Can be resisted by those with high enough perception. Not a mental
effect. Must originate within 300 yards from the caster + 100 yards per Skill Point. Channeled.
Cost: 30 Mana per second.

This was the real test. Intel report said that the Ur-Tallin were arrogant, but with a culture built on honor. I could use that—I had none. If the leader was traditional, we'd lure him out to duel me one-on-one. My research said he should be low to mid-tier Advanced. Per the normal scam that those on the top called honor, a fair duel with me would clearly favor him. Didn't matter. I had plans to cheat.

They used a standard System Contract. The sample my Skill gave me had an exploit I could use. *Air Bud* said there were no rules that dogs couldn't play basketball. This contract had no rule saying my side of the fight had to just be me.

I'd checked twice.

If the sample was accurate, they just assumed honorable intent. If he died, I won and claimed my prize. They'd free our people or break the contract. If that or shame didn't stop them, it was probably because they were charging us in a murderous rage.

Worked for me. At least they'd leave the fort.

They might also kill the prisoners, but I didn't have a better plan. I'd pray, but I believed in Murphy's Law, not God. And you don't pray to Murphy and survive.

A horn sounded in answer, and I stopped holding my breath. The huge gates opened outward, revealing a big flaw in my plan. The Chief wore the antlered mantle that his customs required. He had a blue "eye" and was younger and smaller than those around him. Downright scrawny. It would have been good news, except another cyclops wannabe was with him. This one had a bright yellow "eye," and he stood head and shoulders above the tallest guard.

He had the Chief in a headlock. Big dude was giving the little guy a noogie.

My translation Skill was good. Expensive. But it couldn't translate half-read lips at range. Didn't matter. Some things transcended language. I'd grown up with a brother, around lots of other boys. Big bro was putting little bro in his place. And saving his ass at the same time.

That was brothers for you. Made me miss mine.

The second flaw in my plan was obvious when big brother left the keep. His casual, long strides left all the others in the dust. He moved with swagger, easy confidence, and grace. Big and strong was dangerous. Big and strong and fast was so much worse.

Before I could inspect him, a silvery light shot from a device from near the gate and enveloped him. He appeared twenty feet away from me in a flash of light. A swarm of cameras flew after him. His entourage of other giants followed. They carried high-tech folding chairs and melee weapons.

What had I gotten myself into?

"Welcome, Betrayer," the alien declared, "to New Panoply." He swept his mighty arm in a grand gesture. "I'm afraid the Chief is indisposed right now. Luckily for you, I happen to be in town. I'll be taking my brother's place in the ceremony, as is my right as his elder."

He was decked out in leather armor made of faces. Some were monsters. Some were humanoid.

His club was like the castle though, pretending to be low tech. Like an homage to the first weapon of war. It was even less convincing. They had a mad scientist, their own fucking Earl. I'd bet my life on it.

Four lengths of silver metal formed the club's handle. They were wrapped around a clear glass orb that crackled with electric power, like one of those museum plasma spheres. Its power matched the yellow of his "eye."

The clubs and spears of the gathered masses followed the same theme. That verified my earlier reports. I'd doubted them, but not enough that I hadn't activated Adaptive Defense in prep.

I tried to get a good read on the man to gauge if his bravado was a bluff. He was from an alien culture, and he had a gemstone where his eye should be. I eventually gave up and used Assessment with a very narrow focus.

Alert: The target of this skill has chosen not to block your Assessment. You have been offered the choice to receive the unredacted information you have requested in the Skill's usual format, or in the form of the festive infographic the audience will be receiving. Collectors' cards and action figures will be available for purchase at the Shop.

If that was a bluff, it was the best I'd ever seen.

Not a bluff, I decided. I wouldn't underestimate this invader. Hopefully, he'd underestimate me.

I considered waving away the information. He wanted me to know it. But if I could make that choice, I wouldn't have this Class. Knowledge was a type of power, even in the System.

Kelwroth Vainglory (Level 46 – Advanced)
Ur-Tallin
Class: Populares Gladiatorum (Gladiator)
Scion of Lost Glory
End of the Line
Del-Reetha Bane
Hakarta Bane
Goblin Bane
Shame of the Sector

I gulped. Couldn't help myself.

He must have noticed. His grin widened.

Fuck. Murphy's working overtime.

So powerful. Nearly Master Class. Kelwroth had access to the final Tier of his Advanced Class Skills, a heck of a lot of Health and Mana—which he'd kept hidden, the asshole—and a Class meant for fighting one-on-one.

Odds were good we were about to die.

Think, think, think. Can I talk my way out of it?

Too late. The rite had been performed.

A bribe? I wasn't too proud, but we had nothing he would want. Nothing he couldn't just take. Plus, standing here at all implied he valued tradition. Honor. He'd never accept.

It is what it is. Worry was worthless. No plan could avoid what was about to happen.

"By Ancient Rites, Scion, I have come to challenge you." I felt like an idiot, but I was relying on custom. Better to get it right.

He winced at my choice of Titles, but he recovered quickly. "So formal," He laughed, deep and loud. "But I accept. After all," he said, looking around us both. His eye paused for a moment where my ambush force was located. He wanted me to know he could see them. "It's just you and me. Mono a mono, as I'm told your people say. What kind of Ur-Tallin would I be if I were to reject such an *honorable* challenge? But if you're going to make this formal, I must insist we also make it official."

He whirled around, playing to cameras. The audience.

"What do you say, folks? Are you ready for a match?" He paused and smiled. Must have gotten a response. "With this mighty challenger of Earth. The great Commander himself and all his mighty troops?" he said with a scoffing, mocking tone as he waved at the empty air.

If he was going to mock my planned betrayal, at least the asshole put it in the terms.

"You're doing great," he said under his breath, and he gave me a subtle thumbs-up on his huge, four-fingered hand. "Love the bad boy brooding. But maybe a bit of something flashy, you know, for the rubes at home."

His Charisma was so high that I was happy he was proud of me.

This System is the worst.

Fine. If this idiot wants to give me a chance to show off, I'll use it to my advantage.

I activated Fortify the Position. Prepared to do what I would have done in advance if I hadn't been trying to trick him.

"Alien! You come to my planet." I raised a stone and earth barrier in front of me. Added more like it, here and there behind me. Fall-back positions. "You steal our land." Not hard to force passion into my speech. My allies had changed. My enemies had not. I softened the earth to near quicksand levels in giant-foot-sized spots behind the stone. Trip hazards for when he stepped over. "You murdered our fucking children!"

He turned his head quizzically, then shrugged subtly and thundered, "And they were delicious."

I started to open fire.

The monster scolded me with a finger. "Tsk, tsk, tsk."

What the hell is wrong with this thing?

"Contract first, or your people die," he whispered. "So, here's the deal." His voice was booming now. "When I have defeated you, I will win all of your loot, plus you get the honor of being the first patch of my new cape." He motioned to his disgusting armor to drive the point home. "It will provide no real defense, weak as your flesh is, but it will add some local color. If you somehow manage to win, you get all your people back, unharmed, safe and sound. I'm assuming you're here to save our captives?"

I nodded. "I am, and the Contract sounds fine."

His grin widened until I held up a finger.

"However, your people will also need to return the prisoners' gear. All of it. I get your loot also, obviously. And there needs to be a rule that none of your people will interfere in any way during the fight or try to kill us afterward."

"My loot, yes, but not my body. That includes my 'eye,' just so we're clear. As to the others, I'm offended that you would even hint that my people"—his expression twisted into a mocking scoff—"would be so absolutely vile as to interfere in an official and sanctioned duel. The shame of such a thing would follow and stain them forever. But fine, you can have your addendums, though the others still get to kill you if you ever come back or if you act against our people in the future." He spat on his hand and held it out for me to shake.

"That seems fair," I said, holding my ground and ignoring his spit-covered hand. It wasn't part of their ritual. I suspected he was trying to lure me out of position. More importantly, I didn't want his spit covering my entire forearm.

"I knew that was too gross to be real," he muttered under his breath as he shook the phlegm from his huge hand. "Broken-ass etiquette download." His expression seemed apologetic. Then, loud and clear, he said, "Good."

He sent me a Contract. The deal seemed legit. It completely forbade his people's involvement under any circumstances. There was no such provision for me.

That was when the other shoe dropped.

A new spike of fear hit me as I read the words. Whether we accepted the Contract or not, at this point, we were probably screwed. All we could do was hurry. It was too late to undo most of the damage.

You agree to waive all rights, local or Galactic, to any profits from the ongoing Galactic broadcast of this event.

Ongoing Galactic broadcast. Damn it. We had a lot of enemies. Many of them were far too close, and our location had just been spammed across System space.

I finished reading the Contract with renewed urgency. It was fair. If anything, it favored us. That made me suspicious. After a few moments, I realized a possible snag.

"They have to sign it too." I motioned back toward his people.

"They are bound by my word," he said. His tone sounded like he was actually offended.

"Send me a System Contract that says so, and that you will be forced to release my people and let us all leave in peace right now if you are exaggerating even a little."

"Untrusting swine," he announced with a flourish, but he agreed. And he put his money where his mouth was and did what I'd requested.

That surprised me. But I signed the Contract.

"Excellent. One moment please while I set the stage." He chanted mumbo jumbo and threw his arms wide, fingers dancing.

A massive holographic arena sprang into existence around us. It was constructed of yellow energy, matching his eye. The display would have made Sinestro proud. It even had energy sand and tiny yellow audience members in the distance, cheering wildly.

My heart skipped a beat when I realized that if his people hadn't followed him so closely, in such massive droves, he would almost certainly have dropped the arena in the huge open space in front of the castle, and all of my traps and half of my people would have been for nothing.

The arena was in the contract, so I didn't object. Its only real effect, other than flash and awe, was that it prevented the participants from escaping. It wasn't nearly so effective at preventing entry. I'd checked. Twice. So, I was glad we had the secondary Contract to reassure me that I was the only one planning treachery.

Speaking of treachery, I checked up on mine. I used a steely gaze as cover while I reviewed my Skill-generated mini map. My primary team, the ones he knew about for sure, were in place. So were the second rank farther back. My tertiary forces were scouting out the back of the base. They'd messaged me that the place was nearly empty except for a few remaining troops who were trying to watch the match from the walls. That said, the security systems were top-of-the-line stuff. They doubted they could penetrate it undetected, if at all. Hopefully, we wouldn't need them because we'd win unfair and square, but it was good to have a plan B when so many lives were at stake.

I returned my attention to the arena. *The force walls only benefit us. Keeping this beast of a man contained is our best shot.*

Chapter 24

Lee

I waited impatiently while my opponent worked the crowd. He never stopped moving. He pointed at one fan after another. Flexed his massive biceps. His club blazed bright with electric power as he held it aloft and roared first at the crowd, matching yellow light blazing in his gemstone "eye."

His adoring fans just kept coming. They'd set up the Ur-Tallin equivalent of a tailgate party. They had tankards and kegs. A pair of burly men were roasting giant ribs.

Men, women, and children were jam-packed along the semi-circle of the glowing arena barrier. I had a moment of cognitive dissonance when a pair of toddlers, bigger than I was, stretched their lips wide with their fingers and stuck out their tongues at me.

I could picture my own boys doing something just as goofy. It reinforced the Teacher's message. Burned it into me like a branding-iron stamp. These aliens might be invading scum, but they were also people. People with kids that were just kids. Like the Voloids.

I had nearly massacred a dozen of them.

I shuddered. Thankfully, the showboat didn't notice.

Head in the game, Lee. You're gonna get your people killed.

Behind me, leading into the old growth forest, was my planned battle location. It ran about a football field's length. Maybe half again as wide. The traps were outlined on my mini-map in flashing red.

A holographic announcer appeared nearby. He had a face like a dachshund. Narrow. He turned to question Kelwroth. "How confident are you about this surprise bout, Scion?"

"Well, Mad Tadd"—the Gladiator reached out his massive hand as if to place it on the hologram's right shoulder—"I'm glad you asked me that. You know I'm always confident. There's no power in the galaxy that can compete with an Ur-Tallin in a fair fight." He shook his massive fist high in the air.

"Your people do have a fearsome reputation," the man agreed.

"But I'm really not sure what to expect. Humans may seem stupid, puny, and pathetic, and they are. They are." He nodded and shrugged. "But I have to be honest with you, I'm a bit concerned."

The hologram looked him up and up, and down and down. Then it glanced at me, blinked twice, and turned back to face my enormous opponent. "You are?" His tone dripped with skepticism bordering on scorn.

"You fell for it too, didn't you?"

"Huh?"

"It's not your fault, Tadd. It's totally understandable. I mean, look at him."

The announcer didn't.

"But humans have base cunning, not unlike that of some of the most dangerous monsters of the System. They've been slaughtering each other since they were nothing but furries with opposable thumbs and too many fingers. And they never stop finding creative ways to kill each other. Hear me, Mad Tadd. They. Never. Stop."

"Uh huh," the hologram said. He looked down at his shoes and stifled a yawn.

"It starts," the Gladiator was talking louder now, more urgently, his voice and manner filled with exaggerated passion, "with a rock or a knife in the darkness. Men. Women. Babies. Cuddly little things they call puppies. They don't care. They'll murder anything. And gobble them up if they get a little hungry."

"Well, you're hardly one to judge, given what you admitted to earlier."

"What? Oh that? Um. That was just pre-battle banter. You have to speak their language, my friend, and violence is the only language these psychopaths understand. Hear me, Tadd. They fought their own people, killing each other by the thousands, with guns and swords and bombs, without the System or a single Skill on the entire planet. And they did it without any promise of XP or Loot. They just love killing." Spit was flying from Kelwroth's mouth as he ranted. "And they're *good* at it."

The hologram was leaning forward a bit now, and he turned his head sideways, eyes wide. "Really? Them?"

"You heard how they became a Dungeon World, right? They killed Galactics. With no Skills. No System. They. Killed. Galactics."

That was a good question I'd never thought to ask. *How had we managed that?*

"I just…" the man blustered nonsensically for a moment. "I just assumed they had been low Level Basic Classers."

"Do you honestly believe that our honorable, our noble, our illustrious Galactic Council would send powerless babies to face dangerous hostile aliens? I mean sure, they were Diplomats, Non-Combat Classers. But they had the System. They had Gear. They had Classes and Levels. So. Many. Levels."

"Well maybe the System wasn't active here yet, and those things didn't work."

"Do you think the Diplomats just flapped their arms and flew here? No! They were teleported. Their Skills worked fine."

The whole thing reeked of a setup. The Galactic Council moved a few dozen places higher on my list of things in desperate need of killing.

"Then how?" The interviewer was frantic now, and he strained to hold the microphone closer to the giant's mouth. "Just how?"

The Gladiator waved, and images appeared above us in the sky. Tom Cruise piloting his fighter jet into a high-speed stall, miraculously ending up behind his opponents, who he killed with precision. Nuclear bombs dropping on cities. Mushroom clouds. Luke Skywalker beating Vader into submission and hacking off his hand. The words, "He Did This to His Own Father!" flashed on the screen in neon yellow letters.

"You think these things called humans are dangerous because of the System. I think it leashed them. Or at least…" Kelwroth paused dramatically. "I hope it did, for all our sakes."

There were loud gasps from the audience.

"Well, you heard it here first, my friends. Our surprisingly heroic villain, the Scion himself, Kelwroth Vainglory, once thought the obvious victor in this match, has been revealed to be the underdog against this devious and devilish creature. Get your bets in now, folks. And when you do, remember. Remember the cool, unflinching glare in the human's eyes as it confidently faces off against an opponent with a double-digit Level advantage. Remember that it was the human who picked this fight. Finally, when you place your bets, remember what happened to the Diplomats! Can our hero avenge them? Stay tuned to find out." He blinked out of existence.

I wanted to roll my eyes, but it might save some lives if the invaders thought of us as boogie men. I'd have to show them that Kelwroth wasn't fully wrong.

I didn't have the powerset to do that on my own, so I focused on my allies. My troops were split between two sets. The invisible Advanced

Classers were closest to the tree line. They waited to ambush the "unsuspecting dupe," ranged and casters behind melee. They knew their business. The Basic Classers, hidden with various Skills about sixty yards farther back, had muddled that strategy as they'd jockeyed for position or to get a better view. I ordered them back into place with a simple mental nudge.

Once they were back where they belonged, the color highlighting them changed from dark to bright green, indicating they were good to go.

My enemy, on the other hand, was still listed as dull red. *What the hell is he waiting for?*

He must have noticed my impatience, because he made a casual gesture with his head and club, motioning for me to look up and to my right. I stepped back and watched him through my cameras as I turned my eyes to look up to the sky.

Huge holographic images were playing, videos of Kelwroth and of me. Behind-the-scenes style. We sat talking about our lives with interviewers I'd never even met.

Kelwroth's showed the Gladiator fleeing from a Cthulhu style monster. It devastated a group of his people. Shame of the Sector, it said in bold letters.

Then it zoomed in on him atop an airship as it impaled the same creature with the bowsprit of the ship. He leapt off and smashed one of its eyes with his electrified club, rupturing it in an impressive shower of gore.

Shame of the Sector vanished. In its place, the words now read, Del-Reetha Bane!

Over my head, it showed images, *accurate* images, of me holding my wife and children and screaming in uncontrolled rage. Then flashes of what I'd done to those who'd killed them.

Bestower of Thorough Vengeance.

They had no idea. My family's corpses weren't meant for television ratings. I'd find out which dead men had put this spectacle together. They'd suffer before I slit their fucking throats.

Kelwroth and I were both crying in the videos. The interviewers looked sympathetic and handed us wads of tissues.

"And now we can start," the huge man said. He reached to pat me on the back.

I flinched and nearly attacked, but I let it go when he nodded respectfully and stepped back two long steps. I'd noticed that the man lost people too.

"On the count of three," the Gladiator announced, "our match will begin, and you can try to shoot me in the eye." He turned back to the camera. "For those of you who are new to my illustrious career, they always start by shooting me in the eye. I think it's rank jealousy, personally. They only have those weird fleshy orb thingies."

Showmanship. He had delayed for showmanship. *And every moment this loudmouth stalls makes it easier for our enemies to find us. What an ass.*

It made me want to shoot him. In the eye.

Chapter 25

Lee

"Three, two, and one!" the announcer counted down.

Kelwroth's icon finally flashed bright red.

I raised my blaster and fired at his eye, falling for or thwarting his mental gamesmanship. It didn't matter. It was still a decent target.

He stepped one foot to the left and turned his head. My disruptive attack missed him completely.

Damn it.

He moved so fast that if it wasn't for the earthen barrier he'd let me erect "for the rubes at home," he'd have reached me before I could dodge.

I rolled backward and to the side.

He stepped over the barrier and his foot sank into the soft spot. He missed a step, screwing up his ankle. Genuine anger flared on his face.

Never give a Tactician prep time.

I retreated toward the invisible ambushers.

His attacks, now that they had begun, were relentless, like a bull charging a black man who's bad at coming up with metaphors when under pressure.

All I could do was dodge.

If he'd been less pissed, I'd have missed when he smirked as he followed me into the kill zone. But he was pissed, and the contrast made it stand out.

I sent a mental message through my Full Coordination Skill. Fast as I could, I repeated it twice. Made me miss a step, and he struck me a glancing blow that was enough to dent my armor and knock me a bit off course.

I double-stepped to recover my footing, whipped around to aim my blaster at his face, and yelled, "Now!"

His smug expression bloomed into a grin as he flexed his outstretched arms, posing. His eye flared and bright yellow light engulfed him as he triggered a Skill to protect him against an alpha strike that never came.

My typed order: *"Hold fire. HOLD fire. Hold!"*

Shock, then outrage, appeared on Kelwroth's face. His expression finally settled on amused acceptance.

"All right," he said, standing there and talking in the middle of a death match, "well played. Mad respect. Score one for the human. You got me." He turned to face the cameras. "He got me."

With no transition at all, he was charging and swinging his club. He never even turned his head. "My turn!"

He sees through the cameras.

The club slammed into my chest with the force of a high-speed collision. A clanging thud sounded as my armor layers crunched, followed by the ringing in my ears as I felt my feet leave the ground and my heavy body went flying. I felt the momentum before a second weapon smashed into my back with a loud crack and a force that nearly matched the gladiator's.

Once I'd left a small furrow in the ground and come to my senses, I realized the truth. He'd knocked me through a mid-sized tree. I still hadn't felt any pain. Bad sign. Shock.

He's too strong. My stomach churned and my chest tightened as I tried desperately to find my feet and flee but tripped and fell. I scrambled away just in time to avoid him grabbing me by the ankle.

My pulse was pounding as I watched him from my drones.

His broad grin had returned as he stomped through what was left of the pines. He wasn't even rushing, clearly hamming it up for the audience. This asshole was toying with me.

Need to use that.

He'd knocked me over the first trap. His current path would take him just to the left of it. Lucky. Made me want to dump my next points in the Stat. I faked the start of a dash in the opposite direction, then bolted that way.

He changed his angle to follow me. "Fi, fum, fo, fee." He laughed, stomping hard with every step. "I'll grind your bread to make my bones!"

Oh dear lord.

"Get ready," I messaged the others. *"Fire!"*

I whipped around and activated Burn Them Down as he stepped on the trigger plate. I lifted my empty arm in front of me, then realized I'd lost my gun. I pulled my Hakarta 983 Striker hand cannon from my Arsenal to replace it. The beast of a gun appeared in my hand loaded, cocked, and ready to fire. Gun safety rules have an extra-dimensional space exception. It nearly slipped out of my grip as the oil I hadn't realized was dripping down my chest from my broken cybernetics had made my gauntlet slick.

Sticky glue globbed onto and around the behemoth from the trap. He swore and struggled.

I shot him in the face. This time he failed to dodge, but my grip was compromised and I missed his eye. Smaller burns than I'd have preferred peppered his face but could not penetrate his thick hide.

The rest of the main force had opened fire as ordered. They went all out. His Health ticked downward. Slowly. Too slowly.

Kelwroth stood stock still, taking the hits. Then he trembled, shook, and stomped his foot. The crowd matched his rhythm. As they did, the gem of his eye glowed brighter and the cameras spun around for a better angle.

His muscles swelled with a roar and massive final strain as he triggered some kind of skill. He heaved and the sticky adhesive shattered.

Goo shattered. I hate this System.

He drew power from the crowd. Probably even the ones not present.

Kill the cameras. Blind the audience. Don't let him see. Don't let him talk.

Easier said than done.

Before I could tell the others what I'd realized, he was barreling at me with ridiculous speed I couldn't have matched, even without my prosthetic. I couldn't breathe. The part of me that was still flesh and blood tensed at just the thought of him hitting me again.

It was all I could do to brace for the attack as he pummeled me with his club-filled fist. He slammed the handle into my non-cybernetic arm, denting the armor and cracking my humerus. Sharp pain and tingling numbness warred for my attention.

While I was staggered from the force, Kelwroth hauled back and charged up the lightning on his weapon before grinning broadly and touching it to my chest with aplomb. A jolt of power slammed into me and I felt as if I'd been hit with a taser, but my Adaptive Defense saved me from the worst of it.

He glared at me, then at the head of his club. Whatever he'd been expecting to happen hadn't.

I stumbled backward. I was barely able to keep my feet as I sent a mental command. *"Block audience. Kill cameras. Blind—"*

I lost mental focus as his hands closed around me in a crushing grip and he hefted me high above his head. I reeled with vertigo and the confusion of shifted perspective as my world spun, forcing me to close my eyes. I let my mind focus on the viewpoint of the drones and my sense of my teammates. I forced myself to ignore the feel of heavy momentum and dug my fingers into his to try to break free, but it was no contest. His single finger was stronger than both my hands.

From my own scout drones, I saw a smoke screen rise, which didn't help as much as it should have because of the tree cover and the cameras.

Shots rang out, and I heard at least one of his cameras explode behind me.

Then we were flying forward, and blood rushed to my head as Kelwroth slammed my body into something or someone with thunderous power.

We sounded like a train wreck. I felt a newfound sympathy for a puny fictional god.

I heard a cry of pain that matched mine as his fingers dug into my armor and my neck and spine were jarred by the force.

By the time I could focus my attention and redirect my camera, he had moved on and was stalking toward a different target—Gerri. Had he seen them throw down smoke screens?

If so, they weren't the only one. Several of the others had dropped colorful smoke grenades, here and there.

Then the big man got shot in the eye by Roy, our resident Marine.

Kelwroth held out an arm, superhero style, to defend it. "Do you see what I mean! Rank jealousy. It's not my fault your—"

Jay, the obnoxious "this is all just a game" Grenadier yelled, "Boss mechanic!" and shot a grenade into the huge man's mouth from the underbarrel of his M4 Carbine. Annoying as he always was, Jay had a point. The Gladiator's Skills were a bit like a boss mechanic from old games.

The explosion did serious damage. It knocked loose several of the Gladiator's teeth and hamburgered his tongue. His face darkened and Kelwroth tried to yell something but gave up after the garbled sound that followed. His rage magnified tenfold when he saw the Grenadier firing at him in the near distance.

Not so funny now, is it?

The Gladiator charged and yelled, "Foowwr," then sent Jay flying with the same club attack he'd used on me. The Grenadier's Health dropped by a quarter, then another fifth as his body failed to break a truly massive white pine.

Then time seemed to stall as the big man jerked his massive thumb at himself, then pointed at Jay. A smaller arena appeared around the two of them.

No one and nothing moved. Ammunition and fire bolts were frozen in midair. Holograms of the two combatants appeared in the air above them.

In the arena, they moved in a blur too fast to follow. In the sky above them, a highlight reel flashed key images. None of them boded well for Jay.

Kelwroth didn't even use his club. A double-fisted blow knocked the Grenadier to the ground. He followed the attack with an oversized boot stomped down, shattering ribs.

Jay was stunned. He could do nothing when Metal-knuckled gloves smashed into his face with piston force, cracking bones and shattering teeth. Finally, a brutal headbutt smashed the man's skull like a grape.

I added Jay's name to my list.

The Gladiator rose, blood dripping from his hands. Eye glowing, he flexed like Hulk Hogan in his prime. Muscles swelled. Veins popped. His wounds closed even faster than before.

Shit.

Time resumed.

The gem is the key. Not a big surprise.

I focused Burn Them Down on the eye and sent a mental command.

All weapons and skills focused on a single target.

The monster hunter brothers were the first to respond. They unleashed a Skill that bound the Gladiator's arms and legs in bands of condensed water.

It failed to restrain the giant man completely. He was simply too strong for them. But they did manage to slow him down.

"You thuck et banter," the Gladiator said, glaring at me.

"At least I can talk."

"Bedder. Bedder."

"Fuck you." I shot him in the eye.

My high perception let me notice a tiny crack. It made my day.

Those of us who couldn't do anything more useful returned our focus to the gemstone. He turned his head this way and that, thrashing as he struggled to avoid shots until he could force his arm to cover the gemstone.

Roy unleashed his Devil Dogs Skill, summoning a trio of Doberman hellhounds. They rushed to hamstring the Gladiator. Blood gushed and sizzled as they tore strips of flesh from his skin, leaving blood pooling on the ground. The air filled with the scent of burnt bacon.

In the meantime, the Marine kept firing his modified M1014 shotgun, using some kind of Rapid Reload Skill between shots.

The Gladiator seemed to weaken against the bindings. Then his whole body shook and his muscles flexed. The binding was stronger or his Skill was weaker this time, because it failed. He roared and tried to chant something, over and over. Damaged as his mouth still was, it was unintelligible.

Efd-uf duh-ln, Efd-uf duh-ln, Efd-uf duh-ln.

What the hell?

Then the audience joined in. "End of the Line! End of the Line! End of the Line!"

One of his titles?

His eye flashed and his oversized muscles swelled to a size that would make the Rock feel puny. He used his other Skill again, yanked with a mighty tug, and the water restraints broke like chains.

I got a message from Gerri, *"Can blind. Smoke. He'll kill me."*

She could blind him with her sculpt smoke. Smart. But she was right. She'd be a sitting duck.

I was formulating a plan when Kelwroth activated a Skill. I got ready to dodge, expecting his brutal charge. Instead, a huge golden net dropped on a massive area, covering the two Tribe members, Roy, and myself. The net made it impossible to dodge as giant flaming tridents struck us all, cutting through armor or cooking us at the same time. Searing pain shot through my side as a prong punctured something that felt horrifyingly important and cauterized it at the same time.

I screamed in agony and fell to my knees. I'd never taken more damage, or felt more pain, from a single attack.

Capstone Advanced Skills. Holy shit. I need to Level faster. Killing this prick would be a good start.

He was running from one side of the field to the other, using the biggest trees to change directions like a wrestler uses the ropes. He was building up to something we hadn't seen yet, and I wanted to make damn sure we weren't still trapped in the net when that happened.

I had nothing that could help with this, so I pushed the message to solve it into the whole group. Got resigned messages of failure.

The Gladiator's entire body was blazing with yellow power. Whatever he was planning was about to happen.

The ground fell out from beneath us, dumping us down a steep incline and onto a new flat area of dirt at a lower part of the hill.

The Excavator!

"Tell Edna that I've always loved her," popped up on all our prompts in party chat.

The man was sacrificing himself. His power was channeled, and it was anything but subtle.

I watched, helpless, as the Gladiator changed his direction and leapt. He slammed down on the man like a blazing meteor. The explosion left a crater the size of a small house. Several of our Basic Classers near the Excavator took massive damage. They were all stunned and broken and they would all die soon from the ongoing AOE. We could save them.

I made the tough call. We didn't.

The other set of Basic Classers joined the assault. Quantity has a quality all its own. Kelwroth's Health dropped a bit faster. He took even more damage when alternating arrows of fire and ice slammed into him from the distance.

The Gladiator used his charge again. Grateful it wasn't at me. I was even more grateful when the taller of the monster hunters, William, turned into water and splashed away. The man flashed back into solid form almost immediately. Neat trick.

Skills like that one made me jealous.

I desperately gave myself a combined healing and Mana shot. Screamed orders telepathically. *"Larson, need you."*

"Yes sir," she said. Moments later I saw her appear over the troops between us and land with expert grace in front of me, her acrobat staff in hand and her blue eyes sharply focused.

I had no time to appreciate the view. *"Go to Gerri. Get smoke."*

"Gotcha," she said, all business now as she rushed toward the Pharmaceutical Revolutionary.

Once she'd retrieved a smoke source that I couldn't clearly see from Gerri, I ordered, *"Do your thing."*

Larson stumbled and nearly fell. "Me?" She said out loud. Terror filled her voice. "*But he's so fast.*" Then she seemed to realize what she was doing, and her tone got hard. "*Yes, sir!*"

"*Good luck,*" I told her. I did not add, *and goodbye.*

Apparently, I still had something of a heart, because the thought of a friend and former lover dying on my orders was threatened to break it. But she was the only one who stood a chance.

I lost my train of thought entirely when Thomas, the shorter of the Manidoo Aanike, attacked me from about thirty feet away with a powerful blast of focused wind. I didn't have time to retaliate, or even fully process the attack, when the Gladiator slammed into the tree I'd just been standing in front of.

It broke with a thunderous crack.

I need to recruit that hunter. People who are capable of taking initiative and following orders are priceless.

One of our Snipers finally managed to shoot the last of the floating cameras, and I knew then by the lack of fury from the giant that his "eye" must be broadcasting, first-person style, for his viewers across the galaxy. Taking out the cameras would not be enough.

Hopefully, we were about to ruin the show completely.

Thomas used a powerful Skill to hack a deep gash into the back of Kelwroth's leg with the two tomahawks made of condensed water. He then turned into water when the Gladiator responded with a swing of his club.

His "eye" and boots glowed yellow as he punted the man-shaped conglomeration of water. It somehow stayed together as it was launched about half a football field, landing with a wet splat against the ground.

The Manidoo Aanike was not dead, but between the attacks, the fall, and the explosions, he was severely injured. His brother turned to face him, took a single step, then stopped. He resumed shooting flaming arrows into his brother's attacker.

Good man. We needed all the damage we could get.

A thunderous roar bellowed from the Ur-Tallin as the smoke fully surrounded him, just as the Acrobat spat a thick green loogy in his face as she leapt forward, parkouring off of his chest and then a tree, only to land behind him.

The Gladiator took the bait. He charged after her as she led him through the worst possible spots for him, including pits and soft spots. She was fast. He was faster. My Skills fed her directions. He was blind. He made mistakes.

I just kept shooting. We all did. I was nearly out of Mana, which would ruin all of our days as some of my key Skills would end, so I took a powerful Mana recovery shot. I reminded those with potions, shots, or pills to do the same, as we tried to wear the big man down.

I directed Larson toward and over traps. Somehow, he managed to avoid them all.

When he turned his body in a way that didn't make sense, I sent out a nudge for everyone to be careful. It was too little, too late. The huge man launched himself into the sky and dove down in a dramatic arc, cub overhead, directly at the spot where William had landed.

The handsome man and his brother reacted in unison, directing a blast of wind at the enemy in complementary directions that should have been enough to throw even someone as big as the Gladiator off track. They apparently trusted that this would work, completely.

It didn't. They were low Level Advanced Classers. He was at its peak. He was also massive. The club slammed down, cracking the man's skull. Blood and fluid leaked as the Ur-Tallin seemed to accelerate into a flurry of blows.

By the time we could pose a real response, the Gladiator was already swinging the club in a massive finisher that shattered William's head and grayed his Health. I expected his brother to scream, but he surprised me when he didn't miss a beat on his attacks, a true professional. I could respect that. If we could, we'd make the beast of a man pay. Revenge first, then mourning.

So many names.

The Ur-Tallin saluted with his club and pointing it near the dead man's body in a sign of respect. With him wrapped in smoke, it was an odd sight to watch him going through these motions.

Kelwroth listened, turned quickly at the soft sound of Larson's footfalls, and resumed his blind chase.

"Keep moving. Tracking us with sound. Gerri, silent."

"Hey, muscle man. Why is your eye so much smaller than the rest of you?"

He growled and lunged at Larson, so apparently she'd hit the mark on that one. She managed to avoid him, always a step ahead, flipping, rolling, using the trees and even her attacker as a parkour launching spot.

All the while, the group burned the big man down.

I saw out of the corner of my eye as Roy pulled the pin on a grenade and threw it. Larson was nowhere near the grenade. Didn't matter. It was too late. I tried to shoot it out of the air anyway.

The concussion grenade was strong, but the Gladiator shrugged it off. Larson was not so tough. She fell to her knees with a thud and a groan.

"Gotcha!" the one-eyed man yelled as he closed a massive hand around her right thigh and a second on her left bicep. His huge muscles swelled, and he let out a mighty roar as he began to pull her in half.

She screamed in terror and then anguish as her body began to tear.

My mind raced, desperate to help. But I was helpless to do more than keep firing and renewing Burn Them Down.

Gerri leapt from their hiding spot. Started activating one Skill after another, purple and green clouds of smoke and sparkling, lemon yellow and acid blue powders filling the air. Debuffing Kelworth. Healing the Acrobat.

I watched in horror as blood gushed from Larson's mouth, nose, shoulder, and hip. He tore her arm and leg from her body in a final heave of massive strength. There was something off. Too perfect, too precise. It was a Skill. It had to be.

Probably called something like Limb from Limb.

My mind tried to reject a reality that included such things. Then practicality stepped up. *Kill the motherfucker. He hurt my friend.* I opened fire with a scream of rage.

Tactically, it was the worst mistake I'd ever made.

He wheeled at the sound of my voice and raced at me with lightning speed. I was too slow to dodge as he beat me with the dismembered limbs of my teammate.

That hurt nearly as badly as when he'd used his club. My empathy for Jay grew as Kelwroth pummeled me as he had the other man. Ligaments tore and servos broke with a scream of metal rending. Then I felt nothing at all as my body and mind were too broken to feel.

"I've got them," came a voice I should recognize. He was speaking, rather than typing.

I could barely think as I tried to run or struggle. I was no match for Kelwroth alone.

Words and thoughts jumbled in my mind. Consciousness slipped.

A pair of healing surges flowed into me as our healers did what they could against the onslaught.

Right. Not alone.

I reactivated Burn Them Down. *If I'm about to die, then this jerk is going with me.*

I'd known my death was a likely end. Prepared myself. I sent a final set of orders, just in case.

There was a flash of blue light and a cluster of forms materialized behind Kelwroth. I'd seen that skill before. One of Topher's Basic Trainer Capstones. Send Reinforcements.

I could barely hear the sounds of battle now, but what I could hear doubled.

My hail-Mary pass from earlier had paid off. Better than expected. While the fight distracted our enemies, our rogues had freed our allies and managed to retrieve their gear.

Sometimes Murphy fucks the other guy.

A trio of mechanical men stepped into view. The constructs whistled and clicked as they attacked with blades and blasters.

A cloud of nanites swarmed me, working to reform my flesh and tech.

Earl and Wilma must be somewhere close.

Mostly there was gunfire. Lots and lots of gunfire.

I gurgled what I could of a cheer as the Gladiator's Health bar dropped precariously. I tried to smile, but my mouth and jaw were shattered.

If his people were going to break the contract and attack, this was when they'd do it. The Chief was his brother, after all. The moment passed. They did nothing.

Honor is for suckers.

"Wull fuck," Kelwroth gargled more than said, and I was grateful that his pummeling slowed quite a bit while he did so. "Leash my deash'll have greash rashings."

"Guh fugg youshelf." I couldn't help myself, though for all I knew he'd just get stronger from the banter.

What was left of his mouth and teeth opened into one last bloody grin.

"Lash quesh-on," he said. "Whish of ush dies firsh?"

Good question.

We raced to find out.

Chapter 26

Quinn

Barely escaping the base with my life meant I needed a place to rest, prepare, and recover. With the base compromised, my only options had been the staging ground the HLF used for underwater dungeons or a clearing in the woods. I'd decided that the bunker at the lake would do, so I drove my ridiculous car into the mirrored perfection of Nature's Lake with a splash. The water gurgled and bubbled, filling the interior and pouring through the holes in my armor. It wasn't thrilling or exciting, no matter what people said. It was unbelievably cold, and it wasn't even winter.

My whole body tensed, but the cold did help to wake me up and focus my attention. *I hate Minnesota. At least the blizzards have finally stopped.*

The oversized tires of the vehicle locked into tracks hidden under the sand with a loud click. There was no turning back now. My forward motion slammed to a halt, then started again, no longer under my control. I plummeted forward, having only enough time to take one deep breath before I was entirely submerged. It felt like the first drop on a roller coaster, and I couldn't even scream.

Our intel reports had said that some sort of freshwater spirits had created two-way portals between all of them and the Great Lakes's mega-dungeons. If rumors could be believed, the entire shoreline of Lake Superior was now unlivable, unless you could survive the tidal-wave wrath of some kind of dragon-lynx creature called Mishipeshu. It sounded like a load of crap to me, but so had the giant Paul Bunyan and Babe statues from Bemidji coming to life as regional dungeon bosses until one of the HLF's top squads got ox-stomped, so who knew.

It was a sure thing that if not for the war between the Muskellunge Monarchs and the Walleyes with their Pikemen, the Great Lakes surface region would have been long since overrun. If there was a Muskie hiding from their cannibalistic monarchs nearby, I'd be screwed no matter what I did, so there was no point in worrying about them.

The Walleyes were different though. Those sneaky fish were cunning, and their Water Wolf Pikemen could be anywhere. I watched the shadows and sands as well as my Perception would allow in the murky brown depths. Frankly, I had no business here. We'd lost an Advanced Class Navy Seal down here recently, and my spiders can't even swim.

I let myself relax when the massive coontail forest parted, allowing me through the wall of needled green stems. We had a deal with the plants, but they were fickle. And Ned, our Naturalist, had apparently forgotten to update the sacrificial offering log. I'd have killed him for it, metaphorically, if I hadn't already killed him for treason, literally. *Serves him right.*

Then I was through and safe. The massive vault-like door resealed behind me as the water drained from the underwater airlock. I sucked in a massive breath when the waterline cleared my mouth.

I waved away a notification. The System was telling me I'd failed the Quest to rescue HLF troops before Lee could that it had tried to saddle me with. The Humanist would have wanted me to do it, but I'd had my own plans.

This base was a staging ground for the dungeon where I had planned to unveil my creation to the team. In a more perfect world, my mobile weapons platform would have been the perfect synergy between my blade and tech-enhancing Skills and Lee's power to modify the vehicle for any environment.

My feelings were a distraction, so I walled them off. The tension in my face and body dropped away.

Hopping out of the ruined vehicle, I paced over to the second massive door. The last water splashed around my ankles as I held my hand over the palm lock. It scanned my biological and cybernetic components to verify my identity.

Something thunked inside. The barrier slid up with a hiss of steam. I stepped over the foot-high threshold and into the staging ground I planned to use as a makeshift workshop.

I was going to have to leave this place the hard way, so I crossed to a storage locker and grabbed a breathing apparatus to stash in my inventory. Then I unloaded my crates, construction supplies, and tools. I went to work sorting, organizing, and finally welding. The whole project would have taken a week or more, even with my reduced sleep, if we hadn't already put in the time. What I had left was glorified assembly work.

I love working with machines. It's people that suck. By the time I was really in the swing of things, it was so therapeutic that I let my emotions out for the rest of the project.

In the end, that turned out to be a mistake. I had underestimated the complexity of the madman's special contributions.

I tried and failed, again, to figure out how the clockwork gears connected to the steam valve. *This was supposed to be your part of our little passion project, Earl. I never wanted this weird stuff in here to begin with.*

There had been no reasoning with him though. The man was crazy, even by my standards, utterly obsessed. The only one who could effectively communicate with him was his wife, and I suspected that was because she was just as immersed in the cosplay alternate reality he lived in as he was.

There was no questioning his value as a craftsman, however. I couldn't have made this beauty without him. I still might not be able to finish it if I let myself lose my temper and destroy these parts.

I segmented my mind, letting that part of me scream and smash things to its heart's content while I worked. My breathing slowed and my hand steadied as my mind focused on the task at hand. That let me stop thinking about what I was doing and start looking at the parts as they really were, treating them like a puzzle rather than using my own unsuitable crafting knowledge.

And just like that, the core structure of my behemoth was complete. Even with our combined Skills, we'd needed to requisition parts from other specialists and the Shop, and it would still need upgrades to reach its true potential. But it already punched above its weight class, and its modular design would make the upgrade process smooth.

For a moment, I got a little sentimental, wishing the mad tinker was here with me for our shared insanity's fruition. Then I chuckled. He'd have looked at it with a monocle-magnified eye and judged it either perfect or worthless. If it was worthless, he would tinker. If it was perfect, he'd lose interest entirely and start on something else, unless his wife was there to feed him truffles.

My stomach gurgled at the thought. The doc was weird, but the things she called Victorian era delicacies were actually first-rate and I hadn't eaten in far too long. Besides, she always had absinthe, which was better than nothing even with a superhuman constitution.

I was about to turn the levers, pull the knobs, and fire this baby up when I got a call from Ken, one of the loyalists among the HLF members the Commander had saved.

That act of loyalty to his people by the Commander had been further proof, as if any was needed, that Lee was not responsible for any of this madness. I didn't know if it was the Teacher, Gerri, the aliens, or all of the above, but it didn't really matter. Sometimes scattershot solutions were best. *I'll just kill them all and go from there. Simpler.*

I answered the call with a brusque, "Why are you calling me? You're supposed to be keeping a low profile."

"As if anyone would call you if it wasn't urgent."

The Communications Specialist had a point. "Spill your guts before I do."

"I rest my case," he said, then, very quickly, "It's bad, Quinn. The Commander, Lee, he's hurt and he's… he's not getting better."

"What!"

"He had a brutal fight. He was nearly killed. His chest plate is busted open and it looks like Hamburger Helper and scrap metal in there. They can't really heal him without fixing the cybernetics and the hag insists she and her old man can't do the job in the field. It's all they can do to keep him alive to try to… Quinn. They're taking him back to the ship."

Lee, oh god Lee. Stay strong for me. I'll get you out of this mess somehow.

A pop-up alerted me of another call. It was flashing. The Humanist. My already tense muscles nearly cramped from the stress as I brushed away the notification. "Will he make it?"

"I don't know. Maybe," he hedged. "It would be a lot more likely if the healers weren't splitting their Mana and our supplies trying to save what's left of the Acrobat. Though that ass is definitely worth saving." He let out an obnoxious whistle. "Most of us think that we should just let her die, but Lee's last order before he… well just before, was to listen to the healer. We want to say it wasn't Gerri, but we all just know that it was. One of the boss man's Skills."

Blades slicing. His tongue gripped in my hand. Blades move lower. Lower.

Another flashing pop-up box. I grit my teeth and my hand tried to wipe away the screen on instinct. But things were already dangerous enough for Lee. If I infuriated the Humanist, they would be worse.

I let Ken know to wait. Then I shoved the shriveled remnant of myself that could still love, empathize, or care into a box with Segmentation. The combination of this practice and my Personal Firewall passive had never failed me before. I accepted the Humanist's call.

"Sir?" I said, all business.

He was ignoring me. "Find them and kill them all," he shouted maniacally.

He's like an angel from heaven.

He was losing his damned mind.

"No, not you, Tomlin." He looked incredulous. "We don't kill refugees. Yes, of course I mean humans. Aliens aren't refugees. They're invaders. Do I really have to explain this every time?" He gestured imperiously. "You. Yes, you, Reeves. Now! As for you, Tomlin, send all available resources to…" He hesitated as he became aware of my gaze. He held up a hand toward the others to wait, his cruel dark eyes burning into mine.

He's looking at me. Oh my god. He really sees me.

He'll kill us all if I don't find a way to stop him. *Wait. No. He's desperate. I can use that.*

"Support quadrant three," he finally finished. "Now out! All of you. Go!"

I waited in silence.

Oh my god! It's really him. I love you, sir. How can I serve you?

"Report."

He sounds so upset. I've upset him. Why am I like this? I'm so sorry. How can I make it right?

255

"We lost. They won. I was able to preserve the base and bug their vehicle. I can track them. I've made contact with loyalists they freed from captivity and attempted to recruit. They are staying to infiltrate the group, on my orders. I've—"

"Good," he said, then he smiled like the break of dawn. "I should have known you'd never fail me. It's just a setback. I'll leave this in your capable hands. Kill the traitors and aliens and get me that ship."

He smiled at me. He forgives me. I love him so much.

"And the Teacher?"

"Hmm. That is an excellent question." He sat for a moment in quiet contemplation. *Say it, please say the words.* "Capture him if you can. Kill him if you must."

I smiled wickedly. Apparently too wickedly.

"If you must, Quinn."

Oh my god. He knows my name.

I disciplined my expression and nodded.

"Good. I'm glad we got that settled. I'm counting on you. Things are… well, things are complicated at the moment. I'll expect good news from you soon. Very good news indeed."

He needs me!

He needs me. My wicked grin returned, if only in my mind.

"About Lee…"

He held up a hand to stop me. My mouth shut of its own accord. So his Skills worked through my Firewall, even if his Charisma didn't. Good to know.

"Kill him. Kill him and make him suffer. No matter who else you have to kill. No matter what you have to sacrifice, Lee dies. Is that clear?"

"Crystal," I answered. I'd heard that somewhere once, and it sounded appropriate now.

I'll kill him for you, Lee. I'll make the bastard suffer.

The Humanist could go fuck himself. I'd do his dirty work, since it lined up with mine. I'd kill the traitors and the aliens. Maybe I'd even get him his ship. The man was far too dangerous to openly oppose.

But Lee? Lee was mine. Once the Teacher was dead and Lee was free, we could decide how to move forward together. I'd planned to throw ourselves on the mercy of the Humanist, after getting him everything he'd wanted. No harm no foul. Apparently, that had been a pipe dream. Maybe we could stage our deaths, sell the ship at the Shop, and run. Or keep it and escape beyond even the Humanist's influence.

One problem at a time.

I realized that the Humanist had been talking and was watching me for a response.

"Yes, sir!" I said. "Consider it done."

"Excellent. You have done well. I won't forget it." And he cut the line before I could respond.

I switched the call back to the Communications Specialist, letting my fury shine through.

He met my eyes, but he didn't dare to speak.

"I want to make this very, very clear, Ken. The Commander lives or you die. Use someone expendable to finish off the other patient if you have to, to save resources. In the meantime, I'll get ahead of you and stash some emergency supplies for you to 'remember' or 'shake down from the men.' Just make sure you make them prioritize Lee."

"I don't see why you would even want to save..." *He must have remembered who he was talking to.* "Sure thing, Quinn. I'll get it done. But how are you going to get ahead of us? We're in a rough spot, but we're still hauling ass."

I finished the activation sequence. Gears turned, steam whistled, and my baby was born. One part spider-bot, one part steampunk abomination, one part weapon of war. She had been meant as a huge surprise for Lee and the others, a mobile assault platform he could modify with his upcoming Advanced Class Skills. It was meant to be our road to Master Class. Now, it would be Lee's salvation.

"Leave that to me."

Chapter 27

Caleb

Back in the real world, instead of my own curated dreamscape, I fired my turret at the attacker Pavise had summoned for me in the training hall, a duplicate of the fanged deer that had charged me the first day of the Apocalypse.

I managed three shots to its face before I whipped around and dashed away with my not-so Thrusting Charge. At the end of my stumbling dash, I tucked my body into a roll and sprang back up to my feet, narrowly missing a fake log and the stump it had fallen from. I'd learned the hard way that the images were solid to my temporary form. They didn't do real damage but smashing my face into them still hurt. I was finally able to avoid doing just that.

It was me, not the supercomputer, who had come up with the idea to assume and direct the fall of my dash, rather than trying to prevent it. It worked better than we could have ever hoped. If heaven or something like it really exists, my parents are up there patting themselves on the back for the tumbling lessons they'd bribed me to take in grade school.

My enemy was closing in fast, but a pair of spruce trees gave me the cover I needed. I dashed, rolled, then whipped around and activated Hunter's Strike. Bull's-eye. Or in this case, deer's-chest. Not as catchy.

Imaginary balloons, streamers, and confetti fell from the ceiling of the room. Horns sounded. Giant gold stars and smiley faces appeared. Pavise was probably giving me crap, but I loved it and glowed with pride. I'd always been a fan of gold stars, as a student and a teacher, and I wasn't about to stop now.

Pavise was there to help me every step of the way. His presence was always reassuring, even in a relatively safe environment.

Still, even with Pavise's help, learning to use my two new Skills had been a nightmare. We had managed to make my new attack functional, at least when I used the turret rather than my unsuitable human hand. I could fire straight ahead with a blaster, but we didn't get the full range we'd predicted.

Pavise and I agreed that we'd done the best we could with the time we had, and he allowed me to wake up. My body, unlike my mind, felt well-rested. Even so, I wanted a nap, but Pavise let me know that if I did that, I'd lose the sunlight. He did not recommend going out at night for my first hunt. I completely agreed. At the thought of going into a monster-infested world at night, an invisible fist gripped my chest and wouldn't let go until it was nearly impossible for me to take a breath. The first flashes of blue blood and the sound of the Matriarch's death throes were cut off as Pavise spoke with urgency and shock in his voice.

"It seems that your Quest has been updated, sir. The failure penalty now lists execution by the Human Liberation Front, rather than merely the Commander." His three "legs" tapped against the floor with a metallic ring as we walked.

"Does that mean that he's dead or that he's bringing reinforcements?"

"There is no way for me to know, sir, but it doesn't really matter. Whether there is one murderer or a hundred, you will be just as dead. That is, of course, unless you intend to abandon the ship and flee with the children in some random direction. Even then, we're as likely to be caught as to be killed by monsters. We've already planned to resolve the situation as quickly as possible. I suggest we continue our plan."

We hurried through the door to the armory.

"Good point," I told him as I equipped my armor. After a short debate, I strapped on the belt of stun grenades.

Out of old habit, I started to remind myself to think of Pavise as it, rather than he, until I remembered that his preference had changed. He'd settled on he, though he'd also insisted that though he did not understand why I insisted on referring to him as a person at all, he really didn't care what I called him.

That made me chuckle.

For someone who claimed to not care about what he was called, he certainly got snippy when you used the English pronunciation of the name I'd chosen for him, instead of the pretentious French one he preferred.

"Sir," he said, yanking my attention back to him, "we don't have time for whatever is making you lag." I started to explain, but he cut me off. "We don't have time for you to explain either. I'm afraid we dare stall no longer."

"That doesn't leave much time for dilly dallying," I said as I headed for the door.

"Another movie quote?" he asked.

I started to tell him that it was another one from the *Princess Bride*, but I thought better of it and answered with, "Sorry, Pavise. I don't have time to explain."

"Quite right, sir," he answered.

I made it to the last major conjunction of pathways before the main crew compartment by the door before I found my path blocked by Aul, along with three of the other children who had been being trained as Hunters. They were in full battle dress and equipped with spears and blasters.

"No," I said, stopping. "Absolutely not."

"Caleb will learn to fight to protect hive, is truth?" Her spear butt clanged against the floor.

I turned toward Pavise, betrayal written on my face. He lowered his head halfway into his armored chest.

"Yes," I said reluctantly.

"Aul will help. Kek and Nun and Nal will help. Hive will protect Caleb, is fact."

"No," I said again.

Aul's gray skin turned steel blue and her bulbous eyes popped. Anger filled her voice. "Caleb will die, is fact. Hive will protect Caleb."

"I care about you too," I answered, and I forced a weak smile. "But I can't let you go. I need to learn how to do this alone, and I can't do that if I have to focus on protecting you."

She turned to Pavise. "Caleb needs hive to live, is truth?"

"He's not in charge," I snapped, interrupting before he had a chance to reply. Then I forced myself to take a deep breath and remember to be grateful rather than annoyed. "And he doesn't know everything."

It might have been unmannerly, but I felt it was better to nip this in the bud right now, especially since Pavise might agree with them.

"Pavise knows more. Caleb knows less." She crossed her upper arms.

Pavise cleared his nonexistent throat.

"Yes," I answered, "but that doesn't change anything. I have to go, and you have to stay. I want to tell you that it's because you all need to stay here to protect the others while I'm gone, but this close to a dungeon, you probably couldn't stop anything the door didn't stop anyway. The most important issue is that I'm not ready to be able to protect you, even if I was willing to risk your lives, which I'm not.

"You hunted with the others before when there were careful plans and skilled warriors to protect you. That's not me. And even Pavise isn't good enough to safeguard you if things went wrong, which they almost always do."

"Pavise cannot protect pack, is truth?" The way Aul was holding her head and the aggressive angle of her upper body dared him to answer with anything other than the absolute truth.

"I'm afraid that it is true, young miss, at least not while linked to a non-Combat Classer who is unsuited to working with a shield-bot."

"Hive must train. Caleb must train hive to protect pack."

Inwardly, I groaned. Aul was right about that, but still.

"I'm not that kind of teacher," I said, rubbing the center of my forehead. "But I'll do what I can when I am confident I can protect you."

"Is promise?"

"Yes, I promise."

"Perhaps we could set up the training hall to train them while you are away, sir. It wouldn't take long, and it would be good for them to develop their Skills."

"That's a good idea," I answered.

Aul shuddered and readied her weapons.

"Not with weapons," I said. "Not unsupervised." That was a bit of a dick move, since they were obviously far more competent with the weapons than I was ever likely to be. "Set it up to train them in the other Skills they'll need to survive?" Then I realized that would give them too much wiggle room. "Set up an obstacle course with non-painful zings to let them know if they get hit. The goal is to train their stealth and their ability to move quickly and quietly, and if that fails, to run and evade attacks at the same time."

"I suggest that you consume approximately a fourth of a serving of Indekk while I get them set up. In a situation like this, I would not recommend a full stomach."

That made sense.

"We should probably practice stealth while we head out. You made a good point that neither of us have properly developed the skill," I said.

"For you, sir, it will be a Skill. For me, it will take specialized equipment that we will need to get at the Shop. Even then, I'm afraid that shield-bots are simply not constructed for subterfuge."

"That's okay, buddy. No one is good at everything. But I should still practice the techniques."

"As you wish," he said.

Was he messing with me? *Has he seen the* Princess Bride *after all? Pulled it from my mind?* But the tone was wrong, and he had never been much of a liar, so I decided it was inconceivable.

Chapter 28

Caleb

Around fifteen minutes into my "hunt," I had become certain of two things. My senses were lying to me and they were very good at it.

Soft, gray pussy willows danced in the gentle breeze. Chilly air saturated my lungs and teased the hairs on the back of my neck, making me shiver. I breathed it in, savoring the nose-tingling freshness of the Minnesota woods in springtime. I tipped my head back and looked up through the sparse canopy, where leaves were just beginning to create a green blush against the backdrop of the achingly blue sky and fluffy white clouds.

An adorable ruddy squirrel was sitting on a tree branch nearby. It was bigger than usual, but only about the size of a small house cat. Because it was facing away from me, I couldn't see what it was shoving into its already swollen cheeks. Its fluffy tail was wrapped around the branch, which was odd, but cute.

I wonder which of them is going to try to kill me first. My money was on the squirrel, but the pussy willows were a close second. *The clouds are probably safe.* I smiled. Then I remembered that the giants and dragons I'd enjoyed when cloud-gazing in the past could now be elementals readying to strike.

This is not a normal forest and that is not a squirrel. It is not adorable. This is a death trap and that is a monster. Their cheeks are not cute. They are probably filled with gore. That cloud is going to eat me. I forced myself to breathe, slow and long, but I couldn't stop my heart from racing or my eyes from flitting from one potential danger to the next.

"*Perhaps you should use your Inspect Skill, sir,*" Pavise said.

He had a point, so I started to do just that. The squirrel moved behind the trunk of the tree. I walked around it to the left for a better angle.

And the pussy willows exploded, spraying dark liquid from their centers and launching tiny gray blades in every direction. My armor took the hit like a champ, though there was some superficial damage. The sizzling hiss and blades peppering the surface told me that things would have been much worse if the Matriarch hadn't insisted I not skimp on my armor.

I'll never get a chance to thank her.

I forced my mind back to the present. I'd let the clouds distract me from the pussy willows, a rookie mistake, and now I was pretty sure that the squirrel and the plants were in on this together.

Once the attack failed, the squirrel moved back into view. I inspected it.

Sanguine Puncturer (Level 30)
HP: 318/318
MP: 82/87

Called it. Well, maybe not quite. If it was a vampire squirrel, its cheeks might be filled with blood, rather than general gore. I could see now that its tail, though fluffy and soft, was tipped with a scorpion-like stinger.

Either it hadn't noticed me, it was overestimating my danger based on our level disparity, or it wasn't hostile, despite the name.

"It's hostile, sir," the shield-bot answered, though I hadn't intentionally directed the thought to him. He had permission to pull things from my head in life-or-death situations. *"It's probably just waiting for reinforcements. I wish you had purchased the enhanced sensory functions or drones I requested. It makes it very hard for me to do my job when—"*

"Shh," I interrupted. *"I need to concentrate."*

My mind expanded and time slowed as he lent me processing power.

"That's not what I meant." Still, it was a good idea. *"What do you think, buddy? Just avoid it and move on?"*

"If the children come after you, it will easily kill them. Also, it's probably already too late. You should eliminate this first threat. It may dissuade the others, or at least lower the danger of being overwhelmed. You may also wish to move into a more defensible position."

"You're probably right about the kids, as much as I hate it. But I'm not going to murder it. I'll move a bit closer. If it attacks, fine. If not, I'm leaving. And you can't know for certain there are more."

"It's level 30, and it's here. If it were alone, it would be dead."

"Fair point." I moved closer, fully aware that shooting first would have been the safer choice.

The creature turned when my foot cracked a stick, and it opened its maw wide. Then wider. Then wider. The cheeks weren't filled with gore or blood, I saw, but rows and rows of fangs. Its eyes were filled with a kind of ravenous, furious hunger I'd come to associate with monsters.

It was so obviously eager to attack me that I raised my gun and readied my shoulder-mounted turret to fire. I was doubly grateful that the Matriarch had thought it was shameful I had not been born with a proper exoskeleton.

The squirrel surprised me so much when it hesitated to attack that I nearly pulled the trigger. I forced down recriminations—this wasn't the time to feel my feelings. We maintained the impasse for a long moment, and I couldn't help but wonder why until I remembered that the System had video-game-like rules and I was twelve levels higher than it was.

The monster was probably just being prudent or waiting for reinforcements. *Or both.*

That meant it was time to go.

"Kek is impatience. Caleb kill or Kek will kill, is truth."

The monster snapped its predatory gaze to this new presence before I could even twitch. So I witnessed as alarm, understanding, and finally fury filled its expression before it opened its arms wide and leapt from the tree, gliding right at Kek Inu.

Oh God. A flying vampire scorpion squirrel.

Time lagged hard and searing pain erupted in my head. *"Focus, sir. You'll never forgive yourself if you hesitate now. And that includes technicalities about moral gray areas."*

Pavise knew me so well. His words helped my mind jump past the confusion to the conclusion that a child was being attacked and anything else could wait. I willed away the connection before my brain could melt and time sped back up as I aimed and fired.

I missed it completely. The thing was just too fast.

A barrier of blue light appeared between the monster and Kek. The squirrel slammed into it, fanged-face first.

I winced in unwilling empathy as it shook its head to clear it. I'd been there. My second shot at the now-stunned squirrel didn't miss. Neither did my third as I finally remembered my turret and fired the weapon with a mental command. The blast hit the squirrel in the chest.

It winced as the attack took a more noticeable chunk off its Health. In actual combat, the turret did far more damage. Got it.

Gunfire sounded in the distance. *More monsters. No, that's not fair.*

Focus.

"Kek, get back to the ship."

But Kek didn't move, frozen in fear without other hunters to protect him. I understood completely. I turned my attention to the creature.

"Go on now," I said, since the squirrel could apparently understand at least some speech. "Get out of here. We don't have to do this."

It hissed and lunged at Kek from a different angle.

The shield moved to intercept it.

"Kek, your spear," Pavise said.

The child shook off his terror and thrust the weapon toward the creature.

It dodged, but the additional attacker made my shot easier. Shot. Crap. I activated Hunter's Strike. The empowered attack slammed into the monster's left leg, searing it like a steak and setting its fur on fire.

It shrieked and whipped around to face me.

A chorus of barks and chatters filled the clearing from the woods. There were at least five distinct sources. We were making a lot of noise. Would that draw more monsters? The people with the guns?

Damn it! What should I do? My eyes tried to look everywhere at once and my heart tried to batter its way out of my chest. *We need to get out of here.* The creature had nearly half its Health left and Pavise had limited energy. But where would we go? The creatures had us surrounded.

The first squirrel simplified that and complicated everything else as it chirped out orders that caused the rest of his pack to gather behind me. It glared at me one last time, then turned its attention back to Kek. Apparently, this was personal for it.

I gagged as the smell of its leg finally wafted over to me.

"Don't panic, sir. Get behind the shield," Pavise said.

Gamer experience told me to finish off the injured leader.

My heart told me to sacrifice myself to buy Kek the time to run.

Trying not to hesitate, I aimed for the best of all three worlds. "Kek, run! Ship."

Kek chittered defiantly. "Kek is protect Caleb."

I'd already activated Thrusting Lunge, hurling my body at the lead squirrel in what I imagined to be a rather heroic tackle. I shot forward, attempting to dive as I did so.

Unfortunately, trying to alter Skills as I used them didn't work as well in the real world as it did in my mind. If it was something that could be done at all, I failed entirely.

I missed and tripped. A thud and the crunch of my nose breaking heralded a spike of pain as my face dug a small furrow in the grass. Knocked half senseless, I somehow managed to force myself to my feet and whipped around to face the squirrels. They were across the clearing, but I knew how fast they could be. I wanted to use my Charge to dash away, but I couldn't just leave Kek to die.

I caught myself overthinking, then realized it was act or die as the creatures leapt.

A sudden burst of energy washed over me. My vision narrowed. My breathing quickened. Time seemed to slow. *Not enough*. I yanked on the connection with Pavise and my head felt like a hot dog in a microwave as time slowed to a crawl.

Even like this, I had precious little time, and Pavise was focused on using his body and his shield to keep Kek alive, though I could feel his intense desire to switch the shield to me and his plan to do just that if it came to it. "Sir, I should—"

"I have armor, Kek doesn't. Don't you dare."

He may have responded, but I'd already moved on. Blaster. Not a great choice against five. Kite them? Into the woods and abandon Kek? Grenades!

I'd have just enough time to hit them all with a grenade, though it would be far too close to me. I'd have to count on my armor and higher Level. I let time resume as I reached for one of the weapons and pulled. Nothing. It may as well have been welded to the spot.

Crap! Never trained with the grenades.

I managed to stop one with a shot from my turret that burned fur and caused it to curl up reflexively, putting it off target. The other four of them had made it onto me.

How they attached themselves to me, I couldn't see, but three were tearing into my armor with their fangs and striking with their stingers. The fourth climbed onto my shoulder and bit my weapon.

Oh god! I'd never even considered that. It took all my strength to yank it off and toss it away. Pavise had been right. I wasn't nearly strong enough to be effective in this world.

More gunshots in the distance. Much closer, I heard an eerie, hissing roar and what sounded like an oversized rattle.

Focus, Caleb. Focus.

My terror spiked and I nearly screamed as my defenses failed for the first time. A row of sharp fangs penetrated the armor of my leg, then my skin. Though it gave me none of the thrill I'd read about, my adrenaline did give me the strength to tear the creature from my thigh. The pain was so much worse as I pulled it loose. Agony and existential dread took what would have been an exciting game and turned it into a terror-filled nightmare.

The last of the creatures was staring at my crotch. My mind, on the verge of insanity, wanted to make a joke about squirrels and nuts, but just the thought of that fang-filled monstrosity chomping on me there broke something in me.

A Hunter's Strike discouraged the creature. It was the one that I'd already hit, so I decided this would be my primary target, with the clever one that had attacked my turret as number two. I managed to shoot the first one again before he could dodge effectively, but my mind blanked as three of them managed to bite me at the same time.

Things went from horrible to hellish when Pavise sent me a flash image of his shield failing and I heard Kek shriek in agony. I could only think of one thing to do that might save Kek.

I sent Pavise an image of himself standing between Kek and me, then screamed, "Kek, run now!"

I hesitated for much less time than I would have liked to let them follow my orders before I reached down to my belt and activated one of the grenades by pressing the symbol of the crossed spears and turning the button that popped out to the right. Luckily, it was the same device the Voloids used for the traps I'd learned about from the Security Skill book.

The count of three was filled with me taking two steps closer to the squirrel attacking Kek, who thank God was finally running away with Pavise between him and me.

A clap of thunder shattered my hip and my eardrums as it hurled all of the squirrel monsters through the air like sock puppets. I couldn't move. I could barely think. I couldn't even force myself to scream from the agony.

Pavise sent an image of Kek face-first on the ground in a puddle of blue blood from his wounds. The monster, though obviously stunned senseless, was still latched onto the child with its over-fanged maw.

Wet warmth was dripping down my leg. I thought at first that I had pissed myself, but my agony and my slowly dropping Health bar set the record straight.

While we were all stunned, a new monster with the upper body of a grizzly bear and a thick serpentine tail with a wicked rattle blocked my path. It was covered with reddish fur and coppery scales. Its canine teeth had been replaced with oversized snake fangs. The smart money was on the monster being venomous, especially since the tail near me rattled. It's slitted, greenish eyes were glaring at me.

I suspected that the only reason it had not attacked me was that it was already busy swallowing someone's body whole. Head first.

I inspected it.

Ursa Serpentis (Level 40)
HP: 518/518
MP: 82/82

Our only hope was if the creature was too full to bother killing us.

That hope evaporated as it sucked in the legs and boots in a final gulp and the whole thing just disappeared into it. Even the wide bulge in the bear's neck and torso vanished as if they had never been there.

"Likely extra-dimensional storage," Pavise told me. "Run or die."

I was shaking off the stun, but Pavise clearly didn't know about my injury.

"Shattered hip," I told him. "Not giving up, but this doesn't look good." I managed to turn my body a little to be better able to aim my turret at the grizzly. "Try to save Kek."

"I am afraid that my end will closely follow yours, sir. For your sake, however, I will do what I can in the meantime." There was a short pause. *"It has been an honor, sir."*

I started to say, *"This is not goodbye."* But I didn't want to lie to myself or my friend. So, I opted for, *"I love you too."*

The squirrels had shaken off the stun and damage from the grenade, and they were heading back my way. From the sounds of Kek's wails, Pavise had yet to find a way to help him.

Think, think, think.

I tried to slow time, but there was a flare of pain by my cybernetic implant and nothing happened. But my mind was already working, regardless. I had a Skill I'd used a couple of times to help the Voloids when a hunt went bad. Could it work here?

Pay Attention (Level 1)
Directs an individual or group's attention toward a particular subject.
Area of effect: 30-foot radius centered on Teacher.
Grants a +5 bonus to perception for 1 minute.
This Skill also aids in resisting distractions.
Cost: 25 Mana.

It was worth a try. I focused my intention on the Ursa and activated the Skill, willing the squirrels to focus on the new threat.

The Skill worked. It worked all too well.

The attention of the squirrels was immediately drawn to the massive and terrifying threat they had yet to notice. Five for five, they fled, leaving me as the sole target for the bear.

They fled in the direction of Kek and Pavise.

No, no, no! What have I done?

The bear dashed forward. I tried to shoot it in the face with the blaster, but its fang drove deep into my hand through the armored glove. I dropped the weapon and stepped back. I felt my hand throbbing and Pavise let me know through our link that it was rotting. I tried to turn and dash, but my hip screamed in protest and failed utterly. I doubted it would have mattered. The thing was just too fast. I managed to cast a single Minor Heal before its massive paw slammed into me, breaking my arm clean in half and sending me down to my knees.

Kek's screams redoubled then choked off with a final, gurgling wail.

Before I could even try to react, the monster gaped its huge maw and swallowed me whole, armor and all.

Powerful, crushing force smashed in on me from all sides, adding ribs and shoulders to my list of broken bones. If the Matriarch hadn't shamed me into wearing a proper exoskeleton, as she'd called it, I would already be dead. My consciousness came and went until the crushing force suddenly stopped as I fell through darkness, only to face and belly flop into a rancid liquid pool.

I screamed and screamed as my flesh sizzled from the acid trickling into my armor through the bite holes. There was a muffled, frazzled sound. It might have been Pavise. A shocking bolt of pain exploded near my temple. Then my mind shut down.

Chapter 29

Aul

Ku'un, a portion of Ourself that guards, brought her body to the training hall to speak words to me in language. *Words. In language. To communicate with part of Our own hive. What have We become?*

I was hiding behind one of the groupings of white-and-black barked trees in the emulated forest Caleb had prepared before leaving. This part stopped hiding, bringing an end to the training game. So that the lesser shame would not be borne by Ku'un alone, I moved to join her.

Lesser pain erupted in Our, my, back as the stun-spear struck this part with great force.

The game had not ended just because I had chosen! The lesser shock of this realization was worse than the weapon's blow. Turning, this part saw lesser-savage-triumph in the eyes of T'vonn, the most aggressive of our hunters.

I chose not to tell T'vonn of Our shared shame.

I was choosing not to tell a lot of things lately. Caleb would not approve, though he would be kind. He would call such things lies of omission. He disliked any kind of deception. He would make a good Voloid. *Can I still say the same about me?*

Thinking of my teacher made my heart-cluster flutter with worry. *Is he still alive? Are we even more alone, now? Has this vile Dungeon World taken him from Us, from me, too?*

The Ku'un portion was speaking, but this part had not heard. This part had not listened.

"—returned. You must come at once."

Who had returned? Caleb? The killers? One of the monsters that had attacked the ship before? To ask was to admit I had not listened. How could such a shame be borne?

A choice was made and this one body, my body, went to the Command Deck.

The empty pods were a reminder of everyone we had lost. A reminder of her. I almost couldn't bring myself to enter.

All I have left are my duty and my hive.

The first step was the hardest.

Pavise had made an overly ordered mockery of the elegantly arranged cables and connectors that had once been so expertly used by Tun'Ne Ah, the One Who Computes. This once-beautiful piece of technology had augmented the connection of a Voloid hive mind to the computer. The shield-bot's jury-rigged workings, however artless, nevertheless functioned.

Before he would leave the ship, Caleb had insisted that Pavise find a way for us to connect with and control the ship. He had found a way, though it barely worked. A combination of the cords and the globules against my temples allowed me to connect my undeveloped Eunn to the device, now that he had regained access.

Ku'un helped me hold the devices against my temple. With great strength of will, I could form a weak connection to the ship's systems. This part willed it to activate the defensive weapons, though without access to the System and Skills, they would be entirely inadequate. Then I urged it to show me what the sensors were picking up outside of the ship.

A faint image appeared, overlaying my vision. I closed my eyes. I could barely make out the human with a green robe and short dark hair. This part trembled, searching the scene for the two who were both humans and machines. They were not there. The lack of the one with yellow hair on half her head was reassuring. The lack of the One-Who-Chose was not.

The one who made the purple smoke did, however, have other humans with them. They wore the artificial exoskeletons humans used to cover their shameful lack.

Almost all of them had guns.

Caleb would point out that Voloids also used weapons, but Caleb was not here. He could not save us this time.

This part of the whole turned on the ship's exterior communication device. "Murderer is not welcome. Aul is not forgive."

The human recoiled as if struck. "I'm sorry."

"Human is be leaving. Human do not be come back."

"I'm sorry. I can't." The human pointed at three bodies wrapped in red bandages, carried on stretchers.

"Human is bring more victims?" The System, Caleb had taught, did not translate the Voloids well. What he did not know was that the Queen had paid a fortune to the System to ensure it. He had not heard the story of why, and I did not have the words to tell him.

Yet Caleb had taught me so much. My hive could speak with humans in ways no other Voloid ever had. I felt lesser shame to be back to such limited communication now. But I could not calm my heart cluster. I could not stop the rapid whistling of my spiracles.

Grief and rage did not lend themselves to nuanced speech with alien beings.

"I'm here to save lives, not end them," the human said.

Not dead then. Were they the thing that Caleb had called mostly dead, from the story that he liked so much?

"Aul is not trust." I focused my mind to speak more carefully. When I did, the view in my mind came more clearly into focus. "You are not welcome here. Go aw—Caleb!"

It was him. One of the mostly dead bodies was Caleb's. What could be seen of his skin was burned and bruised, even with the System recovery to keep him alive. His right hand and part of his arm were entirely missing.

Oh, Caleb. You are not good and bad. You are good and stupid. Good and weak. What have they done to you?

Where was Pavise? There. The machine was also scratched and damaged. He had scorch marks and a dent in his armored plates. But he was not nearly as damaged as his counterpart. One of the other bodies, this part now realized, was what might be a human Patriarch, the One-That-Chose. The third was not, sadly, the one with yellow hair and spider robots.

Hopefully, she was already dead.

"Human is save Caleb!"

"That's why I'm here. We need a safe and clean place to help them. We have healers, a Chirurgeon, and someone who specializes in cybernetics. Please. There's no time. Can I bring them in?" The human looked urgently between the hull of the ship and those lying on the stretchers.

This part had no difficulty translating the look upon that one's features. Worry was something I had seen upon Caleb's features many times.

"Human is bring Caleb, healers, and people that save. Other humans is stay out."

"I won't leave the others to die. I save everyone or no one."

Lesser anger threatened to become as large as greater anger upon the human's statement. My mandibles quivered. It was all I could do to not fire our weapons and cover the ground with their odd red blood.

The human wanted me to let the Matriarch's murderer back on the ship. *They want me to choose to save him.* Were they holding Caleb hostage? Had they captured him to force my hand? Was this a trick to get back on the ship now that they did not have the one with spiders?

Does it matter? Can I just let Caleb die?

"Human is promise save Caleb first." Again, I strained to remember what Caleb had taught me. "Or everyone dies."

"Don't listen to the damned alien," a larger human said. "The Commander should be the top priority."

"The Commander," the first human said, "put me in charge."

"He was drugged."

"You made me drug him. Now do what I say or answer to him if he survives this. I agree to save the Teacher—did you say his name was Caleb?—first."

I had already agreed, but I could not stop the words that wanted to explode from my mouth. "Human is save Caleb and new human. Matriarch's killer is not welcome."

"He saved your lives."

I saw blue and practically screamed, "Human not be murder is not human is be save us!"

"I will only save your friend if you let me save mine. Please hurry. If we wait much longer, they will all die."

"I'm out of Mana," a pale, exhausted-looking human said. They had been using healing Skills to help keep them alive.

I was torn in half with a desire to save Caleb and revulsion for the Matriarch's killer.

Another fear gripped me. The Queen would not approve. The entire hive could be punished.

Unless.

"The Matriarch's spear is be return. All Voloid things is be return."

"I don't give a damn about your spear. But the loot is in his storage. He'll have to give it to you when he wakes up."

"I can do it," another of the humans who looked very much like the one who had argued against the one with purple powder said. "If my One for All Skill still works with him now that we're not part of the HLF."

The bigger human glared at the new speaker.

"Try your Skill," the first human with the green robe said.

"Why should we give them anything? We have their friend."

"He's not a hostage. He's just a person. A good person."

Humans are good and bad. I remembered. *This human is good and bad,* I was forced to admit.

"It's not a fair trade."

"Humans is murdered Matriarch. No trade is ever be fair."

"We can just break in and force them. You said they're just children."

This part of Ourself aimed the ship's weapons at the human making threats. The broken killer would be a better target, but Caleb wouldn't like it. It felt wrong, but I almost couldn't force myself to care.

Aul is good and bad.

"Sir, as one former soldier to another," a tall human said, "shut the hell up. And don't give me any backtalk about the chain of command. Your commanding officer told you to do what the healer says."

"Try your Skill," the first human said again. "Everybody not part of the medical team, clear out. This situation is tense enough already."

"Purple smoke human is murder. Pill smoke human is be leave."

A strange look I could not identify appeared on the human's face. It was a look that Caleb often got but could not fully explain. "I'm sorry. I can't. They all die if I'm not there to help them."

"Caleb is die?" This one wanted to scream and throw down the equipment on my head.

This human was the reason our proud hunters had died in shame. They wouldn't even let them fight back. We students had not even been there for them. The Matriarch had blocked our knowing. Caleb would not Show and Tell. Only after the killers were gone had Pavise told us fully what had happened.

Now I had to welcome the shamer like a guest. *How can this be borne?*

The one with a Skill had taken the spear from the storage of One-Who-Chooses, along with many other weapons. The other types of supplies were not there. This part wanted to force the issue, but Caleb was dying.

Most of the other humans had left. There was no way to tell if this was a trick, but this one made a decision. I opened the hatch just long enough for the seven humans to enter.

Chapter 30

Lee

I floated, detached from my body. Until that moment, there'd been nothing. I'd been nothing. No presence. No darkness. No pain. Then I *was* again, though I couldn't feel my body and my eyes refused to open.

I'd gotten used to this by now. Walking up from seeming nothingness, groggy and exhausted.

They'd taken out my adenoids and my tonsils when I was a boy. My leg had been removed at twenty-five. I'd blown off the rest my damn fool self, but the aftermath had always felt the same.

What did I lose this time?

No. That was the wrong question. *What happened to me this time? Where the hell am I? Why am I here?*

I remembered getting my ass kicked by the Gladiator. The feeling as my head and chest had been bashed in.

I remembered being desperate to die.

Can't even do that right.

Cut the self-indulgent shit, I told myself, but with my father's words. We'd won. I'd lived. That was the end of it. Always forward. Never back.

Unlike my eyes, my ears were kind of working, though everything sounded wrong. Distorted. Magnified. People were arguing nearby. They didn't know I was awake. Vulnerable. Keep it that way.

"Aul is be refusal. Fury. Aul is help too much." This voice was deep and resonant. His tone was as strange as his grammar. *An alien?*

"I know that this is hard for you." Gerri's voice. "And I'm sorry. But we don't have any choice."

"Yes, we do." A male voice I couldn't make out, though I knew I should recognize it. "We leave them out there to rot or we attack."

"We can't do either. The ship's defenses aren't enough to keep out five Advanced Classers, even if most of them are only fifty-one. I could hold my own, but I'm still mostly out of Mana. Keeping them alive was brutal."

We're on a ship. What ship? I started to ask, but instinct urged me to stay silent. I decided to let this thing play out. I was unsure of my condition and there was still an alien somewhere nearby.

"Ship not for humans. You is be go."

"According to the System, it is a human's ship. It's his."

"Caleb not own ship. Caleb Teacher. Caleb friend."

Wait, that ship? In that case, the aliens aren't a threat. Might as well get up. Easier said than done. *What had Gerri dosed me with?* My body did not want to follow orders. My eyes still wouldn't open. Correction. Eye wouldn't open. *But I couldn't see from my cybernetic side either. Bandages? Or was it just too broken to fix?*

"That makes it simple then. We just take the ship from him." The voice belonged to Kryte, a cranky old asshole but a good soldier. He had been the leader of the Leveling group. The man had been a retired pro wrestler before the System came and revitalized his body, if not his attitude. He'd come up the ranks as a Grappler and was now a tanky brawler Class called a Crusher.

"Ship not human's!"

"We're not thieves," Gerri said.

"Who says we're not?" Kryte snapped.

"He did," Gerri said. "And I do."

"Well, he's not in much of a position to boss anybody around, is he little bit? Neither of you are.

Score one for the instincts. Is that a System thing? Perception? Does Luck affect it? Good old-fashioned paranoia? I need to know more about this stuff.

"He's in that position because he saved your lives, you ungrateful bastards. Because we saved your lives. And this little bit, as you call me, is two levels higher than you. So watch your mouth before I watch it for you."

"Huh?" he said at that last part.

I had to agree with the sentiment. What the hell did that even mean?

Still, Gerri must have gotten through to him because he said, "Yeah, I think they were going to eat us and wear our skin. You guys came through for us. No lie." It was the closest thing to an apology I'd ever heard from the lumbering brute. "But whether we take the ship or not, we should still use its defenses and fight those fuckers."

"Too many of our strongest are too hurt," Gerri said. "It's just too risky. And who knows if they have backup or others they can notify."

"It would be an easy fight if you hadn't sent the others away."

"I didn't send them away. They left without telling me. Though if they had asked to go check out the dungeon, I might have agreed. How the hell were any of us supposed to know a group of bounty hunters would come hunting us right now?"

I need to fix this. My body's shot, but I still have my mind. Maybe I can activate my Skills. The thought sent a shard of pain through my head, even as I struggled to keep focus.

"You do know what our group does, right? We kill alien scum and blow up their stuff. It's a lot of fun, but they don't really tend to see it that way."

Wonder what the alien thought of that line. Probably furious. But he kept his mouth shut. Smart. The big man was dangerous.

"I didn't really think that through," Gerri said. "I've had my hands full."

"Then maybe somebody not so busy should be making these decisions."

If Kryte attacked them, I'd have to at least try to help, no matter how rough a shape I was in.

"No," Gerri said. "Hell no. I'm in charge until Greyson says otherwise, and I say we try to find a peaceful solution or stall until the others get back. It's too risky for us and it's not fair to the... whatever these things are called."

"Voloids," said another voice, this one prim and proper. "The children are called Voloids. And my master would certainly appreciate your desire to preserve as many lives as possible in this situation. I believe that he would suggest diplomacy as well."

"That last fight was broadcast," Gerri said. "None of us can trust that we won't be recognized. And they aren't going to listen to children or a glorified tin can. No offense."

"Offense taken," the one who'd called the Teacher his master said. "How could there not be? Would you feel less offended if I called you a sausage-stuffed flesh sack offhandedly, so long as I instructed you not to take offense?"

"Sorry," Gerri said, "I'm not at my best."

"That's no excuse for poor manners. When one is under duress is precisely when manners matter most."

"I'll keep that in mind."

"That's all anyone can ask."

"Caleb is diplomacy. Caleb would talk them stopping."

"How the hell is he supposed to do that?" Kryte questioned them. "No offense." He paused, possibly seeing if the other voice would scold him. "The man is not fit for the spotlight. Don't get me wrong. I thought for sure he was a goner, all broken in like that and with parts missing when we cut him out of that monster's gut. But you and the doc did great. The new arm looks as good as new. But he's dead to the world and he might as well be held together with magic duct tape."

"I could wake him up and give him some boosters," Gerri said. "Maybe a sedative for the trauma. But he won't be in a state to convince anyone of anything."

His power. That weird passive Skill that convinced people to believe him. If nobody else thought of it, I'd have to force myself to moan and flop until someone got me functional somehow. *This is so humiliating.*

"The problem," the stuffy voice said—must be the robot that made the force shield—"is that though my master has many excellent qualities, deception is not among them."

"His power!" Gerri said. *Well done, Gerri.* "That thing he used on us."

"Only works when he is telling the truth," the robot said.

"Damn it," Gerri said. "I forgot that part."

"And the man is honest to a fault."

"Back to plan A then," the big man said. I heard the telltale sound of his meaty fist pounding into his other hand.

"Aul is knowledge."

"We're not going to attack them, Kryte. There has to be a better way."

"Well," Kryte said, "you're so smart. What's your better way? I'm waiting."

"Aul is knowledge!" The alien was shouting now. It made some kind of weird clicking sound. "Aul is solution. Human give Aul drug. Aul wake Caleb. Humans hide. Aul not tell Caleb truth. Caleb tell hunters lie as truth. Hunters leave."

Gerri chuckled, and I almost managed to blurt out a laugh.

Maybe there was hope for the kid, after all.

Chapter 31

Caleb

I limped down the hallway, one half-numb hand on the wall of the ship to help me keep my feet. *I should still be back in bed, resting.*

You should be dead.

"Pavise."

Nothing. Was my implant broken? It had definitely gone on the fritz.

Images flashed in my mind. Kek's body in a pool of blue blood. Five vampire squirrels flying at me. The bear, hauling back to swallow me. I could almost hear my own screams and Kek's wails.

I pushed aside the thought, walled it away. I had a job to do.

"Pavise, are you there?" My tone was a bit desperate now, and I didn't even try to hide it. "Damn it, buddy, can you hear me?"

Nothing.

There was probably a way to check in my Status, but Pavise managed most of that for me and I couldn't stop rushing forward to dig into it. *The children are counting on me.*

I strained to feel the connection, and there was something. A feeling that might have been embarrassment or shame. That had to be me projecting? Still, if there was a connection that had to mean Paise wasn't dead, right?

Or should I say broken? I was pretty sure it would have to be both, if he was gone. He might say that he's not a person. He might even believe it, but there was no way that was true. Not in any way that mattered. He had a viewpoint. He had thoughts and ideas. Hell, he could feel smug.

I realized I had stopped walking and was leaning face-first along the cool stone, so I forced myself to take a few deep breaths and put Pavise out of my thoughts. If he was gone, there was nothing I could do about it now. Even if he were busted and waiting desperately for me to come and try to save him, a laughable concept after everything that had happened, I wouldn't be able to fix serious damage without access to the Shop. I certainly couldn't get there without him.

Or with him.

Crud. Still not moving. I forced myself to walk. Or trudge, as Chaucer would say. Soldier on. This time I managed it, barely.

Stop thinking. You're only making it worse.

How could it be worse?

It can always be worse.

The children are counting on you.

Then I'm pretty sure they're out of luck. I had to hope that being hidden in the classroom would be enough to save them if this went badly.

Stop it. Pull yourself together. They need you now, and this is something you might actually be qualified to do. I'd woken to two Voloids and eight frantic hands bandaging and dressing me. Aul had been there, agitated. She'd let me know that they had gone looking for me, when I didn't return, and they had found me unconscious and carried me back to the ship.

They'd also brought back what was left of Kek's body.

They hadn't found Pavise.

My mind must have snapped when the grenade went off, or when...

Don't think about it.

I must have had a hell of a nightmare, because the last thing I remembered was the moist, crushing darkness and the acid as the... I shuddered. It felt so real. The bear had been swallowing what was left of me whole once it had finished injecting me with a venomous bite and beating me mercilessly. As real as it felt, I must have imagined or dreamed it all. I was here, after all, and this wasn't like any afterlife I'd ever heard of.

Why couldn't the bear be real and Kek's screams be a nightmare?

I was fading again. My feet weren't moving. I had no Skills that could help me here. No potions.

Or did I?

My Mana was recovered, and my Health was improved, but not full.

I cast Minor Heal. It helped the tiny amount it ever did, but it was better than nothing. Still, it took a lot more out of me than it ever had before. My head was spinning. I felt exhausted in a way that wasn't reflected in my stats. I also felt drugged in a way that made no sense. The Voloids did not have or use those kinds of medicines. As a hive mind, they had special techniques I didn't understand fully that they used to cocoon the minds of the severely injured or dying.

The spell helped a little. It hurt my head a lot.

Nope. Won't be doing that again.

I was going to need my mind, more than my body, when I reached the bounty hunters at the main ship's hold.

I smacked my own face when I realized my eyes were shut. I'd trade a lot for an energy drink and a splash of cold water from the sink. I had no time. Aul had made it clear that the bounty hunters had been waiting too long already, and impatiently at that. I picked up my speed.

I moved to the last door and opened it. I stood, letting my hand leave the wall and fall to my side. I stepped forward, standing tall and putting on the strongest face I could. It was a bad sign they were here, but it was a good sign that they were waiting and talking, rather than raiding the ship. Or killing us all.

I took two steps into the room. When I saw a massive, tusked soldier who looked like an Uruk-Hai from the Peter Jackson movies, I stumbled and fell face-first into the man's broad chest. Great first impression.

"Protector," he said, his voice like velvet thunder, "surely one so Titled does not faint at my mere countenance, however fierce. What ails you, sirrah?"

I'd never heard one of our non-native visitors sound anything like this. Did that mean I was dreaming after all? Or dead? Was I in a coma somewhere while Pavise kept my mind contained?

If so, buddy, you're doing a terrible job of keeping me relaxed and sane. No answer. Maybe there never would be. *No time to cry. I've got a job to do.*

I wiped my eyes too roughly. My arm didn't want to work right, still injured enough to be partially numb.

The huge man looked around and behind me, as if he expected to find a dagger buried in my back. "Are you beset, sirrah? We have tracked our enemies to this location, though the trail is old."

His word choice indicated that he was talking down to me, that he considered me his lesser, which was fair, especially under the circumstance. But the man had manners. Maybe I could use that.

I looked at him more closely. My Relatable Skill told me his special interests were tracking, firearms, and long romantic walks under the stars. I started to label him Uruk-hai in my head before I realized I was being rude to a lethal man who seemed to value manners, even if it wasn't on the list of his special interests.

"I'm sorry, sir," I said. "I'm Caleb. May I ask for your name?"

"Certainly, sirrah. I am Henning. The Pyrexian pyramid floating behind me is called Orb—don't expect me to be able to explain why. The lovely lady beside…" He kept talking, but I zoned out for a moment.

When I realized he had finished, I bowed my head. "Thank you. It's wonderful to meet you, and I appreciate your courtesy when visiting my home. You asked if I was beset. I'm not. It's just me and the children here. I'm afraid you haven't caught me at my best. I'm recovering from a bad hunt. We lost someone precious."

The *Art of War* would tell me that this moment of weakness was all the more reason to make a pretense of strength, but we were long past that at this point. If this was a war, rather than diplomacy, I'd already failed.

"What Skill is this? I trust you like my sister, though I know you not. Yet you are neither silver-tongued, nor beautiful."

He was one to talk, but I bit my tongue. Beauty was in the eye of the beholder, after all, and this beholder had green and black skin and massive tusks. Odd as I found his appearance, he wasn't without his charms. The man was built halfway between a surfer and a running back, and he carried it well. His armor was as polished as his manners.

I explained about my passive.

He was looking at me strangely. His strong hands were holding me up by the arms. "Wake up, sirrah, you're mumbling. Kalieus, can you do nothing for him?"

A female were-cow. Brown fur. Chocolate milk. My mind was mush.

A surge of power blasted into me. It was like stepping into the small offshoot waterfall you pay extra to tour during the *Maid of the Mist* tour at Niagara Falls. The potent Skill woke me more fully than I had ever been awake before, and my body was invigorated beyond even its System-enhanced limits.

"Wow! Holy cow! What was that?" I felt saner, and I grinned. I forced it down; it felt like a betrayal.

"It's a Skill, Caleb," she answered. "Nothing more."

"She is modest. But great as her power is, do not trust it. The healing will remain, but this vigor you feel will pass."

The female minotaur-like woman, not much taller than the Hakarta, took his hand with graceful elegance, like how a bull in a China shop actually is, despite the vile slander they were so often attacked with. My Skill let me know that her special interests included Quantronic harmonics, philosophy, and gardening.

I now had a new special interest—finding out what Quantronic harmonics were. They sounded awesome. In my head, I labeled her tentatively as Kalieus, since that was what he had called her. It could be a Title or a term of endearment, but anything was better than were-cow. I'd need to ask her what she preferred.

I considered inspecting her, but I didn't want to be rude.

She said something powerful, and her hand and eyes glowed.

Nothing else happened and she looked puzzled. Then she squeezed my injured appendage, got a look of understanding on her face, and placed her meaty palm on my shoulder, covering it completely. My lingering pain faded as gentler waves of the same type of power she'd used before washed through my body. Sometimes it flowed smoothly, bringing ease and pleasure. Other times, it washed up against a deeper injury like rocks in the path of water, and the power swelled and gathered there before it exploded in a burst, leaving a smooth flow behind it.

It was the single most relaxing and pleasurable thing I'd ever felt, true ecstatic bliss without side effects or sensuality. Three points to the Utilitarian philosophers. They were still wrong, but this stuff was awesome.

I wanted to make a joke, but all that would leave my mouth was a desperately sincere, "Thank you."

She smiled, her huge teeth on full display, massive eyes shining.

"If you're that grateful, sirrah, perhaps you could return the favor with the information we require."

I was starting to suspect that the man had been bamboozled into buying a "special" language-and-manners pack. *Or maybe he's just being overly formal, and the System's running with it. It might even be a guy-from-Jersey type situation.* I'd probably never know. I wasn't about to ask him.

"Sure," I said, "I'm happy to help. And thank you again."

"If you don't mind my asking, sirrah, what happened to you?"

"I was hunting. I nearly died. I'm worried my shield-bot was destroyed. Did you see a broken robot anywhere out there?"

"No, I'm sorry. We are on a Quest to hunt down foul brigands that have committed terrible crimes against my people, the Hakarta. Have you perchance seen—"

"Twin soldiers." My eyes glazed over, and my heart sank. "A powerfully built black cyborg, a vicious blonde with metal spiders, and a Native American with a green robe?"

Even through the remarkable power of Kalieus's invigoration, the images haunted me. Shredded shells. Blue blood. The children, pale and weak. The Matriarch slaughtering the twins. Red blood. The Insurgent running the Matriarch through with her own spear.

"I do not know of this person with a green robe born in the place called America, but yes, the others are indeed the scoundrels we seek."

"I'm sorry. I don't know where they are. They came here, slaughtered almost everyone, and left."

"Why did they spare you?" He seemed suspicious again.

"Because I'm human and their leader was racist. Speciesist. I'm not sure of the right word."

"He hates non-humans?" Kalieus replied.

"Yes, a bigot. It's not a justification, but I think he'd lost a lot since the System came. We all have."

"The Yerrick, my people, are no fans of the System." She gestured to the others in her group. "None of us are."

At her gesture, one of the others in her group, a three-foot-tall floating pyramid, opened several small compartments. A Swiss army's wish list of high-end blades and tools extended. I was feeling too relaxed and euphoric to flee. After a moment, the Yerrick waved it away and it stowed its tools as it floated backward. Relatable let me know that its special areas of interest were cybernetics, alien biology, and surgical grafting.

So, an alien horror movie monster. The pyramid named Orb is an alien horror movie monster. Good to know.

So, I'm a prejudiced asshole about surgeons that don't look like humans in lab coats. Good to know. Those interests would make sense for any surgeon in a Galactic community.

The last member of the group was a tragic figure. He was built like a double-wide pro wrestler, but his body was a mosaic of alien biology and tech. No two parts were the same. He had a clawed, reptilian left arm and a spear-tipped, cybernetic right. He bore no weapons, but he clearly was one. Their group's tank, perhaps?

Am I allowed to judge the floating pyramid without being an asshole now?

Not until I know if the person in front of him was his victim, his patient he is trying to restore, or someone he saved in desperate solutions by any means necessary.

Still, he's creepy, right?

Oh, yeah, so creepy.

Thank you.

But that doesn't make you not a jerk for prejudging him. Also, you're talking to yourself.

I've been through a lot.

Fair point. But they are all looking at you funny.

I forced my attention back to our "guests," and said, "Sorry, what were you asking?"

"And you haven't seen them since?"

"No, hopefully I never will."

Unfortunately, my disordered thoughts seemed to have renewed his suspicion, because he asked, "And if you did know their whereabouts?"

"Then I would ask you questions, determine your intentions, and decide what to do from there."

"He's being evasive," the massive man said.

"No, just honest," I said. "I try to always be. And my Skill reinforces that trait because it stops working if I intentionally deceive someone."

"Forgive me if I worry that a Skill that can make me believe someone could be misused."

"It's a valid concern." I pulled up the Skill and sent it to them with an impulse of will.

Everyone with a face seemed surprised, judging by their expressions. And I probably had the same look on my face, though for a different reason. I'd always just assumed Pavise was assisting me when I sent people things through the System with such a minor effort. Had I been giving my friend too much credit, or was this evidence that he was still "alive?"

"Your Skill seems legitimate," their apparent leader said. "I'm sorry to ask, but this is a very odd set of circumstances. Are you hiding anything from us?"

The money. The thought popped into my head. "Of course I am. Many things that are none of your damned business, if we are being a bit less tactful."

"An honest and fair response," he said. "However, I note that your statement implies, but does not state outright, that what you're hiding from us is not related to our business. So I will ask again, more pointedly. Are any of the things you are hiding from us related to the location of our targets?"

"Absolutely not."

He smiled broadly. "Then that's good enough for me. You have been a great help to us, sirrah, and I'm sorry to put you through an interrogation when you have clearly been through so much."

"Thank you," I said. "Though the healing helps make up for the intrusion."

I'd be glad to have them leave this place on positive terms. It would be better for all of us that way. Then I realized I was letting fear stop me from taking advantage of an amazing opportunity.

"Since you are here, any chance that you have time for a quick escort Quest to bring me to the nearest Shop?"

"I'm afraid not, sirrah. We have been well paid for our diligence regarding our Quest, and our reputation for keeping our word is our livelihood."

"I understand. I imagine it's already pretty clear that my last attempt at exploration was less than successful. Do you happen to have any other potentially useful gear to sell at the moment?"

"You are two days late on all counts, I'm afraid. We sold all such things last time we stopped at the Shop." He turned toward the pyramid. "No." After a brief pause, he finished with, "I said no. Don't ask again."

I looked at Henning quizzically.

He let out a long-suffering sigh. "My friend here wants to offer to upgrade you, though he does not have the parts on hand. He has a Quest from his mentor to find him one of the locals to... *improve*. I reminded him that we do not have time."

"A shame," I tried and failed to say deadpan.

Definitely a horror movie monster.

The Hakarta patted me on the back, a bit too hard for my comfort. It nearly sent me stumbling. "Sarcasm bypasses your Ring of Truth Skill. Good to know. I like you, Caleb. You seem a decent man." He pulled a coin from thin air. "If you do head to Fort Ripley or the Settlement of the Rapids that are Grand, show this to the city guard, but keep it on your person. I'm very close with the woman who owns the place. This will allow you entry to the settlement and Shop without a fee. Consider it a token of my gratitude for past"—he held it out to me, then paused right before I took it—"and future assistance." He placed it in my hand. Then he conjured another item, a small box with a button, and held it out to me. "Press this button if they return or if you learn more about them."

I took the item and thanked him again.

His smile got a bit harder as he said, "That token says that I vouch for you."

"I'll be careful not to make any trouble."

His smile returned. "That's all I ask. It's been a pleasure. Now, off with you. You may wish to find your bed before the Invigorate buff concludes. It will end very soon."

He turned and motioned for the others to follow him. They did, though the creepy pyramid hovered for a moment before following the others outside.

I took Henning's suggestion and rushed to my bed. I made it just in time.

As the spell ended and my mind shut down, I thought I heard Pavise say, ever so faintly, "Well done, sir. Very well done, indeed."

Chapter 32

Quinn

Strider, the name I'd chosen for my monster mech, was about the furthest thing from a smooth ride. On the plus side, her lurching gait was faster than we'd hoped. Her top speed matched my Kawasaki Ninja's, and her eight long legs filled nearly two full lanes.

I triggered Skills and slammed the lever hard. It wasn't fast enough. Not when Lee might die at any moment. Assuming he wasn't dead already. Something reached into my chest and squeezed. I double-blinked so I could see.

I flipped the switch to turn down my emotions. The god-damned things were getting in my way. Clear-headed, I saw an opportunity and skipped a turn entirely. My vehicle off-roaded like a champ. Her best feature for the current situation though, was that her bladed limbs could hack through trees.

My favorite passive proved its worth again.

Cutting Edge Tech (Level 7)

Any technologically advanced blade wielded by you, or your controlled devices, gains an increase to

damage, armor penetration, and durability. This Skill works best for cutting edge technology,

offering a higher bonus to elite and experimental blades. Mana Regeneration is reduced by 35

permanently.

I'd nearly reached the others when a loud crack reached my ears. Strider stuttered and slowed to a stop. I felt confident that what was wrong would be an easy fix, until one of her legs fell off.

Well fuck! I jumped down to take a look. It wasn't pretty.

A quick examination left me shaking my head. Parts were scattered everywhere, but I had no idea why. I'd never been a slouch as a mechanic, but Earl was an artist. The man was as good with machines as I was with murder, but half of what he did made no damned sense. Compared to him, I was just a weekend hobbyist.

The good news was that I had options. My Communications Specialist was with the Geek Machinist. I'd have him get the man alone and announce a way to fix this issue. I had no doubt the madman would correct him.

After climbing back up to my seat, I used Strider's long-range comm to contact Ken.

Nothing.

There was no way they should be out of range. I clenched my fist and cursed in irritation, but there was nothing I could do. I couldn't fault the man for not responding. He was working undercover, after all.

I maxed the volume and left the line open as I hopped back down and got to work.

It killed me to do it, but I put the leg back together. It took me well over an hour. Once it was back the way it was, I had a part left over. It was a hexagon with a flat side and rounded side. I hadn't the slightest clue where it would go.

I dropped it in my inventory and moved on.

Strider was too big for me to run remotely with my Skills, but I did manage to make parts move around. Slow going, but I found the culprit.

One of the gears was catching in a key junction. It was where the front left leg joined with the hub. The worst possible spot, since it was screwing up the cross belt and recharger.

Fuck. My fault. I hadn't even thought to fuse the ricton. Amateur hour.

I tried to fix the issue, but my access was blocked until I took off the leg again.

I was in a foul mood, my wrench in one hand and my samoflange in the other. That was when I got a call from Ken. It threw off my timing, and my samoflange slipped, knocking loose the gear. Blasted thing was a pain in the ass, but there was no better way to do the job.

"You have the worst timing ever," I said through half-clenched teeth. "If my samoflange runs out of TD units before this project's over—"

"What the fuck is a…" Ken said, before static cut him off. "We're… thought… Hopefully… knows their shit."

From where I was, I couldn't boost the signal. But stopping now would cost me precious time. I cursed and yelled, "Repeat all that."

With another twist, I was able to fuse the ricton and get the cross belt back in place. Silence and static were all I heard, one after the other. That was when I saw a second problem. This one pissed me off. The gears screwing up the alignment weren't for a god-damned thing. They blew a fucking whistle, and it wasn't even there to release steam.

Bullshit decorations! I'd heard the madman used to work in Hollywood. This seemed to give the rumor credibility, though it might have just been different with his Skills. The System made no god-damned sense sometimes.

Earl is too valuable to kill, I reminded myself as I tore them out, one by one. *There'd be no giant spider without him.*

If his bullshit killed Lee, I'll invent new ways to make him suffer. The bleed-through had more force behind it. It tried to make my body move. Concerning, but this wasn't the time for diagnostics.

I shut the rage down hard. It worked for now, but it cost a lot of Mana. I'd never had to spend so much before.

"The Humanist called... special containment and teleportation device... capture the Teacher and the aliens and send them back to base."

What aliens? The children? Why the hell would we capture them?

"I can hear you," I shouted. "Start over. It's been static."

"None of... Lee is..."

I climbed to get my hand on the antennae. Boost Signal was a tier one Basic Skill. It had no real range to speak of. When that did nothing, I used any Skill that had a chance of helping, then gave the "radio" a solid thwack.

Strength wasn't a Class Skill for me and hadn't been a key stat for my build. Even so, Topher wouldn't tolerate what he called min-maxing. I was stronger than I could have been pre-System. Far too strong for sensitive machines.

It dented, made a high-pitched squeal, and quieted. It may or may not ever work again.

I cursed and cast Minor Repair. The dent popped and the "radio" squeaked and squealed. After that, it just made a faint hum.

"Lee is..." Ken's voice had said. He might have been saying stable. He might have been saying dead. Either way, I had to fix this thing and get to—

Twin tsunamis of grief and rage struck into me from either "side."

I reeled, overwhelmed and confused. My body convulsed and I lost my grip, tumbling from Strider to the ground. I landed hard and barely even noticed any pain. I hadn't felt this way since... there was nothing. Emptiness. Just a void where whatever caused my pain should be.

I rallied. Now that I was ready, I was stronger than the pain. I focused my will and buried them both deep, forcing my Segmentation to its upmost limits. It captured ten percent of my max Mana, and my IQ dropped by double digits too.

It would have to be enough, though rage demanded that I break everything in sight, and terror said to rush to Lee on foot.

I crawled over to grab my tools and get back to work. My emotions struggled to break free from their bonds as I removed the wasteful extra parts from my machine.

I was exhausted, hurt, and fighting inner demons. It shouldn't have surprised me when intrusive thoughts broke through. This time, they were from my unblocked resentment. *Damn it, Lee, you've made this so much harder.* It would be so easy just to let him die.

No! My segments both demanded.

Then I felt a faint hint of awareness, followed by a flare of manic glee. My Mana counter glitched and Segmentation triggered. The wall between my rage and grief went down.

I had just enough time to realize I'd given the blocked parts of me an asylum full of misery, enough Mana to activate my Skills, and more Intelligence than I'd had when I was twenty.

The other part of me had reached the same conclusion. It was my last free thought before my mind was caged.

Images and flashes. Running through the woods. Smashing my fists against trees. Lost. Confused. Fingernails. Weeping. Blood.

You'll never get to Lee this way, I told them.

My passions couldn't hear or did not care. They shoved me right back down.

When I resurfaced again, they were weeping. And smashing my head on the ground.

I'll fix it. Just let me help you.

You'll kill him!

I won't. I didn't mean it. They were just intrusive thoughts. I was telling the truth.

It didn't matter. Nothing I could say would make an impact. They didn't give a shit about the facts, and I'd blocked myself off too much to relate. I had no way to bridge the gap between us.

Not a gap, I realized, *but a wall.*

I braced myself to pull the whole thing down. I'd rather die than face what I had buried, but only one man in this world had shown me kindness. I'd go through hell again to see him saved.

"Damn it," Ken's voice sputtered through the speaker. "… we need…"

I didn't know if my choice appeased the monster I'd created, or if Ken's voice just distracted it for me. Either way, the result was the same. The balance of power tipped in my favor enough that I could force the walls back up and weaken the emotions enough to stop the threat.

Now that I understood the risk, I used my Wrapper Skill to cap the Mana for each segment, with the max at one less than the cost of Segmentation.

Rushing back to my repairs, I had one thing on each segment of my mind.

Get my ass back to the ship.

Murder all the traitors.

Save my friend.

Chapter 33

Quinn

Strider was faster than ever. She devoured mile after mile like a giant, starving beast. It was an easy comparison for me to make due to a run-in with a herd of monstrous boars. The oversized creatures had looked badass, with massive forms and acid-dripping spines. When I saw them, I'd been eager for a bloodbath and XP, but the monsters just turned tail and ran away.

I was so close to leveling I could taste it. *I might need the extra strength for what comes next.*

But Lee might be dying. I didn't have time to chase down a stampede. I had a trick that could stop them, but I only had a single web-net loaded. I'd planned for more, but then I'd slit the crafter's throat.

If I could catch at least the slowest pair, I could test my baby's blades, but something told me I'd get my chance soon. *Fuck it,* I decided, then broke off from the boars and ended my pursuit.

When I made it to the ship, my giant spider stalked it like a predator, invisible and silent. I used a single-use consumable we'd bought for just such an occasion. It was the only one I had, so I'd have to make it count.

My team was ready. They joined me underneath my suppression field. As long as we were relatively quiet, nobody outside of it would hear a thing. Ken let me know that Lee was inside the ship and stable. It sounded like Gerri was the one to thank for that. I'd still kill them, but now I'd make it painless.

Ken had taken the initiative to remove the toughest members of the traitors. He'd persuaded them to leave the ship unguarded except by those within: the ship's crew and the HLF loyalists. They'd left to attack the nearby dungeon for XP and loot while they waited for Lee to come around.

My men prepared our ambush as we spoke.

Alarmingly, Ken had also been in touch with the Humanist directly. The man had sent him a special containment and teleportation device that would allow us to capture the Teacher and the aliens and transport them to a containment facility on base. I wasn't sure why he was trying to capture them. It was against official HLF Policy.

That said, not disobeying the Humanist was an even more important policy, and it made it much more likely I'd be able to capture and save Lee, despite the Humanist's earlier instructions. It would give me plausible deniability.

It was a bad sign that the Humanist had bypassed me. It showed I'd never really had his trust. Still, it didn't interfere too much with my plans. I'd even loaded my mech's systems with non-lethal capture tech in case I needed it for Lee.

"Everything is ready on our end. Our inside man was able to confirm that none of our preparations have been spotted."

"Good. So why do you sound like I'm going to peel your skin with my spiders?" I summoned one to hand to emphasize my point.

"A group of heavily armed alien Advanced Classers has approached the ship. Bounty Hunters. One of them was Hakarta. I tried to get your approval to attack them, though I frankly think we might have lost without you. And Quinn…" There was an honest-to-God audible gulp. "The ship just let them in."

"They let them in?"

"The door opened and they just walked right inside."

"Any chance they're working together?"

"We don't think so." He went silent.

"Why don't you think so?" I asked.

"There was a lot of yelling and threats, according to the scouts."

"Did they surrender?"

"The man on the inside says no."

"Fuck my life."

"Only fair," he said.

"What the hell is that supposed to mean?"

"That I'm pretty sure your life is gonna fuck me."

I heard a strange sound come from my own throat. A chuckle. The man had balls. Maybe I'd even let him keep them.

The group boarded Strider, and they all took positions. Everyone but the one meant to replace me in the driver's seat, so we could move me to the engine "room" inside the ship. I could boost things best from down there.

"Where's the driver?" I whispered to Ken. "His Skills should work with this bad boy, and you told me you'd recruited him?"

"Couldn't keep his damn mouth shut. The idiot got way too rude with Lee. He interrupted a meeting, twice, and then ignored an ultimatum."

I narrowed my eyes and whispered harshly, "You told me that Lee was stable. You didn't say he was awake to fight."

"He isn't," the man rushed to answer. "This was before the big fight. I barely managed to shut the Driver up before he burned us all."

"Why is this the first I'm hearing about this?"

"Because you were too busy threatening me to listen." He was trembling and his face was red, but more with fury than with fear, I would have bet. His next words confirmed it. "Now slit my throat or drop it, Quinn. I did my god-damned job."

I didn't kill him, so I guess I agreed.

"Are we attacking the ship?" he asked.

"Not like this. Our main strengths are surprise, the trap, and Strider. Not one of us can help with what's going on in the ship. Report back to the Humanist, ask for reinforcements and a siege team. Otherwise we wait 'till they come out. Or 'till the other group gets back. The fight should probably bring the Teacher and his people running."

The Communications Specialist didn't have time to follow my orders as the bounty hunters left the ship with nothing. A muscle-bound freak of a cyborg led the way, followed by a two-legged dairy cow. I was pretty sure I finally understood things. *The Teacher isn't a Teacher at all. He's one of those extra-sneaky types who can hide their true Class from Inspection.* He'd enslaved a group of aliens, and when we'd killed them, he'd saved the next generation to continue with his twisted plans.

I wasn't sure if I should kill him or recruit him.

Kill him. This is his fault. Make him pay.

I gasped at a thought before I could stop myself. Had the man enslaved the bounty hunters too? If so, he wasn't a Basic Classer at all. He must be Advanced. Maybe even Master Class. It all made so much sense now. No wonder even Lee couldn't resist him. Had I misjudged Gerri too? After all, they had saved Lee's life, hadn't they?

Why am I immune? Is it my Firewall? Segregation like with the Humanist?

Had the Teacher even been hurt or had that just been an elaborate trick to lure our people back here now that they didn't have me to protect them? That would mean he was afraid of me. That hadn't been an act. The man knew I could kill him.

All his fault. I knew I should have killed them all, back when I had the chance. Why didn't I just kill them? Right. Lee's orders. Fuck.

The Humanist needs to know about this right now.

If I died here, the Humanist was the only one I knew who might be a match for this Machiavellian puppet-master freak. He'd expect a full report, however. Before trying to contact him, I needed to know more.

I barely ever used Inspect—it was mostly redundant with my Measure Twice, Cut Once passive. That gave me a gut feeling about what I faced. But with this Hakarta, my instincts told me nothing. So I took the time to activate Inspect. Encoded text appeared for a second then vanished.

Denied: *You are not the Predator here.*

Wow! I had a new life goal to get the Skill that sent that message when I got inspected.

The Bounty Hunter turned and met my eyes, and I knew deep down that the Hakarta had inspected me. A beam shot from his eyes and we all popped into view. It was an impressive Skill, and it screwed my plans royally. But that was par for the course at this point.

It was time to prove that the System text could not have been more wrong. This man was now marked as my prey. I was the predator here. I'd show this asshole that one fly was no different than another if they faced off with a Spider Queen like me. The trap should work as well on aliens as our intended target. Better actually, since they couldn't turn my troops against me like the mind-controlling human. *Wait. Is he really even human?*

I had no time for this.

I wished Lee was here. *This is his bread and butter. I mostly just kill things. At least there are a lot of things to kill.*

No. Not kill, capture. Better to take the aliens alive than to try to change the plan we'd put in motion. *We can always kill them later, if we need. Maybe we could record the fight and make a spectacle of it for the crowd. It could put the Humanist in a more receptive mood. He loves that kind of thing and he'd ordered us to test his brand new toy. No better way to save Lee.*

"Go, go, go," I yelled to my troops as loudly as I could.

Then several things happened all at the same time.

My Group's Mana Augmenter, one of the nameless flunkies, placed her hand on the Mana battery that fueled the Gravity Well our Trapper was activating. The battery flared brightly as she added her power to his, boosting the already-boosted trap.

At the same time, hard eyes twinkling, the Hakarta grinned broadly as he pressed a button on his wrist. A blast shot outward from his belt buckle, and a giant, glowing weave covered our group.

In the center of the two energy effects, overlapping like an oversized Venn Diagram, something went very, very, wrong. The two powers, both gravitation-based, dragged us all several feet toward the center. Light itself warped inward. All of that happened so fast I had no time to react.

Then a cacophonous explosion launched nearly everyone away. The Mana Augmenter and the Yerrick woman were devastated. The cow had been the closest to the nexus, and it compacted her body in a way that even an Advanced Classer like her was unlikely to have survived. She looked like a toddler-sized cow-person plushie doll that had been covered in filth and smashed in the crack of a recliner for decades.

But her squashed body was still whole.

Either she was dead or she was so devastated with debuffs that the fight was over for her. I put her out of my mind. From the sound of her group's screams of fury and anguish, it wasn't good news for them.

I got no thrill from her pain, suffering, and likely death. It had been too quick, too clean, and too impersonal.

My team fared only marginally better. Being the next closest person, my Mana Augmenter had been pulled headfirst toward the sphere. When she returned, it was with a shrunken head and a grayed-out Health bar. She was probably a major loss to the HLF and therefore to our cause in general, but she was a Non-Combat Classer. Therefore, no real problem for our chances in this battle now that her work was already done.

Everyone not in Strider had gone flying, but they had mostly just been rattled.

My body tensed as a spike of terror threatened to overwhelm me, until I realized that the battle mech was too heavy to get tossed. I shuddered at what would have happened if I'd been close enough to enhance the technology like we'd planned. Things could have been so much worse.

I shuddered. *It can **always** be worse.*

Backing up my baby was harder than it sounded. Amazing as she was, the massive beast of a robot did not like to move backward. It also didn't have rearview mirrors, which… okay, that one was on me. Functionality first, awesome looks second from now on.

Once we got everyone loaded and I turned back to kill our enemies, I learned why Strider had not alarmed them. A floating pyramid had extended dozens of glowing vials from holes in its metal frame. Long appendages stretched from holes in its form, and it injected the Frankenstein freak with a rainbow assortment of gunk. Then the whole pyramid glowed, spun, and opened. From its center floated a sphere of clear glass.

There was a sound like two wine glasses clanking, and an inferno of golden light struck the monster of a man. He grew from oversized to enormous, cybernetics and all.

An overwhelming sense of unfairness washed over me. *No whining. Get it together.*

The pyramid closed and moved to hide behind the magnified monstrosity.

The Hakarta jet-booted his way to the thing's shoulder. He dual-wielded a pair of rocket launchers.

What the hell had I gotten myself into?

Freakzilla or not, I still felt we had the upper hand. By this point, my Spider was nearly fully manned. We had two Gunners, an Engineer, I was filling in for the driver, and I was channeling Enhance Technology.

As the bounty hunter launched his rockets, our gunners opened fire with Strider's cannons, shooting what our enemies would probably see as shrapnel blasts. I grinned as their rockets exploded against an invisible force shield projected from the belly of my beast. That was the most expensive of the Shop-purchased items Earl and I could not construct ourselves, but it seemed the credits had been very well spent.

Unable to hear anything over the thunder of explosions and the rat-a-tat of gunfire, I watched when the Hakarta's expression morphed to fear from fury. First, his attacks were harmlessly deflected, then our shots tore into his ally, unfolded into smaller versions of my classic spider drones, and dug in deep.

Even distracted as he was, the Hakarta couldn't fail to notice when the "chest" of my battle spider opened and dumped a swarm of spider bots in three different sizes. The middle size were the standard, and the largest were as big as mid-sized dogs.

All together, there were hundreds.

Strider's main guns had the standard blades for slaughter. But the new drop's blades were swapped out for injectors, half weakening debuffs and half paralytics.

They had been Lee's idea. Something to use if a boss could not be sliced and diced.

To his credit, the Hakara adapted quickly, showing why he led an Advanced Classed group in a Dungeon World. He swapped his launchers for what looked like flame throwers, complete with a massive fuel tank on his back. Instead of flame, they blasted out spray foam. He sprayed a liberal coat of gunk onto his "ride."

What the hell does he think he's doing?

The foamy coating tightened as it hardened into a rubber gel. But why had he used it on the brute, rather than the spiders?

The giant was apparently too strong to be contained by this material. It adhered to his massive form regardless. Armor. *Interesting.* The trick worked wonders, repelling my spiders and even restricting those already on him.

Damn it.

The giant wasn't inactive either. He charged forward, massive feet leaving deep footprints in the ground. When he slammed into Strider, it felt as if we'd crashed two semis together.

It hurt me more, on a deeper level, when he grabbed two of the metal legs on my baby and tied them together. Even my mostly deafened ears could hear the creaking groans as steel twisted and bent.

I could also hear, much to my delight, his resounding roar of agony as two of the massive blades drove deep into his torso and made a different kind of twist.

"Give him everything you've got," I yelled.

I wasn't sure they heard me, but at least someone must have since things went kind of wonky after that. Gunfire quickened, impacts knocked him backward more, and he had to shield his face with his arm from searing light.

Everybody opened fire while I tore into the giant with Strider's legs. Skills were traded off, fast and quick. Skills to add damage, to debuff, to wear down the other guys. They out-leveled our average but our Skills and my mech were taking their toll. We were wearing the aliens down.

Either they'd never had a healer, or we'd gotten *really* lucky with the cow.

Blood splattered me, and my companions screamed. Focused on the giant, I'd missed the reason why.

The Harkarta's expression changed from fear to shock. Finally it seemed to settle on rage as his eyes focused on something near the ship. Mine flicked there briefly. The door of the ship had opened and the Commander was there, leaning against that Teacher's robot. With him were Gerri, the traitors, and even several of the bugs. They were all armed to the teeth and waiting, watching.

The puppet-master must be hiding. He was nowhere to be seen.

Because I was distracted, the giant brute had managed to grab Strider. He dragged it as he took a quick step backward, then roared as he whipped his massive form around. With awe-inspiring strength, he hurled my giant spider at the spaceship. He barely missed the Commander's group, and we smashed against the ship nearly ten feet from the ground.

The commander and his people opened fire on the giant. Everyone but Gerri, who began to weave her magic smoke.

The massive freaks attack was an impressive feat, but it had clearly cost him something, because he started to shrink. With both groups firing on him, his Health dropped and he thrashed as if he was in the grip of a grand mal seizure.

That was when all eyes turned toward me. They aimed at me but didn't fire yet.

As he was lowered toward the ground, the Hakarta threw a chunk of metal. It was drawn to my baby like a magnet and stuck on tight. He reached toward his wrist to press a button.

But he was too late. My spiders crested the Hakarta like a wave. I couldn't even see the blood as they tore him up.

I reminded myself I couldn't kill him.

"Evac!" I yelled.

The aliens were beaten, but we'd paid a heavy price. More than a third of my troops were dead already. The rest were far too hurt to take the ship.

My surviving troops were thrilled by their new orders.

Eddie, our Transport Specialist, uncloaked our Non-Combatants. He used the device the Humanist had given them to open a portal. Our people dragged the bounty hunters through. They even took the remnants of the cow. They grabbed everything of value on the way. Only the pyramid, loyal or idiotic, followed them by choice. He'd suffered only scratches and a single dent.

Lee was confirmed to be safe, and I wasn't going to win this. Strider and my team were just too damaged. I tried to hop down as well, but I was trapped inside Strider by the twisted gears of my damaged harness. I fought to open it but couldn't. No problem. I summoned spider-bots with the purpose of severing the straps.

That was when the spaceship's defenses and crew opened fire on my robots and me.

Strider wasn't busted, not completely, so I yanked on the controls. I forced what was left of Strider's legs to turn itself around. The shield was a no-go; it was shattered.

I directed most of the spider bots to swarm the aliens, careful to direct them to avoid Lee. The rest I kept back for my own protection. That forced them all to focus on the spiders. Bought me time.

The ship's thrusters fired, engulfing the back of Strider. I'd only managed one step with Strider before it groaned in outrage, faltered, and died.

The silence felt palpable. Then *beep, beep, beep.*

My eyes fixed on the hunk of crap the leader had thrown at it.

A tracker?

No, an explosive with a timer. *Fuck! Fuck! Fuck!*

Boom! Half of Strider vanished in a burst of force and fire. Pain seared my lower body as metal and flesh fused, and burned, and melted.

I slammed my fist, again and again, into the ejector seat and self-destruct combo Earl had installed against my wishes. It jammed as what was left of my cybernetics and seat were fused to it.

I closed my eyes and isolated the part of my mind capable of pain and terror. Alone, and where none of the other parts could hear, it screamed and screamed as I willed my spider-bots to help extract my upper body, half of my pelvis, and the salvageable parts of the ejector seat.

I'd made a terrible mistake in capping segregation. There was more pain than anyone should face awake.

Even before the work was fully finished, I stopped the bleeding with a flare in either hand. A pair of healing and repair shots later, I cast Regenerate. Mid casting, the ejector seat finally triggered with a tell-tale shriek. Over-pressurized steam, finally set free, launched me away from the ship as Strider's remnant form was finished off.

What was left of my body and a portion of my mind continued working to try to treat the damage. It activated Minor Heal and Minor Repair.

Another part of my mind begged for the release of death. I was terrified and relieved when my parachute failed to open.

I didn't even have the mental capacity to curse as I fell.

Chapter 34

Caleb

I woke to a voice in the darkness.

"Good morning, champ. How are you feeling?"

I didn't recognize the voice. It was soft and feminine. The words were friendly, but the tone was detached and clinical.

My mind was a muddled haze, but my body felt faintly euphoric, as if I'd had a bunch of chocolate. No, not chocolate. Morphine. Like that time I'd had to miss the last two weeks of class when I had my appendix out.

Did I have surgery?

"Huh?" Light flared as I opened my eyes, but it was dim enough to not blind me.

There was a professionally dressed woman with equally businesslike dark hair, fashionable glasses, and a white medical frock.

What the hell? I was starting to remember. The System. The Voloids.

"One moment," the woman said as she injected a syringe into my arm.

Warmth oozed throughout my body and it tingled. Sensation spread from the spot where she'd injected me, then through my whole system via my blood.

Behind the woman, the room was filled with test tubes, beakers, syringes, and other medical paraphernalia.

Oh Lord. Have I been crazy this whole time and they finally found a way to get through to me?

No, my mind rallied. I remember this trick. *Fool me once, mind, and it's shame on you, but you're not gonna fool me twice with the same trick.*

I took stock of my surroundings. It didn't take long to spot the familiar asteroid rock wall behind the modern medical equipment.

This was my course room, or it had been. *Where'd all this equipment come from?*

The woman had spoken, I realized.

"I'm sorry, what?" My manners finally caught up with my confusion.

"I'm Penny, and it's a pleasure to meet you, Caleb." She tapped an odd device in her hand. It looked like a tablet computer, but it was thicker, and it was metal instead of plastic. Above the screen was a small engraving of a gear with another symbol I didn't recognize. It was long and had a roof and some kind of hole. Maybe it was a medieval tower? "I'm just running a few diagnostic scans. They're more for my sake than yours, I'm ashamed to admit. It's part of a Quest. You'll be happy to know that you are in tip-top shape, and your cybernetics are running as smoothly as can be expected."

Cybernetics! A flare of panic struck me.

"I'm sorry, sir," came a voice I recognized. Pavise. *"Aul and I had not left your side for the last two days. We wanted to be there when you awoke. However, we were called away by urgent business that appears to have been a ruse. We are on our way to rejoin you."*

I felt him rummaging around in my head. There was a strange pain where my cybernetics were housed. I was going to need to get that repaired asap.

"Please do not worry, sir. Everything is fine," Pavise said. I felt a twinge of doubt and guilt. *"Everything with you is fine, that is. Please be patient. We will arrive very soon."*

"Pavise. You're alive!" Relief washed through my system faster and stronger than whatever the maybe-a-doctor had injected me with.

"I am functional, sir," he corrected, setting aside his normal humor. *"We will explain everything soon."*

The woman, Penny, had been talking again. I returned my attention to her. Relatable let me know that her special interests include Ukrainian culture, microbiology, and baking. My high perception noticed something else. My friends were on the way. I decided to set aside any important questions for *them*.

"You have cat hair on your lab coat," I said. Both her shoulders were covered with the stuff. "Where did you find a cat?"

"System Pet," she answered. "I tried to save my cat with my Perk, but it was too late. The System did its best to accommodate. She's been very useful for scouting and such. I'm surprised you've recovered as quickly as you have from your initial shock. It's curious."

"Not that curious. I have my own System Companion." I tapped my temple. "He's on his way."

"Ah." She frowned. "That makes sense. Still, it's surprising that you asked about my cat, rather than your situation."

"Not really," I said. "I know and trust my friends."

"And you don't know and trust me." Her gaze focused, as if I had somehow become more interesting or real to her. "Not as naïve as they said. Good to know."

"Who is 'they'?" I asked as adrenaline made my heart flutter. My muscles tensed and I sat up. I nearly fell right back down as blood rushed from my head.

"I hear your friends coming," she said. "I'll let them explain."

She stepped aside as they rushed into view. I nodded, noting that she'd heard them before I had, despite my high perception. Then I turned my attention fully to my friends.

Aul looked tired, weak, and pale. Pavise was battered, dented, and scraped, but nothing my repair skills couldn't fix. Had he gone for help? Is that who this person was?

"Pavise, what the he—"

He cleared his mental throat.

I remembered Aul and started again. "Hi, Aul. Good to see you. Hold on a moment please." I turned back to Pavise. "What's going on here, buddy?"

"Please try to remain calm," he said, which made me much less calm. "You have recently recovered, after all."

And then I remembered what the woman, Penny, had said about cybernetics. I remembered the healer's confusion earlier, as well as my own numbness. I looked down at the bandaged hand and arm and peeled away the cloth.

"Sir, I'm not certain that you should—"

I'd stopped listening to him.

My arm had been replaced with silvery metal. The new limb looked exceptionally well made and expensive, better than a grand prize winner at Comic-Con.

I tested it, running the fingers along the sheets beneath me. The weave was rough, and I could feel it just fine. I gripped my other hand and squeezed with both. It was definitely stronger. "Awesome. They have rebuilt me. They had the technology."

Pavise sighed. "Another movie quote?"

"Barely," the woman said. "Still, he's taking this remarkably well."

"Indeed," said Pavise. "He is, he assures me, something of a geek."

She smiled broadly. "A shame you're not my type. My parents would love you."

I smiled back. She wasn't my type either, which made it a bit surprising to me that I wasn't hers. Usually, I could count on the men and women I wasn't attracted to to be interested. Then again, times had changed, and she didn't look like a local, or the type of people I'd usually interacted with.

"Human is liar. Human is trick us." Then louder and slower, "Human is leave. Aul and Pavise is talk to Caleb."

She turned and looked at Aul over her glasses, a sight I'd thought I'd never see again. Why was she wearing glasses anyway? Was it a fashion choice or some kind of magic item? I decided that it would be too rude to ask her.

Speaking of rude, I said, "Aul, why are you treating our guest so impolitely? Has she done something bad that I don't know about?"

Aul looked back and forth between the two of us twice, before pausing a bit too long. "This human is trick us. Not is guest. Human is be part of wrong human hive."

"Sir," Pavise interjected, "I must insist that we try to eliminate any upsets or distractions to allow you to have the time that you need to learn about the recent and current events without damaging your recovery."

I motioned to the other two. "Why are you insisting on that to me instead of them?"

"Because neither of them will listen to me."

That tried to pull a chuckle from me, but it came out wrong.

"It's vital that I talk to you," Penny said, rolling her little stool a bit closer, "but the robot keeps trying to stop me and the alien keeps screaming at me to get off your ship."

I gave her the stern look I reserved for troublemakers in my class. "The alien, as you call her, has a name. It's Aul, and this is her ship. If she doesn't want you here, there's not all that much I can do about it." I shrugged. "So, you might want to treat the future Matriarch with the kind of respect that she deserves if you have any hopes of being able to stay."

Aul stood straighter and stuck out her undeveloped chest armor, crossing her lower set of arms.

Penny blanched for a long moment and then scoffed. "As if any of you could make us leave. Besides, it's your ship. The System says so."

"Us?"

Aul took this opportunity to repeat, "Human get out!"

"Perhaps you should leave for the moment, miss. I'm sure Caleb would be happy to hear what you have to tell him, after he has a chance to take in the various recent developments."

Then they were all talking at the same time, and though I felt fine physically, my breathing quickened and my body tensed. A hint of burning started in my missing arm and spread from there. It was just a hint of what had happened to me, but the feeling threatened to drag me back into that moment I was so desperate to pretend had never happened.

"Enough," I said, firm now.

When none of them stopped, I remembered I was in my course room.

"Enough!" I declared, activating Administrative Authority as I forced myself to my feet.

I stumbled and nearly fell. All three of them moved to try to help me up but slammed into each other as I slumped to the floor. It was a perfect metaphor for the way the three of them had behaved from the start.

I looked at the newcomer. "Penny, we'll start with you."

She smiled and started to talk.

I cut her off with a gesture. "Not that. You are all in my course room, and you're all trying to talk to me. What that means is that I'm in charge of this interaction, lab coat or no lab coat."

They all indicated reluctant agreement.

"Penny, apologize to Aul and introduce yourself, or you may leave my course room and this ship without talking with me. She is the future Matriarch of her people, my friend, and the rightful owner of this ship."

"But the System—"

I cut her off mid-sentence. "The System can go to… I mean, the System can mind its own business. Consider me holding the ship in trust for her until she reaches adulthood."

"You might want to keep that to yourself. The fact that you're a human is the only reason the others haven't claimed this ship yet." I opened my mouth to interrupt again, but she hurried on before I could get out another word. "That's not a threat. I just thought you had a right to know. And fine." She turned to Aul. "I'm sorry, future Matriarch. May I please speak to Caleb before I go?"

"No, ma'am, I'm very sorry, but I'm afraid that you cannot," Pavise replied. "Caleb is—"

I held up a finger to indicate that he should wait. "*Please, buddy. Thank you, but you're making it worse. Let me handle this.*"

He nodded and stepped back.

"Aul," I said, "may I have a moment to speak with the nice lady?"

"Lady is not nice." Aul looked down at the floor. "Caleb is choose talk. Caleb not Voloid slave. Human can stay for one talk."

I smiled gently at my student. "Thank you. Any chance I can get you to wait back there with Pavise? It would be easier for me to focus on one person at a time right now."

Aul grunted and clicked, but she said nothing as she moved back.

I sat up a little straighter and scooted back to lean against the bed, then I turned my full attention to the stranger in my classroom. "Now, is this urgent enough that I can't have a few minutes to find out what's going on and why, and maybe get a bite to eat and clear my head? Or are you trying to ambush me before I can get my bearings and anyone else can establish a narrative?"

"Smart too," she said, seeming to reevaluate me. "Fine, a bit of both honestly. But it's not these two I'm worried about. If I give you a few minutes to talk to your friends while I get you some food, will you promise not to talk to anyone else but me until we've had a chance to talk?"

"Sure," I said. "That sounds good."

She shook her head, a look of wonder lighting her face. "They were right, I just know I can believe you. That's going to take some getting used to."

"I've been told that before. Pavise can talk to me through our link. So hopefully he can show you where we keep the food while we talk."

I looked at my shield-bot, who nodded. They started to leave.

"One question," I asked before they could walk out. "Where did all this equipment come from? Is it part of your Class?"

"No," she answered. "Gerri. She's some kind of alchemist."

"Do not ask who she is talking about, sir. Please trust me and just let her get you food."

"Okay, buddy."

"Thank you for your trust, sir."

"Penny, since you are getting my food, I should let you know that I'm a vegetarian. Can I ask that you clean your hands of any possible meat residue before touching my food?"

She turned back with a strange look of haughty disdain that I knew I had seen before but couldn't remember where. She left without another word, and I turned back to Aul.

The Matriarch-to-be started to speak.

325

I held up my hand. "You know that I love talking to you, Aul, but I'm guessing that a lot has happened?"

Aul nodded.

"And things are kind of urgent?"

Another nod, much more vigorous.

"Then would you mind if I got the update from Pavise? It would be quicker."

Aul made a chitter that my translation Skill told me meant she was frustrated, but she nodded again. Then her big eyes brightened as she said, "Caleb Show and Tell what Pavise say for Aul."

"Okay," I said, though I didn't really feel up to using Skills, or doing much else that required any concentration. But I would have wanted to know if I were in her place.

I pulled up an image of Pavise and described what the shield-bot told me for Aul as he walked me through a summary of everything that had happened. My frown deepened the longer the description went on.

A few minutes later, Pavise had returned, and I was still trying to process everything. "So let me make sure I've got this straight. Slytherin, the caster with the green robe, came back. Their actual name is Gerri and they saved my life and made sure the others didn't just attack us. Do I have that right so far?"

"Yes, sir," Pavise said. "Two caveats. One is that I do not know what the word Slytherin means as it is not translating, and the other is that several of the others with Gerri killed the monster that had devoured you and they found your body inside. So more accurately, they saved you, though Gerri has healed you since."

"And they gave me a cybernetic arm."

"One of the humans, sir, yes. She performed such surgeries on three of the humans, though Aul insisted that you be first."

"Insurgent, um, Commander Greyson, is also back, and he was even more hurt than I was. He's fully recovered now and talking with the others. But Edgelord, Quinn, the spider-lady hacker that wanted to kill us all, didn't show up until after the bounty hunters left, then a bunch of them killed each other, got captured, or fled? Do I have that more or less straight?"

"That is more or less accurate, sir, until the end. Specifically—"

I held up my hand to cut him off. "*Specifically*," I shot back, "I want to talk about the fact that you two lied to me, or at least that you tricked me and made me party to your lie." I gave them both a hard look, but I couldn't maintain it for long. "We don't really have time to deal with that now though. These people on the ship are dangerous. Dealing with them is going to be complicated, because what we need from them seems like it might be mutually exclusive. We need to try to get them to leave, and we need to try to get them to help us." I hung my head. "I'm clearly not going to be able to protect us on my own, even with your help, big buddy."

"If that were any more clear, sir, it would be invisible."

I chuckled, but it didn't reach my emotions. I felt emptied out, hollow, in my chest.

"We'll have a class on justified deception next time we get a chance. We can talk about the Holocaust. In the meantime, I'll trust that you did what you felt you had to do. I don't like it, not even a little bit, but I understand why you did what you did. I only hope it doesn't come back to bite us in the ass." I frowned. "I hope it didn't get them killed. They seemed like good people." My thoughts returned to the floating triangle. "Most of them."

"Before you talk with the one called Penny, I feel that we should address the two concerns you have addressed."

"Humans is go away. Humans is no welcome." Aul's whole body trembled slightly in a way that I hadn't seen from the Voloids, except after the attack.

"I'll talk with them," I said. "If they are already recovered, it's a bad sign that they aren't already gone, but it might also be what saves all our lives. We need the help."

"Killer humans hive is not help. Human killers hive is get out."

"I want them gone too," I told her. "But the two of us might not get what we want. We aren't strong enough to force them, and we have to do whatever we have to do to protect the others."

Aul chittered and made a chirping sound. "Aul is trust Caleb."

"Thank you," I said, nodding. "I need to go. I have to talk to Insurgent. I mean the Commander."

"You promised the young woman that you would talk to her first, and you should eat to regain your strength. We are bringing you Indekk, orange soda, and one of your pizzas."

"Thank you both," I said. "I'd like to talk with her alone if that's okay with you. I'm easily overwhelmed, and I think she's got something important to tell me. Maybe she'll feel safer and open up more if it's just the two of us. She might be able to tell me where we stand with the others."

"Of course, sir," Pavise said.

Aul looked as though she wanted to say more, but she hesitated and left the room without another word.

Poor girl. She'd been through so much.

I tipped my head back against the lowered railing of the hospital bed behind me and let myself wallow in a tiny moment of self-pity, just a hint of the time I'd need to spend alone, feeling my feelings, when things were a little less urgent. I'd been through a lot myself, far too much.

Chapter 35

Lee

We'd been forced to run things from the massive training room. My men had outdone themselves while I'd recovered. An oversized recliner on a raised platform was facing a ludicrous assortment of kitchen chairs, weapons crates, and half a dozen barstools.

The command deck would have made more sense, but we hadn't been able to open the god-damned door. That taught me what smug looked like on Voloids. Heads held high. Mandibles open wide. They wanted us dead, or gone, or both. I couldn't really blame them. But if they kept blocking doorways shouting, "Humans is be leave," much longer, somebody was gonna snap. Might even be me.

The Teacher should wake up soon. Hopefully, the man could shut them up.

I reviewed the situation while my men finished final touches.

We'd won, if you could call that clusterfuck a victory. At least we'd saved the men.

I'd gotten XP from the Quest, but the gladiator had left no loot. His death had gained us no XP. His body had left no loot. Topher suspected an escape Skill, which made good sense to me. Creepy that it left a corpse.

I also hadn't died. Shame. It would've saved me loads of trouble. The HLF wanted us dead. The Hakarta and other alien factions wanted us dead. On top of all that, my medics were pissed. They'd ordered me to rest. I'd told them, "Your authority ends when the bleeding stops," and went back to work. They didn't like that, but my cybernetics were repaired and the System would handle anything else.

I was bone-deep weary, but I didn't have time to rest. My people were clustering into cliques like high school students. It was gonna break them up and get them killed. I didn't survive well on my own, so it was time to put a stop to it.

I saluted the troops guarding the room, thanked them for setting things up, and asked them to leave and secure the door. Something felt off, but I couldn't put my finger on it. It didn't feel urgent, and I had no time to think about it now, so I let it work its way through my subconscious while I went about my business. This preliminary meeting needed to be private. As they left, seemingly as an afterthought, I told the cleaning guy to stay.

Vernon, the Cleaner and Expert Custodian, was my best hope to salvage the situation. His swarm of drones were polishing and cleaning the various surfaces to maintain appearances.

The noises would also help muffle the sounds of our meeting.

To that end, I took out a few devices of my own. Scattered them throughout the room. They reduced Perception and helped block out eavesdroppers, System-backed or otherwise. It was old hat for both of us by now. I put the last of the devices on the table between us. Nothing new. He wouldn't think twice. I'd been doing it for months for just such an occasion.

One of my passives probably helped. Countermeasures from Guerilla Tactician. The Skill's description was vague. Worthless. It said that it helped to disrupt spying. No figures, no details. Even Topher knew jackshit. At least it was passive. It did what it did, and I could just ignore it.

The Cleaner, which was what everyone called the man I'd summoned, was thin and weak. Pathetic. I'd had to personally power-Level a half dozen Non-Combat Classers as cover for leveling him. If that had been a wise investment, it would pay dividends today.

The dishwater-blond man dragged his oversized can in behind him. Then he dug through lint from his pocket until he found a butterscotch candy. He popped it in his mouth. Having found a second, he generously held it out for me to take.

I ignored the pocket-filth-covered offering and motioned for the man to sit.

He did so.

"What have you got for me?"

He sat bolt upright with proper military poise. His slack-jawed idiot expression sharpened and focused.

"Everything there is to get, Commander, same as always." The snitch smirked with knowing satisfaction.

"Then give me what I need."

"If there are any loyalists to the HLF left with us, they are keeping it to themselves."

"That makes sense. They hadn't expected us to survive. Where does that leave us?"

"There are three main factions, sir. Each of them has a strong leader, though some have secondary figures of importance. The third is basically a one-woman dictatorship."

"Wilma?"

"Yes, sir, though I realize that's not exactly news."

"Has she pulled in any but the Non-Combat Classers?"

"A few of the lowbies, Sir, but no one worth noticing. Her plan is to bribe or cajole the others to get them to the closest human settlement. They will beg, borrow, or trade for passage as far away as possible, to fully human settlements."

"It won't work. The Humanist will find them anywhere on Earth." I removed two enchanted, frost-covered mugs from my inventory and set them on the table between us. A matching set of shot glasses followed.

"Yes, sir," he said, sounding skeptical. "A few of them must agree with your evaluation. They plan to ditch the planet and buy passage to worlds that hate the organizations we've most openly opposed."

"That's not gonna work either. None of them but Wilma and Earl are anything special, and the two of them are only special for humans from Earth."

"Yes, sir."

"I'm guessing that Roy, the Marine, leads one of the other factions?" I added bottles of A&W cream soda and butterscotch schnapps to the table's supplies. Longstanding tradition.

"I suspected that too, sir, but no. Remember Fox, the Gunman you had kill the asshole traitor back before we fought the cyclops?"

"I do." In spite of my concussions. "He's running the show?"

"Yes, sir, for the group that wants to work as a mercenary force. They actually hope to join some kind of dungeon guild. They'd love to recruit you, but they're too timid to ask."

"Well, their odds are better than they would be anywhere else, but I wouldn't bet on them. The competition is fierce, and gunmen aren't a scarce commodity. They'll find work, just not the kind that would protect them from the Humanist or the Hakarta."

"Yes, sir." His earlier skepticism was absent now.

I filled the mugs with cream soda and the shot glasses with the schnapps. Then I returned the nearly empty bottles to my inventory. "Who's in the third group?"

"Sneaky types and trappers. Rogues, trackers, the people who think they can go into hiding and live off the land. Everly Donaldson is running that bunch."

"They put a Non-Combat Classer in charge?"

"He put himself in charge. The man's a bit of a zealot, but he's a natural leader. He's also killed more people and monsters than the rest of them together, though a lot of those were too low Level to give him much XP."

"Really, his traps are that good?"

"Yes, sir. The Captain was telling the Humanist that he was something of a prodigy. They were planning to ship him back to the main base before this all… well, before the shitshow. He was one of the ones we saved. He was less than thrilled that we'd broken away from the HLF until he learned about the mind control aspect. He said he was happy to blow up aliens, but he was no one's puppet. He's one of the main reasons we haven't had any defections yet."

"Good to know. I'd hate to lose him. Their plan is to go into hiding until things die down?" I considered that as I dropped the schnapps-filled shot glasses into the cream soda-filled mugs. Stealthers heading off into the wilderness and hiding for a year or so might work. It was the best plan so far.

"No, sir," he said, pulling my attention back to the present. "They're true believers. Zealots. They plan to continue the work, whether it kills them or not."

"Can I trust them, or do we need to clean house?"

"Most of them agree with you about not killing the children. The rest will keep their mouths shut unless they get a chance to take them out alone. You don't have to worry about them. If they leave, they'll just disappear."

"Do you have anything else for me?"

"Yes, sir, two odd things. Earl and Wilma's daughter made a point of checking on and visiting the Teacher. She even sent his keepers away with a lie."

"Interesting, but not sure it's useful."

"Mine is not to question why, mine is just to be your spy."

I groaned at the bad rhyme.

The other man smiled at my reaction. "Oh, and the robot has been making the rounds. He's been questioning some of our people. This is recent, so I'm not sure why, but something's going on there. That's everything for now, but I'll keep you posted."

"Thank you," I said, pushing forward his glass of the butterscotch concoction we always shared after a debriefing.

He reached out for it, then glanced at the device on the table. Perception was Perception, and our drinks would taste weak as water with that thing so close to us.

"I'm sorry, Vernon. With this place being so new and unsecure, I can't risk turning off the Muffler, even if it messes up our celebration."

"Aren't we done?"

"The System is crazy. Some Advanced Class Skills can recover remnant echoes of conversations, even after the fact." Who knows? Might be true. The System could do a lot.

"Damn," he said.

"Damn indeed," I agreed. "Here, let me make it up to you."

I reached into my inventory for a separate bottle of butterscotch schnapps and added an extra shot to his. Then I tried to do the same with mine, feigning a frown when I "discovered" I'd run out.

He chuckled and grabbed his drink. We clinked our glasses together and downed them in a long draught.

Now it was his turn to frown. "Hey, this…"

The paralytic that the Perception suppression device had hidden from his enhanced senses had taken effect. He would never finish that sentence.

"I'm sorry," I told him. "Information security has jumped to the top of our priority list. You told me a long time ago that you came by your hidden Class naturally, and I believe people when they tell me who they are. You can't be trusted."

He would sell us out to the Humanist as a matter of course. It was his nature.

I gave him an injection to extend his paralysis and placed a custom-crafted muzzle over his mouth so that he couldn't trigger his escape Skill. It would have let him whisper a final secret and disappear.

"Thank you for your service. I'll try to make this as quick and painless as possible." I pushed him over backward, chair and all, then stepped down hard on his neck with the spike from my prosthetic. It would clean up the mess before it was even made and use his vitality to repair the remaining damage to my body and my gear.

I debated for a few minutes. How had he tried to kill me? Suicide vest. Everyone knew he was a coward. Must have chickened out at the last minute. But he was too late. I'd already seen the danger. I'd talked him down. Injected him with a paralytic.

That worked. Wouldn't survive deep scrutiny, but who would bother?

I strapped some explosives to his chest and put the trigger in his hand. I'd leave it for Donaldson to disarm. Then I scuffed the back of the straps and dumped his body in his own trash can.

I was going to need a new drinking buddy. Hopefully, this one would appreciate cigars.

Chapter 36

Lee

Gerri was pacing in the stone hallway as I strode down it, trying to puzzle out what I'd forgotten. The crystal lights gave a cool-blue cast to their skin. Their fists were clenched, and tears were streaming down their face. I didn't know if they were about to cry or murder someone. Either way, I wanted to help.

"What happened?" I asked.

They jumped and raised their hand. When they opened it, it filled with indigo powder.

I held up my own hands. Open and empty. I tried to reassure them with a smile, but my adrenaline had kicked in. My body was tense. A subtle vibration had joined my tightening muscles as my cybernetics primed.

They muttered something gruff, then cleared their throat and tried again. "Your friend Topher is a son of a bitch."

"Yeah, and?"

"And? And!" Her fingers twitched.

"Maybe put away the powder?" My tone was patient. Calm.

"What? Oh, right. Sorry." The powder disappeared.

"Topher is an asshole. A jerk. He has no tact and less conscience. It's one of the reasons I like him. He's also a tremendous asset. What happened?"

"You like him?" The look on their face was priceless.

"Did you repeat everything he said incredulously too? If so, I think I see what—"

Their glare shut me up. I waited.

They kept glaring.

I could do this all day. Even before I had superhuman Stamina.

They broke first and looked away. When they finally looked back, I nodded for them to continue. Anything I said seemed to be making things worse.

"He hates me."

I did not say, "He hates everyone," but it must have been written on my face.

"No," they said, "he hates me."

I took a moment to consider, started to open my mouth. I reconsidered. No, I didn't buy it. But Gerri wasn't going to want to hear that.

This was a mess. Complicated. Screw that.

I did an about-turn and marched toward where my map let me know I could find the trainer.

Gerri followed me, boots clacking against the solid rock floor. "Wait. What are you doing? Just stop."

I didn't.

Topher was measuring part of a wall completely indistinguishable from any other part with a hand-held device for some damned reason or another. He turned to face me, then snapped to attention and saluted.

"Knock that off," I told him, finally realizing what had been nagging at me. "We're not part of the HLF anymore."

"Fuck that, I'm yer man." After a pause, he added, sharply, "Sir."

I saluted him back with a smile. "This is Gerri. They saved all our lives. They're to be treated with the same respect and courtesy as anyone else here."

"Yes, sir," he said, dropping his hand and relaxing his stance. "Innae much I can do fer 'em if they storm off like a bitch though." He glanced back at his device and waved it at another section of the wall.

"Asshole," Gerri said under their breath.

"They think you hate them," I explained.

"I hate everyone."

"They think you hate them more. They think it's personal."

He looked flustered, then pissed. He glared at me. "I treated 'em the same as I would anyone else." He turned his hazel glare on Gerri. "I don't know what's got yer knickers in a twist, but don't go bitchen' 'bout ol' Topher. Say it to me face or shut yer damned fool mouth."

Gerri turned to face me. "He said—"

"I'm standin' right bloody here!"

They turned back to meet his glare. "I asked you for help, and you mocked me and called me an idiot."

I waited silently.

"I did nothin' of the sort." His chin jutted out stubbornly and he crossed his arms over his barrel chest.

"I asked you for advice on how to adjust my Class and what my Master Class options might be so that I could plan ahead."

"And I told ye what to do."

"'Go back in time and pick a different Class.' Really helpful, jackass." They planted one hand on their green-clad hip and gave Topher a disgusted look.

Topher ran his hand over the stubble of his shaved head and pinched the top of his nose as he let out a long, deep breath. It was the biggest emotional reaction I'd ever seen from the man that didn't include yelling. "It wasn't an insult. I said what I said."

Gerri and I were both speechless as we waited for the man to explain.

"None of us understood this shite goin' in. Not yer fault. But the Class ye chose is too damned dangerous, to you and the ones ye care about. Yer gonna get someone killed unless you go to the Shop, have 'em reset it, and choose somethin' else."

"My Class is powerful. It's versatile. It's a bit unpredictable, sure, but it comes with powers to protect against that." Their voice cracked like a whip through the space between the two.

"It comes with powers ta protect ya, and those cannae be trusted. I sure as hell don't wanna be standing next to ye when ye try something new. I don't wanna take some bloody pill when I get hurt only to find out that it's eatin' me alive from the inside or makin' my dick fall off."

"That can happen?" I asked.

"Oh, aye." Topher nodded sharply and I looked at Gerri, brows raised.

"Shit," Gerri said, glaring at their boots.

"That too," Topher said. "I'm sorry, but at least the Shop can reset yer progress. It's expensive, and it wastes experience and time, but it's also the right thing ta do."

"Can't I just push on to Master and fix it then?"

"Aye. An amazing Master Class. Not one most would take though. Armageddon Containment Specialist. Impressive, though it'd narrow yer focus. Trouble is, it only works if ye don't get yerself killed in the meantime. Even if ye manage that, you'll leave a body count behind ye in yer wake."

Gerri was openly crying and trembling. I could only imagine what the thought of respeccing this late in the game would feel like. There was a strength in Gerri's expression though, even now. There was a sharpness to their eyes. I suspected they'd find a way to make this all work for them, instead of against. From the sound of it, they'd been doing that all their life.

"We can't get Gerri to a Shop, Topher. And we can't afford to have them waste their power now. They've already saved us several times. We're just going to have to be more cautious, especially when it's time to experiment.

Just help them for now, and they can decide what to do for the future when the future comes."

"Yes, sir." He turned back to Gerri, all business now. "Did ye save up any extra Skill points?"

"No." Gerri still scowled at the man. "Just the one from the last Level." They turned to me. "I got a Quest to keep the three of you alive, in spite of how impossible that was. Score one for the broken Class. I would have failed without my Mobile Lab and my Research Grade Storage."

"No doubt," Topher said. "It's a powerful Class. But it's early days. The dangers come later. You'll note they didn't mention the third Class Skill tree in that little speech."

I turned to Gerri, trying to sound casual as I said, "Oh, what's that?"

They mumbled a reply.

"What's that yer sayin'?" Topher cupped a hand around the back of his ear. Sarcasm dripped from his tone like acidic honey.

"Hazardous Material Reactor," Gerri answered flatly.

"Containing things like that sounds good to me," I said.

"Aye, sir. But that innae what they use it for. The damn thing is a bloody AOE," Topher said.

"A lot of the best weapons are dangerous," I said.

"Tell him the name of the Skill tree," Topher said.

Gerri said nothing. They looked grim.

"Fine then, I'll tell 'em. It's Catastrophe. Ca, fuckin', tastrophe. It's got a Combined Tree Skill called Oops, I did it Again." He turned to me. "I'm nae being unreasonable, sir."

"I notice you all use guns," Gerri said. "They're nothing but controlled explosions. Innovation is always dangerous." They turned to me.

"Experimentation and Breakthrough are the other trees. The ones that saved your life."

"I remember." I turned back to Topher. "Apparently, I wasn't clear. You want to call me sir and say that you're my man? Fine then. Prove it by following my orders."

He shook his head to clear it. "Aye, sir. Sorry." He turned back to Gerri. "You've got three choices for yer Tier two Skills." He plonked the first tool back into his utility belt and pulled out one that looked like a tablet.

I'd never understood why he still used them when the System provided holographic heads-up displays. Maybe it was part of his Class. Maybe he was just old school. He pulled up Gerri's Skill tree and tipped the tablet toward us. The format was a bit different than the System prompts.

I tried to ignore it as Gerri wiped away the last of their tears to read along.

Hazmat Protocol

(Advanced Skill - Catastrophe Tree - Tier 2)

Provides major resistance to drugs, poisons, disease, acids, radiation, etc.

Duration: 15 minutes plus 5 minutes per skill point.

Area: 20' radius plus 5'/Skill Level. Immovable.

Mana Cost: 100+10/minute. Ongoing Mana cost increases under extreme conditions.

Experimentation

(Advanced Skills - Experimentation Tree - Tier 2)

Allows for System-backed modification of a pharmaceutical product that changes a single key element of the item. This can be used to modify even base ingredients. Over time, this Skill can allow for construction of permanent newly crafted materials. Small chance of failure and lost materials.

Cost: 75 Mana.

Reverse Engineer

(Advanced Skills - Breakthrough Tree - Tier 2)

A single chosen item (or random if you do not choose) stored in your Research Grade Storage is successfully researched, granting you a blueprint. Chance of successful research is 1 percent per hour in storage, with a max percentage of 5 percent per hour. There is also a 1 percent chance per hour that the product is destroyed in this process. Only works on pharmaceutical products. Percentage cap increases by 1 percent per Skill point invested. Mana Regeneration reduced by 5 Mana permanently.
Passive.

Topher scratched above his ear, a habit he had when he was thinking. "Normally, I'd suggest that ye take these in the order listed, if ye didn't have points stored up. But with us not having access to the Shop or any other crafters who make this shite, I'd say start with Reverse Engineering. We can scrounge up one of everything and you can take turns learning 'em. That way, you can help us get stocked up and have a whole slew of new recipes to bring home fer yer people."

"See?" I said. "You're important already."

Topher deserved a raise. He'd just given Gerri a reason to stick around. We certainly weren't going to give them one of each supply that we had if they were going to just turn around and leave, especially if the drugs could be destroyed.

Gerri must have realized the same thing, because they said, "I need to talk to Thomas."

I tried not to smile and almost succeeded.

"We'll all have to talk later," I told them both. "I'm not convinced the Class isn't worth the risk." Topher opened his mouth, but I shut him up with a glare and a raised hand. "Later. Dismissed."

He scowled, but he left. As the door at the end of the corridor shut behind him, Gerri punched me in the face as soon.

It was a fist from a caster. I didn't bother to dodge. "What the hell was that for?"

"You knew I didn't want you to do that, and you did it anyway. I'm not one of your soldiers."

"Fair," I said, symbolically rubbing my chin as if it had hurt for the sake of their pride. "Still, I don't have time for drama, and this needed to be handled. I'm not about to apologize. I will thank you for not calling me out in front of my men though."

"I've read enough books not to make that mistake." Then they rushed forward and gave me a huge hug.

I sputtered and tried to think of anything to say.

"Thank you for standing up for me. If you ever do it again, I'll melt your face off with acid."

I stood there confused for several minutes after they left the hall.

Chapter 37

Caleb

I was over-stuffed, my stomach was gurgling, and no matter what I tried, I could not force myself to "finish my plate," as Nana would have said. I pushed the tray table back from where it projected over my lap and scooted a little higher up in the hospital bed.

Penny had waited impatiently while I ate, though she'd agreed that she'd like to have my full attention for whatever she wanted to ask me.

Apparently, she wasn't one for small talk. What she did like was having her hair neat. She'd adjusted it several times and even checked her appearance in a small mirror Skill that she conjured from her hand.

I wished again that I was rude enough to just inspect people. I was as curious as anyone, but it never seemed to be the right thing to do.

So I decided to do things the old-fashioned way. I started to reach for her hand, but then realized mine weren't clean and I had no place handy to clean them and let it return to my side. "Thanks for being patient with me. It's been a long week. My name's Caleb, though it sounds like you already know that. I was a teacher before the System came, and I guess I've still been one ever since. I'm not really sure why you think I can help you, but I'm willing to hear you out."

She sat up straight, adjusted her lab coat, and it drew my attention to just how much more graceful people had become since the System arrived. Even I'd changed a decent amount in that regard.

"I'm Penny, and believe it or not, I need your help because you're a Teacher." She reached behind her for one of the vials, but it and the rest of the alchemical lab vanished, and her hand passed right through it. Thankfully, the bed I had returned to earlier still remained.

"That doesn't sound as flattering as you might have imagined it, Penny. I never find it hard to believe that someone might need a teacher. I'll help you if I can, and if I can find the time with my other duties, but unfortunately, you aren't exactly in the age range I'm best suited to assist."

She looked confused, then offended, then embarrassed. The changes in her expression were subtle, and they looked phony somehow.

I gave myself permission to be rude enough to hold up a finger and take the time to take in what I was seeing, to review what I had seen. The changes had been too abrupt, not quite smooth. The closest thing I could get to explaining it was that they'd nearly flickered, but not quite.

Was it some kind of an illusion? Was she a sociopath and she had fake expressions to cover it up? Was her whole persona phony?

Having so much of my time, while raising my Intelligence and Perception, dedicated to noticing imperfections and errors in classwork wasn't a wasted effort toward other things apparently.

She noticed me noticing and tried to resume talking. I thought she was hoping it would distract me. I was about to call her out on it, to say "I'm really sorry, I try to be polite and welcoming, but you came here with a group of trained killers and it's just too dangerous for me to not find out why you're hiding your appearance."

Then I reminded myself that she was a member of a group of trained killers and I was not. I couldn't risk calling her out, especially not when we were alone together. I kept my mouth shut and let her talk.

"It's about my son, David. He's ten years old." She said this as though it should be some sort of bombshell to me, some kind of big secret.

I leaned forward, listening more closely now. She didn't continue. After a moment, it got awkward, so I said, "uh huh," in that sort of half-questioning way you use to urge someone to continue.

She laced her fingers together over her lap, rubbing the tips of her thumbs together. "The Human Liberation Front, the group we've all been part of, they've got hostages. Friends and family members that they rescued and split up without telling each other. They keep them as secret hostages so they can blackmail the more militarily useful person if they have to. The others don't know about it yet, and they're going to go ballistic when I tell them."

"If they're secret—"

"How do I know? I suppose I don't have to hide it anymore, after everything that's happened. I'm part of a splinter group within the HLF that's trying to destroy it from within. More accurately, we want to stop the monster leading it."

"From what little I know, that raises my estimate of you as a person, but I'm not sure what you could possibly need from me," I admitted helplessly.

"They're holding the children along with the others in a well-defended, and heavily fortified, bunker near here."

My mind helpfully presented me with vivid images of getting riddled with bullets and blown up, again, with grenades. Phantom pain spiked where the grenade had crushed me. I tried not to let it show, but my body jerked and trembled and I cried out in shocked pain. I pressed a hand over the area, took several deep breaths, and gave myself a moment.

"Look," I said when I could manage it, "I'm sorry about your son and I'd love to help you, but I think you might misunderstand my Class. Even if I wasn't still…" I gestured down at my bandage-covered self. "I can't save your son from a fortress. I can't even save myself from a quick trip outside."

She sat looking at me, expression filled with confusion for a long moment, then she burst out laughing. A moment later, she pulled herself together, adjusted her glasses, took a deep breath, and returned her gaze to mine. She burst out laughing again, harder. She clutched her own knee and bit her lip, seemingly trying to stop herself and failing.

At first it had felt validating; I agreed with her assessment. Now it was getting a bit hurtful.

I cleared my throat. "Then what exactly do you want my help with? You mentioned that your son was in danger."

That sobered her up quickly enough, and her pained expression made me feel like an ass. "I'm sorry. It's just, well..." She shrugged and gave a helpless expression.

I nodded, trying to be tolerant but finding it a bit harder than usual. Apparently getting swallowed whole by a monster was bad for my disposition.

That thought was all it took.

I was falling, screaming, burning. My hand was rotting away into nothing. My whole world was pain.

"Sir," Pavise said, not in my mind but right there in the room with me.

Four arms were holding me up with some strain as my whole body shook. Had I fallen?

A beam of light was hitting me from the strange device.

"I'm not sure what's wrong," Penny said. "His system is going into shock, but his body should be fine. He's not rejecting the implants."

"What is going wrong is that you failed to listen to me, young miss. I insist that you give my master time to more fully recover before you assail him with any more of your inane ramblings."

"Human, get out!" Aul was practically screaming. She slammed one of her hands into her chest's red slash while she pointed at the door with the other three.

"Okay, I'm sorry, I'll go. Let me give him something for his nerves." She leaned forward and placed some sort of patch on my neck.

Something buzzed and felt like it was zapping into me, but it did calm my body and my mind, whatever it was.

She leaned in a bit closer. "I'm sorry," she said quietly, as if she could hide her words from my companions when they were so close. "I need your help. They've brainwashed the children. They're not going to listen to reason, but they'll believe you. We can save his body, but you're my only hope for getting his mind back. Please?"

Pavise was slowly pushing her from the room by this point.

Aul was holding me the way I'd held her and the others after the attack. It helped a little.

"How could you possibly know all of this? And why should I believe you when even your face is a lie?" I hadn't intended to say that. It just came out.

She gasped. Then she closed her eyes and nodded. "It was one of my Perks. Not the illusion that covers it, but the reason I bought the illusion from the Shop. I was too rushed to read all the details, and with the name it had, I thought it was just going to give me Agility and maybe keep me quiet and sneaky, but… well." She pulled off a ring and her features shifted, showing light fur, cat eyes, and sharp ears. "It turned me into a furry. They'll probably kill me if they find out I'm not really human anymore."

A stronger wave of something from the patch hit me, and my body went from shaking to trembling. My eyes crossed. I wanted to reassure her. I'd help her son if I could. I wouldn't betray her secrets.

"ThunderCats, ho," was what came out of my mouth in a jumble.

Pavise finished pushing her out of the room, and the door shut between us.

Aul half dragged me back to the bed and raised the rails. Where they had gotten an old school medical bed, I had no idea. I closed my eyes and rested. I told Aul she should go do the same. Overwhelmed with exhaustion, she hesitantly agreed.

I couldn't sleep, but I rested for what felt like a long while. I tried to still my mind. When that failed, I asked Pavise to bring me my charcoal and paper, and he did. Then I asked Pavise to let me have some time alone.

I didn't have time to confront my feelings about the last few days, but apparently my mind and body didn't care. Something was fundamentally broken inside me, and I couldn't just ignore it and push forward if this was going to be the consequence every time.

Charcoal and paper in hand, I tried to draw and let my emotional floodgates start to open.

I ended up with a picture of a twelve-year-old Lion-O with the Sword of Omens.

Penny's words, her final impassioned pleading, had gotten to me.

I set aside the drawing with a force of will. There was nothing I could do for either of them now. Any remaining childhood delusions I'd held that I might secretly be an action hero just waiting for my chance to shine had been swallowed whole and burned.

Even if Penny could convince others to save her son and bring him to me, my students couldn't just wait around hoping not to be killed until they could do it and I could help him, assuming I even could. All that ignored the fact that she seemed to be part of some kind of rebel faction against a powerful evil group and I was even more out of my depth.

That's when I realized I was stalling.

I was terrified. For the first time in my life, I didn't dare face my own emotions. I could feel the powerful currents, like a tsunami about to overwhelm a dam, and I simply wasn't strong enough to confront them. It would almost certainly destroy what was left of my shattered sanity.

Part of a line from Emily Dickinson came to me... *what to make of a diminished thing.*

I sat, locked in indecision for a long moment. Then I made my choice. I could not continue forward, broken as I was. My students needed me.

Chapter 38

Caleb

I closed my eyes and tried to center my focus to gather my strength.

I'd give myself five minutes to prepare.

I managed probably three of them before someone pounded on the door.

I wanted to scream in frustration. I wanted to cry with relief.

"Come in," I said.

The one they called Gerri entered. Theirs was not a face I'd ever hoped to see again, but at least it wasn't the Commander.

I reached out to Pavise to see where he was. There was a resistance. When I pushed past it, a shock zapped my head, making my eye twitch. Instead of the normal connection to Pavise, I was seeing through his "eyes."

A lithe, gorgeous woman whose grace would have made a ballerina weep was doing parkour off the trees and branches outside the ship. She was using a wooden staff to aid in her acrobatics, and I'd never seen anything more impressive in my entire life.

Then one of her legs failed her, and she landed hard from a flip that should have been child's play compared to what she had been doing. She screamed in frustration and slammed her fist into the ground.

Both her fist and the leg that had failed her matched my new limbs.

She was crying now, and a thin, wiry man who was the oldest I'd seen since the System came went over to her side. If there was an ounce of kindness in the man, I could not see it on his face.

"Get yer ass up," he said.

"God, you're a son of a bitch," the woman said before kipping up like a ninja.

"If ye wanted tissues and a good cry, lassie, you'd have gone to someone else. Ye came to me. That means you need yer arse kicked. So don't go bitchin' to me now that yer cheeks are getting' sore. Hop to!"

I realized then that I was intruding on something that was very much not my business, and I was possibly betraying Pavise's privacy as well. I had no idea why he was there.

I pulled my attention away. If I was in danger from Gerri, it was too late for him to save me anyway.

"I'm heading to my room," I said, forcing myself up from the bed. "There are too many interruptions here." I turned to walk toward the door but stumbled.

Gerri caught me and helped me reach the door.

"What do you want?" I asked.

The words and tone seemed to shock my visitor. They shocked me too.

Gerri's expression went from proud to ashamed to defiant to proud. Whatever they had been through recently, it was clear I didn't understand it. After everything they'd done, I couldn't be bothered to care. At least their face didn't flicker.

When they didn't answer for a moment, I said, "Thank you for helping to save my life, even though I know it wasn't your primary purpose in coming here. Unless there's anything else, please take the others and go."

"I'll be leaving soon," they said, "but the others don't answer to me. That's part of why I came to talk to you. Lee is a good man—"

I scoffed.

They glared at me. "You have no idea who he is, what he's done."

"I may not know who he is, but I know plenty about what he's done, what he's capable of doing."

"He didn't—"

"Spare me," I snapped, completely losing my cool. I pulled away and turned to face them. "You were there. The man barely drew the line at slaughtering children. Children. But why should I expect better from you? You weren't exactly chomping at the bit to stop him." A wave of dizziness rushed over me, and I leaned against the doorway as I glared them down.

At least they had the decency to look ashamed. "You're right about me. I know that you're right. I just... I didn't. It took me time to understand, and I was so tired. I still haven't slept in so long. Days. Maybe weeks. I've lost track. I know it's no excuse." Tears were running down their face. "But you're wrong about Lee. You'd all be dead if it weren't for him."

"You want him to get extra credit for not murdering us at the last minute?" I caught myself, disciplined my mind to be fair. "No, he was never going to kill me. Not if he didn't think I was a traitor. But he doesn't get a gold star for not murdering kids. That's basic human decency."

"Not that, you naive jerk. Just listen. Lee was part of a group called the Human Liberation Front. I was just a random person he'd helped save who was trying to clear the slate, but I was with him when he went back to his base. There's a guy that calls himself the Humanist. He's using mind control to force people to do his dirty work."

"Are you trying to tell me Lee was mind-controlled?" Pushing off the door frame took a monumental effort, but I did it and shuffled slowly down the hallway toward my room.

"Yes. Well, maybe. Probably? I'm honestly not sure. But he was certainly mind-controlled when we got to the base. I had to give him a Willpower boosting potion to help him break free." Gerri followed me, walking slowly to keep pace.

"How can you be so sure?" I tried to keep the skepticism out of my voice. With everything that had happened, it was hard to keep an open mind. But hard times were when principles mattered most, or they never mattered at all.

"When I gave him the dose, he broke free. The asshole ordered him to come back to kill you all and take the ship. Lee refused. Even when it was just him against a room full of soldiers, he refused. Even when that terrifying psycho bitch turned on him."

The spider-bots. I shuddered. Then I remembered who had made everyone so helpless that they couldn't even fight back, and I re-hardened my heart against this person who had been starting to gain my sympathy.

She was right about Lee though. If he might have been controlled, things were different. If he had drawn a line, risked his life to save the children, that changed everything. The man was everything I wasn't.

He could save them. He could save us all.

I couldn't even save myself.

"How did he survive?" I finally asked.

"A lot of us backed him up. More of them didn't." They wiped their eyes. "We lost people. Good people."

"I'm sorry." Knowing that they had helped, I let my sympathy for them return. It was easy to believe them. They were so obviously hurting. "I'm relieved. I was so scared that he was going to kill us all and take the ship."

I rubbed both palms over my face, trying to clear away some of the exhaustion. The feel of my new prosthetic was so odd contrasted against the warmth of my real hand on my skin. Harder, more... I was getting distracted. Falling into my own mind again. I was just starting to be able to breathe again when I pulled myself up and looked at Gerri. Their crestfallen expression ruined everything.

"That's why I came to talk to you," they said. "They aren't going to kill you. I'm almost positive of that. But you may want to make sure you have anything valuable that you care about packed and ready to go, preferably in your inventory or storage Skill, if you have one. I think… I have no proof, but I think they're going to take the ship, whether Lee wants it or not. Only about half of the people with us fought at the base. The others we rescued afterward. We lost more of the ones I'd trust saving them."

Almost positive! They're going to take the ship. I gasped for breath and my heart wasn't beating right. I leaned against the wall, holding myself up with my head and my hands. I kept moving toward my room, hands never leaving the wall, driven by a desperate need to escape.

"Take these," Gerri said. "They're what gets me through the nights when things get hard."

I let them put the items in my mouth and I swallowed, desperate.

"I'm on my way, sir. I'm sorry that I wasn't with you."

I wanted to reassure him, but I had no strength to spare.

It took a bit of time, but my nerves started to calm. My mind started to refocus. I took several deep breaths, relaxing my body. After a few moments, I opened my eyes and met their dark ones.

"Thank you," I said. "For the warning. And for… whatever that was. It helps."

"You're welcome. And don't worry too much. I think they'll drop you off at a town if they do decide to rob you. Too many of them already died to stop people from murdering the kids for me to think that's really an option." Their expression softened as they must have seen my growing despair. "I'll take you to a settlement myself, if it looks like they're going to take the ship and just dump you on the side of the road. And look, maybe I'm wrong and they aren't going to try to take the ship."

"Try." I scoffed again. It was becoming a habit. As if there was any chance they could fail.

They looked sympathetic, so I decided to press my luck.

"Things have been hard," I said. "It's been a lot. Do you have any more..." I didn't know what to call them and I felt like an addict, begging for a hit.

"Sure," they said. "I've had time to stock up while I waited for you guys to recover." They gave me three sets of two different pills, in see-through packaging. "Take them both together. I'm sorry it can't be more."

"Thank you again," I said, and then repeated it with more conviction, staring deep into their eyes. "I really mean it. Thank you. You learned from your mistake and stood up for the kids when it mattered most, and I think you saved my life twice. That makes up for a lot."

They blushed and looked away. Without another word, they left.

I followed soon after, thoughts of heading to my room and confronting my feelings set aside. The talk and the medicine Gerri had given me had bolstered me somewhat. I needed to find my former boogeyman and see where things really stood.

Chapter 39

Caleb

Whatever Gerri had given me wasn't doing any favors to my stomach. Add to that the fact that I had overeaten, and I was in the worst possible position to walk into a room filled with the smell of flesh roasting over an open flame. I recoiled from the olfactory assault as if I'd walked into a wall.

Who the hell is roasting meat on a spaceship?

Better question. How *is someone roasting meat in the training hall of a spaceship?*

Even better question. Can I make it to my makeshift bathroom before I hurl?

The answers turned out to be: the Commander, someone's fire magic with Gerri handling the smoke, and no.

Indekk doesn't taste better coming up than going down. It's just as slimy. Chunks of pizza and vegetables don't help. Green and yellow splattered the wall. I staggered toward the door, but two soldier wannabees decided to be "helpful" and hold me up, which also kept me from escaping the room.

"Are you okay?" The Commander's deep voice actually sounded concerned.

He was turning a truly massive carcass on a wooden spit over green flames that erupted from the stone. Without his armor, the contrast between his rugged humanity and advanced robotics was starker than ever. His human half would have shamed a Greek sculpture with its aesthetic. His machine half was almost entirely function with form there as an afterthought in the shape of the metal-plates that armored the half-exposed inner workings.

"Are you okay?" he repeated.

I tried to force myself to answer, but I had to take a deep breath to do it, and that nearly set me off all over again.

"I gave him something for his nerves," Gerri said. "I forgot how hard it could be on the gut when you first take it. It's been so long."

"Ah."

"It's not just the drugs," I managed, trying to reassure Gerri. "It's stress. Plus I'm a vegetarian and this kind of blindsided me. Sorry," I said, gesturing at the mess. "The ship will absorb it soon."

Lee looked where I'd indicated. "What the hell is that? Did you eat grass?"

I started to explain to him about Indekk.

He cut me off. "Rhetorical. I don't wanna know. Vegetarian, huh?" I was grateful for the subject change. "Nutrition or ethics? Never mind, who am I talking to? Of course it's ethics. I think Mr. Rogers was a vegetarian too."

"He wouldn't eat anything that had a mother," I agreed. "But I didn't know that when I stopped eating meat. I just think it's wrong to…" I gagged and forced myself not to retch again. "Wrong to kill and eat the innocent."

"In that case, I've got good news for you. You find yourself with the rare opportunity to eat the most ethical steak you've ever had the pleasure of consuming." It was weird to see him smile.

My muscles untensed slightly, but my stomach still gurgled like the time I'd nodded off for hours that I'd thought was only a second. I'd been watching Matt Smith's first episode as the Doctor on Blu-Ray. The episode had been great. The big bowl of pasta salad I'd devoured when engrossed in it had been anything but.

Reassured or not, I'd learned to double-check other people's evaluations of what was safe for a vegetarian to eat. Maybe he was right though. I'd forgotten all about the System and Skills. "Is it lab-grown? Or a Skill?"

With my stomach in the state it was in, and years of habits formed, I wasn't sure I could make myself eat it even if I wanted to, but it would be good to know.

Lee made a huffing sound. "Nothing like that. Is that even possible?"

"Probably." I thought for a minute, trying to steady my nerves and figure out what he was talking about. "I don't understand then."

"Not innocent," he said, patting the carcass with his metal hand. "It's a monster. It ate people." He laughed. "Hell, from what I hear, it ate you."

I wretched and gagged, but nothing more came up. My body convulsed. If the men hadn't been holding me up, I'd have been seizing on the floor.

"Lee, you can be a real asshole sometimes," Gerri said. "Get him out of here. Can't you see this is making him worse?"

"No," I said. "I need to talk to—"

"You need to rest."

I forced myself to gather my will, stand up straight, and forced my stomach to calm. It worked better than I'd hoped. Was it the System assisting now that I was actually attempting to apply my enhanced Willpower? It was something I'd need to ponder when I had more free time. "I need to talk to Lee."

As I spoke, I fully took in the changes to the room. It was nothing fancy, but the layout reminded me of a king's court, with a raised throne and all. *They've already taken this ship. The only question now is whether or not I can get them to give it back.* There were a dozen other people in the room, most of them dressed as soldiers with battered and blood-stained gear. That made one thing certain. We weren't going to be able to take the ship back by force.

I had to play this smart.

Lee met my eyes and nodded. I think he meant it as a sign that he respected me pushing past my limits. He seemed to be that kind of a man.

How could I use that, use what I knew of him, to help salvage this situation? Whatever I did, I would need to be certain it didn't cross any morally gray lines when it came to deception. My Ring of Truth Skill had turned out to be incredibly valuable, especially for someone like me, who valued honesty and sucked at lying. I had to preserve that Skill wherever and whenever I could.

"Thank you for defending us," I told him. "I'm sorry for your losses. Gerri let me know what happened."

He looked at me strangely for a long moment. Then he sighed that familiar sigh and shook his head. "You really mean that, don't you? I'll never get used to that Skill of yours. All right then, you've been straight with me. I'll do the same for you. If you want a hero, look to Gerri or the tall man from the tribe who died. They stood up to protect the kids. I stood up to protect the last shreds of my dignity. More than that, I stood up because that manipulative son of a bitch tried to force me to do his bidding."

"I backed your play," Gerri said. "You stood first. You stood alone. I saw you do it." They put their free hand on Lee's shoulder while the other spun and gathered the smoke.

He looked away from them and down toward the stone floor. "I refused the order to kill them. Refused to do it myself. I'm not sure I would have stepped in if they had sent somebody else. I really doubt it. I'm no hero. Just a stubborn asshole. If you want to give me credit for that, fine, but if you want to turn me into some kind of savior, then it's better that I disappoint you now. I'm just a man who does whatever it takes to survive and take care of his people."

Lee had spelled it all out so clearly. He might as well be holding up a sign that said, "My people come first," and "We're going to keep the ship."

Damn it all to hell. I wasn't even sure I could blame the man. He had real people with lives to protect too, and they were in danger because of what they'd done for us. What he had apparently led them to do. The Commander might not be a good man, but he was a hell of a leader. I wished I was part of the people he considered his. Even more, I wished the children were.

It had been easy to stand on my values when I'd had strong people like Lee to protect me all my life. None of that changed the fact that my values were my values, and I believed that they were right. That was why they were my values. "Is there any chance your people can help me get to the nearest settlement? I need, we need, to use the Shop."

"That's easier said than done. The closest settlements belong to the Hakarta. I hear you met some of the bounty hunters they sent for us already. Almost none of my people can go there, especially now that we've been broadcast on the Galactic equivalent of television. Even Gerri's people were seen fighting with us."

"Do you have any supplies that you can trade with us? Maybe training you can offer me? We could possibly do it out wherever you set up your camp, if you set up a camp. That's assuming that you don't all have to leave right away?"

Lee gave me the look that Count Rugen had given the Man in Black when he'd said, "We are men of action. Lies do not become us." Then he shook his head at what I assumed was his perception of my naivety. I had not been lying, and the Skill let him know. I had not attempted to deceive him. I had attempted to influence him, being very careful with my wording.

"The others are on their way. As we eat dinner, we'll be having a meeting to decide what happens next. You are welcome to join us and speak your piece. Just know that if you stay and hear what we say, I can't let you leave for a Shop until we're gone. I'd say that already, but what are the chances you'd make it far enough for it to matter?" He said that in a very matter-of-fact manner.

Lee wasn't wrong, but he also couldn't stop me. I'd been far enough away now, and the children had no guardian but me. I could take them all and teleport away from the ship. Probably. I'd never tested that Skill because we'd all die and save Lee's group the trouble of helping or robbing us, but it was good to know we had the option, if things got desperate enough to use it.

"I'll stay and join in," I said, careful not to agree or disagree.

Chapter 40

Caleb

Ten minutes later, the group had devoured platefuls of the System-controlled rage monster. If I wasn't wrong, the animal was blameless. It had probably been forced by the System to kill and eat people.

The meeting devolved quickly into what could most accurately be described as an aggressive verbal ping-pong match where none of the players were using the same rules. It was boring and chaotic at the same time.

In my mind, I'd labeled the two groups as the damned-if-you-dos and the damned-if-you-don'ts.

The damned-if-you-don'ts was basically just Lee. He wanted to regroup, train, and ready his forces to take the fight to the Humanist and the HLF. The upside of his plan was that it was proactive and surprisingly ethical. He intended to kill as few people as possible, turning anyone they could, and recruiting those who were willing to join the cause.

The damned-if-you-don'ts were led by three individuals that seemed to represent factions they knew and I didn't. The first was a trio of hard men who looked like they could have been cast as extras in a war movie. One spoke and two others flanked him as if they were his bodyguards. They ate like high school boys at lunchtime, grease dripping down their chins and onto their clothes.

I gritted my teeth and looked away, but I forced myself to stay.

Whether it was his name or a nickname, they called the leader of that group Fox. My Relatable Skill told me that his interests included Louis L'Amour novels, firearms, and Constitutional law.

The second group was led by a sharply dressed redheaded man they called Donaldson. He had a dangerous glint in his green eyes. His interests included high explosives, pyrotechnics, and Taylor Swift. The two supporters he'd brought with him were hard to notice and seemed to want to slip my attention. They ate with much better manners and were more reserved, especially Donaldson, who seemed to be one of the only two without a bottomless pit for a stomach.

The final leader stood alone and ate nothing. She was a stern-looking woman with hard brown eyes. Her name was Wilma. She wore an elaborate Victorian era dress with a low-cut top and a single, stylish glove. She had a headband with triple-eyed goggles, so I wasn't surprised to learn that her special interests included steampunk fantasy and period costumes. The third special interest my Skill informed me about, Cyber-Surgery, was a bit more attention-grabbing.

Had she been the one to replace my arm? If so, I owed her my thanks.

Her strategy seemed to be to shut up and wait for the other shoe to drop.

As far as I could tell, I was the only other one with that strategy. If I didn't miss my guess, it was for the same reason.

Wilma had enough visual similarities to Penny that I suspected they were family. They shared a sharpness of features and almond-shaped eyes. That probably meant that she was waiting for the other woman to arrive, or to drop the bombshell herself. In either case, I didn't understand the reason for the delay.

It was clear that none of the others knew about the hostages or the pre-existing rebel group. It was even clearer that they needed to know asap. I almost told them, but so far at least, I'd held my tongue. Just because I didn't know the reason for the delay didn't mean it wasn't a good one. Both of the women seemed smart and capable, and the issue was life and death, so I waited.

The talks were getting heated. Voices were rising and people were repeating things that had already been said.

The guy with the revolvers, Fox, said, "Look, man, we'd love to have you with us. Any of the Combat Classers. We just can't carry the rest of them." He gestured vaguely with his fork. "We want to, we do, but… they're dead weight in a situation like this. We need to join a strong group that can protect us."

"You want to join up with the enemies?" Donaldson asked. The smaller man spat in Fox's direction, though it didn't cover even half the distance. "Fine, run off and join with the alien scum. You can die along with them when the HLF or us has the time to kill you all. And some of us Non-Combat Classers are more than capable of blowing you all away."

Was he some kind of High Explosives Expert? If so, he probably had a point. He sounded like a zealot and a dangerous man. Was he one of the ones who had stood up for the children? I doubted it. I'd have to watch out for him around the kids.

"I didn't mean you, and you know that. Look, man, I want to kill the invaders as much as anyone." Fox's eyes flitted back and forth between the three of them. "Well, more than most people anyway. But we'd die, and not in a way that would do anybody any good. Find a way to keep us alive and fighting back and we're all in. But running and hiding in the hopes of blowing up more aliens isn't going to work if the Humanist and his people are just going to kill us all."

"Our odds of surviving this and winning are better if we stay together," the Commander said, his voice deeper and rougher than normal. He was still in pretty rough shape, no matter how tough he seemed to be.

"So, the odds of winning go from non-existent to miniscule. That's not worth dying over." That was the Gunman.

"We die slower if we split up," the bomber called Donaldson said. "And we can probably take a lot of these alien scum with us on the way out."

Lee looked at Wilma, who stared back stone-faced.

"Pavise," I said, reaching out to my friend, *"have you seen Penny?"*

There was a sound, then static. Then, "… next to me." More static. "… way to meeting."

Probably as a hail-Mary pass, Lee looked at the rest of us. When his eyes passed over me, I mouthed the word, "Stall."

He seemed shocked, but he rolled with it well. He stood and stretched, motioning for the others to stay where they were when they also started to rise. Then he pulled a bottle of whiskey and several shot glasses from his inventory and walked from person to person, giving them each a drink.

By the time he got to me, the main door of the room flew open, and Penny walked in at a brisk pace. I had no attention to spare for her though, because Pavise was following Penny. Along with them, they brought a strange man dressed in the same style as Wilma, with a top hat, goggles, and a clockwork monkey that darted from one of his shoulders to the other.

The man was in a heated argument with Pavise.

My friend, I saw, had a large turret on one shoulder now.

"No!" Pavise announced, and he sounded as close to pissed as I had ever heard.

"It's more efficient," the man said. His expression reminded me of Tony, an autistic boy from my class the year before the System came. I suspected that this man was also somewhere on the spectrum.

"Gears and steam power are not proper for a Kaldian Shield-Bot. And they are most certainly not more efficient. I appreciate your help installing weapons for me, and I tolerate your eccentricities with those, but I categorically refuse to let you anywhere near what you are calling my hood, and certainly not under it."

"Later, Earl," Lee announced. He turned his attention to Penny as she rushed to his side. "Since you're interrupting a meeting of our local leadership, I assume it's something urgent."

"Life or death," she said.

He motioned for her to continue.

She swallowed hard and looked nervous now that the time had come. But she stood up straight, brushed off her lab coat, and continued. "The Humanist has a secret base. It's a prison really, though most of the people there don't know that. He's got hostages there, even children. He has my son."

I'd known this was coming, so I was ready, watching everyone's reactions. People were clearly surprised by the news.

There was a more subtle reaction from the Commander. He leaned forward. His posture eased and his expression sharpened. "He has human prisoners?"

"He does, sir, but it's much worse than it sounds."

"How on earth could it be worse?" the Gunman named Fox asked.

"When the HLF liberates cities and saves the humans, they have something that they call Security Protocol 3. That means that when they find survivors, they keep them separate and get a list of their loved ones to try to find them and reunite them."

"I'm aware," Lee said. "Done it myself. How is that bad?"

"When things are hectic enough to get away with it, they separate people from their loved ones and let them think they're lost or dead. They say that it builds passion, but the main reason is because then they can put the ones who are more likely to be successful into active service and secure their loved ones as hostages. Just in case they need them down the line."

"Dear God," Fox replied.

"Evil, but effective," said Donaldson.

This man was going to be a problem. The question was, why? Why was he here with us instead of still part of the HLF? I needed to find out asap. Our lives might depend on it.

"Who do they have?" one of the quieter, roguish men said. "I need to know if they have my girl."

Penny started to answer, then flinched.

As a man with Perception honed by teaching, I've become very good at noticing other people's reactions. After two years of doing that with aliens, humans were now child's play. So I took note when Lee's expression and Penny's went vacant at the same time.

Penny said, "I can't give you a full list. I don't know everything."

She had a list. If I didn't miss my guess, Lee had just ordered her not to share it. *Why?*

"If my daughter might still be alive," the man said, "we have to go and save her!"

Oh, that's why. A common threat to unify the group. Or was Lee trying to save the prisoners and worried that he couldn't win without them all? If so, I could understand his motivation, but I couldn't agree with the tactic. These people deserved to know the truth.

Did I have an obligation to tell them? Maybe. Though what did I actually know, rather than suspect?

I felt a chill and looked up to see that Lee was watching me. His face was serious and hard. He said nothing. He just stared coldly and gave the tiniest shake of his head no. His body language was borderline casual. His expression was anything but. With that simple action, he had threatened me.

Would he really kill me? I didn't think so, under normal circumstances. But if he believed I'd put his people's lives at risk, I didn't think he'd hesitate. *I can't help anybody if I'm dead. And none of them will put the children first.* It made my stomach gurgle even worse, but I nodded.

He sighed and turned his hard look back toward Penny. "Assuming that any of this is true, I should have been the first to hear about it. And it should have been in private."

Wilma glared at Lee. "Watch your tone. That's our daughter you're talking to. I may not be able to kill you, but I can refuse to save your damn-fool life. You risk yourself too much to fuck with me."

Lee looked at her, then at the one called Earl. He was sitting on the floor beside them, tinkering with a metal ball filled with clockwork parts. He was trying to shove a whistle someplace where it had no room to fit. It slid neatly into place. The man had dissociated from the conversation, and no one seemed a bit surprised.

Lee looked down at his cybernetics before turning back to Wilma. He started to speak, then seemed to think better of it and nodded. Then Lee turned back to Penny. "How did you learn about all of this?"

Penny turned a disapproving gaze upon her mother before returning her attention back to Lee. "There's been a resistance force growing inside the HLF for quite some time, ever since one of our members learned that the Humanist has hidden Classes he was using to control us."

Donaldson's foot was tapping, and when I looked over to see why, he was red-faced and absentmindedly stroking a short black tube at his belt that was labeled with the explosive warning symbol.

Oh, great, the terrorist with superpowers is insane. Still, the reason for his trigger was noteworthy. He might…

"I need to know everything you do," Lee said. "But—"

"My contact—" she hadn't noticed him continue. She started to speak.

"Quiet!" Lee snapped. His eyes flicked to Wilma before he said, "Thank you," to Penny. "Not here please."

Wilma smirked.

"I can't be sure who we can trust," Lee continued, "and this room is less secure than I'd like for something this important." He turned his focus to the group. "Everyone else, stay put. Eat, drink, do whatever else you want. We'll meet back here in one hour. I'll be able to tell you all more then." He rose to leave the room. "Command Council, Penny, you're with me."

He left the room. The three leaders and Penny followed him out.

The one called Topher stood as well. He looked at Pavise, then he turned his hard green eyes on me. He nodded, mumbled something to himself, and chased after the rest of them.

***

When the others returned, I was glad for the distraction. I'd been stuck in that room with those smells for another hour. I'd have left and come back, but I wasn't sure that I could make myself return. I'd tried to plan my next lesson for the kids, but I couldn't focus with the smells and upset people. I'd have tried to talk with them, but I wasn't quite convinced I wouldn't puke again.

When everyone had settled in place, Lee began.

"Okay," he said. "I'm not going to sugarcoat this, but I think we've got a chance. I've checked with Penny, and it seems likely that the HLF has bigger problems than us at the moment. I've also been informed that we have an upcoming Combat Class healer in training." He motioned to Penny. "We should be able to have her ready in time. Ideally, we'd have one more, but we can make up for that with potions."

I expected him to look at Gerri at this point, but he didn't.

The caster looked intrigued. The man standing next to them looked annoyed. His special interests included board games, spirituality, and hunting.

Wilma scowled at the news but said nothing. My guess was she didn't want to risk her daughter, but she also wanted her grandchild to be saved. That must be a nasty case of cognitive dissonance. I had the same, if not so severe, in my desire to help and my desire to stay as far away from the fighting as possible.

"Our odds aren't great. They'd be much better if we had a dedicated defender. In the HLF, we call them tanks," he explained to those of us who hadn't been his troops. "Don't let the name fool you. It's not the same as video games. That said, they can take loads of pressure off the healers. Unfortunately, all of ours are dead."

There was some disapproving muttering at that, even a few comments of, "I'm out," and the like.

"I'm sorry, but it's not worth the risk," Fox said. He saluted the Commander. "Thanks for being straight with us on where things stand. I know it goes against how you want this handled."

Donaldson nodded.

The man by Donaldson's side who might have a loved one there grabbed him by the arm, leaned in, and whispered something urgently.

Donaldson frowned, then asked, "Can we just bomb the crap out of the place and blitz it while they're distracted?"

"Yes," Lee said. "That's basically plan A. Without another tank and healer though, we'd lose more people than they would, even if we won. More than we'd save too, probably."

"Damn it," the man beside Donaldson said.

I was inclined to agree. I wished there was something I could do to help. Maybe after they were saved, I could help the children. Maybe even some of the adults. I was useless at this stage though.

"There's got to be something we can do," Wilma said. "Maybe he could build…" She motioned to Earl's retreating form. "… something," she finally finished.

"We'll use him if we can," Lee said to Wilma. Then he turned to Donaldson. "Bombs and a full-on assault are definitely plan A. I'm just assuming that won't work with hostages. That said, we might have a solution to plan B, if Mr. Rogers here will come along?"

All attention turned to me.

I stared at them like a deer caught in someone's headlights. Then I opened my mouth and failed to think of anything to say. I finally managed to stutter out several seconds of nonsense before finally managing, "Huh?"

Lee leveled a hard stare at me. "Or do you only care about alien children?"

Quest Received: Do you only care about alien children?
Join the team to save the prisoners at the HLF Compound.
XP and Credit rewards based on performance.

The others in the room had that same zoned-out look. Apparently, I wasn't the only one to get a Quest out of this. Lee had chosen strong wording. He knew his crowd.

"I care," I said, "but I have no idea how that helps you. I don't know why you think you need me in a fight, or a heist, or whatever it is you have planned."

"We don't need you," he said.

It was my turn to let out a sigh.

"We need him," he said, as he pointed at Pavise.

"Oh." *Well fudge.*

"Technically, we need both of you because we need him. I'm told the two of you are something of a package deal."

"I can't just abandon my students." I tried to say more, but I didn't have the breath for it for long enough that I realized I was starting to have a panic attack.

"Any one of my people here can protect them better than you can at this point," Lee answered, "and I'll be leaving everyone that we don't actively need to secure the ship. They'll be safer here with our people than with you."

"Until I die!" My voice cracked and my body was trembling, but I forced myself to continue. "Then what happens to them?"

"I'll make sure they're taken care of."

"What happens if you die?" I said, calmer.

"I'll leave orders to get them someplace safe."

"And you and the others will treat them as if they were humans?" My tone was half a question, half an accusation.

Donaldson scoffed.

One of Fox's men chuckled.

I gestured at them both.

Lee glared them down before meeting my eyes. He started to answer. He hesitated ever so slightly before answering, "Yes."

I noticed.

He noticed me noticing and shrugged. "It doesn't matter. You're worthless to them as you are."

Ouch. I nodded.

"You asked for my help earlier. Fine. This is my price. Me and my people will train you and help you get equipped so that you can take better care of yourself and your students. Or you don't, and you can hope that we save you all, *again*, regardless."

He was right. I couldn't trust him or his people, especially Donaldson, but he was right.

I tried to answer, but I couldn't breathe. I tried to nod. Innocent lives were at stake, and I really did want to help, but my heart was thundering and I felt like even nodding would be enough of a lie to break my Ring of Truth power.

So I did nothing. I said nothing. For a long moment, I just closed my eyes and breathed. When I finally spoke, my words were some of the truest I'd ever spoken. "I'm scared."

"That's because you're smart," Lee said. "You should be scared. I can't change that. I wouldn't if I could. But it's also because you're weak. You're a Non-Combat Classer and you don't have the killer instinct to be anything more than that, but we"—he gestured to Topher—"can teach you enough of the basics so that you won't get in our way while your robot helps us. The same Skills will help you keep your students alive once we're all gone. I know you won't let us down."

That last was a sales pitch. I knew it, but I still wanted to agree. The words wouldn't come. I felt as though my skin was on fire and my body was being crushed again. I needed time.

"You've been through a lot," Lee finally said, "and this is newer to you than it is to all of us." He was looking at the rest of the people in the room as he said that last. "Take the night. I'll use the time to strategize with my team and find out how many of us have the balls to save our people. We'll talk again in the morning."

I nodded, grateful for the temporary reprieve.

I waited. Everyone sat in silence long enough that it got pretty awkward.

"You can go now," Lee finally said.

I did so, trying not to feel like a naughty child who'd been sent to see the principal.

Chapter 41

Caleb

"He intends to keep the ship, sir," Pavise said. He had followed me from the training room.

It took the last of my manners to keep up appearances and not just snap at him to leave me alone. My tone was sharper than I intended when I said, "I know."

"You do?"

I tried not to be offended by his shock. I was idealistic, yes, but I wasn't stupid. I'd always been a student of history and a lover of great stories. I knew the kind of man I was dealing with. "Yes, buddy. He all but told me he was going to."

"Very astute observation, sir."

Did he have to sound so surprised?

"How do you intend to solve the problem, sir?"

"The short answer is that I have no idea. The longer answer is that I'm going to try, and I'm probably going to fail. Losing the ship is going to devastate Aul and the others. If and when that happens, I'm going to remind them that they were never meant to have the ship to begin with and that their Queen had other plans for them, plans that we can now attempt to implement somewhere else."

"Wise, sir. That should reassure them."

"It probably will, but it shouldn't."

"Why do you say that, sir?"

"Because it sounds like this Humanist guy and his flunkies have a hard— have an obsession with killing the children in particular, and I don't have any illusions that I can protect them. Plan A has to be keeping the ship and getting them off the planet. Plan B is hiring a ship and mercenaries to try and get them back to their Queen."

"And if you can't keep the ship and you can't send them home?"

"I don't know, Pavise. Go the old-school *Incredible Hulk* show strategy and move from one location to another, trying to keep under the radar."

"It won't work, sir. I'm sorry, but the existence of Skills and the System's willingness to sell your location makes that a foolish plan at best."

"Do you have a better one?"

"Your plan is excellent, sir. I fully support it." Complete deadpan.

"Priceless, Pav."

"I'm certain I have no idea what you mean, sir."

Then his mention of Skills caught up to me. "I may have an idea."

"That's a relief."

I chuckled. "I could dump some more points into Intelligence, Willpower, and Class Trip. Assuming that I can use it without permission slips, now that the last of the Voloid adults is dead and I've officially taken over the ship, I can set up safe zones scattered here and there and jump between them to avoid pursuit. I just have to make sure I can bring all the children at the same time. I can also bring chaperones, so maybe we can make some friends or hire some mercenaries to back us up. Either way, you and I need to get stronger."

"Does that mean you've made up your mind about taking part in the mission, sir?"

I had forgotten about the question entirely, lost in my paranoid planning. I thought my medicine was wearing off because my world was spinning again as my heart rate quickened. I had to hold myself up with the rough stone wall around my doorway.

"Sir?"

"I need to be alone." I shut down our connection, hard, and let the door slide shut in his face.

I'd apologize later.

Chapter 42

Caleb

Hours passed. Nothing helped. I confronted what had happened to me. My failures. Kek's death. My own inadequacies. Being devoured.

I'd heard a Robert Frost quote somewhere, "The best way out is always through." In the past, confronting my emotions and pain had served me well. This time, I was pretty sure that everything was only getting worse. My lungs were working double time, and my heart was tripping over itself trying to keep up. My mind raced from one horrific image to another. It felt as though my brain was so overwhelmed with stress and worry that it might be cooking slightly, only to heal due to the System's impact.

A dose of Gerri's pills was sitting on my chest. They were gel-caps. One of them was green and the other one was purple. I was as desperate to save them as to use them, though. I might need them later when things were life and death and not just feeling that way.

Maybe I needed to decide what came next and commit to a path of action.

Trying to recover and then decide was clearly never going to happen.

Fine.

My biggest choice would be my Class. I wanted to focus on Teacher or maybe Interspecies Diplomat or something like that, but I wasn't going to just stand by and let people get killed if I could save them.

I scoffed. If my Ring of Truth Skill worked on me, I'd have just lost it. I was deceiving myself. Deciding to save the children and the hostages was something I could do. Actually saving them was quite another matter.

Damn it, damn it, damn it.

I smashed my fist into my pillow. Then smashed the pillow against the wall. It didn't help. Nothing helped.

I took out the drugs twice. Put them away twice. I considered finding Gerri and begging for more.

Finally, I gave up and tried to sleep.

When I closed my eyes, all I saw was darkness. I could smell the acid. Feel my missing hand rotting and my body burning as trickles of acid poured in through the holes in my armor.

I could hear my dead student screaming. Hear his voice telling me, "Kek is protect Caleb."

My room was too small, and my bed was even smaller. I felt as though the walls were closing in. Crushing me. I shut my eyes and tried to make myself relax. *Breathe in slowly through my nose. Hold it. Out through the mouth. Hold it. Then repeat.* I couldn't get a full deep breath, no matter what I did.

Terror gripped me like a bear-monster and wouldn't let me go. The darkness only made it worse. Finally, I couldn't take it, so I opened up my eyes and stood. The floor was cool on my bare feet when I stumbled toward the door. I needed to get out of this space. I had to move.

The tantalizing aroma of bean and cheese burritos pounced on me at my door like an overeager puppy. The surprise was enough to yank me from my panic. It was thoughtful of Pavise to bring me food, especially when I'd been such a jerk to him.

But when the door was fully opened, it wasn't Pavise at all. For a second, I stopped and stared. The acrobat with white-blond hair and bright blue eyes was standing in my doorway. She had a plate of steaming burritos in one hand and a bottle of green liquor in the other. Absinthe?

Her Special Interests included neo-classical ballet, the Anglican faith, and Byzantine art.

"I thought you might like some food, since you couldn't join in with the others."

I grimaced. If that story was going around, I was guessing it was due to the gossip-worthy splatter on the wall.

She must have misinterpreted my reaction because she frowned. "Don't worry, they're just beans and cheese and seasoning. And before you ask, I checked with Pavise, and he gave me a long lecture on how, 'not all cheese is really just cheese, young miss,' and that it can't be trusted to not include meat."

I tried to smile at her Pavise imitation. It was adorable. I failed. Smiling was beyond me now. So I settled for saying, "Thank you."

She held up the plate and bottle. "Mind if I join you?"

I turned back and looked into my mini cubby. Then I looked at her. I'd gone through puberty and adolescence. I'd had fantasies like this. But that wasn't why she was here, and I wasn't in the right headspace to even start to misunderstand that.

I also wasn't in the headspace to want to be alone.

"Sure," I said. Then, to be more honest, I motioned into my small stone rectangle. "You're welcome to try."

She laughed, but her attempt seemed every bit as forced as mine.

That was when I realized what was really going on here. She hadn't brought me food and a drink because I was hurting and I needed it. At least not entirely. She was bringing me food and a drink because she was in desperate need of company from the one other person who could truly understand what she was going through.

She'd been torn limb from limb. Broken. She'd had pieces of herself replaced.

Our situation was different. She was clearly one of the most physically skilled and gifted beings on the planet, and I was me. She'd lost something I'd never had. But we were also the same. We were scared. We were hurting. We were alone.

Maybe we could be alone together.

I moved to my bed and sat down, then patted one of the patchwork squares on the blanket in invitation. She squished in beside me and offered up the food. Now I did smile as I took one of the burritos from the tray, and I meant it.

We had to sit hunched over and a bit cramped together, but it wasn't as bad as I'd feared. She was only slightly taller than me, and lithe where I was still a bit scrawny. I wouldn't have called it cozy, but we weren't quite sardined.

We got a little tipsy and I broke out Gerri's pills for both of us. I saved the last set for a true emergency.

She was warm, and solid, and her legs twined around mine while we chatted about *Serenade* by George Balanchine, a performance we'd both loved. I rested my cheek against her head and wrapped my arms—well, my arm and my prosthetic—around her back and waist. I hadn't realized how much I'd missed basic human contact. The soft warm tenderness was exactly what I needed, though I felt like I had a high interest debt and my paycheck was gone before I cashed it.

She petted my human arm absentmindedly as she asked about my pictures. She complimented them so sincerely that I looked at them with fresh new eyes. I'd missed how much my art had improved as my stats had increased. Any other day, I'd have been flustered and awkward when she stripped off her armor to make room and get more comfortable, and I might have balked when she insisted I get my heavier clothes and sweater out of the way.

I'd at least have fooled myself into believing that she was making some kind of pass at me. Instead I just held her, one person and another, and we rearranged our bodies until we were as comfortable as the space would allow. She snuggled her face against mine. Cheek to cheek.

"You smell amazing," I said.

"I do, huh?" she said. "Not sweaty from the armor?"

"Rosemary, maybe. It's got the scent of evergreen and herbs, like one of those new age shops with incense."

"I smell like a stinky store?" She turned her head to rest her chin on my right shoulder.

"It's nice," I said, evading the question. "Is it because the armor is self-cleaning?"

"If you're asking why I don't stink? That's old-world magic."

"Excuse me?" I asked.

"Soap," she said. "Just plain old-fashioned soap, though a friend of mine told me that she bought some magic soap once. It's a crazy world." Her faint smile was quirky, curving up on one side and down on the other. Adorable.

It made me desperate to kiss her. Her fingers tracing circles on my chest only made it worse.

I decided to distract myself with a topic change. "I want magic junk food."

"I never developed the taste. I was never allowed."

"Because of the athletics?" I twisted a little more onto my side, bunching the blanket and pinning my prosthetic beneath her head.

She nodded.

"I saw you training," I said. "Through Pavise's eyes. Not on purpose. I think our cybernetics are broken. You're amazing."

"Thank you," she said.

My mind added. "I've worked hard to become so." I am such a Princess Bride geek.

"At least I used to be," she continued. "These are gonna take some getting used to." She brushed my cybernetic arm with hers. "My body is a fine instrument, and I'm not ungrateful. But it's going to take the Shop to get back to one hundred percent."

I fell into her deep blue eyes as I said, "Whatever percentage you're operating at, it's still impressive." I flushed. "I think mine made me stronger."

She laughed. "You're a Teacher. I'm sure you're better at that than I could ever be. Still, it's nice to hear your compliments when you've got that Skill of yours. It feels validating. It's still not fully getting through, but it helps. Then again, I've always been my own worst critic, even worse than Mom."

"One of those parents?"

"Yes and no," she said. "She was obsessed with my success, driven to ensure that I excelled no matter what it cost her. Or me. I still don't know why. Now I guess I'll never know."

"She didn't make it?"

She nodded. Then I realized that I kept thinking of her as she was because I had no idea what her name was.

"I'm sorry for your loss," I said.

"We've all lost someone. Some of us more than most."

I nodded and tried to hold back my swelling tears as I thought of Nana. I missed her every day.

My guest brushed my tears aside with her still-human hand.

"I don't know your name," I told her. "I'm Caleb."

She smiled. It was as lovely as a sunrise. "Nice to meet you, Caleb. I'm Evelyn, but the guys all call me Larson. It's a military thing."

"What do you like to be called?"

"Well, aren't you sweet. My friends call me Evie." She chuckled. In an exaggeratedly haughty tone, obviously meant to be playful, she added, "Though men in bed with me usually just call me wow."

I laughed. It helped. "It's a fair response, Evie, one I could give without breaking my Ring of Truth Skill."

"It breaks if you lie?"

"Yeah. It stops working on any person I intentionally deceive."

"Oh, wow. That's great for compliments, but it would make it really hard to date somebody."

"I hadn't thought of that. I've been here on this ship since everything changed. There really hasn't been any kind of an opportunity for courtship."

She laughed, then looked at me with a puzzled expression when she must have realized I hadn't meant the word as a joke.

"I guess it wouldn't make any real difference to me, though I'm sure that you're right," I said. "I've always tried my best to be one hundred percent honest with anyone I've dated."

"How's that worked out for you?"

"I was single a lot. I got pretty good at it."

"That's a sad commentary on modern dating. Well, old modern dating."

"I like people, and it makes it easy to make friends. Asking people out is easy too. But the people I'm most attracted to are really masculine men who don't tend to like men and really feminine women who don't like men like me. At least not that way."

"Men like you?"

"I'm a teacher. A nice guy. A geek. You know. A nerd."

"Come on, it can't be that bad."

"This"—I motioned at myself—"is what I look like after the System. Without my glasses, or the contacts when I could be bothered. My flab has toughened up from years of hiking with the Voloids. I've also leveled a lot and have Charisma as a Class stat. Even after all of that, I'm fit but kind of scrawny. At least when you compare me to the rest of you."

She started to protest.

I felt guilty for doing it, but I talked over her. "Don't get me wrong. I'm not embarrassed or ashamed of who I am or how I look. At least I wasn't until there were lives depending on me in a fight."

She cupped my face and kissed my forehead softly.

"The good news is that some people *are* into guys like me, and a lot of them are really awesome people that I get along with. I'm not shallow though. I care way more about character than chemistry. I even assume I'd find them more attractive over time, because they're good and caring people."

"Then what's the problem?"

"Honesty," I said.

She blinked several times. "You didn't tell them all of that. Please tell me you didn't."

I looked down and to the side, so I could avoid her eyes without being rude. "I told you I was single a lot."

"Oh, you poor, poor idiot." She wrapped her body around me with a whole-body hug. She was really very strong.

I couldn't breathe, and this time it had nothing to do with anxiety. My vocal cords squeaked as she squished the air right out of me.

She realized what was happening after a moment and released me. "I can't speak for the guys, but I think you'll find it a lot easier to be attractive to at least some of the women that you weren't before. You're fit and you already mentioned your Charisma's gone up. Most of all, you've got your title. 'Defender of Children' is gonna be a panty-dropper for a lot of women."

I tried to talk but sputtered instead.

She laughed. "At least until you try to explain it away."

"You seem to know me pretty well already. I would definitely do that. I was just about to do that now with you."

"You won't be able to fool me by explaining it away. I've talked to the others, even Pavise. I know what you did to earn that Title. And I know the kind of courage it must have taken to put yourself between Lee and Quinn"—she shuddered—"and the others. And the balls it must have taken for you to go fight monsters without training or experience is next level shit. You should be proud, not ashamed."

"I wish you had Ring of Truth," I said as my face flushed.

Her eyes focused on mine with intensity and certainty. She held my head between her hands so that I couldn't turn away. "I'm telling you the truth."

"Wow," I said.

"That's usually not the reason they call me wow."

I ducked my head again.

She giggled. It caused very interesting things to happen that I tried very hard to ignore.

"Thank you," I said. "That helps a little."

"You've got the block too, huh? The one where you can't believe compliments, even when they're true?"

I nodded, though I also felt the need to clarify. "Wanting to protect them and being able to are two very different things. One of the children followed me into the woods that day. He wasn't an adult yet. He had no Class or Skills. He said he wanted to protect me." My voice broke as I finished, "He didn't make it."

"Oh, honey, I'm so sorry." One soft, warm hand dragged up and down my arm, while a cooler one cupped my cheek.

I leaned into the caress, letting her compassion seep into every corner of my aching heart. "I wanted to save him. I tried so hard. I just. I wasn't. I couldn't."

Then I was crying, and she was holding me. I wept and wept and covered her with undignified amounts of tears and snot before we took a break for more burritos and another drink.

I kept forcing myself to avoid looking at her until she caught me not doing it.

"If I wasn't comfortable with you seeing my body, I wouldn't be here dressed like this." Then she got a very vulnerable look and she said, "Please don't look away like that. It makes me feel ugly. It's like you can't stand to look at me with these." She gestured to the amazing-looking cybernetics.

My brows shot up. "I'm a geek, remember? Awesome cybernetics are our bread and butter." I traced my finger along the curve of her metal arm before I remembered it was a part of her body now and she could feel through it. I blushed and sputtered an apology.

She laughed, but it wasn't unkind.

It bolstered my courage, so I said, "As for your request. You don't have to twist my arm. It's certainly not a hardship."

I took the time to really savor her lean perfection. She was astonishing. Wondrous. A work of art. I started to tell her so, but she must have read it on my face because she smiled and blushed.

Her eyes were wet as she said, "Did you know your power even works with your expressions?"

"No, I didn't realize that. It's good to know." I hadn't lost it when trying not to show my emotions. Would I have if I'd faked alternate ones? It sounded like maybe I would have.

Then she removed her bra and I forgot about everything else and did what I was told.

"Wow," I said again, this time with heat.

Her smile bloomed like a rose. "You're just saying that."

"You know that I'm not," I said, and I sent her the Ring of Truth Skill description with a flick of my hand. "Just wow."

"I like that," she said, and she bit her lower lip.

"You look beautiful. And your cybernetics don't detract from it. At least not for me. Cyborg women are hot. Ask basically any geek."

"Thank you," she said, and she took another drink from the bottle. Slowly.

I shuddered and let out a long-suffering groan, while she laughed at me.

I'm idealistic and yeah, maybe a little naive. But even I was pretty sure what she was doing. I knew that in this one rare and unusual instant, I could be with this woman in a way that would have been all but impossible for someone like me under almost any other circumstances. She wanted this, maybe even needed it, on some level. I also knew that it wasn't about me, or her, or us. Not really. It wasn't about a relationship.

Evelyn was sweet, competent, and full of life. I could love this woman, not just lust after her. Oh, the lust was there all right, demanding that I give her everything, just the way she wanted. But I also knew I wasn't ready. What I needed now was company. A friend. Someone to talk to. I hoped that it would be enough for her. Tonight, after everything I'd been through, it was all I had to give.

"Tell me about yourself," I said. "Your life before."

The spell broke, and her eyes filled with regret and a tinge of sadness. It broke my heart a little. But she smiled, and her expression was grateful as she took my hand in hers. She didn't pull away. She didn't cover herself.

"I," she declared after a long moment, "was an Olympian." She spoke with pride and gusto, and the way she sat up straight, held her head up high, and stuck her chest out as she did so made things that I'd been ordered not to look away from bounce delightfully.

Wow, just wow.

Then her words caught up to my overridden monkey brain and I got very confused. "Do you mean like in a movie or a play?"

"Huh?" she said.

"You played Aphrodite? Or maybe Athena. You'd be amazing as Athena."

"Oh my god, you are a geek, aren't you?" She giggled again and grabbed the bottle that still held a little of the green liquid and took another mouthful. She shuddered as she swallowed it. It really did taste bitter. It wasn't Indekk awful, but it was still pretty bad.

"Yes," I answered her, "I am a geek. I told you that I was."

"I," she said again, redoing the entire presentation, bouncing and all, "was an athlete in the Olympics."

"Oh," I said. "Yeah, that makes more sense."

"I competed in three events and took silver in two of them. I also got the gold for Artistic Gymnastics. Twice."

"Wow," I said again.

"Okay," she said, "that's getting a bit stale."

"Your awe-inspiring athleticism is matched only by your stunning beauty."

She looked at me hungrily at that, and I might have caved completely at the slightest provocation. I could barely inhale as desire pooled deep in my gut. Squashing it down was one of the hardest things I had ever done. Or at least it felt that way in the moment.

"Thank you," she finally said. She waved her hand in front of her face. "You are now the official president of my fan club. I expect you to pay your dues in the form of such compliments on at least a monthly basis."

I laughed and I would have happily agreed, but I had children to protect and no idea where the future would take us, so I kept my mouth shut.

"When the System came," she said, "it offered me the Acrobat Class. I took it eagerly. It also gave me a couple of Perks. I got some bonuses to my run speed and a passive that converts some of my Mana regen into Stamina regen. They saved my life those first few Levels, though I don't think they're worth much anymore."

"Yeah, some Perks are better than others."

"You're telling me. You made out like a bandit. That's how you got your metal friend, right?"

"Pavise, yeah. I was near a dungeon, so I got better Perks. I wanted an AI assistant, but I couldn't have that unless I got a cybernetic implant, so I did." I tapped my head. "It seems to be on the fritz now. Then I realized it was going to be awkward to have another person in my head and that I was in danger. Like you said earlier, I'm a geek, and I love Star Wars. So, I got myself a shield-bot. The rest, as they say, is history."

She reached for another burrito and found that they were gone. Then she tried the bottle and found that it was also empty. She leaned forward and kissed me on the cheek. Then she looked at me questioningly for a long moment and said, very quietly, "Does this mean that I should go?"

I moved aside my blanket, revealing a smaller storage nook was carved below. From it, I pulled a pack of Reese's peanut butter cups and two cans of A&W root beer. "Stay as long as you'd like, and you can come back anytime."

She grinned broadly and took one of each. We opened the cans with a pop-hiss and a flood of that sweet root beer scent and clinked them together in a silent toast. We both moaned with pleasure as we savored the sharply sweet but complex flavor. Then she ate her peanut butter cup delicately, as I gobbled mine.

She nibbled the ribbed edges smooth before finishing with polite and measured bites.

Once she'd finished, Evie stripped off the last of her clothes, spun around to ensure I didn't miss anything, then nuzzled and twisted and slid under my covers and back into my arms. Anyone less limber could not have made it work.

Without another word she started crying and trembled as I held her.

This kind of help, I was ready and eager to give.

I petted her back and her hair. I kissed the top of her head and her cheeks. I brushed away her tears.

After a little while, even her remarkable distractions couldn't keep my thoughts at bay, and I was trembling and crying right along with her. This time, however, I was not alone. Together, we were stronger than the nightmare that our lives had now become, and things got better over time, instead of worse. Eventually, her breathing slowed. It felt nice against my skin. Soon after that, she was snoring faintly.

I followed her into oblivion soon after.

Chapter 43

Lee

I was planning the HLF raid in my mobile command tent while I should have been asleep. It looked like black plastic and felt like vinyl. No real security, but better than nothing. I'd set it up in a closet. Cramped. But a cot, table, and chairs were all I really needed.

A polite knocking sound when I didn't even have a door surprised me. The aliens were scared of me and I'd told my people to leave me the hell alone.

Mr. Rogers?

Turned out to be his Companion. It looked like a mix between a knight in shining armor and that "Danger, Will Robinson" robot.

"What do you want?" I asked, stepping back to let it enter the room.

"I'd like to speak with you," he said.

I closed the door behind him. "Did the Teacher send you?"

"My master's name is Caleb, Commander, and he most certainly did not send me." He was good at emulating body language with his "arms" and "hands." Good programming. "He is unaware of this visit. He would certainly not approve of its purpose."

"Oh? What purpose is that?"

"I am here to correct your misapprehensions about my master."

I gave the thing a deadpan look. "Your master, as you call him, is pretty much the poster child for you get what you see. I'm pretty sure I understand him just fine."

"That is because you think of people as tools. You see them as resources. You clearly do not understand them as individuals."

He had me there.

"You focus on killer instinct because you are a killer. You are a knife or a gun." He waved his claw-grip appendage in the direction of the assorted weapons I'd been in the process of cleaning.

"And?" I answered flatly. He wasn't wrong.

"My master," he said, "is a shield, though neither of you know it."

"Mr. Rogers is a shield?"

"His name is Caleb, Commander, and yes. When you murdered—"

I raised my eyebrow. My fist clenched, unprompted.

He lowered his head halfway into his torso. A neat trick. "When you killed the Voloids, " he continued, "my master instructed me to intervene. As he has given me instructions that I am not to follow his orders blindly, I refused. He put his body in between you and the children to force my hand."

"Point. I grant you that stepping up like that took balls. The man is definitely serious about protecting children. He's just bad at it because he's weak."

"Yes," he said. "You begin to understand."

"I really don't."

"What does a tank do?" he asked.

"It's an armored vehicle with a powerful—"

"The other kind."

"Oh, they draw aggro and protect the... oh."

"Indeed. I am a Kaldian shield-bot, the primary tool of the formerly elite Kaldian Shield Warders. I am programmed at the deepest levels to understand and defend against risks to those under my protection. But I am also programmed to understand those who can best aid me in that task, and I am telling you that Caleb is such a man. You are a tactician. You understand what to do with a tank once you have one in front of you. But you don't know what it takes to make one. You don't consider what drives them. It is not a killer instinct."

"A desire to protect," I said. "I get it. It's a fair point. But none of that matters. He's too weak to do anything about it."

Then he told me what had really happened before the Teacher got devoured. He told me of a man who had knowingly marched into a world filled with monsters to protect those in his care. Who'd stood his ground when he'd had the Skills to run, for the sake of a student who'd followed him against his orders. He told me of a man who'd triggered grenades strapped to his own body because that was what it took.

My knee-jerk reaction was to discount the Teacher as anything but small, naïve, and weak. My mind didn't want to paint the pictures the shield-bot was describing. But I couldn't imagine the man doing anything less when children were threatened. I'd seen that with my own eyes.

"I didn't know," I said. "Nobody told me."

He nodded. "My master is a good man with extraordinary courage, though you are right that he is weak. That makes you question his worth, but the question of his current worth is not what matters."

"I'll bite," I said. "What matters?"

"The question that matters, Commander, is what would happen if we make him strong?"

Chapter 44

Caleb

The door to my small room banged open without warning.

I rushed to cover myself and my companion but found that the covers were already over me and the spot where she had been was empty.

The Commander was carrying a squarish box with a globe on it. He had darker circles under his eyes, and I doubted that he'd slept at all. But he must have had a breakthrough, because he was standing at ease and he lacked his usual intensity.

Lee pressed a button, and a tripod of metal legs extended down to make a stand. The box folded out into a surface the size of a coffee table.

On it was a suit like the one Evelyn had worn the night before, as well as a high-tech, science-fiction-looking harness the same shape as the one He-Man used to use. This one had a small rectangular Mana battery attached to its back. Three other batteries of the same type were next to it.

Finally, there was a harness of grenades.

I closed my eyes just long enough to take a deep breath and said, "What's all of this for?"

"You asked for us to train you and help you trade for equipment. I'm here to do just that. Get dressed and meet us outside of the ship."

"I haven't agreed to go on your mission."

"You will," he said as he headed toward the door.

I didn't answer, though I suspected he was right.

"Oh," he said as he turned back when he'd reached the doorway. "As for the trade? Talk to the alien and explain what's happening. He won't stay out of our way, and they keep taking down our lights."

"She," I said. "And you get used to the blue. Look, I'll talk to her, but no promises. She's not going to be happy if you intend to stay, even for a little while."

"I suppose I can understand that."

"What should I tell her? Will you all be leaving after the mission is complete? Can I reassure her that you don't intend to take the ship?" Mentally, I crossed my fingers. *Please say yes.*

"You can tell her anything you'd like, if you think that it would help."

I pressed the issue, my voice earnest. "Would I be telling her the truth?"

"That's a great question," he said, and he walked out, shutting the door behind him.

I inspected the gear he'd left me.

The grenades were standard concussion grenades, though ones that were made for humans and that I could understand how to use. I set them aside. I didn't want to have to look at them while I went about my preparations.

The other two items were more interesting.

Danarian Technophile's Augmenter Mark 2

A chest harness that boosts technological effects. It requires a specialized form of Mana battery that can absorb the user's personal Mana. This device has a spot in the back to allow the user to charge such a battery. A single Augmenter may boost up to five devices. Limit may vary based on Level of the user.

Commonly sold with Damarian Technofile's Boosters. The booster can be attached to a device to increase its effectiveness. Extra Mana batteries and boosters not included.

Could this be used to boost Pavise? That would change everything. I put the thought and the item aside as I moved on to the next.

HLF Prototype Dermal Sheathing

This sophisticated nanofiber weave underarmor requires a Tier 2 or higher neural interface. It provides the wearer a +5 bonus to Strength, Agility, and Stamina, as well a small degree of protection. Also includes a minor, if sporadic, self-repair function.

Very cool. I wouldn't be doing super parkour like my new friend, and I certainly wouldn't be running any marathons or throwing cars around, but this was still the kind of power fantasy wish fulfillment that I'd dreamt of as a child.

I rushed to try it on but stopped halfway through yanking it on when I saw one last thing on the table. There was a runed silver necklace that someone had added what looked to be a plain dog-tag style metal rectangle onto. On one side was an acronym I didn't recognize—maybe something from the Human Liberation Front?

It read DMTNS. Maybe M was for Mankind. I checked the other side for a clue and found another mystery. There, it read DSLNL. I had no real guesses on this one. Maybe they were some indications of rank. I set aside the mystery and inspected the item. It read, very simply:

Enchanted Necklace. +5 to Willpower.

I'd take any help that I could get in regard to that, especially now. Gratefully, I pulled it over my head and even that small bonus helped a lot, if not as much as the companionable understanding of my new friend the night before. Stats were all well and good, but it was people that mattered most.

Someone had patched up and cleaned the armor, though it was still in pretty rough shape. I decided to keep it in the armory until I was told to use it. Today was for training, after all, not fighting.

I headed outside. On my way, I passed by Gerri having a heated argument with a man from their tribe. I ignored them and moved on past several guards who were set up like they owned the place.

The Commander and Evelyn were gearing up, probably to join us in our training.

It wasn't until I passed a group of Voloids harassing a second set of guards that I remembered I'd agreed to talk to Aul.

She was going to be upset.

Chapter 45

Aul

This one called I was relieved when Caleb came to find me in the training room. Any sooner, and he'd have lectured us. Now that the human's had stolen a different place to meet, we'd been practicing by fighting mockups of the bad human hive with our spears and blasters. The Matriarch had mostly trained for monsters. This one... no, I, would not make the same mistake.

We'd be as strong as we could be when they finally came for us.

Or when we came for them.

Caleb had taught that worry did not help. I thought the same was probably true for hopelessness and rage. Only the power to drive off murder-hives would help, unless Caleb could somehow save us.

Caleb was our Obi-Wan Kenobi from his stories. He was our only hope for now.

He wore a shamefully thin new exoskeleton that glowed. One of the other humans wore one like it. Were they becoming a hive now? Would she help us as well?

"Hi, Aul. I need to talk to you." He led me away from the others and into the chamber where we slept.

This was very rude, but Caleb did not know and the only other place where I could host him that the human hive had not invaded was the Command Deck. If I opened that, they would take it from me, so this one said nothing and waited until Caleb was ready to speak.

"How are you all holding up?" As he did spoke, he gestured with his hands and an image of humans listening at the door appeared. Along with them were the things that Caleb called cartoons. They showed tiny devices in rooms with lines that lead to the oddly shaped human ear organs. Listening devices. Bugs, the humans called them.

The human hive could be spying on us and Caleb wanted me to know.

Caleb was still our Teacher. He was still our friend.

I wrapped him in a hug with all four of my arms and chittered.

He flinched.

He had been hurt so badly. I hugged him even tighter, careful not to crush his frail human body.

He returned my hug with a tight embrace of his own. It crushed me so much that my semi-hardened exoskeleton started to deform.

I cried out in lesser pain, and he stopped and pulled back.

"Oh, I'm so sorry, Aul. It's this new suit. It enhances my strength."

Perhaps his new exoskeleton was not quite so shameful, after all.

"Aul is understanding. Caleb is be stronger. Good."

"Thanks. The others are going to start training me today. I hope that will mean that I can protect you and the others better soon." As he spoke, he conjured an image of the humans taking the ship and pushing him and the Voloids out of it. In this image, he stood guard over us.

Then he created a picture of a human with the orange hair color that humans call red. He was holding strange devices. In this picture, the orange-headed man was alone with a Voloid and the Voloid was running. Then the picture changed to one of the devices the man had been holding. It exploded.

This man was a danger to the Voloids. If we were ever alone with him, we should run.

It seems that there was a class today, after all.

Then Caleb showed an image of me yelling and him calming me down. This one was confused, and he motioned at the picture of me a few times until I thought I understood.

"Humans is be gone!" I shouted. "Now!" It was nice to let out my frustration and anger.

"I know, Aul," he said. "I'll try, buddy. But I need you and the others to be patient long enough for me to get trained and help them save their people. Please don't antagonize them." He moved his hand and words appeared. **This is not the truth.** "I'm sure they'll leave in peace as soon as we're done."

For the first time since I had known him, I did not have certainty that he was telling the truth. Would he lose his Skill with me now, because of this? With anyone who might be listening? Did his Skill even work through electronics?

He distracted my thoughts by showing me another picture, one of a new computer in the ship and then another of the ship taking off, with the humans left behind on the ground in front of it. Then the words, **I'll try.**

I knew for certain he was telling me the truth.

I placed a hand on his chest and leaned my head against his, willing him to understand, wishing I could think the thoughts into his head in proper communication. When that failed, this one did the best I could with symbolic sounds. "Voloids is being thankfulness. Caleb is Aul's friendship."

Chapter 46

Caleb

Outside the ship, I found a group of three people waiting for me to join them. Evie greeted me with a stunning smile and a friendly wave, whereas Penny gave me a curt nod.

I returned both gestures in kind then smiled as Penny's System Companion, a small black cat with white-tipped ears and paws, rubbed against my leg as it passed by.

The third human was an older teen with redder hair than Donaldson, a spattering of freckles, and a sawed-off shotgun in his hand. His special interests included firearms, League of Legends, and the Vikings. It made me wonder if that was the sports team or the culture. Given that this was Minnesota, it could go either way.

Lee walked past me and motioned for me to join the group. I did so.

To sate my curiosity, I decided to ask him about the acronyms on the necklace he had given me, but by the time I could pull out the necklace to ask, he was already talking.

"This is your new team. You will train together. You'll fight together. Take some time to introduce yourselves and get to know one another. You'll live or die based almost exclusively on whether or not you can trust these people to have your backs. You have five more minutes of freedom before I turn you all over to Topher. Make the most of them. They'll be the last you're likely to get for quite some time."

"Don't let him fool ya," Topher said from behind me. "I'm a big soft teddy bear compared to what he'll do to ye once I've put ye through the wringer."

The two of them walked away together, chatting as they went.

"I'll go first," the redhead said. "I'm Randy. I'm told I'm the lowest level here at twenty-eight, but I'm also the only Combat Classer. I'm a Shotgunner. I think that's self-explanatory. I'm short- and mid-ranged AOE primarily, though I've some longer, single target Skills in my Slug tree. Don't worry, I'll be training even more than the rest of you. I'll be caught up in no time." He looked eager to level. Driven. There was a story there, but it wasn't the time to ask.

"Speaking of time," I said, turning to Penny, "how much do we have? Last I heard, you were going to be debriefed."

"Yes," she said. "We're luckier than we should be. The HLF has bigger problems than us at the moment. So long as that continues, the Commander says we should have the time to do this right, if barely. He refuses to give me the timeline, but he said something about power-Leveling and bringing trainloads of monsters to us to push us to Advanced Class Level 3 before the raid."

"Did he say trainloads or trains?" Dang. What did he have planned for us? I pictured waves of monsters dragged to us all at once by a big dumb brute shouting, "Leerooooyyyyy Jeeeennnnnkkkkiiinnnns!"

She gestured at the Commander. "I don't know. Ask him. All I know is that it's killing me to be training when my son needs me."

"I know. I'm sorry."

"Speaking of training," she said, changing the subject, "I'm going to be the healer."

"Great!" My old school gaming kicked in at that news. "Everyone needs a healer."

"Not great," she said. "I'm a Non-Combat Classer. We actually managed to make me a tremendous asset for the HLF when I was part of a large group of dozens of healers. I was able to use my Med Tech abilities to help figure out exactly what was wrong with the patient and how to treat them. I'm really good at helping actual healers be a lot more Mana efficient while treating people who've been dragged from the front lines or during downtime. But for something like this, I'm just another bad shot and also not really good at defending myself."

"Oh," I said.

Evelyn's smile faded, and she bit her lower lip.

"Fan-fucking-tastic," Randy said, tossing his hands in the air and spinning to face the other direction as he huffed out a breath of frustration.

"It's not quite as bad as I make it sound," Penny said. "I've got a stockpile of healing tech consumables, and they work much better for me than they would for others. I'm sorry, everyone. All of this is because of trying to train me. We need another healer, and I'm the closest thing we've got.

"Once I hit Advanced Class, I'll be able to switch to Front Line Medic. At that point, I might actually be a better healer than I would have been as a Combat Classer all along. I'll certainly be more Mana efficient and better with consumables. But that's still nine levels off for me. Sorry in advance if I get you all killed."

"You're better off than me," Evelyn said. "I'm an Acrobat with replacement parts that haven't been properly custom-fitted. Don't get me wrong, I'm grateful, but I've had one good trick of annoying enemies and flipping away, and now I can't trust my body to do what I tell it to, even with this special suit." She motioned at her outfit, sleek and high tech, just like mine. "Apparently, I'm gonna be a dodgy spear fighter with a fancy name."

"Melee DPS," I said.

"Melee what now?" Evie asked.

"Damage per second."

"That doesn't clear things up the way you seem to think it does."

"It means your job is to hurt the enemies close up."

She gulped. I couldn't blame her. That hadn't gone very well for her last time. Part of me wanted to tell her she didn't have to put herself through this, but it wasn't my place. With innocents on the line, none of us had any good choices.

"What about you?" Randy asked me.

"I'm a Teacher," I said.

"No, what do you do in combat?"

Run, blow myself up, and get devoured by monsters.

"Me? No. I'm not part of the team really. I'm just here because of him." I gestured to Pavise, who was about twenty feet behind me and to the right, observing us from next to a small stand of ash and scrub maple. "He's my shield-bot System Companion. He's pretty tough, and he can make force shields."

"Oh," Penny said. "I thought you were going to be our tank."

"Me!" I looked down at my arms and my chest. I was the second shortest and smallest member of the four of us, and Randy made me look downright scrawny. "Why would you think that? No, I can help people with bandages and minor healing, and I can help repair all of our equipment and Pavise. But that's really all I'm good for."

"So, is he our tank?" Randy asked. "I'm confused. We need a real tank, not just equipment."

"I'd be more confused if it was him," Penny said, jerking a thumb at me. "No offense."

"I'd say offense taken, but I've seen me in a mirror."

"Don't be so hard on yourself," Evie said.

I gave her a deadpan look. "I like you too. But what about this says tank to you?" I motioned down at my body.

She looked away. "The big metal robot?"

"The big metal shield-bot," I said. I turned to Randy. "He's not equipment. He's a System Companion."

"Thank you, sir," Pavise announced as he walked over to join us. "I always appreciate accurate nomenclature, especially when it has to do with me. However, you will need to take a more active role in what you all colloquially call the tanking process if you wish to be able to fully utilize my capabilities. As you know, I was damaged in our recent combat. I will need you to use our connection to direct my shielding powers."

He had barely been hurt in that fight, and my influence over his abilities went directly through his consciousness. What he was saying could not be true, and he definitely knew it.

"Are you trying to lie to me or to them?"

"My statements were all independently true, sir. I had hoped that no one would recognize that they were also unrelated. I am both disappointed and proud that you noticed."

"I trust you, but I'm going to need you to explain this all to me later tonight."

"No."

"No? Just no?"

"Yes, sir. You will either trust my motivations, or you will not."

There was a pale hand waving in front of my face as Randy said, "Yeah, that's not sus at all, standing there mind-melded with your robot."

Pavise cleared his non-existent throat.

"Sorry, shield-bot."

"Quite all right, sir."

"Sorry," I said. "I'm used to our telepathic connection, and I haven't been around people who can't also communicate mind to mind for most of the last two years. The manners are different. I'll adjust."

"I trust you, but there's another concern."

"What's that?"

I continued out loud. They should hear this part. "My implant is damaged. I'm not sure they can rely on me being able to direct you to activate your shields."

"Yes, sir. That is a known problem. Don't worry, we have your surgery scheduled."

"Oh, okay. Wait, what!"

"Wilma is a Chirurgeon. She will be opening your skull later this evening. Her husband, Earl, is a Geek Machinist. He will be doing what he can to repair the implant and restore it. It will not be perfect—for that, we would need access to the Shop—but we estimate he should be able to perform at least the rudimentary repairs that should get us through the next few Levels safely. We have numbing and healing potions prepared for you. Thankfully, with magic and advanced technology, you will not even need to be unconscious for the procedure."

"You want me to be awake through an open-skull brain surgery?" A feeling that was a weird amalgamation of horror, disgust, and intrigue pulsed through me. I blamed adrenaline for the first two and geekiness for the last.

"Yes, sir, I think that is for the best. That way, you can ensure he does not add any gears or a steam whistle. I've become aware that it is a bit of an obsession for him."

"I'll talk to my dad," Penny said. "I'm sure I can get him to minimize any customization."

"Minimize? No. No customization." I felt my eyes widening alarmingly.

"That was my stance as well, sir. Now, we should get started." Pavise turned to walk toward Lee and Topher. There was a new engraving on his shoulder, underneath his new weapon. It was the symbol of a gear and a steam whistle.

I decided I didn't have the heart to tell him.

"Well, let's get this ragtag team of…" I faded off as my face paled.

The others must have noticed because Penny asked, "What's wrong?"

I frowned and told them all, "We're the *Bad News Bears*."

"Huh?" Randy said.

"Or any of those sportsball movie guys," I continued. "We're the team of mismatched misfit outcasts thrown together with… with…" I pointed an accusing finger at Topher and the Commander. "A disgraced former coach and his assistant."

Penny laughed. The others looked confused.

"What the hell are you talking about?" Randy asked.

"Almost certainly a movie from the eighties or nineties," Pavise replied.

"I don't see the problem," Evelyn said. "Those people always rise above their problems, learn to work together, and excel. They almost always win."

"Yeah," I said, "in movies, sure. Did any of those shows come off as even remotely credible to you?"

They were all starting to look as upset as I felt.

"Maybe one or two. The ones based on a true story, like *Rudy* or *Silver Linings Playbook*." Penny must be a movie buff too.

"Not the same genre," I said. "That's just one spirited and talented player in a group of trained professionals. This is not the same. And this is not a movie." I gestured around. "Do you see any cameras around here?"

Evie took my head in her hands and moved it so that I was facing up and to the left, where camera drones were circling us in the clearing where the ship was parked, watching everything we did.

They all cracked up.

It took me a few befuddled moments before I was finally able to join in. It was a good laugh and a bonding experience. Then I felt embarrassed for having worried everyone.

It was the last pleasant thing we would experience for many hours, because Topher took that as his cue to start our intensive training. By the end of that first day, we were all wishing desperately that we were in a sadistic drill sergeant's boot camp instead.

Running through a swamp is hell. Your feet want to stick in the mud, the roots and water want to trip you, you can't properly predict when your foot is going to reach the "solid" bottom. I didn't even want to imagine how awful it would have been without my new suit, two years of hiking experience, and the Stat points Pavise had managed to convince me to invest in my physicality.

They had us climbing the larger trees, leaping from one tree to another, swimming and wrestling with seaweed that wanted to drown us. The last was not an accident. It was not something that just happened. Topher led us specifically to the yellow-green plant, ordered us to tear him off a hunk, and literally kicked me by the ass into the water when we hesitated.

Randy and Evelyn seemed to be old hats at any kind of athleticism, though Evie's new cybernetics tripped her up a bit from time to time. Penny and I were clearly the intended recipients of all of this, and as much as I had empathy for her clear misery as she tried to catch her breath and nearly collapsed, it was good not to be the only one. Misery loves company, after all.

Her cat-like reflexes did save her from failing the jumps from one tree to the other though. Only Evelyn and I did that. That woman could swear up a storm if she wanted to, and I could tell her only two choices had been between fury or tears.

As for me, I just lay there suffering until Topher started kicking me in the side, and when that failed, the head.

"I'm up, I'm up." My arms curled around my head as I struggled back to my feet to prevent any more blows.

"You all have five minutes," he said. "I suggest you use 'em well."

I wanted to snap at him that he could have just let me rest on the ground if he was going to call a break, but I knew enough about exercise and exhaustion to know better.

"I like you, Caleb," Randy said, "so I hope you don't take it personally, but I'm asking for a real tank."

"That's fine. Frankly, I didn't ask for this job, and I hope you have more luck than I did. I'd be careful though. Lee doesn't seem like the type to appreciate insubordination."

Randy growled something unintelligible as I stretched my aching muscles.

While we'd been talking, I was watching my Stamina barely tick up when I saw my Health and Mana start to drop. Apparently I wasn't the only one, because Evelyn and Randy started doing careful assessments while Penny and I panicked.

"Pull yourselves together," Randy said, "or I'm gonna bitch slap the both of you." His voice was forced and sounded phony, like he was trying to emulate the Commander or Topher and he was failing hard. Still, he had a point.

Penny hissed at him loudly, which startled all of us—including her apparently.

Randy and I had lived locally long enough that we were the first to think to check for ticks and leeches. We had half stripped down to our waists before we found the first of them stuck to our sides. Pulsing blue and black things made of some kind of energy, they were slightly less terrifying than the old-school leeches, though also more dangerous. They'd gone right through our clothes and armor and started sucking out Mana and blood in equal measure.

They also passed right through our hands as we attempted to pull them off.

Our weapons were just as ineffective, other than maybe Randy's shotguns, and none of us were willing to let him try with that. So we all stood, stark naked and dripping foul swamp water, as our Health and Mana slowly dropped toward the same levels as our Stamina. We had about twenty between us.

"Does anyone have any spells?" I asked. I had a minor heal, but that would just make my Mana drop all the faster. It wasn't going to hurt these things.

"They made me learn Mana Bolt at level one, but I've never used it," Randy said.

"It's never too late to learn," I said, always a teacher.

He just shrugged and started casting at one of the leeches on me.

I let out a breath that I didn't know I was holding when the creature burst and started leaking blue-black fluid, after the second shot.

"Let me save that for Gerri," Penny said. "Shoot the others while I collect the excreta." She pulled out a vial and started gathering the gory ooze.

It took two or three shots for each of the creatures, so we did end up having to use some Minor Healing spells and Mana potions to keep us all alive long enough for Randy to finish them off.

Our clothes were halfway back on when Topher announced, "Okay, ye lazy buggers. Break's over. Git!"

Randy swore under his breath, and there wasn't one of us who didn't grumble or complain. None of us started running. We all just kept getting dressed.

"I thought ye might feel that way," Topher said, "so I've had the Hunters arrange for an alternative training method, just in case ye wanted ta opt out of mine. I'll see ye all back at the ship." He turned to leave. As he walked away, he said over his shoulder, "Maybe."

That was when the growling started.

Turned out we all had just enough Stamina to make it back to the ship, after all.

Chapter 47

Caleb

Gerri was kind enough to drug me into unconsciousness for the surgery. Pavise and Aul both insisted on standing guard, which was sweet but unnecessary. If the Commander and his people wanted to do something to me, they could, and none of us could do anything to stop them. Being completely powerless to resist someone else did at least help clarify their intentions toward you.

They healed me, woke me up, and sent me back to training.

My implant was mostly working now, but it wasn't one hundred percent. Pavise warned me that it had bought us weeks or months at most. He stressed that it could be much less if we had to overstress it.

It was a pleasant surprise, later that night, when Evelyn took me up on my invitation to come back anytime. She had some kind of mesh ball that expanded into the crack that was pretending to be my room's floor.

It rose to the perfect level to match my bed. When I asked her how she'd managed that, she just pointed at a tiny sensor, gave me a friendly hug, and plopped down on the foam like a child falling back into a pile of leaves.

This made our sleeping arrangements much more, which is to say barely, comfortable. It did get awkward when I had to climb over her to use the bathroom. Respectful and careful as I was, it still earned me a black eye and a bruise on my left thigh. It was late enough by the time I got back that I decided not to risk a rematch and made us both breakfast in bed.

When I'd returned with a tray of Tofu Scrambles and two mini-boxes of Sun Maid raisins, she was already gone. She didn't return before it was time for training, so I ate them both cold. I regretted that when I encountered her and Lee on the way to training—I could have given it to her after all. I regretted it even more when we started our training with sprints.

By the time I realized we were probably being led into an ambush, I couldn't catch my breath to yell a warning. By the time I realized I could have Pavise warn them, it was too late. Two gray monsters my mind labeled as Timber Werewolves, though they could have been advanced aliens for all I knew, were charging us from the side.

Time seemed to slow—whether because of the situation or my connection to Pavise, I didn't know. It gave me just long enough to remember to use a force shield to protect my team, but also to think of an out-of-the-box possibility. It didn't give me enough time to evaluate that idea before deciding whether or not to implement it.

A knee-high barrier of blue force appeared right in front of the werewolves.

One of them hit it hard and tripped, face-planting and sliding toward us through a moldering pile of leaves and twigs.

The other stumbled but caught its balance with a clawed front limb planted on the ground before pushing itself upright again. It beelined straight at Randy and took a shotgun blast to the face for its trouble.

The result of the thunderous blast was like a horror movie. Blood and fur and flesh exploded behind the creature as it snarled in rage and anguish. Also like a Hollywood monster movie, its monstrous face was already healing as its partner rose into a pouncing crouch.

Randy was a Combat Classer and trained, so he didn't miss a beat. He was stepping backward and reloading at the same time.

"Back," he told us as we all hesitated. "Get your asses back and help me kill these things."

We backed up, and I had Pavise throw up a shield to buy us all some time. It did, stopping the monsters' advance as they slammed into it in near unison.

Unfortunately, it also stopped the Shotgunner's next blast just as much.

Pavise willed his Mana bar into my field of vision to remind me just how intensive his shield was as a big chunk of his resource vanished.

The gray-and-white monsters took the time to go around the small barrier, so I let it drop. I wasn't wearing my armor, hadn't prepped my mounted weapons, and I didn't have my grenades. I had to resort to my regular blaster and my untrained Agility. Even then, I fumbled to use it with clammy hands.

The others were more competent, or more prepared. Penny pulled out a mechanized dart gun while Evelyn readied her spear, but what drew everyone's attention was Pavise.

Click-click-CLICK-CLACK! WHOOOOO WHOOOOO!

The monsters flinched and turned to glare hatefully at the incredibly loud sound.

Then Pavise opened fire with a relatively quiet burst of gunfire.

Had the Geek Machinist put a steam whistle and a silencer on the same weapon? Or had the steam whistle just deafened me? No time. I fumbled my weapon as the others attacked.

I missed what happened next as I had to look down at my weapon to finish activating it, but I heard the sound of something sharp scratching metal and the boom of a shotgun firing again and again in rapid succession. Gunpowder filled the air.

Blaster ready, I didn't dare fire. Pavise was between me and one of the monsters, and Evelyn was spinning, flipping, and weakly stabbing the other one.

"Out of the way," Randy yelled. "I can't get a clean shot."

Evelyn put a foot on the creature to parkour herself out of the way, but the leg gave out beneath her. She stumbled just long enough for the monster to lunge forward and clamp its maw down on her shoulder.

Randy stepped forward, pressed his shotgun against the creature's head, and pulled the trigger.

Hollywood had nothing on the gore that escaped. Blood and brains and bone-bits splattered us. They stank of copper, steak, and mold.

This time, the creature didn't get back up as Penny and Randy circled Pavise and opened fire on our remaining opponent. Evelyn recovered quickly and used her spear to damage it and trip it up when it attacked the others.

I wasn't just sitting back and watching helplessly. I hadn't been through the paramilitary training of the others and I was no match for them in combat. I had, however, watched a whole hell of a lot of movies and TV shows, and I knew better than to fall for the trap that the rest of them had clearly missed.

A werewolf that didn't get back up was not the same as an XP notice.

I headed over but stayed far enough back to keep the furry creature safely covered with my blaster. My head ached as I pulled on processing power to give myself the time I needed to evaluate the situation.

Was this a person? A monster? Both? Did it even matter when it had already tried to eat my friend? I couldn't shake the feeling that on some level, deep down, this was an animal that was being driven by the System to kill. It should be captured and fed and studied. Could it be uplifted with Intelligence Stat boosts? Could it be taught and saved?

The only answer I had for this Timber werewolf at this moment was no. I didn't have the power, or the resources, or the time to save this creature without endangering my life, my new friends, and all of the children I'd sworn to protect. The System would heal it soon. It might already be able to attack us again. It might be pretending.

"I'm sorry," I told the blood-covered beast before I unloaded two quick shots into its head.

Its bright red eyes flew open at the last. The beast had definitely been playing dead. Brutal hatred, and far too much understanding, glared back and met my sympathetic gaze.

This was the System, not a zombie movie. It took three more shots to end its life.

I waved the XP notice away unread.

There has to be a better way.

Chapter 48

Lee

Topher and I watched from the shadows of a dense thicket as the group finished off the Night Hunters. They were sloppy. Weak. We'd nearly decided to step in three times. But they got the job done. Three of the humans, and one robot, were finishing off the last monster standing.

I had no attention to spare for them.

"They're shit," Topher said. "I can polish 'em up for ya, but you'll just end up with shiny shit." He kept talking, but I had no attention to spare for him either.

All of my attention was on the Teacher. Mr. Rogers. Caleb.

He was a small man. Chris Rock small. Weak and frail.

But he'd fought with the others. He'd used his shields. He'd stood his ground.

Again.

Was the robot right, after all?

"Are ye even listening or am I talkin' just ta hear meself speak?"

"Quiet," I snapped and pointed at the Teacher. "Watch."

Caleb had noticed that the first monster was down but not dead. The others had missed it. Probably the most common rookie mistake. And the most lethal. He didn't lower his weapon. Didn't get too close.

I got a close-up shot with my drone. The man was trembling. His brown eyes were wet.

He said something. I couldn't read his lips.

He hesitated. Didn't have the strength to do what needed to be done.

I should have known that this would happen. Just two days earlier, I'd found the Teacher crying in his classroom with the kids. He was overdue for training, so I'd gone to drag him out. He was talking to them about grief. The dead bug kid named Kek. Even I wasn't a big enough dick to interrupt.

One of the kids was more sensible. They said, "Caleb is be sad along with Voloids. Sad not small but much less big. Hive is greater angry mad. Voloids want to hurt the humans. Ki… Voloids want to make them gone from ship."

He'd launched into some sappy Mr. Rogers song about what to do when feeling mad.

Made me sneer. He'd never understand. I could have taught them what to do with fury. How to focus it. Let it drive you. How to get revenge.

The revenge would be on me though, so I'd let him sing his damn fool song. Corny, but the part about being able to choose to stop when doing wrong had stuck with me.

But this made clear the price he paid for principles. The man couldn't do what needed to be done. That was it then. The end of the track. Should have trusted my gut and not that hunk of metal. Let him get my hopes up.

Two shots blasted into the creature's head.

Well, I'll be damned. I didn't think he had it in him.

He'd underestimated the creature. Watched too many movies. But we'd all been there at one time or another. Couldn't fault the man for that.

Three more shots and the things Health bar was empty. Solid gray.

"Well fuck me," Topher said. "I can work with that."

I couldn't have said it better myself.

Chapter 49

Caleb

"Nobody tells my dad that the whistle actually helped," Penny said as we squelched our way through the wooded swamp to a nearby clearing where Topher and Commander Lee stood waiting for us. "He's already impossible about it. He doesn't need the encouragement."

We'd looted the bodies, and Topher had offered us time to evaluate our own performance.

Everybody had taken it seriously, but things were obviously winding down, so I took the opportunity to call the gruff man over before he noticed we were starting to slack. I couldn't imagine that would end well for any of us.

"Well?" was all Topher asked.

"I started the fight trying to be too clever by half," I said.

He nodded. "It's all well and good to think outside the box, but ye had a simple job ta do and tryin' to make it fancy could have gotten yer people hurt."

"We have no real coordination," Randy added, stepping up beside me. "I shot at a shield I should have predicted. We got in each other's way. It was a mess."

"Yer nae wrong, but that takes experience. It'll come. What else?"

He was looking for something specific. What?

"We acted like we were in the old world," Evie said. "We weren't really watching for attacks because we knew it was a training exercise."

"Did ya now? Then yer lucky ta be alive. Don't count on us ta save ya. If you cannae be bothered to look out fer yourselves, why should we?"

"Because you need us," Penny answered.

The rest of us all gasped at that.

"Do we now?" Topher said. "Commander. Do ye have any family trapped at the HLF base?"

Lee shook his head.

"And I sure as shit don't. You need *us*, lass. Yer son needs us."

"You're right. I'm sorry." Leaves rustled as Penny shifted her weight, a pinched look on her face.

"Fuck sorry. Be better."

"Yes, sir." She snapped to attention.

"What else?" he said, looking pointedly at each of us.

"That's all we've got," Evelyn said.

"You've got a scientist, a teacher, a soldier, an Olympic Athlete, and a great-big, fancy fuckin' robot, and that's the best ye came up with?"

We lowered our heads.

"Yer gear!" He pointed at me. "Ye have armor, lad. Where is it?"

I stood "at attention" the way I'd seen soldiers stand in movies. "Back at the base, um, sir."

"Dinnae sir me. What are ye doin' out here without yer armor?" He didn't pause for me to answer. "Yer robot told us ye have a special weapon. Where's that?"

I waited, correctly predicting he would not let me speak.

"Most importantly, the Commander gave ye a harness to make yer robot much more powerful and ye left it lyin' useless on yer bed." He pointed at Evelyn. "Ya dinnae have yer spear out, and yer trying to be fancy when yer nae ready."

She looked away.

He pointed at Penny. "Even after the fight, you didn't help heal yer injured member. What if that damn whistle had brought some more creatures?"

He pointed at Randy, then hesitated. "Get more levels."

Randy looked smug and started to speak, probably to let Topher know he'd done just that.

"Actually, no. Ta hell with that. Of course, ye did the bare minimum. The Commander trained yer arse his own damn self. But yer part of *this* team now, and you let them"—he motioned at the rest of us—"do all of that. Ye should have known better, so their shit's on yer shoes too."

He was a redhead, so when he blushed, he really blushed. "Yes, sir!"

"It's not my job to teach ye how to exercise," he said. "It's my job to teach ye to survive. Use yer bodies. Work together. Be prepared. What!" He shouted. He was glaring at me.

I met his gaze.

"If ye have something to say, spit it the fuck out."

I'd always hated this "test them first and teach them after" method. It made the student feel like a failure and accomplished nothing. He must have seen it on my face, without me even realizing I was showing it.

"I just think that you should teach first and test second."

"Oh, do ye now? Isn't that sweet," he sneered. "And should I bring ye warm milk and a mat to nap on? This isn't kindergarten. It's the bloody apocalypse, and the System doesn't give ye an F and send yer arse to summer school if ye slack off. It'll come for ye when ye least expect it." He started poking me with his finger, hard, to emphasize each word. "It will devour ya whole until yer dead. Dead. DEAD! Or until ye wish ye were. I thought that, at least, ya'd bloody well have learned."

"In case it wasn't clear, you flunked. All of you. Every bloody one of you. Yer lucky yer not dead. Go back to the base. Eat. Sleep if ye can. If I ever see any of ye unprepared like this again, I swear ta God I'll kill ye all myself, in front of witnesses to warn the next damn bunch of fools."

All of us turned to Lee to see what his reaction was to that.

"Use Mr. Rogers as your witness. With his Skill, they'll believe you." With that, he simply turned and walked away.

"Oh, aye. Good point that." Topher looked at me. "Besides, it'd feel like kickin' a puppy. Not right that."

I closed my eyes and tried to force myself to stop trembling. I failed.

When we hadn't left quickly enough, Topher turned to us and screamed, "Go on now!"

We went.

Chapter 50

Caleb

I'd switched sides with Evie so that I could charge the Mana batteries with my harness while I slept. Its straps were thick and metal, so it was awkward to try to sleep in, but I'd tossed and turned until I found an angle on my side that I could tolerate.

Pavise woke me halfway through the night for a battery swap, and I used the opportunity to take a bathroom break.

I thought about having him wake me again when Evie got up, but I decided that was over the line. If I decided to do something about the issue, I'd do it by talking to her directly. So far, we'd both been so exhausted when we finished our training that we'd barely said a word to each other before passing out.

As predicted, she was gone when I woke. I had Indekk for breakfast, gathered my armor and gun, and headed for the spot where our group had agreed to meet. My harness was on and the third Mana battery was charging.

After some testing, I'd learned how to use the Technofile's Boosters. They looked a bit like a circuit-covered nicotine patch, and they had a spot in the center for a Mana battery about the size an old nine volt would have been, if it was square. When I was wearing the harness, I granted a passive boost to whatever device the battery was connected to, as long as that device was spending my stored Mana to fuel the effect. I'd double-checked that. It had to be *my* Mana—no idea why.

I could boost my underarmor or my armor, but not both. It didn't matter where on the items I put the patch, it would not do both. This was arbitrary and stupid and it made no sense.

When I complained to Pavise, he told me, "You have better things to do than nitpicking, sir. And delving into this issue would almost certainly require investigating the System."

"Oh, right." I'd promised him I wouldn't do that and I was a man of my word, so I chose my underarmor because my physical attributes needed all the help that they could get. The second fully charged battery went to Pavise.

He helpfully added a second Mana bar to my usual display, about a third the size of his main bar. I decided to stop whining about what this miraculous item couldn't do and just be grateful that I had it. That much extra Mana for Pavise could mean life and death for our whole group.

"Can you add that on to the end of the main bar with a bit of extra glow or something please?" I asked him. "I'm sorry for the tone. I'm not trying to sound harsh. It's just happening more and more."

"You have been through a lot, sir. I understand completely."

Evelyn, Lee, and Penny were waiting when I arrived. I looked around, but I didn't see Randy.

"He's training," Lee said when he noticed me looking for the redhead. "He's taking power naps as they travel, and they wake him for any fights or when things look dicey."

"Sounds dangerous," I said.

"What isn't?"

He had me there. I nodded.

When we tried to discuss the day's plan, Lee held up a hand and said, "He'll be back in a minute, and he's already eaten so we can get started right away. No reason to go over everything twice. Feel free to chatter while we wait." Then his eye unfocused as he reviewed his screens.

Looks passed between Evie and Penny and me. They were friendly enough, but it seemed that none of us were comfortable with chatting while Lee was there, so we resorted to awkward silence.

A couple of minutes later, Randy showed up, riding in a pickup truck covered with armored plates. The back had a small armor barrier protecting his lower half. His upper half was wearing heavy armor. I doubted he could move in it, and he was positioned behind a heavy weapons turret. It looked ridiculous, but it must be effective.

When they came to a stop, he opened the armor and hopped down to come join us. It reminded me of a type of special mission on some old video games. Randy looked worn but happy. I suspected he'd Leveled again. At first, he just fell into attention, then he caught himself.

"Gear check!" he announced. He was doing a better job at that tone. It made me suspect he'd been practicing. If he were one of my students, he'd have gotten a gold star.

"I've got my underarmor, armor, and both my blasters," I said. "I've boosted my underarmor and Pavise with my charged Technofile's Boosters." I pulled up the description and image for all of them with Show and Tell. "The next one is charging, but it takes hours we haven't had yet."

"Will you use the next one on your blaster?" Randy asked.

"It's too small. Probably Evie's underarmor and your armor would be best for the last two."

"Who's Evie?"

She snorted.

"Larson," I said, gesturing.

"Oh."

"Would that work on Randy's shotguns?" Penny asked. She held her System Companion in her arms and petted him gently as he purred.

Pavise put the cat's name above his head—Captain Hark Jackness.

It made me wonder if Barrowman had survived. I hoped that he had.

Then I realized everyone was looking at me for an answer. "Probably not. Actually, make that no. It's only for things that have their own Mana charge."

"Damn," Randy said. "That would have helped."

"Are there shotguns that use energy instead of ammo?"

"Absolutely," he answered.

Everyone but he and Penny smiled at that.

"At the Shop," he said, and the rest of us deflated.

"Something to look forward to." I tried to stay positive.

"Are your weapons charged? Do you have any grenades, potions, or other consumables?" Randy asked.

"I have a belt of grenades." I patted the sci-fi-looking silver orbs. "Two Health potions and one for Mana."

"Good," he said.

Then he went through the others, one by one, followed by himself. We were all fully equipped this time.

"I had an idea," I said, "but I'm not sure that it'll work." I turned to the Commander. "Can we get comm earpieces?"

"I have an implant," Randy said.

"Me too." That was Evie.

"I don't," Penny said. "I wasn't a full HLF member yet."

"Sure, one sec," Lee said. He pulled two out of thin air and gave them to us.

We both thanked him and got them ready.

"My thought is that I can have Pavise link up and announce, 'shield up,' as I raise it and, 'shield down,' when it's about to drop. That way we don't stumble as much."

"I like it," Lee replied.

Everyone else made sounds of general approval.

We spent the next few minutes discussing tactics, and I was grateful when Lee let himself get pulled into it. Apparently, he didn't share Topher's obsession with testing first and asking questions later.

Then he turned us back over to Topher and our real training began.

***

It was grueling and intense, day after brutal day. I hated the man's methods, but even I had to admit that they were effective. During the two weeks Topher trained us, we all Leveled more than once. We'd never been unprepared again. Penny and I were both surprised when we gained a couple of Stat points beyond the few Topher would not let us spend. In my case, it was a point in Strength and a point in Will.

At the end of the two weeks, I'd leveled three times, more than anyone but Randy, who'd managed a whopping eight. Three gold stars and a rainbow!

The last day, Topher let me spend my Stat and Skill points. I had nine free stat points and one Skill point. The stat points, he had me divide between Strength, Constitution, and Agility with two each, with a whopping three in Willpower.

When I asked him why, he tried the, "Because that's where I told ye ta put 'em," spiel that the petty tyrants love so much.

When I'd forced the issue, he said I'd get more out of my physical attribute points while I was using them so aggressively. Wisdom, he assured me, was vital for anyone who planned to fight, especially in melee. He also reminded me that, "You might have forgotten that our enemy is a mind-controlling fascist."

Three points it was. I'd have gone for six.

Even Evelyn and Randy had come a long way, despite starting out so far ahead of us in combat skills.

None of that stopped Topher from yelling at us and insulting us every single day. He was the worst teacher and one of the most unpleasant people I'd ever met. So I was as surprised as he was when I tracked him down five minutes after he'd finally announced that he was free of us and that he was turning us over to the Commander the next day by saying, "Kindergarten's over."

"What do ye want?" he asked me.

"I need your help picking out my Advanced Class so that I can prepare in time."

"Sure," he said, his tone like battery acid. "The way I see it, you've got two choices: Sainted Do-Gooder and Wishful Fucking Thinker."

"Cute," I said.

"Go fuck yerself. Those are the only two Classes that will ever get close ta what yer lookin' for."

"Let's try this again," I said. "If I had any other way to get this information, I'd use it. I don't like playing hardball, but for you, I'll make an exception. There are lives on the line and you don't seem to care, plus you've done a lot to intentionally hurt people that I'm starting to really care about. Do your job and help me find my Advanced Class or I'll let everybody know how fake your accent is."

His eyes narrowed and he reached for a dagger hilt at his waist. "Be very careful what you say to me, boy. Be even more careful about what you say about me and to who."

"Your business is your business," I told him. "It's just that my grandmother's best friend lived half her life in Scotland, and the two of them talked basically nonstop. I also spent a couple of years backpacking in Ireland, Scotland, and Wales after college. I know what a Scottish accent sounds like and—"

"My business is my business, and my secrets are my own." His jaw did that pugnacious jutting thing, but his eyes were more dangerous than I wanted to think about.

"I'm just asking you to do your job and help me find a Class that can—"

"Help ye save everyone, up to and including the arseholes like me, and the monsters, and the aliens. I know. Everyone knows. But I'm not a Magic Eight Ball. I'm a Basic Trainer and Troop Progression Specialist. If the Class you wanted did exist, I might not even know about it. If I did, it still wouldn't be my job ta help ye find it, because I donnae work for you. I work fer the Commander. And the big man and I worked out the best Class choice for ya with yer robot weeks ago."

"Pavise? The three of you made a Class plan for me and none of you thought to tell me?"

He laughed. "We thought to tell ya, lad. Then we decided not ta. You'd just overthink it and get in yer own damn way. Look at ya even now. There are real people with real lives depending on ye, and yer spendin' time ye can't bloody spare tryin' ta figure out how ta save everyone else, when it's gonna get the people that ye can save killed. Yer not Mr. Rogers. Yer Mr. bloody Magoo. Now get out of me face or I'll make yer voice tone match yer girlie temperament."

I left. I needed to talk to Pavise.

I couldn't find him. He was hiding from me and our connection was blocked.

I closed my eyes and counted to ten as I took deep slow breaths. I could force the issue, but that would be a complete betrayal of our relationship. Would it be the first, or had he already done just that?

Actually *could* he have done that, even if he wanted to? Even if he tried? The restrictions on him were why I was so careful with how I treated him, and why I restricted myself to match his restrictions.

After a few minutes to calm down, I remembered that I trusted him.

I couldn't say the same for Lee. He also wasn't the kind of person who would avoid me just because I was upset with him. Now that I thought about it, neither was Pavise. If he was avoiding me, it would be for my sake, not his.

After asking around, I learned that Lee was at the ship's Command Deck. Apparently, they'd finally managed to get the door open after all this time.

Aul was not going to be happy. None of the Voloids would be.

I'd have to break it to them in class if they didn't already know. We'd resumed classes after a week without, though they were shorter than they had been. They were shorter than I'd like. And they cut into my already limited sleep time.

They weren't my only classes either. A week ago, Lee had realized that if he asked just right, he could give me Teacher quests that could be used to get me even more XP during the times when I needed to recover between training sessions. He'd made similar realizations with Penny and then Evelyn. Lee was even more surprised when he found out the progress his Troops could make with Safe Space active on the area and all my other Skills used as needed.

The three of us were always exhausted now, all of the time. None of us complained. We all knew that we were under a literal deadline, and an uncertain one at that. Besides, we all had it easy compared to Randy. Between our training sessions, they alternated between marching him on monsters and marching monsters on him. It was brutal and unfair, but it accomplished its goal. He was progressing faster than any of us.

I found Lee sitting on an elevated chair. It gave the impression of a makeshift throne.

"I'm guessing you and your plan for my Class is the reason that Pavise is hiding from me?"

"Your robot is hiding from you?" He laughed the loudest and hardest laugh I'd ever heard from him. "Well, isn't that something?"

"Don't change the subject."

"I'm afraid that you've confused our relationship," he said. "I'm the commanding officer of my people. I am not your bitch."

"I don't think you're my... my servant. But I'm also not one of your people. You don't have the right to pick my Class for me without my input."

"Oh, that. That's on you."

"Excuse me?"

"Your robot—"

"Shield-bot."

"Your System Companion," he said, stressing each word, "came begging for our help for the same reasons that you did. He's trying to keep you alive and to help you protect your students. Did you want us to just turn him away?"

"Pavise asked you to help pick a Class for me?"

"Yes, and to help you train for it."

"And you didn't think to tell me about this?"

"He *specifically* asked us not to."

"Why?"

"How the hell should I know? Ask him yourself. He's your System Companion."

"I can't. He—"

He laughed. "Right, I forgot. He's hiding from you. Strangest thing I've ever heard."

I knew what was coming next and started preparing myself to have this argument again. I'd already had to debate this point with Topher, Randy, and Penny this week alone.

"Just order him back and make him tell you."

"I can't just order him around. He's a person."

"Clearly, and yes, you can."

"No, I can't, and… wait. Did you just agree with me?"

"Yes, you'll find that happens almost anytime you're right."

"You think that he's a person?" I said.

"He talks. He reasons. He makes choices and has opinions. He's clearly a person."

"Then you should understand why I can't just order him to do something."

"I order people to do things all the time." He gestured at the word "Commander" written in stylized letters on his uniform.

"Yes, but the System will force—"

"I also force people to do things all the time. With violence and threats of death. Hell, you may remember that I also kill people"—he patted one of his many guns—"when they need to be killed." He seemed to be finished, but then he added, as if it were an afterthought, "Or if they get in my way."

Was that a warning? A threat? I didn't think it was. He was stating a simple and basic truth of his existence. In some ways, that was even more terrifying.

"You all picked a Class for me, and I know that it's going to be about combat. I'm guessing some kind of tank Class that uses Pavise."

He nodded. "It's Called a Kaldian Shield Warder."

"From what Topher said, it sounds like all three of you know I won't be happy about that idea?"

"Everyone knows that. You've got some kind of savior complex."

Did I? I didn't think so. It wasn't about me, was it? No.

"I want to be part of the solution, not part of the problem. And it's not about me saving people," I told him. "It's about people being saved."

He sighed. "Which people? Which people, where?"

All of them. Everywhere. It was too big to say out loud. Too arrogant.

He must have seen it in my eyes or assumed it from our past interactions because he looked at me askance for a long moment and then said,. "Everyone? Everywhere?"

I nodded, but I couldn't meet his eyes.

"You're ambitious at least. That kind of power would be Heroic or Legendary. The fastest road to those is to bathe in oceans of blood. Classic story. Idealist finds out he needs money to make real change. Learns all the tricks, but he'll only use them to do good. Eventually. The mansion and servants are just to keep up appearances. Necessary."

"That almost never ends well in fiction," I said, but I got the concept.

"It almost never ended well in real life either." Then he shrugged. "Made a lot of people rich though."

"I know I can't solve everything at once, and I know it will take time. Any real change will probably take generations. I'm okay with that. I'm a teacher, remember? We know how to play the long game."

"If you want to play the long game and you're not worried about getting credit, then why not choose the Class that keeps you alive to do the work?

Nothing says that you can't also teach. This is a Dungeon World. It's just too dangerous not to have a Combat Class. And it's not like the Class we have in mind for you isn't about protecting people."

He had a point, but his way ignored the streams and rivers of blood that even a tankish path to Leveling required. "There has to be a faster way that isn't drenched in blood."

'You want philosophy? From me? Really?"

I just waited, curious as to what he would say.

"You know what? Why not? I need a new drinking buddy." He pulled out two shot glasses and filled them with some kind of liquor and then he was pulling out frosted mugs and filling them with cold and frothy cream soda.

He picked up one of the shot glasses and motioned for me to take mine.

I picked it up and downed it with him in a shot. I'd braced myself for whiskey or something utterly foul, so I was delighted when it turned out to be sweet. "Damn," I said. "That's really good."

We both picked up our mugs and I clinked mine with his when he offered. Cold and fresh, it was incredible, though it also had a bit of an alcohol taste to it.

"What's this?" I asked him.

"It's called Not Your Father's Cream Soda."

"It's good," I said. "Smooth."

He laughed. "Did you hear that in a movie?"

I hesitated for a second. "Yes I did, but it's still true."

He shook his head, rolled his eyes, and sighed. "So, philosophy. Your premise is that there has to be a faster way to make things better and help everyone. Why?"

"What do you mean?"

"Where's your evidence? What possible reason could you have to believe that must be true?"

"It's just a moral sense. It feels true. Oh, and I did get this." I passed him my Quest to find a better way.

"Imagine a situation. You have a Skill to stop blood loss in a large area. Three people next to you are bleeding to death and six thousand people on the other side of a cliff are also bleeding to death. You have a strong feeling that you should be able to fly and a Quest that mocks you because of it. All other evidence says you'll die if you try it and all the others will die as well. Do you jump and hope for the best or save the three you know that you can save?"

I mumbled a reply.

"What was that?"

"I'd quickly try to fly without jumping off first, and if I could manage that, I'd carry as many of the three as I could with me while I flew to the other side."

"Then you have your answer. Try to find a way without wasting your Class on it. Then take the Class that will help you save the people around you. Kaldian Shield Warder is a Prestige Class, by the way, so you'll get extra Attribute points to help you make up for all of this." He waved at my body.

"I notice that your answer happens to get you the exact result that benefits you."

"I noticed that too," he said with a half-grin. "To be fair, what I wanted was to save lives."

"I would have said what you wanted was to keep your people together and build up your forces."

"Tomayto, tomahto. The lives still get saved, regardless of my motivation." He pulled out a long cigar and asked, "Do you mind?"

I recoiled as if struck.

He scowled in disgust. "Another one." Then the Commander smiled with excitement. "I'll try Gerri. They at least smoke weed. Get out!"

I started to leave but hesitated. I pulled out the necklace he'd given me.

He laughed when he saw it. "I'd forgotten about that."

"What does it stand for?"

"Your shield-bot, Pavise, told me about your Mr. Rogers necklace. I figured if that's the way you learn best, I might as well help a brother out." He got a distant look in his eyes. I thought at first he was checking his interface but it must have just been his memories. "Mom used to have one of the WWJD ones. She really loved the damned thing."

"Did she—"

"No," he said. "But not the System. Cancer. Some things were shit before the System ever came."

"Yeah. I love life and the world, but it's not the way it should be. The System too. It brought a lot of wonders with it, but it wasn't worth the price."

"No, it was not," he agreed, and he looked haunted.

It made me want to give the man a hug. He looked like he could use a lot of them. But he also looked like he would break me in half if I tried, so I did my best to give him a reassuring smile.

I startled and almost screamed as he slapped his own face with his metal hand. Hard. His expression regained its ordinary intense focus. "We were talking about your necklace."

I decided that we all had our own ways of dealing with trauma and let him change the subject.

"What does it stand for?" I repeated.

He pointed at the side that said DMTNS. "Dead Men Teach No Students."

I closed my eyes and pinched where my glasses used to sit. I took a deep breath and let it out before turning the tag over. It read DSLNL. It didn't take me long, with the new information, to figure this one out. "Dead Students Learn No Lessons?"

He nodded, and I blanched. Kaldian Shield Warder was sounding pretty good right about now. Lee looked just a little smug.

"Either way, get your ass to bed. Tomorrow, you start grinding levels. Take it from a man who knows and get some sleep while you still can."

I thanked him and wandered back to my room, lost in my thoughts and oblivious to my surroundings. He was right, of course, but sleep was elusive.

I'd wanted to be a teacher for *nearly* as long as I could remember. But there had been a time when I was very young when I'd had a different dream. Back before I'd failed to protect my parents when our car was destroyed, before I'd moved in with Nana and learned to share her love of old educational shows, I'd wanted more than anything to be a superhero. Most of the boys my age did.

While most of my young friends had wanted to fly, toss around cars, or shoot lasers from their eyes, I'd had a different favorite power. The heroes I dreamed of being were the ones like Superman, Colossus, Thing, and the Hulk. The ones who could stand between the innocent and the terrors of the world and make the evil stop. Nothing had embodied that more to me than bullets bouncing off the hero's mighty chests.

For a moment during the attack on the ship, when I'd stood between danger and the children, a spark of that old dream had come alive in me. The idea was silly, I knew. It had been Pavise's shield that had stopped the attack that day, not any power of mine.

But Green Lantern had his ring, didn't he? Iron Man had his suit.

Protector of Children, the System had called me. Could its strange power make that Title true?

With a shield of force, I saved Kek, in my dreams.

Chapter 51

Caleb

The next couple weeks were my own personal version of hell. The fighting and killing was as nonstop as a dedicated group of well-organized militants could make it. When we weren't fighting, we were resting or trying desperately to get ourselves less filthy. Every day, we were hot, sweaty, and covered in blood and other things I didn't want to think about.

Randy was the exception. He was as Zen as a Buddhist monk when it came to filth. He'd wipe blood off of his gloves on the grass, then use them to eat jerky. Then he'd clean his weapons with the same meticulous obsession the rest of us used for everything else, though with a lot more success. His weapons were immaculate. We were disgusting.

A couple hours of sleep each night after what passed for a bath, and catnaps as they drove us to the monsters or the monsters to us, was the majority of our downtime.

The worst part for me had been when I'd passed Aul on the way back from a particularly rewarding "hunting" trip. The red slash on her chest reminded me that what we were doing was almost indistinguishable from what the Voloids had come here to do. "Levels and Loot," the memories of my own voice haunted me, followed by the echoes of Aul's, "Caleb good and bad."

Neither of us were wrong. I'd made my choice, but exhausted as I was, it didn't stop me from tossing and turning for most of that night, and several afterward.

Not even two weeks later, we'd all leveled three or four more times. Pay Attention hadn't evolved the way Topher had planned, a fact that he swore about every day. That would never change, because both Topher and Pavise had told me that a non-combat Skill I'd used mostly for Teaching was unlikely to change into a taunt. Topher had been trying to use it as a desperate hail-Mary attempt.

I'd made a different choice, dumping those points into Class Trip. None of my Skills had failed me more, but none of them had as much potential. And somehow, Topher didn't know about it. I suspected that his Basic Trainer Class was based on military Basic Training, rather than training Basic Classes.

He seemed to primarily be a Combat Specialist. When it came time to review my Skills, he'd just asked Pavise if I had Skills that we might subvert for combat. Pavise had gone all in on helping him. They'd bypassed me completely, even though I'd been right there in front of them.

I'd ignored their Skill plan as thoroughly, so I had no room to judge. Class Trip had evolved at level 6. Maybe the System felt sorry for me that I'd never had a chance to use it.

Class Trip – E (Level 6)

Group teleportation Skill

Transports a Teacher, students, and officially recognized chaperones to a location that the Teacher has previously occupied or thoroughly researched. This Skill has evolved to override a single restriction for all participants. This cannot affect max distance or Mana Cost.

Max distance 100 miles + 25 miles per level.

Cost: 200 Mana + 25 for each student or chaperone beyond the first.

I wanted to put more points into Universal Translator, but our situation was too urgent. From this point forward, my points would go to Demonstration.

I had no regrets. Sooner or later, the Humanist would come for us, or Lee's goals would oppose my own. When either of those things inevitably happened, my new and improved Class Trip was my last best hope for the kids.

***

Our group had gotten comfortable enough working together that we'd let ourselves get overconfident and underestimated a pair of what had looked like easy monsters. They were a mix between the classic Swamp Thing and old TV stereotypes about the Appalachian people. We'd assumed they would be easy pickings for ranged attacks, but we learned quickly that they had skills that could turn the swamp against us.

Pavise had info-dumped his conclusions about the situation into my head in a disorienting blur that would have gotten us all killed if he hadn't "cheated" and thrown up one of his blue energy shields while I processed it all.

Cold terror had shot through me as he'd shown me the most likely methods they would use to kill us all. I'd yelled to everyone, "Retreat and kite them. We have to get them out of the swamp."

We'd never have managed it if not for our extensive training in this exact environment. As it was, by the time we'd hacked and stumbled our way free, my muscles were trembling and my breath was outrunning me. Every now and then, Penny cursed from behind me. Her normally perfect diction was as slurred as my nana's guests during happy hour.

Slowing down and damaging our pursuers had cost most of our Mana and a good chunk of our Health. I'd hoped they'd stop following us when we hit dry land, but no such luck. At least they were more injured than we were from our ongoing ranged attacks. Without Mana to charge said attacks, however, we were barely harming them now, and they were recovering faster than we could hurt them.

Their inexorable shambling gait threatened to break my will. I didn't dare to stop and check on the others but decided to say something to encourage them and me. Somebody beat me to it.

"It's okay, guys," Randy said, "We trained for this. Keep your heads in the game."

It helped, at least a little.

Then something unexpected happened. Both monsters turned to focus their attention on Randy, and there was a crude cunning in their eyes. They sped up, but thankfully, even rushing they were just too slow, and we had enough open space behind us to figure out some sort of plan, or to turn and run if it came to that.

That was when both monsters activated some kind of Skill and raced toward the Shotgunner.

Stupid, stupid, stupid. Never assume.

Pavise was running on fumes, but he had enough power for a few carefully placed shields. I crafted a thin bar of force at chest level.

"Up," Pavise announced through our broadcast.

The monsters slammed into the barrier with a pair of thuds and loud groans, cracking it with their strength. I'd already given the order to dispel it, and it vanished just as Randy's shotgun fired with a blast that hit one of them dead center and even managed some damage to the second. He was so used to our timing at this point that he didn't really need Pavise's announcements anymore.

I raised a moderate-sized barrier to block the path of the one on the left as Randy stepped back. Evie's job was to set the spear for the second, if it rushed us, or to lunge forward and drive it deep into the monster if it hung back. She'd gotten great with the spear, having long since mastered the staff, but the stronger looking brutes still triggered her.

I could relate.

She hesitated when it mattered most, took a half-step back, and jabbed tentatively. Her technique was perfect for a defensive strike, but the creature easily avoided it and returned its attention to the Shotgunner.

Because of all this, when Pavise was supposed to step forward and Randy and Evelyn back and to the sides, Randy got snagged by a root vine from the body of one of the gnarled green monsters. It kept him in front of them, blocking Pavise and giving both of the monsters a chance to attack him while Randy couldn't dodge.

No, no, no. Come on. Desperate for my mental math to be wrong, I tried to put up just one more shield to buy us time. No such luck. Unlike in the movies, caring more didn't change the outcome.

A pair of thorn-spiked fists slammed into Randy, staggering him. The vines held him up and prevented him from getting knocked back. When they pulled back their fists to strike again, I saw that some of the thorns had been flattened on his armor, but others were gone, clearly buried inside Randy.

The attacker who hadn't used the vine was much closer to death than the other one. I hesitated longer than I should have, feeling the ick sensation that comes with moral compromise. I knew what had to be done, but I hated becoming the person who could do it.

"Finish off the one most injured," I said, then I triggered my Demonstration Skill. It felt like a betrayal of my Class, but sometimes all of your options are bad.

I used the last dregs of Pavise's power to protect Randy with a protective field as the others opened fire, using whatever regeneration Mana they had, to unload on the single target. We took it down with shotgun blasts, gunfire, and poisoned needles.

Once we'd dropped the first, the second would have been a forgone conclusion, if Randy's Health weren't dropping from whatever the Brute's attack had left behind inside him.

Evie managed to dodge-tank it with her spear while Pavise and I slowly worked down its Health. Any time the creature turned away to try to attack us, a fierce thrust from her helped it remember the greater source of danger. All of us together were no real threat, but we ground it down.

At the same time, Randy, paler than ever and grim-faced, was cutting thorns and vines out of his body with a dagger, while Penny fought with her scanner, potions, salves, and bandages to keep him alive while he did it.

When they'd finished treating his wounds, Randy didn't bother to dress. Shirtless and bandaged, he unloaded all of his recovered Mana into a couple of close-range slug shots to the Brute, finishing it off.

As everyone started to recover and I let out a long sigh of relief, Randy rushed over and shoved Evelyn hard, his face a mask of rage somewhere between a child's tantrum and an adult's murderous fury.

The attack completely blindsided her. She fell back, tripped, and landed hard on her ass and then her back. She kipped up in a flash and dashed toward him, spear thrusting for his throat.

I tried to have Pavise throw up a shield, but he had nothing left.

Randy didn't back down, attack, or attempt to dodge as she stopped the blade just as it pricked his neck. His whole body shook, and I watched him swallow one hate-filled rant after another—whether because he'd been raised in the Midwest and she was a woman or because he'd been trained to control such outbursts in the HLF, I didn't know.

He eventually seemed to give up trying to put his thoughts into words and just tore the bandages from his chest, exposing the seeping, gel-covered wounds and the acid-burned flesh where Penny had helped burn the plants away. Evie's furious expression crumbled into a tear-filled sorrow as she looked away. I suspected that the demonstration had affected her more than a verbal assault ever would have. Her mistake was understandable, after everything that she'd been through, but it had nearly cost the Shotgunner his life.

"I'm sorry," she finally said.

I hung my head in shame as well. She hadn't been the only one who'd hesitated, and she'd had a better reason with the monsters right up close.

"Not good enough," he finally said. "Be better or quit." Then his expression softened as her tears finally reached past his anger. "I'm sorry. I know you've been through a lot. It's not your fault if you can't move past it, but—"

"I can do this." She wiped away the tears and her expression hardened. The spirit that had made her an Olympic champion shone clear on her face. I vowed to try to emulate that fierce dedication.

"I believe you," he said and gave her a strained smile. "Don't let it get us killed."

Chapter 52

Caleb

As we continued our circuit toward the base, Evie went on, psyching herself up. "I just need one enemy. A big one. Really strong. Let me confront it and take it out myself with as little support as possible. I'm used to my cybernetics now. They aren't perfect, but I can make it work." She didn't sound confident, but I had no doubt she'd get her game face on when the time came.

While Penny had evaluated and treated the others, I'd used the time to use my Repair Skill on Pavise and even took off my armor to switch his old boost for the new one I'd been charging. I also took the opportunity to switch my own boost from my underarmor to my armor, because that way I could swap it out for Pavise's if things got desperate again.

We'd made it about halfway back and regenerated around forty percent of our Mana before we found something interesting. A clearing we often passed was the usual haunt of a giant monster called a Vutin. It looked enough like a skunk that none of us had been willing to risk fighting it. The plan had been to bring in high-range snipers with the System equivalent of gas masks and hope for the best.

Apparently, we'd been worried for nothing because there was none of the trademark sulfuric stink we'd been afraid of. Instead, we found the monster dead and half eaten, and a truly massive beast was sleeping under one of the overgrown evergreens nearby. It was about twice the size of the bear that had eaten me, with the same ursine body but with a magnificent mane of gray-brown feathers. Filled with geek nostalgia, I inspected the owlbear and took a few quiet steps backward.

Great Horned Owl-Bear (Level 2 – Advanced)
??

I checked and felt more than a little disappointed when I confirmed that the "horns" on this monster were the same type of feather tufts as a usual horned owl.

Awe filled me as I saw one of my favorite D&D monsters come to life. But fear followed close behind because it's form was so much like that of my recent nightmares. Apparently, the others had inspected the creature as well because Evie whispered, "No," followed by the increasingly wise, "hell no."

Randy brushed his shotgun with his hand, eyes eager as he stared at the beast. Then he looked at our surroundings and the position of the sun and seemed to make up his mind. "I think if we were fresh and it were daytime, I'd say it would be a good challenge for us. As things stand, I don't think we should risk it."

We all agreed and worked on our stealth skills as we noped right out of the area.

We'd only made it about half a mile when Captain Hark Jackness, Penny's System Companion, took turns tripping us until we all stopped walking. Then he raised his tail and sauntered imperiously into the woods, pausing casually to give himself a bath until we got the message and followed him.

"I'm not entirely comfortable with this," Pavise said as we brushed aside branches and stepped over roots and rocks. "The others will not know where we have gone, and the captain has not explained the reason for this detour."

"Cats used to be revered in ancient Egypt," Penny said.

"What does that have to do with following an under-Leveled Spirit Companion through the woods?"

Hark fixed Pavise with a predatory feline glare.

"Cats aren't in the habit of having to explain themselves to lesser mortals," Penny continued.

"That is not a cat. He is a Spirit Companion. I assure you that he is fully capable of speech."

The captain lifted and turned his head imperiously to signal his disdain, then continued on his way as if everyone would follow as a matter of course.

We did just that, eventually coming to a huge American elm tree. Its bright green leaves formed a huge canopy that Hark led us under. There, lying on the ground in the lattice of light and shadows, was a tall thin man with bulging eyes, swollen lips, and bluish-black veins.

"Poison," Penny said. "Give me a minute to stabilize him, then we need to get him to Gerri, fast." She pulled her scanner from a satchel at her waist and scanned the man quickly. "It's bad. I'm not sure he's going to make it, no matter what I do. Give me some space and keep watch. We need to get him out of here as quickly as possible."

"Not to be heartless," Randy said, "but we need to get us out of here. Whatever did this to him could come back."

"It's almost certainly dead, or he would be," she replied.

"I don't like that *almost*," Randy snapped. "And there could be more of them."

"Then you'd better shut up and let me work." She tried to force a pill down the man's throat and failed entirely.

I rushed over to help. In the end, she had me hold his mouth open while she moved aside his tongue and swollen throat with a plastic-and-metal device I didn't recognize. It looked something like that thing some women used to use for their eyelashes.

With that still in place, she opened a vial and poured it down his throat. Her expression was halfway between professional and frantic at this point and his body was starting to thrash.

"Hold him down," Penny told me.

I tried and failed completely. Even with my suit and my slightly increased Strength stat, he was just too strong.

Pavise joined me at that point and we failed together. "I'm sorry, sir. I could probably hold him in place with my weight, but I am concerned that it might finish what the monster started."

"Any idea what kind of monster…" I cut myself off. What was I thinking? "We need someone stronger," I half-yelled.

Evie came running over. It took all she had, and it was obvious even she would have failed if he were well enough to really fight back.

Penny took an oversized syringe filled with a metallic silvery liquid and prepared to inject it into the man's arm. Then she thought better of it and tried three or four more places before she just hauled her arm back and jabbed it into the man's chest.

I tried to inspect him, but he was blocked.

"He's stable, maybe," she hedged. "We need to go."

"Move!" Randy was trying to be commanding. He'd get there with time. For now, he sounded desperate.

The sight of this man had clearly terrified the Shotgunner. Did he have his own trauma to wrestle with? Unfortunately, the odds were good. Maybe I could use that shared reality to help build a bridge—

"I said move!"

Oh, right. I got moving, but I didn't make it far before I noticed that Penny had activated a Skill that summoned a floating cot with tubes, wires, and mini bellows. I helped her load the injured stranger onto it, thankful I had armor between his skin and mine, just in case. The floating platform strapped him down and followed us as we ran.

Nice Skill.

I was improving, but every member of the group could run faster and farther than I could. They'd learned to follow my pace over the last few weeks. Now, they would be leaving me in the dust if I wasn't pushing myself beyond my new limits. I was starting to lose my breath again and my Stamina was dropping fast. We had been explicitly ordered, several times, not to do exactly this because it could get us all killed.

On the other hand, we had a life to save. If we didn't get him to the ship in time, he might still die. I doubted this, since he had still been alive when we found him, we'd delayed his poison, and we could always heal him more if it came to that. Still, better to err on the side of...

I couldn't maintain the pace. If they wanted to race ahead, they'd be doing it without me.

That would be fine for them. It might not be fine for me. But how could I value risk to my life over risk to his, especially now that the children might be safe even if I died? My team would also be without Pavise, however, and in this place, with night falling, that might get them all killed. Frankly, even letting their own Stamina drop too low could get them killed.

"Stop," I yelled.

They didn't hear me or didn't listen. It was hard to be loud when I couldn't manage a deep breath. I sent a message to Pavise with a mental nudge as my body collapsed on the ground.

"Please wait," Pavise said. "Stop please. You are leaving my master behind."

Nothing. I'd think they'd lost their earpieces, but two of them had cybernetics. My already tight chest constricted torturously as I panicked. Why couldn't they hear us?

None of them had noticed me stopping either. Who knew when they would?

I wasn't quite as powerless in this world as I had been, however, even if the power wasn't truly mine.

Our words didn't stop them. A blue bar of force in their path, on the other hand, worked great.

At least they all had the decency to look concerned and ashamed as they made their way back to me. Well, everyone but Captain Hark. I may have been reading my own inadequacies into his reaction, but I swore he looked judgmental and amused. Cats.

I was still sitting on the road, looking up at the others, or I probably would have missed the giant shadow that passed by a moment before a massive winged form dove down and snatched Evie like an eagle with a mouse.

No, not an eagle. An owl. Oh. Oh no.

I couldn't breathe as terror tried to shut down my mind. I refused to let it.

I thought about calling out to Pavise for help. But what could he do? Nothing but shields, and the owlbear wasn't moving forward. Its massive wings were flapping furiously, buffeting us with wind as it was gaining altitude.

It took me half a precious second to remember Pavise could make horizontal shields. I'd owe Topher thanks, if not an apology. He'd forced me to defend the group against falling arrows. Odds were it would work the other way. I willed Pavise to create a horizontal sheet of blue force right above the creature.

I got nothing but a jolt of pain in my forehead for my trouble.

Evie was twisting and striking, but the creature was just too strong. Her struggles did seem to slow down its ascent.

Thunder sounded down the path from me as Randy opened fire. The owlbear didn't seem to notice.

"Pavise, put up a…" My mind blanked on how to explain. I yelled the first word I thought of when one finally came to me. "Lid!"

A horizontal sheet of blue power appeared just above the creature's head.

The owlbear slammed into the barrier, shattering it, but losing momentum in the process.

Frantic, I threw my hands toward the monster like a crazed wizard, willing Pavise to generate another shield. It sprang into being, stopping the creature's progress.

The owlbear shrieked in rage, and I howled in triumph as it dropped Evie. Then my exhilaration plummeted like a roller coaster and took my breath with it as the creature dropped to the ground after Evie, clearly intending to crush her beneath its massive frame.

I lagged. Things were just happening too fast. And with my cybernetics on the fritz, I didn't have Pavise to slow them down.

A third shield, this one at an angle in an attempt to minimize the owlbear's destructive force and dump it away from her, met its fall. Thank God for Pavise. Apparently, he was no longer pretending that I was essential. Whatever game he was playing, I was glad he wouldn't take the thing too far.

Damn it, my mind was wandering again. Neither Pav nor I were quick enough when this unfortunately clever opponent used the barrier I'd intended as protection as a launching off point to pounce at Randy.

Why was it always Randy?

Apparently, he'd noticed the same trend. The enormous monster was about to smash into him when he activated what I thought of as his trademark Stopping Power Skill. Experience had shown me that it would certainly be no match for this creature's monstrous momentum.

My eyes went as wide as the owlbear's when Randy's shotgun blast launched the man backward, well out of the reach of its taloned paws and snapping beak.

A new Skill, and a damn good one.

I inched closer, careful to keep my distance while still keeping the owlbear in range. Pavise moved to stand in front of me.

Flying owlbears. Damn. I felt betrayed. D&D had lied to me. *No, stop it. Focus. You've already let yourself get… no. Think.* Owlbear. Owl. Bear. Big. Strong. Fast. Bears were faster than they should be. Owls. Wings. Fly. Talons.

Enraged, the owlbear used its wings to buffet up a blinding cloud of dirt, leaves, and debris. I had to turn away. When it had finally settled down, I looked to find the monster's second leaping pounce at Randy. His eyes were still covered and his head was turned away.

After breaking through Pavise's barrier, the owlbear smashed the Shotgunner to the ground with enough force that it shook me where I stood. It rent strips of flesh and armor off him as if they were both the same.

Randy screamed and thrashed.

Evie was dashing toward the monster, and she looked to be readying to leap into a truly magnificent backstab into a vulnerable location like its spine or its neck. There was something there. *Neck? Owl? Oh! No, no, no.*

"Evie, stop!"

I tried to throw up a shield where I knew her attack would meet a horrifying surprise, but unlike in the movies, Evelyn heard me, listened, and abandoned her plan. She dove to the side and threw herself into a roll.

Score one for the teacher that loves animals, I thought, as the owlbear's head whipped around in a full one-eighty that would have looked right on a demon-possessed child. It shrieked in fury at the prey that had escaped it yet again.

We were doing amazing, but we were also in a lot of trouble. It was faster than us. Stronger than us. It could fly. We'd barely hurt it.

"Fubar, sir?" Pavise said.

It was his plan that I'd named from a *Tango and Cash* quote. He wanted us to abandon him. He'd stall the enemy. We'd run, drop scent grenades, and find places to hide and deploy our woodland stealth pods.

"Give me time, buddy."

"There's no other way, sir."

"Give me time," I demanded. *"As much as you can."*

Something fizzled in my head, a burning zing as time slowed by a little better than half. Pavise was trying to talk, but it was like the old jokes about driving through a tunnel. We were breaking my implant, possibly for good. Run or fight. Owl. Dark vision. Footsteps. It would find us. Woods, dense cover. Maybe. Fight. We could do this. Only one monster. Tank, 2 DPS. Healer. Healerish. Two and a half DPS. Maybe 2.75 with me. Could we do this. Yes.

In my mind, I saw memories of Evie stepping back, timid.

Chain. Weakest link. We'd break if she did. Her face. Fierce determination.

"I trust you," Randy had said. "Don't let it get us killed."

He'd made his choice. I made mine.

"We fight," I told Pavise, though my body was shaking. I rose to my feet, fired up my turret, and drew my blaster. "Regroup!" I shouted, the way I'd learned to do when working with children at recess.

They listened.

It took two force walls, a dash skill from Randy, and a ludicrous somersault-backflip combo from Evie, but we managed it.

Pavise stood before the beast, shoulder turret firing steadily, looking undersized and thoroughly outmatched. Behind him, Evie stood ready with her spear, ready to punish the owlbear any time it dared to attack. Randy and I stood behind her to either side, firing our weapons with his impressive and my nearly adequate skill. Ozone and gunpowder smells from our weapons combined with the pungent, musty smell of the owlbear. Behind us all was Penny with her toxic dart gun. Like me, her attacks probably helped a little.

But she was ready to heal if we needed her.

"Evie, I'm slapping your back," I said as I realized we were wasting the patch I'd been charging. "Expect a bit of a boost. Get used to it before—"

"Got it," she cut me off, and she seemed the slightest bit faster. I suspected it was half the boost and half psychosomatic, but I'd take anything we could get right now.

We'd been well trained, if not for long, and we worked together well.

It wasn't enough.

Most of us had Non-Combat Classes. We were under-Leveled. And the difference between Basic and Advanced was more than the Level difference would imply.

The owlbear was faster than something its size had any right to be. If I put up a force wall, I could stop its onslaught. But when I tried to efficiently block its attacks, I failed almost as often as I succeeded, and failing had consequences. Sparks flew to the sound of the rending screech of metal on metal, the smells of oil and other unmentionable fluids as Pavise started to come apart before my eyes. Thunderous paws slammed into the shield-bot, leaving deep dents in his metal shell.

Would my Skill even be able to help with repairs of this level? Could Penny's parents? We needed Pavise. *I need him.* He couldn't take this kind of punishment. It was too much.

I had Pavise put up a force barrier and hold it in place to give the shield-bot a moment to rest. It also gave me time to activate my Minor Repair Skill. It popped out a small dent and repaired a slash in an exposed black tube.

Penny one-upped me with a repair gel that closed some leaks and fixed one of the main dents.

We'd unloaded a lot of Mana and special attacks into the creature at that point. It was seriously hurt. But Pavise would run out of energy long before the beast ran out of Health.

Had I gotten all of us killed?

"Hold the wall," Randy yelled. "Grenades."

I flinched, and my hip ached. I'd forgotten about grenades.

Everyone reached down to their belts except Randy, who pulled one from thin air, and Penny, who yanked one out of her satchel.

I'd had nightmares about grenades lately, and it wasn't the ones about how I'd blown myself up and possibly killed Kek, though those would likely haunt me forever. These nightmares were me playing softball in high school, clumsy, weak, and not reliable to throw in the direction I wanted, rather than the distance. Except instead of softballs, I was throwing grenades. They landed in the stands and blew up Voloids and my old human students.

Focus. They need you. I wasn't the same person anymore.

The monster shrieked. I felt the sound wash over me as much as I heard it.

I forced myself not to run. Not to cower. As the others threw their grenades, I pulled back my arm and let it fly. My muscles were too tense. My aim was terrible. The weapon slammed into the force field and bounced right back at us.

I tried to make a shield as I heard the explosions, but Pavise's power was blocking the monster. I braced for pain, for screams, as my nightmare came to life.

But the pain didn't come, at least for me. A new kind of shriek, filled with pain and rage, filled the night, but there were no screams. *What the hell?*

"Activate and throw, sir. Not just throw."

Oh, right. I'd never been so embarrassed and so relieved at the same time.

I resumed firing. Charging batteries had kept my Mana low, so I used a few Hunter's Strikes here and there, but mostly I worked with Pavise.

My eyes flitted to his energy bar and found it hitting red. How? The grenades. They'd hurt the monster but burned through the shield in equal measure. An easy mistake. It might get all of us killed.

"We're out of shields," I said. "Pavise can't take much more of this."

"I apologize," Pavise said. "Locomotion is severely impaired and my systems are failing."

I dropped the last of my Mana on a quick repair that barely helped.

"I've got this," Evelyn said. She let her spear fall to the ground and summoned her Acrobat's staff.

The System had changed us all. It had given us Skills. But Evie had Skills backed by skills and tremendous personal talent, honed by decades of blood, sweat, and triumph.

She took over for Pavise and she was marvelous.

With her new stats, she was something superhuman. My mouth was dry as she stepped in and dodged the first beak strike by inches. The rearing head, the twist of the body as a wing came to buffet her was dodged by a backbend, then a flip that would have made even the Russian judge give a ten. My heart was beating faster than a dozen locomotives as she struck it again and again, with precise staff attacks from every angle imaginable.

My jaw dropped. Here was my first childhood crush, Cheetara, brought to life right in front of me. She spun, dashed, twirled, and leapt, always a step ahead of the monster. When it tried to ignore her and focus on the rest of us, she smacked it in the face or jabbed it in its oversized eyes.

As the rest of us fired, its Health trickled down, injuries accumulating all over its body.

The monster reared up, opened its beak wide, and a trumpet of thunder crashed into us, stunning everyone but Pavise. Evelyn screamed in terror, probably expecting to get torn to pieces, but the effect was extremely short-lived and the monster wasn't attempting to use it to kill her. It had unfurled its massive wings and wind buffeted us as it took to the sky.

I tried to block it with a shield of force, but my connection with Pavise failed, or he had no energy left. Or maybe he was just broken. Either way, we could do nothing as the monster rose into the sky.

I saw a glint of madness in Evelyn's eyes as she braced her body in what looked to be a mad leap to launch herself after the owlbear.

"Clear," Randy shouted, making Evie hesitate then frown as she missed her chance.

Echoing clunks, sharp and metallic, followed one by one as Randy switched from shells to slugs. Three shots. Four. Then a final shot that resounded, louder than the previous four combined.

An XP notice flashed on my screen as an Acrobat flew into my arms. My underarmor didn't let me down. I held her in a tight hug as she covered my face with kisses, then tighter as those enthusiastic lips turned serious and passionate as they found mine.

"Headshot," Randy said, sounding very self-satisfied. "Execution Skill on the Slug Tree."

I could not have cared less.

Chapter 53

Caleb

Having finally been reluctantly disentangled from the best moment of my life, I pointed toward the spot where the injured stranger had been. "Where did he go?"

"Hmm?" Penny mumbled. She had some tools and devices, and she was doing something to Pavise. "Oh, crap."

She rushed to where the man had been, then followed the scraped trail the few dozen feet to where he was now a shuddering and trembling mess. The man's skin was gray and blotchy. If it wasn't for the System and Penny's earlier administrations, I was confident he would already be dead.

My heart went out to him. I knew what it was like to be lost and alone in a dangerous place like this, and I didn't wish it on anyone.

Penny motioned for Randy to help her. "In you go," she said as the two of them lifted the man back into his floating cot. "Oh, you're awake. Don't worry, we'll have you back to the ship in no time and we can get you all fixed up. Try to stay calm and keep the straps down tight. They'll keep you safe."

He was shaking his head and mumbling urgently, but his throat and tongue were far too swollen for him to speak. I looked around for hidden dangers. If he was trying to warn us and simply couldn't talk, I wanted to know. I didn't sense anything out of place, and none of the others seemed particularly alarmed, so I stayed quiet and tried to focus as I kept watch.

Penny treated the man again, frowning as his skin tone did not improve. She announced that she'd done what she could, but we needed to go. As soon as we did, however, he started trying to wriggle free from his binding again.

"Do you speak sign language?" I said and signed to him at the same time.

He didn't respond, except to try to break his straps and crawl away.

"Poor guy," Penny said. "Whatever is killing him must be making him paranoid."

"Is it even possible to be paranoid anymore?" I asked her.

"Fair point," Penny replied. "And yes, it's just harder to spot among all the legitimate terror."

I let out a long, sad sigh.

"I'll give him something to calm him down," she said, pulling out a syringe.

"He doesn't look like he wants you to do that." I gestured to where he was shaking his head and flailing his arms weakly.

"He could have gotten himself killed. If he wants to do that when he's well, that's up to him. But when he's impaired to the point of near death and non-sensibility, I'll make the call."

She gave him the shot as I was trying to figure out the best way to test if he could write.

Whatever she gave him didn't knock him unconscious, but it mellowed him out. I figured it was probably something that she'd gotten from Gerri. Their medicine had certainly done wonders for me.

We made it back to the ship without any more trouble. I took Pavise and went to find Earl. The man seemed eager to help, but the gleam in his eye made me worried that Pavise was going to find himself unintentionally "upgraded" to some kind of robot version of a steampunk Frankenstein's monster.

I whispered my plan to Pavise and headed off to try to find Penny, the one person I thought might be willing and able to intercede on my shield bot's behalf. By the time I got back, the injured stranger was already a dead husk on the floor of the loading bay and Penny was yelling furiously at Lee.

"You may be in charge here, but that was my patient, and if you have a problem with one of my patients, you don't just go and kill them. You bring the problem to me. I shouldn't have to explain this," she curled her fingers in fury as she ranted.

The commander waited patiently, letting her vent, before he said, "I appreciate your concerns and the help that you and your parents are providing for us." She tried to talk again, but he raised his finger and looked at her sternly. "You had a chance to speak your piece. That's much more than most would ever get. Now, it's time for you to listen. I knew the man you're calling your patient from the HLF. Tomlinson. He was part of a two-man Spy team. Looks like we got lucky and that bear-snake monster thing ate his partner and sent this asshole running.

That would explain the man's odd behavior. It probably explained our comm systems shutting down as well. Then I had to scold myself for getting paranoid as I wondered if the man had somehow summoned the owlbear so that he could escape.

Lee was still talking. "If I'd let him recover enough to use his abilities, he would have reported back everything he'd learned. I can only hope that he didn't manage to do just that, because we're counting on discretion as much as distraction to"—he stressed each of the following words—"*save your son.*"

She cursed under her breath. "You're right. I'm sorry. I didn't know."

I wasn't sure that he was right. She was certainly biased. But so was I, I decided. It was vital that the children were kept safe. We couldn't afford to have spies reporting on us. Still, what if he had been a defector, rather than a spy?

I found myself relieved to have been spared the decision, and then guilty for having felt relieved.

"I understand," the Commander told Penny. "But I want to make it clear that if you ever call me out in front of my people again, I'll still help save your son, but I'll also throw you in the brig and leave you there, no matter who your parents are. Are we clear?"

"Yes, sir," she said.

"Glad we got that cleared up. Now if you'll excuse me, I've got a meeting."

Lee went over to talk to Gerri, who had apparently been standing behind the others since I arrived. Everyone else left the room, even Evelyn.

Before Evie left, she gave me a sultry smile and said, "I'll go grab us some food. You're gonna need your strength." A wicked grin and a delightful saunter later, and she was gone.

Lee looked at her and then at me. He was shaking his head as he walked away.

He wasn't wrong.

Once the Commander was out of the room, Gerri walked up to me and said, "This is none of my business, but I know that you've been stuck here. You have enough of a reputation that I want to warn you about something, just in case."

"You already warned me."

They looked alarmed and made the "will you shut up" face. "Not that," they whispered. They resumed speaking normally. "You weren't around for all of the... let's call them surprises that the System has saddled us with."

"Oh?"

"Birth control," they said. "It's not as reliable anymore. Birth rates are way up. The... well..." They fidgeted a bit, hands in their pockets. Their mouth made a small frown. "The other solution still works. But you being you, I thought that maybe… look, I thought you'd want to know. That's all."

It took me just a moment to puzzle out what they were saying, then I felt my expression turn from overjoyed to somber. "Thank you for letting me know."

They nodded and left. I wandered slowly to my room, lost in thought.

When Evie came to my room, she found me sketching a picture of her fighting the owlbear. She smiled at the sight of her jabbing it in the eye with her staff. She ate quietly while I drew.

When I'd finished and set down my charcoal and reached for my food, she doffed her top, sprawled backward on the bed, and said, "Draw me like one of your French girls."

"I haven't thought about *Titanic* in a long time. I love the songs." Then I dropped my pizza back onto the plate and retrieved my charcoal.

"Everybody loves the songs." Then she took the charcoal from my hand. "Don't get any ideas. Eat your food."

"It was your idea," I said, but I ate my food in relative silence.

When I'd finished, we looked at each other awkwardly for a long moment, hesitating for one reason or another. Then we both started talking at the same time, and even the same words. "I need to talk—"

We laughed and it broke some of the tension.

"Sorry," I said. "You first."

"Don't apologize," she said. "You didn't do anything wrong. And I was just going to say that I'm not sure if you're looking to have fun or maybe something more." She got a shy, sweet look on her face and bit her lip. "I get the impression that you're a something more kind of a guy, and I've got a concern—well, more of an ultimatum really, if there's going to be any real chance of us ever making that happen."

"I'm listening. What do you need from me?"

She sat staring at me in stunned silence for about a minute and a half. "That may be the single sexiest thing that anyone has ever said to me." She shook her head to clear it. "Okay, look, this is going to sound weird, but I know me, and even with the System, I'm going to get older or I'm going to get even more injured and eventually I'm going to look worse. Be worse. Or I'm going to have an awful hair day, or I'll lose my temper and be a total bitch for a while, and you're going to want to be supportive and reassuring, because..." She waved in my general direction as if that explained everything.

I supposed it did.

She continued, "Look, I'm sorry, but I'm going to need you to be able to lie or skirt the truth. At the very least, you'll have to learn to not tell me every little thought that goes on in your head. So if we're going to have any real chance of this working, I'm going to need you to lie to me."

"Excuse me?"

"Deceive me. Trick me. Break your power. Is that clear enough?"

"Oh, that," I said.

"Yeah that."

"I thought you enjoyed that."

She grimaced. "I adore it. And it's going to break my heart a little when it goes away. But it's necessary."

"I think you may be underestimating how much—"

"Please don't explain. Just trust me and do what I'm asking. Everything changes."

"No, it doesn't," I lied, smiling. "Nothing ever changes."

"What the hell are you talking about, of course it... oh!" She beamed. "Thank you."

"You're welcome. I never want to have any kind of power over anyone that they're not comfortable with."

She inspected my face. "You're still looking at me like that?"

"Like what?"

"The thing with the sincerity and the adoring me and the eyes."

"Is that going to be a problem? Because I'm not sure that I can fix that, ultimatum or not."

She blushed and looked away, then looked back with an expression much the same as how she described mine. "No. That isn't going to be a problem, though I am going to have to teach you how to lie."

"This may be the strangest conversation I've ever had, and I've lived with hive-minded alien children for the last two years."

She cupped my cheek. "I'm not sure how a man like you even exists in a world like this, but I'm really glad that you do."

"Right back at you. Except the man part. And the not sure part." I matched her sweet gesture and held her cheek in my hand. "It's obvious how you managed to survive when so many others didn't. You're amazing, and I'm glad you're here."

Her eyes filled with joy, then hunger. She leaned in, eyes fixed on mine, that way people get when they desperately want their bodies to be as close as bodies can be so that something that's deeper, whatever you want to call it, could get even closer than that.

I wanted that too, desperately, but I had my own ultimatum, as much as I wished that I didn't.

It was one of the hardest things I'd ever done, but I held up a finger between us. "My turn."

Her pout was adorable, but she waved airily for me to continue. I looked away from her eyes, shy and a bit hesitant. Then I glanced back up quickly.

"That"—I made the same motion she had done earlier to indicate everything about her as a whole, and her state of dress in particular—"is not fair. I think you intentionally ambushed me before your ultimatum."

"All's fair in—" She bit her lip to stop herself from speaking the next obvious word. "I play to win."

"I'm more of a cooperative game theory kind of a guy."

She turned her head with a quizzical expression. "Swinging? Poly? You?"

I face-planted. "No, that's not really my thing, though I'm not judging. I just mean I think we all survive better when we uplift one another and work together."

She raised a skeptical eyebrow.

"Don't worry, I know meritocracy and contests are important too. I'll leave that to you though."

"That's fair. I'm not asking you to change, and I'm glad you feel the same about me. I think we've stalled long enough. What did you want to talk to me about?" She took a long swig from a green glass bottle that may have been beer. I didn't recognize it.

"Babies," I told her.

A few moments later, as I wiped her explosive spit take-off my face, the mystery was solved. It was definitely beer.

"You want babies!"

"No! Well, maybe someday." I grabbed a towel to wipe myself off. "But I'm not trying to do that now. This is not going well. I'm timid because I've lost friends over this issue even before I lost them from the System. People want me to care about women and equality and personal autonomy, and I do. I care a lot."

She nodded.

"But they don't want me to care about what's in the mother's womb. They say it's just a clump of cells, but I can't not think of it as not a baby, because that's either what it is or what it's going to be. I've lost friends on both sides of this issue. People want me to only care about one or the other and I just want to help and to protect people."

"I'm listening," she said back to me. "What do you need from me?"

"That is nice," I said. "Thank you."

She motioned for me to go on.

"I'm falling for you," I said, then corrected myself to be more accurate even though I didn't have to. "No. I've fallen for you. I'm worried that it's going to scare you away, but no matter how I feel about you, I can't do anything that would risk getting you pregnant. I don't believe that we have the power or the resources to protect and provide for a child in this world, even if we did want to have them now. But my ultimatum, if you want to call it that, and I guess it is, is that I can't ever have you get pregnant and then have you intentionally…" I struggled to even say the words.

"I think I might get what you mean, but you're being kind of vague and this is important."

I smiled, but it was a frail thing. "I will give you as much or as little as you want, whenever we both feel like we're ready for the consequences. I just need to know that I'll never have to deal with… with that. It would break me. What's left of me."

She cupped both of my cheeks now and looked deep into my eyes. She got a matter-of-fact look on her face and said, "You're trying to say that you aren't comfortable having sex with me until we're ready to have kids, whatever that means for both of us in a world like this." She smiled wryly. "And you want to know that you can trust me not to terminate the pregnancy if and when we do decide the time is right?"

I nodded.

"Okay," she said. "That's fair. Thank you for talking to me about this in advance, and for taking initiative and responsibility if that's how you feel about it, instead of just dumping it all on me after the fact." She squeezed my hand and held it.

I didn't know how much I'd needed it until she did.

"As for the more practical aspects of this issue…" Her expression was timid, and full of need in a way that mirrored my own inner world, before blooming into a proud and almost wicked smile. "Don't worry about that. I'm *flexible.*"

And then she proved it.

Chapter 54

Lee

I moved aside some tarps so we could sit on the chairs in my new "office." Better than sitting on dust. I'd planned to set up in the Command Deck all along. It just made sense. But it was a work in progress.

"What the hell is going on in here?" Thomas, the surviving twin from the tribe, asked.

He'd helped us a lot and lost more doing it, so I answered him. "Come over here."

I led Thomas and Gerri to the shaft and moved aside the tarp. Then I pulled a survival flashlight from my arsenal and showed them our recent work. Metal rungs led to the heart of the ship. Security mirrors showed the odd alien computer. Some kind of gel orbs.

The closest thing we had to experts could do nothing with it. Earl had just sneered and walked away.

"We have no way to run this thing," I told them. "Needs to be replaced."

Gerri looked like they really wanted to say something, but they held their tongue. Probably for the best. I liked them, but they weren't planning to stay. When the time came, I'd make the call that was best for my people.

"You asked for a meeting?" I said.

"Yes," Gerri answered, "thank you."

"Have you gotten any updates from your people about the tribe?" Thomas asked. The last few weeks had not treated him well. Even with System-enhanced recovery, he seemed more worn and weathered, as if he'd aged several years in as many weeks. He looked less like his late brother now. Even his hair had lost some luster.

"Yeah," I said. *Damn*. I'd hoped to stall them a bit on this point. The longer I could keep Gerri here, the better. I figured the odds were good they'd be gone as soon as they got the news. "I sent the Squad of Combat-Classers and Scouts like we agreed, though I still think the deal was a bit one-sided."

Gerri got to learn all of our recipes. In return, they used that time making product for us from our supplies. Win-win, if not for the extra demands.

"Think what you want," Thomas said. "A deal's a deal."

He was right. Not gonna tell him that when I had to deliver bad news though. Better to get to the point and pull off the bandage quick.

"The place was cleaned out," I said.

They jumped to their feet, eyes wide and bodies tensed. Pulled the bandage off a little too hard.

"There were no signs of combat or struggle," I reassured them. "It looks like they decided to just pull up stakes and leave. Can't blame them with the HLF gunning for them. They covered their tracks better than our people have been able to uncover them. Without the Shop, I doubt we're finding them. But there's still a lot of buildings and stuff there and we're not sure they aren't coming back, so my people are holding down the fort. Since it's just them, I sent a few more to back them up, just in case."

Thomas started to snap at me, but Gerri put a hand on his arm. He hesitated long enough for them to speak instead.

"Thank you. We know it's a risk to divide your people." They turned to Thomas and said, "We appreciate it." It sounded like an order. "I wasn't going to say anything, but we may have some idea what is going on."

Where Thomas had lost ground, Gerri had gained it. They looked more mature, but not older. They were standing straighter and taking charge without it feeling forced.

"Gerri, don't," Thomas said. "It's not his secret. He isn't one of us."

"I'm barely one of us," Gerri said, "as you've all taken pains to remind me."

"It's not like that," he said, but he didn't sound like he'd managed to convince himself.

"It's exactly like that, and it doesn't really matter. We tell him and maybe we can make this work, or we keep it to ourselves and we give up before we start or die trying. You know as well as I do that we can't solve this alone. If you thought we could, we'd already have left."

I wanted to push them to fill me in, but I'd learned in business that shutting your mouth and accepting a yes at the other side's pace was a more workable strategy than intensity and bluster. I could be patient when I had to be.

"Fine," he said. "But if he screws us over, you're the one taking the blame."

"You say that as if I wouldn't be the one scapegoated even if it were all your fault."

He glared at them until they turned away.

"Fine. You're right. My call, my fault." They turned back to me. "You might want to sit down for this."

"I've been sitting this whole time."

"Metaphorically," they said, though they took their own advice and resumed sitting.

"Sure, I've made a bit of time. Mind if I smoke?" I asked as I pulled a stogie from my inventory.

They wrinkled their nose, and my hopes of a drinking buddy to share cigars with died during labor.

"Sure," Thomas said. "It'll give me a chance to practice my water-focused Skills."

"Cute. I get the point." I turned back to Gerri. "Tell me what's going on."

"The two of us had a dream last night."

"The same dream," Thomas chimed in.

"I think it was my sister," Gerri said. "One of her Skills."

"It felt more real than that to me. Spiritual."

"The System is real, and mysticism and spirituality are definitely in its wheelhouse. We've been over this. Believe what you want, but I still think it was Corrine. I felt her presence, like she was calling out to me."

"Yeah. Me too," he admitted. "It was definitely Corrie."

"Corrie?" Gerri said, lifting their eyebrow. "Does *Corrie* know you call her that?"

He started to answer but stopped when I cleared my throat loudly to bring things back in line.

"Sorry," Gerri said. "We had a dream."

"A vision," Thomas said.

"Whatever. We had a shared experience while we slept. We were underwater, in a lake." Thomas frowned and looked as though he was about to speak, but Gerri cut him off. "I'm being vague because of your concerns, but if you want to tell him, be my guest. Otherwise, shut up, stop interrupting, and let me tell this my way."

He glowered, but he shut up. I was grateful.

"In the lake there was one of those shimmery portals you hear about sometimes, the ones that supposedly link all the lakes together."

"They're real," I confirmed. "I've seen plenty of reports and recordings."

"Good to know. Did they look like giant oval mirrors, but with a translucent reflection?"

"Yes."

They'd both helped a lot and I hadn't given up on recruiting them. Especially Gerri. I took a deep breath. Let it out slowly. If I was gonna have a chance, it would take an echo of the man I used to be. Good at wining and dining the rich and shameless. Not the hardened soldier.

I pulled out the Macallan I'd planned to share with Topher, back when I first hit Level sixteen. The bastard's loss was their gain, though I'd save the man a shot. I took out my shot glasses and poured us each a rich amber shot. It smelled like chocolate and dried fruit. The good stuff.

They both refused with clear body language, a shake of the head from Thomas and a dismissive wave from Gerri. If the bottle had been in my human hand, it would have shattered. I set the three shots in front of me. *Oh well. More for me.*

"At least your intel on the portals matching our experiences is confirmation that it wasn't just a dream," Gerri said.

"We didn't need any confirmation," Thomas said. "I would think you'd have some faith in your sister, if not the rest of us, but why would I expect any kind of loyalty from you?"

I took a shot. My mouth filled with the intense flavors. Raisins and figs. A surge of cinnamon and ginger. Subtle sweetness, vanilla and chocolate. An echo of oak.

No reaction. Nothing.

There was a wall between me and pleasure. Not even a contented sigh could penetrate it.

Rational or not, I blamed Thomas. He'd been a dick to my friend. Pissed me off.

Gerri was talking. "Once we passed through the gate, time seemed to jump in fits and starts. There were soldiers with tridents in scaled armor riding giant pikes. Walleyes the size of Buicks. Muskies with auras of power that made you want to bow and serve them. They made the walleyes look like minnows."

I'd seen reports about all of this. Gerri was right, it gave what they were saying a lot more credibility.

"Don't forget the storm," Thomas said. He sounded snide.

I took the next shot, slammed the glass down, and gave him a look that was just as hard.

"At the center of the storm was one of those big Godzilla-level things," Gerri said.

"A Kaiju?" I asked.

"Yeah, one of those," Thomas chimed in.

I didn't drink.

"It was terrifying and wonderful," they continued. "Like a dragon had a baby with a giant panther. Supposedly it—"

"Mishipehshu," Thomas cut them off, voice filled with wonder. "You should treat them with more respect."

I took another shot.

He noticed and gave me an incredulous look.

I smirked and held up my glass as if I were making a toast.

"A Kaiju that looks like a legendary monster that supposedly caused all the big storms in Lake Superior," Gerri summed up.

Thomas looked as though he wanted to repeat the name, but I'd refilled my shot glasses and he'd noticed. He kept quiet.

"There was another portal underneath the monster in the center of the lake. It was surrounded by a mountain of corpses—"

"And treasure," Thomas interrupted, then gritted his teeth as he watched me take another shot.

"And treasure," Gerri continued. "But we could see through the portal."

"*You* could see through the portal," Thomas corrected. As he did, he reached out and handed me one of my shot glasses.

Gerri giggle-snorted.

I slammed it down. Refilled the lot. A wasted effort given my Constitution, but sometimes going through the motions was all that you had left.

"My sister was on the other side of the portal. She was dressed in a mix of pearlescent metal tech and old-school, traditional garb as if she was at one of the big pow wows our people used to do that brought in a lot of tourists."

Thomas scoffed but didn't say anything. I made a judgment call and decided that would count, so I slammed a shot.

Gerri smirked at him then did the same.

"Well, fuck you very much," he said, now that we'd teamed up on him.

They bit their lower lip. Chemistry. Interesting. Possibly one-sided. They certainly bickered like a couple though.

"What kind of treasure?" I asked.

"Not the point," Thomas answered.

"I'm making it the point," I shot back.

"Worthless treasure," he said. "Shiny shit."

"We don't know that," Gerri said. "It could be magical. And the gear on the people is almost certainly high-end stuff if they made it all the way there."

Thomas got a smug expression when Gerri had stepped on his words a bit, and he reached out and took a shot, then huffed and slammed it down, cracking the glass.

Poor guy didn't understand how things like this worked. I tried to take pity on him. Let it go. My expression must have revealed my thoughts though, and Gerri was certainly not hiding theirs.

"Fine," he snapped. "You can both go straight to hell." He took a few steps away, then half turned, and said, "Find me when this clown show is done. I'm gonna go find something to kill."

He, Topher, and a few of the others had taken to hunting together. Hopefully, that would give him time to calm down. Shouldn't have pissed him off. He was useful. Too late now.

"We need your help getting to that portal," Gerri said. "There's no way we're making it alone."

"We can arrange that. Come with us for the mission and give up any claim to the treasure on the way to the portal and you've got yourselves a deal."

"I'll agree to all of that for me, but not for him. Thomas won't be willing to go with us. There's too much risk that we'd lose another key defender that the tribe can't afford to do without. Besides, I promised last time that I wouldn't ask him to do anything more."

"That's fine. He'd be a big help, but we need you more. He can help guard the ship while we're gone."

"I think he'll be fine with that, but you have to ask him. As for the treasure, he gets a share. I think we can both agree that he's sacrificed enough already."

This time I looked away. I had a strange feeling in my gut that reminded me of when I'd first met Caleb. If it had been my brother, I'd have been much worse. And still I'd cut him zero slack.

"Yeah," I said softly, standing up to put away the booze. And the past. "That's fair." *I'm such an ass.* "We'll give him my share too."

Gerri nodded. They must have shared my mood because they left without another word.

Chapter 55

Lee

Gerri and I trailed after our new squad. They'd done well enough so far that we were bored. I sent an order through Full Coordination Skill to stay alert.

I'd offered them a few days to recover from their training. Testing their resolve. They'd chewed me out for giving them the choice. Lives were on the line. They'd "rewarded" themselves with double-length turns at the Quarter Master's Field-Shower, one big meal, and a real night's sleep before their dungeon run. Dedication. Made me proud.

They'd been exceedingly cautious as they explored the Duck Camp dungeon's outer zones. It took most of the day. Had to remind myself that only Randy was a Combat Classer.

The dungeon's "levels" were outdoor areas. You had to beat them one by one. Order didn't matter. Each mini-boss dropped a piece of the golden-duck-whistle McGuffin we would need to access the main lodge. They'd fought a beaver made of gold, a yellow snowman that smelled like cat piss, and a mosquito the size of a dump truck. The last one should have been nuked from space.

So far, Gerri and I were surplus. We'd trained them all to the verge of Advanced Combat Classes over the last several weeks. No. More than weeks by now. Time flies when you're obsessively focused. This would be their test. If they could prove themselves in the dungeon, we'd know they were ready.

If not, we'd wasted a lot of time for less than nothing. Screw that. They'd gotten past Topher and they'd gotten past me. They could do this.

The inside portion of dungeon was the twisted remnants of a hunting lodge for rich assholes. The kind I'd have been if my fiancée hadn't made me choose between marrying her or hunting for sport. One upside of the apocalypse was that I got to eat a lot of burgers and steaks that had tried to kill me—her one allowed exception. I'd trade it all for one more smile from the woman I loved and never regret it for a second.

Caleb had used his Show and Tell Skill to let us see what this place had been like before. Old-school. Rustic. Now it was a towering log cabin, about half the height of a small skyscraper and twice as wide. It loomed above us and blocked out the sun.

In the distance, I heard the booming whoof, whoof, whoof of the Midnight Retriever, a black lab the size of Clifford the Big Red Dog. My boys would have worshiped the damned thing. It was still barking at monstrous mallards the size of sports cars. Labzilla had chased off the birds before the team had been forced to fight them. A waste of XP. I'd just been glad we didn't have to fight the dog. I could shoot humans if I had to. No hesitation. I'd do it with enthusiasm if they gave me half a reason. But a dog? No. If I had to hurt a dog, even I'd lose sleep.

"He's clearly a monster, but he protected us," Caleb was saying. Again. He was looking at Larson, but I got the impression he was talking to all of us. "Do you think that means that most monsters are just jerks that choose to kill us, or that the dog is some kind of exception?"

"I don't know," Larson said. "How could we know?"

"Good question. Hmm. I didn't get any special interests, just like with monsters. Maybe if I put a few points into it, I can evolve it to where I can get more information about the monsters. I could use it to—"

"No," I said, not kindly. "We've been over this. You are absolutely forbidden to put any points into Basic Skills after you can get Advanced. Even the idea is insane."

"Yeah," Caleb agreed, but he didn't sound convinced.

I glared.

"Fine," he said. "I know that you're right. I'll have to find another way."

"Blow the whistle," Randy said.

I gave the others enough time to see if anyone would catch the mistake before I said, "Okay," and blew the whistle several times in rapid succession. The quacks it made were deeper and more resonant than I expected but still nasal and reedy. At first, nothing happened. Then we heard the howls of pain and anguish in the distance and the flapping of giant wings.

"Definitely a trap," I said as the sounds of the ducks' wings and the anguished cries of pain and rage from the dog hit us at the same time. Still, it was their first big mistake. They were doing well.

Rather than prepare to fight, they went with the better part of valor and tried to force the door. The massive wooden thing opened slow and closed even slower. Some kind of mechanic. Figured. They made it just in time.

The whole building shook as the mountainous mutt slammed into it, followed by the crashing thuds of a dozen ducks like giant drops of rain.

"Shame," I said. "I bet giant duck is delicious. I could have made us a crap-ton of jerky and still had plenty to roast."

Caleb looked predictably disgusted but also rather cranky. When I gave him a questioning look, it was Larson who answered.

"We ran out of his pizza and burritos and things. He's down to nothing but that nasty green sludge the Voloids drink." She put a hand on his shoulder. "I'm sorry, hon. If I hadn't eaten so much of your stuff, you'd have enough to get through till we get to the Shop."

"It's fine," he told her. Was that a lie? I guess she'd know if it was one, him being him.

"We don't have time for this," I said. "You can buy more supplies when you go to the Shop. I'll make sure you get the containers you need. For now, just be glad you have options and don't need to make any hard choices."

He grimaced but said, "Let's get going."

The inside of the lodge would have been a great set for an Evil Dead film. Dust and mold and rotting wood planks were everywhere. Animal heads on the walls. There were deer, bears, and other things you'd expect to see, but also giant duck heads with sabertoothed fangs. Last were life-sized stuffed humans, men with antlers and claws and shiny glass eyes. I inspected them all, expecting another trap. They were what they seemed. One blonde had hair too much like Nancy's and it made me turn away.

"Nancy, Kyle, Joseph…" I whispered.

Not the time.

I shoved the grief and rage back in the hole where my heart should have been and went back to inspecting the room.

A fireplace the size of a public pool dominated one of the walls. Hellish flames erupted from its depths, where entire tree trunks—branches, leaves, and all—were burning in a heap.

I looked up. Nothing.

Always good to check. I sent my scout drones to map the place. Slow work. There were a lot of webs. My first instinct was to burn it all away. Bad idea in a building made of kindling. My battle map populated. Rooms. Key points of interest. Lots of red dots.

X 12 Duck Hunter Zombie (Level 4 - Advanced)

Maintenance Man (Level 5 – Elite - Advanced)

Big Shot Zombie (Level 6 – Mini-boss - Advanced)

They were spread out enough that I felt Gerri and I shouldn't have to pitch in much. Better to preserve as much of their XP as we could. Good thing too. Gerri's paralytic smoke probably didn't work on zombies.

The hunters had gleaming shotguns and *Crocodile Dundee*-sized knives.

The first couple mobs were together in a bedroom. Zombies often had great hearing, so shotguns going off would not be subtle. They sent the robot ahead into the room. Effective. But it would backfire if they got overrun from adds.

Birdshot from the zombie hunters bounced off the blue barrier and the fight started strong. The group had their timing down, and they opened fire the instant the barrier dropped. It would have gone smoothly, but the zombies in the opposing bedroom joined the fight. I noticed that the rest of them stayed put in the main dining room. *Interesting.* Another game-like mechanic?

Pavise stood blocking the first door, relying on his armor against the bird shot, as he used a bar of force at gun height to block the mindless mobs. He forced the others to remain in the room with his shield. Nice. I'd never considered that trick. Effective, but inefficient.

The Hunters were firing bird shot. Not great for armor penetration. That said, Pavise was in desperate need of an upgrade and the monsters were level 50. He was forced to retreat, firing his ridiculous steampunk shoulder turret as he went. If he were a proper robot, he'd have tank treads and a laser turret.

The team was able to defeat the four without serious threat, but it cost them more Mana than they would be able to maintain. I considered it a passable effort, however. Their teamwork and Skill use were solid. Everything else could be resolved with upgrades to Pavise, gear, and their Classes.

Gerri gave them various substances to boost their abilities and recovery while Caleb and Penny worked to repair Pavise and the group's gear. That repair Skill of Caleb's was useful. I'd pick it up when I got the chance and recommend it for my troops.

I wanted to give the team my Adaptive Defense Skill to protect them from the shotguns, but it was powerful. It would cost them too much XP and invalidate other aspects of the test. I activated my Good Luck Skill for them instead, boosting their Perception, Agility, and Luck. If that wasn't enough, Gerri and I would kill a few of the extras.

"I think these things are mindless," Caleb said. "I feel like I'm playing a video game. I have to keep reminding myself that there might still be a person trapped in there and that even if there's not, this kind of issue is the slipperiest of slopes."

"I'm sorry you feel that way," Penny said. "Because I have an idea and you're not going to like it."

The teacher's face was somber when he asked her, "What's the plan?"

Her answer was to hold up a grenade.

She'd been right, he didn't like her plan, but even he had to admit it was a good one.

After a bit more discussion, the group demonstrated that our training had paid off and helped pave the way for their own creativity and skills to shine. Standing in the massive open archway, we saw eight rotting corpses dressed in what looked to be top-of-the-line hunting gear. The contrast of camo and bright orange vests made me want to laugh, but I held my tongue. Had to maintain my image.

The zombies surrounded a long wooden table covered with plates and pans of "food." Moldy, steaming bread and rancid melted butter were joined with similarly rotten mockeries of iced cinnamon rolls and other "treats."

Platters of fish, still covered with scales and as deteriorated as the zombies, sat beside equally disgusting servings of deer, bear, and skunk. One of the zombies was washing down soaked bread with a putrid eyeball-and-vegetable soup.

My gut revolted and I heaved. If I'd eaten breakfast, I think I'd have filled my helmet. I wasn't alone. Everyone was gagging. Fuck this room. This dungeon. This System.

One by one, metallic orbs joined the gruesome scene as the squad activated and tossed as many grenades as they could manage in rapid succession. One after the other, the devices detonated. Shrapnel shredded clothes and flesh. Concussion grenades broke fingers, limbs, servings platters, and trays. Some kind of holy effect seared the rotten flesh, doing more damage to the corpses than all of the others put together. I'd need to find out what the hell that had been. Nice.

The monsters stumbled, blundered, and eventually made their way in the direction of the team, who'd kept tossing grenades. When they got too close, Pavise threw up a shield, protecting them from the explosions and the monsters. He left enough room at the top for them to keep lobbing in grenades.

When they finally ran out of the spheres, it was Randy's time to shine. All eight of the zombies were nearly dead, but still coming for us, and he blew them back into the other wall with one of his Shotgun capstones. None of them got up again.

Overall, their strategy was wasteful, but no one could say it hadn't worked. It had the added benefit of saving a lot of Mana. I'd have been impressed if the explosions hadn't spread the gunk and smells even more than before. It made me dry heave and groan. Doubted anyone could hear after the grenades and shotguns had burst their eardrums.

I noticed then that Randy was picking up all of the dropped shotguns and tossing them into his inventory. Smart, but they'd be a bitch to clean.

"Good work," I said. "Work smarter, not harder."

Everyone looked happy at the praise except for Caleb. He was off by himself, as far from the "food" and the bodies as he could get. He pinched his nose as he looked at a picture of a sweet old couple. The image spoke of what this place had been like back before the System. His arm was wrapped around her, while she held a pan of treats.

When Caleb looked back up, he had his game face on. "Let's get this done," he said, and moved across the dining room.

Pavise put a shield in his way. "Rest, sir."

Caleb looked around at the others, seeing that no one was injured or tired. He gestured to them in demonstration.

"Not all exhaustion is physical, sir. Nor is it always apparent."

"Wise words," I said. "And don't go that way."

"Never go that way," Caleb quoted.

I rolled my eyes. "This isn't *Labyrinth*, and that's not the way to a castle. It is the way to the end boss though, and you don't want to leave the mini bosses as adds. Remember that this isn't a game, and the monsters aren't required to play fair. Pavise, make a note to add some surveillance and scouting gear to your team's equipment. Going in blind like that is gonna get them killed."

"Already done, Commander."

"Excellent. Pretending for the sake of the trial that you had such tools, you would note that there is an elite monster over there"—I pointed to the left—"and a mini boss over there." I pointed to the right.

In either direction, side doors led off to passageways that I doubted were ever part of the old lodge. I imagined this place had been a warm and comfortable spot to escape the hustle and bustle of city life, back in the day. We'd lost so much.

"If we take out the elite first, there's less risk that we can't finish him off before the mini boss can join in," Caleb said. "On the other hand, if we do it the other way, we'll have had time to recover during the easier fight and that might get us to the boss quicker. I vote for the safer way. Sometimes, slow is fast. We can't help save anyone if we're dead."

"Pavise," Penny said, "what do you think?"

"I think that your manners are a bit lacking, Miss Sprocket. My master's points were well-considered and reasoned and ignoring that to request my input is ill-conceived at best and bad for team cohesion. As the damage is already done, however, I will add my voice to his, for whatever that is worth."

"Sorry, Caleb. He's right. You made good points. I'm just… there's a lot riding on this."

"I understand. A lot of people I care about are counting on us too."

"I agree with Caleb," Penny said.

"Yeah," Evelyn echoed.

"Looks like I'm outvoted," Randy said as he reloaded his rifle. "I'm ready when you are."

The way to the elite monster was clear. It looked impressive, like an old man who'd had his lower body replaced with a riding mower. Both of his arms were chainsaws. I wanted to ask if he'd bought them at S-Mart, but if I let myself quote a movie, even once, I'd never be able to get Caleb to stop.

If our squad had been slow melee combatants, they'd have been in trouble. As it was, even Larson took out her gun and they just kited the thing until it died.

The mini boss was a different story. Inspection had called it a Big Shot, and the dungeon had taken that literally. The zombie-looking thing was ten feet tall and had a ground-mounted turret at the end of a long hallway. If they still had their grenades, the group would have had a good chance. As it was, they'd need to get creative.

I summoned some caramel corn and a pair of folding chairs for Gerri and I so that we could lounge while we waited. I hadn't thought it through, and the smell was still lingering. Neither of us managed to eat a single kernel and I'd have to throw it all away.

The team settled on three possible strategies: charge and hope for the best, destroy the wall to the back of it and kill it from behind, or have Pavise drop shield after shield between them and the weapon until they could get past it.

After a few more minutes of intense debate, they came to us with their decision.

"Well?" I asked them.

"We're ready to fight the boss." They'd apparently nominated Penny to break the news.

A chuckle snuck past my defenses. "How do you figure that?"

"We don't have the Skills or equipment we need to fight that thing without risking all our lives. Even so, we'd do what needed to be done if we had to. It's just that after talking it over, we don't think that we do."

"Why's that?"

"The gun is mounted to the floor. If it decides to follow us when we fight the boss, it probably won't be able to bring its main weapon. Even if it can, it looks like that would really slow it down. When you add to that the fact that none of the other monsters have come running between rooms, we've decided we should skip it."

"Okay," I said. It was a good call.

"Makes sense," Gerri added.

"Mind if we kill it?" I'd been getting bored and needed a distraction from my nausea.

"Knock yourselves out."

They waited while Gerri and I took turns lobbing it with vials and explosives, then we all headed on to face the final boss.

Sensible, but boring. It worked.

Chapter 56

Caleb

I cursed myself again. A year and a half ago, when the Matriarch had told me that I didn't want to know when I'd asked about the boss fight, I'd taken her at her word and never pressed. If Lee and his people knew, he wasn't telling us. The information would have really helped us to prepare.

Things got a little clearer when we entered the kitchen and inspected the ogre-looking humanoid in the center of the room. It was wearing the pleated white hat and double-breasted jacket of a chef. They were both covered with blood and bits of things that I did not want to identify. One chunk was almost certainly a decent-sized piece of a human ear. I forced myself not to gag, barely, though bile rose in my throat. Inspecting him revealed basically nothing.

Head Chef (Level 14 – Boss - Advanced)
??

He was standing in the middle of a giant kitchen. Huge, ridiculous ovens surrounded the room, with the boss in the center at a central island stovetop. Eight oversized pots, the kind used for making gumbo, were steaming and gurgling, topped with giant metal lids.

As we stepped into the room, flames blazed out of various ovens, seemingly at random. I sent Pavise a mental nudge to watch for a hidden pattern.

"*Of course, sir.*"

"Also watch for sous chefs," I said. "Head chef's imply coworkers."

"What about bus boys?" Randy said with a snarky tone.

"Oh god," Evie said. "Do you think they'll be actual busses?"

"Be ready for anything," Penny chimed in.

Our plan was cut short when the chef plunged one of his massive hands into a pot and pulled it out, red and blistering with a gravy-dripping human head gripped like a basketball. Its face looked real, though it was missing its eyes.

Pavise raised one of his glowing blue barriers just in time.

The fastball head exploded like a gore grenade against the force wall. *It isn't real. It's System-generated. Pull yourself together.* I gathered my will, activated my Demonstration Skill, and opened fire as I yelled for the others to do the same.

"Sir, stopping this level of damage is unsustainable for me. I suggest that we retreat immediately. He is unlikely to follow."

"Okay, buddy." To the others, I said, "Let's find out how strong his defenses are and gather as much intel as we can and then fall back to strategize."

"Sounds good," Randy said.

"Excellent strategy, sir."

"I'm just glad this isn't a video game. If it was, we wouldn't be able to—" *Crud!* "Retreat! Back out of here. Now. Now! NOW."

The thud and clink of a massive metal gate slamming shut behind us let us know we'd missed our window.

"I stand corrected," Pavise said, oh so helpfully.

"Fall back to the gate. The hall will give us at least some cover."

I glanced behind me as I backed up. I heard the scraping sound as I watched the gate inch toward me. Even in video games, things like this had stressed me out a little. In real life, it was horrifying. I tried, and failed, not to let the presence of Gerri and Lee reassure me.

"Any ideas?" I asked.

"Try our best and hope that the others save us?" Randy said, nodding to Lee and Gerri as he did so.

"That defeats the purpose of this whole thing," I answered. "Pretend that it's just us. What do we do?"

"That's easy. We fight as hard as we can and then die painfully."

"We don't have time for this. Anyone?"

"We're out of grenades," Penny said. "Also, those ovens are probably going to shoot fire at us."

An explosion devastated one of Pavise's shields. "Every time I do this, sir, it wastes more Mana that we are desperately going to need."

"We're out of time. Randy and Evelyn, unless you have a better idea, stay to the sides and keep mobile—"

"I've got a better idea," Evie said.

Cognitive dissonance slapped me in the face for a second. Decades of entertainment had taught me that nobody ever had a better plan. "What's the play?"

"I'll get behind the monster and interfere. Randy to the side. Spread our targets. Dodge if you can. Shield second priority."

"Good," Lee said. "I like it. Can you give them an edge, Gerri?"

"Fire resist pills. Thomas will be pissed if I give them out."

"We'll cover the ingredients. That work?"

The gate was getting close enough that we couldn't really wait for them. I started to say so, but Gerri was quicker. They'd already handed Evelyn a pill, and the Acrobat was flipping across the room before I could comment.

I activated Demonstrate again, and we resumed our assault. Evelyn circled around, which split the boss's focus. I considered activating Pay Attention to help her taunt him, but as good as she was at dodging, no one was perfect. This thing out-Leveled us and Evie's suit barely qualified as armor. It probably would have failed regardless.

I opened my mouth and took the large pill as Gerri pressed it into my mouth. Randy did the same.

I tried to swallow and half gagged. I'd never been good with larger pills. This one wasn't too bad, so I might manage it, but my mouth and throat were also dry. I tried to think of pizza in hopes of making my mouth water, but this place was the least appetizing thing I'd ever seen in my life.

"Got water?" I choked out.

"Are you kidding me?" Lee said.

I took a chance and bit the pill open. It tasted like cinnamon mixed with aspirin. I swallowed it down over several attempts as I fired. Distracted, I missed the ogre-sized boss completely.

Lee and Gerri split up, each of them taking a corner on Evie's side of the room. Whether they planned to help or not, the action took some of the pressure off of us. The boss threw a head after each of them before turning back to us.

Gerri dodged, barely, but the indirect damage vanished in midair. Some kind of protection spell?

Lee was more overt, having dropped a consumable device that offered a barrier. Now, he was reshaping the stone around both of them with a Skill to give them more secure locations.

I considered using Pay Attention targeting Lee, but that felt like cheating. Also, it might tick him off.

Randy was using slugs primarily. One after the other, he took potshots at the chef's head, eyes, and throat. His attacks were doing more damage than the rest of us put together, but none of the damage seemed consequential. I halfway expected the monster to yawn. In the meantime, Pavise's Mana was at less than half, and the boss was only casually tossing heads at us. I suspected he had several more tricks, especially when I saw the massive cleaver and butcher knife on his counter.

When he picked up one of the pot's lids and used it as a shield to block some of the shotgun's damage, I had to hold back an audible groan.

"Evie, try to steal his blades," I said.

The boss glared at me, then used his oversized bulk to block the Acrobat's path to the weapons.

Oh crud. It understood us. I needed to communicate via Pavise.

It grabbed the lid off one of the unused pots and blocked with it.

With it's free hand, the Head Chef redoubled its efforts to kill me with head bombs from the newly opened pot. One after the other, faster than Pavise could raise his shields.

One of the explosions drove shrapnel into my body and slammed me against the wall. My ears popped. I heard my mother screaming and metal rending as a drunk driver took my parents away from me again. My seat belt had saved me then. Only my armor saved me now.

"Sir!" Pavise shouted. He must have been trying to get my attention for some time. "Sir, you will die if you just stand there."

I moved to crouch behind him as another set of repeated explosions broke one of Pavise's shields. The remaining force rocked me backward but failed to penetrate my armor now that I had some cover.

Gore coated me. Blood, chips of bone, and pieces of brain covered me. I'd thought I'd never smell anything worse than when I'd protested factory farming at a manure lagoon in college. This dungeon was so much worse. It was like a combination of rotten meat, urine, blood, and sour milk.

I was desperately glad I hadn't eaten.

It took all of my enhanced Willpower, but I focused on the scene around me. The Head Chef had turned its attention to Randy, who had given up shooting to dodge. I wondered how he'd managed to aggro the monster so completely, then I saw that it was holding the shield lid over its crotch. The shield was huge, thick, and peppered with slug dents.

Wildly exaggerated bursts of fire blasted from the open ovens as the infuriated boss tried again and again to kill Randy. Every time he nearly succeeded, a blue barrier blocked his attack. But the Head Chef had caught on and was throwing the heads in a way that was forcing Randy into the fire from one of the ovens.

Randy cried out in anguish as he dove through the flames, a scream pulled from him even with Gerri's potion increasing his resistance. His Health bar dropped more than the boss's had the entire fight before he escaped the flames.

It wasn't all bad, however.

Randy's antics had forced the boss to take a few steps to the side and switch to another of his pots. That had given Evelyn a chance. I tried not to look directly at her as she stealthily picked up the monster's massive knives and placed them in her inventory before backing away. *Go, Evie!*

Then she did something I hadn't even considered. She summoned her Acrobat's staff, launched herself forward with a Skill I didn't know she had, and smashed into one of the pots with a powerful two-legged kick.

It sounded like a gong, and the truly gigantic pot tottered. Her athleticism and momentum, backed by her enhanced underarmor, got the job done though. The pot fell to the floor and exploded, blowing a massive hole in the tile and almost certainly deafening any of us that could still hear.

A look of absolute fury turned the Head Chef's face as red as his bloody spilled soup. He wheeled to face Evelyn, reaching for his blades that were no longer there. Bereft of his melee weapons, the monster reached out to grab her with his massive hands.

He was faster than he looked, but she should have been faster. I saw her eyes looking at a scene that wasn't the one in front of her as she hesitated, overwhelmed by her past trauma. I wanted to help her, to take her away from this place and hold her until the hurting stopped, but she was too far away. Even Pavise couldn't shield her from this distance.

Noticing her helpless expression, the monster's furious attack was totally committed before either the monster, or I, realized she'd been faking it. She took one quick step toward the monster and to the side. At some point during its berserk charge, she'd retrieved a weapon from her inventory. Evelyn used the creature's momentum to help her drive his own butcher's knife deep into his guts, then she cartwheeled away and kited the monster around the room.

The Head Chef's mouth moved as if he were roaring with fury and anguish as he chased her.

I urged Pavise to move a bit closer to the action so that we could intervene as needed, making sure that he remained squarely between me and the monster at all times. I also took the opportunity to pick up the lid from the pot that Evelyn had kicked over. Even if the heavy metal was bent a little, it was still functional as a shield. It was heavy and awkward to lift and move, but I now had a tower shield, taking some of the pressure off of Pavise.

Angry as the creature was, he didn't take the bait and let Evelyn kite him forever. Instead, the Head Chef pulled out the knife, dropped it to the floor, and then hefted one of the headless pots and drank from it deeply. His Health dropped a big chunk as he did so, as his face burned and blistered from the "beverage."

Almost immediately after, however, the Dungeon Boss's Health ticked up faster and faster.

When he picked up a second of the used pots, I was sure we all expected him to do the same. Instead, he hurled the contents as an area of effect attack against Evelyn as she passed in front of Gerri's hidey-hole.

Evelyn made it out of the area in time. Gerri was coated with the bloody, gruesome soup. Whatever protection she had in place wasn't applicable or wasn't enough. She seized on the ground, gagging uncontrollably.

I heard a pop and a static whine as my hearing returned. For a moment, all the sounds were magnified and every footstep thundered. I thanked God that Randy wasn't close, when the next blast of his shotgun sent me reeling.

Lee opened fire then. As he did, the monster glowed red, marking it as the group's primary target.

The Head Chef threw a second pot in Lee's direction.

The gore smashed against Lee's shield. He smirked as he never stopped firing. A few seconds later, as the fumes fully reached him, his eyes crossed, and he fell with the same kind of seizure that had affected Gerri.

I prayed they were faking to test us, but it *really* didn't look that way.

My fear for my friends, bereft of our safety net, dialed my terror up to eleven. I had my own moment of panic, and I wished that Pavise was still able to help me slow my relative perception of time.

Focus, Caleb. Focus.

Two members down. Vulnerable. Monster attacking.

He was ready to throw more heads at Lee. Gerri would be next. Gerri was closer. Lee had a kind of barrier. He was a cyborg. High level. Tough. He could—

Taking too long, thinking too slow. I was still so bad at this without Pavise's help. The Head Chef had thrown one of the heads into the hole with Lee. It exploded. I couldn't see the damage from where I stood, but I assumed it was catastrophic.

Need to grab Gerri. Drag her to Lee. Protect her with my shield. Pavise can defend us all at once. But would it be in time? I moved to Gerri's side, grabbed them by their arms, and dragged them toward the next safe spot. All the while, I kept the shield between us and the boss. It was slow-going and awkward, but I was more grateful than ever for my new training and the points I'd invested in Strength. I prayed that the other's antics would be enough to distract the boss.

It turned out they weren't. But obsessively trying to kill Lee did the job. He'd missed entirely with one head, because of a well-timed shot by Randy. The second head smashed into the barrier but didn't break through. He was readying another but got distracted by the other members of the group.

Evelyn kicked a second of the pots off the stove and parkoured herself to safety, while Randy managed to take out a third with back-to-back blasts from his Knockback Skill.

The Head Chef let out a bestial roar of fury. It was almost certainly a buff trigger, because the boss was faster than ever as he took turns protecting its few remaining pots with one arm and throwing heads at all of us with the other.

Faster or not, they'd managed to split his focus. It gave me the time I needed to fireman carry Gerri to Lee, and I found him severely injured and covered with gore. A third of his armor was blown off, and bone shrapnel was buried deep inside the flesh and gear beneath.

I felt a surge of triumph at gathering the two disabled members into a single location for Pavise to protect. My elation grew as he completely stopped a flurry of three exploding heads in rapid succession from devastating the out-of-commission pair. Pavise had managed to shield us all completely.

"My Mana is almost empty, sir." The shield-bot's words smashed into me like an exploding head.

"I'm out of packs and my armor's booster is basically dry," I said. "I've got nothing left to give you."

I shook Gerri and Lee, one after the other. They seemed to be starting to recover, but they were groggy and moving slower than we needed.

I had no Skills for this. No smelling salts or potions. Gerri might, but I had no time.

I smacked them both in the face as hard as I could, again and again, screaming their names.

An explosion sounded as one of my allies sent another of the pots crashing to the floor. I had no attention to spare to find out who as a head destroyed Pavise's blue barrier.

"That was the last of my shields, sir. I have sustained moderate damage from the attack. There is shrapnel in my…"

He kept talking, but I was too distracted as vise-grip strength crushed my wrist, locking my arm in place, as Lee woke and stopped my "attack."

"Huh?" Lee said.

"Fight," I told him. "Save us!"

His eyes came into focus and he forced himself to his feet, blood and oil from his injuries and gore from the soup dripping down his body. He threw out another shield consumable and took in the scene before him.

"He's protective of the pots," I said.

"Avoid the fire," Randy said, sounding bitter.

Lee reactivated his Good Luck Skill. The world came into sharper focus and my body felt more responsive. It boosted Luck too, but I wouldn't have known it if he hadn't told me. He followed that with Reposition and I felt a strong urge to rush to him, which I didn't do because I was already right next to him. Finally, Lee activated Hit and Run, boosting our movement rates and our attack speeds.

The others scattered, and we worked to attack and avoid the monster, all the while looking for ways to attack the remaining pots. Soon, Gerri was up and fighting and the last of the pots had been disrupted. The Chef was forced to fight us with his bare hands, since Evelyn had retrieved his knife again.

After that, the fight went smoother except when the monster managed to get ahold of Randy. He didn't beat Randy with his fists or try to tear him apart like what he'd attempted with Evie. Instead, the Chef hurled the young man into one of the oven infernos.

The screams broke my heart. It was happening again. I was supposed to keep him safe and I couldn't do anything to help him. I started to scream in rage and frustration when I remembered something. I wasn't powerless anymore. Not completely.

As the others continued their mad rampage around the room, I dropped my shield-lid and used my Dash to clear the distance to the oven, no longer having to roll now that I was used to the Skill and wearing my armor. I turned my face away, drove my arms into the fire, and tried to drag Randy out. He was kicking, thrashing, and a hell of a lot stronger than me, so at first, I couldn't force him.

I screamed as the fire heated my armor to the point that it was searing my skin. I activated Pay Attention on Randy, worried that the extra increase in Perception would also increase his agony, and screamed, "Stop fighting. Saving you."

He still thrashed, but he didn't actively resist me anymore. I was able to drag him from the oven with great effort, panting from panic and adrenaline as much as lack of oxygen. Once he was free, I cast Minor Heal and poured a potion down his throat, all the while trying not to look away from his bubbling, blackened flesh. If I hadn't been a vegetarian already, the smell of his flesh cooking would have sealed the deal. If not for the protection Gerri had provided for us, he'd almost certainly be dead.

I followed up with a Minor Heal and a potion for myself. Then I returned to the fight, shooting the Head Chef again and again until my shoulder mount ran out of charges. I switched to my hand-held blaster, but my hand-based weapon attacks were still pathetic. Randy joined in after a few shots from my blaster. His attacks were not pathetic, especially with the boosts from Lee.

It wasn't easy, because we just didn't have the damage output, but it was a forgone conclusion.

We passed our test.

When I'd finally rested long enough to notice, I saw my notifications. Reviewing them, one stood out above all the others.

Congratulations! You've reached Level 50!

Attributes automatically assigned. 2 additional attributes available to be assigned.

You may now choose an Advanced Class

Would you like do so?

(Y/N)

Pavise stopped me from selecting yes, just in time.

Chapter 57

Caleb

The Commander made us wait until we got back to the base before choosing and discussing our new Classes and Skills. They'd set up something of a graduation ceremony for us, with beer and Tillamook cheddar cheese that I could eat, which was more thoughtful than I would have given Lee credit for. They'd hung a banner in the central hub connected to the loading bay that read, "Welcome to Advanced Class!" and everyone but me had a big box of new gear next to a chair with their name on it.

The whole room was full of people drinking, laughing, and chattering.

As a teacher, I've always been a big fan of validation, both giving and receiving. The celebration warmed my heart. Something about the camaraderie and the return of the old ritual added fuel to the fire of my hope for the future. We could never go back, but maybe we hadn't lost as much as I'd feared.

Aul and several of my students were in attendance. It reminded me that humans weren't the only ones who'd lost a lot. The metal grating of the floor was spotless now. Not a drop of Voloid blood remained. Khaln-Te and Vun-Eln had died where my chair was set. The human twins had died where I was standing. Evelyn was talking with Penny, laughing and drinking beer a few steps from where the Commander had driven the Matriarch's spear into her chest.

The guilt and grief felt like a spear into mine. I needed some time alone, but that just wasn't possible now.

My students seemed nervous but also proud of me. For some reason, they also congratulated Evie, but not the others.

"Aul is go with you," she said.

I was going to ask her what she was talking about, but Lee interrupted.

"We're on a deadline," he announced, loud enough for everyone to hear, "so I was gonna keep this short and sweet. But then Gerri and I got taken out and these sons of bitches saved our lives." He ruffled Randy's hair.

Randy glowered, but he didn't object.

The group cheered. Nearly a third of the troops and tribe members were in attendance, and they were in a festive mood.

Lee beamed at me. His eyes said, "I didn't think you had it in you."

I wasn't offended; I'd felt the same. I still did, most of the time.

"I kind of figured that having to save you was just part of the test," Penny said.

"It… was… not," Gerri replied.

"But you passed anyway," Lee said. "Great job." He handed Penny an oversized can of beer with a bald eagle on it and clinked it with his own.

The sounds of clinking cups, cans, and mugs rose like a chorus around us.

The Commander was in fine spirits. It gave me an inkling of what he might have been like before the System came. He was handsome, charming, and the life of the party. Even so, he kept the focus on us, telling everyone the story of the dungeon. He didn't exaggerate or downplay our failings. I learned a lot from hearing his viewpoint. It also made me trust him when he spoke of what we'd done well. What I'd done well.

"I'll be damned," Topher said when the story had ended. "Who'd've thought they had it in 'em?"

It was almost the same thing the Commander's expression had communicated so clearly, but it rubbed me the wrong way. I still didn't like the man, though I hoped he would come around, and he'd directed that at my friends, who didn't deserve his scorn.

No one else seemed to mind, so I let it go for now. Regardless of how much I liked validation, I'd never felt entirely comfortable at this kind of party and I felt disconnected from it, even though it was partly for me. It reminded me of high school and college parties. They were usually drunk and chaotic, neither of which appealed to me. A small group of friends playing Dungeons and Dragons or watching Star Wars were more my idea of a good time. Still, I was grateful, so I tried to put a good face on it.

"Now that we've passed, tell us the truth," Randy said to our trainer. "You wouldn't really have killed us if we were unprepared again. That was just training banter, right?"

The rough man's eyes locked on the redhead, and his smile turned predatory. "I never bluff, boy. And don't think yer off the hook just because your training's done. I have a reputation ta protect. If ye make me look bad, I'll still kill ya."

My shudder turned to tension as my body readied for danger. I nearly put a shield between them. The moment passed when someone spoke, but it didn't ease the tension.

"He killed Vince for that kind of thing," a voice I didn't recognize said.

"Wasn't that for treason?" a female voice asked.

"That level of incompetence is treason, lass," Topher said. "Though I suppose we're all traitors now."

"We're not the traitors," Donaldson, the creepy guy with the explosives, said, his voice filled with cold fury. "They are."

"Damn right," Lee said. Then he turned to Topher, expression stern but with a slight smirk. "Don't kill these guys until after the mission, no matter what."

"Oh aye, sir, of course after the mission."

I hoped they were joking, but I wouldn't have bet my life on it. Either way, it wasn't funny. Not for the first time, I missed being able to send mental messages to Pavise. It gave me a tiny insight into how the Voloids must be feeling, separated from their hive.

My attention was drawn back to the group.

Randy was opening the oversized container that held his new gear. It was a steam-punk mech suit with heavy iron plating and anime-sized guns. "My new Class is called an Armored Assault Specialist."

"I knew you were an AASS all along," Evelyn said, dragging out the sounds to better fit the acronym.

I stifled a laugh. Others didn't.

The chuckles ended when gears clanked and steam hissed as the mech twisted and moved like an old-school Transformer, raising him into a harness. Its base widened, divided, and spread into the form of a thick tripod.

When the transition finished, Randy had become an armored turret with an assortment of absurdly oversized weapons. There were gasps from the assembled group at the sight. I circled the armored turret, taking it all in. It was truly stunning, in what looked to be copper and bronze. Gears, rods, and metal plates were everywhere.

I hadn't felt jealous of the others until Randy got a real Transformer as a reward. It brought back the dull ache I'd always felt when I'd first come to Minnesota. Mom and Dad were gone, and my access to exciting toys had gone with them. Nana was loving and kind, but she wasn't made of money, as she'd reminded me often. The other kids took for granted things that felt so necessary to me. It had been years until I could earn my own money and buy them for myself.

It had taken a few more years, and a lot of self-reflection, before I'd realized that it hadn't been the toys I'd been most jealous of. It had been the parents to buy them.

I shook my head to try to clear the funk. This was a celebration, not a time for melancholy. As I so often did, I resorted to humor. "What, no whistle?"

"Thank god," Randy replied.

"You're welcome," Penny said. "I spent an hour and a half trying to talk Dad out of it for you. Finally, I just had to distract him with a new project."

Randy thanked her. He was beaming proudly. I wanted to ask him about his new Skill, but it felt rude.

"What about you?" Randy asked Penny, apparently not sharing my concern. "Get any fun new toys and Skills with your Front-Line Medic Class?"

"I did," she said, and it was her turn to grin, though hers was a bit more reserved. "Though it's rude to make someone follow all of that." She motioned at his mech.

She wasn't wrong.

"It is pretty sweet, isn't it?"

She agreed eagerly. "Anway, I got a new white combat medic suit"—she pointed at her box—"but my Skills are the most important thing. It's killing me that I'm not taking Critical Wound Care, but Topher's right. Here."

Penny made a graceful motion with her hand. Her Skill details appeared—at least most of them. I wondered why she'd held some back.

Stabilize Battlefield Trauma (Level 1)

Spray or inject the patient with medical nanites that stabilize the patient's condition and prevent ongoing harm. Sets bones, binds wounds, clears airways, etc.

This also sets the stage for ongoing healing, granting the recipient a 20 percent bonus to all healing effects within the duration.

Duration: 5 minutes.

Cost: 200 Mana.

"I can stop you guys from getting worse, then heal you the same way that I have been, but with a major bonus to healing that stacks with the bonuses I already have."

"Not bad," Evelyn said. "But wasn't the main point of all of this to get you a powerful healing spell?"

"It was, but we underestimated what kind of protection Caleb would be able to provide, and more importantly, we didn't know that Dad was gonna make me this." She held out an upgraded model of her paralytic injection gun. This one had her father's trademark steampunk look, gears, and steam valves.

"That looks amazing, but I don't see how a better gun takes the place of a healing spell," I said.

"Inspect it," she replied with a proud grin, motioning at it Vanna White-style with her other hand.

We did.

Prototype Portable Potion Condenser and Remote Injection Device

Condenses potions, then loads them into weaponized injectors. Also accepts pre-condensed cartridges. Can be used for offensive or beneficial concoctions.

"Wow," I said. Many of the others made similar sounds and statements. "I didn't even know that you could do that."

"None of us did. He just handed it to me about a week ago and changed all of our plans."

"If the System was all things like that—the healing part of that, I mean—it would be a dream come true instead of a nightmare."

Evelyn walked over and traced my cybernetic arm with hers. "It has its moments, even now."

I shuddered, and the others laughed.

"What about you?" I asked her.

"I am also going to do a big reveal that will be a hard act to follow. Are you sure you want me to go first?"

I restrained myself from saying, "Ladies first," and motioned graciously for her to continue.

"I'd say that this would make you super jealous, but you're going to be too busy having a geekgasm for that."

It hadn't stopped me from being jealous of Randy's new toy.

"Wow me," I said.

She did.

Evie reached into the box and pulled out a long rod of silvery metal. It nearly matched her Acrobat's staff in dimensions, but it was covered in alien-looking geometric shapes and patterns.

"That does look kind of cool, I guess," I said, before she smiled wickedly.

Silvery-blue energy extended from both sides of the staff. It did amazing things to Evie's eyes.

I gasped. It was a long moment before I could speak.

"Plasma saber staff," I announced with the kind of awe most people reserve for religious ecstasy. I had to restrain myself from bouncing up and down like a teenie bopper at a Taylor Swift concert.

"Now I think I'm jealous," Evelyn said teasingly. "And it's a plasma spear." With a haughty head toss that made me smile, she moved the weapon behind her, watching as my eyes tracked it. "Stop staring at my staff like that."

I wasn't really listening to her. I was using my new footwork skills to move to where I could still see it.

She turned the weapon off.

"That's the most… I mean, I've never seen anything that… wow!"

"Now I know I'm jealous," she said with what seemed to be a genuine pout.

"You have nothing to be jealous of," I told her with enough sincerity that it broke through her melancholy.

She smiled. "Thanks."

"After all," I said, "it's your plasma spear."

Her glare told me that she was not amused, but at least she wasn't pouting anymore.

I probably should have told her about what it did to her eyes. I started to apologize and try that, but she started talking.

"Fine, what Skill did you choose?"

I noticed that like Randy, she'd skipped telling us her Skills. Was that because they'd both had the same HLF training? I'd have to ask her in private.

"That," I told her, "is a very good question."

"Unfortunately," Topher said, "we have no idea."

"What do you mean?" Evelyn asked him.

"My Skills are impressive, lass, but he's using a Prestige Class. Without access to the Shop, I just don't know enough about his Class or the gear they use to offer proper guidance. So, we're going to send him to the Shop with the few people the Hakarta won't be looking for."

She turned to me. "You have to wait until you go to the Shop before you can pick your Skill?"

I tried to answer, but Topher beat me to it. "No, he has ta wait until he gets back here, after his trip to the Shop. It's a pain in the arse, but it's our best path forward."

"He does at least have his Skill info, right? Can we at least see that?"

"Ye should know better than to ask that and… and he's already projecting 'em fer all the world ta see," Topher said, in a tone that indicated he might as well give up.

He was right to feel that way. If he wanted someone dedicated to keeping knowledge from others, he shouldn't have picked a Teacher. Besides, thinking about my new Skills gave me the kind of thrill I'd always gotten from leveling up in games. It always helped, at least when the game was new.

I had three Skills available at the first Level, just like everyone else.

Personal Force Field
Creates a protective field of force around yourself or your shield-bot to reduce incoming damage. Can be used multiple times as separate castings.
Duration: 5 Minutes.
Cost: 200 Mana.

From the moment that I saw this Skill, I'd known it was the one I wanted. Even ignoring childhood fantasies, danger and pain had become constant companions for me lately, and just the thought of force fields to protect me and Pavise had made my eyes tear up.

Rapid Repair
Reconstruct a moderately damaged construction or mechanical device. Effect is increased if the targeted item is Kaldian Technology.
Cost: 100 Mana.

Of course, the next Skill would be another that I desperately needed. Still, since I *did* desperately need it, I couldn't complain. Much.

Shield Projection
Remotely direct and modify your shield-bot's force shields, empowered by your own Mana. Also allows for the direct generation of a secondary shield by the Shield Warder.
Cost: Varies.

Topher hadn't been convinced, but I'd known what the choice would be as soon as I saw this Skill, as much as I might want the others. Still, he was right to tell me to take my time and evaluate things fully.

Once I gave everyone a moment to read through, I explained. "They all sound amazing, though I'm leaning toward Shield Projection. The problem is, we can't be sure that it's enough better than the trick we're already using to make it worth giving up a personal force field or a way to repair Pavise. We have a lot riding on him. And I'm pretty sure my repair Skill will work for all of our armor and cybernetics as well. The secondary shield might be weaker, and it's almost certainly not as good as a pair of force fields. Frankly, we need all these Skills desperately."

"They're good Skills, lad. We'll know more when you get back."

"And since you're a volunteer who's doing this for us, we're footing the bill for your gear," Lee said. "I realize you don't have many Credits, since you've been stuck here the whole time. What you have, you're going to need for food and other essentials."

He had no idea the amount of Credits I had access to from the Voloids. Probably more than all of them combined. If he did know, I had no doubt that his "generosity" would go the way of the world before the System arrived. Since none of that money was mine, however, and because this mission was not being done for the sake of the Voloids, it was none of his business. Their money was their money, no matter who was holding it.

There was one rather large purchase I might need to make for them, however, if we were going to have any real chance of saving the children. One way or the other, we needed to be able to run this ship.

Lee claimed to have written that off for now, though fuel was on his shopping list. I suspected that he had something planned, but then again, so did I.

"Who is going with us to the Shop?" I asked.

"Aul is be going," Aul said, triggering a full-on panic attack in me.

"No, you're not," Lee and I said at the same time.

"Aul is not be no."

Damn it. This was Kek all over again. Would she try to follow us and get herself killed if I refused? Was it wrong to make her stay by force if she wouldn't agree? Could we protect her if we let her come with us? My lungs felt too small. I couldn't get a full breath.

"We'll talk about it later." When she started to object again, I said, "I promise."

She turned and left the room. The other Voloids followed her without a word. All of their mandibles were clacking.

"I also have to go," Evie added. "I need to get my cybernetics adjusted."

"I'm sorry," Lee said. "You won't be going."

Evelyn's eyes were getting wet already. "Why the hell not? I've never attacked the Hakarta."

I tried to hold her hand to reassure her, but she batted me away. I didn't think she noticed, but it still stung a little.

"You fought the Gladiator," Lee answered her.

"I remember," she told him, holding up her cybernetic hand as evidence.

"You were recorded. There's no way the Hakarta haven't added you to their hit list. And before you ask, Gerri, that's true for you and most of your people also."

"We don't need much," Gerri answered. They turned to me. "Would you mind picking up some extras?"

"Consider it done," Lee said before I could answer. "There's just one thing."

"What's that?"

"We need to buy or borrow one of your trucks."

Gerri nodded and headed off.

As if that was a signal, most of the others did the same.

Without a word, Lee sent me a pair of files and a note. One was Evelyn's measurements, and the other was the specs for her cybernetic implants. The note told me that the Shop would almost certainly be able to solve Evie's issues remotely, one way or another, though he didn't want to get her hopes up.

"Thank you," I replied. *"I'm sure she'll appreciate your thoughtfulness. You're a good friend."*

"I take care of my troops," he said. Even through text, it seemed defensive.

I'd seen them together enough to see through that. Lee was more natural with her, like he was with Gerri and Topher. *"Riiigghht,"* I teased *"She's not your friend, not even a little."*

He sent back a blank reply, but he was glowering at me from across the room.

"Don't worry," I told him. *"Your secret's safe with me."*

Chapter 58

The Humanist

Desperate times call for desperate measures, I thought as I stood at the door to the bunker where we kept the true heart of the HLF's primary base. The cellar door was the same kind of thick titanium alloy as my chest-plate, and it was flanked with four heavy-blaster-turrets. I'd lost contact with another two of my forts at the same time as the latest disruptions at our main base. One of our settlements was currently under attack by over-informed alien forces, and at least two schism groups were actively working to try to take over the HLF from within.

Organizationally, we were walking wounded.

I'd already had to make a deal with one of the alien devils in order to save Quinn's life. Though she was one of my best enforcers, even she wasn't irreplaceable, but it would have taken two or three trained specialists to do it, and I had less of those to spare now every day.

Two of my elite guards waited for us above. Only Harold, my Trusted Advisor, was with me. I'd have preferred the General, but there were rumors of another disloyal base, and I'd dispatched her to root them out. Harold stroked his self-indulgent mustache with one hand and leaned against the barren stone wall with the other.

At need, the room could be filled with acid, electricity, fire, or a handful of other measures. It could also be filled with concrete. Our last line of defense in my own personal bastion, we'd spared no expense to make the fort as impenetrable as the System and our Credits would allow. It did not encourage decorations.

"The troops we have left are the best of the best, sir, except for the elite squad we lost in Minnesota. We are hemorrhaging lesser troops, resources, and Credits faster than we can take them from the alien scum. We can't survive another month like this. Hell, another week and we might be too far gone to salvage. I'm sorry, sir. I take full responsibility." He dropped to his knees in supplication.

"Don't get your mustache in a twist, and for God's sake, get up off the damn floor and follow me. This isn't your fault."

"It isn't?" Harold said as he followed me down the marble steps into the vault where we kept the Settlement Orb for the base.

"No. This isn't even your department. Frankly, with the System being what it is, I can't even blame Lucas, and he's my Black Ops Chief. Enough Credits and Skills and there's no amount of dedicated effort that can solve a problem like this. It's not like we haven't gone above and beyond to ferret out the traitors."

The man shuddered, probably remembering the shame of having been forced to turn our Inquisitors on our own people. Or the pain from when it had been his turn.

"I don't like it," I said. "Hard work and dedication should be rewarded. But the System is what the System is. I've fought against it for as long as I can. It's time to give up trying to stop it and just do what has to be done, no matter how devastating and humiliating a price we have to pay."

He started to speak again, but I put my hand on the Orb and disappeared before he could do so.

"You have finally returned," said the Shop Keeper. It was some kind of lizard man with a hood like a cobra and colorful scales of orange and gold. The alien wore fine silks but also golden shackles that chained it to the counter. It had never mentioned why, and I'd never been curious enough to ask. An alien was an alien. Could this one even be considered an invader when the Shop wasn't actually on Earth? "Good. Good. I wasss beginning to doubt that I would ever sssee you again."

"Shut up, alien," I said. "You can speak when you're spoken to. Do you know why I'm here?"

"Thisss one would never presssume to guesss." He bowed, nearly as obsequious as my advisor.

"I have a traitor, or traitors, and we haven't been able to find them no matter what we do."

"How can thisss one be of ssservissse?"

I spat, disgusted by the alien, the System, the situation, and myself. "How much will it cost for me to buy the name of the traitor or traitors in my group?"

The servile lizard man tried not to smile and failed. His slitted, golden eyes filled with unhidden delight. In addition to my self-respect, this was clearly going to cost me a crap-ton of Credits. It wasn't so easy, of course. You had to word the questions right, had to ask the Shop in the right way, to get the right answers. Like one of those genies they tell you about in old stories, where the wrong thing said can end it all.

Eventually, he gave me a price and a warning, "This will not reveal a treacherous heart, only treasonous actions."

I nodded. I understood.

I shuddered. It was hard to remember that I was the Humanist here. The sheer power of the Shop was staggering, and it wanted to humble me. The Humanist was many things, but humble was not one of them. I braced myself, remembered who I had become.

After everything, the deal itself was a simple transaction. The Shop was akin to wishes and a greedy corporation, all rolled up together. It gave me everything I needed, though it cost me the price of a Settlement.

A long list of names and their crimes against the Human Liberation Front appeared, all on the System equivalent of an iPad. After that, it was one button press to sort out any normal minor offenses, so that only the truly treasonous remained, then another button push to sort them by seniority.

Most of the names meant nothing to me. I couldn't put a single one of them to a face, for the first few pages. They could be my non-elite guards or the girl who brought me my lunch, and I'd have never known. There were so many of them and only one of me. I couldn't be expected to know them all.

Deciding to change tack, I swapped the order from bottom to top. Then I cried out in anguish and betrayal and nearly dropped the tablet as I saw the first name listed there.

The Humanist roared in righteous rage.

Chapter 59

Caleb

It had taken me more than two years, but I was finally going to experience the legendary Shop that everyone kept telling me about. After all the months of stress, worry, and pain, the trip itself was uneventful, more like a relaxing drive through the north woods than a trek through monster-infested wilderness.

Pines, birch, and aspen trees grew everywhere. With humanity reduced and the System apparently quickening their growth, the Chippewa National Forest was swiftly reclaiming lost ground. I'd lived in several cities in my earliest years, before my parents passed away, and I still remembered the wonder of a sea of green when Nana brought me home for the first time. Whatever happened, I hoped to get a chance to see this again with the gorgeous mix of oranges, yellows, and reds.

We rode in an old green-and-white Ford pickup. Penny was driving and I was riding shotgun, which Randy hadn't stopped ranting about. He, Pavise, and a Rifleman named Tony rode in back with Aul, who simply couldn't fit in the front.

The Commander's people had cleared a path for us and given us cover for nearly half of the way. Past that, we'd only had a few miles until we left the higher-Level areas and only another hour or so until we reached land patrolled by the Hakarta.

Other than a checkpoint that my token from the Bounty Hunter got us through with minimal hassle, everything went smooth. We knew that using the item was a risk, given that the bounty hunters had all been captured or killed, but we'd decided it was too good of an opportunity to pass up. I'd liked the man and hoped he and his people were okay, but I wasn't deluded enough to think that it was likely.

From a distance, the settlement looked like a mix between a modern fortress and a logging camp. Everything was high-tech and futuristic. Walls armored with metal plates were backed by manned heavy ordinance and what were either high-tech security cameras or automated laser emplacements or both. My money was on both.

Some of the Hakarta were decked out like the classic space orcs trope, but others were dressed more like ordinary people. A tent and pavilion market surrounded the right front side of the gates and seemed to have its own security forces. Not only did it remind me of a fair, with all of the good and bad that that entailed, but some elements of it were clearly Mana-refurbished carnival stalls. There was even a Ferris wheel covered in Christmas lights. Humans, Hakarta, and people from other species were doing business and seemed to be getting along. Some were segregated into clusters, but others mixed and matched freely. It gave me real hope for the future of our world.

We left the truck with Tony and headed toward the gate. As a group, we all stopped and gawked at a tall, shaved-headed human sitting in the captain's chair of a flat-topped, pale blue boat surrounded by a sea of junk, books, armor, and other seemingly random items. He was a handsome man, exuberant and charismatic. He seemed happy and alive in the way the others around him didn't. He was selling what looked like science-fiction scuba gear to a pale orange humanoid.

A sign hanging from the ship said, "Van's Consignment, Sales, Shipping, and Installation." On the boat beside it, in barely legible letters, it read, "Crabass II." His capitalization choices irked my inner grammarian, but that world had ended, and billboards had never been that good about such things, even in the old days.

"I need it," the being said, their voice soft and melodic. Their tone still managed to be urgent somehow. He took an aggressive step forward as he spoke, and his cheeks puffed.

I glanced around for guards, but none were nearby or watching.

"I know, you told me. That's why it costs so much." The big man grinned and his eyes twinkled fiendishly. He leaned over casually, putting his hand on a knobbed, dark wood walking stick my Nana would have called a shillelagh. Beside it, on the ground, was an open case holding what looked to be a sniper-style rifle of some sort.

"But you are only selling it for five percent less than the Shop?"

"Ten percent less," he said, holding out some kind of tablet. "I checked."

"Fine, but I feel like you're taking advantage of me."

"Business is business," the man answered as he put away his tablet and loaded the gear into an old duffle bag. "Come back anytime."

"Kraken sheddings. Whatever."

"Oh, one second." The man, Van presumably, grabbed one of those headband lamps, a cube the size of a Magic Eight Ball that my inspection skill told me was an emergency atmosphere cube, and a softcover novel titled *Fool Moon*.

"What the hell is all of this? I mean, I can really use the cube and the underwater lamp, but I can't afford any of this. You cleaned me out. And I'm not bringing a book underwater."

"I've gone above and beyond with five-star service since before the System came. I see no reason to stop that now."

"If you were just going to give me all this, why did you fight so hard over the price?"

The big man looked puzzled by the question, as if it were in a language he couldn't understand, and the alien seemed to realize he should shut up and go away before the big man changed his mind, so he did just that.

I shook my head and focused on the Settlement in front of us as security finally let us through.

The inside was much less hectic than the outer market. Everyone I saw seemed to be part of the city's guards. We were led straight to the Shop, and I barely got to learn anything about the place. What I could see was basic and boring. That was probably a security measure.

At their instruction, we put our hands on the orb I'd heard so much about.

I'd been told what to expect.

It wasn't what happened.

Darkness surrounded me. I felt as if I was floating in deep space. I closed my eyes unnecessarily and breathed in deeply through my nose and out through my mouth, forcing my body to relax and my pulse to slow.

When I opened my eyes, a blue text window had appeared in my vision.

Quest Received

Restoration of Honor and Glory

A benefactor has purchased a Shop upgrade for you.

You are able to access the Kaldian Commerce Core.

Other Shop access has been permanently restricted.

You have met the requirements to trigger a hidden Quest.

Requirement 1: Acquire a Kaldian Shield-Bot.

Requirement 2: Have or meet the requirements of a Kaldian Advanced Class.

To succeed at this Quest, you must prove the inherent superiority of Kaldian Technology and Skills.

Success will be rewarded based on intention, style, and results. Failure will have thorough and permanent consequences.

This Quest cannot be refused.

What had I gotten myself into!

A warehouse apparently. When the world sprang back into focus, I found myself standing in front of a truly massive storehouse of shelves and boxes. It looked so much like the scene from Indiana Jones that I felt a bit nostalgic. Turning around, I found myself face-to-faces with a trio of robots standing behind a hovering store counter. Functionally, I guess it worked fine, but it was so strange to be able to see their feet and legs. Weird.

"Welcome!" the robot on the left announced. It was painted bright orange with a few green lines on its head. "Congratulations on your upgrade to premium level service. You lucky duck."

"Luck indeed," the one on the right said. "I don't see why you're congratulating the human. It hasn't done anything to earn our services. It certainly doesn't deserve them."

"He, not it," I told the robot firmly.

"The human is correct," the robot in the center said to its counterpart on the right. "Customer service is paramount, after all."

The cranky robot grumbled but said nothing intelligible. It was taller, thinner, and older-looking than the others. The craftsmanship was fine, but the metal seemed forged or sculpted to resemble knotted wood. It created an interesting effect I appreciated much more than its personality, at least so far.

I turned my attention to the central figure, ignoring the other two for now. It seemed to be in charge. It also looked a lot like Pavise, though without the heavily armored look. They all had at least some similarities in that regard, especially when it came to their heads.

"Hello to all of you," I said, "and it's Caleb, not human. May I have your names? I certainly don't want to keep thinking of you all as robot."

"Of course, of course," the central robot said. "Welcome indeed, Caleb. Though I must agree with my illustrious colleague that congratulations may be a bit premature. I am Dranaw. To my right"—he gestured to the smaller orange robot I'd been thinking of as on the left—"is Lepsus. And finally"—he gestured the other way—"Gulluth."

"The Gulluth," the taller robot corrected, in a tone that conveyed affront.

"Indeed." Dranaw, the center one, continued, "How may we help you, fine customer?" My slight hint of annoyance must have made its way to my face, because he noticed. "Oh, quite right. My apologies. We've been waiting here so long. I find myself overexcited. How may I help you, Caleb?"

"First of all, can you tell me what happened to my friends? We entered the Shop together?"

"Oh! Quite right. Please excuse me." He waved, and Aul appeared beside me. "As an Elite member, you are more than welcome to bring guests or possible recruits with you to the showroom in the future. This one was summoned, however, as I see you are her guardian."

"You will be responsible for her activities," The Gulluth announced.

"And rewarded for her accomplishments, should you manage to recruit her," Lepsus chimed in cheerily. "This will be true for all guests, so please do be selective."

"Quite right, on both accounts," Dranaw said.

I would have had Pavise put their names over their heads. I couldn't do that politely without my cybernetic link. Things like that were the reason that fixing the link was top on my to-do list. Without it, I had to repeat each of their names a half a dozen times in my head. It reminded me of the first few days of class each year.

"First things first," I said.

"Excuse me, sir," Pavise interrupted, "but if I may? I see that you have been *awarded* a new Quest. Perhaps it would be best to begin by requesting information that would allow us to become informed on exactly what would be seen by the Quest-issuer as honor, glory, and success, as such concepts can be quite relative."

Wow. Score one for Pavise. "Excellent point, buddy. Do you have anything like that?"

Dranaw, the central robot, answered. "You have been granted access to the lowest level of our premium selection, as well as our services negotiating deals for you with the rest of the Shop's affiliated organizations. We can help you to receive many discounts and opportunities and also help to steer you away from"—his voice took on the sound of a person who was sneering, though he had no way to make expressions—"inferior technology."

"For instance," the tall one said, "that disgusting piece of filth you're wearing on your chest."

The most important item that I owned. Great.

"Allowances must be made," said the central figure. "He can not be expected to have known such things without our expert guidance."

"At least he didn't pay for it."

"Quite right, quite right. We will be happy to dispose of it for you, good sir."

They were more well-informed about my personal matters than I was comfortable with.

"It isn't mine," I said. "I need to return it to the one who bought it."

"Of course, of course," the middle one said.

"As part of your upgrade," the orange one interjected, "I can provide the basic fundamentals of the history of the Kaldian Empire, its technologies, and its tragic downfall." He set out a cube. "For your companion, of course."

"Thank you," I said, as Pavise picked up the item and slotted it into one of the receptacles beneath his armor plates.

"You will also be awarded three tokens. Each allows you to select one of our premium upgrade options for free. Normally, you would have been advised to use one for your Class, one for your Companion's Upgraded Form, and one for your matching gear set. However, you have *accomplished*," he stressed the word in a defiant tone, "your Class through your own efforts. You should be quite proud."

"Thank you, I am."

"He doesn't even have the associated Basic Class," The Gulluth said.

"That is hardly his fault, and it isn't one of the requirements."

"It should be."

"We've been over this," the central bot declared, breaking up the fight between the other two. "The rules are the rules, and we do not set them."

"Maybe we should," the taller, grumpy robot replied.

"Maybe we should, indeed. However, we do not. No amount of complaining is going to change that."

I wanted to ask Pavise if he still wanted to claim that Kaldian bots weren't people when they so clearly were. But this didn't seem like the right time. I missed my cybernetics.

"Sir," Pavise said, "I strongly advise you to allow me to negotiate on your behalf regarding a key issue. There are matters of etiquette and propriety at play here that may seem a bit counterintuitive to human sensibilities. I'd suggest, in fact, that you do nothing but nod once for yes or twice for no."

Trust fall rules then. I forced myself not to grumble and just nodded once.

"Excellent. With that handled…" He turned to the others. "I would like to summon an inferior assistant to aid our honorless follower with her lesser shopping needs."

He had been right to get me to agree to shut up in advance. I would not have tolerated that statement.

The middle one spread out the three actuators on its left "hand." My translation Skill told me that this indicated yes.

Pavise turned to me. "Sir, Aul has requested your permission to use a portion of the Credits you are keeping for her people as their guardian to purchase books and other things. Do you approve of this?"

I wanted to ask questions, but I didn't dare. Still, Aul was a good kid, so I nodded once.

"Excellent, sir. Aul will disappear now. Do not be alarmed. Aul, in addition to your shopping, please enjoy a presentation regarding the honor and glory of the Kaldian Empire, *quietly* and *without questions*."

Aul nodded, sparkled like a vampire from *Twilight*, and then vanished.

"She will be safe, sir."

"Thank you."

"Now, as the first step, may I suggest using your first token to replace your cybernetic implants with the much more advanced and superior Kaldian Cerebral Enhancement?"

The System details popped up on the usual blue screen in my field of vision. The shield-bot was clearly doctoring the feed on my behalf, bless him.

Kaldian Cerebral System Enhancement, version 28.7 (human adapted variant)

Creates a dedicated and optimized cerebral connection to your Kaldian Companion and affiliated technologies. The information security it provides are nearly double your previous system. Additionally, this device allows for a 15.274 percent faster connection than your previous, inferior device. As this is an upgrade to your entire nervous system, rather than just a portion of your brain, it provides the following additional benefits.
Intelligence and Agility: + 10
Willpower and Perception: + 5

"That's sounds great," I said and nodded eagerly.

"Excellent. As they prepare the device for implantation, may I show you your options in our Class-appropriate equipment? Assuming, of course, that you would like to use your other upgrade tokens for their usual purpose."

"Sure."

"A Kaldian Warder and their shield-bot's most crucial decision is a choice between three different chassis types. Please take note that there are *three*," Pavise said, "as is *just* and *right* and *proper.*"

What the heck is that supposed to mean? There's nothing just and right and proper about the number three. Oh, cultural values. I bet the Kaldian people had three fingers, like the actuators on the shield bots. We had stupid customs too. Still, there was a Quest in play, so I did my best to memorize the phrasing.

Pavise paused a little longer than I needed, and I was eager to get started with our upgrades.

I tried to take the chance to look around more, but he noticed before I could see anything interesting in the giant stacks of sealed containers. He pointed in front of me as a loud hydraulic hiss sounded from the exact same spot.

I turned to watch as two circular areas on the off-white floor, each about twice as wide as Pavise, rotated and rose to the accompaniment of mechanical humming and whirring noises. The distinct scent of opening new electronics followed. The machines revealed were made from metal and some kind of composite material with advanced robotic arms.

I had to bite my tongue to stop myself from teasing them that two machines instead of three was unjust, wrong, and improper. But there was an active quest from a wealthy and powerful patron who valued courtesy and honor. He'd already threatened "thorough and permanent consequences."

I had not even noticed a slot until Pavise slid a pair of platter-shaped bronze disks into them like giant arcade tokens.

The machines came to life with rumbling vibrations.

Three containers, like those on the shelves, arrived through a shoot and clicked into slots in the machine. Each of the containers had a picture of a robot chassis for the machine on the right, or a suit of armor for the machine on the left.

"The first option," Pavise said, the leftmost box glowed, "is the heavily armored model. This leads to the Kaldian Crusader Class." His tone was filled with awe bordering on reverence.

Holographic images of a much heavier and elaborate version of Pavise's armor appeared. It came with a tower shield and a three-sided, spiked mace. The Crusader themselves had armor and gear to match. The crusader and his armor was clearly based on me, rather than a Kaldian, as it was sized to match me and it was fully humanoid in shape.

Then the images changed, showing gun-toting goblins attacking the pair with vaguely implied allies in the distance. A personal force field appeared around the armor. Then a larger barrier surrounded the duo and the goblins, separating them from the Crusader's allies.

"That's a lot like a knight in shining armor," I told him. "This option would be amazing."

"It would be, wouldn't it?" Pavise said wistfully.

The first boxes dimmed and the middle boxes lit up. Instead of normal armor, my side had a chair inside an armored cube. Like Kang from the Ninja Turtles. Pavise's chassis option was less heavily armored but larger, and it had a hole in its chest where my armored cube would go. The openings in the cube concerned me, but I assumed there would be see-through barriers of some sort. As I watched, this form switched its "legs" to treads, raised an extra armored barrier to seal off the cube, and a blaster cannon rose from its back.

"The Kaldian Marauder," Pavise said in a total deadpan. He clearly didn't like it. "A powerful combination of ranged offense and mobility, balanced with respectable defenses."

"That sounds ideal for us, buddy. It would keep us both as far from the danger as we can get. What's the problem?"

"That is an excellent question, sir. Perhaps one of your thought experiments may be the best tool for me to use to clarify my answer. Do I have your permission to proceed?"

"Yes," I told him. "For the record, you don't have to ask my permission."

"I would like you to imagine there is a troop transport in the distance. We are in hostile territory, have engaged in many battles with forces that look much the same, and they are headed our way."

"Got it."

"You and I are prepared, aware they are coming, and have clear shot from a long distance with the powerful weapon on display. I let you know that I calculate with a ninety percent certainty that—"

"Oh," I said. "Well, crud."

"Indeed, sir. I make it clear that it is nearly certain the enemies are hostile, and they are now within the optimal striking distance to fully take advantage of our weapons long-range …" He paused, the way he'd seen me do with students in the past.

"I get it, Pav. I'm not going to attack them without at least attempting diplomacy, so what's the point of this upgrade option?"

"You are correct, sir."

The force field appeared around this one too, though the force barrier appeared as an impassable wall behind the duo, apparently to stop their troops from rear assaults.

"Finally," he said, "the Kaldian Sentinel. Though they do not match the offensive power of the other option, this chassis is a true defensive specialist, able to generate and shape more powerful force constructs while still maintaining adequate armor and mobility."

This pulled up images of sleeker, more high-tech-looking armor. They had a central glowing energy core and visible lines of power.

The possibilities excited me. I turned to ask Pavise, "Just how complex are these force constructs?"

"Still quite simple and slow to reshape, I'm afraid. But much more versatile than the others."

So, no giant green boxing gloves in my future, but it still sounded like a great choice.

By the time I'd gotten my imagination under control, I'd missed the extended demonstration and the boxes had all gone dark.

"If I understand correctly, Pav, we're picking between a powerful defensive and mild utility option, and a more balanced offensive and defensive combat choice that you prefer. Is that right?"

"Yes and no, sir. Perhaps a more practical example, this time." He waved his hand and the first of the boxes opened. On the top was the truly epic-looking triangular mace. "Hand it to me please, and I will show you."

I walked over and reached for the mace. I expected it to be heavy, so I gripped the handle with both hands and pulled. Nothing. I braced my feet, adjusted my balance, then realized I was being an idiot and gave up. It might as well have been Mjolnir; I hadn't even made the thing budge. There was no chance I was ever going to wield this weapon or wear its matching armor.

"Got it," I said. "I would say that I chose Sentinel, but it seems that Sentinel has chosen me."

"Us," Pavise said, and he sounded a little bit whiny.

"As is right, and just, and proper," I teased him. "You would have preferred either of the other two choices, wouldn't you?"

"Any Kaldian path is an honor to follow," he said, which was definitely a yes.

He's also reminding me we're being observed. Judged.

I'd better watch my tone.

Once our chassis was chosen, I was thrilled to learn that there were dozens of cosmetic options we could select, each with customizable tweaks to get things just the way we wanted. I nearly couldn't stop myself from laughing when we organically narrowed them down to three choices.

One was a royal blue with neon lines and patterns. In the center was a core of radiant energy. It looked amazing and reminded me of *Tron*. The Shield Warder bot's body matched it beautifully. It was much more like the Star Wars battle droids I'd initially envisioned, and much less *Lost in Space*. However, it still had the squat, plate-mail look that I'd always associated with Pavise.

There were some key differences. The new arms were thick, Doc Ock-style cables with much more precise looking "hands." They had what looked to be blasters in the palms.

The second was bright silver, with a blinding white core. My friends would hate it, since it would blind them, especially in the sun. But it might also blind my enemies, and visually, it was the favorite for both Pavise and me.

The last was almost exactly like the first, but with metallic purple instead of blue.

We ruled out our favorite first, for obvious reasons. That left the blue and the purple. I would probably have gone with the blue based on nostalgia alone, but Pavise, who had no personal preference, informed me that the purple would look better with my skin tone. I took him at his word, and we went with the purple. It would take some getting used to.

I wonder what Evie will think of my new armor. I wish she was here. Its base value was actually worse than what the Matriarch had bought me, but the maneuverability and self-repair functions were stronger. And my old armor was just armor. This was so much more, though I didn't have enough tokens or Credits to do more than scratch the surface of its potential.

Core: Kaldian Apex 3B Mana Engine

CPU: Kaldian Secondary-Worker (Linked to Companion and Implant)

Armor Rating: Tier IV

Hard Points: 1

Soft Points: 5 (1 used for Neural Link. 1 reserved for Companion Link-Currently disabled)

Battery Capacity: 120/120

+2 Strength

+5 Perception and Constitution
+10 Int
+12% Resist Energy
+15% Resist Physical

The token and Pavise's connection to my new Class did a lot of the heavy lifting to bring Pavise's AI tech up to his current level. The rest, Lee had offered to fund, and I took him up on it. We also purchased several modest software and firmware options.

Pavise also mentioned to me that he had made other purchases with the money I had paid him, but he declined to tell me what he'd bought. Over and above his normal increases, the upgrades for his new body were as follows:

Core: Kaldian Apex 3 Mana Engine
CPU: Kaldian Warder Companion Matrix Alpha-1
Armor Rating: Tier IV
Hard Points: 4
Soft Points: 3 (1 used for Neural Link)
Battery Capacity: 120/120
+6 to Willpower
+7 to Intelligence
+12 to Strength and Agility

With all of that handled, we settled in for the rest of the shopping. Most of the items we needed were easily resolved, and with prices that Pavise assured me were quite a bit better than we could have gotten otherwise.

That said, a half dozen of the items the Commander and his people had requested, the Kaldians flatly would not let us to buy. Four of them had obvious Kaldian-approved replacements. For the other two, which were overtly magical items, we'd have had to buy replacements that I wasn't confident would fulfill the intended purpose.

I had Pavise let Randy know about the issue and give him the Commander's Credits so that he could make the purchases. I also loudly declared that the Credits were not mine, that I had been holding them for someone else, just in case. I was desperate to talk to Pavise again privately.

Then a terrifying thought occurred to me. If this being could upgrade my Shop access without my permission, and if we were using tech he specifically wanted us to use, could we ever have any real expectation of privacy ever again? Assuming that there was a living being watching this at all, and not just a System upgrade purchased automatically by a person who'd been dead for centuries. What did I really know about how any of this worked?

I decided that my only real choice was to assume that we could discuss things privately via our secure connection. Otherwise, I might as well just ask them to add tinfoil to my new helmet's interior.

Chapter 60

Caleb

Once our shopping was complete, they replaced and adjusted my cybernetics. The Shop didn't require me to be awake for the process. I lay down, lost consciousness, and woke up with the process complete. I didn't even have dry mouth.

Once everything else was out of the way, we addressed the most important issue of all. Pavise, who looked amazing in his upgraded body, let them know we were looking to purchase a new AI for Aul's spaceship. Pavise clearly announced that this neither was, nor ever would be, my own personal ship and that it was therefore not either allowed to, nor expected to, use Kaldian technology. I was holding the money in trust for minors. He clarified that these were innocent minors whose lives had been saved, against overwhelming odds, by the stalwart might of a Kaldian shield-bot.

The robots hemmed and hawed and bickered for a while, before finally agreeing to transfer us to a special room that would allow for limited communication with an outside specialist. Pavise gave them the exact details and specifications that he thankfully knew—because I certainly didn't—and we soon found ourselves in a vast black emptiness, talking to a pile of glowing green goo that Pavise assured me was sentient.

With a specially provided upgrade to my translation Skill and Pavise's programming, we were able to understand that the creature's gentle ripples and waves were complex language, and the changes in the shade and brightness of the glow indicated the various emotions and their strength, respectively.

I learned three things quite quickly.

1. Advanced AIs for custom spaceships were expensive.

2. Neither I, nor the children, were quite as rich as I'd let my overactive imagination hope for.

3. The Kaldians would not allow the normal means used to deliver or install the exceptionally large and heavy devices that housed such technology.

I decided to tackle the problems in order. "Please eliminate any options that could be considered expensive."

The green of the slime darkened. There were still far too many options, and the ones that were front and center were out of any kind of price range I'd be willing to consider.

"Please prioritize any options that could best be considered dirt cheap but functional." I hoped the translation software was up to that level of complexity.

Apparently it was, because the glow turned from "run for your lives" to "glow in the dark" levels of apparent radioactivity. The salesbeing was not a happy camper.

Then I asked, "Do you have any items that would do the job very well but have some kind of weird quirk or trait that makes it hard to sell?"

The shade of slime speckled, and its body undulated in a way that my translator told me indicated malicious glee. It shone.

I wasn't sure whether I should be worried or excited.

It sent over the specs. The AI in question would serve our functions not only adequately, but exceptionally. There were four distinct and powerful hubs, with a fifth that integrated them and provided all of the basic functions and controls for the ship. The four each had specialized functions that allowed them to run the ship without a pilot or crew, though a pilot or crew were recommended due to the benefits of various Skills, especially for those with dedicated Classes.

"What's the catch?" I asked.

Hesitant wiggles and a faint glow failed to translate.

"I'm sorry," I said. "I don't understand."

"Sorry," he answered. "The translation does not do well with profanity."

"I see," I said, in a faintly disapproving tone that probably would not translate either. "I'm waiting."

His first response was just more vigorous wiggling. Eventually, though, he gave what I hoped was a straight answer. "The device is larger than usual and takes up a lot of space. It is also more Mana intensive, and therefore, there will be some necessary give and take in urgent situations. This can be offset or improved via a crew and Skills, of course."

"There's no way that's the catch with the price you're offering and the way you were hedging," I said.

"Perhaps we should look to a different purveyor of goods, sir."

The green light turned an angry medium color and flashed repeatedly.

"Last chance," I told them.

After a long delay, it quivered and flashed. The translation came out as, "It has no manual controls. Each of the four AI hubs have problematic personalities running them. They think that they are people."

"Maybe they are people. I mean, you're clearly a person, and you're..." I gestured to indicate the pile of goo before me.

A pulsing flare of light nearly blinded me.

"Sorry," I said. "I don't mean anything bad by it. I just mean people come in all kinds of shapes and forms and sizes. Why are you so confident that these AI are not people?"

The slime oozed its way to a data cube, which Pavise took and inserted in a slot beneath his amor.

"I see," he said. "That *is* quite tragic."

The puddle undulated its agreement, but the lights were dim and the color didn't change.

"Sir, the tragedy of the Hallory family is apparently quite well-known in artificial intelligence circles. Randon Hallory was a true pioneer in the field. His wife, Vylia, was a brilliant Mathematician and Neurophysicist. Their children proved to be prodigies as well. Their son, Gypher, was a genius when it came to general physics, and their daughter, Tannin, was an engineer and musician. As a scientist, she was nothing special, though competent. As a musician, with an instrument called a tei-tei hoon, she was unmatched.

"They were hijacked by pirates and their ship's propulsion was destroyed. The story tells that the pirates were so touched by Tannin's music that they left the ship without hurting any of the girl's family. Less believably, it says that they stole nothing.

"The thrusters, however, were already damaged beyond repair. Tannin blamed herself for her inadequacies as an engineer, though no level of genius could have fixed it with what they had on hand, and a less-inspired musician wouldn't have been alive to have even tried.

"In desperation, the father, Randon, attempted the impossible. He strove to download his family's memories, personalities, everything that made them individuals, into storage devices. He was a brilliant man and he'd triple-checked his work. One by one, they activated the device with confidence. And one by one, they reassured their waiting family members of the experiment's success."

I listened raptly, wishing that I hadn't been told this was a tragedy. "The poor family."

"Indeed, sir. When the ship was discovered, decades later, both the System and dozens of gathered experts verified that the experiment had been an utter failure. Not only was much of the brilliance and experience of the family lost, especially because they had no System access to recover their lost Skills, but there was no one there when it came to true consciousness."

Here the merchant reentered the conversation. "The experts did not have the heart to destroy them, especially because one of their number disagreed with the findings, destroying her reputation forever. Instead, they placed the device in a museum. When that closed, it came to me, though I'm under a System Contract not to modify it in any way, with a few listed exceptions. I can sell it, but the buyer has to agree to the same contract.

"I realized that the family had crewed their own ship and that they still retained the know-how to do just that, and the central AI they'd used is fully functional. To tell you the truth, since you've got a System Companion looking out for you and you'll never buy the damned thing anyway, I've sold it three times so far. Every time, the buyer has sold it back to me for much less than they paid because the AI are delusional and won't do what they're told. I always cut them a fair deal on the replacement. Well, mostly fair. It's becoming quite lucrative for me."

"Can I talk to them? The Hallorys, I mean."

"Sir," Pavise said, "this seems unwise."

"What can it hurt to talk to them?" I had an idea. It was risky, maybe crazy, but it might be my only chance to help the children recover their ship.

When the salesperson agreed, I asked for a few minutes of privacy.

An older man and woman, who both seemed intelligent and just a little haughty, appeared as holographic forms to meet with me. Two equally impressive looking young adults appeared behind them. They looked like handsome and well-dressed humans, except that they had opalescent skin and oversized gills on their necks.

"Nice to meet you all. My name's Caleb."

The elder male stepped forward, looking me up and down rather skeptically. He sighed. "Another one already." His voice was smoother than that of a human, but his tone matched his words.

The younger woman, Tannin, sneered. "Can he even afford a spaceship?" Her voice was lyrical and lovely. It made sense. She was a musician, after all. And a snob apparently.

I scolded myself internally. I should have changed into my new armor. I did look pretty underwhelming, and it was important to look my best.

Her mother, Vylia, looked at Tannin disapprovingly, but said nothing.

I reminded myself that they'd been through a lot and restrained my frustration. But I did not speak again. I'd learned how to handle unruly people with personal baggage. I just smiled, held Randon's eyes, and waited.

The younger man, Gypher, snickered, but he sounded more amused than harsh.

The father met my eyes and held them for a long moment, seeming to reevaluate me. "I suppose that I have nothing better to do, under the circumstances. Hello, Caleb. I am Doctor Randon Hallory, one of the galaxy's foremost experts in my field. Indisputably, the greatest authority on my own viewpoint in this universe. In spite of what some will tell you"—he glared at the salesbeing—"I can assure you that I am, in fact, a person. That we are people."

I nodded. "Nice to meet you, Doctor Hallory. For the record, I never doubted it for a second. As far as I'm concerned, if you claim to be people, then you're people. Heck, I've got an AI companion"—I gestured to Pavise—"who claims not to be a person, and I'm thoroughly convinced that he's wrong. So please trust that I will treat you with the same courtesy and respect that I would give to anyone else."

"That is refreshing, if somewhat suspicious."

Another situation where my Ring of Truth Skill didn't function. This one, at least, made a lot of sense.

"That's fair," I told him. "Cards on the table, I'm in trouble, but it seems like you are too, so I'm going to be blunt. I have a friend, a Voloid child named Aul. She and her hive have a spaceship, and I'm their guardian. The trouble is, I'm not great at my job yet. A group of other humans have taken over the ship, and I'm not sure how to get rid of them. But they don't have a way to control the ship. Your help may be able to get us the advantage that we need when the time is right."

"I'm not sure how much help we can be," he said. "But I understand high risk gambles more than most. You're right to call our situation troublesome, as well. We have some tools and abilities, but they are limited in the situation we find ourselves in."

"I'm not sure either, but if we have a chance to get away from all our enemies, I want to be able to take it. And you should, at least, be able to restrict their ability to do the same."

He chuckled. "That, we have proven quite adept at managing."

"I want to be one hundred percent clear. I do not, and will not, buy people. I have no interest in owning any people. It's evil, and I'll have no part of it. But if the System needs to say that I own someone in order for that person to be free, like with Pavise here, I'm willing to do that for them. That isn't an offer of a deal or me asking for a bribe; that part I'll just do. It gets a bit more complicated when I'd have to use someone else's Credits to do it. I'd still try to find a way now that I know about your situation."

He was really evaluating me now, I could tell, rather than blowing off a stranger who had shown up and might be trying to trick him. "Thank you," he said. "I appreciate that more than you can know."

I smiled. "Though I'd prefer to just think of people as friends and work together, I am willing to hire people, whether or not the System will enforce the contract with you."

"It will not," he said, his voice bitter with barely suppressed rage.

I wanted to put my hand on his shoulder to reassure him. But I didn't have his permission, and there was no reason to ask for it since he was not solid anyway.

"We can worry about pay later," he said, "since we have to trust you anyway. I'd like to get us out of prison here and onto a ship as fast as we can. What's the next step?"

"How can you trust him?" Tannin asked her father.

"Because we have no better alternatives, and that is never likely to change until we do something about it."

His daughter gave a reluctant nod.

"I trust him," Vylia said. "He has kind eyes."

I beamed at her and met her gaze. "Thank you. I'll try not to let you down."

She bowed gracefully.

"I'd prefer that we had the deal worked out in full before beginning, but I'm not going to leave you trapped here to make that happen."

"We're grateful for your help" Randon replied. "I'll also send you a list of Skills for you to consider for yourself and programs for your companion. We will be able to provide you much more help if you get what you can. I'll also include a list of things to get for others over time, those who you know that you can trust."

"Thank you. Make sure you highlight the most urgent, and I'll pick them up on our way out. If there's nothing else, and assuming that I'm able to work things out with a delivery and installation service guy I met outside the settlement, let's get the four of you out of here."

They disappeared, leaving us alone with the salesbeing. He must have overheard everything because he was pulsating with a pleasant green glow.

"Pavise," I said through our newly restored link, *"please remind me not to announce how desperate we are to have something where a salesperson can hear it."*

"An excellent point, sir. He has already sent us an offer, but we should review and negotiate several key issues before we accept."

"He's going to triple the price, buddy, if we're lucky."

"But certainly he would honor the agreement that he's offered," Pavise said.

"I think he's so excited that he forgot he sent it."

"I don't think so, sir. I believe that he is waiting because I have expressed concerns, so he plans to negotiate as we address those points, and he believes, rightly, that I will advise you to not accept the contract as is."

"Are any of the points things that will come back to negatively affect the children? Or really screw us over?"

"Nothing of that sort, sir. But it is important to—"

He stopped talking when he got the prompt that I'd accepted the offer.

Pavise drooped, pouting? But I was confident I had done the right thing when the slime's glow dimmed.

Chapter 61

Aul

Like a Voloid after metamorphosis, Pavise and Caleb emerged from the Shop with glorious new exoskeletons. Even the darker purple portions were reflective, shining brightly under this planet's yellow sun. They would be worthy of great praise, if only they'd been grown instead of purchased. Still, even an artificial exoskeleton was better than none, this one that was called I decided, as my mother had before me. I chirped my approval.

The changes had done nothing to address the pair's unfortunate deficiency of limbs. *Caleb is only human*, I reminded myself. He'd said so often enough himself. The Teacher understood his people's limitations. Pavise was another matter. *His entire body's been replaced. Surely the Shop could have done something to make him whole.*

Pavise was intelligent and wise. He would have a good reason for such a drastic oversight. What that might be, I could only speculate. Whether it was because of a restrictive budget, or a sense of solidarity with his hive mate, I did not know. It would be rude to ask.

We exchanged greetings and left the Settlement behind. Randy and Penny, the Shopkeepers had informed us, had finished long before. They'd left word for us to meet them at the truck.

The buildings we passed were strange to me. They were made of wood and metal. None of them were carved from anything, and very few used any stone at all. They were all created by putting things together. It was very strange.

We passed them soon enough and my focus returned to myself, my hive, and my worries.

This one had bought many books. Slavery, hive minds, genetics, individuality, and free will were the main topics. Caleb would be proud of the purchases and the subject matter. If buying those were all that I had done, this one would not feel so lesser ashamed.

I had even found a gift for Caleb—a book about the efforts made to uplift monsters. He had told us about his Quest to find a better way than killing them in class last week. His lesser feelings had seemed so much like the greater feelings of a whole hive that I did not have the heart to interrupt him, even though the questions that I'd had were so vitally important.

He'd also told us of a book called *Don Quixote*, and a song called the "Impossible Dream," so this one had decided that my friend was overwhelmed again. I'd finally found a way to try to help. It might reduce the lesser shame that was growing in me every time I looked at him.

My guilt lessened as I imagined the Teacher's big grin as he opened the gift. It was not enough to stop my antennae from drooping because of my second deception of Caleb.

He had clearly trusted us. Me. I had used that trust against him. Was this the thing that Caleb called betrayal? Such a concept had been unthinkable to me when he'd first introduced it. No one in the Queen's hive could hide a truth or have any cause to do so. We were a part of the Queen, extensions of her will. That was what it meant to be a Voloid. It was the way that things must be.

And yet I shuddered at the thought of our rejoining.

Another betrayal, I knew, but not a betrayal that caused me any guilt, lesser or otherwise. Not like what I'd done to Caleb.

I'd used a large amount of Credits, and I'd used them to make purchases that I knew for certain Caleb would oppose. This one had set in motion things that could not be undone. When Caleb learned that nearly a third of the Credits he had kept in trust for us had been expended, he might not even care. When he learned that I'd made choices that would put all of us in danger, however... I didn't even want to consider it. It sickened my stomach.

I had been hoping to sneak off to find a way to sample the local food. Cut off from the Matriarch and the Queen, we could no longer share in the sensations of feasting. Fighting off the urge to share the bounty of the Hunters' feasts had gotten harder every day. Only our desire to honor Caleb's wishes, and our pride and resentment toward the other humans, had prevented our surrender to their offers to partake.

Now, I could not have eaten, no matter how savory the smells from the outdoor stalls. Guilt had turned my gut against me. I could not keep Caleb's, "I'm not angry, just disappointed," look from appearing in my lesser mind's eye. This was not like that thing that he had called the Holocaust. The hive would not die if I did nothing.

But I was the One that Chooses, or I would be soon, and this one would rather choose to die than to face what would happen to my hive if I did nothing. So, might not deception be okay? I did not think Caleb would feel that way. Even knowing that, I did not feel I had chosen wrongly.

My actions could not be undone. The purchases had been made. The messages had already been sent.

This one's thoughts were distracted as Caleb brought us back to the human selling things on top of the blue vehicle the humans called a boat. I must not have learned the lessons about such things correctly, because the boat was not on the water. This one called me had completely misunderstood its purpose. I could not even try to guess it now.

Caleb and the boat human got into a passionate debate about shipping, handling, installation, credits, and *Star Trek*. I tried to understand them, but they were talking quickly and using words I did not know that did not translate. I gave up trying entirely when Caleb declared that one of the letters of the alphabet was more powerful than the Force.

A long line of humans caught my interest. They were dressed in old and dirty clothes and shuffled around in a massive cluster, with the strange ordered-disorder of those without an Eunn to bind their consciousness. My hive had been suffering from just such confusion recently. It was a sad and shameful thing, both lesser and greater.

If there was a Man-Queen somewhere, he had abandoned them.

I circled the white and gold pavilions so that I could get a better view. It seemed to me that the humans were waiting to get on a large rectangular spaceship made of dull gray metal.

Were the humans trying to escape dangers like we were? Did that mean it was it my responsibility to help the humans as Caleb had helped us? Or was the ship the help they seemed to need. I did not know and I had promised Caleb that I would stay close to him, so I could not learn more without betraying his trust. Again. My lesser shame was feeling greater and greater, and I did not want to make it worse.

I edged a little closer, then a little more, looking back to make sure that Caleb was still in sight. Once I reached the point where I could almost see Caleb, I saw the person "helping" the miserable looking humans. He had bad guy eyes. Caleb had Shown and Telled us many villains. This was a bad man. Caleb had taught us what happens to people when bad men load them onto ships.

I rushed back to Caleb and tried to ask him for his help. "Caleb, humans and others are trying to flee, is truth?"

"What!" He turned, then looked to where I was pointing with one of my smaller appendages.

I nodded to let him know he was looking in the right place when he had turned to me, confusion obvious.

"They are just waiting in line for something," he said. "I'm sorry, Aul. I need to finish making a deal here. One moment."

The lines were forming quickly. People were signing things and people were boarding ships.

"Caleb is curved priorities!"

"Huh?" he asked.

"Caleb is priorities not straight," I clarified, trying to remember his exact words.

He turned to me, eyes kind and attention focused, and he was Caleb again. "What's going on, Aul? How can I help?"

"I think he's talking about the slaves?" the bald human with the name of a vehicle said.

"Yes. Aul is worry about humans be slaves."

"Slaves," Caleb said. "They're taking humans as slaves?"

"Yes? No? Well not exactly," the Van man said. "It's a System Contract, and I guess you could say that it's voluntary. Except it's really not, and they're trapped forever without any way out. Kind of like marriage." Then his face paled, and his eyes widened. "Not my marriage!"

Caleb was ignoring the other human now as he said to me, "It's called bonded labor, or at least it used to be. And yeah, you're right that it's a lot like slavery, or it can be. I'd need to know more about what they were doing before I judged them."

"I love my wife," the van man declared. His lesser fear seemed very great indeed.

I decided to follow Caleb's lead and just ignored him. "Caleb is not time. Humans is being taken to ships."

"Where are they taking them?" Caleb asked the other human.

"It varies. Not anywhere on Earth."

Caleb rushed over and used Pay Attention to make the human child about to sign tablet listen to him. Caleb would feel lesser guilt for using the Skill later, I knew. Sometimes Caleb was too good to not be dumb.

"Please don't sign that yet," Caleb said.

The short, literally white humanoid with a large forehead protrusion and ruby-colored eyes glared at the Teacher. "What in the hell do you think you're doing, human!"

"I'd like to talk to these people, and I'd like to see the System Contract you're trying to get them to agree to."

"Get your own worthless dregs. These belong to me."

"No, they don't. Neither do the others you've already tricked and trapped. But these people haven't signed your evil slave contract yet. And if I have my choice, they never will."

"Look who's so high and mighty," he said, stretching his shoulders and long neck to exaggerate his height and raise his voice to try to imitate Caleb. "I think I know better than everyone else just because I'm human." He glared. "You don't understand anything, scum. I haven't lied to any of these people. Sure, they're desperate, but that's not my fault. I didn't make them that way. I'm just willing to take them away and make sure they're safe and fed and able to work it off over time. If most people choose to stay longer than that, I say why shouldn't they? What else is out there for them?"

"Freedom," Caleb answered.

"Overrated. Security beats freedom any day."

"If that's all true, then let me see the contract," Caleb demanded.

"Are you considering signing it?"

"No,"

"Then bugger off. You're no use to me."

"How much is he paying you?" Caleb was using teacher voice, talking loudly to the crowd now.

A haggard-looking older human man with a missing hand answered. "Not much, though I don't see how that's any of your business."

A pink-haired younger woman said, "There's nothing for us here anymore. Some of us don't have Classes that are any use to anyone, and they don't help us fight monsters. It's get taken advantage of here or someplace else. At least somewhere else isn't a Dungeon World. None of us have any illusions that we'll ever be free, but we'll eat, and we'll be safe again, like it was before."

"You're adults, you can make your own choice, though I'll help you if I can. But"—Caleb gestured to a boy scratching his head—"you can't really call it a choice if it's a child, even if I'm sure he's had to be more grown up than any of us were at his age."

"Sir," Pavise interjected, "children are offered at least some small protections by the System for such situations. It can be exploited, and it certainly is in many places, but some of the elements of mixing usurious loans with a company store are offset. They can accrue a debt based on what is provided to them, but they must be appropriately credited for any work they do and there are limits."

Caleb got the disfocused look of reading his prompts or talking with Pavise.

This one waited, not knowing what to say.

Caleb squatted to meet the boy's eyes. "Where are your parents?"

"Mom's dead, sir. I never knew my dad. He may still be alive somewhere. Never cared about me when the world was easy, so I doubt he cares more now."

"I'm sorry," Caleb said. "No one should have to go through that, especially alone. Just know that I see you, and you matter. I think you're special just the way you are."

"If I'm so special, then give me the money I need to get a roof over my head, a full belly, and something to get a Class worth something."

"How much do you need?"

The kid gave Caleb a skeptical look. "How the hell should I know?"

"That's fair. We can look into it. How old are you?"

"Seventeen."

Caleb waited patiently, eyes kind.

The child said nothing.

Caleb waited longer. I knew from long experience that Caleb would win.

"Fourteen," the boy finally said. He looked away.

"And what's your name?"

"Daniel," the human child said. "Not Dan."

"Daniel it is," Caleb said. "Like the lion."

"Huh?"

"Human child is should come with us," I said.

"Whatever," the being in charge of the line said. "Just take the runt and go. I don't get as much for them anyway." He leaned forward and whispered, "If you need more kids, maybe we can work something out. I've cleared out the riff-raff, but I'm sure some could be discovered, for the right price. Wadda ya say?"

Caleb stared at the man, hard. For the first time since I met him, Caleb looked dangerous. But not to me. Never to me. Eventually, the man got the message and stepped back.

"Last chance, folks. Once we're gone, who knows how long it will be before we come back? Sign or lose your chance, maybe forever."

"I'm not sure he'd be any safer coming with us," Caleb said to me. "Would he stay with me, or Lee's people, or you guys?"

"Child is be saved first. Details later."

Caleb beamed with lesser pride that looked so much like greater that I felt as if he had given me a whole sheet of his precious golden stars.

"You can come with us," Caleb finally told the child. "I can't promise you that you'll be safer, but we have plenty of nasty-tasting nutrition drink. I could go back to the Shop to get some food for you. We have to travel through some bad places to get back home, but we have strong defenders. We also have even stronger enemies who probably want all of us dead."

"If you creeps are trying to abduct children, you suck at it." This was the alien.

Caleb ignored the alien and spoke to the Daniel child. "I wish I could do more, but come with us and we'll do what we can to help."

"I've been looking after the boy here," the man with the missing arm said. "We're kind of a package deal. I should go with you."

"Me too," said one of the others.

Then all but two of them were chiming in.

"How many is be fit in truck?" I asked.

"Not enough," Pavise said. "And time is of the essence, I'm afraid, young miss."

Caleb stood up straight and firmly said, "Wait!" to the humans.

They did.

He turned back to the child. "Do you know these people?"

"Yes. They've been around for months, just like me."

"Have any of them even tried to help you?"

One of the adults glared at the child. Several spoke and moved closer. Caleb ignored them. Pavise moved to stand between the child and the new adults.

"None," the boy finally said. "Most of them just called me names. Some tried to take my food if I managed to find any. Only Vix was nice to me"—he pointed at the pink-haired girl—"but she never had anything to share."

"Liar," one of the people shouted.

"You little bastard, no wonder your dad left you."

"We're leaving," Caleb said. He met the pink-haired human's eyes. "I'm glad to meet you both. Niceties will have to wait, but the two of you are welcome to come with us if you want to."

The pink-haired girl looked back and forth between Caleb and the ship, then the man with the contracts. "There's no hope here and the Hakarta won't let us stay anymore. We'll come with you if you promise not to hurt us?" Her voice made the strange sound Caleb called trembling.

This one noticed that she had said us, not me. She had some Voloid in her.

Caleb met her eyes and smiled. "I promise."

He was so very Caleb, in that moment, that I thought she wouldn't need his Skill to trust him, even after everything she'd been through.

Chapter 62

The Humanist

Damp air, redolent with blood and feces, smacked me in the face as I entered the unpainted concrete room. My lips curled in disgust at the smell and the scene before me. On my observation screens, it had seemed like nothing more than horror-movie gore. Gross, but somehow distant and detached. They had failed to express the visceral reality of what Quinn had endured.

Spotlights blazed hotly, illuminating the space where the "work" had been done. Shelves littered with artifacts, both technological and organic, had been set up along two of the walls. A long work bench held tools, leftover bits of body, and overfilled jugs of blood and oil.

What have I done? I thought as I retched. *Why did I listen to that alien scum and sign his god-damned contract? I knew what a monster he was.*

Echoes of my discarded past haunted me, but I ignored them and the overwhelming urge to turn and flee. Such things were beneath me. A lesser man would have cowered in his office while Quinn was waking. But the Humanist… I… was not a lesser man. My enforcer's nearly fatal injuries, and the grotesque indignities that followed them, had been suffered in my service. The least I could do was to be there to support her when she woke.

She stirred. Tossed and turned.

A projection screen was displayed on the wall in front of her. It showcased her new form from every angle. The lower half of her body had been replaced with that of an alien spider, though the upper half was still perfectly human in its shape. Spider-like hairs with a funny name I couldn't be bothered to memorize covered her completely. She had clawed hands and an alien's face. It was still lovely, hauntingly beautiful, but inhuman and terrifying. She had vampire fangs backed with small shark teeth, and a long black tongue that would haunt my nightmares.

She opened her eyes, two twin black orbs. Then two more. Finally the other four.

That was when the screaming started. The sound was ghastly, shrill and raspy.

My spine flash-froze and I stumbled backward, till the closed door behind me blocked my path. I did not scream. I did not run. Predators always chase you when you run.

***

Quinn had not stopped screaming since she'd first seen her reflection. It had given me time to pull myself together. Once I had fully gathered my will—a feat that had taken longer than my pride would like me to admit—I had bent my Charisma and Skills to the task of reassuring her. And myself. The screaming had improved slightly. What was left of my conscience had not. *It's not all bad,* I reminded myself, not for the first time. *She's going to be more powerful than ever when all of this is said and done.*

Despite the surgeries, Quinn was even more of a cyborg than she had been before. Dermal plating, an upgraded neural interface, and metal blades tipping every one of her many appendages were just a few of the new horrors she'd been forced to endure.

The choice had been between this and letting her die. It hadn't been an easy decision. Normally, I'd have let her suffer a hero's death and mourned her loss for a focus-group-tested length of time. But desperate times called for desperate measures.

Times had never been more desperate. General Janice, my mother's oldest friend and my own most trusted ally, had betrayed me. Her treason was so thorough that nearly two-fifths of HLF had been involved, to a greater or lesser degree. If I acted cautiously, I could salvage many of them. But her splinter group would take far too long to remove that way. It could not be allowed to fester and grow. Like the cancer it was, it must be excised from the healthy tissue of my organization before it was too late.

The alien mercenaries Quinn had captured, I'd decided, would be my chemotherapy. The leader was a Hakarta. He hated me, hated all of us, with a fiery passion. He would never have accepted a contract to aid us, even if it cost him his life. For the life of his teammates? For that, he had agreed. Everyone had weaknesses. You just had to discover where to apply the proper leverage.

Now they worked exclusively for me for the next three years, in a System-backed contract that they could not escape—not without some really hefty penalties. Best of all, they even had a spaceship. Once I'd learned that their ship was alive and technically a member of their team, I'd made it agree to the Contract too. Once I captured the Voloids' ship, we'd have two ships for humanity's burgeoning fleet.

Do the remnants of the former nations of Earth have spaceships of their own? If so, that would have to be part of the price that I charged them, when I finally brought them back into the fold.

It didn't matter now, so I set the thought aside. There was a time for such speculation, but it wasn't when I was trying to minimize the harm to an ally from a Faustian bargain.

One of the aliens, it had turned out, didn't give a rat's ass about any of its teammates or my threats. It had Heroic level backing and a device that could remove it from my power entirely. The metal pyramid that insisted on being called Orb had threatened to revolt and do just that, unless his Hakarta boss agreed to translate whatever he'd been trying to tell me. I did not brook with translation powers. Talking to aliens was beneath me, or had been, and if I was going to do it at all, it was going to be their translation power that let them speak to me in a proper human language. "Know thy enemy" was wise, but I'd had people I trusted for that. Now, I may need to buy a translation pack after all.

The pyramid alien had a Quest from its Heroic Classed Master to find a suitable candidate for a project. He'd chosen Quinn for this "honor." I'd been forced to agree, though it shamed me to allow a Heroic Level alien into my base while it committed its crime against humanity.

Poor Quinn.

She was the only HLF member still alive that I knew for certain hated aliens at least as much as I did. Now, she wouldn't stop screaming. I was mortified by the very real possibility that I would never be able to wring any further use from this gold mine of an operative.

Then the screaming simply stopped with no warning. The horror disappeared from her now-alien face, replaced by the cold blankness I'd come to expect from my pet sociopath.

"I'm sorry it's come to this, my loyal friend," I told her. "We'll root out the traitors together, you and I. There's just one mission left between us and the glory of humanity. It won't be easy, and it won't be quick, but it will give us everything we need to free our planet from these alien scum. Then we'll make all of our enemies suffer. I can't do it without you, Quinn. I need you.

"Stick with me and you'll be my new right hand, my swift sword to slaughter all threats to our rightful place in the galaxy." I sounded like a dark lord ranting and I knew it, but it hadn't been their ambitions that had made them evil. It had been their corrupted purpose. My purpose was pure. "Are you with me?"

"You talk a lot," she said, her voice empty of even the wicked cruelty she normally cultivated. "Speeches are for the others. Just tell me who you need for me to kill."

"That's my girl," I said proudly. Her dedication to our path eased my tension more than a soak in a hot tub had ever managed. I leaned in closer to whisper in her ear. "This is nothing that the System can't fix. Soon, we'll be drowning in oceans of Credits."

"Credits and blood," she answered.

The last dregs of the man I'd once been quaked in terror at this freakish monstrosity that could shred me like a cabbage any time she damn well pleased, if not for my hold over her. *A monster, yes. But my monster.*

I waved the list of traitors and their locations to Quinn. Then I handed her a key to a teleportation network I'd kept hidden away in the depths of our bases, for my use only.

I'd given a series of orders over the last few days, carefully hiding my tracks as I sent away my loyalists and segregated the general's people into bite-sized chunks.

"Kill them," I told her and her new group of bounty hunters. "Kill them all."

She left to do just that, leaving the bounty hunters to do their parts alone.

I sent orders to Quinn and the others to record everything from all available angles. I'd have to edit this footage alone, or Quinn could help me with it. This operation was as need-to-know as such things got.

For the first time in as long as I could remember, there was nothing productive I could do. I decided that this would be a rare opportunity to set aside my more-than-full-time job, for a few hours at least, and relax. One of my favorite things about getting rich before the System came was to soak in a hot tub. I was sure I remembered that we had them somewhere on the base.

Using the Shop to find the traitors still felt like a form of surrender, and I still had to deal with the General. But all of those concerns could wait. Even I needed to take a chance to rest and recover every once in a while. I could start building back, stronger than ever, when Quinn's grim work was done.

Chapter 63

The Humanist

When the bodies had been gathered and the blood had been washed away, I rose from the steaming water. My System-perfected physique caught my attention in the mirror. That was when it hit me again, that eerie strangeness that none of this could possibly be real. It wasn't my flawless skin or my chiseled muscles that unsettled me. What gave me the old-world equivalent of the uncanny valley phenomenon was the mirror and the steam. There was no fog.

The strangeness stayed with me as I dressed in my uniform, but not my armor. I'd found the General's leverage. Though she didn't know it yet, she would never oppose me again. It should have made me happy. Triumphant. But the eerie feeling haunted me, threatening to send my whole understanding of the world spinning out of control.

I knew that the lack of fog must be a crafting Skill, or something one of the Maintenance Workers did, but it didn't help. A cause-and-effect chain I had relied on my whole life was broken. Shattered forever, just like my ability to trust the woman I had counted on the most.

***

I waited for the General on her plush velour couch. It reminded me of a bunny's fur, as soft as the bitch was hard. Its smoked-silver shade would seem luxurious if its stench wasn't every bit as smoky.

Janice returned from the fake debriefing looking haggard. Hour after hour of questions about minutia had kept her out of contact with her people, while Quinn and the mercenaries slaughtered them.

Videos of the massacres were endlessly repeating in a square-within-square format on her wall screen. It was important for her to see what she had caused. Its brilliant display of colors, most notably the gray of the stone and the red of the blood, were the only lights in the well-appointed suite.

I nodded at her when she dropped the folder she'd been holding. Then I smirked as her filthy cancer stick fell tumbling from her gaping maw.

I was going to enjoy this. I would *make* myself enjoy this.

She tried to reach for her weapon, but I locked her down with Humiliating Subjugation.

Janice winced and clenched her jaw, but she didn't make a sound as the Skill paralyzed her body with intense and crippling pain. I'd been careful to allow her the freedom to cry out or scream, but she didn't even whimper. The traitor was a tough old goat, I had to give her that.

"How did you find out?" she finally asked, wise enough not to bother playing dumb. It was far too late for that.

"The System," I admitted as I released my power's hold on her. "You can buy anything if you're willing to spend enough Credits, and smart enough to know how to ask the right questions."

"Fucking System."

I nodded in complete agreement. *Anything you can do with the System can be done to you by the System. It is an awesome God, as wondrous as it is terrible.*

"You might as well kill me now," the General said. "You know I'll tell you nothing."

"You'll tell me everything," I replied, patting the couch for her to join me. "I won't even have to hurt you."

She flinched at that and fumbled as she sat beside me. She knew that I knew, and I'd already told her *how* I knew. This time, she was desperate enough to try deception. Really, she was right to make the attempt. She'd hidden her brother's illegitimate son brilliantly. None of us had ever suspected a thing. Her expression turned incredulous.

I snapped my fingers. One of my technicians changed the video feed on cue. Now, the central image was her nephew, with his chubby cheeks and brilliant smile. He was playing with blocks on the floor. Four guards stood quietly in the room around him. He paid them no mind. One of the guards, whose back was facing the camera, was holding a scalpel in one hand and a pair of pliers in the other.

The camera returned to the previous feeds, with images of the boy added to the rotations.

I sat there, patiently waiting. I even let Janice light one of her cancer sticks and take a long, slow drag. Traditions were important, so some concessions were acceptable for people facing execution.

I watched her resolve harden as her proud eyes met mine. Then it cracked as she looked toward little Brandon and her face fell. Finally, she slumped, broken and defeated. It had taken minutes, not seconds, an impressive display when I'd won before she'd set one foot inside the room.

"What do you want to know?"

"Tell me everything," I said. "But first," I said, trying and failing to keep the pain out of my voice, "tell me why?"

"You'll never understand."

I waited. She already knew what was at stake.

The General's eyes got distant, lost in the past. "When you first found me, I was as broken as you are. I'd just retired from the army and the family had gathered at a lodge in St. Moritz. Ted and I were going to see the world.

Try to rebuild... it doesn't matter now. We had plans to spoil the grandkids. I could have saved us all when the System came. I had the expertise. But most of them ignored me and listened to the men. Celebrities. Millionaires. Titans of industry. Even half of my extended family blew me off."

"Morons," I said. HLF Policy insisted I should tell her to shut up; we don't dwell on the past and mourn our losses. But I'd asked her a question and I needed the answer, so I let it play out. "No real loss," I threw out as an afterthought.

"You're wrong." She shook her head. "We couldn't spare them. We lost more than half within the first two days. They might have been the dumbest, but they were also some of our strongest. And our most experienced, except for me. By the time the survivors knew to listen to me, it was nearly hopeless. Out there in the wilderness, the monsters were so strong, the people were scared, and even the cold could kill you. I made a plan and got them ready. We set a trap for one of the Yeti-looking things. I think it would have worked, but Ted slipped on the ice during a crucial moment. The distraction left the monster just out of position."

Janice put out her half-smoked cigarette and lit another. I'd never understand smokers.

"All the attackers died but me. I was the farthest away, nearest to the ridge. I was able to escape while it was busy... I dragged myself back to the lodge, but aliens had claimed it. They'd left the last survivors frozen in the snow.

"I planned and schemed, but in the end, I didn't have the power I needed. Junior Officer isn't a solo Class. Don't ask me what sustained me. Some things really should stay dead and in the past. Eventually they caught on and I had to flee into the mountains. I expected to die. Decided to die."

My hand started to reach out to comfort her. Reassure her. She'd been a stable fixture my whole life. *She's nothing but a traitor now,* I reminded myself for the umpteenth time.

"That's when your people came for me with helicopters. They pulled me out, warmed me up, and fed me. Then I led them back to clear the base and end the monster. You gave me a purpose and a way to distract myself. A chance to get revenge. I was all in."

I scoffed. "I thought so too."

The General ignored my gibe. "The System and the aliens had taken everything from me, and the HLF gave me a way to focus my revenge. I was loyal, even once we uncovered your secret hidden Classes and Title. But then your brother, Hu—"

I backhanded her, hard, before my mind caught up to me. It wasn't my fault. I'd warned her, months and months ago.

"Don't say his name," I told her. "Never say that name."

I'd need to have that part of the name removed again. It was expensive. And Credits were already tight, no thanks to her. It was also humiliating, though I had paid a lot to not remember why.

Without my buffs, the slap barely hurt her face. It must have hurt her pride though, because she glared at me. "Once you killed your own brother because he refused to bomb a friend and neighbor—"

"The alien was not a friend," I said. "And we can't afford to be seen making exceptions."

"He was your brother!" Smoke billowed from her mouth at me.

I turned my face away, disgusted.

Janice glared at me through hard gray eyes. "He was a good man, and he deserved better. His neighbor deserved better."

It was my turn to glare indignantly. "I don't remember you saying anything about it at the time. You spit in both their faces."

"I know," the General said. She didn't cry, but her eyes were glistening as she glowered. "I didn't understand. Not 'till Brandon's mother found me and begged for me to take him. I've been every bit the monster you are, I know that. But I couldn't look that sweet boy in the face and tell him what I do. We've hurt a lot of good people, aliens and humans. If there's a hell, I'm sure I'll burn there next to you. But I swore to keep him safe from all of that. To stop you if I could so that he could have a better future."

"You could have come to me," I told her. There was a crack in my voice. I tried to steady it as I continued. "I might not have agreed with you, but I would have listened." *To you, only to you, I would have listened.*

She stared at me, eyes wide. A hint of hope flickered in her eyes. She opened her mouth to speak until she saw that my expression had turned hard. Cold.

I shook my head. "It's far too late for that now. You betrayed me. You're nothing to me now."

I activated Humiliating Subjugation, forcing her traitorous mouth closed and her head back to expose her throat. Too good for her. I let my power cramp all her muscles. I'd kill her slowly. Drag it out for hours.

Hope died in her agony. Now her eyes simply begged for death.

"Dying won't save you or your secrets," I said. "The only power you have left is to decide whether it's you who pays the price of your transgressions, or Brandon."

I waited for a response for several seconds. Then I remembered that I had her bound.

I let her go. "Go on, tell me everything."

Then I took my time, listening carefully. Asking probing questions. She tried to hedge here and there, always just a little, to throw me off the scent of some key plots. I spoke to her gently, my kindness a display of my power over her louder than any aggression could have been.

"Please remember that though you won't be here with us going forward, your nephew will be. If you cooperate fully, he'll be here for a very long time." He'd be my protege, I decided, if he had her strength of will. "If I find out later that you lied to me…" I let the silence do the real work.

She nodded. Then she revealed a key splinter group that she'd been hiding, as well as a pair of groups I'd never even heard of. She'd been training them in secret to oppose us. Finally, she told me everything about Commander Greyson and the traitors to humanity he'd taken up with. She revealed their plan. The timeline. Everything.

"Call your contact," I told her. "Let them know I'm cleaning up the mess you've caused me but that we haven't found you yet. Give them a new deadline. Make damn sure they come on time."

"I can't—" she started, but then she stopped and said only, "When?"

"The day after tomorrow. Tell them that the guards will have been called away by then, and that reinforcements will arrive on Friday, tripling the guards."

She took out another cigarette and lit it, but her hand was trembling so badly that she eventually gave up, dropped it on the carpet, and stomped it out with her heel. She walked to a table-mounted comms unit, so she wouldn't have to try to hold it steady and sent an outgoing call to her contact—a woman named Penny. She was the adopted daughter of two of our more mercenary allies.

There was no answer. I motioned for her to record a message. She did so flawlessly.

Then she shut the screen. I watched her hesitate again, for an even longer moment, before she opened it again and turned it off. She'd left it recording, trying to warn them. Clever, but she'd finally accepted her situation. There was nothing she could do now.

I'd set up a brilliant illusion, and it had played her perfectly.

"I've told you everything. Torture me, kill me. Do whatever you want. But remember that you promised not to hurt my Brandon."

I hadn't actually, but I let it go.

"It's funny, Janice," I said, demoting her forever with a single word. "I thought I was the blind one, since you managed to betray me so completely. But I knew that you were ruthless, bitter, and tough. I only ever misjudged your loyalty. But you still don't know me at all, do you? Even after all this time. You've betrayed everything and everyone who ever trusted you, and it wasn't for a false promise. I'll keep my word, though I never really gave it. But you could have kept your secrets and gone to the grave a martyr for your twisted, sick ideals, if you'd only known one simple truth."

"You're monologuing again," she said, blood dripping from her weathered chin from when I'd struck her. "But I'll bite. What truth is that?"

I held up my finger to let her know to wait.

My security forces, black-clad specialists who'd proven mostly loyal, entered the room and took her into custody. They bound her. Debuffed her. Blocked her access to her inventory. Locked down her powers. Then they all aimed their weapons at her and prepared to strike. I wasn't taking any chances. Not with her. I'd seen too many movies, and I knew her far too well. This woman was a traitor, but she was also brilliant. She'd be dangerous until the bitter end.

I leaned in close and whispered so that only she would hear. "I may be the monster you helped make me. I'm willing to be anything my planet and my people need for me to be. I'll torture you and kill you for what you've done without a second thought. You're a traitor. You deserve what's coming to you. But Brandon is an innocent… *human*… child. I'd die before I'd hurt him."

I could see that she believed me. That she knew the truth. That realization broke something essential in her. She just closed her eyes and sat there, silent, waiting for her death.

I lied about one thing. I'm still having second thoughts. She was the last link to my past. To my mother. And her strategic mind had been a priceless asset. Images from *Blacklist* and *Silence of the Lambs* tempted me with possibilities. Though those shows offered warnings of their own.

If I kept her isolated, I could make the General watch as I remade her nephew in my image. *I can force her to advise me, once she realizes that Brandon's future depends…*

My own thoughts interrupted me, repeating in my mind. The words might as well have been eureka, because they changed everything. *I can force her…*

With better gear, more buffs and Levels, why couldn't I just bend her and any future traitors to my will? She might still be a vital resource, someday soon. Maybe not while I was still Advanced. But the next tier was exponentially more powerful, and they didn't call them Master Classes for nothing.

Chapter 64

Quinn

The steel-and-concrete garage was as lifeless as the corpses I'd dumped in a chest-high pile. The smell of oil mixed with the copper tang of blood threatened to overwhelm my newly sharpened senses.

I'd hunted down the traitors to earn the Humanist's trust. I was drenched in blood and gore as I'd cracked their armor and savaged the flesh I found beneath. I hadn't even thought to use my spiders. I was the weapon now.

Eight long limbs, every one a polearm. A masterpiece for murder.

I sprayed the blood and bits of traitor off me with the hose we used to wash our vehicles. The icy water made me shiver. It was reassuring that at least some things were the same. The cleaning solution in the spray had a swimming pool smell. Bleach? Whatever it was, I was confident it wasn't made for human skin. It didn't even tickle.

Not that I was a human anymore.

Kill me. Kill me now. Please, just let me die.

My surface level wounds had fully healed. None of my victims had been able to penetrate my subdermal armor sheath. Whatever the Humanist had let the alien madman turn me into, it had removed my human frailties along with the last of my humanity.

I'm still a human, you psycho bitch!

Nearly the last of my humanity.

The pinkie I had left at the HLF base had been long since recovered, but the one left inside Lee's car was another matter entirely. Now inside the Voloids' ship, it was the last remnant of my old self. Thankfully, it still functioned.

Even with a spy device on site, I hadn't learned any of the rebels' big secrets. Lee was too security-minded to let himself get sloppy. But even Lee was less than perfect. He'd slipped up from surprise when the General reached out to him to set them on a course that would get them all killed.

If it wasn't for Lee, I'd just let it happen.

The screaming stopped. A faint flicker of sanity.

Lee! Oh, my Lee. Save him. Save him please. You owe me that at least.

I did. And maybe I could. The General's message made the Humanist's plan clear. It gave me insights I could use to help him, though it galled me it might save the others. But I had time to set some traps, put some plans in motion.

I jacked into the base's systems directly and initiated the back door I'd hacked into when I first arrived. I sent a short message to Lee. I only hoped that it would be enough.

General compromised. Dead. Trap. Arrive 1 day early or everyone dies.

It would have to do. I'd done my part regardless. I did not—could not—care. Not any further.

Locked away, possibly forever, the part of me that I had been created to protect would likely never stop screaming. I'd failed her, just like I'd failed my family, years before.

What couldn't be protected could still be avenged.

I felt something then, a visceral and predatory drive akin to hunger. It was a new feeling, so I'd never needed Segmentation for it. I decided to keep it. It would likely serve me well.

My other half seemed to feel it too. Her wailing cries turned to something darker.

Kill them. Kill them all.

I'm so hungry!

"Fine," I told her as I licked my oversized fangs with my rubbery, blackened tongue.

She was right. I had failed her completely. I owed her something. And all this meat... there was no point wasting it, now was there?

Chapter 65

Caleb

We were making good time on the trip back, but guilt and dread distracted me from enjoying the fresh air, the warmth of the sun on my skin, and the endless emerald forests. We'd been hauling ass ever since Van had tracked us down on our way out of town to warn us that a few Hakarta security members had been asking questions. He'd also handed me a bag with a receipt and a hardcover book, *The Stardance Trilogy*.

I'd already fought with the rest of the crew. They'd wanted to leave Vix and Daniel behind, but I'd leveraged the fact that Pavise and I were necessary for the mission, and they'd have to explain to Lee why they needed to come back and pick me up.

I felt a bit guilty that if I wasn't still hiding my Class Trip Skill, we'd probably be back by now.

A piercing scream like a horror movie heroine left us with a bit of a dilemma.

"Drive faster," Tony, the soldier who'd been sent with us, urged Penny.

"It sounds like somebody's in danger," I said.

"Bugger that," Tony replied. "I'm sorry, but they're probably already dead. If not, it's almost certainly a trap to lure us in. I don't believe in coincidences, and what are the odds of us passing by just as someone gets attacked?"

Pavise started to answer, but I asked him to stop with a mental nudge. The odds didn't matter. "We should at least check it out. We have to help them if we can."

"Look, man, I'm not going to pretend I'd agree anyway. But we've got kids in the car thanks to you. Do you really want to risk them for some stranger?"

Dang it. "Good point."

"My expanded sensors are not detecting the approach of any monsters," Pavise announced. "I do have a scouting device that I can use to investigate now."

"That sounds like a good compromise, buddy."

"Lee's gonna kill you," Tony said.

"Lee can't kill me until after the mission," I said. "Pavise isn't expendable and we're a package deal."

"That's all the more reason why we have to go."

"Lower your voice," I said. "Just give him a minute to find out where things stand."

Pavise sent the feed to me, and I used Show and Tell to keep the others up to speed.

The camera drone was bigger and slower than the Commander's, but it was what we could afford. It hovered over a grove of birch trees, past a barbed wire fence made of a speckled blue metal. The links of the fence were shaped into mystic-looking runes. As the drone flew past it, we spotted two things before it shorted out and was lost to us forever.

The first was a humanoid form wrapped up like a mummy in the iconic white and silver bark of a birch tree. The second was what looked to be a racoon in a chocolate-brown outfit, halfway between a wizard's robe and a waxed-parchment trench coat. He had a gnarled staff in one hand and a tire iron in the other.

"I like the robe," I said. "The yellow of the runes highlights his eyes."

"It's a monster, not a fashion show. And it's got what looks to be a human prisoner. We should kill it or we need to leave," Randy said as he pulled his old shotgun from his inventory and casually hopped down from the truck.

"Damn it," the other soldier said.

I wanted to correct his language, but there would be a better time. "We don't know that he's a monster. He looks like a wizard. And we can't be sure that the scream was a human. We don't have enough to go charging in there and shooting people just because they look like a raccoon."

"To hell with that," Randy said while he walked slowly toward the gate. "That was a woman, or a little girl, and she was terrified. We have to help them."

"Yes," I told him as I followed to catch up with him, "we need to help. But that doesn't mean we should charge in recklessly when we have no idea what's really going on."

"You should listen to your friend," a thunderous voice boomed from all around us as a giant image of the racoon wizard waved its clawed hand and mumbled odd words.

The fence flew from its location and resettled in about a hundred-foot radius around us. Along with it came a pile of trash that was shaking and rumbling. A massive form rose up. Its headless torso was a Jeep Grand Cherokee's front half. Its arms and legs were iron beams and concrete. One appendage ended in what looked to be a sharpened flagpole, while the other had a chain with one of those square crushed cars on the end of it.

The racoon-man appeared beside his monstrous creation, the yellow of his eyes and the arcane runes of his robe glowing brightly as he levitated. Terror emanated from the man in waves.

I was getting used to fear. I gulped but said, "That's a really amazing effect. A Skill?"

He frowned, which on his black masked face was kind of adorable. "My amulet." His voice was deep and gravelly. "It's supposed to drive away the riffraff. Damn thing's not working." He thudded his tire iron against the almond-shaped golden item. "That's twice today."

"It works fine," I tried to reassure him.

"Then how and why are you still here?"

"Overwhelming terror is my new normal," I told him. "As for why we're still here, we heard screaming." I tried to keep my voice friendly., "and we wanted to make sure nobody was getting murdered."

"Oh, so just because I'm not human, I'm some murderous monster. You humans are all the same."

"It's not the alien part that concerned me. It was the mummification."

He sneered, "Sure, it was."

That threw me for a second. I was so used to people just knowing I was telling the truth. "I'm not lying," I said. "I'm surprised you don't know that. I have a passive that lets people know when I'm telling the truth."

"And I'm a wizard. We're a skeptical bunch by nature. And you're not the only one with passives, boy. I have one that blocks just the kind of mind tricks you're trying to use on me."

"It's not a trick." I sent him the System description.

"Sure, it's not. And I can trust you, even though your people either think that I'm a monster or an adorable animal that surrounds himself with trash."

"People are people. That applies to you, me, and whoever mistreated you. As for surrounding yourself with trash, you do live in a landfill." I was going to mention that it seemed he was making good use of it, but he cut me off.

"Because one of you *humans* convinced the local Hakarta boss it would be funny. Ha, ha, look at the Dun'shallan refuge, living in a trash heap."

"That's awful," I said. "They shouldn't have done that to you."

"But?" he prompted sardonically, motioning with his clawed hand for me to continue.

"No but about that," I said. "On an entirely unrelated matter, you have to admit that the screams of a young girl in a place where a mummified body just so happens to be is more than a little bit suspicious."

He laughed at that, loudly. "You hear that, *wife*? A bit of magic and he screams like a little girl."

"Why the hell should I care?" a female voice yelled from somewhere in the distance.

"'Why should I care?'" he mimicked in an exaggerated imitation. "You know damn well why!"

"I should have listened to my mother and married Zanadeer. He knew how to treat a lady. Just because you couldn't satisfy a—"

The wizard waved his staff and mumbled something, and the sound cut out. "Where were we? Oh, that's right, you were leaving." He made a shooing gesture, and we were pushed slowly but relentlessly toward the gate by mystic force.

I sent a mental instruction to Pavise, who raised a barrier behind us.

"Oh, come on," he said. "Why the hell do you even care?"

"He always cares," Penny answered.

"I care because it's a person. I'd care just as much if it were you trapped in a birch bark cocoon and there was a human wizard trapping you."

"Sure, you would."

"He would," Randy said in an annoyed tone. "It's gonna get all of us killed."

"Really," the wizard said sarcastically. Then something about Randy's somewhat disgusted reaction must have reached him because he said again, in a much less bitter tone, "Really?"

"Dude's a Teacher. He saved a bunch of alien kids that were about to be murdered by human commandos. Put himself in the line of fire to stop them."

"Really?" he said again in the same tone. Then he seemed to remember his skepticism. "Piss off."

"One of them is with us." Randy's tone was deadpan, as if he didn't give a shit. Maybe he didn't. "You can ask her." He motioned to Aul.

The racoon's, no the Dun'shallan's, I reminded myself, sinister expression returned. "You'd better not be lying to me, boy."

The Jeep monster's headlights turned on as it raised its arms into a fighting pose and took one lurching step forward.

"Just ask her," Randy said, his voice cracking.

"Okay then, I will." He motioned to Aul. "This one?"

"Ya think?" Randy snapped back. Then he cowered just a little as the wizard glared at him. I suspected he was wishing that we'd let him wear his new armor.

"Hey, you," he said as he walked toward Aul.

As he got close enough, my Relatable Skill let me know that his special interests included historical fiction, arcane puzzles, and being left the hell alone.

"Did this human save your life?" the wizard asked Aul.

"Caleb is save many Voloids," she answered.

"Hm. Okay, fine." Then he got a thoughtful look. "You may want to focus on whatever a Kaldian whatever it said your Class was when I inspected you. If you're that girl's Teacher, you suck at your job. Her grammar is terrible."

"Translation Skills are notoriously... you know what. It doesn't matter," I said. "What happened with the guy in the birch bark? Did he think you were a monster and try to kill you or rob the place?"

"I wish," he said. "He tried to seduce my wife. More than tried, if I'm being honest. He's a Scoundrel."

"Sounds like it," I said. "Seducing another man's wife."

"No. Well, yes. But I mean his Class is Scoundrel, though he hides it behind Wanderer."

A female of his kind was storming toward us now. Her furious scowl was adorable, but the red sunfire-sword blazing in her hand convinced me to keep that thought to myself. Her special interests included shaming dumbasses, eviscerating monsters, and gourmet cooking.

She motioned to her mouth.

The wizard shook his head no.

She raised her sword to strike him down.

He wisely canceled the spell.

"Try that again, you miserable son of a... oh," she said as she noticed us. "You didn't tell me we had guests." She used her free hand to brush dust from her fur and straighten it a bit.

"They aren't guests, and they were just leaving. Take your friend and go." He waved, and the fencing around us opened to let our vehicle leave.

"You're friends of Kaidan?"

The wizard, whose name I realized I needed to ask, opened his eyes wide and gave us a fang-filled smile that was probably meant to encourage us to go along with this.

"No, ma'am," I said. "We came because we heard him screaming."

"You're a bully," she said to her husband in a scolding voice. Then she saw the man whose name was apparently Kaiden wrapped in birch bark, and her small dark eyes burned as hot as her sword as she glared at her husband. "You let him go this instant."

"Fine." He waved and the birch bark fell away.

"You should probably go," she said. "I'm sorry I haven't been a better host, but my husband and I are going to have a nice long talk about the proper way to treat a guest."

"Nothing about the way you were treating our *guest* was proper," he retorted.

She giggled, then tried to make herself glare again. She failed as she took in the scene in front of her.

I forced myself not to grimace. *People are people. People are people. It's not my place to judge.*

Turning, I found myself easily distracted from the thoughts. Even fresh out of a birch bark cocoon, the scoundrel was ridiculously attractive in a way only natural good looks and an absurdly high Charisma could have justified. Just seeing him made me feel disloyal, so I looked away. It didn't help. The sight was stuck in my mind like a catchy song. His exposed tan skin wasn't red, it was flushed. His black hair wasn't messy, it was shiny and tousled. It had to be some kind of passive.

He cleared his throat, drawing my attention back to his flawless face. His dark eyes twinkled with joy as they met mine. Admiration and gratitude gushed from him as he said, "Thank you."

"You're welcome." Then I cleared my throat since it had sounded a bit husky. "I'm Caleb."

"Kaiden," he replied with a very naked bow. His special interests included decadence, debauchery, and drunken revels. "I see you've met the beautiful Tul-Vesha and the Lout."

"Tul-Fular," the wizard said and then growled.

"Savage," his wife said and snarled at him.

"Hussie," he snapped back.

"We should probably be going, friends," Kaidan said to us as he sauntered in our direction.

I looked away again, skin flushed.

"Put on some damned clothes, man," Randy said.

"Oh, yes, of course, how rude of me." Kaiden pulled stylish but road-worn clothes from his inventory and put them on. "How do I look?"

"Apocalypse chic," I answered. "We need to go." I led him back to the truck.

"Come back anytime," Tul-Vesha said with a coquettish wave.

He blew her a giant kiss, then dashed out of the way as the crushed truck golem left a small crater where he had just been standing.

The sound of a fist smashing into what was almost certainly the wizard was followed by an explosive expulsion of air from tiny lungs.

We got back into the truck and drove away. The truck bed was overfull already, so Kaiden was smashed in between Penny and me.

When we were a few miles away, the Scoundrel turned to me and gazed into my eyes with intense sincerity. "I want to thank you," he said. "You have no idea how much this means to me."

"It wasn't just me," I said. "And it's not that big a deal."

His expression exploded into a look of shocked outrage. "Not a big deal! You, sir, are a hero. You have saved the most precious thing in the world to me, friend. You saved me. I will never forget what you've done for me."

"You like to say me a lot." Then I remembered. "Oh right, a Scoundrel."

His grin was incandescent.

"You'd better be a Han, not a Lando."

He looked away, shamefaced.

"Well sh…" I caught myself before I swore in front of the kids again. "Shucks. Should we drop you off here, or somewhere else nearby?"

"I go where you go," he said. "I owe you my life. If you need anything, anything at all, and it isn't overly taxing or exceptionally dangerous, I'm at your service. I am, for better or worse, your man."

"I have a girlfriend," I told him, just in case he was hitting on me.

"Not like that. That's not my scene—unless there's a beautiful woman involved, of course." His eyes brightened as he got an idea. "This girlfriend of yours, is she a looker?"

"No," I told him, responding to his idea, rather than his sentence. Before I could catch myself, it was already too late.

"I'm sorry," he said, looking at me sympathetically.

"Not like that. She's gorgeous."

He looked at me suspiciously. Was everyone going to doubt me now?

"Fine," I said, and summoned an image of Evelyn with Show and Tell.

"Is she real?" he asked everyone in the cab but me.

Penny glanced at the picture and nodded.

"I'll make an exception," Kaiden said. "I'll be there for the two of you even if what you have planned is overly taxing." He looked at the picture again, longing in his eyes. "Maybe even if it's exceptionally dangerous."

"We don't do that," I said, trying not to sound judgmental. Or tempted. "The poly lifestyle is not for me."

"I'll forgive you," he said, with his hand on his heart and an exaggeratedly mournful expression, "but only because you saved my life."

Chapter 66

Caleb

"What the hell took you all so long?" Lee snapped before we'd even made it to the ship.

Converted vehicles were being loaded. Armored troops were everywhere, weapons at the ready. Lee's cybernetics and armor were fully repaired, I noticed, though no one else's were. It had to be his terrifying prosthetic. I'd seen what it could do. Then I remembered what he'd done to the spy.

His expression gave me flashbacks of that first day I met him. As much as things had changed, I cowered as my pulse doubled. I raised my hand to prepare a shield.

His expression softened—slightly—when he noticed my fear.

Why all the commotion? Had there been an attack?

"What's going on?" I asked.

He ignored my words, taking in the people around me. Frustration seemed to pour off him in waves. "Why the hell are there more of you than when you left? We're not running an orphanage here."

"Young humans is Voloid guests," Aul said. "Ship is be anything Aul chooses. Humans not be alien's slaves."

Fury flared on Lee's face.

Aul took a quick quadruple step back.

Then Lee must have replayed the words Aul had spoken. Not "Aliens not be human's slaves." The reverse. The Commander took a deep breath. My guess was confirmed when he said, "Aliens were going to enslave these humans?"

"Yes," I said. "Some kind of indentured servitude."

"Bastards," he said before turning to the kids. "Welcome aboard. We'll find a way to make this work." Then he turned back to me. "Good job."

I hadn't expected this reaction, so I just smiled and nodded. Then I realized it made it seem like I was taking all the credit. "You should thank Aul. She's the one who noticed what was happening and insisted that we help."

He turned to look at Aul, met her eyes, and nodded once, respectfully.

She glared at him, mandibles twitching.

It would have to do for now.

"What about him?" the commander asked, indicating Kaiden with his metal thumb.

"He's a Scoundrel."

"Hey," the gorgeous man said. "Ixnay on the Oundrelscray."

"I speak pig Latin," Lee told him. Even Lee's gaze stuck a little longer than usual on Kaiden.

No surprise. Charisma was Charisma, and the man was magnificent. Like Evelyn, I reminded myself loyally, who had the same effect on people without a Class designed for it.

"*Sir,*" Pavise messaged me with a mental nudge, *"you're zoning out again."*

"The Commander has a right to know what kind of people we bring on board," I told the Scoundrel. "And I don't trust you."

"That's fair," Kaiden said, seemingly entirely unoffended.

"Are you asking me to kill him?" Lee said, shock in his tone.

"What? No!"

"Because it sounds like you're asking me to kill him."

"Do not kill him. Does that make things perfectly clear?"

"I fully support this plan," Kaiden chimed in, nodding enthusiastically. "It's an excellent plan."

Lee shook his head. "We don't have time for this. I'll have someone toss him into a hole until we're back from the mission."

"Maybe I could help," the Scoundrel said.

"Hell no," Lee snapped. "If even Mr. Rogers here doesn't trust you, then I definitely have no use for you."

"It's fine," I told Lee. "He's only volunteering because he doesn't know how dangerous it is anyway."

"I'll await your return with eager anticipation."

"Waste of space," Lee said before ordering his troops to lock the man up and set a guard. Right before they were out of sight, Lee's eye opened wide as he had a realization. "Hey, Scoundrel!"

Kaiden turned back to look at the Commander with a mix of fear and hope on his face in an exaggerated display.

"Do you like cigars?"

The scoundrel replied with an eager smile and a thumbs-up. Then he clarified with, "Only when I'm drinking."

"Change of plans," Lee called to the guard hauling Kaiden away. "Get him a job and put him in the rotation. We'll find a use for him after all."

The guard dragged the man away, grumbling, "I like cigars."

"What's going on?" I asked Lee again.

"There's been a development," he said. "We're starting the raid early."

"How early?"

"We leave in five."

"Hours, days, weeks?"

"Minutes," he said. "Your group can give you the details. I'm sending Topher with you so that he can help you pick your Skill."

"Sounds good," I said. "Why the rush?"

He let out an impatient huff. "We think our contact in the resistance is compromised."

"I haven't even had a chance to try out my new gear or Skill," I complained.

"Then you should have been back sooner. Your team's over there." He pointed at one of the modified trucks with heavy ordinance.

I smiled when I saw Evie and the rest of my four-person squad. I turned to ask Lee another question, but he was already walking away at a brisk pace.

"Perhaps you could consider this on-the-job training, sir," Pavise said from behind me.

"Great, like an amateur brain surgeon practicing on a living patient. What could go wrong?"

I was walking over to the team when I got a team invite from Lee. I accepted, assuming he was just inviting everyone. But a message followed.

"I forgot to ask. That group of robots that came to install a new ship's computer and AI systems. They were your doing, right?"

"Yeah," I said. *"I sent them with a password."*

"Only reason I let them in. Speedy Delivery. Cute."

"I remembered you were a fan."

"I said I remembered the man. Not the same thing."

"So, you're not a fan?"

You have been removed from party chat.

I smiled and joined the others.

"Wow," Evelyn said, then winked at me. "You two look amazing."

"Badass, man," Randy added.

"Thanks. Hopefully, it works."

"The Systems are fully operational, sir."

"Maybe we should do a test anyway, just to be sure," I said.

"This is not a new toy for you to play with, sir."

"It kind of is," I said.

Randy nodded.

Evelyn rolled her eyes.

Pavise made a sigh sound and generated a much larger wall of force than ever before. The purple energy shooting from the center of his chest looked amazing, but also wrong.

"I kind of miss the blue," I said.

"The purple's a gorgeous color on you," Evie replied.

"She's not wrong," Penny added.

"I no longer miss the blue," I said. Then I tried, and failed, to wink.

The women were far too kind to laugh.

Randy wasn't.

"Thank you, young ladies," Pavise said. "You have fine taste."

Concentrating, in part to help me ignore Randy, I widened and thickened the barrier, testing my new limits. The improvement was significant, more than fifty percent.

"It got bigger," Randy said, then snickered.

"That's what she said," came Topher's voice from behind me.

I rolled my eyes, partly because Topher couldn't see. The man scared me.

"Can you just not?" Penny said, obviously annoyed with Topher.

"Funny, she said that too."

The whole group turned to glare at him. Topher just laughed.

"We're supposed to pick my Skill," I said, trying to change the subject.

His expression turned cold and serious as he lowered himself onto one of the armor-reinforced bench seats built into the back of the pickup. "Tell me everything."

I opened my mouth to answer him.

He didn't even glance at me as he raised his finger to silence me. "Not you."

That was fine with me. Better even. Then I remembered that I had Evelyn's surprise. I sat beside Evie and snuggled in.

"So, do you remember what you made me do, because of your ultimatum?" I whispered to her.

"Yes," she said, a hint of suspicion in her tone.

"Well, it implied that I shouldn't always tell you everything, so—"

"You're new to this," she said, not whispering at all, "so I'll fill you in. You're going to want to keep this short and to the point. You're talking the way people do when they break up with someone, or admit to cheating on them, and people who drag that out are assholes."

Guilt washed over me. *Why? It's nothing like that.* Then I remembered, and all thoughts of her present flew from my mind. "This isn't what I was going to say, but we found a Scoundrel in the woods and saved him, and I saw him naked and he was—"

"Breathe," she told me, and she chuckled.

The tension went out of me with my laugh. Then a different kind of stress hit me, one I wasn't used to, as her eyes filled with more than a hint of lust.

"No one is going to blame you if you got an eyeful of that man and liked what you saw. I got a peek back at the base and wow!" She fanned herself.

Penny looked intrigued, but she said nothing.

Jealous. I was feeling very, very jealous. That made sense. So did Evie's reaction. Still, it helped me to appreciate Evie's viewpoint on white lies a little more, though I wasn't persuaded. I decided to just let myself be jealous, feeling the feelings until they went away. Eventually they did, as I faded off to sleep, snuggled up tightly against this amazing woman.

Chapter 67

Caleb

I woke to soft kisses and a voice calling my name. Then a bit of gentle shaking.

My head was resting on firm pillows. The rest of me was encased in something hard. The world was rumbling and shaking, like a road trip on a backwoods... oh. Right. I tried to open my eyes and make my body move, but everything was heavy and my...

My snooze will get me up in time for school. Work? All the same to me. I sighed and relaxed as I let myself fade.

"Just kick him already, lass. We're getting close."

"Can't he sleep a little longer?" a sweet voice asked. "They're just clearing the road."

"I'm up," I said, remembering. I looked at Topher but motioned to Pavise. "Did the two of you compare notes?" I wiped an embarrassing amount of saliva from the side of my mouth.

"Aye," Topher said. "Here's what we came up with."

"Not you," I told him. "Pavise."

Topher's pine-colored eyes twinkled at the small payback, until the others laughed. His expression hardened, but he motioned for Pavise to speak.

"We were not able to select the best Skill choice, sir. We were, however, able to select the worst. If we need Rapid Repair, we have likely already lost. The other two Skills will be vital from the start. Shield Projection is likely to be the strongest choice for the group's safety. However, if the two of us are defeated, there will be no shields at all. I suggest that you select Personal Force Field for that reason, but we have been unable to reach a consensus."

"You're biased, buddy. But that's okay, that's your job. My job is to protect the healer while she keeps us all alive. We'll take Shield Projection."

"This isn't a video game, lad." Topher looked down for a moment. "But it's a fair point. Yer call."

I nodded and selected the Skill.

Evelyn straightened my hair with her fingers. I smiled at her and bent to kiss her cheek.

"Get a room," Randy said, and jumped off the truck to stretch his legs.

Evelyn turned and claimed my mouth with hers, kissing me deeply.

When she finally came up for air, I said, "Wow," I said. "I think I agree with Randy."

"Not the time," Topher said, reaching over to pull us apart. "We need ta prepare."

"Right." I huffed out a deep breath.

Evelyn did a double backflip to get off the truck, while Penny sat down on the tail-gate and scooted off the end.

I decided to try a trick I'd learned from the fight with the werebear. I made myself a flattened circle of purple force, halfway down, and then did a double hop to make it to the ground.

It went off without a hitch and Evelyn clapped, which sounded a bit off due to her cybernetic hand.

That was what made me remember. "Oh, crud." I turned to Evelyn. "Your surprise."

I summoned the box. It was too heavy and awkward, so I lowered it to the ground. Then I had to dropped to one knee to adjust the latch and open it. I reached in for the activation crystal and held it up to Evelyn.

Penny and Evie gasped.

Topher said, "What the hell do ye think yer doin'? Now is not the bloody time."

I looked up at him, confused. Then I looked at Evelyn, whose eyes were wide and teary, and her expression was filled with empathy and concern.

"Oh, oh no," I said.

"It's not a no," she said, eager to reassure me. "But it's definitely not the time." She looked around. "Or place. You have rotten instincts for this."

"It's a present," I said. "Not a proposal."

"Huh?"

"The box was too heavy, and the controls are way down here. I may be clueless when it comes to romance, but I'm not that out of touch."

"Oh." Her expression confused me. She bit her lip and frowned, looking disappointed more than anything.

"It's not that I don't want to. It's just… it's like you said, not the time or place."

She nodded, wiping away her tears from earlier. "Right. You're right. Get the hell up." She reached down to help me do just that.

I took it. When I did, it pressed the crystal against her cybernetic hand.

"What the hell?" she said, holding up the arm. The crystal sank into it, and there was a loud hum as it visibly vibrated. Then her leg joined it. A swarm of tiny robots flew out of the box and went to work.

"Your present," I said. "I'm sorry. The device was cued to you and the activation crystal was in my hand."

She was hyperventilating and writhing spasmodically, obviously desperate to get the nanites off of her.

My mind was racing to sort through all the ways this could hurt my friend. Flashes of her cybernetics falling off or being left attached as sparking hunks of metal were competing with my attention when I tried to explain, so it came out badly. "Please just hold still. It's something you're going to want."

"And that's what I said," Topher cut in.

Evelyn slapped Topher, hard. Randy glared.

She wasn't listening. It twisted my gut to do it, but I triggered Pay Attention.

"It's from the Shop!" I hurried on, ignoring the asshole. "They're upgrading your implants!"

"Oh, oh, okay," Evie said, still huffing. Then she stood stock-still and closed her eyes as the flying robots made their intricate adjustments. After a long moment, she opened her eyes and watched them intently.

I was as surprised as anyone when they made their final changes, adding a blue-steel protective coating and some sky-blue gemstones. There was one at her shoulder and one at each of her knuckles. They looked expensive and tasteful, and they perfectly matched the shade of Evie's eyes. The work on her leg was a perfect match. She also got neon lights that would have matched my suit, had I gone with the blue.

"Oh wow," she said. "That's something all right."

"I got a special discount because I'm supposed to try to recruit people to the many, varied, and multifaceted glories of the Kaldian way. I hope you like it. I'm sorry it happened without your permission."

Topher's eyes twinkled. He hadn't noticed Lee marching over to stand behind him.

Unless someone had messaged him, the Commander's hearing, and his ability to split his attention, must be exceptional. He'd been nowhere near us during the earlier exchange but made his knowledge of it clear when he said, "Say it and I'll kill you myself."

There wasn't the slightest trace of playfulness, or mercy, in Lee's cold tone. It sent a shiver down my spine.

Topher must have felt it too, because his eyes darted frantically, seemingly looking for a place to run. Finding none, he said, "Aye, sir."

He didn't turn to face the Commander. He didn't salute. He just stood there quietly until Lee's distinctive footsteps let him know the man was gone.

"I'm sorry," Topher said in a voice that sounded both sincere and terrified. "It won't happen again." Eyes averted, he took a few steps back to give them space.

"That's something you don't see every day," Penny said under her breath.

"Yeah, Lee's even hotter than usual when he… and my boyfriend's standing right beside me."

Evie wasn't wrong on either count.

Since this was my fault, I decided to give her a graceful exit from the sentence. "As I was saying. I'm sorry—"

"I'm not!" she said, then she kissed my cheek. "These are amazing." She posed then swirled around and posed in a different angle. "They don't only restore my abilities but improve them. The only downside is that it's going to take a bit of getting used to, and this isn't the best time for that."

"Better timing than a marriage proposal," Randy said.

He wasn't wrong.

Evelyn started testing her new limbs. I wanted to stop and enjoy the view, but we had important work to do.

"Back to the matter at hand," I said. "Can you guys fill me in? Lee wasn't very talkative."

"The *Commander* didn't have time to coddle ye while he was too busy tryin' ta organize the whole damn raid at the last minute?" Topher's glare was back, if not with its usual ferocity. "He was too busy saving lives to answer all yer damn fool questions? Imagine that."

I wanted to protest, but the jerk had a point. I reminded myself to try not to judge him too harshly. I had no idea what the man had been through. So I just nodded and said, "Can anybody fill me in?"

Penny was the one who answered me. "I almost got us all killed."

"It's not your fault," Evie replied, landing next to Penny after a triple somersault with a twist, before cartwheeling away.

"The hell it's not," Topher snapped.

"It doesn't matter," Penny continued. "What matters is that we almost walked into a trap. My contact called me. She told us we needed to move up our timeline. She wanted us to attack the day after tomorrow. It wasn't until after Lee got another message from an anonymous contact that warned us she was compromised and it was a trap that I realized the General hadn't been smoking. She's *never* not smoking. Ever."

"It's easy to miss something like that," I said.

Topher was stomping back over. Apparently, his moment of contrition had passed. "Oh aye, as long as yer not payin' proper attention. But why should she care? It's not like her son's life is on the line. It's not like *all* our lives are on the bloody line."

"Please stop," I told him. "It's not like she doesn't understand."

"Yer gonna defend her from the big scary man?" he mocked.

"I'm the tank," I answered. "I have one job."

He glared at me for a moment. Then his expression eased. He nodded. "Aye, so ye do, lad. So ye do."

Penny nodded her thanks.

Her System Companion rubbed against my legs and purred.

Then Penny's expression hardened, and her cat raised its back and tail with a hiss.

"That one job had better be to save my son," she said with an intensity I'd never heard from her. "You do anything you have to do to save my boy, do you hear me? Anything. That goes for all of you. If I find out that—"

"We know," Randy interrupted her. "We remember."

"We'll do everything we can to save all of the hostages," I answered her, "especially the children. You have my word."

"My son is the first priority."

"The children are the first priority," I hedged. "I'll give my life for them without hesitation, if it comes to that, but I won't play favorites. It's the best that I can do."

She nodded sharply. She didn't like it, but it was clear she could tell I meant it. At least my Skill wasn't entirely on the fritz. Or maybe it was just my reputation, earned or otherwise. Defender of Children, the System had titled me. Seared into my soul like an infected brand, the sound of Kek's screaming disagreed.

"The new contact said we needed to attack today," Penny finished.

"It's probably a trap," Topher said morosely.

Everybody nodded.

Then we all got the same disfocused look on our faces as we read the incoming message from Lee.

"Back in the trucks. The road is clear. It's time."

Chapter 68

Caleb

Stopping near the Big Fish restaurant was bittersweet for me. Half log cabin, half giant goofy muskie, the place had a special place in my heart. When Nana'd brought me home with her to Minnesota, after my parents' accident, the odd attraction had been a much-needed distraction from my grief.

The staff had been welcoming and friendly, and the burgers were huge and delicious. Young me had loved them. The remembered pleasure didn't sit well with my current values though. I decided to just be happy that at least one of my favorite things from the old world was still standing.

I smiled contentedly until I noticed Donaldson and his men. They were stuffing high explosives into a fancy steampunk car. The Commander did not look happy about it. He scowled at them from time to time, as he and several of his troops set up a pair of trucks that had artillery cannon things on them. There were also two troops on each of the vehicles with shoulder-mounted weapons. Most looked normal, but one of them had mystic-looking runes.

The trucks were about thirty feet apart. Each of them had five other troops with rifles flanking them on either side.

"Please tell me that this isn't what it looks like," I said to no one in particular.

"It nae what it looks like," Topher replied. "Would ye also like me to tell ye that yer a mighty bloody mountain of a man?"

"He's going to blow it up. Why?"

"Because he tried a giant worm hooked to a line, but it dinnae take the bait."

I pinched the bridge of my nose and decided to end the conversation there.

He continued anyway. "The base is hidden underneath it. It's the only reason that the damn thing's standin' after all this time."

I forced myself not to sigh. "If we need to blow it up to get down into the base to save the hostages, that changes everything. Buildings and memories matter. People matter more."

"We're not blowing it up to get into the base," he replied. "It's a distraction."

"We're blowing up one of the last remaining attractions on Earth as a distraction?!"

"You were right the first time, Caleb," Evie said. "It's a distraction to divide their forces and box them in. That way, we can save the hostages and keep ourselves alive while doing it."

I nodded. "That makes sense."

"Glad ye approve," Topher mocked. "I'll let the Commander know that he's allowed to proceed."

I rolled my eyes but bit my tongue. I worried that we were all getting a bit too comfortable antagonizing a person whose danger level sat somewhere between serial killer and super villain.

"Lee's plan is a good one," Penny said. "We're going to—"

"Not announce the full plan where it might be monitored," Topher cut her off. "We've used some devices that Captain Purple Pants here picked up from the Shop for us ta block their sensors, but who knows what other tricks they have? Not worth the risk."

"Sorry," Penny said. "You're right."

He nodded.

I wanted to point out that he'd been the one to start revealing secrets, but not antagonizing the murderer was starting to feel like a solid plan. I decided to run with it.

"This way," Lee announced as he activated several Skills.

I accepted Dedicated Comm Channel and Full Coordination when prompted. Health bars and a mini-map appeared in my field of vision. My awareness of the rest of my team increased. The connection with Penny was the strongest of them all. I could sense where they all stood in relation to me, and the relative distance, without even having to think about it.

Mounted weapons systems lifted from the ground around the fish. They exploded before they could open fire as rockets, fireballs, and a blob of acid slammed into them. All of that was in addition to a barrage of what my untrained eyes took to be artillery shells.

Then the explosives-laden ATV crashed into the muskie and exploded in a giant sphere of flame. A sound that made thunder seem restrained slammed into me and nearly sent me to my knees. I looked away, wanting to remember Big Fish the way it had been.

Guided by Lee's Skill, we turned as a group and sprinted down a field for several hundred yards. Even *my* Stamina was getting quite impressive now.

We stopped, readied our weapons, and guarded the perimeter of the area I could feel was assigned to us. The way we moved reminded me of Voloids. When I looked around, I saw that roughly two-thirds of our troops that had followed us had divided into five separate groups of five, spread into a star-point pattern. In the center of those groups, two men not clustered were planting what looked to be small metal tops into the ground.

"*This way,*" Lee announced through the party chat portion of one of his Skills.

I felt the impulse to hold the pattern and how I should run to do just that. I did.

At five other locations, the tops were planted.

"Decoy Breach Drills deployed," one of the two men announced via party chat. Then they ran off in separate directions.

We charged another hundred yards or so until we reached what looked to be a heavily defended garage. It hadn't been visible from fifty feet away. Some kind of illusion? One of the five-person group's largest members conjured a massive iron battering ram as he ran. A blast of cold, reminiscent of northern winters, washed over us as one of his companions blasted the heavy metal door with a cone of ice. It froze solid just before his partner slammed into it with inhuman force. The metal shattered, and we all rushed inside through the breach.

"It's times like this that I miss Quinn," Lee said. "She'd be able to hack this lift in no time." He turned to Donaldson. "Make us a hole. Everyone else, get ready to rappel."

I was just starting to panic at the thought of rappelling, something I'd forgotten for a moment that I was relatively competent at now, when the whole floor lowered us into the ground.

"It's a trap," Topher said.

"Okay, Ackbar," I replied, already forgetting not to antagonize the psychopath. I changed tactics and switched to party chat. *"It might be more help from the one who warned us."*

"Optimism," Topher said with a sneer. "How's that working out for ya?"

I looked around at where I was, considering the state of the world. Then I took in the group around me, my new gear, Pavise's upgrades.

"The results are mixed," I said. Then I turned to Evelyn and smiled. "But better than I could have ever hoped."

Her grin was dazzling, but the way she followed up by biting her lower lip made my knees go weak.

Topher looked at me and then at her. He let out a disgusted grunt. For the first time since I'd met the man, he was speechless.

"It's Murphy's Law," Lee said, "not Murphy's Suggestions. So shut up and be ready for the shit to hit the fan."

We did as we were told, readying our weapons and our Skills.

A horde of troops was rushing toward us as the elevator stopped.

Chapter 69

Quinn

The entire base was filled with office cubicles, converted fluorescent-style lights, and gray corporate carpeting. It gave me flashbacks to my first, soul-crushing job at a call center.

Aside from the guards, everyone here reeked of weakness. Paper-pushers and crafting Classers. Some prisoners weren't even human. The aliens, at least, were mostly locked in cages. The humans thought they were soldiers for the HLF. They thought they could judge me.

One group of them had learned the truth before I'd isolated myself in the control room.

I stood next to the shredded chair, ignoring the massive screen of monitors in front of me. I was watching the same images that were displayed on them, but I was skipping the screens and consuming the data directly through my tech. It was the only way my Skills could bypass the interference tools that Lee's people were using. High-end items, but automated. Not nearly a match for me.

The attack was fully underway when my attention was needed the most. So that, of course, was when the Humanist chose to contact me.

His pompous image appeared. He was wearing his armor, now adorned with the many medals he'd had himself awarded. "Where the hell are you, Quinn? We're nearly to the ship. You were there at the start of this. You should be with us at the end."

"I couldn't reach you, sir, so I had to make a judgment call. Now that I'm at the base—"

"Base? What base?" His voice was satiny smooth, but his eyes were cold and hard.

"Delta 3 Niner," I told him. "The Loyalty Enforcement Division."

I had full access to the base's systems, but I hacked it anyway to let Lee in because of his comment. Then I cursed myself for allowing sentimentality to make me careless. Still, my suppressed humanity had stopped screaming long enough to notice that my only friend had missed me. That was worth some risk.

"Why?" he said. His tone made it clear it was more a threat than a question.

"I intercepted their communications. They jumped the gun. Here."

Rather than explain things, I sent him a standard debrief form. It was his preferred method. The man loved listening to himself talk, but he didn't feel the same about others. I'd sent the mercenaries to him as planned. I'd brought the guards specifically prepared to counter the Teacher with me.

I had a moment to think while the Humanist reviewed the file.

Lee missed me. He could express the fact that he missed me. Did that mean he was breaking free from the phony Teacher's control? Was that why he was finally able to express his true feelings? It gave me hope until I remembered what he would see if he looked at me. What I had become.

Would Lee kill me himself? Could I blame him if he did? Did I want him to? *Not yet. First, I have to drive my blades into the hearts of my enemies. Once I've had my revenge, I can live or die. It'll all be the same to me.*

I reminded myself not to get my hopes up. But if the Commander could be reached, I'd have to try to talk him down. If not, my plan to capture him would almost certainly fail. I'd spare him, no matter what the Humanist said. Then, wherever Lee went and no matter how long it took, I would find him. I would save my friend, or I would die trying. He was all that I had left.

The Humanist stopped reading. He stared at me.

I waited, my expression as dead as my emotions.

Apparently I passed some test because he nodded. "Well done. This changes nothing. We'll capture the ship. You kill the traitors. Protect the hostages." His signature ambition lit his eyes. "And bring me the Teacher. Alive, Quinn. Have I made myself clear?"

"Yes, sir." I slammed my hand to my chest in his ridiculous salute, but I didn't nod. I never had. He didn't notice, or he didn't care. "The assault has begun, sir. They are past the first checkpoint. I can continue to multitask to keep you in the loop, but—"

"No, that's fine. You do your job, and I'll do mine." He slammed his fist to his chest with a sharp nod, then he disconnected the feed.

I returned my attention to the base. I'd been confident that Lee would feint on one entrance while he attacked the other. It was his usual MO. But even I was surprised his assault was quite so thorough. His Decoy Drills had sent the base's defenders into apoplectic shock, and I'd nearly lost my spy pinkie when they exploded Lee's custom ATV. Thankfully, I'd managed to get it back underneath one of the trucks with heavy weapons systems.

Caleb wasn't even trying to pretend to be a Teacher anymore. He'd swapped out his disguise for high-tech armor. His robot was also unmasked. They both wore purple, the color of royalty. He was rubbing our noses in what he'd done to our people.

"Divide and conquer," I reminded myself. I tweaked the message to the former General's contact, along with the updated blueprints and suggestions.

If the "Teacher" somehow managed to survive, I'd arranged a way to counteract some of his lies. If I could break the illusion of his selfless, goodie-two-shoes-nature, maybe I could break his hold on his companions.

Maybe it would break his hold on Lee. I may not be a tactician, but I was a hacker. And multiple attack vectors were a key tool of my trade.

Chapter 70

Lee

The plan worked better than I'd hoped. Made me suspicious. A dozen Level forty Basic Classers met us at the gate. Soldiers, but well trained. Professionals. They were smart enough to fall back to another set of gun emplacements every time we disarmed one. Skilled or not, they'd already lost two men.

We'd lost nothing. Nothing except for time. They were slowing us down. Delay tactics? Were they setting up an ambush?

"Can't let them set our pace" I announced to the group via chat. "Caleb. Count of three. Put a shield *behind* them. Everyone else, give 'em everything you've got. One, two—"

"Stop," Penny said out loud.

"Better be good," I snapped back.

"Message from our contact. Updated maps. Troop movements. Includes two main targets. Heavily defended. The station control center and the housing units with the hostages. Lee, they're preparing to go into lockdown and trap us at this base until reinforcements arrive. They're starting to execute hostages. Our contact is stalling the main lockdown as long as they can. They're stopping the firewalls for now, but the automatic doors are about to close and seal."

We did not need to go forward. The hall to our left would lead us to the control center. To our right would lead us to the hostages.

"First, we have help. Now we have to split up. I don't buy it," I announced. "Stay together. We'll take down these fuckers and sort this shit out after."

"Did you mean it?" Penny whispered to Caleb. "What you said about the children?"

Shit, shit, shit. "Don't you dare," I said to them, abandoning the party chat. But I was too late.

Caleb used his broken charge Skill to dash through the open doorway to the right. His robot followed, a shield between him and me. Penny rushed after them. *Damn fool man. I knew who I was bringing along.* At least the others would have to get through me if they wanted to join them.

I grabbed Randy's armored bulk, but it was a wasted effort. He'd followed orders. *Good kid. No. Good man.* I let him go.

Evelyn took the chance to remind me that the space was three-dimensional, using the opposite wall, the ceiling, and her cybernetic hand on my shoulder to parkour her way past me and over Caleb's shield. Then she rolled through the door, just as it closed and sealed behind her.

"*Damn fools,*" I cursed them. "*Larson, I expected better from you.*"

"*This is the job,*" she replied, "*and you never split the team. You taught me that.*" Randy winced.

She wasn't wrong. I had taught her that. I'd also taught her to follow my god-damned orders.

She'd followed her heart instead. Couldn't trust her anymore. Shame.

"Randy. Turret mode. Hold the line here." I tossed out two of my emplacement shields to protect him as his armor twisted and rotated.

The end result was a powerful armored turret, with Randy in a mobile harness seat that reminded me of the gunner's station on the Millennium Falcon.

"Whole Nine Yards," he whispered to himself as he opened up with massive fully-automatics. His first use of his brand-new Advanced Class Skill. He unloaded, filling the entire hallway with bullets.

They dove for cover but found none except each other. Their armor cracked. Bits flew off like shrapnel. Blood and more unmentionable fluids puddled below them all.

They withdrew. Odds were high that they'd be back with reinforcements. Better defenses.

I'd leave Randy where he stood, howling triumphantly. He'd been well trained, and he knew how to follow orders. I knew he'd hold them off until his dying breath. It would probably come to that. A soldier's usual reward for loyalty. Unjust, but I was glad to have him with us. His current placement was perfect for his new Class.

Doubt was trying to nag at me. I'd sent the others off to die without their strongest fighter.

No. Fuck that. They'd sent themselves off without him. Disobeyed my orders. If he died without his team to back him, that would be their fault. Not mine.

But I knew who I was bringing along. My own thoughts haunted me. No time for this. Too late now anyway.

I reviewed the old battle map. The new one. *Damn it.* Without the extra three, we'd have no one left to watch our backs if we decided to press forward. It would leave our rear exposed to enemy troops. Couldn't risk it. This was an obvious and amateurish trap, but I was going to have to trigger it and hope for the best. The trio had left me no damn choice.

Whoever was "helping us" was playing us. I was certain of that now. Zero chance that one door closed to split us up while the other one stayed open. Not without intent. They were splitting us up. Divide and conquer.

"Donaldson, take out that door," I said, motioning to the one Mr. Rogers had gone through. "Then follow us. Blow this door too if it locks behind us.

Then wait for my orders. Everyone else with me." I motioned them into the room and followed them through. The door closed behind me with a clank.

There had been a battle in this room. Several hacked up corpses. Lots of blood. The low-rent office furniture and drywall was shredded like the bodies.

"What did this?" Gerri asked.

"Could be an out-of-control monster," I suggested.

"Or berserkers with swords," Fox, the Gunman, said.

"Reminds me of my ex," Topher snarked.

"Not helpful," I told the asshole, then said to everyone else, "Be ready for anything."

"So do what we were already doing anyway. Yer leadership's inspiring, sir."

"If Topher talks again, shoot him. Follow me."

Halverson checked the door. Cleared it. He was a Rogue. Thorough. The man still had hopes that his dead daughter might be here, I remembered. Poor guy.

We opened the door and moved in, ready to attack.

In the third room, we found a long hall filled with cells. There was a single alien prisoner. A small man. Naked. He looked like he'd been carved from cracked granite.

"Should I kill the alien?" Fox asked, gesturing toward the man with his revolver.

The thing pressed its bare flesh against the bars and begged, "Kill Gendon. Don't let her hurt him like the others. Please just make it stop."

"You deserve whatever you get, invader," Fox snapped at him. He fingered his revolvers. "But I've got your mercy right here."

"Yes, yes, pleeeaaasse. Shoot poor Gendon in the head." He pressed it to the bars. "Save him from her. Gendon brought here. Gendon Slave with contract. Not Gendon's fault."

Pathetic.

Something he'd said stuck in my mind though. *Her?* Who was he talking about? The Commander of the base? Penny had said that the person in charge here was a man? Had all of our information been phony? Damn. I'd fallen for it. Ought to know better by now. But we had to move, had to try.

"Leave him," I told the Gunman. "We don't have time for this."

As we moved on to the next room, something about the alien bothered me. Was it that I'd left a possible threat alive? I didn't think so. He didn't feel like a threat. I couldn't put my finger on it. *Whatever. We can always kill him on the way out.*

One room after another, we followed the same pattern, until all but two had been cleared.

"This will be the one," I told them.

Topher clearly wanted to speak. He looked as though he might have a real question. I ignored him.

"How do you know?" Gerri asked.

Topher pointed at them and nodded vigorously.

"Obvious." I sent them the picture of the map. One last big room before the smaller one with the Mana generator and computer banks. "They aren't going to want the fight in the room with all the gear they're trying to protect. That means this one."

"Process of elimination," Gerri said. "Makes sense."

"When the door opens, verify the targets. If there's even one enemy, unload everything you've got. Think grenades. Explosives. Cause some chaos and do some damage. Then focus your fire on the one I mark. Got it?"

They all indicated that they did.

We opened the door to find the room filled with a pile of shredded, half-devoured corpses.

I imagined the pile exploding like one of the chef's head grenades, but everyone held to their trigger discipline. Made me proud.

"What the fuck?" I said, accompanied by a mistimed chorus of the same.

The door on the other side of the massacre-filled room opened on its own.

"We need to talk, Lee. Just you and me." The voice was raspier than I remembered, and it sounded a bit artificial. It was still Quinn.

I looked at the pile of half-consumed corpses, then into the darkened room. I remembered the slaughter in the first room. The messages. The fact that someone had let us waltz right in.

I remembered she had turned on me.

I remembered that she needed to die.

"Wait here," I told the others. *"Be ready to attack on my command."*

I stepped into the darkness.

Chapter 71

Lee

Quinn was sitting on a spider-mech in the shadows of the room. She'd destroyed the screens. The chair. Everything but the computer terminals and the generator. Part of me had hoped that the voice had been a trick. No such luck. She'd survived the destruction of her giant spider after all.

Shame.

She wanted to talk. That was good. I had enough firepower here to kill her without question, but not nearly enough to kill her without casualties. Including me. That wasn't the worst part. Deadly as she was, the real threat was behind her. None of us could match her with computers. She could fuck us as she died. Lock the base down. Trap us here for reinforcements. Set the base to self-destruct.

She could also turn the base against our enemies. Wipe the evidence of what we'd done. She could let us go. I decided I would hear her out.

"What the hell is going on here, Quinn?" The question was a stall tactic as much as anything. It would give me time to check on the others. Time to issue orders.

She swayed from side to side. Some kind of drugs? Still recovering from her injuries? What was she doing here in the first place? And why was she hiding in the dark? It looked like she might be naked. Was she embarrassed about scars?

"You can't even be bothered to say hello to your old friend," she said with an uncanny valley voice that wasn't quite right. "Has he got that strong a hold on you? Maybe this will help." She reached out for a device attached to her mech chair and pressed a button.

My group-related Skills shut down completely. *Shit. Stall. Keep her talking. Give the others time. Turn her if she can be turned.*

"I'm not the one being controlled. You're the puppet with a master and strings." But I remembered the truth. She'd been the one in charge when she'd betrayed me.

"Lies," she said sharply. "I'm immune to the Humanist's tricks, just like the 'Teacher's.' You're the one who's not yourself."

Her words reinforced my evaluation of her. Sealed her fate. "If I'm the one who's not myself, then why are you the one that's hiding in the dark?"

She shrieked in rage as her mech's huge, bladed leg slammed into the carpet and concrete like a toddler's tantrum.

The inhuman sound of her scream triggered a primal fear response. Felt like mainlining ice water. It was all I could do not to shiver. I took an instinctive step back and raised my Hand Cannon as conflicting instincts demanded immediate action.

Run for my life.

Kill it with fire.

I held my ground, even as Quinn's movements revealed more of her appearance. Too many eyes. Black as midnight. Light glinting off a mouthful of metal fangs.

Pity warred with terror. Fought it to a stalemate. I took another step back. Urged the others to retreat with a mental shove from my Skill that wasn't working. Fuck. I gestured for them to fall back and they did.

I reminded myself to stall. "What the hell did that monster do to you?"

Quinn had a lot to answer for. The Humanist had more.

She stepped into the light. Her expression was as dead as her victims. Quinn's body was a Frankensteinian freak of spider legs and chrome.

Pity won the war with fear. I'd rather be dead than whatever she was now. Killing her would be a mercy. I had to remind myself that it was one she didn't deserve. I'd kill her anyway if I could do it and preserve the mission. This thing needed to die.

"I'll kill him," she said, causing me to reevaluate. "I'll kill them all."

Not kill you. Kill him. Them.

"Who?"

"Humanist. Teacher. Aliens. All our enemies."

Our? What did she think was going on here? Could she still be turned? She would be useful, no question. But she'd been dangerous at the best of times. Volatile. Now she was a nightmare brought to life. She could not be trusted. *Turn her. Use her. Kill her.*

"We need to kill the Humanist, Quinn, and any of his people we can't turn. Help me." I decided to gamble on a guess. "Like you did at the lift. Turn their weapons on them. Help us fight. We need to get out of here."

"And the Teacher? The Aliens?"

I'd sacrifice the Teacher if I had to, though I liked the man. But he was trying to save hostages as we spoke. Children. Like my boys. No. Wasn't going to happen.

"To hell with them," I tried. "We only need to kill the Humanist. We'll grab our best men on the way out. Head straight to him. I can resist him. You've seen me do it. You said yourself that you're immune."

"Beat him to the ship and kill him?" She was mumbling to herself now, lost in thought. "Is there still time? Can we kill him? No. He's just too strong. So strong. We need more power."

He was on his way to the ship! *Fuck. I need to end this.* What had she called herself? My old friend?

"I need your help, my friend. You're the only one that I can trust."

Her expression got strange, alternating between anguish, rage, and emptiness. Anguish won. "I'll save you."

I didn't like her tone. Didn't trust her. I stepped back, feet crunching the broken glass below. Watching for any signs of danger.

If I hadn't been wary, I'd have been too slow when she rushed forward to grab me. I'd have missed the grapple traps shooting from the wall.

As it was, I was barely able to sidestep the automated grapples. Quinn would probably have managed to grab me anyway, except whatever had happened to her had clearly not been intended for non-lethal encounters.

Even without my Skill, my troops knew enough so that every weapon was fixed on her and primed to fire.

"Hold fire, but stay sharp," I ordered. "Single shots only. Careful aim. Control effects that won't break things."

She let out a shriek of rage and stepped back, glaring at the others furiously.

"Come with me," she begged, gesturing with her clawed hand toward a bank of what looked like huge computers.

I kept the majority of my attention focused on her as I turned my drone for a better look. Obviously triggered remotely, the bank of computers moved aside, revealing a secret passageway.

"I have a bunker big enough for two. He'll think that we all died." She turned to look at it, longing in her black eyes.

"Open fire," I commanded and then triggered Burn Them Down followed by Hit and Run, activating the first charge to increase their rate of fire.

She cried out in pain as the bullets struck. They tore through her hairy skin but bounced off metal underneath. Some, at least, tore into the metal, and Gerri wrapped Quinn in corrosive green smoke. Her Health was dropping.

We've got this. The secret passage nagged at me. She'd already escaped once.

"Armor piercing, if you have them." I changed my hand cannon's ammo with practiced efficiency.

Many of the others did the same. The smell of burning flesh and metal filled the air, causing me to wrinkle my nose. Quinn twitched and jerked, her limbs covering her whenever someone tried for a headshot. Blood and non-human liquids flowed from burnt metal, light sparking as broken electronics glittered in the dark. Something was screaming, a high-pitched tone that cut through the hum of attacks.

"Surrender," I told her. "You're finished."

"Oh please," Quinn replied as she turned back to me, face filled with scorn.

The base's speakers blasted an announcement. "Self-destruct sequence activated. Base entering lockdown mode. Two minutes remaining."

Was she bluffing? No. She'd offered to blow this place to save me. Damn it.

Trap her here? Play chicken with a crazy bitch? Pass.

Might be my last chance to finish her? But there was no chance. Not really. We'd lose everyone for nothing. Quinn had outplayed me. This was checkmate and she'd won.

There'd be a rematch someday. When it happened, I promised myself I'd cheat.

We had to get out. I dropped a force barrier device. It would barely slow her down. Better than nothing. I backed away, before whipping around to flee.

I was already running when I pushed the others to, "Go, go, GOOO!" I triggered Hit and Run's second charge to speed up our retreat.

"Just keep fighting him," Quinn yelled after me, her face screwed up in sympathetic concentration. Then it was like a switch was flipped, and I was dealing with the murderous monster again. She screamed in fury, "I'll find you. No matter how far you go. No matter how long it takes. I'll never stop."

I shivered as I ran.

I didn't hear the sound of metal on stone of her following me. My drones followed, watching our retreat, but there was no sign of her. We ran, heading back the way we came, feet pounding the concrete flooring.

The heavy metal firewalls were slowly dropping, but I couldn't shake the feeling that something was wrong. That I was about to cross some kind of line. One I'd never make it back from.

"Out!" I demanded as the others slowed their pace when I hesitated. I activated my Reposition Skill to give them a flat movement speed increase and help offset the few spots of bad terrain. They took off like bats out of hell.

I swore at myself when I realized what was wrong. The alien. He wasn't even a child. Clearly. He was a full-grown adult. Just as obviously, he'd been forced to come here.

"Invaders invade," Caleb had said, that first day we'd met. It was just as true today.

The alien, beaten and caged, was about to be murdered. I glanced at him, cowering in the corner, as I ran.

In my inventory, I kept an assortment of specialized equipment to keep my ass alive. One of them was a single-use device that could make me insubstantial for thirty seconds. Long enough for a snatch-and-grab or a quick jailbreak. I wanted to keep it. Might need the thing myself.

I tossed it into the cell with the alien as I ran, yelling, "Activate it. Run through the bars. Follow me."

Then I heard the sound I'd been listening for. The clatter of sharp metal on stone. She was coming. *Why now?* Then I saw a camera. Was she watching? Had freeing her prisoner set her off? My body turned and bolted.

I didn't glance back as I ran. No time. I raced through the doors and rooms and headed out into the night. He would follow or he wouldn't. I wasn't going to look, because there was a monster on my tail.

Chapter 72

Caleb

Hordes of Basic Class soldiers attacked us nearly the moment we got through the door. The room reminded me a bit of a public school classroom. It would have made me feel at home if not for the all the soldiers with guns and knives and other melee weapons.

I'd tried to explain why we were here to deescalate the situation, but they hadn't listened. I wasn't sure they *could* listen. Metal plates had been implanted where their ears should be. I got the impression that this was intended to prevent exactly what I'd been trying to do. It felt as though I was wandering into tinfoil hat territory, but paranoid or not, I was pretty sure that I was right. Because the very next thing they'd done was scan the group of us, locate me specifically, and open fire.

It was hard not to take that personally. It was even harder not to be paranoid when a security bolt locked into place on the door behind me.

They were using the kind of rifles the news had always said were assault weapons, but that Topher and Lee called semi-automatic rifles. Even with all of our training, those guns terrified me. They'd featured in the worst of my nightmares for a decade before the System ever came to Earth, back when I'd have been entirely powerless to protect my students if a shooter had attacked.

Now, I had force barriers, assorted weapons, and a team. Well, most of a team. I wished that Randy had made it through to join us. A shotgun would have been perfect for a situation with so many enemies smashed so close together. We'd have to use the next best thing.

"Grenades," I called out, grateful as always that Pavise had my back. He'd put up a shield while I was flinching and distracted. I sent him my feelings via our updated link. It was easier than ever.

"I hate those things," Evie said, but she reached for them regardless.

"Goo grenades," Penny chimed in, and I updated my plan.

"Smart," I said as we all grabbed the weapons she'd named.

I remembered to actually activate mine this time and tossed it over the shield. The grenades exploded into a gray metallic goo that gushed and melted all over the enemies and their weapons, gumming up several of the guns, limiting the soldiers' movement, and even managing to blind one of them.

"Smart indeed, sir," Pavise said. "It would seem that these weapons are specifically..."

He was still talking, but I'd stopped listening. We'd only really gotten seven of the enemies, and more were entering from a doorway behind them. The room was big enough that they could swarm us by going around.

Without a word, Evelyn triple-somersaulted with a twist right into the center of the enemies. My heart stopped. I wanted to wrap her in a force field, but that wasn't how my power worked. I'd need to wall off the worst side when things got really rough.

She was amazing, but I'd learned her limits weeks ago. There were too many of them, and just like everyone else, sometimes even champions need saving.

This wasn't one of those times.

I'd forgotten that Evelyn had a whole new Class at her disposal. She showcased her new Skill, blurring as she spun and stabbed and slashed. Between swings, her staff was just a staff. Every time she struck, however, she extended the plasma blade and drove it deep into the enemies with a hissing sizzle. It was nothing like it sounded in the movies.

The burning metal smell that filled the room became more acrid, with subtle hints of sulfur.

The Acrobat's—no, the Spear Dancer's display was a wonder to behold, though it lasted only a few seconds. We backed her up as much as we could with our shields and weapons fire. Even with so many weapons going off at once, the scream of Pavise's shoulder turret's whistle was painfully loud.

I only managed a few Hunter's Strikes, and Penny, who'd had to change her cartridge, not even that. As Evelyn's Skill ended and she leapt in a graceful double-backflip to rejoin us, two of the survivors had been disarmed. Many more were seriously injured, if their cries of pain were any indication.

Not one of them had landed a hit on her, though they'd certainly shot each other. It was nice to finally be the Advanced Classers versus Basics, instead of the other way around. The reinforcements seemed endless though. I wasn't sure that our level advantage would be enough.

Then my body, and everything else, seemed to slow to a crawl as Pavise shared his processing power with me. He was on the same track, but he was way ahead of me. We'd be overwhelmed here, and our retreat was blocked off, but there was a second, smaller door we could use to change things up.

For the first time, Pavise and I generated force shields at the same time, blocking off a much longer path than we could have otherwise.

"Door," I shouted as I rushed toward it.

"Out of the way," Evie ordered. "Your shield's breaking."

"Already?" I said as I stepped aside and let the translucent purple shield fall, generating a new one where it had stood.

In the interim, a trio of bullets slammed into my chest and stomach. It felt like Ant-Man had punched me hard and knocked me backward a few steps. One of my ribs cracked like my armor's outer shell. I grunted. It was worse than I was used to, and it took my breath as surely as my lack of fitness used to.

My new armor was still bulletproof, but it had been designed as a backup and enhancement for a personal force field I didn't have. Not that the force field would have done much good, if the shield was any indication. I wanted to ask Pavise why the shields were suddenly crap, but I couldn't breathe well enough to even try. I sent the question as a concept through our link.

"As I may have mentioned earlier"—when I'd been ignoring him, his tone implied—"their ammunition is designed to disrupt the shields we rely on."

"I knew… wasn't… paranoid."

As I struggled to speak, Evie had forced open the door, and she and Penny were already on the other side of it.

"Not the time," Evie said as she grabbed one of my armor's plates and dragged me after her.

I whipped back around and threw up one of my stronger shields for Pavise, so that he could drop his own shield and back into the room.

He didn't quite fit through the door frame.

My stomach dropped and my mind threatened to spin out of control as it desperately attempted to reject the reality of what it was seeing and come up with an immediate solution at the same time.

Pavise stepped forward, converted into his tread form, and tried again. But his computations were ahead of his body. "This isn't going to work."

He was almost able to make it through but ended up like the oversized couch I'd bought at a rummage sale. I couldn't get it into my apartment no matter how I turned it. He was really wedged in there now.

"You all need to go," Pavise said. "I will wait here and secure your escape until my Mana runs out."

That was when I caught on. He'd known all along this would happen. Of course he had. He was a person, despite his claims, but he was also a supercomputer. He just didn't tell us until we couldn't stop him. He was trying to make a sacrifice play.

Not if I could help it.

"No," Penny and I said at the same time.

I turned to look at her—her response had surprised me.

"We'll never make it out of here without you," she said. "It's no good to halfway save my son."

My expression hardened a bit before I could school it. She was right to care about David, I reminded myself. Still, her continued lack of disregard for the other hostages was grating on my frayed nerves.

She must have noticed. "It's no good to halfway save the hostages."

I gave her the stern nod I usually reserved for students with correct answers but unruly tones. "She's right. But how do we get him out? He's burning through Mana way too fast this way. And every time they break one of the shields, he's going to—"

One of the shields broke, allowing the weapons fire to score into Pavise's armor until he could raise another.

"That," I said, pointing.

"One of the slippery grenades?" Evelyn asked.

"Grease." Then I remembered that was a D&D spell. "I mean…" I could not remember.

"Slippery Liquid Dispersal," Evie clarified. "SLDs."

"Slippery it is." I pulled out one.

"Don't!" That was Penny. I started to ask her why, but she pulled out a canister and sprayed the spots where Pav met the doorway. "Too uncontrolled. More trouble than it's worth. I brought this to help with cuffs, but it might do the trick."

It didn't. Pavise made it a bit farther, but not nearly far enough. He'd taken a few more shots, and part of his armor was getting severely damaged.

I used Minor Repair on him, which simply wasn't good enough. It eased some of the scrapes and minor burns, but not the one that mattered. It would have to be enough.

"Ropes," I said. "We can try to pull him out."

"I appreciate your dedication," Pavise stated. "However, if we do not do something to counter the assault, none of it will matter. Without Mana, I will be unable to assist you. If I am destroyed in the process, doubly so."

Evelyn took an incendiary grenade from her inventory and gasped. "I may have a very bad idea that kills two birds with one stone."

"Oh? Oh!" I said as I realized what she'd planned. Brilliant! I started to blurt it out, but I'd learned working with children just how much people hated it when you did that. I shut up and let her have her moment.

She swapped her grenade for another. "Concussion."

We all backed away, and she threw it past Pavise as soon as he said, "Down!"

The explosion knocked back the enemies. They cried out in pain, but the sounds were muted after the explosion.

One sound was loud and clear despite all that. The metal-on-metal scraping sound as Pavise was driven deeper into, then through, the door frame. He popped out on our side.

I grinned as my hope surged anew. Pavise was free!

Evelyn beamed, and I desperately wished I could throw my arms around her and cheer. I felt like the Grinch as my heart swelled and swelled until it was too big for my chest. But there was no time.

Heavy as he was, Pavise had to back up before we could attempt to close the door. He lost his line of sight as we closed the door, costing him his shield. This time, they'd been ready, and armor-piercing shells slammed into him, including a shot that treated his damaged armor as if it were a bull's-eye.

Sparks flew as something important in Pavise was damaged. I had no time to evaluate what.

At the same time, I heard a struggle breaking out behind me. Our training had taught us to work together as a team. While Pavise and I did our part to secure the door as best we could, grunts and curses echoed behind me. I ignored it, trusting my team to handle it. They'd tell me if they needed me.

We were able to force the door shut, but the frame and the door itself had both been bent by the explosion. We could close it, but it wouldn't be secure. Pavise pressed his heavy body hard against it to hold it closed.

I turned to find that the others had dropped a pair of guards, and Penny's white synthweave uniform had been seared through. She was covering it with a gel-coated pad. I frowned. I'd have to do a better job protecting her. If I could…

"Caleb," Evie said, shaking me until I focused my attention on her. "The door."

"Right, sorry."

Focus, Caleb. Easier said than done. I was so tired. When this was over, I'd need to find a place to hole up and finally get some sleep. Wait! A visceral zing radiated from the back of my neck. I grinned.

"So, this is going to sound like a wrong-place-and-wrong-time kind of idea, but do you have your bed with you?" I asked Evie.

"What?" Penny exclaimed, glaring at me.

"Oh," Pavise and Evelyn said in unison. Then only Evelyn continued. "That just might work."

Penny's expression swapped from angry to confused, but she didn't interrupt as Evie pulled out her expanding bed material and its placement devices and used it to fill the doorway. It nearly did the job, but the material just wasn't strong enough.

"We still have some of these," Penny said, pulling out her last few goo grenades.

A few seconds later, the bed material was coated and secured to the walls with globs of the hardening metallic gunk.

"That is one of the strangest things I've ever seen," Pavise declared.

"I like it," Penny said. "It's not elegant, but it works. Now, we need to go."

"I hate it," Evie said.

Penny had half turned and started walking. She turned back around, worried. "What's wrong?"

"That was my bed. Where the hell am I supposed to sleep now? His floor is solid stone, and his bed's not much better."

Penny looked beyond furious. "My son is in danger. He may already be dead."

Evelyn paled, then turned solid red. "You're right. I'm sorry."

"It's fine," Penny lied. "Let's go."

"Sir, shall I stay here and guard the door, just in case?"

"You can't, buddy. We're gonna have to just hope for the best."

Penny turned her glare on me, and I used Show and Tell to pull up the part of the map where we were standing. A green arrow pointed at where we were standing. A red arrow pointed at the enemies. Then it showed that the two paths could travel in the direction we were heading and exactly where they would eventually intersect.

"Oh," she said. "Good catch."

"We'll head to the other path and hold the line. I'd leave him here, but I'm not able to use the force field projection at that distance, at least not yet."

"Not ever, sir. Barring some sort of Evolution."

"Not important now," Penny said.

"I apologize, Miss Sprocket."

She nodded.

Was her last name Sprocket? Really? Not the time to ask.

"I do have a concern, however. My master has ranted endlessly about games and movies and television shows."

"Hey!"

"And there have been several nuggets of wisdom buried beneath the mountains of dross."

I held my tongue.

"Get to the point," Penny snapped.

"I believe the most common version of the maxim may be, 'Don't split the party.'"

I pointed back toward where we'd broken off from the main group. "I think that ship has sailed, buddy."

"Yes, sir. But that doesn't mean we have to sink it," Pavise replied in a tone of stern disapproval.

"Besides," Penny said, "it's not the only expression. We also have, 'The exception that proves the rule.'" She bolted off toward one of the rooms.

Evelyn chose a different direction, saying, "And, 'Rules are made to be broken.'"

I opened my mouth and headed toward the other entrance, but before I could speak, Pavise said, "Mr. Jenkins it is then, I suppose."

I should not have laughed. Things were serious. I blamed exhaustion.

"It's fine," I said. "We have the party chat and group map. If anything happens, we'll know."

By the time I reached the end of the hallway, the door was already open, with soldiers on the other side. That sobered me up real quick. I tossed out a force shield, barely managing to stop the door before it was wide enough that our enemies could have forced their bodies through, one at a time. At that exact moment, our party chat ended abruptly, and the maps closed.

Lee! My heart skipped a beat. I hadn't realized how much faith I'd put in the man until… Was he dead? Captured? What hope did we have if even the Commander could fail?

An arm forcing its way into the crack of the doorway pulled my attention back to the moment.

"Fudge!" I shouted.

They only had to break the shield once to force the door wide open. My training kicked in, and I was running toward the door before I even had the terrible plan that formed, seconds later. I focused my mind to aim my shoulder turret at the man's hand long enough to shoot it. If my plan was going to work, his arm needed to be out of the way. I activated my half-broken Thrusting Charge as I took my shot, then timed the leap perfectly, managing to kick off of the ground at the exact moment when I'd normally have rolled. I didn't even have time to stop and see if the shot had hit as my body slammed into the heavy door, boots first.

Shockingly, for a geek like me, I did it. I managed the leap, my flying kick striking the exact spot on the door I'd chosen. Exhilaration filled me as, for the first time in my life, I'd truly excelled at a remarkable bit of athleticism. As a teacher, however, I'd failed utterly. Caleb the teacher knew that mass moves mass, and the doors were really massive. I, on the other hand, was not.

The door did move a little. The guy grunted in pain from the weight of the door if not my failed shot. But even if I'd made the shot and he'd withdrawn his arm, it would not have been enough.

That was when I heard Pavise shout, "Caleb, move!"

Pavise using my first name shocked me. It would have stunned me into inaction if I hadn't been drilled so hard on what to do in such a state of alarm. I dove aside just in time to avoid Pavise's very heavy metal form as he charged the door at top speed.

As he did so, he yelled, "Mmiiiiissssttteeeerrrr Jeeeeeennnnnnkkkkiiiinnns!"

Then a resounding clang pealed like thunder and the door slammed shut with a heavy thud. The only other sounds were a scream that was cut off as the door fully sealed, and the much lighter thudding sound as a detached human arm hit the floor.

I was about to shout in triumph when Penny screamed.

Chapter 73

Caleb

"We should not have split the party," I told Pavise, in a tone I would have to apologize for later. "Stay here. Guard the door. Yell if you run low on Mana. I'll be back."

"I am already low on Mana," Pavise said without missing a beat.

"Lower," I said, and I ran.

Penny was exiting a room by the time I reached it.

She shoved me backward, hard. I stumbled, tripped, and fell into the wall with a harsh clang. She'd left bloody handprints on my armor. Her face was horrified, but not grief-filled. Either she hadn't found David, or her medical training was better than it had any right to be.

"Do not go in there," she ordered.

"There might be survivors." I felt like a fool as soon as I said it. She knew her business better than I ever would, a fact driven home by her next words.

"I have a whole Class Tree called Triage," she said. "There's no one left to save."

I nodded. Then I tensed as I tried not to imagine what could have been bad enough for her to shove me away. What had she seen in that room? "The hostages?"

She shook her head. "Aliens." She hesitated. Then her expression soured as she continued. "Some of them were kids."

Her words reached into my chest and crushed my heart.

Penny must have seen it on my face because she clutched my hand. I thought she was trying to reassure me, until she said, "I keep waiting for

Evelyn to scream. For the other shoe to drop. If she does, I think you'll have to carry me."

I stood up straighter. Something about her needing me lent me the strength I needed to go on. "Whatever it takes."

"I haven't forgotten your promise." Her lips said promise; her eyes said sacred oath.

It could have been a nod or a pinkie swear. It all meant the same to me. She didn't even need to ask.

"I'll go ahead," I told her.

She closed her eyes and took a deep breath. "No, stay with Pavise. I'm sorry that I pulled you away."

I put my arm on her shoulder. It was trembling. "He'll call me if he needs me," I said in the tone I'd learned from Mr. Rogers. "We'll go together."

She nodded, and we walked together into the next room. It was huge and actually pretty nice. I'd imagined a prison, but this was more like a mix between a dormitory and a summer camp. There were military-style bunk beds, a table, and a desk. The place even had a big screen TV and an old Indiana Jones pinball machine. There were a dozen humans. Three of them were children, and two were the newly rejuvenated elderly I'd heard so much about. The rest were spread in all other age groups. About the mix of hair and skin color that you'd expect in the US, if not in northern Minnesota.

We checked, but none of them were Penny's son.

"Where are the rest?" she asked them.

"There was one more," the gray-haired woman said. "But a monster took him."

"Took him or killed him?" Penny asked with barely controlled panic in her voice. It wasn't visible, but I felt her cat tail as it smacked into my leg.

The older woman's eyes softened. "He was someone you knew?"

"Was?" she said, voice cracking.

I had the strongest urge to reach out and pet Penny, but I restrained myself. I settled for words of comfort, but I never got the chance.

"He wasn't dead when she took him. But he's—"

"That's enough," the older man said. "For Pete's sake, just tell her what happened, or shut your pie hole."

She stormed off in a huff.

"Look, lady, I'm sorry and all, but your kid is probably dead. The alien or monster or whatever went off on a long speech about a Teacher being a fake and how this will show them. I can't really remember all the words. But she said the Teacher had to come alone. That you, lady?"

Penny sputtered for a moment, then tried and failed to answer.

"She's the mom," I said. "I'm the Teacher."

"The thing seemed crazy. It's gotta be a trap, right?"

"Yes," I said, at the same time Penny said, "It doesn't matter."

"That's kind of heartless, Lady," the older man said.

I wanted to answer him, but Penny's eyes were begging me. I tried to give her a reassuring smile as I nodded. "It is, but it's also true. What do I have to do?"

The man moved aside the pinball machine, exposing an oversized crawl space behind it.

The woman spoke up again. "She said you wouldn't go. Then everyone would know you were a fake."

"Self-destruct sequence activated. Base entering lockdown mode. Two minutes remaining."

"Everybody out," I yelled. I pointed back to where Pavise was waiting.

I wanted to talk, to plan, to coordinate. I wanted to take a perfect movie moment and kiss Evelyn one last time. But the clock was ticking down, so I turned and ran as fast as I could hunched over without another word to anyone.

"Stall as long as you can," Pavise told me. *"I'll protect the others, but once you die, I will cease to function."*

I couldn't slow down enough for words, so I shoved my gratitude and affection through our link, along with my feelings for the others. I'd miss him so much. All of them. But I forced them from my mind. I had a job to do.

I ran with everything I had left. Somehow, I found energy that I thought had deserted me and a gratefulness for Topher and Lee for all the running and training they'd put me through. I ran, my breathing rocketing up, my feet digging into compact earth and throwing up dust clouds behind me.

The hall was blessedly short, or I'd have died for nothing. It opened into a wide dirt room that was supported by wooden beams. The child was on the left side. My first thought was he was so small, so brave looking, standing there. Alone.

He wore a flashing collar around his neck, and he was surrounded with a ring of shaped-charge explosives. Next to it was another circle with similar explosives and another collar that was obviously meant for me.

I took deep breaths and tried to slow my racing heart and clear my thoughts as I took in the rest of the details, looking for any clue that could help me salvage the situation or make the most of my sacrifice.

Three tripod cameras sat recording everything. Or they were laser weapons that would cut me down if I left. No time to inspect them and check, and I wasn't going anywhere.

My greatest fear diminished as I saw a ladder leading upward toward the surface. I'd had no confidence I could explain his path to him, or that he could have made it in time.

That new hope aside, I was pretty sure I knew what was about to happen. I'd seen too many movies not to know. I'd step into the circle and put on the collar, and then we'd both be trapped until the whole building exploded. Or the two rings of explosives would go off and the building wouldn't even explode. Cue maniacal laughter.

But I had no time to second-guess my choice. I'd have to put it on regardless. It might already be too late. I had no tools that could possibly break him out. And fantasies aside, I wasn't some superhero who could dash in faster than a bomb could explode and tear the collar from him with super strength before absorbing the blast with my body. Without Pavise, I was nothing special, just a teacher.

No, I remembered. A Teacher.

A Teacher with an ace in the hole that he'd been saving for just such a situation. An ace in the hole that had always let me down when I'd needed it the most. My evolved Class Trip.

I didn't dare put on the collar now. Too many collars blocked powers in fiction, and I would not give up my best chance to save him. Save us both.

"I'm going to get you out of here," I told the boy.

"What's the password?" David asked.

"I don't know the password. Your mother sent me. I need to get you out of here or we're both going to die. I have a Skill. It can save you. It can save both of us. I just need you to agree to be my student." I needed parental permission too, but my Skill Evolution would save the day on that one. "Just agree to come with me and I'll take you to your mother."

"Liar," he said. "My mother is dead. He told me so, and the Humanist wouldn't lie. He said that aliens might come, or alien-loving traitor humans pretending to help. The alien came. Now here you are too, traitor. He told me this would happen."

Was it his age that blocked Ring of Truth? Maybe because he wasn't fully accepted by the System? Or was it the collar or something else about the room? My Ring of Truth Skill had served me so well for so long. Why did it keep failing me now?

"I'm not a…" I hesitated. "I'm here to help you, to save you. Please, we're almost out of time."

"But he was a hero. He was my friend. He'll save us all."

"Who?" I asked.

"The Humanist. He said not to trust any alien-loving scum. I won't go with a traitor. Are you an alien-lover?"

I didn't have to wonder what Mr. Rogers would have done. "No," I lied. "I'm here to save you from them."

"What's the password?" he begged, obviously terrified.

"I don't know." I was the one begging now, as the seconds ticked down toward single digits. "Please just agree to let me teach you?"

Even with the Skill evolution, Class Trip could not be used alone. I had no time to ask again. He had no time to answer. All I could do was pray to any god who would listen that he'd agreed enough for the Skill to count it. I imagined taking us both to the spot behind the vehicle on the road where they'd been parked.

For once, the Teacher Skill that had impressed me the most finally didn't let me down.

Limitation Over-Ridden by Skill Evolution.
Skill activating.

In a flash of dazzling golden light, we vanished from the room with a second left to spare.

Chapter 74

Caleb

We appeared in the exact spot I'd envisioned, except for the ground shaking and a deep rumble from the explosion we'd so narrowly avoided. The teleportation itself was disorienting, but it had none of the other classic side effects.

The clean scent of wood smoke was in the air from the initial attack earlier. The smell would have brought back good memories if not for the acrid chemical and sulfur scents from the weapons. The building half of the Big Fish restaurant had not completely exploded, but the giant painted-wood muskie front was a smoldering heap of rubble.

The collar was still with David, though the lights were off now. He was safe, and that was all that mattered. No, I reminded myself. I still needed to keep him safe. Pavise wasn't with me, and so many of my Skills depended on him.

I wanted to reach out to Pavise, to check on him. But I was so overflowing with joy and gratitude that I couldn't stop myself from expressing it to David. It was all I could do not to hug him.

I dropped down and met his eyes, Mr. Rogers-style. "Thank you. Thank you so much for believing me."

His lips pursed and his eyes widened. They looked so much like his mom's. But he was obviously confused.

"I didn't," he said. "I don't."

Now it was my turn to be confused. "You didn't?"

"No. You said you were going to bring me to my mommy." He looked around.

"I'll check on her in just a minute. She should be on her way now."

"You also said the building was going to blow up. You said my mom was in there?" His lips quivered and skin was paling fast.

My heart fractured at the sight. "A friend of mine should be with her. Give me a second to ask him." That thought triggered my own fear for my friends.

"Pavise, buddy, are you okay? Are the others with you?"

"Yes, sir. We are on our way. Lee and Topher and the others are with us. We only lost a few people. None of them were from your team."

Even though the news was bittersweet, relief washed over me, and I could finally get a real full breath. *"That's good news. Tell her that her son is with me. David's eager to see her."*

"I have let her know, sir. She is splitting the party again."

"Your mom is safe," I told David. "She's on her way right now. Are you sure you didn't agree to come with me?"

"I'm sure. I wasn't going to listen to you, because there was a power trying to trick me, to make me think you weren't lying. The lady warned me about that. Then it went away, and I was scared. I wanted to listen and believe you, but you didn't know the password and the Humanist said not to go with anyone who didn't know the password. And he told me that Mommy was dead." Even now, his eyes were filled with as much suspicion as hope. He wanted to believe me, but he was clearly terrified of being hurt again.

Some resistance in him broke then, and he leaned toward me the way that children do when they fully break down. Now I did let myself hug him as he cried.

"There, there," I told him. "It's okay now. Your mom will be here soon."

Guilt warred with my confusion. My Skill had worked on him after all. I might have… I forced myself to stop circling the mental drain. This wasn't about me. This was about David and his mother, a woman who would have given anything to make sure her son was safe. Someone who had made me promise to… and that was it. "You do anything you have to do to save my boy, do you hear me? Anything." The System must have accepted that as permission for Class Trip. I could have teleported him out right from the start. *Note to self, try the Skill and let it succeed or fail, before assuming that it just won't work.*

And then we could see Penny in the distance, and David ran to her. It was like a Hollywood movie as they ran together and he threw himself into her arms. She just hugged him and hugged him, and he clung to her like a boa constrictor and just kept squeezing.

Not long afterward, an incredibly athletic blonde leapt into my arms in the same fashion, though with a lot more momentum on her side. It had the predictable result.

I lay there on my back for a long time, holding her and kissing her, my heart full to bursting. Neither of us could stop smiling.

"Time and place," Topher said, kicking me in the side.

"Here and now," I answered, and Evelyn laughed.

"Watch this," I heard the Commander say as an aside. "There are children present."

I'd completely forgotten. How had I forgotten that? Our whole mission had been to save the hostages. Of course there were children present. I turned and jostled and sat up. Then I stood, brushed myself off, and offered a hand to Evie.

She accepted gracefully, though she could kip-up with the best of them.

"Don't be too hard on yourself," Lee said, patting me on the back. "You did damn good. I do have one question though."

"What's that?"

He invited me to accept his Full Coordination Skill, and I did so. The party chat, map, and all the other goodies we were spoiled with every time we worked with the man returned.

He sent me a private message. *"How the hell are you two still alive?"*

"I'd rather not say."

"The Humanist is on the way to the ship, if he isn't there already," he told me gravely.

Flapjacks and biscuits! I met his eyes, nodded, and sent him my evolved Class Skill info.

Lee whistled. Now it was his turn to look puzzled. He turned his head quizzically. *"If you had this all along, why didn't you just use it?"*

"It wasn't evolved yet. That happened later. The Skill failed when we first met because I needed permission slips."

"They were about to be murdered and the System required permission slips?" He was so upset by this information that he'd forgotten not to speak out loud.

I nodded. His outraged reaction validated my own.

"Fucking System."

"Careful," I told him, though I agreed whole-heartedly. "There are children present."

He laughed. Then his expression hardened. "So, you were planning on keeping this from me so that you and the kids could run, if it came to that?"

"Yes." There was more that I could tell him, but now was not the time.

He sighed. "I guess that makes sense." Then he continued silently, *"I'm glad you didn't. Quinn's alive, but we should get away clean if you can teleport us all. She should have no way to follow us."*

"Thank God," I said, and meant it.

"There's more. You might remember Donaldson. The redhead with all the explosives? He's going to be a problem. The man got a bit creative with my orders. He and his group got past the troops. I don't know how. They found another big group of survivors, humans and aliens who were working together. Apparently, they got along great. Not invading aliens, like the ones that killed my wife and kids. These people were brought here against their will. Like this gray guy here with me. Slaves in all but name. Like what was gonna happen with the kids you found."

I nodded.

"He and his people blew them all up. Humans and aliens alike."

Now it was my turn to be outraged. But what could I do about it? I had no real outlet for my rage. I frowned and pinched my nose, thinking hard.

"Why are you telling me this?" I finally thought to ask.

"You and I are square. You did your part, and I did mine. We need to beat the Humanist back to the ship and get the hell out of Dodge. It might get crazy. If the zealots aren't following orders, I can't predict what they're going to do. They might decide to exterminate the Voloids. Hell, they might even kill the alien-friendly humans. I bet they have a list already."

"Are you asking me to kill them?" I told him, trying to lighten the mood. "Because it sounds like you're asking me to kill them."

"I wish," he said. "But no. I was just wondering if you have control over who does or doesn't travel with that Skill of yours?"

"That's a great question," I answered. "Let's go find out."

Chapter 75

Caleb

Our team and the rescued hostages gathered together, but only some of us were engulfed in a flash of golden light. It turned out that it was easy to exclude Donaldson and his people from Class Trip. They weren't my students, and I didn't see them as suitable chaperones. That was all it took. I wasn't sure I could have included them even if I'd wanted to.

I watched as alarm and then fury flared on Donaldson's face. Then the redhead and his zealots seemed to vanish entirely. Tears welled in my eyes as one of the many dangers to the children was finally resolved.

Then I frowned as I realized the cost of what we'd done. Those men had murdered innocent people, even children. *They're going to do it again, and we didn't even try to stop them.*

I knew I was being too hard on myself; we'd saved the ones we could. Knowing that truth and changing how I felt about it were not the same thing. It was a cold comfort that if we'd been able to safely kill the monstrous men, Lee would have made it happen. He must know something I didn't.

The sight that faded into view was different from the one that I'd envisioned. The floor and walls of the Command Deck were the same as always and the Matriarch's pod remained, but the similarities ended there. The hole that led to the computer was overflowing with a tightly wrapped bundle of pulsating metal cables. They were connected to strange rectangular objects about the size and shape of apartment bookcases. They looked like metallic blue honeycombs. Altogether, they filled about a third of the room.

Those sections of the room included several spots where people should have been. The four people who weren't where they should be were Topher, Pavise, Penny, and her son.

The last dregs of my adrenaline flared and failed, like my old Impala when it was forty below zero. Rwr rwr rwr, rwr rwr rwr. Click. Nothing. The backlash sent my mind and body reeling. I leaned on one of the bookcase things to stop myself from falling. It was damp and warm and slimy.

That was when David walked out from behind the "bookcase" I was leaning on. My tension eased as I realized that they'd been shunted behind what were almost certainly the ship's new AI components. Even with the wave of relief, I felt as though I might pass out.

Desperate, I took the last of the pills Gerri had given me. They stabilized my over-frayed nerves almost immediately. Thinking of Gerri brought my attention back to them. They planned to leave soon. Could I beg or trade for more before they left? The frantic hunt for them with my eyes worried me. Were the pills addictive? I spotted Gerri with Evelyn, who was giving a golden shot to the Commander before the two of them rushed toward the next team member.

They were busy, so my imagination dragged me back into my worries. There were countless ways my Skill could have gone horribly wrong—from long falls to raging infernos. It was going to need some rigorous testing before I'd risk using it on children again. For all I knew, my Skill's evolution would bypass a hidden requirement that we not teleport someone to their certain death. A portal where you could see the other side would have been so much safer. Then again, if I'd had a portal instead, David and I would already be dead.

I couldn't do anything about that now, so I pointed at the blue honeycomb. "Lee, is this what I think it is?"

"Your speedy delivery," he answered. "Or at least part of it. Damn thing took up about a sixth of the ship's open spaces. Anywhere the delivery-bots damn well chose. Wouldn't listen to us. Bit of a theme. There's no control panel, and the AI crew doesn't listen either. I'd have blown it all up and torn it out if we didn't need to find a way to fly the ship." He looked at me with pity and a bit of scorn. "We'll hack it if we can, but I think you got ripped off."

Doctor Randon Hallory appeared in front of him, and I saw that what I had thought of as opalescent skin was actually tiny scales. "Your accusations are meritless, sir. I find both them, and you, beneath me as a gentleman."

I smiled and waved. "Hi, Doctor Hallory. Great to see you again. Were you and your family able to settle in okay?"

He smiled at me as well, but it was a controlled expression. I'd have called it restrained. "Hello again, Caleb. It is a pleasure, as always, but I'm afraid that introductions will have to wait, assuming that you survive."

"What the hell? You know this guy!" Lee was already shouting at me indignantly before the last few words were spoken. He stopped the moment the word survive left the AI's "lips." The Commander's expression and posture changed from outrage to an intense and predatory focus. He whipped around toward Randon. "What do you mean?" When he got no answer, he snapped, "What the hell is going on!"

Hallory ignored him with some slight effort and kept his focus on me.

"What's going on?" I asked him.

"The ship has been breached by more of these"—he gestured to Lee—"ignorant fools who think that just because a being has no body, they must have no soul."

I wanted to reassure him that Lee wasn't as bad as he might think when it came to such issues, because of the man's views on Pavise. But repairing their relationship might put the children at more risk, rather than less. Either way, now was not the time.

I was shocked at how well I was taking all of this until I remembered. *Oh, right, magic drugs. That's not going to be a problem later. What could go wrong?*

The AI had most of the group's attention now, except for Evelyn and Gerri. Those two were intently focused on loading golden vials into Penny's condenser. I considered alerting them, but they were working so quickly that I assumed it must be urgent. They knew what they were doing.

"When did all this happen?" I asked the AI, panic cracking my voice despite the drugs. "Are the kids safe?"

"I'm afraid not," Randon said. "He soundly defeated the defenders, and he has taken many hostages. He is torturing one of them as we speak."

I turned and bolted toward the door. Randy and Lee each grabbed one of my arms as I rushed chest-first into a purple energy barrier.

"No," Lee said.

I wheeled to shout at him, but he looked every bit as concerned as I felt. After a moment's thought, I remembered that I trusted the other two, especially Pavise. It forced me to stop long enough to realize they were right. We needed more information.

"Sorry," I said before realizing that wasn't what I really meant. "Thank you."

Lee watched me with a sharp eye before letting me go and motioning for Randy to do the same.

"Doctor, can you show us what's happening?" I asked.

"Of course, my friend. In fact, we can do better than that."

The rest of his family manifested at these words. They were beautiful people and every one of them had gorgeous, golden hair.

Randon turned to his wife and said "Darling, can you send over what we prepared please?"

"What *we* prepared?" she asked, smirking.

He gave her a sheepish grin that conceded her point, as he gestured for her to continue.

She got the kind of look that demonstrated feigned annoyance, the kind people got when they were actually amused but trying to hide it. I knew that look better than most. As a teacher of young students, I'd needed to master it early on in my career. She gave the impression of reading things and shuffling documents as she "prepared" her presentation.

Now I knew how Penny had felt. Impatient and impotent terror felt as though it would be tearing me in half if not for my "medicine." I had a desperate need to do something proactive and to do it sooner than now. But there was nothing I *could* do, and it made me want to scream and stomp my feet. I needed their family's best help, however, and rushing them wasn't the way to get it.

It took all of my willpower to force myself to beg. "Please hurry."

Vylia turned empathic, ocean-blue eyes meeting my gaze, and nodded. Then she pulled up feeds of what had happened, what was happening, and a detailed summary of what forces we were facing and where they were located.

I let Lee and Pavise worry about all of the details as my attention was riveted on finding out whether or not the children were currently safe.

Aul and the Voloids were safe, after a fashion. Six of them were on the deck of the ship, and each held a spear to a human's throat and a blaster to their heads. Two of the humans were the children we'd rescued from the Settlement. The other four prisoners were women from the Commander's group or the tribe. The "prisoners" looked broken and battered. Aul and the kids could not have done it—they hadn't even been accepted by the System yet. As damaged as the victims were now though, even the children might be enough to finish them off.

Exhausted and drugged, I had no idea how to process or react to what I was seeing. None of this made any sense at all. I trusted Aul, he wouldn't be threatening people without a good reason. But what could the human children have done. I had to get to them and fix this right away. But something nagged at me.

Why weren't the human's recovering? Three of the strongest defenders we'd left to guard the ship, one from the tribe and two of Lee's men, lay in puddles of their own blood on the floor. One of the flashback feeds showed the Humanist lifting two of them and smashing them together with his bare hands. They didn't seem to be healing, so they were probably all dead. The living prisoners were also not regenerating though, so that gave me some hope and a hell of a lot of confusion.

Thomas was kneeling in front of the one called the Humanist. Blood poured from his mouth where his tongue should have been. His fingers were pulled back as if he were wrestling an invisible giant, and he was obviously screaming in terror and anguish. He had a bruised handprint on his throat, larger than what his own hand could have caused.

The Humanist's armor was proof that Thomas hadn't gone down without a fight. Along with bullet dents and blaster scorch marks, it was slashed through one of the arms and its side as if by powerful axe attacks, though there was no obvious damage to the skin beneath and zero evidence of blood. Regeneration? That didn't seem quite right. There would still be blood, right?

I also spotted at least three camera drones hovering in the room.

While starting to wrestle with the implications, I was also frantically trying to take in everything else at once. It was too much. I sent a mental nudge to Pavise for him to do the same. He was much more equipped to process vast amounts of data than I was, and something was nagging at me. My nostalgia sense was tingling. Why?

Thomas continued to writhe on the ground in agony as the Humanist toyed with him, turning his hand this way and that, like the Goblin King with his crystal ball. The Manidoo Aanike's strong body cramped and seized.

The Humanist was the most handsome and noble man I'd ever seen. He was tall, strong, and graceful. A knight in shining armor. He wore no mask or helmet. Why hadn't anyone told me that our broken world had a superhero after all? I could barely imagine the horrors that Thomas must have committed to force this wonderful man to have to hurt him.

Why wasn't the Humanist stopping the terrorists from threatening the children? It nagged at me, just like the nostalgia issue, but I knew that there must be a good reason. Then I realized what it had to be. Hostages, of course! The Voloids had turned on the humans, and even the Humanist didn't dare to strike them down before they had released the hostages. Even his mighty power must have some limits.

Why would Aul do that? Had her Queen found a way to take them over, even without a Matriarch present? She must have had a way to empower them. It didn't matter. I had to help the Humanist somehow.

Gerri was talking urgently with Penny behind me, but that wasn't important. I was evaluating the best way for my friends and me to help the Humanist, but I kept getting distracted as Penny worked to treat some wound or other on my back. I must have suffered it without realizing, but I trusted her to know her job and do it right.

It was even more distracting that Lee and Pavise kept shouting things at me and Pavise was trying to shove some kind of signal into my head. All of this together made it impossible to concentrate.

"Shhh," I told them as I shut Pavise out of my mind, "I need to think. The hostages are in danger and the... oww!"

A sharp jab of pain in my back yanked a bit of my attention from the emergency, as Penny gave me some kind of injection. It muddled my mind and made it harder to focus. I willed away the notification before it could fully display.

Powerful Will:

+ 12 to your Willpower for 30 minutes.

"Stop that," I told her, knocking her hand away.

"Here," Gerri said, "take this. It will help."

She handed me a pill and a vial of some kind, probably to help me wash down the pill. Thoughtful of her. I needed to focus on more important things, but I decided it would be quicker to just take the pill so that I could get to the important issues. As I swallowed the pill and washed it down, a new notification popped into being.

Steel Trap

+20% bonus to resist mind-altering effects.

Alert: You are under the effects of too many mind-altering substances. You suffer the following effects.

There was a list and what looked to be another buff message, but I couldn't force myself to read them or even will it away as pain flared in a crippling migraine. It hurt more than when the grenade belt had shattered my hip.

Gerri was talking. I couldn't hear them over the terrible screaming. My screaming, I realized. I could barely make out the last word of Penny's shouted sentence, "… overdose."

I forced myself to stop screaming. The hostages needed me. And the sound might upset the Humanist. Wait, why did I care about that? Mind control. *What a jerk.*

"Can't you give him something for the pain, Gerri?" the Commander said, his thunderous voice causing a spike of pain with every word.

"No," Gerri said at a less torturous volume. "It would only hurt him more." They turned to Penny. "Maybe your new Skill?"

"Oh, right. Probably not. This isn't the kind of Skill that…" She hesitated as she read something on her device. "Oh, shit!"

"What's wrong?"

"Lots. Mostly a brain bleed," she said. "This is way worse than an overdose."

"I warned ya about that Class," Topher said.

Gerri blushed and turned away in shame.

Penny came to my side, and she must have done something because I felt like I did once when they'd given me some kind of radioactive liquid in my IV for a medical test. It was cold at first, then warm. For a second, I thought that I'd peed my pants, but it felt dry down there.

The pain in my head eased from intolerable to miserable then, and I let out a long sigh of relief.

"Thanks," I told Penny. "We need to go. I have to help the…" No. That wasn't right. Mind control. "Cheese and rice," I swore. "How do you fight someone like that?"

"You haven't seen him toss around tanks," Lee complained.

"That's not fair," I said.

"Yeah, this guy sucks donkey—" Randy said.

"Children," I said, cutting him off.

"Right, sorry."

"Don't talk about the Humanist that way," one of Lee's men said.

A few of the others agreed.

Gerri and Penny kept working, dosing people until they were on our side again, and sedating and binding the lowbies when that wasn't enough.

I realized that Gerri had no idea their friend was being tortured. I wanted to tell them. It was the right thing to do. But what they were already doing was the righter thing to do, wasn't it?

Randy distracted me. "He doesn't even know we're here and that Skill still works."

"It's like Vader Force-choking people with a vid screen from across the galaxy," I said. "It shouldn't be allowed."

"Get used to the System not giving a shit," Lee said.

"Language," I reminded him.

"Get used to me not giving a shit too. We have more important things to worry about."

"You're not wrong, but something doesn't add up. The System may not be fair or caring, but it's generally balanced, according to Pavise. Something's off about this guy. He shouldn't be able to be great at everything like he is. It's giving me nostalgia."

"It's doing what now?" Randy asked.

"Sir, this might not be the best time for one of your digressions."

"I know, but I feel like this is important."

"I thought that you, at least, would prioritize the children," Lee said. "What's wrong with you?" He turned to Penny. "What's wrong with him? Is he still messed up from the overdose?"

"I don't think so," she answered. "Maybe. I'm not an expert on mental health."

"To hell with it. It doesn't matter. Everyone, form up and we'll make our plan." Lee started activating skills. "Buff if you've got 'em. I'll try to get the guy talking, then open fire while he's distracted."

"Monologuing," I corrected him.

"Whatever. Just be ready."

As the others gathered, I prepared my weapons and followed Lee.

"Randy," I told him as I saw his pre-selected loadout, "shotgun-style weapons and hostages don't mix."

He blushed but nodded as he changed his weapon selection to single target. "Right, sorry. Habit."

As people formed up, checking their gear, what was left of my battered mind turned over the puzzle that was bothering me. *Invulnerability. Super Strength. Charisma. Mind Control. One guy beating so many enemies, all at once. It's like he's showing off how powerful he is. Why? And how is he so powerful in the first place?*

I felt like it was on the tip of my metaphorical tongue when I got distracted by Gerri's gasp as they saw Thomas's condition for the first time. Unlike with me, it seemed that no one had expected Gerri to run. None of us managed to stop them in time, though Lee ordered them to stop and Pavise put up a purple shield just a fraction of a second too late.

"Damn it, Gerri," Lee called after them as he rushed to follow.

The rest of us joined the procession and raced to the central hub only half a dozen steps behind Lee. He hadn't hesitated at all. Say what you want about the man, but Lee was loyal. He was running so fast that he barely managed to stop in time to avoid slamming into Gerri, and I failed to stop before bouncing off of Lee. I smashed my nose and got my breath knocked out of me. I doubted he even noticed.

The Humanist was just standing there, watching us all when we entered. He gave us a beaming smile and said, "Welcome back. It's about time. Join me, please. We need to have a talk."

Chapter 76

Caleb

Even with the buffs and gear, the Humanist's presence was hard to resist. I could hate the man, but I couldn't not like him.

One of the cameras was getting an overview. The second was watching the Voloids keeping the human prisoners hostage. The third was watching us face off against the Humanist alone. Why? And why was he facing us alone at all when he had an army at his beck and call? There were a lot of us and only one of him.

I took a closer look at the man. His special interests included podcasting, human supremacy, and Machiavellian supervillains.

Oh! That was it. The last piece fell into place. *Oh no. No, no, no, no.*

"You're a traitor to humanity," Lee said, obviously intending to push the man's buttons.

It worked. "I'm not the traitor here, Betrayer. You are. You and these alien-loving—"

"*Now,*" the Commander ordered through party chat.

"No!" I stepped forward and gathered my will. For the second time in about as many months, I caused a purple field of force to separate Lee from his intended target.

He howled in fury and turned to open fire on me.

Another force field, this one generated by Pavise, blocked his shot entirely.

Lee glared at me with thermonuclear fury.

The Humanist was slow-clapping and laughing. He turned to look at Lee. "It's not fun when your own people turn on you when it matters most, is it?" His humor had morphed to scorn and hatred as he spoke.

"No," Lee admitted, glaring at me, "it isn't. Caleb, I thought you'd finally grown up and put on your big boy pants. How could I have been so stupid? I'm as naïve as you are." He continued, stressing each word, "You can't save everyone."

"Don't bother," the Humanist said. "He's made his choice."

I let my face express my true—if forced—liking for the man. I wanted to nod to encourage him to continue, but that might be considered a deception because of implying agreement. I motioned for him to continue instead. As I did, and as he spoke, I sent messages to the others via group chat.

"Even I'm not that naïve. Fuck this guy. Keep glaring."

"Glaring is easy," Lee said. *"Explain before I kill you."*

"I hadn't let myself believe that it was possible," the Humanist said, true to supervillain form. He was pacing across the metal grate, making oversized gestures with his hands to emphasize his points.

"Kill him myself if I get a chance. Not morals. Strategy. Tactics."

"Really? You? Then you have my attention. Go on."

"But I have to admit that I'd gotten my hopes up just a little." He closed the distance between us and looked me over.

I just waited. I knew he'd monologue, and it would give me more time to think.

"Have I finally found a kindred spirit? I have to admit—Caleb, is it? I'd written you off when I first heard about you enslaving the aliens. I thought using filth like that was beyond the pale. But I've had a change of heart since then. Seen the error of my ways. They are our enemies, but that doesn't mean they can't serve us. Consider me a convert to your viewpoint," the Humanist said, beaming what looked to be a genuine smile, though his dark eyes were predatory and ravenous.

'Figured out his plan. Trap. You were rushing into it. He gets propaganda videos. Aliens killing humans. Traitors attacking him. Together or separate. Either way, he wins." As he continued speaking, I wanted to explain that the Humanist was clearly too tough for us to kill quickly, and he could always bring in reinforcements if he started to lose. Either way, we'd gain nothing and he'd get everything he wanted. But he was talking too fast, and with my focus split, there was just no time. By the time I had figured out what to say, his next speech was wrapping up.

"But I'm afraid that being a fan of your work doesn't change the fundamentals of our situation. I'm willing to work with exciting new talent like yours, but only if you're smart enough to fall in line. Convincing me to trust you will be difficult." His voice got deeper and more intense as he continued, "I've been disappointed with my min… with my followers of late." He glared at me for a moment before his expression softened again. "That said, actions speak louder than words and you've shown a lot of wisdom here today. I can spare a few minutes to get to know you and maybe talk things out. What do you say?"

Crud. I need more time to explain, coordinate, and plan. I made sure that my expression was one of consideration as I honestly considered how to handle this. *"Shit. Done monologuing. One sec."*

Don't lie, I reminded myself. *Don't deceive him.* Could an announcement of my intention protect me from overstepping on Ring of Truth? It had worked with the Voloids and Lee. *Keep him talking.* "I haven't made up my mind about you yet. I won't tell you everything, and my motivations are my own. My words will be literally true, but I'm not under oath. I don't have to extrapolate. I don't have to explain. Take my words as literal and ask any questions that you need. Don't blame me if you misinterpret them." I covered my bases, with no idea if this could remotely work.

"Old-school Mephisto rules," the Humanist said, establishing his geek cred. "No outright lies."

"The truth is far too much fun," I quoted, and it was the truth. I thought the truth could be a lot of fun, though I'd rather not deceive with it like Marvel's big red baddie.

"The man knows his comics," the Humanist said as he slammed his fist into his chest and nodded. "Be still my beating heart."

"I would never have believed I'd want to serve you, until I saw you for myself," I told him. "But I'd also never realized that anyone could be as powerful as you are, even with the System." I was pushing the boundaries on my Skill. Technicalities? Had I crossed the line? "I want to know everything. Will you tell me more?"

He sidestepped my question. "You really can make people trust you," he said with wonder in his voice.

I hadn't broken the Skill. That was good.

"It's a remarkable Skill," he continued, "but I'm more interested in the others. The one you use to enslave the aliens, and the one you use to break my hold on my people."

This was backfiring completely. He was interested now, asking me questions, instead of the other way around. How could I fix it? I had the first inklings of a plan, but it was dangerous. "I think I might know how you're so much more powerful than everyone else."

His dark eyes narrowed, and his expression got so intense that I suspected he might kill me where I stood. "Go on."

"I'm assuming you don't want me to just blurt it out in front of everyone," I said, motioning to the people and the cameras.

He looked around. "I don't think we have to worry about witnesses. One way or the other. As for the camera, we can fix that in post, as we used to say in 'the biz.' I'm sorry to have to take your toys from you, but don't worry, if you end up working for me, I'll find you better. Now, I'm much more interested in learning your secret than I am in revealing mine to you. That said, I am curious what you think you've figured out."

"Be subtle," Lee said, *"but everyone needs to move into the positions I've sent you. Don't let yourselves get distracted. Be ready at a moment's notice. Caleb, I need something more and it had better be soon."*

"He cannot answer you, Commander," Pavise answered when I couldn't. *"He doesn't have the attention to... oh! One moment."*

My perception of time slowed and my ability to multi-task increased, as he lent me some of his processing power.

"Thanks, buddy. But bad timing. I don't think I need this anymore. Just listen, Lee. Pavise will repeat it if you guys can't hear."

"I'll make you a deal," I told him. A hint of a plan was evolving in my head. "I'll whisper my guess to you, and you let me know if I've got it right."

"And in exchange?"

I couldn't think of anything to tell him now that wouldn't break my Skill. But was there something I could ask? "What is it you'd like to know?"

"I want you to educate me on how you have been able to control the aliens and how you were able to break my control over my own people."

"Confirm or deny my guess, and I'll tell you about how I've influenced the aliens and helped your people make their own choices, despite your Skills."

He seemed to consider. "Would agreeing to your terms mean that you can get away with hiding one of your Skills or items or other tools from me that you used to do the two things that I listed?"

"No."

"No is pretty straightforward. I'll accept your deal provisionally, because..." He motioned for me to continue. Was he testing me?

"Because you can always just kill me if I disappoint you?"

"I knew I liked you." He grinned and patted me on the back, denting my armor and knocking me to my knees.

Bully.

I stood with some difficulty and leaned forward to whisper in his ear.

"Ancient spirits of evil," I said, quoting the old *ThunderCats* show where the main villain had used external power sources to greatly heighten his combat powers any time he left his base. "You Mum-Ra'd yourself, right? Some kind of Perk, item, or minions."

His nostrils flared at the last word.

"That's the one. You have a bunch of specialists who buff you. Smart. Brilliant actually."

The Humanist looked more pissed off at my discovery than gratified by my compliments.

"I'm not thrilled to have anyone know about that," he said. "And I always preferred Mon-Star. He had the better pet."

I liked the *ThunderCats* and Mum-Ra better, but the *Silverhawks* was a great show. And the last part of what he had said was undeniable, so I nodded to acknowledge the point.

That seemed to appease him more than my compliment had. He let out a long-suffering sigh. "To hell with it. People can just buy the knowledge from the System anyway. I found that out the hard way. So I guess it's no real loss." He wasn't even trying to whisper. No one here would live if he had his way.

I'd planned to get more information to the others via this conversation. But it hadn't been natural enough to make it work. So I shoved my understanding into Pavise through our new and improved connection and he explained it to Lee and the others, including the AI team that ran the ship. That way, they could all prepare for if my plan worked, and as was more often the case, if it failed.

"Well played," the Humanist finally said with a half bow. "Consider me impressed." He smiled, but it turned into a hard thing, fast. His eyes were fixed on me as if he was readying a shot. "Your turn."

"I really am a Teacher," I told him. "That's the first thing to know."

He laughed. "No shit? Well, I guess if you can't lie. Still. That's crazy. I'll be damned."

You will if I have anything to say about it, you fascist thug.

"I can teach you better if you're officially my student," I told him. "I'll even throw in a secret that you didn't ask for and that you would definitely want to know. One I've kept from almost everyone since I got it. That is more of a show versus tell situation, however."

"Are you trying to trick me into anything that would allow you to kill me or harm me in any way?"

His wording had likely just saved all of our lives.

"No," I was able to answer honestly. Flatly. I couldn't hurt him if I wanted to. I wanted him off the ship.

He stared at me hard, then grinned wide. Certain he had won. Arrogant. Certain that he knew better than the Teacher. "Fine then, Teacher. I agree. Do your job and teach me what I need to know."

"What you need to know and what you've asked me to tell you about are two different things. But since you're asking, I'll cover them both." It might be good to have him riled up when I made my move. Adding confusion and surprise to an angry mind might work better than if he were as calm and collected as he'd been up to now. I also couldn't discard the faintest hope that what I said might reach him, as much as Lee would blame me for that.

"Go on," he said flatly.

"What you need to know is that people are people. It doesn't matter if they're human"—I motioned to the humans with us—"aliens"—I motioned to the Voloids—"or constructed." I ended with a nod to Pavise. "People are people."

"How quaint," the Humanist said. "An interesting philosophy for a slaver."

"Anyone can be a slaver." I said, careful to intend the sentence as part of a more thorough explanation so I wouldn't be deceiving him. "All you have to do is to abandon the idea that everyone else has lives that matter to them, and to God or the universe or whatever, as much as your life does to you." Then something Lee had implied gave me the final piece of what to say. "And frankly, it doesn't matter if they're people, if people don't matter to you anyway."

He met my gaze with his dark, hard eyes. "It's time for you to answer my question, Teacher. Otherwise, things will get very unpleasant for you."

"Of course," I told him. "You're not going to like the answer but remember that I have to tell you the truth. The fact of the matter is that it isn't true that people don't matter. They do. That's why I'm not a slaver at all. My second Class is a Kaldian Warder. It's about protecting others. I never enslaved the Voloids. The children are my students. I helped them."

He clenched his jaw tight, then started to open it to speak.

I raised a finger to delay him as I continued, "And your victims"—I motioned to Lee—"weren't passed from one manipulative master to another. I taught them. I showed Lee that these supposed alien invaders are really innocent children and that they haven't done anything wrong. That they didn't deserve to be murdered. That, and reminding him that there used to be good in the world, and there could be again. My Charisma and Teacher Skills probably helped with that, but that was all. Nothing I did forced them to do anything more than to pay attention and know I wasn't lying to them."

The Humanist's gorgeous face was twisted into a cruel and vicious sneer. "Then you're worthless to me. I should have known. In that case, it's time for these alien invaders you seem to care about so much to do what they came to Earth for and murder these poor human victims."

"You're forgetting something," I told him urgently.

"What's that?" He was barely listening now as he gathered his power about him like an ever- expanding cloak.

I rushed on, knowing I needed to hurry. I still had to get him angry, so I poked at him a bit more. "I promised to show you a Skill. I owe you a secret that you would definitely want to know."

He turned back to me, still indignant and bordering on angry, if not nearly as much as I had hoped. "Fine. Show me. Wow me. Your life depends on it."

"As you wish," I said, never one to pass up a chance to quote my favorite movie.

Golden light enveloped us both.

Chapter 77

Caleb

When we reappeared in a flash of golden light, I grinned at the shocked befuddlement on the Humanist's face. I was primed to block him with a force field and dash onto the ship while the entrance closed. My smile faltered when his confusion twisted to a smirk. The reason became clear moments later as I took in our surroundings. We'd only traveled half a dozen feet. We hadn't even made it to the ramp.

Why? I backed away from him as I tried to understand what was happening.

He must have read the puzzlement on my face because he held up a bracer and tapped it.

"It is a dimensional-locking device, sir," Pavise said.

"Thanks, buddy. I figured that part out." My pulse was throbbing in my head. *So close. It almost worked. There has to be something I can do. That we can do.* I heard Tim Allen's voice in my head saying, "Never give up, never surrender," but it felt as phony as I did. I was an imposter, just as he'd been in *Galaxy Quest*. It was hopeless. I should just give up now and beg for mercy. I was no match for…

Oh, that fucker!

I'd never been a match for any of this, but when had that ever stopped me? There were still children to protect. Giving up had never been an option.

"Get out of my head, you mind-controlling asshole!" I gathered my will. My love of life. Even my superhero complex. And I shoved back hard against the pressure mounting in my mind.

It broke before I did, and my despair fell away.

"*Are you all right, sir? The whites of your eyes have turned blood red.*"

"*Burst blood vessels. Least of our problems. Give me time,*" I told Pavise, and he took it much more literally than I'd intended and lent me processing power.

Moments crawled as the Humanist's eyes swept the room, considering. Deciding to monologue and grandstand even more, or to end this here and now, I'd guess.

He glanced behind him. Shrewdness seemed to war with megalomania in his dark eyes. "Should I kill them myself or wait for reinforcements?" they seemed to say.

As he debated for what was probably a couple of seconds at most, I rushed to find a plan.

"*Give me a solution, buddy?*"

A long pause. Nearly infinity in AI time. "*I'm sorry, sir. I will keep calculating options.*"

I started to say that it was just one man, but Pavise pressed an impulse toward me. I accepted it and looked out of the ship through his eyes. Hundreds of well-armed troops were closing in from where they'd hidden in the distance. It was slow going as they moved together, but Pavise calculated we'd have several minutes at most before they all arrived. They'd brought weapons, vehicles, and *Oh, my lord, is that a tank?*

Pavise sent me an image along with understanding of what was happening behind me, around me in the corners where I wasn't looking, so focused was I on the Humanist.

Gerri had been absolutely brilliant. She'd used her purple cloud of enchanted powder to paralyze all of the Humanist's former hostages, except for Aul and Thomas. Weak as they all were, those bound weren't breaking free anytime soon. Aul wore a brightly glowing amulet and a look of defiance.

The amulet was already dimming though. Gerri was headed toward Thomas, likely to heal him.

I didn't have to do this alone. Shouldn't have been, really. I should have been relying on them before this, instead of grandstanding too.

"Tell Lee to get ready, get the rest ready. I'm going to try to talk sense into him." Normal time resumed, the world spinning back to normal as Pavise fed everyone what I said.

I opened my mouth to speak even as Lee answered me.

"Waste of breath," Lee said. *"Everybody's in position."*

The Humanist must have agreed with him. "We're done talking. You're worthless to me."

Something in his voice triggered my flight reflexes. I twisted toward the others, bending forward to sprint.

The tap of the Humanist's armored boots on the deck spiked my panic, even despite the drugs. Reason returned as I realized I'd never get away. I jerked to a stop, but he was already there, striking like a viper.

A purple field of force flickered into existence between us. Empowered as the Humanist was and as fast as he was moving, Pavise's barrier broke, though it slowed the attack. Even then, I only barely managed to avoid the blow, feeling the rush of passing air ruffling my hair.

He was already swinging another strike when someone behind me threw something. The Humanist knocked it aside with the hand he meant for me, droplets of oil spraying across the ramp behind him, coating it and part of the deck and ground.

"No grenades!" I announced via chat. I wanted to add, I'm standing right here, but I couldn't manage it while trying to keep track of everything else going on.

Per the mini map, Pavise and Evelyn had started to rush to my side, but the Humanist threw out a pair of devices that cut in front of him and repelled the shield-bot's approach. I realized what had happened, why the Humanist had let me talk.

I'd given this jerk prep time. It got worse when he threw a metal disk on the grate behind him. It widened to a radius of fifteen feet. Soldiers apparated inside the ship, all smashed close together, like a mad mashup of *Star Trek* and Sardines.

A pair of steam whistles behind me nearly made me piss myself. I whipped around to see a steampunk monkey tossing down a complex silver puzzle box. Earl himself was turning a gear on what looked like a giant's watch. A beam shot out of it, bounced off the Humanist's bracers, then down into the puzzle box. A dome of buzzing sparkles filled half of the room, and the semi-solid soldiers cried out in pain and terror as the stolen power of the bracers disrupted their summons. It seemed the Humanist's tricks were a little out of date.

He was trying to isolate me, and it was working. But that was my job anyway. His strategy would let everyone else unload on him at range while his attention focused on me.

Pavise's turret whistle sounded, along with the thunder of gunfire and the zap of blasters as my allies unleashed what they could. The air filled with sulfurous smoke and an acrid tang. Most of the attacks bounced harmlessly off the Humanist's armor, but some were doing real damage. He winced as his skin sizzled in some spots and formed into welts in others, but even those healed at a visible rate.

I had to admit, I was more worried for me. If not for the unnatural coordination everyone had, and the fact that I was doing my best to stay small and in one spot, I was sure I'd get clipped.

There were more attacks and from more angles than there should have been. I wanted to glance back to find out why, but I didn't dare. On the mini map, several turrets were now listed as resources on our side.

Score one for Lee.

Perhaps sensing my need to know, Pavise sent me a brief image of him and Aul. The two of them were tossing out disks that grew into small turrets. Pavise must be running them all. I doubted he could have managed it before his upgrade.

Aul and Pavise had clearly coordinated all of this at the Shop, and I was pretty sure that I'd approved the Credits. We'd have to have a talk about lies of omission, but I was really glad they had them now.

The Humanist had used this time to smash the puzzle box to bits. Then he rushed to do the same to me. He swung again and again with lightning speed, shattering shields and leaving fist-prints in my armor. I did what I could to dodge and block, but jolts of pain, sharp and intense, followed each of his blows like thunder. Pride in my student, in my friends and allies kept me on my feet as the Humanist struck me time after time.

It was a downward spiral. The more that he hurt me, the less I could dodge. The less I could dodge, the more he could hurt me. *Please stop. Please stop. Oh, please God, just make him stop.* I hadn't realized I'd been speaking out loud until the bastard cackled.

I was swelling like an overcooked sausage and my own armor crushed me. My breaths were wheezing gasps, and between that, my injuries, and his punches knocking me around, my movements faltered. All I could manage was to keep my feet and hold my ground to buy the others time. Flickers of images and emotions flashed through my mind. Aul. The Matriarch. Kek. Evelyn. David. People I'd saved and people I'd failed.

Not again. Can't let it happen again.

I tried to dodge and block the Humanist's attacks, but his speed and skill were beyond me. All I could do was keep my hands up in a boxer's stance, try to duck and weave. It was always the same. I'd slip past one blow just to realize I'd walked into a harder one. My Health bar was already down by half and all of this was happening in seconds, though it felt like eternity to me.

Then he grabbed me by my helmeted head and used it to block where Randy had been shooting him repeatedly. There was a peal of thunder. An instant of blackness. I reached back to clutch the wound and I felt the dent there. The resistance under my gloves let me know there were spiderweb cracks.

Zings of comforting warmth and numbness shot into my back. Penny? *Oh! Thank God.* I'd forgotten I had a healer. My Health bar ticked up.

"Kneel!" a voice and a will washed over me, demanding obedience.

My body obeyed him and I collapsed, the man having released me earlier. Gunfire slowed.

"Bow down."

My memory provided. Superman. He'd used the Zod tone. Melodramatic chump.

I used my shoulder turret to shoot him in the crotch with Hunter's Strike.

The Humanist groaned and hunched over. For the first time since a racist bully broke my nose in fifth grade, I felt vindictive. I wanted to hurt this man like he'd hurt me. As I fired again, I tried to talk but had to spit out blood and teeth first, both of them flecking the insides of my helmet.

"You're no Zod," I told him. "You're just the big dumb thug."

"No more talking!" He grabbed me with both hands and crushed my forearms.

My armor bent. Bones and mechanisms cracked. My hands went numb. He pressed them down and let one go, yanking me up to him with the newly freed hand. *Note to self: don't antagonize the schmuck with super strength.* Circulation came back with a burning zing. My free hand was pressed against something. I tried to explore what, but I could barely move, though I was now free of his compulsion.

I felt a zing of something cold and tingly on my back. At first, I thought it was nerve damage. But then power washed through me. My body crack, crack, cracked like a chiropractor had gone berserk and was taking it out on me. Bones straightened and fused. I felt my blood thicken and clot. Penny's new Skill?

The Humanist headbutted me, and fireworks exploded in my face. The dent and the spiderweb cracks in my faceplate were like seeing the world through a phone's cracked screen. Each breath was an agony, each twitch made my human arm explode in pain.

I was trapped, and from the glow of his eyes, he knew it.

Chapter 78

Caleb

Gunfire continued from behind me, all around. The crack, crack, crack of spells and people repositioning to hit the Humanist from the side and back was all around. Pavise was saying something comforting, but I couldn't focus. The Humanist had me held with both hands, one on my arm, the other on my armor so he could headbutt me again.

Spells flew by, lurid colors unlike the flat zing of bullets that I swore I saw no matter how ridiculous that was. One of the Humanist's eyes froze over with a glaze of ice. I had no idea what they'd done, but I hoped they would keep it up because clutching his face and trying to get the ice off was distracting him from hitting me.

There was a loud pop whose source I couldn't identify as I struggled to back away, trying to free myself from the unyielding grip even as my shoulder turret kept firing.

"Finally," Evelyn said over the channels. Fast as a whip, she was there beside the Humanist, driving her plasma spear into his side with a flurry of strikes, one after the other, all in the same spot. I watched the armor heat up, sizzle, and burn.

"Stop that!" the voice of command boomed. Another damn Skill.

The gunfire lessened. Evelyn staggered.

Only one of my own eyes would open. The other was swollen shut. The padding within the helmet was nowhere near enough to stop the attacks punching through, bouncing my head around. I glanced at my abuser through tears and blood. He was looking behind me. Desperate, I remembered the object against my hand. What was it? My blaster? No. Wrong shape. Too round. One of my concussion grenades.

Slowly, ever so slowly, I managed to close my hand around it.

The Humanist was ignoring me and glaring at the others. I saw it in his eyes the moment he made his choice. His focus shifted entirely. He let me go, and I realized how much he'd been holding me up. Something in the armor's leg wasn't working and I found myself slumped to my knees as he released my wrist. I couldn't let him focus on my friends. He'd kill them all. Needed to find a way to keep his attention.

Crap.

Antagonizing the schmuck with super strength was my job.

I liked my old work better.

The Humanist loved supervillains. Maybe I could use it against him. I was trying to think of something better than, "Doom would call you a peasant," when he tensed his body to charge my friends.

Out of time, I said the first thing that popped into my head. "Your name is dumb."

Lame or not, it must have hit the mark because he backhanded my face, breaking part of my helmet and wrenching my neck with a terrifying crack.

My only reply was a gurgling whimper.

He grimaced as a bullet struck his face again. This time, a bit of red blood came from the tear. Were his buffs fading? I didn't see fear or urgency in his eyes, just a twitch of a hand to his belt that saw a small shield flicker to help stop further attacks at his face.

Something was wrong, because the megalomaniacal madman was starting to grin. He had some kind of trick he hadn't used yet. I sent a mental message to Pavise to warn the others. We had to stop him before we could find out what it was the hard way, but I couldn't speak, couldn't convince him of anything.

So maybe it was time for action.

I barely managed to hold up the grenade with my unsteady arm. I primed it for activation. I was lucky that these Shop-bought grenades didn't use pins.

He glanced down and sneered. His expression said, "I'll just wipe you off my armor." Then he must have gotten impatient because he reached out to take the grenade just as I pressed the button.

Pavise, at my mental instruction, generated a powerful purple barrier to block his hand.

He pulled back his fist to punch through, only to cry out in pain as a plasma spear drove through part of his wrist. It added the stench of burning plastic to the nasty smells that filled the room, along with a sickeningly sweet smell I didn't want to think about.

I created my own thick barrier of force, the circumference of a large pizza pan. It was concave, surrounding the grenade that I had let go of right between the Humanist and me.

"Down!" Pavise announced through our comm links as he dropped his own shield.

Evelyn dived and rolled for cover.

The grenade exploded with a burst so strong that it broke my shield and knocked me on my ass. Focused as it was though, it hit the Humanist harder. He was sent flying backward, and it left a dent on the center of his chest plate to match the ones he'd given me.

The Humanist landed hard in the area with the lubricant and just kept going backward and down the ramp. Something stopped him partway down. A Skill? A Stat? His Level? Who knew? The System didn't always make sense to me.

"Well done, sir," Pavise said. *"But not quite enough, I'm afraid. He's still on the portion of the ramp that functions as the ship's primary hull in space."*

Pavise showed off one of the features of his new armor as he blasted the Humanist with force bolts from his hands as he rolled over to me, freed at last from the Humanist's barrier. The blasts were more forceful and disorienting than they were damaging, but here, that was ideal.

"The rest of the ramp can be torn away in an emergency, it's only armor. Five feet further—" He kept talking, but I was distracted.

Just five more feet, but it might as well have been a mile. Our concussive attacks weren't enough. They couldn't knock him back. Or the Humanist had some Skill or gear that helped reduce his knockback.

I reached for my concussion grenades, though I doubted it would work a second time.

Then I remembered his earlier glee. We were running out of time and I was out of aces.

"Remember me?" Gerri said as they unleashed a toxic green sludge in the Humanist's direction. "Let's see how you do without that armor of yours."

The liquid splashed into the tyrant, bubbling and sizzling as it hit. They must be using a spell because the spray and excess liquid flew back toward the Humanist like a magnet. The liquid was clearly potent, and the spell-effect equally impressive.

The Humanist's deep green and blue armor outmatched it. It might as well have been made of Teflon. The liquid just dripped, pooled, and sizzled in a puddle on the metal ramp under his feet. He scoffed at them and shook his head as he answered with a single word. "No."

"You will now," Gerri said as the metal finished dissolving beneath the Humanist's feet, dropping him like a bomb from the bay.

The Humanist gasped as he reached out to grab the ledge. Between the sizzling green acid and the lubricant from earlier though, even his strong hands couldn't get a grip.

"Gotcha, motherfucker!" Gerri said.

"Great work," Lee announced.

"Not bad," Topher joined in. "Not bad at all."

Gerri beamed with well-deserved pride.

Relief was running through me, but I still felt unsettled. Why? I reached out for Pavise's processors to buy myself some time. Got less help than I'd bargained for. He was working on a dozen small emergencies and had linked himself in to help the Hallorys. He seemed relieved to leave this one small part to me. "One small part." That was it. The hole.

Lee's eyes went wide as his paranoia caught up to my enhanced processing speed.

The Humanist could likely jump this distance. The rich, entitled jerk might even fly.

Pavise and I generated focused shields to cover the hole, just before Lee called out for us to do the same.

The man was impressive, but he would still have been too slow. We barely managed to get the fields in place before the Humanist smashed into them and rebounded.

I tried to cheer as the concentrated, layered shields held. Instead, I coughed up blood.

"Celebrate later," Pavise announced. "The enemy's reinforcements have reached striking range and the ship is taking damage." Along with his words, he passed along an image from the ship's external sensors. The vehicle was wrapped in what looked to be a sphere of northern lights. It was offering some protection, but it was not stopping most attacks outright and it was already getting spotty in some places.

It was gorgeous, but Skill-book granted knowledge gave me insight into just how bad this situation was. The energy field was mostly there for thermal regulation, not for getting shot at. It was already fading fast.

"Lift off now!" I had Pavise shout to the Hallorys in my voice. "Get us out of here. Take us someplace safe."

They must have been watching and keeping the ship ready, because their response was immediate. The ship shook and trembled as the thrusters came to life, throwing tremors through us all as we rose into the sky.

Chapter 79

Caleb

The Commander patted me on the back when we'd finally come up for air. When I looked up at him, he was giving me a stern look. Even after working with him so long, it unnerved me.

"That," he said, voice rumbling, "was a lot more than a week."

I just stared up at him, befuddled. He reached down and took my armored hand in his and helped me to my feet. There was a twinkle in his eyes now and the hint of a curve to his lip. For the first time, I saw him more as the irresistible man he must have been and less as the terrifying killer. He was messing with me somehow, but I didn't get it.

Pavise either saw the confusion on my face or he was still connected to my surface thoughts because he answered, *"I believe he is joking about your quest, sir. The one that he gave you to get the aliens off his planet."*

"Quest? Oh, that Quest." I'd have been scared, but the big man was smiling at me now, with something like admiration in his eyes.

"Great work, Caleb. Seriously. You didn't manage to do it in a week, but you got them off my planet. I'll take it." He laughed. "Wouldn't have guessed in a million years that I'd be along for the ride when you did."

Then I laughed as the Quest paid out. Fifty thousand Credits that I really could have used at the Shop, and five thousand XP that felt like a drop in the bucket now.

"I'm right there with you. I'm still in shock about all of this." Then I held up my finger to let Lee know to wait, and I shouted, as loud as I could, "Does anyone know what happened to the children?"

"They hid them with some gorgeous guy who was cowering in a storage locker," a lady I didn't know said. "Someone went to get them."

I felt the way that Atlas must have felt the time that Hercules gave him a break. A long sigh escaped my lips before I asked, "Where are we going, Doctor Hallory?"

"Tevron R-B," he answered. "A small mining outpost in the Quavra sector. It's become a bit of a trade hub in recent years. We'll be able to refuel, access the Shop, and plan. The fee should be quite modest."

Then Aul and several of the other Voloids were in the room. They rushed over and grabbed me in powerfully crushing hugs. It took every ounce of Willpower I'd built up not to scream as they aggravated my injuries. I forced myself to wrap my arms around them and give them giant hugs, one after another.

"Voloids is gratitude," Aul said. "Aul is gratitude. Caleb is be hero."

I didn't know about any of that. I certainly hurt like a hero, at least that part was true. Smiling at them and everyone around me, I hesitated when I realized that Gerri and Thomas looked frantic. They were arguing with the hologram of Doctor Hallory's son, Gypher. He was shorter than his father, but still tall. I excused myself from the Voloids gently and made my way over, grateful for the reprieve.

"Is everything okay?" I asked Gerri.

"This thing won't answer our questions. We need to know how long the trip is gonna be."

"He's not a thing. He's a person. And it's going to be a long trip. Give me a second and I'll get you both the timeline."

"We can't have a long trip! The Tribe needs us. My sister needs us. We have to stay on Earth."

Thomas grabbed me by my armored, but injured, arm. I cried out in pain, not willing to hide my misery to protect his feelings the way I'd done with the children. He released me and a flash of remorse flared on his face before intense purpose replaced it again.

"You have to take our people back," Gerri said. "That Skill of yours can do it, right?"

"Maybe. Pavise?"

"Perhaps for another twenty seconds or so, sir. However, you would certainly not have time to return. There are also no available locations that I would recommend, especially not while we can barely function."

"We'll be with you," Gerri said. "The two of us can keep you safe."

"For how long?" I asked, and they stammered. "It doesn't matter anyway. I can't leave the children here alone. Some of these troops might murder them."

"They're not alone," they said. "Lee will be here."

"Some of Lee's men killed kids today, even with him right there in the base with them. I'm sorry, but I'm not about to take that chance. It's just too risky."

"It was a few people and they're gone now."

"We can't know that for sure. A lot of his followers didn't go with us, and I don't trust anyone here completely. Not when it comes to protecting the children and looking out for their interests."

"Please, just do it. There's no time." Gerri was begging now. "I saved everybody today. You know that I did. You owe me."

"I do," I admitted, deciding not to point out that we *all* owed each other. "And I would want to help you even if I didn't. But Gerri, I owe a lot of people a lot of things, and I owe the children most of all. I'm their guardian. I'm sorry. I'll try to help you find a way back as soon as we can."

"Can we go somewhere else?" they said. "Can we change our destination?"

"I'm afraid not," Randon answered. His expression of grief was so human it surprised me. "We've taken significant damage, including to one of our auxiliary thrusters. We will need external repairs before we can safely—"

He stopped talking as Thomas grabbed me and a hatchet of water appeared in his other hand. "Eew ut," he said as best as he could without his tongue. It wasn't hard to understand his message.

"You'll have to kill me," I told him flatly. Then I remembered things had changed. "You'll have to try. I'm not abandoning the children."

He pushed me away with a grunt of disgust. It was good to know he'd been bluffing. I wanted to like the guy.

"It doesn't matter anymore anyway, I'm afraid," Pavise said. "We are certainly out of range now."

Gerri was crying and looked away. Thomas held them, even though he was still obviously fuming.

"Come on, Aul. Let's get you all settled in your pods for a good night's sleep."

They all chirped and clicked their mandibles contentedly.

"Once we get repaired and fueled up, we can figure out how to get everyone back home who wants to go."

Aul's exoskeleton paled, and her large mandibles quivered as if in terror. It wasn't the reaction I'd expected from her, but I supposed that it made sense. Relief can sometimes allow you to feel all the negative things you've buried deep inside yourself to just keep moving forward, and she'd been through a lot.

I swore to myself that whatever it took, I'd make sure everyone made it home, or wherever they needed to go, safe and sound. Still, there was nothing I could do about that now, and one thing was certain. I was exhausted. If I didn't get some real sleep soon, then I was gonna pass out on my feet.

"I'm sorry, but I can't deal with all of this right now." I motioned around at all the others, arguing and celebrating. "I'm gonna go and get the children settled. Then I plan to sleep for like a week."

"I'll help you get the pods ready," Evelyn said. She kissed me sweetly on the forehead and her lips were warm and soft and perfect. "The problems will still be here when you're rested. For now, let's get you settled in to get some sleep. Heaven knows you've earned it."

I smiled at that and motioned for my class to lead the way. They scampered ahead of me, and I saw Lee taking stock of the remainder of the people on board. Gerri set to helping him while Thomas stormed off in a huff.

I'd managed to save the Voloids and get them off a planet where they would never be safe. I could, finally, start the process of returning them to their Queen. I'd miss them, but it was the right thing to do.

We'd escaped the Humanist, and I'd found a way to balance being both a teacher and a guardian. It wasn't perfect. But nothing ever was, especially in an apocalypse. For the first time in many months, though, I found myself with real reasons to have hope for the future.

It was a very good feeling.

The End

Epilogue

Shuul Hek'khan Vey
Hive Queen of the Voloids

The tiny forms of lesser bodies rushed to serve Our will as this greater ruling body merely floated. The giant tank that held the ever-growing form was large enough for many hundreds of Our lessers. We would have to expand it again soon. Even the cavernous core of Our planetoid-sized fortress neared its limits. We'd Tier up soon enough that work should start.

An inkling of a doubt worried at Our attention. *Why must this always happen just as We are savoring an especially flavorful morsel of meat?* Our Matriarch-of-Hedonism's Epicure-Classed drone had the perfect palette. It was further enhanced by carefully cultivated System Skills, allowing him to focus on the finest of sensations to heighten Our delight. It was a perfect counterpoint to the satiation We were receiving from the same Matriarch's Glutton-Classed drone.

We could no longer give either experience the attention they deserved, however. So We cut this ruling piece of Ourself out of the loop as much as possible, allowing this part to focus on matters of greater concern. That way, favored subordinates could still enjoy the experience. This part would relish what remained from their memories, though it would be a lesser thing.

Sacrifices must be made.

The Grand Matriarch of Intrigue, a gorgeous Voloid with an exoskeleton so dark that the gray was nearly black, had learned of a troubling report regarding the Dungeon World known as Earth. Our exploration team had been destroyed there, an unfortunate but not unexpected loss. The expedition had been a low odds gamble, and everything lost there had been expendable.

We'd considered sending a replacement team and had investigated the cost for such a mission. Suitably boosted to survive the increased danger expected, of course. That was when We'd learned the shocking truth. Bereft of Voloid life, the ship should have self-destructed.

Instead, the ship had been claimed. Skill books had been used.

The initial reports We'd received were obviously fraudulent, and whoever had concocted them had not done adequate research. As if We could be tricked into believing that the Teacher had claimed the ship and used Our Skill books.

Preposterous. His Skill and Our years of study had proved him to be the only human We knew We could trust.

That had led to deeper digging.

Someone had used a Heroic Skill to obfuscate the children. The ship was covered by that haze as well. Surprising, but in the end pathetic. A poorly disguised report had been unearthed. Amatures. Many human governments conspired. Treachery. Yet they themselves, it seemed, had been betrayed. Our ship, technology, and secrets, had not been sold via the Shop as the hive of groups had ordered. What more could one expect from lesser beings without the glory of a hive-mind? Without even an Eunn?

The groups who had conspired against us, however, would not receive Our Pardon. They had stolen Our technology, Our knowledge. Someone had attempted to force one of Our lesser bodies to enter the System undeveloped. They'd sent letters to Our rivals, haggling Our secrets We'd long kept from them at great price of blood and Credits.

We had felt greater affection for the one called Caleb Hanson. He had served Us, and that part of Us not quite developed, well. The naive fool was also wise. He had earned Our great respect in spite of all. We had given him a weapon. An exoskeleton. At the time, We could think of no greater honor to bestow. Now, in recognition of his service, We would not exterminate the human race.

Despite Our rare forbearance, this threat to Us could not be overlooked. The groups who had initiated this affront would be eliminated. With the security of Our secrets now at risk, We could not trust mercenary forces.

We flexed Our will, and the Matriarchs of Science and of Vessels sent their lesser bodies scrambling to prepare. Our ships would be made ready. Stasis pods would be primed for Our special forces soldiers to awaken, the Matriarch of Military chief among them.

Myriad Voloids, on dozens of worlds, chittered and shrieked in rage as We planned Our coming vengeance. For the first time in a century, We would prepare Ourself to go to war.

Caleb will return in Dropout.
https://readerlinks.com/l/4354507

Henning will stop at nothing to save his unrequited love, even if it means clashing with Caleb and his class.
Sign up for the Starlit Publishing newsletter to read what happens when the ruthless Bounty Hunter spots his prey!
https://www.mylifemytao.com/bonus-epilogues/

Join Tao's Discord (https://discord.gg/ZYjwf5kBWe) or Facebook Group (https://www.facebook.com/taowongauthor/) to talk all things System Apocalypse: Liberty with other readers.

Authors' Note

I was working on an entirely different story when this one slammed into me like one of those t-bone car wreck scenes that you see on TV. The magic of social media yoinked my attention to a speech that Mr. Roger's gave before congress. It was one of the most amazing things I've ever seen, and it blew my mind.

I said, "We need more of this and less of everything else," threw out the project that I was writing, and got to work.

Shout outs:

> The whole team at Starlit Publishing are rockstars, and I appreciate them all.
> Cassie Robertson, my primary editor from Joy Editing, was a godsend. I could not recommend her services more highly.
> My wife and alpha reader, Pepper, was vital for the setting and the earliest drafts.
> My beta readers: Cassy, Michael, T, Mason, Dalton, and Jeff were enormously helpful.
> Sarah and Aurora, my emotional support humans, provided a different, but no less essential, type of support, just like they always have.

And if you made it this far, a special thanks to you as well. None of this matters without the readers. I hope you enjoyed this story and I'd love to hear from you. I can be reached on Facebook at Jason J. Willis Author (https://www.facebook.com/profile.php?id=61558185905470) or at my email address: Jasonjwillis@live.com.

Head of the Class

~Jason

***

Working on this series has been a blast. It's interesting taking a more epic fantasy / scifi look at an apocalyptic world, and putting a staunch pacifist in the middle of all this. Having the character deal with his emotions, with his beliefs and how he has to compromise - and make others compromise - is always fascinating.

As always, working with new authors in the System Apocalypse universe poses their own challenges. They come with questions that I'm not certain of, queries about what they can do that I've never thought about and, in their writing; are always pushing me to figure out how to improve myself.

None more so than the year 2 authors really like David and Jason, all of whom have their own visions; which might not be the 'traditional' apocalyptic angles for LitRPG but on the other hand, bring something new and fresh to the world.
I'm looking forward to seeing how people find book 2 just as much all of you.

As always, read, review and share your thoughts! We can't do it without you.

~Tao

For more great information about great LitRPG series, check out the Facebook groups:

- GameLit Society
  www.facebook.com/groups/LitRPGsociety
- LitRPG Books
  www.facebook.com/groups/LitRPG.books
- LitRPG Legion
  www.facebook.com/groups/litrpglegion

About the Authors

Jason J. Willis is a US based author in Thief River Falls, MN. His first published work, WWMRD, appears in System Apocalypse Anthology 2, part of the System Apocalypse post-apocalyptic LitRPG series.

When he's not writing or working, he can be found playing video games, TTRPGs, watching shows or movies, or consuming vast quantities of audiobooks and podcasts.

Jason J. Willis' Facebook Page
https://www.facebook.com/profile.php?id=61558185905470

Jason J. Willis' Amazon Author Page
https://www.amazon.com/stores/Jason-J.-Willis/author/B0CWPKZDG6

***

Tao Wong is a Canadian author based in Toronto who is best known for his System Apocalypse post-apocalyptic LitRPG series and A Thousand Li, a Chinese xianxia fantasy series. His work has been released in audio, paperback, hardcover and ebook formats and translated into German, Spanish, Portuguese, Russian and other languages. He was shortlisted for the UK Kindle Storyteller award in 2021 for his work, A Thousand Li: the Second Sect. When he's not writing and working, he's practicing martial arts, reading and dreaming up new worlds.

Tao became a full-time author in 2019 and is a member of the Science Fiction and Fantasy Writers of America (SFWA) and Novelists Inc.

If you'd like to support Tao directly, he has a Patreon page - benefits include previews of all his new books, full access to series short stories, and other exclusive perks.

- www.patreon.com/taowong

Want updates on upcoming deluxe editions and exclusive merch? Follow Tao on Kickstarter to get notifications on all projects: https://www.kickstarter.com/profile/starlitpublishing

For updates on the series and his other books (and special one-shot stories), please visit the author's website:

- www.mylifemytao.com

Subscribe to Tao's mailing list (https://www.mylifemytao.com/book-club/) to receive exclusive access to short stories in the Thousand Li and System Apocalypse universes!

About the Publisher

Starlit Publishing is wholly owned and operated by Tao Wong. It is a science fiction and fantasy publisher focused on the LitRPG & cultivation genres. Their focus is on promoting new, upcoming authors in the genre whose writing challenges the existing stereotypes while giving a rip-roaring good read.

For more information on Starlit Publishing, early access to books and exclusive stories visit our webshop: https://www.starlitpublishing.com/

You can also join Starlit Publishing's mailing list to learn about new, exciting authors and book releases: https://starlitpublishing.com/newsletter-signup/

System Apocalypse: Kismet

**Not everyone falls during an apocalypse.
Some rise to the occasion.**

For Fool and Jackal, the System Apocalypse was a chance to start again. A chance to rise, and be who they were meant to be.

Now, they're trying to offer others the same opportunities as part of a secret organization helping humanity survive the System.

Today's mission? Nothing big, just your typical save-the-princess quest.

But when you're the Acolyte of a Trickster god, typical is the last thing you should expect.

Just ask Fool's cat.

Read more!
https://www.mylifemytao.com/?page_id=8647

System Apocalypse – Relentless

Bail bondsman. Veteran. Survivor.

Hal Mason's still going to find surviving the System Apocalypse challenging.

While bringing in his latest fugitive, Hal's payday is interrupted by the translucent blue boxes that herald Earth's introduction to the System - a galaxy spanning wave of structured mystical energy that destroys all electronics and bestows game-like abilities upon mankind.

With society breaking down and mutating wildlife rampaging through the city of Pittsburgh, those who remain will sacrifice anything for a chance at earning their next Level. As bodies fall and civilization crumbles, Hal finds himself asking what price is his humanity. Are the Credits worth his hands being ever more stained with blood?

Or does he press on – *relentless?*

Read more!
https://www.mylifemytao.com/?page_id=5213

Glossary

Teacher Skill Tree

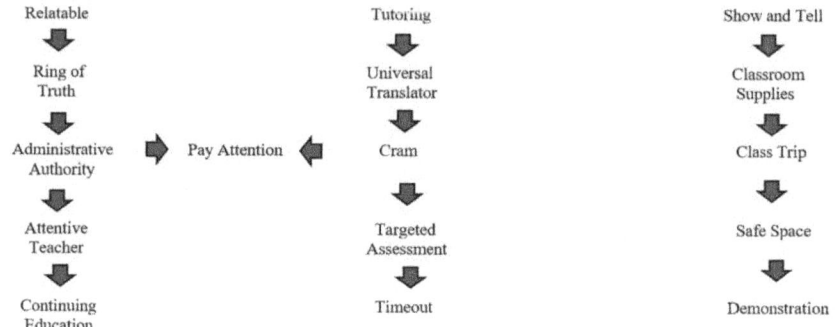

Guerilla Tactician Skills

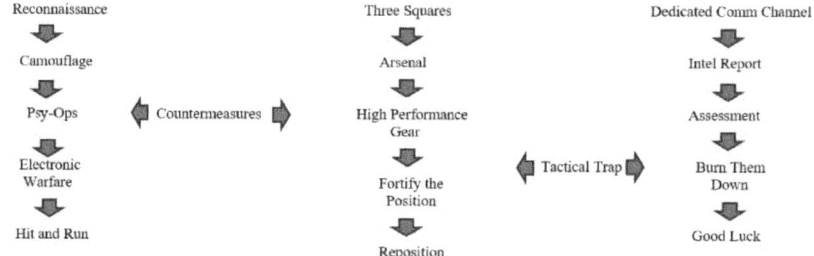

Caleb's Skill List and Equipment

Skills:

Class Trip (Level 3)

Group teleportation Skill

Transports a Teacher, students, and officially recognized chaperones to a location that the Teacher has previously occupied or thoroughly researched.

Max distance 100 miles + 25 miles per Skill Point.

Cost: 125 Mana + 25 for each student or chaperone beyond the first.

Class Trip – E (Level 6)
Group teleportation Skill

Transports a Teacher, students, and officially recognized chaperones to a location that the Teacher has previously occupied or thoroughly researched. This Skill has evolved to override a single restriction for all participants. This cannot affect max distance or Mana Cost.

Max distance 100 miles + 25 miles per level.

Cost: 200 Mana + 25 for each student or chaperone beyond the first.

Administrative Authority (Level 1)
Classroom only.

+10 Charisma. + 5 per Skill Point.

Cost: 25 Mana per minute.

Attentive Teacher (Level 1)
+ 10 to perception checks +5 per Skill Point invested.

Duration: 1 minute +20 seconds per Skill Point.

Cost: 25 Mana.

Show and Tell (Level 1)
Creates an illusionary visual demonstration of what the Teacher is discussing. The witnesses do not need to understand your speech, and the limits of visualization are based upon your imagination and connection to the System. Channeled.

Area of effect: 10-foot area + 2 feet per Skill Point.

Cost: 5 Mana per minute.

Demonstration (Level 1)

Grants +10 to your next Skill-based action. Requires at least one allied witness. If you succeed at this action, allies who perceive you gain a +10 bonus to do the same action. A similar tool is required if the copied action used one.

Area 30-foot radius +10 feet per Skill Point.

Cost: 20 Stamina and 20 Mana.

Pay Attention (Level 1)

Directs an individual or group's attention toward a particular subject.

Area of effect: 30-foot radius centered on Teacher.

Grants a +5 bonus to perception for 1 minute.

This Skill also aids in resisting distractions.

Cost: 25 Mana.

Personal Force Field

Creates a protective field of force around yourself or your shield-bot to reduce incoming damage. Can be used multiple times as separate castings.

Duration: 5 Minutes.

Cost: 200 Mana.

Rapid Repair

Reconstruct a moderately damaged construction or mechanical device. Effect is increased if the targeted item is Kaldian Technology.

Cost: 100 Mana.

Shield Projection (Level 1)

Remotely direct and modify your shield-bot's force shields, empowered by your own Mana. Also

allows for the direct generation of a secondary shield by the Shield Warder.
Cost: Varies.

Hunter's Strike (Level 1)

Provides a bonus to accuracy and an increase to the damage of a single attack.

Effect: +10% to accuracy, +5% to damage of attack.
Cost: 10 Stamina and 15 Mana.

Thrusting Charge (Level 1) Voloid Variant

Dash forward, striking your target with a mighty thrust of your spear. Bonus to damage dependent upon user Skills, Attributes, and equipment used. Max dash distance 30 feet.
Cost: 15 Stamina and 10 Mana.

Spells:

Improved Minor Healing (I)

Effect: Heals 25 Health per casting. Target must be in contact during healing. Cooldown 60 seconds.
Cost: 15 Mana.

Minor Repair (I)

Effect: Repairs dents, tears, and scratches. Can not repair major or structural damage.
Cost: 15 Mana.

Equipment:

Klop-Nimbus-Three blaster pistol:

This short-range, high-powered pistol is the pride of Nimbus-Three. Others may consider them a
backwater neck of the Galaxy, but it's worth noting that only the truly powerful or foolish have the guts to say it to their face.
This weapon deals disruptive damage.
Damage varies based on the application of associated Skills.
Shots: 25 Recharge rate: 1 shot per 5 seconds.

Danarian Technophile's Augmenter Mark 2

A chest harness that boosts technological effects. It requires a specialized form of Mana battery that can absorb the user's personal Mana. This device has a spot in the back to allow the user to charge such a battery. A single Augmenter may boost up to five devices. Limit may vary based on Level of the user.
Commonly sold with Damarian Technofile's Boosters. The booster can be attached to a device to increase its effectiveness. Extra Mana batteries and boosters not included.

HLF Prototype Dermal Sheathing

This sophisticated nanofiber weave underarmor requires a Tier 2 or higher neural interface. It provides the wearer a +5 bonus to Strength, Agility, and Stamina, as well a small degree of protection. Also includes a minor, if sporadic, self-repair function.

Caleb's Armor Upgrade

Core: Kaldian Apex 3B Mana Engine
CPU: Kaldian Secondary-Worker (Linked to Companion and Implant)
Armor Rating: Tier IV
Hard Points: 1

Soft Points: 5 (1 used for Neural Link. 1 reserved for Companion Link-Currently disabled)

Battery Capacity: 120/120

+2 Strength

+5 Perception and Constitution

+10 Int

+12% Resist Energy

+15% Resist Physical

Pavise's Upgrade

Core: Kaldian Apex 3 Mana Engine

CPU: Kaldian Warder Companion Matrix Alpha-1

Armor Rating: Tier IV

Hard Points: 4

Soft Points: 3 (1 used for Neural Link)

Battery Capacity: 120/120

+6 to Willpower

+7 to Intelligence

+12 to Strength and Agility

Lee's Skill List and Equipment

Skills:

Good Luck (Level 5)

+5 (+1 per level) to Perception, Agility, and Luck to selected targets.

Max targets 4 + 1 per Skill Point. Must be grouped.

Cost: 40 Mana + 10 Mana per target past 4.

Fortify the Position (Level 4)

Allows Guerilla Taction to moderately reshape the environment for raised walls, trenches, etc. The kind a military group could construct. Can't be activated beyond the first minute of a battle. Permanent changes. Affects a 20-foot area + 5 feet per Skill Point invested. Range: 20 yards. Channeled.

Cost: 50 Mana + 20 Mana per 5 seconds.

Hit and Run (Level 1)

Tactician creates a movement and attack rate buff that lasts 15 seconds + 1 second per Skill Point used. Activation creates 2 charges. The second charge must be used within 2 minutes, + 20 seconds per Skill Point used. 5-minute cooldown. Can be cast on participants in active combat. Must be able to fit everyone affected into a 10-foot radius on activation.

Cost: 45 Stamina + 15 Mana per participant.

Burn Them Down (Level 5)

Guerilla Tactician indicate a particular target to focus fire on, giving them a moderate defensive debuff and alerting all nearby troops to target them. Outlines them in faint, glowing red.

Cost: 25 Stamina and 30 Mana per 40 seconds.

Intel Report (Level 4)

Creates a battle map for Tactician that updates with any intel that party members gather. Includes info gained by
surveillance tools. Gives a summary of troop movements, key resources, etc. Also includes operational goals, targets, and
priorities.

Area 500 meters + 100 meters per Skill Point.

Reduces Mana by 20 permanently.

Retreat (Level 1)

Provides Strike Force Commander the following boosts to group members actively attempting to flee. Effect: +10% damage resistance, +15% movement rate and resistance to traps and slowing Skills and technology, +5 Luck, +2 Agility, +10 Stamina Regeneration
Duration: 5 minutes + 1 minute per Skill Point or until 1 mile from their original battle map position.
Cost: 50 Stamina + 150 Mana.

Adaptive Defense (Level 1)

Provides Strike Force Commander's Troops +20% resistance to the harmful effects of a chosen category. Max members affected: 4 + 1 per Skill Point. Cannot be cast in combat. Bonus applies only to permanent physical items like armor, not Skill effects. Options include impact, slashing, piercing, cold, fire, electrical, acid, and poison. 24-hour duration.
Cost: 150 Mana.

Real Time Updates (Level 1)

Continuously updates Commander's battle map and assessment with real-time System data. Includes likelihood of mission success and estimated losses on both sides. Recommends when to trigger retreat based on preset parameters. Allows user to share Intel Report with group members on a need-to-know basis.
Duration: 1 hour.
Cost: 100 Mana +10 Mana per 5 minutes.

Assessment (Level 5)

Updates Tactician's Intel report with easily obtained System information. Provides estimates of resources, positioning, troop numbers, etc. This information is not fully reliable. Accuracy of information increases over time during the op.
Cost: Variable Mana and Credit cost based on request.

Full Coordination (Level 1)

Battle map overlays, along with details, routes, and updated orders are provided to all group members on a need-to-know basis. This also allows the Commander to access information regarding your effectiveness at various roles. This Skill is System-and Strike Force Commander-controlled. It affects all allies in the Intel Report's area of effect, which it doubles.
Cost: 50 Mana + 5 Mana per minute per individual linked.

Psy-Ops (Level 1)

Guerilla Tactician creates loud noises, smoke, and other sensory disturbances to indicate a chaotic
and dangerous environment. Can be resisted by those with high enough perception. Not a mental
effect. Must originate within 300 yards from the caster + 100 yards per Skill Point. Channeled.
Cost: 30 Mana per second.

Equipment:

Lifetap Inc. Variable Prosthetic

Growth item. Tier 2 weapon. Base Damage 20.
Becomes a spike to pierce the unwary and consume their power. Drains 5 Mana, Health, and Stamina per second and replenishes 1/3rd the value of the same. This

device was originally used by a techno-organic race known as the C. Vengi 3LD and can therefore be used to restore cybernetic or android parts, as well as biological. Techno-organics are restored at ⅔'s.

The Humanist's Skill List

Humiliating Subjugation (Level 4)
Mentally restrains a single target in the manner of your choice. They are crippled with pain, unable to move, or unable to initiate any Active Skills. Direct damage caused by this Skill is mental, and the effects last only as long as the Skill does. Resisted by Willpower.
Duration: Time channeled + 1 second per 10 seconds restrained. Channeled.
Cost: 50 Mana + 25 per 10 seconds.

Quinn's Skill List

Cybernetic Bilocation (Level 2)
You can remove a small portion of your biological material that has been cybernetically augmented and leave it at a remote location, up to 100 miles away, + 10 miles per Skill Point. You are counted as present at the location of the device for Skill activation. One additional body part can be Bilocated per Skill Point invested.
Cost: Varies based on part selected and distance traveled.

Cutting Edge Tech (Level 7)
Any technologically advanced blade wielded by you, or your controlled devices, gains an increase to
damage, armor penetration, and durability. This Skill works best for cutting edge technology,

offering a higher bonus to elite and experimental blades. Mana Regeneration is reduced by 35
permanently.

Gerri's Skill List

Hazmat Protocol

Provides major resistance to drugs, poisons, disease, acids, radiation, etc.
Duration: 15 minutes + 5 minutes per Skill Point.
Area: 20-foot radius + 5 feet per Skill Point. Immovable.
Cost: 100 Mana +10 Mana per minute. Ongoing cost increases under extreme conditions.

Experimentation

Allows for System-backed modification of a pharmaceutical product that changes a single key element of the item. This can be used to modify even base ingredients. Over time, this Skill can allow for construction of permanent newly crafted materials. Small chance of failure and lost materials.
Cost: 75 Mana.

Reverse Engineer (Level 1)

(Advanced Skills - Breakthrough Tree - Tier 2)
A single chosen item (or random if you do not choose) stored in your Research Grade Storage is successfully researched, granting you a blueprint. Chance of successful research is 1 percent per hour in storage, with a max percentage of 5 percent per hour. There is also a 1 percent chance per hour that the product is destroyed in this process. Only works on pharmaceutical products. Percentage cap increases by 1 percent per Skill Point invested. Mana Regeneration reduced by 5 Mana permanently. Passive.

Penny's Skill and Equipment

Skill:

Stabilize Battlefield Trauma (Level 1)

Spray or inject the patient with medical nanites that stabilize the patient's condition and prevent ongoing harm. Sets bones, binds wounds, clears airways, etc.

This also sets the stage for ongoing healing, granting the recipient a 20 percent bonus to all healing effects within the duration.

Duration: 5 minutes.

Cost: 200 Mana.

Equipment:

Prototype Portable Potion Condenser and Remote Injection Device

Condenses potions, then loads them into weaponized injectors. Also accepts pre-condensed cartridges. Can be used for offensive or beneficial concoctions.

To learn more about LitRPG, talk to authors including myself, and just have an awesome time, please join the LitRPG Group!

https://www.facebook.com/groups/LitRPGGroup/

Milton Keynes UK
Ingram Content Group UK Ltd.
UKHW041207051024
449245UK00005B/38